LOUP GAROU

Howard H. Webb

LOUP GAROU

BY

HOWARD H. WEBB

© 2013

© 2013 COVER ARTWORK BY DAN SANTIAGO

ISBN: 978-0-9897113-0-2

PUBLISHED BY

HOWARD ENTERPRISES

This work is dedicated to the one person who TOLD
me to finish what I started.

Thank you Luiz. Without your encouragement a
dream would have remained a dream.

Book 1
Henri LeBlanc's Memoirs

Prologue

After all this time, it still calls to me, beckons to me.

Certain lands and places, even cities, can have an undeniable hold, a mystical bond, over some people that even time (ever relentless time) can never break nor diminish. These places survive as living, breathing entities, ecosystems, through floods and droughts, through extremes of weather and freaks of nature that, even while perhaps forever altering a landscape, it will adapt, endure and live on. Even when considering that one element, man, who can destroy forever in the wink of an eye, a vision of beauty and mystery that only nature can provide, the land still adapts. And time moves on.

Such a bond was forged between myself and the swamps and bayous of an ancient land, even though commonly referred to as 'the new world'. It captured my soul, my very essence if you will, because it was there that I lived and died and then lived again.

Uniquely, part land and part water, these wetlands, the swamp's wilderness, can beguile and bewitch, it can be a friend or an enemy. To the man, hunter or fisherman, who understands its mysteriously complex ways and does not abuse them, but rather lives with them and adapts himself to them, the swamp, with its many basins, bays and slow meandering bayous, can provide a friendly source of habitat and livelihood.

But to the one who misuses nature's abundance, either through carelessness or deliberate mercenary acts of destruction, the swamp will become their implacable enemy. And so mother nature, protecting herself, will one day rise and reek out her vengeance on those abusers of this wetland which

4

she protects and nourishes in her own unique fashion.

Further and further into the filtered light of the swampland is evidence of this motherland with its own particular vibrant and delicate composition. At once, a harsh and beautiful world, which I first became acquainted with in the latter half of the 18th century; herein reigns nature most profoundly and unapologetically.

In the stillness of a warm, misty spring morning, the scene is not un-dreamlike, of tall cypress forests springing magically from water coated with a thin sheen of vibrant green. With icicles of moss decorating trees and brush, where the air itself seems to be heavy with life. There is the smell of briny water mixed with the heady perfume of wildflowers, floating plants, and fertile earth which can only be reached by shallow boats, where man's destructive presence has yet to be felt.

And on many summer days, as the sun progresses on its track hot and high in the sky, clouds will form and the heavy atmosphere of the hazy afternoon fills with the clean sweet scent of rain showers which help make this wetland such an unique, productive world. The beautiful billowing clouds drift overhead, dark and heavy with moisture, hanging pendulously over the land, lending it an ethereal image of lights and shadows. The rain storm moves quickly, washing over the area giving necessary life, which the tall trees seem to yearn upwards towards in silent prayer.

Then later in the evening as the sun sets, the intoxicating stillness gives rise to a gentle, light breeze that starts slowly, as if called forth by some unseen generous goddess. A breath of wind to cool the swamps and marshes from a long, hot sunny day, engulfing itself all around the many different species of flora and fauna unique to this water-land. And still it calls to me.

The soft, evening wind is but a sweet prelude to the night. As dusk falls and the moon rises, the land and water become active with life. The coolness has inspired movement everywhere. From the majestic tops of 500 year old oak trees, to the deep recesses of dark waters, lies the life and death struggles of the inhabitants. Hunger and survival rule the night. This nocturnal interlude is, by nature's necessity, a stirring of life and (inevitably for all) a silencing of death. The swamp lives upon itself, giving birth, burying the dead. Eternally evolving and enduring.

Perhaps that is why at this time of twilight, it especially calls out to me, for I know it well. I am one of the few hunters who can freely venture deep into this watery terrain without fear. Most who enter, into what I consider as my domain, never return. The few who do are never the same. Legends and myths of unimaginable horrors and demonic doings abound. Wildcats, snakes, alligators, bears all take on some form of supernatural creature of supreme wickedness and evil that kills with abandon, without discretion, with neither care nor remorse. Tales that elsewhere would never be taken seriously.

So here in this untamed country, in the tiny towns and villages, young ones are warned at an early age to stay away from the wet-forests edge or they will be swallowed whole, no trace of them ever to be found. The adults will not admit to each other their belief in those stories, but at night many homes are bolt and shuttered tight, despite stifling, still air, against the dangers that they profess so strongly not to believe in.

It is here in this fertile, naked land that my own story begins. My tale of pain and rage, of sorrow, loss and love, of ultimate betrayal and supreme vengeance, that has made me as I am today. Even time can never release me from my curse, my destiny of eternal torment and wandering, without the security that love can bring, that most men know of. My only constant is the companion of insatiable, searching hunger inside of myself, which only death, God's last mercy, can put an end to.

But even that one coup de grace eludes me, for I and others have tried innumerable times and in many different ways, only to fail.

Listen carefully, for it is calling to me even now, as I write this, calling persistently, constantly. No matter how far I roam, no matter how many years pass by. It beckons me back for it is my home, where I belong, where my cursed self was born.

My blood carries the curse, this land carries my blood.

Loup Garou

PART ONE:
MY METAMORPHOSIS

1

The swamp grew ever dense and dark the further we ventured within, only mere patches of moonlight occasionally filtering through the tall cypresses showing shadowy glimpses of the way ahead. Our men and dogs had been out almost all night and now the animals had caught the scent of what we thought to be a bear. Dawn was fast approaching. I had somehow gotten behind the rest of the hunting party, who rushed in headlong, sure that they were about to surround and trap a huge prize, one of the largest seen in this wilderness.

"Mon Dieu, he's gigantic." "Colossus", I heard their exclamations close ahead. Wildlife was plentiful in this area; wildcats, beaver, foxes, deer, bear, rabbit. All good for furs and meat, trapping and trading, but we had never hunted this deep into this particular basin. Even the local natives seldom traveled this far.

The barking and howling was ever louder and ceaseless. Then I heard shots. I stopped to listen. "C'est impossible!" "He's not going down." More shots, more howls. I cautiously approached. Screams and shouts filled the air, but I could not discern what they said. And then...silence. I paused. What could possibly be happening! I scrambled through the underbrush. The silence was complete and utterly frightening, not even a whimper from one of the hounds. And then it was torn apart by an unearthly, bloody scream that filled me with terror. Then that terrible silence again pervaded the atmosphere. I slowly crept ahead to a small clearing, not knowing what to think.

What I saw in the faint early morning light was unimaginable.

I thought I must be hallucinating. Entrails and body parts were scattered out all over the scene, as if a tremendous explosion had occurred. Four dead men- mutilated men- and twice as many hounds, but I could not distinguish one from the other or recognize any of my comrades. Blood, dripping down from the tree branches above, sounded like a soft rain shower.

I studied the scene dumbfounded, trying to absorb the horror, trying not to retch, when a tremendously loud, echoing howl shattered the diminishing night. I slowly turned towards the sound and thought I caught the glint of two large eyes staring directly at me. Self-preservation conquered my fear. I slowly crouched down and started to move quietly and slowly back the way I came. The moon was disappearing fast and the sun was not yet up. It seemed to be getting darker just before the dawn.

The eyes began coming closer to me, but I could not discern an outline of the beast itself. It was part of the forest.

I shot at it, below those piercing eyes, where its heart should have been, at close range, yet it never winced or hesitated in it's slow and silent progress towards me. I hurriedly moved to reload.

It pounced. Quickly and decisively, with great force. I fell backward on the ground, the wind knocked out of me. After that, all I could see were gigantic sharp teeth, dripping saliva, coming towards my neck. Instinctively, I raised my left arm and the pain was immediate and excruciating as the beast's large snout clamped down on me with the force of a bear trap. I heard bone's snap. My screams must have been hysterical, but I have no recollection.

Vaguely, through the tremendous pain and terror, I faintly heard distant voices; it must have been the remainder of our hunting party which had gone by a different route. I believe I yelled for help. The night was lifting quickly to make way for the first rays of daylight and I managed to see the thing face to face. It looked to be a gigantic wolf!

It backed off to attack again, now clawing at my chest as if to literally pull out my heart. The anguish was unbearable. As I started to pass out, I remember saying a silent prayer for God to please let me go quickly with no more pain. I sensed the beast's warm, foul breath against my neck as he was about to deliver his last blow.

But my last sensation, before oblivion, was that of staring directly into the monster's eyes. They were a deep blue and I had the oddest fleeting thought, a strange feeling, that the eyes were human.

2

Somewhere in my extreme stupor of pain, I saw a vision of an angels face. She was remarkably beautiful with long, dark brown hair to match her large, dark eyes which looked down upon me with utmost concern. Her features, delicate and petite, were so fine as to be chiseled from marble. She had to have been an angel. Which meant that I must be, indeed, dead and now in heaven- or some such place. The vision began to blur and slowly fade away. I tried to capture it, to hold it, but could not. I realized my pain was subsiding. Was I dying? Hallucinating? I closed my eyes and surrendered to a deep, restful, healing sleep. I felt at peace, thinking that if I was to die, at least this beautiful servant of God was administering to me. And I dreamed.

Of home. Not my current home, in the warm marshes of this new land, but of my first home, where I grew up. The only other home I've known. With cool playful summers and cold, sometimes harsh winters. Near a wild ocean much different than the calm warm waters where I now live. Extreme tides were the norm. Here my French descendants had settled a century or more before I was born and here I, Henri LeBlanc was raised with my brothers and sisters, in a large family with many cousins and distant relatives. It was a wonderful, idyllic existence for a young man. Hard manual work, fishing and farming, hunting and trapping, braving the elements, bartering with neighbors and natives; all with beautiful, breathtaking changes of seasons.

There I grew up, learned to provide for our family, made

friends, flirted with girls, lived and led a peaceful existence.
Until the great expulsion.

Here my dream becomes a nightmare as I remembered the atrocities committed upon my people. Forced to leave our homes, to board over-crowded ships bound to places unknown-we were captives, unable to defend ourselves against these soldiers. Families were separated, lovers torn apart and we with no choice in the matter. Chaos ruled as children were lost, torn in the melee, from their mother's grasp, brothers and sisters sent aboard different ships. I heard again the cries of my little sisters mixed with the shouts of orders from the foreign soldiers forcing us to pack quickly and leave.

My father, calmly and quietly had us pray and told us to be brave and to try to stay together. He promised that if separated we would one day be reunited. For everyone to eventually travel to that most southern French territory where that great river meets the ocean. Where distant relations had already settled and where most of those expelled would finally call home.

I saw my mother trying desperately to keep the little ones near her, being whisked away in one direction towards a ship, while I was forced in another direction with a group of young men to board a different vessel. We sailed away watching helplessly, as our farms and homes were being burned and our livestock killed. They made sure that we would have nothing to return to.

History has a number of such disgraceful pages: unfathomable to those who hear of them, unforgettable to those who bear witness to them.

I sailed away that day not knowing where we were heading nor if I would ever see my family again. Only nineteen, I was the oldest of seven with only one brother, two years old, last seen holding tight to our mother's skirt as she tried, in vain, to keep her brood together. All I could do was hope and pray that my parents and the young ones would not be separated and that we would all survive to eventually be together again.

On board with me, among a sea of familiar faces, was one of my cousins, Jean-Pierre, whom I had grown up with and regarded as my best friend. He too was separated from his family. At least we were together.

Our voyages, the desperate situations aboard the ships, the hunger and sickness, has all been passed down into history. Many ports refused us safe harbor. Deliberate delays created by uncaring port officials, only made the situation worse. Many, many died.

I and Jean-Pierre were a few of the lucky ones, surviving well and traveling slowly over sea and land, to that safe place in French territory, that lovely warm and soft wet land named for French kings, as my father had hoped for. Our people settled in the bayous, basins and bays of this friendly, welcome area, making it our own, but Jean-Pierre and I have yet to see or hear of our families. Now, at twenty-one, I have still not given up hope; I look for them in every face and somehow, even feel they are very near. We pray that they are safe and healthy and that one day we will be reunited.

3

Hours (or days?) later, my dreams gradually made way for wakefulness. Through bleary eyes, I saw that I was in a tiny cabin room, lying upon a small comfortable bed, stuffed with cotton and covered in blankets. Suddenly I jerked upright, fully awake, fear making my heart pound, as I recalled my last waking memory. Unfortunately, pain also returned, racing through my entire body. I realized then that I was not yet dead, for only the living can experience pain. But where was I?

I gingerly lowered myself down. Dressed only in trousers, I had what seemed to be clean, fresh bandages around my chest, left arm and neck. Somehow, someway, I had been spared.

As I calmed down, while observing my surroundings (no windows, one door just ahead, a single lantern providing light), the door slowly opened and two women quietly entered the room. One
was young and the other much older, with long gray hair and who walked with a cane. It was obvious she was blind or nearly

so, and she sat herself down on the other side of the room on a wooden bench.

As the young, tall girl approached my bedside, and bent down towards me, I recognized her from my dream vision. She was as beautiful as I had recalled. So statuesque, she carried herself with such grace. With café-au-lait colored skin, toned and unblemished, her brown, almond shaped eyes shone down at me with calmness and serenity.

Without saying a word, she sat down beside me and slowly, methodically, began to undress my bandages. My lower left arm was completely wrapped, a large bandage encircled my bare chest, a small one was on my neck. Blood was on them all. My head and throat ached.

As if reading my thoughts, she knowingly reached for a cup of water on a stand next to the bed and brought it up to my dry parched lips. I swallowed slowly at first, the cool water quenching the dry ache in my throat. I gulped down the rest. She tenderly wiped my lips with a clean cloth and then silently continued unwrapping the bandages.

My hoarse voice broke the silence like a rough saw breaks the silence in the woods. "Where am I? How did I come to be here?"

The old lady was the one to respond, my nurse not stopping from her duties. "I see you are awake." At this, she laughed lightly at herself. "Your friend brought you here. You were nearly dead." She spoke excellent French, but her look and dress was that of one of the natives. Dark-skinned, and with the wrinkles of old age, she looked to be eighty or even ninety, but her voice was ageless.

"Pierre?" I asked. She nodded. Again I asked, "And where is here?"

"A tiny village. Not too far from where you were...found." She paused, "He said your name was Henri?" she asked politely. Sitting on the bench in such a regal, royal manner, she seemed not unlike an ancient ruler, a queen or high priestess. Perhaps she was.

"Yes," I replied. My dutiful nurse was now starting to gently wash my wounds. Strange that they didn't seem to hurt as much as I thought they would. Perhaps it was her gentle touch,

13

like healing magic.

"And how are you called?" I asked looking directly at her.

Her reply was soft and dignified. They were no doubt related. "I am Selena. This is my grandmother." I thought that a most appropriate name for an angel like her. I suddenly wished she would bath me all over. I definitely was feeling better.

She stopped what she was doing and looked down at me curiously. Was she a mind reader? I felt uncontrollably embarrassed. She resumed her tasks.

"How long have I been here?"

"Almost two weeks." Her grandmother replied dramatically. "Your wounds are healing unnaturally fast." I thought that a strange choice of words.

"You were unconscious most of the time, having some very disturbing dreams it would seem." She seemed curious. I wondered, if I told them what I thought I had experienced, they would think me mad.

Selena spoke next, in her soft, melodic voice, while applying some soothing lotion that smelled of flowers, not medicine. "Your arm was crushed and mangled, totally useless. We had to reset your shoulder. It was literally tore out of its socket. We thought that we might have to amputate your arm." She spoke matter-of-factly, but with a young girlish sense of wonder. "We feared at one point that you were dead."

"I dreamed I was." I clasped her hand in mine, briefly, warmly, looking directly into her eyes. "Thank you, I am most grateful."

"It is what we do," the grandmother stated plainly, simply.

Healers. They must have very potent medicines and herbs for me to heal so well, so quickly. My arm was stiff and sorely painful, but I could move it freely. My chest wound, now just a jagged scar across the heart. The old lady's knowledge and abilities must be the stuff of legends.

"Our remedies are very old and sacred," Selena spoke in answer to my thoughts; her voice containing much pride. "Grandma-ma is a great healer, with time-honored cures and knowledge of herbs and potions."

The grandmother interrupted, "How are they? The

wounds?"

"Amazing," was the reply. "They are almost healed. No bleeding. I am re-bandaging them now."

"Quickly," the old lady whispered intently. She stood and looked silently towards the closed door like a sentinel. Had she heard something? Was she totally blind or partially, I wondered. Perhaps her hearing was magnified since her loss of sight. Suddenly, I felt very tired.

"Yes grandma-ma," Selena worked quickly, yet adroitly like she had done this work many times before. She helped me raise up to put the last bandages around my chest. Reaching behind me, we were almost in an embrace. Our faces close together. I could feel her warmth. She smelled of flowers. Roses? I sensed her strength beneath that gentle touch. The moment was over all too soon. She rose to leave and join her grandmother at the door.

But first she reached for a glass on the stand. "Drink this." I obeyed. It tasted slightly bitter, very potent, healing. "You will sleep peacefully now through the night and we will be back in the morning." Her voice left me calm with no doubt that I would do as she said.

She started to leave but stopped at the door and turned back. "I will tell Jean-Pierre you are doing much better. He will be happy to hear that. He has been quite worried." Her reassuring smile stayed in my mind's eye even after the door closed behind them.

And I did sleep well and heavily as she had ordered. My body tired from this ordeal, my mind tired from bewilderment and wonder at what had happened to me and the others out there in that dark wild swamp.

So I slept and dreamt of roses instead.

4

I awoke at sunrise and with a pleasant surprise, found my

friend Jean-Pierre at my bedside in a small chair quietly watching over me. "Pierre," I exclaimed.

"Mon ami." We embraced. "You look so very well, Henri."

"I feel well. Almost as good as new." Jean-Pierre, even though my blood relation, was more fair than I, with sandy, short blond hair and hazel eyes. In contrast to his short, stocky build, I (and my siblings) were tall and mostly lean. At just under 6 foot, I had an elongated torso, long wavy black hair and deep-set coal-black eyes. I had a dark-brown complexion that tanned easily, compared to Pierre's more ruddy, red face that looked like a permanent sunburn. And whereas, I was hairy, with heavy shadow on my face by the end of the day, Pierre was smooth.

He was handsome in his own way, with large features; nose and lips, eyes round and large like a cow's. He was shorter than I by half-a-foot, stout and could put weight on easily. But strong as an ox. He was always the winner in wrestling matches back home. One of his best stories (of which there were many) was how he had wrestled an alligator as large as a man in a nearby swamp, nearly being killed before he conquered the beast and made several pair of boots from his hide!

Together we had learned about this new land and the swamps. About how to live with it and not try to best it. How to appreciate it without destroying it. He was not just my cousin, but my friend. His heart as large and generous as any. After all, we had been through the diaspora together. He smiled across at me, a large, ebullient smile of happiness and relief.

"Tell me Pierre," I had to ask, unable to disguise the urgency in my voice. "When you found me...Did you see what happened to the others? Was what I saw real?" I still doubted my own eyes.

His comforting smile disappeared, and his face turned mysterious. He stood and reacted nervously, pacing back and forth, as if wanting to choose his words carefully. I waited patiently, hoping beyond hope that the others might be alive and I had imagined the attack, but then how to explain my wounds?

He turned to me. "Carnage. No other word for it. Pieces is all that was left. We could not recognize one man from another." He paused, "And you almost the same way, if we had not fired when we did."

"Did you kill it?" He shook his head again. "I swear I shot it point blank."

" But you..you did see it, Pierre, didn't you?" My voice rose with my body. I sat up wanting to hear some logical explanation.

"It?" He started pacing again. "We saw something. Very large, huge. A bear, maybe," he shrugged his shoulders, "a boar?"

"A boar? Impossible! A boar could not have done what it did to me and the others."

"Not one, but many perhaps." He did not sound convinced. He sat back down and looked at me squarely, speaking slowly. "What do you think it was?"

I looked away. "I really don't know, I really don't." Then I looked back at him. I had to confide in him, even if it called into question my sanity. "I had the sense that it was a wolf, but as large as a man. In fact, it seemed..somewhat human!"

"Nonsense!" Pierre abruptly started moving around the room again. He seemed not to be able to look at me, avoiding my stare.

"Pierre, please sit down." I said calmly.

He sat down with a warning, "Don't dare to repeat that to anyone here."

"Why did you bring me here? I don't remember hearing of a village this far into the basin."

"Neither had I. But the oddest thing. Moments after we found you, some old dark native woman with long gray hair appeared out of nowhere with the sunrise. She said she was a great healer and for us to carry you and follow her to this village." He shook his head in wonder. "She may be blind as a bat, but she sure knows her way around." He lowered his voice and whispered, "Voodoo."

"Voodoo?" I exclaimed, laughing as he tried to quiet me. "Now who is talking nonsense."

He relaxed a bit in the chair. "Think about it. Explain how your wounds have healed so quickly? Where are the scars? You were torn all over from claw marks and bites. Your arm practically bitten in two. I saw the bone." The painful memory came back to me. "And how did she come to appear there, so suddenly, miraculously, like a dark angel or priestess?" He whispered the last word poignantly. And again, I thought of my image of her: her bearing, like royalty or even as he said, a priestess.

"Perhaps she has sight." I murmured to myself.

"Second sight," was his response. We both chuckled and relaxed. There was a silence between us for a few moments. No need always for words between good friends. Then I was the first to speak again.

"As for the beast," I began, and he immediately started fidgeting again in his seat. "Remember the tales our grandfather told back home of the half-man, half-beast."

"Those were just that. Tales made up, meant to scare us and keep us from wandering around in the woods."

"But I think he believed in them."

"Grandfather was a crazy old fool. My papa- your papa too- did not believe in his stories. Werewolves indeed!" He chuckled. "Next we will see ghosts and goblins."

He started to laugh, softly at first, then largely as was his tendency. Infectious. We both laughed heartily. Of course, my imagination must be overwrought. I felt relaxed and peaceful again.

We settled into our comfortable friendship. Much of the time at this point we would be passing a rum bottle.

"Well I best be going, mon ami." He stood to leave. "Selena gave orders for me not to overstay my visit. Says you must rest. She is most protective of you." He winked knowingly.

"Isn't she the most beautiful creature?" It was a statement- not really a question requiring an answer.

"My dear cousin, I do believe you are smitten." His famous laughter filled the room. "She will be in later today. Rest now, Henri." He patted me on the shoulder.

Then he mentioned, almost as an afterthought, "And maybe we will find your wolf. Perhaps there is a large pack out there somewhere. That would explain a lot. In fact, one in our group said he saw a wolf's print leading down into the bayou."

"Why didn't you tell me that you found tracks?"

He shrugged. "Only a few in the mud at the water's edge. I could not identify them. Like I said one man thought they might have been made by a large wolf." He seemed to want to dismiss this information, though I wanted to speak more about it.

But it would have to wait for another time. He waved and walked out of the room and closed the door behind him. A pack of wolves? I wondered.

I slowly sat up on the edge of the bed. Time to stand. I had been lying down for over two weeks. I stood up carefully and stretched. Sore and stiff, I shuffled about the room. I was fortunate to be alive; to have the use of my arm. I poured myself some water and drank, slowly, for a long time. I sat back on the bed and thought of Selena and her grandmother. They could be from the West Indies, Martinique perhaps. Selena definitely had French blood in her. Feeling a little dizzy, I laid back on the bed on top of the blankets and thought about my family, my parents. Perhaps they ended up in a village such as this one. Jean-Pierre and I had searched every town we came upon, yet, so far, we had no luck in finding relatives. There were probably other communities like this one that we had not heard about. We would still keep searching, keep looking. Yet in the meantime, I found that this land was now my home. I felt comfortable here. It was a welcome, warm land. You just had to treat it with respect. I fell back asleep to the sound of distant thunder, thinking.. 'Mon Dieu am I hungry'.

5

I dreamed of the sound of splashing water and gentle hands washing my arms and legs with a warm, wet cloth. I didn't want to wake. They were soft, feminine hands that now were bathing my shoulders, neck and chest and I wanted the sensation to never cease. I felt like a child again, until I realized I was becoming aroused. Rather, I dreamed I was becoming aroused. Was this Selena? My dream did not allow me to see a face, so I just surrendered to the feeling. I felt the flow of warm water and her expert hands caress my body. She reached down and stroked my sex.

I awoke slowly out of this stuporous state, my first realization being that I was naked beneath the blankets (my sex stiff). Had the dream been real? My next sensation was the sound of soft rain outside and the sweet scent of wet sycamore. The steady drizzle was comforting, cozy.

But I also heard something else- the sound of muffled voices. I was not alone. Through the open door I could see shadows moving. People- men, were in the next room, in what seemed to be an intense discussion. Their language was a local dialect that I had heard before, but had never understood. They were most probably talking about me. I noticed my bandages had been completely removed; the scars were now little more than scratches. No one would have been able to tell, simply by looking, that I had been horribly attacked, mangled and near death only days ago.

Were the old lady's and Selena's healing prowess that successful? It had seemed only yesterday (was it yesterday?) that even they were surprised at my quick recovery. Was this the matter under discussion next door?

Something told me that I should find Pierre and go back to our camp as soon as possible, despite the appeal of having such a wonderful nurse as Selena tend to me. Some porridge and meat were on the table beside the bed and I had started to eat, when without warning, the group entered the room, silently approached the foot of my bed, and unceremoniously stared down at me.

Three men, obviously native to this wetland, were accompanied by Selena's grandmother. Dressed in buckskin and local garb, the oldest man, perhaps a leader or chief, had frizzy gray hair and showed his strength and ageless wisdom all at once, in the many lines of his face. He stood tall and erect, a male equivalent of the old lady. Only one of the others stood out, in my memory, a young brave, younger than I, who only wore pants, his muscular torso and arms proudly evident. His hair braided back, I could sense something skeptical and guarded in his dark eyes as he looked down at me.

The grandmother waved down at me. I was obviously on

display. See for yourselves she seemed to be saying.

The chief spoke first in slow, stilted, but precise French: "You are feeling better?" I nodded a response. He sat down on the bed beside me, his manner friendly, fatherly and kind. Even so, I felt a deep feeling of anxiety growing inside of me.

Selena's grandmother retired to the nearby bench. With a raise of his hand, the chief dismissed the other two. The young brave began to protest, but with another raise of the elder's hand, he fell silent. They left the room and closed the door behind them.

The chief then began his examination of me. "Let me know if it hurts," he warned as he began to prod and poke. His touch was that of a professional, a man of medicine with knowledge of human anatomy. Firm and steady, he felt for any broken bones, swelling, any signs of tenderness. Thorough, it seemed like a pleasant massage from my neck down to my waist. I wondered if he had seen me in my original wounded condition.

"You have been through much. An ordeal that would have left most crippled- or dead." He looked at me questioningly, as if seeking a response. I gave none. He continued pressing deep into my ribs and stomach while speaking. "I am sorry to hear of the deaths of your comrades. You are called Henri?"

"Yes monsieur." His hands stopped their search and I began to relax. Yet something told me to be wary and not reveal too much to this man, however trusting and kind he seemed. He pulled the blanket over me like I was a child he was tucking in for the night. I had only just met the man, but I knew that he must be extremely intelligent and sage. Knowing the French language so well, a man of medicine, he was perhaps a leader of many peoples and not just one tiny village.

He rose and addressed Selena's grandmother in French. For my benefit? Even though he was the definite leader in this arena, his manner toward her was one of the utmost respect and honor. I suspected that they had known each other a long time and even, perhaps, shared some history between them.

"How do you explain such a complete and quick recovery, madame? Solely from your medicines and expertise?"

She replied calmly, even casually about Selena's and her thorough methods of healing. About what medicines and

21

remedies they had used. Of how my wounds, thought at first to be fatal, were not that deep. Yes, I had lost a lot of blood, but no major arteries were severed. The arm and shoulder was reset easily. No bite marks- she seemed to place particular emphasis on this. She then went to some pains to describe my terrible, resultant fever and consequent delirium and explained that I had been greatly hallucinating and babbling- speaking nonsense. What on earth had I said? What did this man, or the others, know? But most of all, why did she deliberately minimize my wounds and what had happened to me?

"Others say that when his friend carried him in here he was near death. Bleeding to death, with very deep wounds. They say that there were...bite marks from some large animal." The others were probably the two men in the outer room, even now listening in on this conversation.

She replied again in her steady, affirming voice. These 'others' had they actually seen the wounds, washed them, dressed them as she and Selena had done? Had they applied the poultices, administered the necessary teas and herbs to reduce the fever? Yes, I had been very sick and yes, my recovery was nothing short of miraculous. But had not the chief, himself, witnessed firsthand, how her medicines do perform miracles? Wasn't she and her cures in great demand all over this area? Did not people travel great distances to see her almost daily?

Her voice grew more firm as she reminded him of how her rituals and magic have protected him and all his people from storm and flood for all these years. Did not her predictions always ring true? She paused in order to particularly emphasize her next sentence. And was it not her, and her abilities, who helped him to become the great leader of many that he is today, a leader respected and loved? She stopped. There was an embarrassing moment of silence. She had made her point. Pierre must be right. She practiced voodoo!

The elderly man bowed his head towards her, respectfully, knowingly, acquiescing to this serene yet powerful woman. "Thank you for allowing me to examine your patient, madame. Your words", here he paused, but I detected the well-hidden chagrin: Selena's grandmother had hit her mark! "They speak a logic I cannot argue with. I am most grateful." He nodded in my direction and then calmly left the room. Selena then appeared, closing the door behind her. She must have been in the other room all this time. She gave me a quick glance, but sat down next to her grandmother and gently took her hand. She had brought with her a bundle which I knew contained some clean clothes for me. We could hear the three men outside as they resumed their discourse in their own language. The voices gradually faded and all we heard was the now steady pleasant patter of rain. A flash of lightning cast a distorted shadow across the open door. The shower was turning into a thunderous downpour.

Silently, Selena walked over to my bedside. Without saying a word she picked up the bowl of porridge and began to spoon feed me. This is ridiculous, I thought, I am quite capable of feeding myself. But I let her proceed anyway. I wanted this- her closeness, her warmth. To experience her compassion, maybe even her love- I believe that she needed this too. We both knew it was time for me to leave. I was alive and well thanks to them and I would never forget her and her grandmother.

But tonight I must go and not knowing when or if I would ever see her again made my heart ache. And I grasped for the first time in my life, what it meant to be in love.

6

Pacing back and forth in the cabin, gathering strength in my legs and body, I kept trying to make sense of what had happened earlier today. I expected Pierre to arrive at any moment and we were to leave together. The rain had stopped and I could smell the wonderful scents of the outdoors. This land was now my home and little things like a rain shower or a sunset made me feel at ease here, part of and one with this unique land.

But I also sensed, from the reactions of the men who had

been to see me, that I was not wanted here. What threat could I possibly pose? Why would they consider me a danger? A curse? I was under no curse. I felt no different than before. In fact, I was feeling stronger than ever, like I had never been sick at all. That probably happens after a severe illness. I felt renewed and energetic, but sad to leave Selena. I smelled her on the clean, fresh clothes she had left for me that I was now wearing.

Darkness was forming quickly. Where was Pierre? But was it preposterous to think that I was a victim of the supernatural? I hated to think of it. I didn't want to think about it anymore. Put it out of my mind and just go on with my life.

However, I did want to think about Selena. I had never met a girl who captivated my thoughts so. Perhaps if I saw her again, I would have the courage to tell her how I felt. Unfortunately, time and events had separated me from all the ones I've loved and now it was happening again. Hope. Hope was all I had sometimes. Hopes and prayers that I would be reunited with those I love and now I could add Selena's name to the list.

There was a brief knock and Pierre entered. "Mon ami, it is good to see you up and about. You look like your old self again. Not like the pale and bloody clump of flesh I brought back here two weeks ago." Sometimes I hated his way with words.

"Thank God," we both whispered together. He slapped me on the back. "Are you ready?"

"Do you have the horses?"

"Yes, with some provisions also. As was all arranged by your lovely Selena." My lovely Selena! "She and her grandmother were most insistent that I take you from here tonight." He looked at me questioningly.

"Silly superstitions that's all. The villagers here are silly and superstitious. They think I may carry some curse of sorts."

"Do you believe so?" He asked me point blank. "Do you...still believe what you said? That a supernatural creature had attacked you?"

"I don't know anymore. I thought on it all day and it seems more and more absurd in the light of day, but now..at night..I don't know. I suppose it could have been my imagination. It had to have been. Perhaps it was a pack of wolves that..." I reached for my clothes bundle, "Let's forget all this and leave. Let's just leave." I slung the bundle over my shoulder, which contained the extra shirts and breeches, shaving razor and mirror that Selena had left earlier, along with the large knife left on the table.

I blew out the lights and we took the lanterns with us. It was a dank darkness outside, the only light coming from nearby cabins and the stars overhead. No moon tonight. And no activity- strange that. No one was roaming about. Just us. There was the faint smell of roasted meat. I wondered what cabin Selena was in. We saddled up quietly and rode through the village, Pierre leading the way.

There were two horses and one pack mule carrying goods, provisions, our guns and mounds of furs and pelts for trading. The horse provided me was a little skittish at first and I had to use a firm hand with it. People say I have a way with horses. They always were a passion of mine, ever since I was a child. One day I hoped to be able to raise and breed them. It could make a good livelihood. We stopped on the village outskirts.

"Are we returning to our old camp?" I asked.

"Non, I have brought everything we own." He glanced back at the mule. "There is a village, about 30 miles from here, where we will be welcome."

"How do you know that?"

"I just know," he replied mysteriously. We resumed our journey.

"Where is Selena?" I suddenly asked.

"Back at the village, I suppose." He looked straight ahead.

"How do you know we will be welcome?" I repeated.

"Selena's grandmother said so." Well that was good enough for me. He looked directly at me. "And besides I've been to where we are going. I visited there once. Settled by French Creoles." Was there a twinkle in his eye? It hit me that he just might know this land and its people even better than I. He could stay out for days hunting and trapping alone with no companions. And always come back with riches of fur, meat and trophies.

Whereas I would usually hunt with others and only occasionally venture out alone. But that was going to change and change dramatically.

"Also, there may be a surprise waiting for you there. Maybe". There definitely was a twinkle in his eye. A surprise? For me? What could..?

"Selena," I whispered.

"Maybe," he whispered back. "Now be quiet, you love struck fool, until we make camp."

Joy again filled my heart. My prayers were to be answered. Perhaps I was traveling not just to a new village, but to a new life. Hope was again my companion.

7

We camped that night about a mile from the village. We had ridden most of the night over a not well-traveled, boggy, muddy road and decided to rest and get a good night's sleep before entering the small town. Of course, I dreamed of Selena: of seeing her again, of her smile at our reunion, of the scent of her rain rinsed hair. My dreams turned erotic as I felt her legs and her warm, expectant moistness.

I woke just before sunrise, realizing that I must be completely on the mend, for my sexual appetite had definitely returned and even seemed more intense than ever.

I stretched, totally comfortable, in my blankets on the soft ground beneath the glorious oaks. Dawn was beautiful here. The tree branches and moss hung low and heavy with moisture from the previous rains. The heady, yet soft scent of nearby swamp flowers drifted by on a breath of a breeze. We had camped under a canopy in one of the oldest oak groves I've ever seen. Spanning majestically over me, they were a magnificent sight, the perfect way to greet the day. Flashes of early sunshine glinted on their leaves; a jungle of trunks, limbs, and roots; some so huge it would take five men, arms outstretched to encircle them. I felt rejuvenated, ready to move ahead, start a new life and hopefully, that would include Selena.

We had a hearty breakfast of meat, potatoes and eggs before leaving. Our destination was a rather remote, yet sizeable village originally settled by French Creoles but which now includes many local natives, plus a good number of settlers from the West Indies (notably Haiti and Martinique) and even some free people of color. It was not far from a fort on a nearby large bayou, which offered the townsfolk some protection and facilitated trade. It would remind me of the many hamlets which surrounded the forts where Pierre and I grew up. Perhaps here I might finally acquire a home- and someday make a family.

Also, make a living. I was sure of that. Pierre spoke of this place as a thriving, profitable wonderland, based upon the natural attributes of this delta-rich earth; excellent for any crop, supplying timber for homes. A paradise providing plentiful hunting for meat and trapping for furs. Riding towards this new place, I felt elated and had completely forgotten that I had been near death only days before.

As we rode into the village, the inhabitants gave us little attention, as if we had lived here always. Maybe we were expected. And I do believe, one or two of the young girls gave Pierre a secret sly smile. I would not doubt if this was where he disappeared to occasionally.

Looking ahead at a distance, I saw her- unmistakably her- standing tall, shapely and stately, near a cabin nestled into a grove of lovely trees. Her regal nature blended in and was part of the majesty around her. She was definitely a child of this unique land. And when she saw us approaching, this nature turned into one of a child, displaying her youthfulness. With undisguised happiness, she rushed to the cabin's door, telling her grandmother (I supposed) of our arrival, and then turned towards us with a sweet, bright smile, accompanied by those huge, shiny, warm eyes that told me immediately that I was not the only one eagerly awaiting this reunion. How I hoped she wanted to see me as much as I wanted to see her. How I hoped she dreamed of me as I had dreamed of her.

As we alighted, she embraced us briefly, giving each a kiss on the cheek, but I savored the moment. Their cabin was on the edge of the village, near the forest, four rooms square, one of the largest in the village and I at first wondered how could they possibly achieve such a place- the two ladies- then I realized it was befitting a person of her grandmother's stature- a doctor, a physician, the healer of the community. One of the extra rooms, I learned later, was actually a sick room, used for patients if they had to be observed carefully. The grandmother appeared as if on cue, in the cabin's front door. Her bearing struck me again. Here was the source of Selena's regality and statuesque beauty. She must be highly regarded here and I silently speculated just how far her reputation extended. It also occurred to me that, even at her great age, she had a sort of immortal beauty and must have been an extremely beautiful woman at one time. But what had happened to Selena's parents?

Tethering the horses and mule outside, I noticed a small vegetable garden next to the cabin, with a small pen behind that, containing goats, pigs and some chickens.

We were graciously led into the house. Before I could ask if this was all theirs, Selena answered, (again as if reading my mind), "Welcome to our home. It was built by my grandpa-pa as his wedding gift to grandma-ma. Our family has lived here ever since. It was here I was born."

Grandmother had sat down at a table in the center of the room. The cabin was furnished sparsely, with the essentials and little else: A huge kitchen cupboard almost covered one wall, a dining table, a few comfortable chairs, a sewing table, etc. However, there was one particular nice piece that commanded the whole room- a French longcase clock against one wall. It dominated with its presence and its soothing, steady sounds of marking time. I had never seen such a lovely clock. Fascinated I studied it carefully- the white dial, the brass decorated pendulum, the curved pine case.

Selena's grandmother spoke up, "That clock was purchased from a traveling salesman by my husband on the very day of Selena's birth. I wind it weekly and it still keeps excellent time to this day. Perhaps it has part of him with it watching over us," she chuckled. "Of course, it has special meaning to us."

"Of course," I replied simply, somewhat startled that she knew I was studying it. She was probably more aware of her surroundings than most sighted people.

"Sit," she politely commanded. We obliged. "I trust you left without incidence?" Pierre answered for us- we had indeed left without incidence, enjoying a most pleasant ride. He thanked her for the horses and provisions. I also thanked them again, for all they had done for me, adding that we will repay them whatever they wish: in money, furs, goods, even labor.

"We can discuss that later. I was merely doing what I always do when someone needs help or becomes sick." She acted as if she had helped me over a cold, instead of rescuing me from the brink of death. Or maybe she does that routinely? An amazing woman, proud but without displaying it as such. I found myself caring for her deeply.

She continued, "There is an empty cabin not far from here, more in the woods than in the village, very private, which the owner has willingly offered to us for however long you and Pierre require."

Selena added, somewhat hesitantly, as if weighing her words carefully, "It is my hope…our wish that you might stay here…in this village." She was looking down at her hands. "And maybe one day you will… call it home."

My wish seemed to be coming true. Was it time to stop roaming, searching each village, every town for our disrupted family? We wouldn't have to give up the search entirely, but we would have a base- a place to call home at last. And begin our family anew. I looked at Pierre. I received a nod. He was ready to stop roaming also. We had discussed finding a home somewhere, but could not decide where or even when. Now it looked like fate had dealt his hand with this offer. (Besides, I think Pierre had another reason to stay nearby and it wore a skirt.)

So it was all agreed to and my future was mapped out that afternoon. Little did I realize that fate had mapped out my destiny earlier when I had been attacked in the woods and left for dead.

The cabin which Pierre and I shared was small, but hospitable with a fireplace in each of its two rooms. It was only 100 paces or so from Selena's home- a short walk, but through dense trees. Furnished only with a table, chairs and cupboard, it was perfect for us. We promptly moved in.

There was one more household item of interest. In one corner stood another longcase clock, similar to the one of Selena's grandmother's, but more modest in appearance, and this one was not working. Upon close examination, the mechanism seemed to be complete, only very dirty and oily with cobwebs intertwined among the gears. It could probably be cleaned and put into running condition with relative ease.

"Perhaps you can fix it," Pierre suggested. He was separating our things and putting everything in order. We had brought in the last of our possessions. "You always were handy with tools and repairing small objects." Indeed, I had repaired much jewelry and pocketwatches, for family and friends back home (making a small side income) and these clocks intrigued me. If I fixed it then I could present the clock to Selena and her grandmother as a gift, after purchasing it from the owner, of course. I might could even make a profitable hobby out of this, if there were other clocks in the town.

But for now, and the next couple of weeks, our concentration turned to our usual means of living- trapping and hunting. However we added farming to this. The cabin's owner had a small plantation where we would contribute a few hours most every day, helping in the fields of sugarcane, corn and cotton. I learned a lot from the village folk about the town and the surrounding land.

One of the first things I did, was sell my share of the furs and buy a few horses for breeding. Pierre helped me build a corral in a clearing near our cabin. It was as if all my desires were finally coming true. And of course, my most cherished desire- to become close to Selena- was also being realized.

Every evening was spent with Selena and her grandmother.

Dinner was a welcome ritual. And usually afterwards, the old lady and I would share a pipe (sometimes Pierre would join us) while Selena did some sewing or some other form of housework. I cannot remember a moment when she was ever idle.

And some evenings I would go with grandmother to visit the ill, her patients that she would see routinely. In this way I was also introduced into the village. The townsfolk were very friendly and welcoming to strangers and it was obvious that everyone held her in high regard and followed her advice without question. She helped mend broken bones, cured chronic coughs and colds, assisted the old and infirm as well as babies and children, brought newborns into this world and helped those who were dying leave without pain or suffering. I admired her more every day, this blind woman who could see more than most.

The village itself was small, but heavily populated- growing with new settlers and profiting from traders constantly coming and going. They had a town square where open markets were held daily, along with the occasional festival or celebration. A church with a proud steeple stood at one end. A dry goods store and blacksmith shop were thriving. Selena's grandmother even introduced Pierre and I to the mayor; a very friendly, talkative, older tall man who (it seemed to me) was rather over-solicitous to the grandmother, doting on her obsessively when we visited his home on the square. He mentioned the village council voted to install a clock in the tower at city hall and asked me if I would tend it. I eagerly accepted, thinking again that yes, I have found my home.

Selena and I would go for long walks in the warm twilight of the long spring days. We held hands, shared modest caresses and kisses, spoke little, but communicated nonetheless. I was falling in love.

For almost two weeks, I felt a joy so profound and powerful that it seemed surreal. Dreamlike. Like all that happened before this time had happened to some other man. I could not imagine having lived without her and I could not foresee a future which she was not part of.

My days began and ended with seeing Selena. I looked

forward to the next day; longing for her look, her touch. I would rise early, eagerly, most days before dawn, bathe in cold spring water, dress and go immediately to see her. She would be up making breakfast and coffee for anyone who cared to come by before going off to their fields or some other work. I would help in my way. Pierre and I had become part of a family again.

It was on one of these mornings when Selena and I first made love. It had been raining steadily all that early morning, not a storm, but one of those magical downpours that cleansed the air and kept the earth damp and fertile with growth, feeding the bayous and basins with that unique life found only in this part of the world.

She was preparing the coffee, when I arrived, and had not yet started the usual breakfast of venison, eggs and flat breads. I greeted her with the usual kiss on her cheek and felt her tender touch on my face as her response. Only this time we were not able to take our eyes off of each other. I had dreamed last night of being intimate with her and the desire was within me still. Perhaps she sensed it or read my mind. We leaned in close to each other and kissed long and deeply. She allowed me to feel her breasts- so soft and young, yet so firm and supple. Her hair, usually pinned up in the fashion of many Creoles and those of African descent, was today, loose and cascaded down her back. Running my fingers through it- long, straight, dark- I pulled her firmly against my chest. She seemed to melt, relaxing in my grasp, at last giving in to her passion. It was something we had both been wanting, needing, since our first meeting. We ran through the rain, holding hands like innocent children, and stopped beneath a centuries old oak some distance from the cabin where we would not be seen. We undressed and laid down under the dry protection of the tree's thick canopy, using our clothes as a blanket over the soft bed of damp earth and fallen leaves. The scent of her mingled with the early morning, heavy with magnolia and sycamore. We made love slowly and wonderfully and, when finished, we kissed and whispered the magic words to each other...

"Je t'aime."

It happened so naturally and so wonderfully that the actual act was, more or less, unnoticed until we were spent. I had climaxed, but do not actually remember the moment. We just held each other close, concentrating on our longing, our loving deep kisses. The sound and scent of the gentle falling rain mixed with our togetherness giving us a sense of a little piece of eternity.

All my previous sexual encounters had been accomplished through drunken hazes in the soiled beds of women who were proficient in such things. Making love with Selena was as different from the others, as night was different than day.

That morning no one got any breakfast.

Every night afterwards, we met secretly at our special trysting place, beneath that old oak, so majestic, whose large limbs spread far and encompassing, looking down upon us young lovers with nature's approval. Sometimes we made love, sometimes we just caressed and kissed. Then kissed some more. Communicating without words, our joy in each other could not be disguised or hidden. Everyone knew we were in love and sometimes grandma-ma would give me the strangest expression that caused me to wonder if she had guessed what Selena and I were doing late at night.

And so, it was time I spoke with her grandmother. To speak of Selena's and my marriage.

"Tomorrow evening?" Selena asked.

"Yes, tomorrow after dinner," I replied. We were holding each other tight not wanting to part, but knowing we must.

She looked deep into my face, questioningly, hesitantly, "You.. you are sure that this is what you wish?"

"Oh yes, my darling," I replied. "Oh yes. I am certain. I want nothing more than you for my wife. Je t'aime."

"Je t'aime." She gently pushed my reluctant self aside and started to walk away. Selena was usually the stronger one when it came to emotions and control. I touched her arm, she turned.

"And you will say yes?" I asked half-jokingly, half with insecurity.

Her smile and her kiss was my answer.

The next evening after dinner, I spoke with Selena's grandmother over our pipe, Pierre and Selena both excusing themselves for one reason or another, I don't remember. But I do remember that the moon was near to full, high in the sky and that I felt extremely nauseated- ever since sunset. I thought at the time that it must be due to my nervousness at broaching such an important subject as her granddaughter's marriage, to this sweet yet formidable lady.

She was the first to speak: "You and Pierre are still joining us at the festival tonight?" I had forgotten about this midnight festival on the bayou. Selena and her grandmother were looking forward to it because it was an annual ritual in this area, (part voodoo, part catholic- very pagan), and was to be officiated by a supposed true-to-life Haitian voodoo queen. "Of course," I squirmed in my seat. "Of course," I repeated.

Her brows arched over a thick plume of smoke released from her pipe. "You wish to ask me something?" She knew. She knew as surely as I sat there. Did she also know about the oak tree and what happened beneath it? I must be careful with my thoughts, for I truly had come to believe in her and Selena's mind reading abilities.

I hesitated. It was hard for me to relax. My stomach was churning with nausea. I felt beads of sweat on my forehead. She looked directly at me in her not so subtle manner, as if trying to discern something deep inside me with those sightless eyes.

"Go ahead, Henri. No need to be formal. You may be yourself with me." She spoke calmly, I suppose trying to make me feel at ease. It only slightly worked.

"I must ask you a thing of some importance."

"Yes?" she encouraged me.

I drew in a large breath. "I would like your permission…and blessing to.." And then the words came flooding out in a torrent like a dam broke and the waters couldn't be held back. "…to marry Selena. I love your granddaughter very much and promise to give her my greatest devotion and lifelong affection."

My words then started to slow and fade, "I promise always . . "

Showing no surprise, she responded by pulling up a small stool beside her chair near the fireplace, where a small fire burned making the room stuffy. My nausea was growing worse. "Sit here," she commanded gently.

I obeyed. She turned to face me, looking deep with those glassy, unseeing eyes. "I know," she said reassuringly, "I know you will take good care of her."

"And you also," I interjected.

Her familiar, throaty broken laugh relaxed me somewhat. She waved her hand. "This is about you and her. I can tell she loves you deeply." She smiled and nodded knowingly. I wondered just how much Selena had confided in her. Had she mentioned our nightly rendezvous beneath that romantic oak? My stomach and head were both taking a dizzy turn.

"I also know you well, Henri LeBlanc, and know you to be an honest, sincere young man whose word is his honor." She paused and, taking my right hand, clasped it with both of hers. "And you have a great strength, though you do not realize it." I had no time to ponder the odd phrasing of that remark, for she continued. "I would be proud to call you my son. You and Selena have my blessing."

My heart leaped with joy. My first instinct was to jump up, embrace her and dance a jig, but she was really not the demonstrative type, so I just leaned over and kissed her gently. "Merci, grandmother," I whispered.

She chuckled again. "So polite, so formal. You remind me of my French husband and the son we had together. Our only child, a beautiful child. And a handsome man." Her face drifted to some unseen place and time. "Selena's father died at an early age, you know, in a hunting accident, before she was born. And then her mother, of French- African descent," she added, "died a few days after the child's birth, from complications. I could not save her." Her loss of those young people showed profoundly, in this usually reticent, woman. I had always thought of her strength and successful abilities. It had never occurred to me that she would know helplessness or doubt of any kind. She turned back towards me, "I have had to be both mother and father to Selena." Pausing, her blind eyes filled with tears. "And now I have a son again."

My heart wept for her. She stood, "You have my blessing," she repeated. I reached for her and she let me embrace her briefly. She pushed me away, wiped away her tears, quick to replace them with a smile and a cheerful countenance. "Go now..my son," she added the last two words definitively. "We must get ready for tonight. Send Selena in please." She sat back down, close to the warm fire, returning to her memories.

I kissed her gently on the cheek and turned to leave. As I was about to exit, she called after me. "And you must now call me grandma-ma, eh?" Again her short but hearty laugh.

"Thank you.. grandma-ma," I replied. "Until tonight."

"Until tonight."

I couldn't look for Selena. The nausea overtook me. I ran behind the cabin and retched. It was more than just nerves, I felt warm and feverish all over. It must be an infection of some kind. I sat down on the ground for a moment, bathing myself in the bright moonlight, and felt decidedly better. If I did not feel well in the morning, I would ask my new grandmother for medicine. For now, I must find Selena and give her the good news and then we were all to meet for the midnight festivities on the bayou. I hoped I would be able to get through it without becoming ill again. Little did I know that this night's significance was just beginning.

10

The annual festival on the nearby bayou was pagan in nature. Pagan being a relative description. Of Haitian origins, it was, essentially, a voodoo ceremony. Its original purpose, being to ward off droughts and floods, plagues and diseases, hurricanes and tornadoes. I heard tales of powerful Haitian voodoo, its roots tied to Africa. Their ceremonies celebrate with an intensity of drums, fire, magic, dancing and of course, spiritual possession. This night was to be particularly special for the most powerful witch queen in the territory was to preside and would personally bless each of those who chose to be. Midnight was to be the moment when the spirits would inhabit the participants.

The night was clear and the moon bright. As soon as I was outside in the moonlight, my skin began to itch all over. It was as if I were on fire. My head throbbed. I literally felt like crawling out of my skin.

I walked by the corral. The horses were very restless that night and seemed to get more nervous and high strung as I approached. They kept running to and fro and would not come near me even though I held out handfuls of grain. Even the mule was skittish.

"Strange," Pierre's voice was behind me. He joined me at the fence.

"How long have they been behaving like that?"

"All night, I believe. Since about sunset."

"I hope they don't try to jump out. In this state they would be hard to retrieve." Not only were they an investment, but I thought of them as pets. "Do you think there is a wild cat around?"

"Perhaps, but I have been walking around and saw no evidence of predators. They will be fine. Are you ready?" I nodded and we walked away, casually, towards the bayou and the festival. We could already see the night sky, glowing in the distance from the light of the bonfire. There was a faint sound of drums.

"So?" Pierre looked at me inquisitively.

"So?"

"Are we to now make plans for a wedding?"

"Oh yes. Of course..yes!" My headache and the terrible itch had temporarily taken my mind off my happiness from earlier this evening. "She is a most remarkable woman."

"Selena's grandmother?"

"Yes, she now calls me her son!"

He slapped me soundly on the back, as was his usual habit, laughing. "Congratulations, mon frere. I am most happy for you." We walked in silence for a few moments. "Do you know anything about this . .uh. .celebration?"

"Not really. But there is supposed to be a special guest of honor. A true to life voodoo queen. Of some renown I hear."

"I hope she is young and beautiful and puts a spell on me." He joked. He did not take any of this seriously, nor did I actually. But our minds were about to be changed.

"I think most of the villagers think of it as mere entertainment Perhaps a blessing for good crops this harvest."

"With my luck she will be an old crone."

"With your luck," I had to laugh. "You have more luck with women than any man I've ever known." The drums were getting louder as we approached.

Suddenly, he turned and asked, "Why are you fidgeting so, Henri?"

"Oh, it must be a rash or something. I itch all over. It's almost unbearable. I want to climb right out of my skin."

"And into what?" he laughed. "Here take some of this before we enter the camp." He produced his usual flask of whiskey from beneath his shirt. "You are just being nervous. A nervous fiance. It is to be expected. This will relax you."

I hoped he was right, but I had my doubts. We toasted my coming marriage. Then we drank again. "Now come on. Let us see what all this excitement is about."

However, instead of relaxing, I grew more apprehensive, which, as we came closer to the crowd, turned into a severe sense of foreboding- a feeling of nearing disaster. I tried to dismiss it, yet it never completely left me.

We entered the camp not quite knowing what to expect. I recognized many from the village, but there were many more from elsewhere and all were sitting around, encircling a gigantic bonfire. The light from the fire cast an eerie scene. Long shadows fell far from the tall, cypress trees, thick with hanging moss. They stood like quiet sentinels, ghostly onlookers. The drums were a constant throbbing in my head.

We joined Selena and grandmother close to a make-shift stage. Grandmother was one of the few who actually had a chair. Most everyone else was sitting on the ground or standing. Selena and I kissed and embraced. Grandma received a kiss on the cheek from both Pierre and I. "Selena, what is this for?" I nodded towards the platform.

"It is for the ceremony. For the one presiding tonight. A well known healer, with great knowledge in the ways of voodoo. She was born in the West Indies." She looked around conspiratorially and then whispered in my ear, "It is said that she can raise the dead." She seemed serious. But my startled look must have been comical, for she laughed. That sweet laugh full of charm and grace, similar to the wonderful sound of a tiny wind chime. I was glad to see that she was not so serious about all this- zombies and spells and witchcraft.

Grandma-ma smiled at me, "I am glad you came, my son." The sound of that made me feel so welcome, so at home at last. Selena was literally beaming, her cafe-au-lait complexion glowing in the firelight. She seemed to become more beautiful to me everyday. The more intimately I knew her, the more I had to have her, like a drug.

The crowd was all adults. Pierre and I waved and nodded at a few faces which we recognized. There was a lovely young woman, very dark complexioned, dressed in a colorful robe and headdress (as I imagined African women would wear), going around the crowd, and pouring a beverage out to most everyone. As she approached us, Selena produced some cups for Pierre, herself and I. Grandmother was obviously not going to imbibe. It did cross my mind if it was wise for me to drink in my feverish condition. The girl poured Pierre and I each a healthy portion. Selena had only a sip or two. The drink was a potent alcoholic brew of herbs and flavors I could not recognize. Pierre shrugged and drank his down with a gulp. I looked at Selena and she nodded reassuringly. I drank the bitter concoction down and it had an almost immediate effect on me. My head cleared and the mysterious itching started to slowly subside. It left me wanting more.

The drums grew very boisterous and then the queen made her entrance, stepping onto the stage without ceremony. She turned and stood impressively, overlooking the crowd. She was also dressed in many colors of greens, reds and golds, but more elaborately than the young girl, more elegantly. Indicative, I suppose, of her status. Her headdress was folded into a fan shape, gold fabric encrusted with green jewels, shimmering and sparkling in the fire's glow. She was quite tall and moved with such grace that it reminded me of Selena's grandmother and her royal demeanor. She was very dark with large facial features, beautiful and seductive. There were two others, one male and one female, who had come in with her and stood beside her on the stage, one on either side of her. They moved as if in their sleep- no expressions, no unnecessary movements.

They were both beautiful in their respective ways. The shirtless large torsoed man, with dark oiled skin, was very muscular; the girl- young and petite- was light-skinned and had a very curvaceous figure with a rather mature bosom for such a small child. They appeared to not take notice of their surroundings, the crowd or bonfire. They just stared straight ahead, not seeing, not comprehending, their eyes not even blinking. Tres bizarre, I thought. Most probably a drug induced state. The zombies Selena had previously mentioned.

I noticed there were now two girls passing out more of that potent drink. Pierre and I drank more. It stung my throat severely.

The Queen tapped the wooden stage a few times, loudly, with a large golden cane or stick that she carried like a magic staff. The drums suddenly stopped. There was a silent, pregnant pause, then she tapped the floor twice more and the drumming resumed, but this time much faster, in a frenzied manner. The two held in a trance suddenly came alive, sprang from the stage and began dancing, separately, in a frenzy too, but with a compelling coherent manner that amazingly matched the rhythm of the drums. As the drumming increased in speed and volume, their movements also grew faster and more inhumanly intense. Gyrating, almost convulsively, they turned and pivoted defying gravity, springing and leaping. Their heads circled wildly, their bodies twisted and contorted into impossible positions. The girl bent herself backwards, touching her head to her feet as if she had no spine. The man had fallen to the ground and, squirming around, his arms close to his body, he actually began to slither about like a snake.

I thought I must be hallucinating for this was not possible. My vision was becoming blurry. I felt faint. The nausea was returning. It seemed as if the two dancers had changed shapes, had actually become animals, snakes slithering around the bonfire. I was astounded. The crowd seemed not to react. Had they seen something like this before? I looked at Pierre- his look- dumbfounded, mouth agape. I looked at Selena, but she appeared calm as always, in her usual self-contained way.

The drumming had become steadily louder, so that now it was deafening. It must be filling the woods for miles. The high priestess opened a basket on the stage that I had not noticed before and produced a huge giant snake. A python longer than any alligator I've ever seen, thick as a man's waist! The little girl easily, expertly, took it from her- the enormous snake making her seem that much more diminutive. She danced with it. It coiled itself around her, surrounding her, engulfing her. I thought someone should stop the ceremony for surely the creature would crush her, yet no one moved. No one even reacted.

She fell to the ground, the snake encircling her, writhing about her. They seemed to be one. She rose and fell and rose yet again, still moving in that primitive, unique dance synchronized with those insistent, incessant drums. She disappeared on the other side of the bonfire.

I took a sip of the beverage I had left. It was full. When had they replenished it? I drank it down even though I knew I shouldn't. My head was spinning. The night was extremely humid and, combined with the heat from the fire, caused me to perspire uncomfortably.

Suddenly the man-snake was right in front of us, arching his back and neck like a cobra ready to strike. He was so close I could have reached out, touching him. His eyes were no longer human, but had the look of a reptile- cold-blooded, deadly, hungry, inhuman. I had seen the same eyes in the alligators that Pierre and I trapped. His mouth opened and a forked tongue whipped out quickly, shockingly! I wanted to recoil, look away, step back, but I could not move. I was frozen like all the other onlookers. Mesmerized.

Then the fire expanded and grew higher, more intense, like in an explosion. The man-snake had disappeared, but I saw that the girl had danced back around to our side of the fire, the snake still upon her, when suddenly she leaped into the fire! I could hear the tumble of the wood as it caved in upon itself.

Was that the wind? I heard one long wail, not quite a scream, more of a sad mournful sound that rose hauntingly with the fire. And remarkably again, no one reacted. No screams, no anxious faces full of shock. Just that long wail on the wind. Surely she was dying. Perhaps I should do something. But what? It was too late. She did not come out of the fire.

What was this barbaric ritual? I had heard of such sacrifices and shape-shifting ceremonies occurring on the islands where voodoo is basically a religion, but I never dreamed I would be witness to it. And was it...real? What I saw? Or thought I saw?

I shook my head to clear it. The drums were now softer, the fire had diminished greatly. My vision was clearing. Had I missed something? I felt like I had just woken up out of a deep sleep. Or maybe a trance. The high priestess had descended and was going around the circle, spreading her blessings and gris-gris, carrying her staff of gold while a young boy went ahead of her swinging a small pot of burning incense which emitted a great deal of sweet smoke.

I looked towards Selena and then Pierre. They simply smiled back. Had they not just seen what I had seen? I must have been hallucinating from the drink. Then I saw the young girl and the man. They were alive! Back on the stage, standing erect and silent: a pair of statues resembling some unknown Haitian gods. They appeared unharmed. She had not thrown herself into the fire! He was as himself again! They looked as I had first seen them: barely breathing, staring straight ahead, looking into nothingness. I gleamed just the barest amount of perspiration on their faces, otherwise I would have never guessed they had actually moved or danced. They did seem truly catatonic, zombie-like.

Could the dead be made to walk again? Oh what was I thinking? The dead cannot be brought back. But that might would explain the events that I had seen here tonight... I needed a good night's sleep. The fever and nausea was returning. My skin was itching and crawling again and felt literally as if it had a life of its own.

I started to turn to Selena and tell her I was not feeling well and I needed to go home when something distracted my attention. I noticed a tall man on the other side of the stage, standing behind and over a small group of people. He was unmistakably staring intently at us... at me! We caught each other's gaze and he seemed at once, extremely familiar, though I could not place where I had seen him before. Perhaps he was a townsperson or plantation owner I had met on my rounds with grandma-ma. But there was something disturbing about him and his rather intense, even sinister stare. He was a strong, young man with a thick, black mane of hair under a hunter's hat, dressed all in black. He mounted his horse smoothly, nonchalantly, never taking his eyes away from mine as he rode slowly around to our side of the stage.

It felt like he was trying to communicate with me, that he knew me, and knew me well. I tried to look away but could not. It seemed as if he were casting a spell over me. Was he another witch or conjurer come for the ceremony? What would he want with me?

He rode close enough for me to look directly into his eyes and I realized I had seen him before. Those eyes- I had seen before! They were the same set of deep blue eyes, penetrating into my very soul. It was the beast's eyes which I saw! It is he! The Beast has come to haunt me in human form!

With a great deal of effort, I managed to turn away from his glare and when I had the courage to look back, he was gone. Surely this was even more of my imagination playing tricks on me. Tonight had been full of tricks. Voodoo tricks that were not real. That man could not possibly be the same beast which attacked me and killed all those hunters.

I had to leave and lie down. My mind was as sick as my body. I looked at Selena and the others. They seemed not to have seen the man. They were watching, waiting for the voodoo priestess approaching us. Instinctively , grandmother rose from her chair and they greeted each other. She blessed both her and Selena with shakes of gris-gris powder over their shoulders and a cross of ash on their foreheads. Then she turned to Pierre and myself.

She blessed Pierre in the same manner. But she hesitated before me. Her eyes were a startlingly ghostly gray, and she appeared to be very young, but I somehow knew that she was much older. She stared at me silently, intently, searchingly;

then, suddenly she took a step backwards, alarm in her face. She was not exactly frightened (nothing could probably frighten this woman) but she must have seen something in my face that startled her or surprised her. She quickly gathered her regal composure together, before anyone could notice, and reached for my forehead to place the ash with her left thumb.

The intense burning sensation was immediate, just as if she had put a lit cigar against me. I fell to my knees. The priestess quickly turned to grandmother, mumbled something in their French patois, handed the elderly one something from the gris-gris pouch and left. As she passed the stage, her two sleep walking companions instinctively followed, still in their catatonic state.

My forehead burned intensely where she had touched me and it traveled all through my body, racking me with pain. My fever returned tenfold and I knew I was about to vomit. Selena and Pierre held onto me, looking with questioning concern.

"I must go before I faint," was all I could say. I jumped up and ran out of the camp and towards our cabin, stopping only long enough to retch. That sour drink taste in my mouth, burned my throat. My head swooned. I stumbled through the woods on the way back. Just when I thought I would collapse, I found myself home. The moon was shining full and bright. For those few moments, bathed in the moonlight, I felt better. The fever was lifting. Strange to recover so quickly. I still needed to lie down and sleep.

Though first I went to the corral to see about the horses. I don't know why I did, I just did. Perhaps it was the noise they were making. I found them in a terribly nervous state. Entering the corral, I tried to calm them, pet and talk to them as was my custom, but they ran from me, bolting. They were scared of something and would not let me near. One jumped the fence, another tried to stomp me beneath his hoofs, as if in defense or attack. The mule was braying in fear. I heard a howling, loud and close by.

My vision became blurry, but I definitely remember seeing lots of blood, feeling warm blood on my person, tasting blood. I then, must have blacked out; my last memory being that of the full moon above me, peering from behind a storm cloud.

I awoke early the next morning, sore and tired as if I had had no sleep. Gradually I realized, with slowly building horror, that blood was all over my sheets and my clothes were bloody and torn. I checked for wounds, but there were none. The memory of the beast's attack flooded my thoughts. But this was different. This blood was not mine. What had happened last night and why did I have no recollection of it?

I slowly rose and went outside to wash off the mess, hoping that nothing severe had happened. I was at the rain barrel washing my face, when I heard a noise over by the corral. I walked over. It was Pierre. He was standing perfectly still, staring into the pen. I followed his gaze.

There they lie. The horses were dead, each horribly mangled, bodies tore apart, intestines strewn, throats gashed. I stared in disbelief. My investments...even more so, my friends were dead. What could have done such a thing? Only an animal of immense size and strength could accomplish this abomination.

Pierre was looking up and down at me. His eyes wide with alarm. He was noticing the blood on me from head to foot. My hair was coated thick with clotted blood; my fingernails dirty with it. Slowly he spoke: "What happened?...Henri!...What have you done?"

12

"It was the beast I tell you!" We were inside the cabin, I had washed myself of the blood and was changing into clean clothes. "Why would I do such a thing? Destroy the very things I love? My livelihood." I paused, "Besides I haven't the capability, mentally or physically."

Pierre took the clothes outside to be burned. I followed,

trying not to gaze over at the carnage in the corral. It was still very early in the morning. "How do you explain this?" he asked.

"I cannot. The beast! Of course, it was he. Or a...a pack of wolves." My statement sounded more like a question.

"There are no wolves, Henri!" Pierre replied emphatically while making sure each strip of clothing was being torched. He looked up directly at me. "The others and I have been searching the woods and swamps for days now and there is no evidence of any wolves. Coyotes yes, foxes yes, wolves..no." He returned to his chore. I felt weak, my mind foggy, perhaps from the grog last night. I paced back and forth, never feeling so bewildered before. Helpless, like the time when we were expelled from our homeland. "We must bury them."

"What? Oh yes, of course." A grizzly chore, but even in my dazed state I realized no one must see or know of what had happened. And I must be particularly careful to hide this from Selena.

"Quick then, grab a shovel. We will simply say something frightened them and they bolted. We can knock down some of the railings as evidence." Pierre was always so level-headed. And thorough.

We worked in silence for a long while. Far into the woods we dug a pit, so very deep no wild animal or hound from the village would bother them. Carrying the torn carcasses was a ghastly job. Pierre covered his nose and mouth with a bandana because of the stench. I did the same, yet strangely the smell did not offend me so much.

"What was the last thing you remember?" Pierre asked while we labored.

"The horses," was my simple reply.

He stopped for a moment, looking at me. "The horses?" he asked, returning to the task at hand.

"Yes. I remember returning from the ceremony, sick. I heard them racing about. They were terribly frightened of some thing. Much worse than earlier in the evening. Remember?" He nodded. "I went in to calm them, but they would not be stilled. One tried to trample me beneath him."

Pierre did not look up. "You did not see what frightened them?" He paused. "Were they frightened of ...You?"

"Perhaps...Of course not!..I don't know," I exclaimed. "The beast must be back. He had to have done this. The horses must have sensed his presence."

"He?"

"What?"

Pierre looked up from his filthy labours. "He. You referred to the creature as he." Silence followed. For I did not reply, but then he did not expect one. We both knew we were beginning to believe the unbelievable.

We returned to the task at hand, working fast. I wanted to finish before someone came by. Before Selena came to see why I had not been by this morning; to see if I was alright after last night's illness.

As we were finishing up and filling in the pit, Pierre again spoke. "But why only the horses? Why leave the mule untouched? And the chickens and pigs? They are unharmed and are far easier targets."

I had not realized, until then, the complete mystery. Why had our prize horses been killed- selected as it were for death? Leaving the other livestock alone?

We finished quickly and ran the entire way back. The next chore was to clean up the corral. It was soaked with blood and entrails. We turned over the earth, mixing the evidence with mud and manure. The morning was quickly becoming midday. We hurried in our task, knowing that at any moment we could be discovered. Our clothes needed changing- we were covered in blood and dirt and muddy manure and I longed for a hot bath.

We left the shovels behind the cabin and walked around to the front. We saw Selena at a distance, walking on the trail towards our cabin. Pierre quietly whispered to me, "Be careful what you say..and think."

"I'll say we were dressing some deer."

"Good. I'll be changing." He went inside the cabin, leaving his muddy shoes by the doorsteps.

As she neared, she stopped and looked me up and down, her face posing a question. But before she spoke, I answered her thought, "We were skinning some deer." I thought of kissing her as usual, but I was a filthy stench. I hoped for once, she would not try to read my mind.

"I did not know that could be so disgusting a task." She wrinkled up her nose at my sight and smell.

"Not usually- I slipped and fell." I laughed, trying to be convincing. She smiled back.

"Yes," Pierre interjected, shouting out from the cabin. "We shall have plenty of venison tonight."

"Good," she called back. "I will look forward to cooking it. I'll make a gumbo to go with it. We can have a small feast." She turned back to me with a look of concern. I tried to close my mind to her. I thought of our lovemaking, our future happiness.

She smiled again. "I wanted to make sure you had recovered from last night. You were so sick." A pause. "Do you need anything? You are feeling better?"

"Oh yes, very much." I replied. "Like it had never happened."

"Strange," she said.

"Yes, I know. I rose early and felt fine," I hesitated. She was looking past me at the corral. Pierre appeared in clean clothes at the doorway.

"Henri, where are your horses? Have you taken them some...where?"

I was about to reply but Pierre spoke up quickly, "They apparently tore down the fence and ran away. We searched the woods all morning, but there was no sign of them. The rain last night washed away all tracks."

"We are most distressed over it," I replied dejectedly. "They were not only an expensive investment, they were becoming like pets to me."

"I know," her warm, soothing smile was like sunshine. "I could tell something was bothering you. Perhaps they will return." She thought for a moment. "They must have been very frightened. What do you suppose could have happened?"

Pierre again spoke, "A snake..or maybe an alligator. Remember Henri, that alligator that tried to get into the hen house last week."

"Yes..yes," was all I could bring myself to say.

"That is most sad. Poor Henri," she kissed me lightly on the cheek, being careful not to touch my dirty self. "Then I will see you both this evening?"

"Yes," we both responded. She began to walk away, then

turned and added as if an afterthought: "And the mule is still there." She shrugged and continued back down the path.

Pierre and I breathed a collective sigh of relief. He came up beside me, "And now my dear cousin, you had better clean up. We have some hunting to do. Pray we will find the deer that you have already shot!" We both laughed. He was most definitely the best friend and confidante I could ever wish for.

13

Early that evening, over our meal, the conversation invariably turned to last night and the festival. "But what was that drink? It was most potent." I asked.

"Supposedly, a magical concoction, from herbs and fermented mushrooms mixed with alcohol which, when consumed in sufficient quantity will reveal a person's true inner self," Selena answered. "It lowers the barriers we present to the outside world."

"I'll stick with my ordinary, simple good ole whiskey," Pierre patted his pocket containing his well known flask. We all laughed.

"What else did you think of the ceremony?" Grandma asked me directly. She seemed to have been observing me all during dinner, staring right at me with her blind eyes.

"I do not know what to think. I thought…at one point…that the man actually turned into a huge snake, . . . and that the girl deliberately danced into the fire and was consumed." I lowered my voice, "But that is impossible, n'est-ce pas? What really happened? It had to have been an hallucination brought on by the drugged drink, right?"

Grandma-ma's reply was very serious but confusing to me. "A man's mind can make him believe many things, even the supposed impossible. The man's mind made him believe he was a giant python and so he became as if he were a giant python."

I didn't understand. I was truly out of my element. I looked from grandma-ma to Selena to Pierre. They stared down at their plates, pretending interest in their meal, avoiding my gaze. They both knew something more that they were not telling me. I suddenly felt sick at my stomach again. I had eaten too much meat. It had been so good, bloody and rare, the way I had come to like it.

Grandma continued speaking slowly and steadily, trying to make her point. "Yes my son, many men have a beast deep within that, when certain conditions are met, the beast is released and the human side disappears temporarily."

"But I thought you said it was all in the mind!" My voice raised a pitch.

"And the mind is most powerful. If it believes strong enough then anything can happen."

"And a man become a beast? Legends, myths!" I didn't like the direction this discussion was going. It made me increasingly uncomfortable. Physically also. It was becoming very warm inside their stuffy cabin. We needed to change the subject. Perhaps speak of our coming wedding, anything but this. "With all due respect grandma-ma, I for one do not believe in witchcraft and voodoo. It's not rational. Let us talk of..."

"Show him Selena," she interrupted me. "Show what the priestess gave us for protection."

Protection? I was dumbfounded. Protection from what? From whom? It was then I noticed the silver charm hanging around Selena's neck. She unlocked the clasp and taking it off, showed it to me. It was a five-pointed star.

"It is called a pentagram." I instinctively reached for it, but it scorched me at the barest touch, hot as a live coal. I dropped it quickly. My head started to reel. I thought I might fall out of my chair. The puzzled look on my face was surely comical. I noticed Pierre had produced his favorite companion- his flask and he was taking large gulps from it. Not usual at the dinner table even for him.

"What is happening to me, Selena..Grandma-ma?" I sobbed. I was getting sicker by the minute. I held my head in my hands, still burning from the powerful charm. "What are you saying? Speak plainly please!"

50

Selena put her arm around me, caressing my head and hair, trying to calm me.

Grandma was the only one strong enough to speak, her voice quiet, calm, but frank: "We are saying that we believe," She took a deep breath before continuing. "That you were bitten by a werewolf and since you survived....that you may now carry the same curse within yourself!"

What an astounding thing to say! Yet my very first immediate thought as she said this, was my memory of that strange man at the ceremony. The man I thought I knew. Who seemed to know me! The man with those same blue eyes that haunt my dreams still. The same eyes as the beast! The beast they all apparently thought was a werewolf.

I suddenly jerked my head up. What was that noise? A howl. He was calling for me? No it was nothing. I must be going mad I thought to myself. "It's not possible! It can't be. I cannot be like-- That! It's not possible..not possible." I repeated the words trying to convince myself even more than them. I felt that I was about to vomit, I was so nauseated. Selena held me close. Pierre drank some more. Grandma was her stoic self.

"I am sorry my son, but if it is true, tonight when the moon is full, you will turn.."

"NO! NO!" I screamed and jumped up out of my chair. "It isn't true. I am just sick..just sick and weary."

"We think we can control it..if you let us," pleaded grandma-ma. "Please." Selena added. I turned and abruptly dashed outside, Selena and Pierre calling out after me.

I ran far and fast, in no particular direction, just away from that stifling cabin. Fresh air was what I needed. Fresh air and moonlight. No, not moonlight! I tried to stay in the shadows even though when the moonlight bathed me, I felt immediately better, less sick. All I needed was a good night's sleep. And not to dream- of wolves, or of horses, or voodoo queens- nor of strange men with blue eyes.

Somehow, unconsciously, I found myself back at our cabin. The strange itching was again upon me. It was even worse than before- if that were possible. I felt like literally peeling off my skin as if it were clothing. I laid down on my bed, trying to calm my thoughts. I loved Selena's grandmother but she was superstitious. They held wrong, silly ideas. To think that I was a victim of the curse of a werewolf was beyond reason, beyond nature! I was just feverish, needed rest, restful sleep. And dream of something pleasant, something beautiful. Dream of Selena. Or of nothingness. Emptiness. Empty dreams would be just fine.

14

But my dreams that night were nothing if not empty; neither were they of Selena nor were they of a peaceful nature. Tossing and turning, I drenched the sheets with my sweat. I dreamt that I had traveled (walked, ran?) quite rapidly in a short period of time and now was on some bayou, unknown to me, a great distance from the village. I was alone- solitary, looking- hunting for something or someone. I foraged through woods, waded through swamps, in those wetlands that usually make me feel so at home, so comfortable. However, in this dream I was excitable, searching endlessly; and all the while with an odd unaccountable hunger. Then I saw a small light out on the water- a lone man was in his pirogue, night fishing under a full moon. I noticed he became startled at something, began thrashing his oar about in the air attempting to hit some thing, trying to fend off some attack. I saw his face up close. A face of fear- a terrible shock of fear that must have reached down into his soul. Whatever horrific sight he saw was obviously wanting to hurt him, perhaps kill him, yet I could not see the culprit. He reached for a gun. I heard his screams, his shouts for help, but I could do nothing for him- only watch helplessly. I heard his neck snap, his back break. His eyes became dark and wide, frozen dead in fear. Haunting my dream, I looked down and his chest had been split wide open by some great force- ribs and flesh separated in two. I noticed I held something in my hands. It was warm and wet and throbbing. It was a human heart!

I awoke with a start. It was dawn. Birds outside my window were chattering at nothing in particular. A neighboring rooster crowed. My head ached, my limbs sore as if I had not slept again last night.

I put my hand to my head and felt something wet. I looked at my hand- blood! I realized I was only clothed in bloody soaked trousers, my feet bare and muddy. Partially dried sticky blood was on my hands, under my nails, covering my chest. I felt its thickness in my beard. Not again, I prayed. Mon Dieu, not again, please!

How could this be happening? I've been in bed, here all night. Or had I? Some dream, some slight memory hit my senses with alarm- a dream of a full moon and a long journey with a frightened fisherman at the end of it.

Reality hit hard. Oh precious God! I couldn't be the monster that they are thinking of. I would never kill anyone in cold blood. I wanted to cry, I was so confused, so alone. I could not hold back. The tears flowed unleashed, and I was like a scared child. If I were this creature, how could I deal with the guilt of having killed an innocent man; knowing the anguish he must have felt?

After some minutes, I recovered myself sufficiently enough to struggle out of bed, to bath and clean up. I changed the sheets yet again, burning the bloody, dirty ones. I laid down and tried to calm my thoughts.

Perhaps Selena and grandma-ma did know a way out of this. A cure maybe? If I was…that way. If I was responsible for these horrible actions. Why could I not remember? Was my mind deliberately blocking the memory of the last two nights? Memories too violent and foul that to recall them would make one go mad? Grandma said a man's mind could make him do anything- Become anything.

What would drive me to this? I was raised a good man who believed in God. Who believed in right and wrong, in good and evil. In evil. Was there something deep inside myself that was murderous? Did all men have this, that with a certain key it could be unleashed? I thought I might go insane, dwelling on the horrible possibilities.

There was a soft knock on my bedroom door and Pierre cautiously peeked inside the room. "Come in. I'm awake."

He came in quietly, approaching slowly over to me, not saying a word. There was a strange look in his face I had never seen before. Apprehension? fear? bewilderment? No none of these things..or perhaps all of them? He peered at me as if studying me. To see if I was a stranger; someone he thought he knew, but who turned out to be someone else. "I looked in on you earlier, before you woke."

That explained his manner. "Then you saw..."

"Yes," he sat in a chair near me. "Henri," he continued slowly, cautiously. "Where were you last night? Can you explain the blood?"

"I don't know. I had a nightmare. I guess I went outside," I hesitated. "I am positive I was in bed most of the night asleep."

"Non. When I came home from dinner you were gone and I waited up almost all night. You must have returned only towards dawn after I had gone on to sleep."

"Nonsense. You fell asleep and did not know I had returned."

"No Henri. I waited in this very chair until five this morning. You only just came back around sunrise." I didn't know how to respond. Gone all night with no recollection? What could I say? I must have been sleepwalking. That would explain the muddy feet, the tiredness. But where did the blood come from? "Henri," he weighed his words carefully, "do you remember anything of last night? Where you might have gone? What you might have done?"

The nightmare suddenly presented itself to me vividly. Maybe I had been out all night. Perhaps I had seen that fisherman, witnessed the attack on him; witnessed his murder. "I do remember something in a nightmare." Pierre leaned forward listening intently. Do I tell him everything I dreamed or imagined? I had to.

I began with how it seemed like I had traveled for miles and miles, quickly, like I was riding on the wind, but I was on foot. I came to a large bayou, a place I had never seen before, wide and deep like a river. I told him how I could see everything clearly as if it were high noon and bathed in sunlight, though I

54

knew that it was nighttime. I saw and felt the moon. On one side of the bayou was a large marsh surrounded with wild swamp cypress. Here I spotted a lone man in his fishing boat. Then suddenly, unexpectedly, I saw his face up close, and he was frightened of something. Scared for his life. The next thing I remember, was him lying dead in the boat, with a huge, open wound to his chest. "That's when I woke up. Here," I emphasized. "What do you think Pierre? What happened to me last night?"

Pierre got up and started walking, pacing to and fro in the small bedroom. He only did this when he was nervous. Or when he had something important to say. "Henri, I do not know what happened to you, but I must tell you this." Raising myself up in the bed, I somehow knew his news would be distressful. "There was a man, killed last night. A fisherman. He died violently with a strange deep, open wound to his chest." He stopped pacing, but only for a moment. "Much as you described."

I was dumbfounded, "Where?"

"Over 100 or so miles from here. Not far from the coast." He added, "Bad news travels fast, especially..."

"But I couldn't travel that far in one night..on foot!" I snorted.

"No one said you did." He shrugged. Neither of us knew what to say. He was the first to break the uncomfortable silence. "It is said that they found large wolf tracks near the scene."

"But you said there were no wolves here."

He stopped pacing and sat back down looking at me closely. "The talk is that the tracks were not four-legged. It walked upright!"

"Oh My God!" I jumped up. "That can't be true. Rumors. Superstitions. Like you said just talk." I was the one pacing back and forth now.

"How can you say that after all that has happened? After all that has happened to you?" I avoided his gaze. "The men in the hunting party torn to shreds. The attack on you. Our dead horses and now this." I sat back down and held my head in my hands. He continued, "Henri, you know that I am not a super-stitious man, given to fairy tales. But there is only one explanation. There is a beast out there. Something. It could be a werewolf."

55

"Then we must find it and kill it, before it does harm again!"

"Yes, but..." He started to pace again. "..there is one thing we must do first."

"What? What Pierre? Just say it." I think I was yelling. He sat down on the bed beside me. "You think like Selena and her grandmother. You all think I am under some curse and change into...when the moon is full! Don't you?"

He sighed heavily. "Yes Henri, we are all in agreement. We..can offer no other explanation to the strange events surrounding us."

I could not refute him. I had to admit what I was, what I had become. Fate held me in her hands and she had cursed me. Just when I had found the girl of my dreams, fallen in love and planned for a new life in a pleasant place, I find myself in this dire situation. My world was falling apart and I could do nothing about it.

The truth dawned. It closed in upon me with suffocating reality. I was no longer like other men!

I felt insanity looming behind me; lunacy touching my shoulder. Pierre's voice droned on as I sat in stunned silence. "We will all face this together, Henri. Selena's grandmother knows..much magic. Perhaps ways to combat this. To change you. Or to keep you from changing, I don't know. All I do know is that I am your friend and we can fight this thing. You are not alone in this." He looked at me with deep concern, more emotion than he had ever showed me before. But I could say nothing. Feeling so stunned, I was unable to respond in any form. All I could do was stare straight ahead.

He rose. "I have to go now and do some work. We must act in a normal manner. Like we suspect..nothing." He bent down and whispered close to me. "We need to be very careful, Henri. To keep all this secret. No one must even hint about what has happened to you." I looked up at him. The bewilderment, I'm sure, showed in my eyes. I turned my face from him. He patted me on the shoulder, very different than his usual good-hearted slap. I was not the only one who has been changed.

He stopped at the door, "Selena and grandma-ma will be back late this afternoon. I shall return long before sunset. I suggest you just stay inside, rest and..recuperate. Try and get some sleep. Be assured, mon frere, they will know what to do. How to combat this." I gave no response. "Henri, do you hear me?"

I nodded. He left closing the door behind him, leaving me alone with my thoughts. Thoughts that this could not be happening, not to me. It wasn't real; it was..unfathomable. Yet I knew, deep in my soul, that I had indeed, become victim of a horrible curse. Something that I previously believed only existed in books and myths. I found myself longing for a simpler time in my youth, in that cooler clime, when problems were seemingly nonexistent and life less complicated. When there was innocence.

And so, I must face the facts, no matter how strange. I transform into a creature when there is a full moon. Half-man, half-wolf that..that preys on people? How could I live with myself knowing that I might kill, that I may already have killed? If I could destroy the horses, that I loved so much, then all those around me whom I cared about would also be in danger. What could I do? If only I was able to control it. It seemed to control me, leaving me with no recollection of my acts. What could anyone do? What could grandma-ma do? This was surely beyond her capabilities.

I began to think of death. That seemed to be the only answer. The only way to put a stop to this. Either a miracle must happen or death itself: my only alternatives. My mind was going in so many directions at once. Madness showed his shadow.

What was I? Human or inhuman? I felt very human-vulnerable, emotional.

Be still Henri, stay strong, I told myself. I breathed slowly, regularly in order to calm down. What has been done can be undone. A curse put on can surely be removed. If such an evil can occur, then a miracle can also. If it turned out that I was as they thought I was, then ..I will deal with it rationally and with as much dignity as I could summon.

But this one thing I realized, that I knew implacably. If I were an evil beast, an uncontrollable, untamable demon, then I would leave or even take that one final, irreversible act, for I could not possibly live that way, nor expect Selena and the others to live with someone like me. I must do what I must do,

I laid down and buried my head in my pillow and sobbed, letting the scared little boy out again.

16

That day I neither ate nor drank nor slept. The riches and fortunes that I had seen in my future were now but a pipe dream. Dissipating into thin air like grandma's puffs of smoke. What lay ahead looked bleak and unpromising. I was terrified, not knowing what was to become of me, and how this would resolve itself.

That afternoon I rose for the first time since Pierre had left. I must at least show Selena that I was going to try...to try to cope with reality. Show some sign of strength for her sake. Pierre seemed to think that they have a plan or idea about this curse. I would trust their judgment and put myself in their hands..and God's. But if all else fails I knew what I must do. To protect everyone. Everyone that I loved.

They showed up as expected. Selena had a look of worry on her face, though she tried to hide it. We embraced and kissed a little more passionately than was proper in front of her grandmother. She rubbed her body against mine and my desire sprang to life, which totally surprised me, for I had not had any sexual thoughts in what seemed like days.

Embarrassed, I gently pulled her from me and we all sat down at the table. I did not know what to say or how to begin. Thank God grandma-ma spoke first.

"How are you? Did you get some sleep today?"

"Yes, grandma-ma," my first lie.

Selena interjected, unable to hold back, "Did Pierre speak with you? Mention to you what we think has...," looking down at her hands, her voice grew small, "happened to you?" Grandma put her hand over Selena's, not merely to calm her, but to quiet her. The old one was to do the speaking.

"First of all my son, remember, that this has happened

through no fault of your own. Do not blame yourself. We know that you are a good, caring man. You are not the first for this to happen to. The curse of the werewolf is old and more ancient than humankind itself."

"So you think it true. That I am..that way?" I could not find the right words.

"We will know after the moon rises."

"What do you intend for us to do?"

"Mostly observe. Watch you, your reactions."

"But isn't that dangerous for all of you?" I glanced over at Selena.

"I think we can.. 'trap' the curse."

"Trap, but not eliminate." I was not able to disguise my pessimism.

"One step at a time. It is more difficult to remove a curse than to place one, but I assure you it can be done."

There was silence for a moment. Dare I hope to be normal again? "You said my reactions?" She nodded. "Like my reaction to silver?" I noticed Selena was wearing the pentagram necklace. For protection- protection from me!

"Yes, all your reactions throughout the night. Tonight the moon is not quite so full as it has been. It is starting to wane."

"And so its power over me is..?"

"Less? Yes, most probably," was her answer. She relaxed into her chair, smiled warmly and changed the subject. "Have you been outside today? Been into the village?"

"Yes," my second lie. I don't think she believed me.

"Why don't you and Selena take a walk. Feel the warmth of the sun. It is a very beautiful and pleasant day and should not be wasted in this dark, airless cabin." She stood, "So go on you two. I will be alright here. I have preparations to make."

What preparations I wondered, but was too afraid to ask. So we obeyed her as always and went out into the sunny afternoon. Selena had brought some meat and bread and we ate as we walked. I realized I had become very hungry, almost ravenous. We strolled towards the main square of the city and it occurred to me that there was another motive behind grandma's request that we go outside. It was to make sure the townspeople see me. That I was up and about and not sick.

59

That I was a normal man who did not shun the sunlight. That I was a normal man in love.

We held hands, but seldom spoke. We had no need to. Grandma-ma was right- it was a beautiful afternoon. The warm, spring day carried the scent of wild honeysuckle. Gulls cried overhead and high clouds drifted by. A soft breeze rose up from the nearby lake. This was the land I loved. And it gave me great comfort.

People nodded and greeted us as we strode along and I started to feel like myself again. I was happy here with Selena. Proud to be seen with her. We were in love and our happiness could not be contained.

We turned back and headed for the surrounding woods. My arm around her, her head upon my shoulder.

Before we realized it, we were at our special trysting spot. Under that magical centuries old oak tree that had witnessed our lovemaking. Where we had first made love. This place was almost sacred to me. It would always convey a deep sentiment to us both that time could never diminish.

We laid down on soft grass in each other's arms. Saying not a word, we just held each other tight. I knew I would never hurt her no matter what happened tonight, or any other night, even if it meant I had to leave. It would be the most difficult thing I should ever have to do, for she was not just my love, but my strength and I made a vow to myself that I would make her as happy as best I can.

We looked at one another. "Je t'aime," was all we said. A deep kiss and we sat back looking at the light blue sky, not knowing what was going to happen to me- to us. I tried to be mindful and only think- only live- for that moment. I am not sure but I believe that we fell asleep for a short while there; feeling the breathing of the other, close and comforting. It was a tonic for me.

A pinkish glow slowly began to appear on the clouds to the west and we knew it was time to head back towards the cabin. I wanted to convey something of how I felt, but couldn't find the words. To let her know that my love for her will survive anything- even this curse- and I was determined to prove it.

She turned to me and gently placed her hand on my face as

was her way. She nodded, understanding. After all, she could read my mind.

17

Pierre was there at the cabin with grandma-ma when we returned. They had moved the table and furniture to the sides leaving a large empty space in the middle of the room and had marked a very large five-pointed star in chalk on the floor. A solitary chair sat directly in the center. I knew immediately that the chair was for me, but how could a simple chalk outline prevent my transformation?

"As long as you stay within its borders," was Selena's reply to my thought.

"How do you know this will work? Has it been attempted before?"

Grandma-ma replied that her grandmother had told her of the legends of werewolves on the islands and that this was a way of controlling the change.

"The priestess concurs," Selena added. So they had consulted her, but.. "This morning we saw her," was the answer to my silent question.

"Mon fils," grandmother demanded my attention. "You need to be aware that what we are about to do can have repercussions."

"Such as?"

"Great pain," was her simple answer. But there was something more unsaid.

I took a deep breath, "And?"

Selena touched my arm. "It may be dangerous- for you."

I understood. I also understood that this method of control was based only on hearsay, from tales long ago. I could not help but be skeptical. "So you have never actually seen this done before?" As I said this, I realized it was a foolish question. Of course, she hadn't. She was a medicine woman, not a witch.

"Mon cher," grandma-ma's voice grew soft, yet earnest. "I would not ask you to attempt this if I did not believe it has a chance of working."

"Henri," Pierre coaxed. "You must try this. It might be a solution. Even if it is only temporary, you must try for all of us."

"Of course. I will do whatever you think best. I know nothing of such things myself." I deferred to grandmother's judgment, just as I always had, just as everyone did. It was then I noticed the heavy perfume in the room. A thick, heady smell filled the cabin, making me nauseous and dizzy, like an intoxicating liquor.

"That is the wolfs-bane," replied Selena. The small blooming flowers on thin branches were hung everywhere- over the windows, the doorway, in every corner. They were even strewn on the floor, surrounding the pentagram. It reminded me of the heather that grew wild at our old home, but the smell was sickening. Where did they come by this? I never recalled seeing this flowering plant growing in this wet country. "Grandmother got them from the voodoo priestess." Her again! "It grows only in rocky areas, but she has a secret place where she cultivates it."

"She seems prepared for everything."

Selena ignored my sarcasm. "Wolf-bane comes from Eastern Europe. It acts as a retardant. Supposedly repelling one who is under a curse such as yours." I could see why. Their heavy smell was noxious. "Brewed into a tea, the plant is poisonous." She stopped, then added hopefully, "The fragrance might help dull any pain you experience."

Her calm hopefulness was inspiring. So I had to go through with this. I wanted to. I wanted to get this thing over with. And live my life. A normal life.

Grandma pointed to the star on the floor with her cane. "It is nearly sunset. You need to enter the pentagram before the sun sets completely." She was in complete control. I obeyed, entered into the chalk-drawn diagram and took a seat in the small wooden chair. I felt nothing, except the churning of my stomach from the scent of those awful weeds. Selena lit five white candles at each point of the star and then the three of them each took a seat in different corners of the room. At a safe distance from myself.

One last final instruction from grandma: no one was to enter into the circle until sunrise. "No matter what they see. No matter what they may hear." We then sat in total silence and waited.

A few minutes later, I began to itch again like on the previous evenings. It increased steadily as the sun descended. The three of them sat motionless, as if holding their breath, waiting for who knew what. I felt again that sense of dread which was becoming all too common a companion.

A sliver of moonlight streamed through a window and immediately I felt a wrenching pain, starting in my gut and then shooting through my whole body. It felt like I was being torn inside out by some unseen force; some invisible demon's hand reaching deep inside me. I believe I started to foam at the mouth. I had a brief thought that perhaps I had the falling sickness, like the great Caesar. It would be a simpler, rational explanation of what was happening to me.

The pain increased to an unbearable height. I became hot, feverish. My body on fire. A fire that burned internally, yet did not consume. A fire from hell.

I wanted to leave the pentagram. It had to be what was causing the giant painful spasms. I felt as if I were in a cage, trapped like an animal. I couldn't breathe and needed to escape outdoors to get fresh air. The walls were closing in on me, creating claustrophobia. I had to escape, get out of that circle-star. I heard someone scream. Was it me?

I fell out of the chair and it was forcefully thrown out of the star. I groveled on the floor in the pentagrams center. My body wrenched in torment, contorting itself in ungodly positions. I tried to reach out, to crawl out of the circle, but could not. There was something blocking me, preventing me from leaving the diagram. I grabbed my head, it was throbbing so. My heart was about to burst, my body wanting to transform but not able to. Just as the pain reached its crescendo, I collapsed, passing out, my mind going completely blank. I saw only blackness. No dreams or nightmares, not even a single thought. Complete and utter darkness as black as a cave. A cave that leads to Hades.

When I woke, my first sight was Selena's face leaning over
me. How beautiful she was. My first thought was what a
wonderful way to wake up in the morning. Then I realized the
sun was high and suddenly, the memory of last night came back
in haunting vividness. But what had actually happened? I rose
up in my bed, stiff and sore. It seemed like I was endlessly sick
and Selena would always be nursing me back to health.

"What happened last night?" I asked groggily.

"You passed out, but grandma-ma would not let us enter the
pentagram. We could tell you were breathing and I was so
relieved...I thought perhaps you had died."

"I thought I was dying." I looked at her and saw tears in her
eyes. We embraced and let the tears flow freely. I had never
seen her cry. She was still so beautiful. I wiped her face with my
hand. "I am alright now, Selena, I'm alright. I survived the night
and I did not transform." Or? I looked at her closely. "Did
anything else happen after I collapsed? I didn't..."

"No, my darling. You were just like a child asleep. Even
peaceful. Oh how I love you so, Henri."

"And I you." I held her close. "I must thank grandma-ma.
Where is she?"

"Back at our cabin."

"I'm so relieved Selena. But..will I have to go through this
again? Tonight.. next month? Time and time again?" I must
have sounded tired and weak. I was.

"I do not know my dear. All I know is that it worked last night.
And if need be, I will stay in the circle with you. Hold you when
you suffer and..." I stopped her by putting my finger to her lips.

"As long as I know you will not leave me, I can do anything,
my darling." I kissed her long and deep and wanted to make
love to her then and there, quickly and passionately, but I
thought better of it. I started to rise. "We must go to your
grandmother. Tell her..", but this time she hushed me. She rose
quietly and closing my bedroom door, bolted it; she then
undressed in front of me and crawled into my bed, under my

sheets, next to me. She always knew, so easily, what I was thinking.

19

"I'm famished."

"That is a good sign, my son." We were at Selena's and grandma's cabin enjoying a nice large dinner, speaking only of good things; of the future, of our coming marriage. Pierre was saying how he has discovered a group of horses for sale in another village nearby. There was talk about the new rice fields being planted; of how the sugarcane plantations were growing ever larger. We were counting our blessings. And so we laughed and ate, and laughed again. Then after dinner we sat around enjoying the pipe and Pierre shared his flask with us all. Even grandma-ma took a sip!

It had been three nights now since I first sat within the pentagram. Each night I returned and each night became successively less painful, less traumatic. The moon was waning, lessening in its power over me. Once, even a thick layer of clouds helped retard its influence. The last night I did not even pass out. The extreme itching, fever and severe heart palpitations- all symptoms before a transformation- were practically nonexistent. I even ventured out of the pentagram before dawn and nothing happened. I was free of the curse- for another month. However, when the full moon returns, I will at least know what to expect and can somewhat prepare myself mentally (and emotionally) for the ordeal. Perhaps I might even learn to live a normal life in this way. Even one day we might find a cure. Dare I to hope?

The next week Selena and I had a simple wedding in the chapel on the square. It was a gloriously sunny afternoon. The ceremony was short; the bride beautiful; the groom nervous but, oh so proud. The church was crowded full of well-wishers, with standing room only. People came from far away, paying their respects, not only to the happy couple, but also for my famous mother-in-law. Her usual reserve was gone, replaced with obvious joy and happiness and I knew she had the ability to see our happiness also.

Afterwards, followed an outdoor banquet with regional delicacies including: fresh shrimp, crab and oysters cooked a half-dozen different ways; spit-roasted pork, candied pecans, and a type of tiny boiled crustacean which I had never ate before but which were plentiful in the shallower wetlands. Most everyone brought a dish or cake and it appeared to me that the entire village was there; anyone was welcome; everyone was enjoying themselves making merry and drinking rum. Of course, Selena and I led the first dance. She had been teaching me different local dances all week and I had become quite good at it- or so I would like to think! It was a carefree time, sans souci, on a beautiful cloudless day, that would stay with me forever.

The cabin of Pierre's and mine, became Selena's and mine. Pierre moved closer into town setting up house with a rather wealthy family there that had a huge property with a guest house. They also had many daughters- several pretty girls of marrying age which I am sure helped influence his decision. I only hoped he would be careful and not do anything..improper.

Pierre and I still hunted and fished together and we began purchasing horses as planned. We now had an even dozen. Pierre even gave Selena a horse as a wedding present- a beautifully marked paint which she promptly named Porthos. Our next goal was to buy farmland and take advantage of plentiful fertile terrain. I really felt at home in this bayou country and hoped I and my descendants would forever live here.

Selena's and grandma-ma's present to me was something practical yet exquisite. A solid gold pocketwatch on a golden chain! The hunter's case was engraved with a fleur-de-lis pattern and it came direct from Paris. On opening the shiny timepiece, it started to play a tiny jingle. And rather boisterous for such a delicate object!

"Where on earth did you discover such a treasure?"

"One of the shopkeepers from the colonial capital was traveling through. He was so French and so charming, Henri. Perhaps one day we might visit the city, I hear so many intriguing things about it. Read the inscription, darling."

On the back dust cover it said simply, EVERMORE - FROM S TO H. It ticked along strong and happily and came with the tiniest of keys for winding! With a flawless white porcelain dial, the musical watch was undoubtedly very valuable. "Oh my sweet, we are going to be so happy." I promised always to take extra care with it, wind it every day and keep it on my person always, in my breast pocket, close to my heart. It would stay with me for the rest of my days, the dearest gift ever I did receive.

My present to her was very much a surprise, but similar to her gift. I suppose we thought alike. It was waiting for her, on our wedding day when we came home together, our first time to be alone that day, and the first time we were to make love as man and wife. We settled in and I thought she might notice it, for it was working, but it wasn't until later that night, after we had made love for a long evening, an evening filled with incense and candles and wonderful bliss. I had gotten up for a drink of water and when I came back she was sitting up in our bed.

"What is that ticking?"

"What ticking?"

"That ticking." Just at that moment the longcase clock softly struck the hour. She grabbed her nightgown and went into the main room. I had repaired the old clock left there.

"And it keeps time well."

"Oh Henri, it is wonderful. And I didn't hear it all this time." She looked at me mischievously, "I wonder why."

I shrugged innocently. "I fixed it all by myself. It is my wedding gift to you."

"Oh Henri, I do love you so." Her kiss aroused me all over again. She placed a hand upon the wooden case to sense the clock's ageless beating. "This will be a symbol of our marriage, Henri; our beating hearts together, forever." She then turned back towards me and added, beguilingly, "So you can keep a secret!"

"I suppose you were too busy to read my mind in this one thing."

"All I could read today was happiness and...one other thing." With that said, she reached down between my legs and felt my sex. Blood flowed immediately towards her warm grasp. I picked her up, cradling her in my arms and carried her back to our bed."You are right Henri. We are going to be so happy."

20

For a time, our lives ran true and normal like any other young couple in that place and time. But as the days turned into a week, then into another week, that sense of foreboding began to surface within me again. The moon was waxing and I knew that soon the transformation would begin anew and I would have to go through that horrible experience of placing myself in the pentagram. And my new family would have to go through that also.

I had about one week to enjoy a normal life. So we worked during the day; making love at night; still, Selena and I never once mentioned the upcoming full moon.

The first indication that the change was near, was always at night in my sleep. Dreams of blood and death- nothing specific- haunted my nights. I was restless and kept waking. I often thought I heard wolves baying at a great distance, beckoning me. However, there were no wolves, only my imagination.

In the middle of the night I would rise and walk into the main room and check on our clock. I wound it faithfully and made sure it was keeping time well. I always set it to my pocketwatch. Their constant tick soothed me, yet at the same time I realized that they were marking time, and soon I would be sick again. And a danger to my loved ones and others.

On one such night, I sat at the dining table, laid my head down and sobbed silently, though no tears came. I did not want Selena to know, then suddenly she was there, holding me to her perfect breasts, comforting me. We didn't say a word, but held each other tight, knowing what was to come and then not knowing what was to come. There was only one certainty: as long as the curse was with me our life together would be difficult and this curse may never be extinguished completely, with death always nearby. I also concluded to myself, that if I had to, I would end the curse with a silver dagger to my heart; but I blocked that thought as best as possible from my mind, so Selena would not read it.

So we lived for the moment; making love at night, making love on rainy afternoons; making love.

Then one night, I woke suddenly. My heart was pounding and the itching was upon me; my head aching like before. I quickly rose and looked outside. The moon was almost completely full. Thick clouds drifted over it and it was gone. I knew that tomorrow night I would turn and we would have to draw the pentagram and all spend some sleepless nights in pain and worry. I asked the Lord that hard question: Why me? But I received no answer.

21

The next day my cravings were insatiable: for sex; for meat-bloody and rare; vegetables and grains made me throw up. I was nervous and agitated with excessive energy. They all knew it was time.

At sundown we four drew the pentagram within a circle on the floor and lit the candles. No blooming wolf-bane was available this time. Not much was said. Selena gave no sign of worry, but went about the task as if it was just another chore among her many. The only difference was that I noticed she was again wearing the silver pentagram chain around her neck. Where had it been all this time?

I put the chair in the center, sat down and we waited. Dusk came late in those early summer days. The pain seized me quite suddenly and this time it was unbelievably many times greater than before. My veins pulsed and literally, were about to burst. My limbs contorted, tortuously; my body trying to transform, but could not. Grandma sensed the horror that showed upon Selena's and Pierre's faces. I caught a glimpse of their terror as I groveled and groped in agony on the floor, screaming incoherently. They began to realize what I knew instinctively- that this time was different. The moon was at its most powerful and the curse so entrenched within me that if I did not escape from this circle, I would certainly die! Instead of transforming, my body would simply tear itself into pieces.

Selena had had enough and rushed to my aid. She entered the circle and tried to grab my convulsing body. I heard grandma-ma yell, "No, you mustn't! You mustn't!" But then Pierre, also ignoring her admonition, joined Selena and they managed to pull me from the pentagram.

The next thing I knew they were recoiling away from me, their faces showing that I must have transformed almost immediately. I remember rising from the floor and standing, feeling stronger every second. They stared at me, not recognizing me. Looking at me as though I were the devil himself. I remembered everything this time, forgetting nothing. The transformation itself, was instant- completely painless. Like the zombie who had turned into a man-snake, I turned into a wolf-man! And they had witnessed it. There was no denying now what I was, what I had become.

I rushed out of the cabin and into the night. I suppose I must have had some sort of humanity left in me, for I did not attack my loved ones. I do not know. All I recall was I wanted to run and be free from the confines of that circle. To see and feel the moon; to be by myself. And hunt. Half-human, half-wolf, I was capable of thinking and reasoning like a man, but the hunger and behavior was as that of a wild animal. I wanted to kill and eat the raw flesh.

In only a few minutes, I found myself deep in the swamps and the first animal I encountered would be my victim. It was a large mule deer. Though it ran fast, I ran faster. It fell with one swipe of my claws, slashing its throat as if it was paper. I ripped open his midsection and fed on the intestines. The steam and stench rose up at me, but I gloried in the feast.

Hunger, being no longer a priority, I spent the rest of the night in wonderment, fascinated with my abilities- my powers. I remember distinctly the entire night. Running deeper and deeper into the thick swamp; traveling as swift as any horse; other creatures scattered at my approach- night predators avoided me. Even the frogs and crickets grew silent in my presence.

My senses of sight and smell had grown a hundred fold. I saw sharp as an owl for, though the moon was behind clouds, all was visible clearly- even vividly. Every blade of grass, every tree limb heavy with hanging moss. As if it were daylight.

I sensed humans. I cannot ascribe exactly how I knew (the scent?), I just knew. I also instinctively discerned where they were; and so, I came upon a cabin. Without looking inside, I perceived two people- one male, one female. They were asleep. They would have made very easy prey, though for some reason, I still do not know why, I went around the cabin and continued exploring. Perhaps the human side of me prevailed in that instance, but later circumstances would confirm not.

I climbed trees, leaped across streams, swam bayous- all with great speed and agility. And having no fear. The alligators seemed to have disappeared, yet if I came across one, I would be able to kill it easily- no matter how large it might be.

The night was my friend. The glorious night with a bright, full moon. I had no dread of the dark, in fact it was the opposite feeling. I felt at ease, with a joy in the night. I was…comfortable.

I also had not the other feelings that humans have- no tiredness or fatigue. I experienced only strength, immense strength. The mighty hunter in this wonderful wilderness which I called home.

And now I saw it for the first time as a creature of the night; things that no human eyes could ever see- day or night. Nocturnal animals, hunting, foraging. The swamp was as much alive at night as it was during the day- even more so.

Here I was a Lord over this kingdom and no predator or any other supernatural beast could command me. I was undefeatable and I shouted it out. However, the sound that came out was a howling- the howling of a giant wolf- and I was taken aback. Especially when I thought, for one brief moment, that I had heard another wolf's howl in return. But it was only an echo.

I must have traveled for miles around, seeking out areas that

I could not approach as Henri the man. But then day was about to break and I found myself not far from home. The night was being chased away quickly. I laid down in a bed of leaves beneath tall pines and watched the rose tinted sky of dawn while my strength slowly ebbed. And I slept.

22

I awoke with a start. I had distinctly heard footsteps. I listened intently. Nothing. Where was I? Memories flooded back. I had transformed and was able to remember the night and my journey completely. And I had killed, but not humans- that I also remembered. Perhaps, just maybe, I could control this curse and not feel the need for human flesh. Yet even as I had the thought, my hope diminished for I realized that sooner or later I would lose control and...feast. My experience last night was just that, a one night experience and there would be countless more ahead of me.

There was that sound again. It was footsteps! and nearby. My hearing was still acute and sensitive. In fact, all my senses were heightened above normal. A residual effect that I could put to good use.

I rose and crept towards the sound. I was wearing only wet, torn trousers and nothing else, not even shoes. I peered through some bushes and tried to see who it was. I had to be very wary and careful to avoid anyone, particularly any hunters.

It was Pierre. "Searching for me?" My voice, startling him, he quickly turned with his musket raised, pointed at my chest.

"Henri?" He relaxed, cautiously. "Thank God. How...are you?"

"I am fine, mon ami." I hesitated. "So you saw? You saw the..change?"

He nodded. He looked as if he had had no sleep- red, bleary eyes; scruffy unshaven face. "I did not completely think it possible, until last night. I never really believed in curses or the supernatural. But there is no denying it anymore." He stared at me with strong intent. "What happened to you last night? Where did you go? Do you remember anything?" He added, "Selena was beside herself with worry."

"Pierre, it is the most remarkable thing. I remember it all." We started to walk home slowly, being sure to avoid any human contact. My bare feet did not feel the sharp, broken limbs and muddy thistles beneath them. I felt not the slightest human discomfort.

I told him all of what I had experienced the night before. Of my superhuman sight and hearing, of the speed with which I could travel on foot. Seeing for the first time, woods and swamps much farther from here, deep in the wilderness. What would take days for an ordinary man to explore, I saw in one night.

He looked at me with wonder. "You sound as if you enjoyed it?"

"In a way Pierre, yes- I must admit. I never felt more alive, more powerful than last night." His look of wonder turned to worry. I continued, "Do not fret my friend, I realize this is not a blessing. I know all too well the dangers to.."

He interrupted anxiously, "Did you come across any people, Henri?"

"No," I replied, but I knew what he was really asking. I mentioned the killing of the deer and his face twisted in disgust. "I did come across a cabin, but I went around it for some reason." I stopped and looked him directly in the face. "And no- I did not harm anyone." We started walking again.

"That you can remember?"

"Yes, that I can remember."

"So perhaps, you may have..."

"Perhaps, but I doubt it. Not..this time. I can recall everything vividly. I didn't have even a single blackout." We stopped again. "Don't you see Pierre? I might be able to control it. To not feed.."

"But can you Henri? Can you control it? What if the deer had not been there? What if it had been a person instead? Maybe you can control it for one night, but for many nights? How long before the hunger controls you?"

I could not answer that honestly, so we walked the rest of

the way in silence.

When we reached the house, Pierre turned to me, "I must go now. Why don't you get some sleep? Rest awhile. Selena is inside worrying about you. You know Henri, that she loves you immensely..no matter what." He turned and walked away.

No matter what...I was. I finished the thought. Even if I had not killed anyone last night, there were too many unknowns. Even if I controlled the hunger, at any time I might slip and lose that control. I thought of my dead horses and that poor fisherman. Yes, Pierre was right- inevitably I would lose the battle.

But what could be done? Was my death the only recourse? The thought horrified me. I loved Selena and our new life too much to leave her. But if I stayed, wouldn't she and the others that I love be in constant danger? What if I became more and more the animal and less and less the man? These questions were too much for me, for one man to handle. I needed to rest.

Selena appeared at the doorway. Without hesitation she ran to me. We embraced tightly. Suddenly a searing pain struck my bare chest. I pulled back from her. The silver pentagram she was still wearing had carved a scar onto my chest, like a brand. I stormed into the house, into the bedroom and threw myself onto the bed, filled with despondency and disgust. There will always be something to remind me of this curse. Something always to come between Selena and me. We would probably never have a sound healthy life together. Nor a family like everyone else. I never felt more helpless than at that very moment.

She sat down gently on the bed, quietly removed the talisman from around her neck and calmly placed it inside the bedside table drawer, closing it firmly. "I no longer need this."

"What? Selena, I think it still wise when the moon.."

She quieted me with a gentle finger to my lips, then, looking deep into my watery, emotional eyes, said "It is not necessary."

"Why?"

"Because I know you would never harm me. You love me too much."

"Selena.."

This time she interrupted me with a kiss, lingering and

longing. "I will always love you, Henri. No matter what comes. Our love will get us through this. You must always remember that."

"How Selena? How will our love get us through this?"

"I do not know exactly, but we must not give up hope. Have faith…"

"Faith!" I exclaimed. "Mon Dieu!" I turned over on my side away from her. I didn't want to think anymore. I was too tired to reason. "Let me close my eyes and rest for awhile. And not think…about anything."

"Of course, mon cher. Why don't you try and get some sleep." She gathered a small, thin cover over me, as if she were tucking in a child and quietly went to the door. But before she closed it, I apologized adding, "I'll always love you too, Selena. Always."

23

"I heard nothing in the village this morning about any strange occurrences or sightings." We were all sitting around the dining table having a late lunch. "And I went everywhere- the market, the feed store. No rumors or talk." I knew what she really meant- what was left unsaid by us all. That there had been no reports of strange deaths or mauling last night.

Selena was such a God Send to me. So strong and mature for her age. Perhaps because her parents had died early; perhaps because she had been raised by her grandmother- another strong (and wise) woman.

Before lunch she had come in to wake me, by crawling into our bed, naked. We had made love passionately, but silently, saying not a word. Then we just lay there, together afterwards, holding each other and listening to a soft, summer shower.

"So grandma-ma what is next?" I asked as I cut into my usual dish of rare meat. "Do we draw the pentagram again?"

"Oh no," Selena interjected. Then she looked quietly down at her plate. "The moon is too powerful tonight. It would probably be disastrous if we were to place you in there again."

I knew what she meant by disastrous. I smiled at her and placed my hand over hers. "Selena," I spoke calmly, "We must face the fact that all of us may be better off if I were to ..."

"Ahem." Grandmother was about to speak which meant for the rest of us to be attentive. "It is true that to attempt the pentagram confinement again would more than likely be..too dangerous. So we must do something else." In a way, I was relieved. I did not want to again experience that agony. I would sooner die. And the truth is I wanted to live.

"But what can we possibly do?" Pierre's question echoed my thoughts.

"We have a plan," grandmother continued. "There is a large mausoleum not too far from here, where we can lock you in for the night. There you can be free to transform, but not be able to leave."

"A mausoleum? In a cemetery?" She nodded a response. "How is this to prevent me from leaving?"

"It can only be opened from the outside."

"There is no chance of my escape?"

"None."

"I am sorry grandma-ma, but is this practical? My strength when I am… changed is immense."

Selena volunteered, "It was used before for a purpose such as this."

"What? For another werewolf?" I could not prevent my incredulity from showing all too plainly.

"No my son, it was for a different type of creature." I could not help but be intrigued. "Supposedly, sometime back," grandma-ma began her story, "there was a great doctor in this area who conducted grave experiments. And by grave, I mean 'from the grave'." A pause, "He experimented with revivification."

"Reviving the dead," Selena explained.

"Are you serious?" Pierre again echoed my thoughts.

"It is a well known legend in these parts."

"But.." I started to disclaim legends and myths and zombies, but after all that had happened I remained quiet.

Grandmother continued, "It is said that he succeeded,

76

however, he had to keep his creation hidden, for he was untamed, wild, with superhuman strength. A danger to all those around him. So the doctor held him captive in this dungeon-like mausoleum."

"So this man- his creation- was imprisoned in this..crypt?" Grandma-ma nodded. "And where is he now? And this so-called doctor?"

"We do not know," Selena said. Then she added softly, "It is only a legend."

"Ah, but the crypt is there," grandmother spoke up. "With chains in the wall. Marie has taken me there."

"Marie?" I asked.

"The voodoo priestess," Selena volunteered again.

So she was involved in this. Again. Where will all this supernatural mumbo-jumbo end? 'With your death' I heard a voice whisper in my ear.

"Well at least now she has a name," I spoke without respect and immediately regretted it. Yet I continued, "And so the plan is to..what? Seal me in overnight? In chains?"

"No, not in chains, my darling," Selena ventured. She turned to her grand-mother. "He doesn't have to be chained, does he?"

"It will not be necessary. There is no escape from this place once it is sealed."

No escape. The words echoed in my head. No escape from this curse. "How do we know that there isn't a secret panel or escape latch from within? Perhaps the doctor's creation escaped that way or even managed to find another way out?"

"There is no escape from this place," grandmother repeated herself. "I searched the place myself."

"No offense grandma-ma, but second sight isn't.."

Pierre interrupted me, "We can search it ourselves, Henri. Before nightfall." He added almost apologetically, "That way we can be sure, grandma-ma." Even Pierre now referred to her affectionately as a relation.

"Of course, my sons," she replied with like affection. "That is wise. Then Selena and I will join you there before sunset." She gave us a description of the crypt and instruction on how to open it. Then added as Pierre and I were leaving, "Try not to worry, Henri. We may end this curse yet- one day."

I kissed her and Selena both on the cheek and Pierre and I walked outside. How could we ever end it? Did she and the priestess know of a way? Was there something else they were not telling me? I wanted to turn back and ask, but Pierre said, "We must do a few chores and then we can go."

"You have been to this cemetery?"

"Once, when I was hunting in that area. It is in a relatively dry area, not near the swamp. But most of the graves and crypts are still all above ground." He paused, "In case of floods."

I acknowledged with a nod. I had heard that in these low lying wet lands, where floods and torrential rains were common, that on occasion buried coffins had risen to the surface and floated away during storms and floods. So people here mostly entombed their dead above ground in crypts or stone sarcophagus. And now, I will be spending the night inside one of them.

24

We did our chores- chopped firewood, fed the livestock and various routine tasks. Around mid-afternoon, we stopped, washed and cleaned up, then walked for the cemetery. We did not take the horses. Ever since I started to change more frequently, the horses would not let me ride them. They eventually became accustomed to eating from my hand and letting me groom them, but whenever I tried to mount one of them, they would always buck and run. It was just another one of the constant reminders of the curse- that I was not a normal man- not really human, not totally inhuman.

It took a little over an hour to walk to the cemetery which was probably the largest in this area. Most of the surrounding hamlets and villages including ours, used it for their deceased.

"Do you remember which one she said Pierre?" My mind was so full of confused thoughts and doubts, it was a wonder I could remember my own name. I was so glad that Pierre was here; though at the same time I felt guilt at having to involve my friend- again.

"Yes, it has the name Fontenot. It should be the largest mausoleum. Near the center." We found it easy enough.

It was a large receptacle of gray granite and brick with steps leading up to a stone door, flanked by two small gargoyle statues on either side. The arch above the door contained the single name 'Fontenot'.

"But what if someone should come by in the night, open it and release me?" I wondered out loud.

"I will be here outside on watch."

"All night? I cannot ask that of you. Alone here in this ghostly place?"

"It will be all right. I will not be alone anyway." He patted his shirt pocket containing his well known flask.

I wanted to laugh but couldn't. He always was the light-hearted one, even now in this most serious matter. "And tomorrow night? What about next month? I cannot keep asking you for all this help."

"What else can you do Henri? This is what we do for one another, n'est-ce pas? We cannot entrust this duty to anyone else. No one else must know. This is our only alternative." He dismissed any further discussion with a wave of his hand. "No, I will stand guard tonight and for however many other nights I am needed."

"There is one other alternative, Pierre. And I have been meaning to ask you." I made certain he was listening closely before I continued. "It would require great courage from you."

"What is it Henri?"

"There is a silver dagger back at our cabin. If necessary, if I ask you, you must use it and.."

"No Henri, that is not an alternative. No Henri! I will not even listen to your nonsense." He again emphatically dismissed the idea with a wave of his arm. "Besides I don't think, I would … be capable."

"Even if I came at you with teeth barred and claws like nails? You saw what I become with a full moon. You have seen the monster that I am."

"I saw you change Henri, outwardly yes. But I know you, in

here." He patted my chest. "Maybe better than you know yourself. You would never hurt me or the ones you love."

"But that is far from certain, Pierre. I may not be as lucid every night as I was last night. I might not even recognize you. And besides... I have killed at least once already, remember. The guilt tortures me still. It may not be you, but someone else, anyone else who crosses my path. You yourself warned me!" I paused, "If you are truly my friend, Pierre, then one day you may have to help me and end this curse forever."

"Yes, yes Henri," he replied abruptly. "I know, I know. Please let us talk of this later after the full moon passes. Then we can talk, we…we can think more rationally and calmly then. Come let us go inside and investigate this 'sanctuary'. "

By turning one of the gargoyle statues sideways, the cryptic door (a heavy solid piece of carved stone) moved outwardly revealing a small cavern inside. It was easily the largest mausoleum in the cemetery and certainly the largest either of us had ever seen. Whoever built such a grandiose tomb had to have been very wealthy. Was the doctor's name Fontenot? I could not recall grandma-ma saying.

Inside was all thick walls of brick and stone with a few torches along one side. Against the far wall, I saw the chains that had been mentioned earlier. Two above for the arms and two below for the legs. Someone must have been very frightened of something. I wondered to myself if those chains would be able to hold me. There were two large stone coffins in the center.

"Oh Pierre, no..no! I have to stay in here with the dead?"

"It is after all a crypt, Henri."

"Being sealed in a tomb all night is one thing, but spending the night with the dead? Didn't grandma-ma say this place was empty?"

"I do not recall." He paused only for a moment. "Well," he slapped his hands together feigning eagerness, "let us take a look see."

"Do we dare?" I don't know why my voice dropped to a whisper.

"Yes. You want to know whether you will have company tonight, don't you?" His laugh echoed in the chamber and I could not help but smile. He seemed to have no qualms. He was always the adventurous one when we were boys. The one to introduce me to whiskey and rum, then cigars and then women. I briefly thought of my family, wondering where they might be and what would they think of their son and brother now.

"Help me with this lid." His voice seemed so loud within the chamber, tearing through my thoughts. Though the lid was a solid block of heavy granite, we managed to slide it aside easily enough to peer inside. He remarked between heavy breaths, "You are much stronger now..than before." Then added as an afterthought, "Something that you must be careful not to exhibit in front of others."

I agreed silently. We peered down into the sarcophagus; the open door providing us just enough light to see within. It was empty.

"Thank God," I exhaled. We replaced the lid and proceeded to open the other. It too was empty. We sealed it back up.

I looked around, curious. "I wonder, Pierre. Was Fontenot the name of the scientist?"

"I don't know. I suppose so."

"And why is no one interred here?"

"Perhaps the family who built the tomb died elsewhere, far away. Or they moved away. Back to France. The voodoo lady probably knows."

"And that is another question. How did she come to know of this place?" I walked over to the chains, picked them up and examined them. They were extra heavy, thick and strong. Huge bolts fastened them into the wall. A giant key opened the solid, bulky manacles. I thought of a chained gorilla at a zoo. "If she knows of it, then others must also." I paused, my curiosity getting the better of me. "And these chains. The scientist must have been very frightened of his creation in order to resort to chaining him. Afraid for his life." I tossed them back to the stone floor. "Anyway, these were made to hold some thing very strong and big. If the tale is true."

"Why not?" answered Pierre. "A week ago I would not have believed. But now," he shrugged, then continued. "Well let's take a look around for a way out of here. Some mechanism that might trigger the door. Look for a loose brick or stone in the wall or floor. And check the torches in the wall to see if they turn or move."

We inspected every inch of the crypt, examined it by sight and touch, but found nothing that would work the door. In fact, there was no evidence that this tomb had been used at all, for any purpose. The chains and coffins were the only proof of some purpose. Built for what reason? and never used?

The afternoon sun grew dim and shadows lengthened. Voices came from outside. It was Selena and grandma-ma. We joined them. They had brought lanterns, food and blankets.

"How goes it?"

"It goes well, grandma-ma," replied Pierre. "Did you walk all that way?"

She sat down on one of the steps next to the gargoyle that opened the crypt door. "Yes, it was good exercise, but now I must rest," she laughed with her usual chuckle. "Did you find any way out?" We replied that we had not. "I thought as much." She spoke with her usual self-certainty.

"We decided we would all sleep out here, to help keep watch." Selena was by my side, holding my hand.

"Nonsense," Pierre and I both spoke at once. He continued, "I assure you that is not necessary. I will stay awake. Certainly, I would not want to fall asleep here. Some wandering spirit might possess me!" We all laughed a little, but I believe he spoke with some sincerity.

"It would be better for the two of you to go home," I added, squeezing Selena's hand.

"No, we will stay. And help keep this brave man awake." Grandmother spoke with finality and we all knew then, that there was no discussing the matter. Pierre sat down beside her and she patted him on the shoulder, saying "And I will keep away any spirits that may have designs on your handsome young body." We all chuckled, not only at her casual humor, but as much as to bring a little relief to this serious, gloomy situation.

"And you too my son," She nodded towards me. Were those tears in her eyes that could no longer see? "I want you to know that you are a very brave and strong man to endure all of this, mentally as well as physically. And I am so glad that Selena has you for a husband. Non, je ne regrette rien."

"Yes, he is very brave and strong," Selena echoed her grandmother, "and I too regret nothing." As she laid her head on my shoulder, I felt so much pride and joy at that moment I could have entered a den of lions. Confidence swelled within me filling my being deep into my very heart. I was ready for the night and whatever the curse might bring. And hope flickered again- hope that one day we might would lead a normal life and have a normal family.

The sun was setting quickly, so I kissed Selena for a long moment, said my goodnights and entered the tomb carrying a lantern and one of the blankets they had brought with them. I was hungry but could not bring myself to eat the sandwiches they had made.

And I did feel very brave until Pierre closed the door behind me with a thud. Not only did it block out all light, but sound as well. 'Silent as the grave,' I thought. I felt a sudden, very cold chill pass through me and I tried not to dwell on how ghastly this scenario was- to be sealed up overnight inside a crypt! Even though there were no bodies, it was still a crypt in a cemetery.

I also thought, as I went about lighting the torches from the lantern they had given me, how terrible it was for my family to have to spend the night in this cemetery on my account. Which distressed me all the more. I spread my blanket out on the cold, dank stone floor and sat down, waiting for the inevitable.

It did not take long. The usual warning symptoms began and only a few moments later, my transformation was complete. Each time it accomplished itself quicker, with greater ease and less stress upon my body.

I remember a few things from that night. Doing my utmost to find a way out, I scratched and clawed at the door. I combined all my animal senses with human instinct to find a secret release for the door. What really terrified me was I needed out in order to feed. I was hungry- insatiably so. Hunger drove me; the taste of blood and flesh obsessed me; I had to escape. And as the night wore on, my humanness seemed to decrease as my animalistic tendencies progressed.

I began to behave as a wild animal. Pacing back and forth, scratching to get out, howling in anger. I ran into the door repeatedly to open it. I tried shoving against it with my superhuman strength. It would not bulge. This wasn't just a mausoleum. It was an inescapable prison, made specifically to house a beast or some other poor creature such as I.

For hours that night I tried in vain to find an escape. I literally climbed the walls in a frenzy. Finally, growing weak and fatigued, I knew that dawn was approaching. I laid down in a corner and closed my eyes. The next thing I knew, bright light was blinding me. The door was open and Pierre was standing over me.

"Are you alright?"

"I believe so." I stood up and dusted myself off. My clothes were all tattered and torn, my shirt barely hanging on. "Did you hear me last night?"

He shook his head. "Hardly any thing. Howling. Some scratching, growls. But only if we listened closely."

"I really tried my utmost to get out." I paused. "Pierre. I could not control it. An overwhelming hunger…The need! I felt like a trapped animal. Look!" We turned towards the entrance. There were deep, deep claw marks all over the door and wall. "It is remarkable I did not find a means of escape."

"Grandma-ma was right. This is more than just a tomb."

"And how is she?…And Selena?" I looked around. "Did you stay the entire night?"

"Yes, all three of us. They have already gone home. Selena didn't want to leave, but she needed to take her grandmother home. That old one is one strong lady! She protested, but we could tell she was tired and sleepy. You are very lucky to have them, Henri."

"I know." I looked fondly at him. "And lucky to have you also, mon ami." I slapped him on the back. "Did you get any sleep?"

He shook his head. "I don't think I could ever fall asleep here- in this place. A cemetery is not the place to spend the night! Not even as a dare!"

We laughed together. "Then let us go home and get some breakfast and much needed rest, shall we? I am so hungry I could eat a horse!"

Pierre stared at me with shock as I realized what I had said. "Oh madre! I meant that only as a figure of speech…I couldn't, I wouldn't…again." He started to laugh as I became more and more flustered trying to find the right words. Then he broke out in boisterous hilarity at my growing embarrassment. But it was contagious and soon we were both rolling in laughter. A release of tension no doubt, spontaneous and welcome, even in such a somber and sacred setting.

After we recovered ourselves sufficiently, we proceeded to close the door to the tomb and start on the way home, knowing we would be back again tonight.

Selena had some hot hearty venison stew ready for us when we returned. She showed no signs of having stayed up all night- her face, her smile was as bright as always. Perhaps my love for her made me partial and she would always be beautiful to me, no matter what- no matter how we aged.

Grandma-ma had already retired to her cabin. We three ate, then Pierre went home to sleep, while Selena and I curled up together in our bed. Holding her tight, I briefly thought of making love to her, but tiredness overcame me and I fell asleep almost instantly. Which was good, for we had at least one more night of this ahead of us.

25

The next night Pierre was the only one standing watch outside the crypt. It had been agreed that it was unnecessary for the others to join him. I should be alright sealed up inside with no means of escape.

But we were wrong.

I transformed as usual that night, however I could tell the moon was not as powerful this time. Again, I tried to find my way out, and again- I could not. Eventually, sometime in the night, the animal in me gave up and I curled up in a corner and slept.

The next thing I remember was hearing a scratching noise and I immediately thought it must be a rat and my first instinct was to grab it, kill it and eat it. Then I realized I had already transformed back and was my human self again. The moon's influence had waned.

But what was that noise? Where had it come from? If it was a rat, how had it gotten inside?

I heard it again. It seemed more of a grinding sound, than a scratching. Like stone upon stone. I looked at the door, but it was still shut tight. The noise came from somewhere else inside the tomb.

With horrifying clarity, I realized the noise was emanating from one of the stone coffins! As I stared in that direction, through the dim flickering light of the torches, I saw the heavy slab on top of the one nearest me start to move ever so slightly!

For the first time since my altercation that night with the werewolf, I felt true terror! Was I dreaming? Surely so. But I knew I was not.

I could only stand there, my mouth agape, as the stone lid slid further and further open and then . .

I saw long fingers, followed by a large hand reaching out and it singly pushed the slab completely off the sarcophagus with a tremendous crash!

I stood frozen against the wall, not daring to move or react. I expected some thing, some nightmarish creature to appear. A zombie or another monster from hell to jump out and devour me, or worse- put some other even more devilish curse upon me.

But nothing happened. What followed was only silence. Was it a ghostly hand that I had seen? Had we intruded onto someone's sacred resting place? But there had been no evidence of any burial in either coffin.

After more than a few moments, and nothing more happened, I picked up my lantern and crept over slowly and silently to the open slab. My acute hearing heard no noise. Whatever had moved the lid, had had tremendous strength- even more so than myself.

As I neared the opening, I stopped to listen. I still heard nothing. Summoning great courage, I ventured to look inside. Raising the lantern, what I saw was completely unexpected.

Stairs! There were stone steps leading down, down into the earth. A dank, dark smell rose up to greet me. What did it mean? Why had we not seen this before? There had to be a secret panel. Where did they lead? Dare I...?

I thought of trying to get Pierre's attention, but he probably wouldn't hear me. So with conflicting thoughts and emotions, I crawled into the sarcophagus and started down the stairs. Frightened, curious, I had to see where this led- even if it took me to my own destruction. However, I also had a tiny glimmer of hope that perhaps I might find some answers at the end of these stairs. Answers to my own origins, solutions to my curse.

The tiny stone steps (of which I counted forty) ended at the entrance to a tunnel, carved out of the earth, with a dirt floor and wet, damp walls sweaty with moisture. I followed it along expecting at any moment some creature or ghoul to pounce upon me out of the darkness.

Proceeding very slowly while holding the lantern high, I tried to think logically and with calm reasoning about what had happened upstairs and the design behind all of this. It had definitely been a human hand that I saw. Not some ghost or werewolf. A hand connected to an obviously very strong man. Perhaps it was the creature who had supposedly been held captive here. Some one had gone to a great deal of trouble to construct this secret tunnel. But for what ultimate purpose I could not even begin to conjecture.

Had we infringed on his territory? Was he leading me into danger? To become the doctor's next experiment? Or maybe he was showing me a way out?

I then had a terrifying thought. What if it had been the one who had made me? The man I saw at the voodoo ceremony? The original beast. Was this one of his lairs? Was he toying with me- or worse?

But at the same time, I thought not. I had no sense of his presence and for some inexplicable reason I knew that if he was near, I would be aware of it. There was, for evil or good, a connection between us.

The deep meandering tunnel abruptly ended at the foot of another set of stairs. I started upwards (again I counted 40 steps) and in a moment I glimpsed light from the starry night. I blew out the lantern in case someone was above and cautiously continued.

At the top I peered out and detected no one around. I was still in the cemetery. The stairs led out of one of the many above ground stone sarcophagi. It too had its lid pushed off to one side.

I carefully climbed out. Fog was forming in wisps on this humid night and I did not see the moon, nor feel its power over me. Dawn was not far away. I looked about trying to gather my bearings. I was at the far edge of the cemetery, opposite from the main entrance and road. It was a secluded area in the graveyard, with a grove of oaks for cover. The perfect place for a secret entrance to a secret tunnel.

I started on my way back through the cemetery to Pierre and the mausoleum. Suddenly I sensed movement among the graves. Turning, I thought I glimpsed (for the briefest moment) a dim figure: tall and fair-haired running away in the hazy distance, disappearing behind the many statues of angels and crypts that populated the cemetery.

It might have been my imagination, a foggy apparition, but I believed not. I may have seen the very man who had opened the coffin in the crypt.

I briefly thought of pursuing the figure, but I already sensed that he was long gone. Another supernatural creature amongst us? I had so many questions. Had he come to the tomb not knowing I was there? Or did he come to release me purposefully? Rescue me from the prison where he had once been held himself? Or was he a simple interloper who haunted graveyards at night for the thrill and stumbled upon a secret passageway?

I would probably never know the answers, but one thing I did know. I would not be able to use the mausoleum again as a sanctuary from the full moon. It was no longer useful as a means of containment. We would have to think of something else. But what? I was desperately running out of alternatives.

Dawn broke as I neared the mausoleum. I saw Pierre at a distance. He was lying down and I thought he was sleeping, but he jumped up suddenly at the sound of my approach. He had his gun pointed.

I whispered loudly, "It's me. Henri!"

"Henri, What? C'est impossible! How did you..?" He looked

towards the closed door of the crypt, then back at me. "How were you able..?"

"There is a way out, Pierre. A secret panel."

"What?" His disbelief was unconcealed.

"It's true! Amazing but true. Here let me show you."

"But how did you discover it? We searched every inch thoroughly."

"But we did not search every inch of the inside of the coffins." His mouth fell open in astonishment. "Yes! There is an exit from inside one of the stone coffins." I paused and grasped him by the shoulders. "But Pierre, what is really unbelievable is how I came to find it!"

He followed me into the coolness of the crypt. The lid was still off the sarcophagus as it had been when I left. I showed him the stairs leading down into the earth and told him of all that had happened the night before. How it was some one who had opened the panel and shoved off the lid.

We felt all around the inside of the coffin, trying to find some latch or trigger and eventually Pierre moved a loose brick and a panel slowly slid shut becoming the bottom of the coffin.

"Mon Dieu!" He moved the brick again and the panel slid open with the grinding sound that I had heard last night.

"You were right, Henri! This is incredible. Who would have imagined? There must be another way to open and close it from the other side down below." We crawled down into the stairway and quickly found what we were looking for. Another loose stone that triggered the door from deep within.

"What an incredible mechanism," I spoke in awed admiration. "And so this was how he entered."

We closed the panel above us and, saying nothing, I led him down the stairs and through the tunnel, our lanterns lighting the way. "How far does it go?"

"Not very far. To the edge of the cemetery, in a somewhat isolated area."

"But who could have built all this? It is no small feat. And for what purpose?"

"We may never know Pierre. But I thought I saw someone at the other end."

"The one who. ."

"Most likely. For some reason, I now believe that he wanted me to see him." I stopped and turned back to Pierre, "And for me to follow him."

"Strange, Henri. Very strange." He took in a breath sharply as realization dawned. "So he must know about you... and your curse!"

"Yes, He must." I replied simply, turning forward and starting down the tunnel again.

"Do you think it was the scientist or... or perhaps his creation?"

"I can't even guess. Whoever, it took almost herculean strength to remove those coffin lids."

"What if there were two of them?"

"Even then." But I knew there had been only one.

We did not speak again and soon we were at the stairs leading upwards. We exited quietly. The morning sun was starting to shine bright and the heat of the summer day had already begun. Silently, we searched for a secret stone or loose brick that might close a panel and cover the stairs like the one in the mausoleum.

It did not take us long to find the hidden trigger that opened and closed a sliding door which became the bottom of the tomb.

"Incredible," Pierre whispered. There were two triggers: one beneath the panel in the stairway and another above the panel in the tomb itself. "Just like the other one."

"Just like the other one," I repeated.

Without saying anything else, we closed the secret doorway and together, with some effort, replaced the lid on the tomb. I picked up my lantern and started to walk away, lost in thought and ready to go home. I assumed Pierre was right behind me, but as I looked back, I noticed he was still standing beside the crypt.

"What is it Pierre? Are you alright?" I asked him as I turned back. I thought maybe he was simply catching his breath after the exertion of moving the lid. "Come. It has been a long night for both of us. We must close up the mausoleum and go home and rest."

However, he would not say anything. He just stood still as a statue, staring down at the crypt's lid we had just replaced. I

90

followed his gaze and to my horror I saw what had frozen him so.

Upon the lid was carved a name. My name. It read:

HENRI M. LEBLANC
Born October 13, 1735
Died July 8, 1757

26

"It has to be some sort of sick joke."

"It isn't funny."

"Someone knows . "

"But who? How? And when did they leave that carving on the tomb?"

"I think I know."

"There is no doubt that someone has been watching us; observing our actions."

"But again, who? And for what purpose? To scare us?"

"Perhaps. .blackmail?"

"No, I don't believe so. We have to reason logically. "

"What's logical about all this?"

"I think I know who it might be."

"Who then, my son?" We were sitting around the dining table in Selena's and my cabin.

"The one who made me," I was straightforward.

The speculative conversation came to a standstill. "The one?"

"The original beast, the monster that bit me. The other..werewolf." I paused before continuing. "I have seen him."

"When? Where? In the cemetery?"

"You met him? Why didn't you tell us?"

"Please you two. You are allowing your emotions to speak for you. Now then, let Henri speak." Grandmother had to officiate this discussion.

"I never met him, but I saw him. At the voodoo ceremony."

"He was there?"

"How do you know it was he?"

"I do not know exactly, but I could…feel it. All my senses told me so. I am positively certain. And… I am also certain that he recognized me."

"Have you seen him since?"

"No grandma-ma. And for some reason I think- I would feel if he was near."

"Yes, there is probably a connection, a supernatural connection, between the two of you."

"Oh grandma that is mere speculation." Selena spoke somewhat fretfully. She had started to wring her hands together. I reached for them to calm her. She looked at me, her eyes searching for my love. I bent over and kissed her on the cheek and whispered for her not to worry. She relaxed somewhat and summoned her usual composure.

"So he was at the cemetery last night? And the one who opened the coffin?" Pierre asked as he shoved aside his empty dinner plate and took out his flask. Grandma-ma had already lit her after- dinner smoke.

"No. I do not think so."

"But you said you thought he was the one responsible."

"Perhaps," grandmother answered for me, "he had another do his bidding. And someone else carved the lid with Henri's name."

"Exactly."

"Well whoever it is they know all about you. Your full name, your birth date, your...curse. " Selena, though outwardly calm, still could not conceal the tiny quiver of fear in her voice. I put my arm around her. But she continued, "And what of that date for your death? The very day you were attacked! What could that possibly mean?"

I squeezed her and she tried to relax, putting her head on my shoulder and closing her eyes. We all chose to ignore her last question for there was no answer.

I turned to grandmother, "Have you ever heard of some werewolf legend from around here? Some man who might be suspect?"

She looked upwards at the ceiling, seeing nothing in her blindness, but observing everything. Her mind was searching for something, a recollection. After some length, she responded. "Yes my son, I do recall some such tale, when I was a little girl. Many... many years ago. There was talk of some hideous murders committed far south of here near the big river. If I remember correctly, a powerful plantation owner was implicated." She turned to face us at the table. "It was said he was- loup garou."

We were all silent for a moment. Could that man be the same one who had created me? Could he have survived all these years? She had said the words: LOUP GAROU. They echoed with resounding horror in my mind.

"Of course I was very young.. and impressionable. I only remember overhearing my parent's hushed voices at bedtime. I do not believe they put much stock in the tale." She yawned. We were all very tired. It had been a long day and we had accomplished little except worry.

"What became of it?" Pierre asked.

"Nothing as I recall." A pause. "Oh yes, there was mention of a lynching, but that was common then. As unfortunately it still is today." Another pause, "The rumors soon faded."

"I must find him, seek him out." I spoke matter-of-factly.

"What?" Selena sat upright in her chair.

"You can't be serious, Henri!" Pierre exclaimed.

"It is the only way to get any answers to my questions. Perhaps he knows a way to end this curse."

"Why would he help you? Or cooperate in any way?"

"I don't know..I don't know," I repeated myself. "All I know is I must try. For all our sakes." I paused, "If necessary, I will confront him."

"Grandma-ma," Selena turned to the old one. "Tell him not to go. Tell him it would be useless, futile,..dangerous."

"Yes," she replied, "It will be dangerous. However, Henri is right, ma cherie. It may be the only way."

Selena was shaking her head, trying hard not to be emotional. "But like Pierre said- why would he help? He put the curse on you, why remove it? Even if he could.."

"My darling, like I said, I don't know. All I realize, too well, is

93

that this is my last recourse. With him may lie the answers I seek." I cupped her chin in my hand and looked in her eyes. "Perhaps I may even come back normal. And that is worth the risk. You are worth the risk."

"I could go with you?" Pierre offered.

"Non. It would be even more dangerous for you, as a mortal human." Grandmother was firm. "But promise us, my son, that you will not leave just yet. After all we have three to four weeks before the next full moon."

"Of course, grandma-ma." I would agree to anything right now. I was tired of conversation and, glancing out the window at the vermillion sunset, I was ready to go to bed. Ready to take Selena to bed.

"Well then, I must get some sleep. My old bones ache." And with that she rose up, which officially ended the discussion.

"Moi, aussi." Pierre got up quickly and proceeded to follow the matriarch out the door. "Wait and I will walk you home, grandma. Bonsoir, Henri. Au demain. Bright and early, right? We have a lot of chores and work to do. We are behind."

"Yes Pierre. I will see you early in the morning. Bonsoir."

With them gone, Selena and I snuffed out all the lights, undressed and crawled into our comfortable bed together. I knew how she felt: about her fear of the future, her trepidation, her fear for me. I felt it too. I held her very tight and we started kissing. My desire grew with persistence, not to be ignored, and feeling down between her legs, it found her also desirous, wanting.

We didn't speak, our lovemaking saying how we felt beyond words. But as I entered her and we moaned in our completion, I whispered softly to her: "Do not worry, ma cherie. Do not worry at all. I will return. I promise to never leave you. I could never leave you." She embraced me tightly, digging her nails into my back as we reached our climax. And that was only the beginning.

Selena was always convinced that it was on this night that she conceived.

For the next two weeks we were all very busy: working in the fields; tending to repairs about the cabins; Pierre and I hunting, trapping, fishing; taking care of our livestock. In fact, two of the mares were going to give birth. All omens were favourable.

During this time, we built onto our cabin- an extra room for grandma-ma, should she decide to stay the night. I wanted her near Selena while I was gone. The room could also serve as a nursery one day. So we felled a large amount of timber that month, Pierre and I working in the woods almost daily. Timber being plentiful and cheap, neighbors and villagers were always cutting down trees for buildings and every day uses as our towns grew rapidly in population. We would pay the landowner and then select and chop down the trees ourselves.

It was on one of these days that something extraordinary happened which I must relate. For it was an incident that brought home the realization- once again- I was not as other men. I was as different from others as night is from day. Death, even though being my constant companion, was not for me personally.

That sunny hot afternoon, there were a great number of us working in the woods. We all had to be cautious with so many in the same area felling trees. Pierre had wandered off in one direction and I had found a particularly suitable pine and was working fixedly on chopping it down, when I heard a resounding crash overhead. Looking up, I saw a huge tree toppling down fast towards me. Before I was able to react, it fell upon me with a severe thud, completely crushing my legs and hips. The excruciating pain racked through my body sending it into shock, and all went black.

And so, in that moment, as I lay dying or, in that moment of actual death, I had one immediate thought. At last, I would now find peace; that God had finally given me, by chance, his one last final mercy. Suddenly, from high above, I saw myself on the ground, pinned beneath that huge tree. There was a solitary man standing over me, looking for any signs of life; he then ran off. I did feel one single regret: that I would never see Selena again.

But then the vision disappeared, and all at once, I was back on the ground and I actually, consciously, felt the breath of life enter back into me. Inhaling deeply, I realized that the Lord had not been merciful after all: I obviously cannot die by ordinary means like an ordinary man. I might not ever die! I was not human.

Blinding pain flooded back in an immense wave. Without hesitating to think (and with great effort) I picked up the tree trunk and rolled out from under it. Crawling over to a tree stump, I propped myself against it. Even through the fog of pain, I felt my body recovering itself. Remarkably, supernaturally, my bones and flesh were repairing themselves. I thought perhaps I should hide myself somehow, however before I could move, the man who had discovered me returned with others. Pierre was among them.

The man's face turned pale as he stared at me, then at the fallen tree, then back at me. "But you were," he turned to the others, "I would have sworn he was dead."

"Apparently not," someone said as they more or less ignored him and gathered around me with concerned looks. Pierre kneeled down by my side.

"You are lucky to be alive, Henri."

"Yes. Yes I am. It didn't seem to crush or break any bones. Can you help me home?" I wanted out of there quickly before the questions became an interrogation.

"You were pinned under..that," he pointed at the tree. "You were beyond help." The poor man was totally bewildered. He pointed again at the felled tree. "A lone man couldn't move that. I don't see how..." His voice trailed off in wonder.

"Well he's out from under it now."

"Yes," I knew I should speak, say something by way of an explanation, no matter how weak. "I guess I was fortunate to fall into soft earth and leaves and sort of..just crawled out from under the tree. It is all a blur."

"But.." the man was going to argue a point, but I kept talking.

"And of course, the wind was knocked out of me temporarily. And you could not detect any breathing. Who can say? A

96

miracle has probably been performed here today." A murmur of agreement arose among the men. "Help me up Pierre. I must go home and pray with thanks."

Pierre gave me his strong shoulders for me to lean upon and I gathered myself up with his aid and we started to walk away.

"I swear.."

I turned to the man and interrupted before he could speak further. "Thank you, kind sir." I didn't want to leave too abruptly. We must be polite, convincing. "Thank you for bringing me help. It could have been much worse."

"You are lucky, mon ami," Pierre repeated. The man kept shaking his head in confusion; he wanted to protest some more, but doubt caused him to hesitate. "Come we must go, Henri. You have been through a terrible shock." Pierre's last words were a chastisement as we limped away, past the small gathering, into the woods. "Perhaps this is should be a warning to teach us to be more careful and diligent from now on." Then he added, "And not drink while working!" The men grumbled and looked down on the ground with guilt. When we were a few yards away, we looked back and they were dispersing.

We did not speak until we were well out of earshot. Each moment I was getting stronger, my body healing itself, regenerating new tissue. Soon we arrived at the cabin. Pierre sat me down at the table and he then sat across from me, waiting patiently for me to explain what really happened. Selena was not there. She must have been at the market or at her grandmother's.

"Pierre," I tried to speak calmly. "What that man said was true. I did die! I was dead when he found me."

"Mon Dieu," was all I heard.

"It is also true that my legs were totally crushed, useless." He inhaled audibly. "My body can heal itself, quickly and miraculously!"

"Like your wounds from when the beast first attacked you," Pierre was speaking softly as if to himself.

"Even faster now," I paused. "Pierre, I saw myself dead on the ground. My spirit.. or whatever, was above. Then I came back." I paused again. "Pierre- by all counts- I should be dead!"

"Miracles can happen. People see angels and when near

death, tell something similar to your story. It does not mean you were actually dead."

"Honestly, I don't think that is the same as what happened to me." I hesitated before continuing."Remember my mentioning the silver dagger?" He nodded reluctantly. "I believe only a silver weapon or object such as that can kill one like myself. If even then."

"Perhaps," he replied cautiously. "Henri, you are speaking of.. living for all time. Of immortality."

"Precisely," I agreed. "Immortality."

28

"Other men would sell their soul for such a thing." Selena and I were lying in bed together for the night. I had just finished telling her of what had happened earlier that day in the woods and my thoughts on it.

"Exactly. Giving their soul to the devil."

"But you are not like that, Henri. You could never be evil."

I was silent in thought for a moment. "But Selena, I have killed. At least once, uncontrollably. Indiscriminately. Perhaps, the moon brings out that part of myself. The part that a man keeps buried deep within. Then the curse releases it and allows it to surface." I paused. "Perhaps every man has the capability of murder. No matter who he might be. Even if he were a priest." I turned my face from her in guilt and shame.

She caressed my cheek with her hand. "You will return from this journey normal. As you once were Henri. Look at me." I turned to her and saw her beauty, her belief in me. "You will at least know much more than you do now. Answers- not all these superstitious speculations. And, we will work it out together, whether you come back cured or not."

"What if something happens and I don't come back at all? Or what if I do return, but not normal. Perhaps even worse. What if I return...?"

"Evil?" She finished for me, my thoughts having become hers now. "I do not believe that for one second Henri. And you must not either. Deep within you is good not evil. That is the reason guilt plagues you so. In fact," she smiled down at me, "I believe you to have a certain beautiful innocence within."

"Innocence?" I laughed. "Would innocence do this?" I pressed my hard sex against her thigh.

"Why Henri!" her reply coquettish, "You devil you!" We both could not help but laugh. It was a wonderful relief. As was the sex that followed. Our kisses with great longing and passion. Our making love this time very slow and long lasting, both of us knowing I would have to leave any day now. Afterwards, we just lay there in a tight embrace, languorously, catching our breaths; drenched in sweat from the sultry night of sex.

"I think maybe we should change the sheets!"

29

"Porthos will let you ride her." Selena was packing a few of my things into a small bag for my strange, hopeful journey.

"Yes, but she is also going to have a colt."

"I feel it will not be long before I am with child. If not already."

I kissed her. She was taking my imminent departure quite well. The moon was waxing quickly and I could feel its power growing ever stronger, even during the day. I was sure that I would need to leave by tomorrow. "I want to have a family with you very much, my love."

"Do you want a boy or girl?" she asked.

"Why a girl, of course, just like her mother!" She laughed at that. "And I have been meaning to ask you why you gave your mare a masculine name?"

"Oh I don't know. I just like the sound of it." She was humming about the cabin and I suppose, we were both trying hard to show optimism about my going away for awhile.

"Well I do hope you are more circumspect when it comes to

naming our child."

"Oh that's easy. If it's a boy, he will be Marcel. After your father and your middle name."

"And if it's a girl?"

"Why Porthos, of course!" She laughed like a little girl, as I grabbed her and tickled her. I would miss her so. We both fell upon the bed in young laughter and kissed warmly.

A knock at the door stirred us from our reverie. "Allo, anyone there?" It was Pierre coming by to get me for the day's work in the fields. Today we were working one the less wealthy, smaller farms nearby that owned no field slaves. The work was hard and paid little, but we were all now finally able to save money. Hopefully, with a bright future, we would have our own land one day.

"I am ready, Pierre." I called out. "I am ready." I hurried towards the door after having to rearrange myself in my pants first. Selena was able to coax desire from me, even with just a look. "I will see you and grandma-ma tonight, Selena."

"Goodbye you two." She called out after us. "Until tonight then."

Pierre and I walked the mile or so to the fields. "She is happy?" was his simple question.

"Neither of us is pleased I am going, but we are remaining hopeful that the outcome will be..." I searched for the right word, but found none. I just repeated, "hopeful. I am so glad grandma-ma decided to stay with Selena for the time being. Neither one should be alone."

"I am pleased also." He paused before continuing, "Isn't it time for you to be leaving? The moon was nearly full last night."

"Yes, no one is more aware of it than me. But I believe it is safe for me to stay one more night. I will leave in the morning."

He squeezed me around the shoulders and spoke with his usual joviality. "You find it difficult to leave Selena, non?" I nodded with a long sigh. I would miss my dear cousin almost as much as my wife. We resumed our walk, which today was more of a stroll. "You know where to go?"

"I should be able to find him- I believe. It is southeast of here, according to what grandma-ma told me. I will use my sixth sense." I paused in our walk and grasped him by both shoulders. "You will watch after them for me, Pierre? Take care of them? There is the distinct possibility.. .I may not return."

"You will survive. And you will return to us- whole and well. And yes, of course I will always take care of them. It is what friends and family are for. After all I love them too." We embraced. It was to be our last for a long time.

We started to part for he was to work on one side of the fields and I on another. Then as an afterthought, I turned and asked if he had heard if the person responsible for my accident in the forest had been found or come forward. He looked down at his shoes and shuffled his feet. "No, it is strange that. It seems everyone was accounted for in some other area." He looked up. "Perhaps they are afraid ...or ashamed."

"Yes, quite." I waved goodbye and resumed my walk, ignoring his odd behavior. I had much on my mind.

I looked forward to a day of hard work. Sometimes a man can clear his thoughts while performing manual labor. He does not have to concentrate on numbers or pleasing someone. In his aloneness, without interruption, he sometimes can see things clearly and in a more logical manner with less emotion.

There were a few others working alongside me, but we labored mostly in silence- chopping out weeds and gathering cotton. The task was arduous in the hot southern sun, but I had adapted well to this land and enjoyed working it. Feeling the rich earth beneath my hands brought me pleasure. How I longed one day for that which I could call my own.

I saw Pierre once more during a brief lunch break. Afterwards I went to the same owner's rice fields to help with its irrigation. Acadians are natural specialists at this, since we had built superb dikes and irrigation ditches in our homeland where the differences between high and low tides are among the most dramatic in the world. I stopped an hour or two before sunset and proceeded home without waiting for Pierre. I suppose I was slightly impatient to clean up and see Selena for our last evening together.

I was almost to our cabin when I happened to glance up into the bright cloudless southern blue sky and saw. . . large and near, a completely full moon filling the horizon with its presence! I felt its immediate influence. Dropping my tools, I sank to my knees and stared at the moon in disbelief. It had risen early. And with some daylight remaining! It was not expected until tomorrow or even the next day. Why had I not foreseen this happening? Sensed it happening? Why had I not been prepared for this? I had foolishly ignored the signs.

I still might have time to reach the sanctuary, the mausoleum. But non, that would not do me any good, for I know now how to open the secret door. But there were the chains! They were immense and strong, bolted securely and firmly into the wall. Strong enough to hold a gorilla captive. Might they be able to hold a werewolf? I started in the direction for the cemetery.

Only a few paces down the trail though, the first symptoms of the transformation began and I knew I could never make it there in time. Yet I must do something and quickly! But what?

Of course! A pentagram! I could draw a pentagram and place myself in it. The cabin was only a few paces beyond some trees and palmettos. I ran fast, trying to beat the setting sun. I would use the chalk that grandmother left inside. Or if I had to, I could draw a pentagram outside in the dirt. It was my last chance, for I felt the moon's rays on my back.

I looked up at the sky. The sun had all but disappeared, however the moon was hanging pendulously on the horizon, large and bright, reflecting the last golden ray of the setting sun.

It was at the doorstep when I felt the first pangs and doubled over in pain, falling just inside the cabin. There was little time for me to find the chalk marker. I struggled up on my feet, shoving aside the main table in my haste and began to tear through Selena's side cabinet searching for the marker. I had to draw the star and quickly, for my change was almost complete. In a matter of moments I would be transformed.

Then I saw it. Among the kitchen utensils. It was the silver dagger! Without hesitating, I reached for it. The instant burning sensation as I grabbed it actually produced smoke. I threw it down. In the last moment before I changed, I thought that if I grabbed the dagger fast enough and held tight onto it, I would be able to plunge it into my heart. And then I could experience peace. I reached down for it, but magically, impossibly, it flew away from me! Across the room! Seemingly of its own accord, as if some invisible force was preventing me from using it.

But I had no time to think upon what had just happened or what phantom could possibly be interfering with me, for the next thing I knew it was complete- I was transformed. The sun had set, the moon was shining and I was a creature again. A creature loose this time upon an unsuspecting world. And hunger called out to me.

I turned to run out into the early evening before any one saw me, but there in the doorway, was Pierre! Blocking my way with a frozen look of fright on his face. I fell him to the floor with one swipe of my hand, and then with the other hand, I clasped him tightly by the throat, picking him completely up off of the floor, his feet flailing about- just as if this heavy man was nothing but a rag doll. I brought him up close to my snarling face, my huge fangs bared, as he stared in terror and tried to speak but could not.

"Henri, No! Henri!" Selena's voice screamed from behind us. "Henri, it's me Selena." I turned to her, still holding Pierre by the throat. "Let him go, Henri. Let Pierre go!" I looked back at Pierre, his body limp and about to lose consciousness. Then she spoke calmly, with slow deliberation. "Henri, listen. That is Jean-Pierre, your cousin. Now, let him go." I dropped him to the floor. He gasped and coughed as he tried to get back his breath. But I had already fled past her and out the door.

I ran for miles, as quick as lightning, to try and escape the memory of what I had almost done. Even in my monstrous state I realized how close I had come to hurting my best friend. I do not know what would have happened if Selena had not intervened. I certainly was not able to trust myself, and was an obvious danger to my loved ones. If only I had been able to plunge that dagger into my heart! Then this nightmare would be over.

I stopped running and suddenly found myself far away, though near a place I had been to before. Sensing some humans nearby, I stealthily proceeded towards them. Soon, I saw in the near distance, the same home which I had come upon last month- the cabin containing a man and a woman which I had circled about but did not disturb.

The same couple was inside again. Only this time they were

in a very heated argument. She screamed; I heard a glass break. Their fight inexplicably excited me, rousing my appetite. I could not see them, yet knew exactly what was happening. He was in a terribly drunken state; beating her, slapping her around the room. She fell; I smelled the blood. He hit her again, even harder. However, she managed to grab a knife, warning him to stay away. He laughed, advancing towards her. With one hand, he grabbed her arm that held the knife; his other hand encircled her throat in a death grip. They struggled; I sensed her determination to live; and so with one last supreme effort, she succeeded in plunging the knife deep into his stomach. Releasing his grip, he backed away from her, in astonishment, and then fell heavily on the floor. I heard her scream as she panicked and fled outside into the night.

Now it was my turn. The scent of his blood filled me with thirst as I entered the darkly lit cabin. He was face down on the floor, still alive, but barely. I sensed his slowing heartbeat; soon he would be dead. I needed to act quickly.

I turned him over; the knife embedded deep inside him. His eyes were wide with pain, yet they grew even larger in bewildered terror as I drew my wolf's face close to his. He must have thought I was some sort of demon sent to escort him down to hell. Close enough.

It took only a few moments. I bit deep into his neck, eating his flesh, drinking his blood- the one bite almost decapitating him. With my mouth still on what was left of his throat, I picked him up, cradling the dead body in my arms and carried him outside. There was a bog nearby, heavy with summer fog and I disposed of him there. The knife still in him. I felt a certain amount of satisfaction as I watched his corpse sink slowly into the earth where no one would be able to find him. At least not for a very long, long time.

I returned to the cabin quickly, to erase any evidence. She had not returned as yet, and I doubt she ever would. If she did venture back, she would find no body, no blood. No one would be able to detect that a murder had taken place here. She (and others) will simply find that he has disappeared- hopefully, forever.

I left with my hunger satisfied. Remarkably, I had done all

this as a wolf-man. I had thought rationally, acting with reason and purpose as a man would. To be true, I behaved as a cold-blooded murderer- however, uniquely supernatural- an all powerful killer. In fact, I was the perfect murderer for I did not feel that peculiar human emotion called fear.

I wandered about the woody swamps the rest of the night, feeling glorious pleasure in the moonlight and dark shadows. I knew that once morning came I would begin my journey to find the one who had made me. Would he be such as I? Cursed with guilt? Guilt- that other emotion peculiar to humans which I still felt so strongly. I realized that if I ever did stop feeling it, then I was indeed, no longer human.

Even in my transformed state, I felt such remorse for hurting Pierre. If I had severely injured him I would never forgive myself. I had lost control and had to admit to myself that there may be times when the human side would not be able to suppress the beast within, the beast with out. It was all so unpredictable; my wolf's thoughts and actions far from certain.

Tonight at the stranger's cabin I behaved with certainty, with human thought and planning. However- I had to admit- I felt very little remorse (if any) at my killing him. I even rather...enjoyed it. Of course, the man was evil, but did that give me the right to execute him? His wife may also have been evil- a horrible harpy asking to be strangled by a tortured husband.

Mon Dieu! Perhaps my maker can help me deal with these contradictions. Help me, if not to end the curse, then how to live with it without hurting innocents. Perhaps he did not even consider it a curse.

I found myself wondering how he had come to be a werewolf and for how long he had been this way. If there was a cure, surely he would have discovered it and helped himself. Unless..he wanted to remain this way.

And then there was another very big question. Would I be welcome? He has never made himself known to me other than our recognizing each other at the voodoo ceremony. He had made no attempt to speak to me. Perhaps if I had been alone. Yet for some reason, I had the gnawing feeling that he does want me to come and see him. To meet on his land, on his terms. I imagined him greeting me with open arms.

All night I pondered upon these things and more, as I roamed about, a wolf on two legs, with a man's heart and a man's thoughts. (And wearing a man's trousers.) Soon I felt the night becoming day and I headed for home. I had always loved this land, but now, after all my nightly adventures, I had come to love it that much more. I saw and learned of things and scenes that no ordinary human could possibly experience or even imagine. I saw the animal kingdom in all its worldly wonder: hunting, killing, devouring and dying; I saw births and nursing; mating. Life and death in all it's glory. The splendor of trees and plants I had not known to exist. If only I could turn this curse into a blessing, something useful.

Dawn was breaking when I silently entered the cabin, as my human self. Selena had fallen asleep in a chair waiting for me. I gently kissed her on the forehead. She woke, her eyes immediately wide and alert. We fell into each other's arms, holding onto each other ever so tightly, saying nothing for a long moment.

"I am so sorry I frightened you yesterday. I had no idea I could possibly change before sunset." She kissed me.

Our lips parted reluctantly. "Are you alright?"

"Yes. Is Pierre..?" She nodded. I hugged her to myself again. "I am so sorry, Selena." I repeated. "You must tell him for me that I never meant to hurt him. I would sooner die. I would never forgive myself if .."

She pressed a finger to my lips. "He is fine, Henri. And he understands. Believe me he does. You can tell him yourself.."

"No, my dear. I must go now." She looked deep into my eyes, searching. "I must change clothes and leave as soon as possible. It will be a long trip, especially on foot."

She silently, gently took my hand and led me into the bedroom, "Of course, I understand." While I was washing up, she got the duffle bag out and efficiently went about making sure I had everything I needed: clothes, a knife, water, etc. She laid out fresh clothes for me. "I already made some sandwiches for your journey. Would you like me to make breakfast before you go?" Her voice was tinted with the hope that I might stay a bit longer.

"No, I.. I'm not really hungry." I hoped to God that she was

106

not reading my mind about the killing last night. I hated keeping secrets from her, but I couldn't possibly tell her that I had murdered (and feasted on) another human. Remorse and self-hatred flooded my soul, not so much because of my deed, more because I had to keep it hidden from her.

We said our goodbyes at the door. I hated goodbyes terribly. They always reminded me of my family's separation back in our homeland. The family that I have never seen since. And when will I see Selena again? Next week? Next month? . . .never?

"We will see each other again and soon, my darling." She answered my thoughts.

Our clock struck the hour. I had to be going. I glanced at the tall longcase, which was ticking the seconds away. "You will keep it wound faithfully?"

"I will keep it wound faithfully." She added, "Until your return." She then put her hand over my watch that was tucked in my vest pocket. "And you must keep my present near you always."

"I always do, my love. I always will."

Our parting was becoming difficult. I had to leave then or I might not leave at all. I gathered her face in my two hands. Her eyes were moist. "Je t'aime."

"Je t'aime," she replied. We kissed each other as if it might be our last.

As I turned to go, she reached up, caressed my face and said simply, warmly, "Each kiss is as the first."

I quickly walked down the path and onto the road heading south, hoping not to meet anyone on the way.

I would not want them to see my tears.

END OF PART ONE

Loup Garou

PART TWO

MY MAKER
MY MASTER

1

Where the land and the water uniquely join to become one;

Trees grow partially submerged, magically sprouting from beneath dark pools and basins with seemingly no need for solid ground;

There moss drapes heavy and thick from majestic limbs, touching to the ground forming curtains of gray/green, thriving off the very air;

Sheens of vibrant green lie over quiet still depths, sharing space with neighboring lilies;

Where the scents of magnolia and honeysuckle combine to form an intoxicating perfume heady in the atmosphere;

Sunlight forms trellised shadows beneath ancient trees;

There the southern heat builds to an afternoon climatic rain shower, to be replaced by cool evening breezes;

Where nature likes to demonstrate dramatic displays of her power in brilliant flashes and thick streaks of bright lightning, accompanied by powerful drums of thunder that shake the wet earth;

This- this was my land and it had come to be what I call home. It called out to me every night and every day, giving me comfort. Especially so as I proceeded on my sojourn. On a quest to find any answers that might shine light upon my dark nightmare.

And so, leaving my heart behind me with the ones I love, I started my journey of many miles to find the one who made me. I saw, along the way, even more of this lush and fertile land; much more than I had ever known before. Huge plantations of sugarcane; slaves working in fields of cotton; French Creole homes of modest grandeur that would one day grow into huge stately mansions. Signs of wealth, growth and prosperity were everywhere. It was such a beautiful French colony, similar in ways to where I grew up, yet with such a unique and different terrain.

With a different mix of people- French, native Indians, African slaves, free people of color, settlers from Haiti and the French West Indies, the Spanish. And there were new settlers- white ones- that hailed from a British colony near my old northern home. Yes, this was a beautiful place, still a wilderness waiting to be tamed, waiting to be overrun with greed and speculation, which brings its own particular transformations.

Near the end of the first day, I came to that very wide river, the greatest I had ever seen. In one day, I had traveled far and fast, without stopping even once, with no feeling of fatigue. Making sure I was well off the beaten pathway, I decided to camp the night there by the river and undergo the night's transformation. Hopefully, I would not come across any humans and maybe even not feel the hunger, the need to hunt.

Before night fell, I cooked a rabbit that I had caught along the way. And though I preferred the meat raw, I ate it well done, forcing myself to chew and swallow it, along with the bread and goat's milk Selena had packed. It all seemed so tasteless to me. No matter how much I tried to be my old self, it was just not happening. But perhaps the food would retard my wolf's appetite later in the night.

Afterwards, I climbed into the highest tree I could find and watched the moon rise high and bright in the cloudless starry sky. I transformed quickly, effortlessly, yet stayed in the treetop for most of the night. The wonder of the beautiful night held me in awe even in my supernatural state. More so in fact. My heightened senses of a wolf made the sensation ethereal and that much more remarkable. I was literally on top of the world: A king among the animals and I howled with pride and joy into that vast wilderness- my home, my kingdom. The sound echoed for miles around scattering the wildlife below who were going about their nocturnal rituals. The moonlight danced and sparkled on the endless river beneath me. I was in my element.

Later, I climbed down and waded into the water. I swam to the opposite bank and back again, as if to take exercise. I don't know why I did it, I just remember accomplishing the act. The deep current was very strong and only an experienced swimmer could cross it safely. It was strange to realize that such a seemingly placid, slow moving river would be so potentially dangerous beneath. Of course, in my wolf's form it was nothing.

I got out and relit my campfire, though I was not cold. Perhaps it was human habit. It would surely have been a strange sight if someone had happened by and saw me. I probably resembled a primitive caveman, a hairy Neanderthal, poking at the fire with a stick.

All the while, in the back of my mind, deep in the pit of

my stomach, was the hunger. However I consciously, humanly, suppressed it all the night and, miraculously- it worked- I woke an hour or so before dawn, human and soaking wet. Changing into dry clothes, I started again on my journey, following the river south. Yet I knew, that the next night I would likely not be able to control the desire to feed.

There was a busy ferry some miles down the way and I used it to cross to the other side, paying fare with the few coins I had with me. It was crowded with horse carriages and mules; packing goods and supplies; many fishermen and hunters (on horseback); and a few fellow travelers such as I. Nearby villages were growing and thriving, becoming towns with strong economies.

On the other side I abandoned the main river road and traveled on my own, following close to the river bank. The path was seldom used and very overgrown with brush and sharp palmettos. It did not hamper my progress though. I trampled through it easily.

It was then I suddenly fell into a small but deep hole covered with downed dead limbs and rotting wood. I laid there, flat on my back for a moment. The hole was well over my height. I quickly realized there was something alive in the pit with me. And not just with me, but all around me, even all over me: I found I had fallen into a snake pit!

The slithering, writhing black serpents were everywhere and I helplessly felt the same shock any human would upon being thrown into their nest. Frightful madness seized upon me and for more than an instant I experienced the insanity that others must have known when purposely thrown into snake dens for torturous reasons. (Supposedly it is also a cure for those who are insane in order to shock them back into sanity!) My presence of mind came back and I slowly raised up and stood perfectly still, frozen to the spot when...

I realized they were not attacking me. In fact, they

were trying to avoid me, many of them escaping from the hole. Even the devil's own knew what I was and wanted nothing to do with me! In fury, or some other unreasonable emotion, I grabbed one of the largest vipers and choking it, forced its mouth open, wide and white with venom dripping and I plunged its fangs deep into my neck, feeling the poison enter. I threw it down- dead, grabbed another and did the same again. And then another. The last one, before I crawled out of the pit, I forced to bite my wrist. My arteries were full of venom. I walked briskly about the river bank, breathing heavily, making my heart race for I wanted the poison to act quickly. I felt the venom travel slowly in my system, through my veins until..it finally reached my heart and then. . .Nothing!

No pain, no heart attack, no death, nothing. Again, no respite from this cursed agony.

I walked slowly away downriver, trying hard not to think about what had just happened- trying hard not to think at all. Mon Dieu, I asked him, is there no way to end this nightmare? Am I never to know eternal peace- just an eternal life of strife? What if I were to cut off my hand- would my body regenerate a new one? What if I were to lose my head- would I still survive, become a headless demon terrorizing the countryside?

I looked at the river, that wide, old and deep rolling river. So quiet and peaceful, so potentially powerful and deadly when it rages. It must have been here since ancient times, meandering, changing the landscape as it snakes its way to sea. It was timeless- older even than the forests and swamps. Will I grow old I wondered. Will I know eternal youth as well as life eternal?

I stared again at the river. Drowning- perhaps that could be the end of it. Even a werewolf needs to breath, and if the lungs were full of water, what then? What if it occurred when I was turned and not as a man? Death could perhaps come easier that way- or perhaps not.

My head was aching from so many unanswered questions. Soon again, it would be dark and again there would be a full moon. I sat down on a fallen log and made myself comfortable. I looked at my pocketwatch for the time and decided this would be as good a place as any to camp for the night. I ate a little bread and water, but did not really feel like food. I laid a blanket down over a bed of soft leaves and rested for awhile. I was finally beginning to feel some fatigue.

I looked up at the failing sunlight filtering through the leaves of the tree and thought of those magical moments when Selena and I made love beneath that other oak. It seemed like an eternity ago. I closed my eyes and imagined it happening again: Selena and I at our special trysting spot. My daydreams and the sound of the cicadas lulled me to sleep.

When I woke it was already night and it was the sound of crickets and river frogs that filled the air. I looked at myself- down at my hands and feet. This wasn't possible. The moon was full- I felt its light bathing me, shining bright on my face- And I was still human!

Surely I would change at any moment? I waited anxiously, but no transformation showed itself. I had not even the slightest symptom. So then I must still be sleeping and this had to be a dream. That was the only logical conclusion.

But this was no dream. I felt the heavy, humid motionless night air. My back was stiff from the position I had been sleeping in on the ground. I heard a night owl hoot and then heard the squeal of his prey. I stood. The ground beneath my feet was soft and moist. And there was one other undeniable sensation which caused me to realize this was no dream.

I sensed him! The other werewolf. The one who had made me as I am now. I sensed his presence- and he was not far.

I hastily grabbed my things and traveled away from

the river and towards where I believed him to be. I did not understand how I knew which way to go, I only knew if I kept in this direction I would certainly find him.

And how would I greet him? As a wayfarer, a poor simple traveler, come in search of answers? Or do I accuse him? Confront him with what he did to me? Or..let him do the speaking? Surely he must know of my nearness, just as I could tell of his. I was more than certain that he would be expecting me.

I reached a clearing among the trees. A home was just beyond a line of oaks on the other side- his home. Dim lights flickered in the distance. I started across. The ground was wet, marsh-like, thick with mud. Just as I left the shadows and entered into the moonlight, a very large shadow flew past over me, completely blocking out the moon. Glancing up I caught a glimpse of something large flying, low in the sky heading towards my destination. Ten times larger than the largest hawk, it disappeared quickly. It looked like nothing I had ever seen before or could have ever imagined. A gigantic flying beast of some sort. Like some prehistoric animal I had read tales about that lived long, long ago. It resembled... a dragon!

I became dizzy and fell down to my knees. I thought maybe I was beginning to transform, but that was not the case. Gathering myself together, I surprisingly found that I was waist deep in a morass of boggy swamp and slowly sinking deeper. Quicksand! When I struggled to release myself, I only sank quicker and deeper. Soon I was up to my neck. I tried to stay still, to arrest the sinking. But to no avail. Deep down, my feet struck what I knew to be skeletons or carcasses of animals, perhaps even humans, that had been previously trapped here and died.

So this is how it will end, I thought. And so close to finding my answers. I shouted for help, just before I was covered completely, though there was little hope of anyone hearing me. I was too far away from the plantation.

Then came the moment- I was totally covered. I could not breathe, but I also could not die. I let out a silent scream as my body went into a sort of catatonic state- I suppose, not unlike the 'zombies' I had witnessed at the voodoo ceremony.

My thoughts were minimal. I seemed to be aware of only one thing:

I was trapped, and would most probably not die, yet remain in this state until some flood washed over the land and flushed me back out into the world of the living. To my horror, I realized I could possibly stay in the earth forever, never dying, never given a merciful end. A living burial; A living inhumation! Never to find eternal peace, only to suffer an eternal nightmare.

I do not remember how long it took for my brain to shut down into nothingness and the only thing I was cognizant of was a slow, barely perceptible heartbeat. Then some thing reached down, grabbed me by both shoulders and pulled me out of the quicksand in one mighty swoop. Suddenly I was flying through the air past the clearing, over the trees and swiftly nearing the plantation. Dare I to look at what was carrying me!

I looked to one side at what held my shoulders. Giant reptilian claws! I heard the swooshing sounds of large fleshy wings and glancing upwards saw what is best described as a gigantic bat, three times the size of a man. I could not see its face and I did not want to. Though strangely, I had a tiny recollection that I had seen a creature similar to this somewhere, some place- and recently.

Casting my eyes down below, I saw a large home, in the Creole plantation style, lit with life, and the creature was heading for it. It flew down, slowly, to the ground and when near the front of the house, the strong claws released me and I tumbled gently onto a spot of soft meadow-like grass surrounding the mansion.

I just laid there, my eyes shut, so relieved to feel solid

earth beneath me: soft, green, cool. Covered in wet swamp muck, I felt an immense gratefulness to be spared from what certainly would have been an eternal torment. I coughed, spitting up swamp water and tried to gather back my breathing, calmly wondering just what it was that I had just experienced. Had that creature been purposely sent to rescue me?

"Thank God," I murmured.

"No. Thank me."

I unclosed my eyes and saw a man's face staring close down at me. It was his face- the one with the dark penetrating blue eyes! The same man I saw at the ceremony- the one same as myself. His eyes and face displayed no emotion. They seemed blank, 'placide'- showing no concern, no wonderment, no anger.

For some reason I felt safe. Safer than I had felt in a long time. Yes, I was sure I was safe. And this he communicated to me (without speaking!) that I was safe; that I should rest; and yes, he had been expecting me.

I slowly shut my eyes. After two days of traveling miles on foot and my experiences of stressful terror in the snake pit and quicksand, I was beyond exhaustion. I wanted to sleep right there and then on that heavenly spot of comfortable grass. I had reached my destination. My search was over and now I could rest for a time...

I whispered to him, "Merci." And I slept.

2

Waking up in a brightly lit room, I found myself in a most comfortable four-poster bed with pineapple finials, carved all in fine solid mahogany. I lay on lush feather pillows and clean white woven sheets. No mosquito netting. Silver candelabra and wall scones lit up the room. It was still dark outside. The bedroom was immaculately and elegantly furnished with a writing table, a very large armoire, other small tables and upholstered comfortable chairs, every piece carved from luxurious woods. Imported rugs lay on a highly polished wooden floor. Light, white gossamer drapes, gently flowing from a night breeze, covered the ceiling to floor windows that opened onto a balcony. The walls were covered in a subtle, dark gold color. Such wealth I had only beheld in the fine homes of our town officials where I lived. Against the far wall, above a fireplace, hung a portrait of a young man. On the carved white marble mantel ticked a gilt French clock with a statue of an angel comforting an infant in her arms. It struck the hour of one on its tiny delicate bell.

I had not slept very long. Unless I had slept through the whole day and night! I suppose I could have. Nevertheless, I felt completely refreshed. And I knew that the moon outside was full and bright.

Yet I was still human, untransformed. In fact, I was lying naked on the bed completely cleansed and washed. Someone had bathed me during my deep sleep.

I saw that my clothes had been cleaned too, and laid out across the room on a type of settee or daybed. And on the floor beside it was my bundle of clothes and things I had carried with me all that way. And my pocketwatch! It lay open on the small marble-topped table beside the bed. Its tiny tick was going strong. I eagerly grabbed the bright and shiny case. It was undamaged, as beautiful and polished as the day it was given to me. The delicate moon hands registered the hour of one also.

I felt curiously relaxed and at home here- even after my encounter with that freak monster last night (was it last night?). However I also felt a guiltiness at being so comfortable. I walked over to a round wooden table in the center of the room where a pewter pitcher sat, wet with sweat from the cold water inside.

I poured myself a drink into one of the crystal glasses provided and drank it down slowly. Going to one of the open windows, I looked up at the night. Just as I had supposed, the moon was big and shining in a clear sky. Though it was waning, I still felt its power- yet for some reason I had not transformed again this night. Was the curse magically lifted from me somehow? Hope, beyond hope!

But at the same moment, I thought not. Deep down inside of me, I felt the moon having some hold over me, some attraction even. And what is more, the hunger was still with me- that unrelenting desire for human flesh. I was certainly not cured, at least not totally. Something, or someone, had prevented the transformation. Perhaps my maker had the means, the where-with-all to cast an orb of influence about me, about this house, his land.

I put on my trousers and walked onto the balcony and into the humid night. I was on the second floor of this wealthy but modest plantation home. Looking down I saw him, the other like myself, taking a bath in a large wooden round tub or cistern. He, sensing my presence, looked up at me and beckoned for me to join him. I heard his thoughts as if he were standing next to me whispering in my ear. He pointed to the back of the house where I noticed a small wooden staircase leading downstairs.

Surprisingly, I felt no apprehension as I followed the steps down. Most of the house was lit well and (if my room was any indication) it must be full of many fine furnishings. He had to have servants but I saw none of them about. Perhaps he even owned slaves, since he must have land and fields in order to support this comfortable style of living.

I observed him carefully as I approached. This was the man who made me. Though only slightly taller than myself, he had a much larger frame which gave him a lean muscular torso with exceptionally broad shoulders, making his head seem almost small in comparison. He had long, coal black hair, straight, not wavy as mine. And he sported a well-trimmed goatee in the manner of many French and Spanish men of that time.

His features were well-chiseled with a sculpted chin. His eyes commanded my attention. Though deep set, they were immediately noticeable for their arrestingly deep blue colour. Overall, he was a rather handsome, masculine man with a certain magnetism I was not immune to. Again I heard his thoughts- His name was Gerard.

I took off my trousers, with no regard as to who might be watching, left them carelessly on the ground and climbed into the large tub with him. Instead of extending his hand in friendship, he opened his arms with affection, anticipating an embrace. I hesitated only slightly. If it had been any other man I would have simply, shyly, turned away.

We embraced. I remember that the first immediate sensation was feeling his hard stiff sex against my own. Which made me take notice that I too- surprisingly- was just as stiff.

We held each other in a tight grip. I noticed how broad was his back; how his heart beat was rapid and strong against mine. Our eyes locked; our facial hair grazed one another. If he had kissed me, I would have responded in kind, but we did not. We merely stood there for some minutes.

Before we dissolved the embrace, he spoke out loud for the first time- His voice low and melodic, in a whisper deeply masculine, his breath falling lightly on my lips. He was glad I had not come to him in anger. That he had not meant to make me as he was. But now that it was a fait accompli, we were bonded, like as blood brothers- even more so. He realized I had many questions and in time he would answer them and teach me all he knew and tell me of his own history.

We parted and then proceeded to bath and soap one

another completely. I followed his lead. I had never thought of two men enjoying each other physically. If I had, I would most probably have dismissed it as not only improbable, but impossible. However that night I concluded it was not only possible, but it must be much more commonplace than I would have ever imagined. I also came to realize, that in a world of many different types of ecstasy, I had, that night and without fore-thought, made the discovery of several more.

We stepped out of the tub and he began to dry me off. He was right- I had so many bewildering questions. What was that creature? Why had I not transformed with the full moon? And he, unchanged as well! Is he so powerful? Perhaps not only a werewolf but something more! A sorcerer with powers beyond common voodoo? Could he cure me? If so, why has he not helped himself?

With ourselves wiped dry, and again with no regard to curious eyes, he took me by the hand and led me to the front of the house near where the giant flying creature had safely dropped me. There, with the bright moonlight bathing our naked bodies, he told me to gaze upwards. I did.

Suddenly the power of the moon enveloped me. He had been controlling our transformations! Preventing it or forestalling it in some way. Now he released his influence and instantly, we both shifted shapes giving ourselves over to the moon above.

So I had a companion to join me in the night. Gerard must have long been wanting someone to share in this; for some one who is like him. He had to have suffered a loneliness most profound. But now we each had the other to hunt with, to share in this inhumanity.

For we were the same. As human misanthropes, we both knew the isolation- the feeling of being different than others. Being among people, yet being none of them.

For we were the same. As lycanthropes, we had the same animalistic feelings, the same powers and desires-the same relentless hunger.

It was a relief to share this with someone. To know that there was another as myself.

However that night we did not hunt, though the hunger was always with us. Instead, remarkably, we played! Like little pups, we enjoyed one another. Climbing and leaping, we wrestled, tumbled and tussled- nipping and scratching each other in play. He would climb up the tallest tree faster than a squirrel and I would follow. He taught me that I could jump as high as the two story house- even higher. He showed me that the strengths we possessed were even more enormous than I had previously believed; that most anything within our imagination could be accomplished. Except for actual flight, our abilities were practically limitless. Even the quicksand could not conquer Gerard. With a little thought, ingenuity and belief in my powers, he taught me that I too, could have freed myself from that boggy mire.

So for me that was another night of self-discovery. We raced each other- faster than the fastest cheetah; swam through the great river- swifter than the swiftest shark. A huge alligator had the ill luck to come across our path. Gerard chased after it, caught it and pried open its fierce, powerful jaws until they snapped in two. He tossed aside the carcass as if it were a mere chicken bone. We traveled far and fast that night, across his extensive acreage. We did not think of feeding, our only thoughts were of our happy companionship. If we had paused in our adventure, we might have fed, but it would be later, during other full moons when we would hunt and devour together.

The moon was setting: our night had passed by quickly, soon dawn would be here. We returned to the plantation and climbed up the same staircase I had descended earlier. His servants and field hands would be waking soon. He motioned for me to enter the room where I had awakened, where my clothes and few possessions were and once inside, I astonishingly found that I was back to my human self. He too, was now Gerard, the man. We stood naked before each other, (I not knowing what to expect), when smiling, he spoke casually, in a tone I would come to recognize and appreciate as his relaxed hospitable manner. He told me to consider this my room and for me to rest as long as I would like. He would send for me in the mid-morning and then give me a proper tour of this plantation he called home.

He started to leave out onto the balcony, when he turned back and said pointedly, and with some emotion, "I am pleased, mon frere, that you have come to me here. It makes me very glad."

"Moi, aussi" I replied, but he had already exited out the door-window.

I blew out the lights and laid down on the plush bed and whispered out loud to myself,

"I am glad also, mon frere. I am glad also."

3

I awoke to the sound of the clock striking nine. Eagerly, I arose and went over to the brown marble washstand in one corner of the room and proceeded to wash up. I had been provided for: a porcelain pitcher of fresh water, the matching bowl to pour it into, soap and a clean towel awaited.

I ventured over to the armoire and looked inside. Gentlemen's clothes filled the cabinet. Going through them, I noticed they were fresh and clean, not musty smelling like garments that have been stored a long time. They were certainly finer than the clothes I possessed. And they looked as if they might fit myself. I grabbed a white, light linen long-sleeved drawstring shirt and put it on. A perfect fit. Next I tried on a light brown pair of pants- a tiny bit large in the waist, the length a fraction too long, but barely noticeable. I found the matching vest.

Below in the bottom of the cabinet, were a number of boots and shoes, along with men's stockings. I selected a dark tan pair of leather riding boots. Their fit was remarkable. I wondered whose clothes these were. Did they once belong to the young man whose portrait hung in this room?

I walked over to the mantel and gazed up at him. A relative of Gerard's perhaps? He showed no resemblance. This man was fair and blonde, with hazel green eyes, clothed in a fine suit with a high starched collar and contemporary apparel. The portrait, itself, was an excellent piece of artwork. The subject sat straight and dignified with legs crossed, long slender hands on his knees. His face had a subtle look of determination. Overall, the portrait captured a great deal of strength, with perhaps, a hint of delicate aristocracy. Suddenly and oddly, it struck me that this young man was one of the most beautiful men I had ever seen. He reminded me of an angel.

The gilded frame showed that no small expense had been taken. It appeared that a tiny plaque had once occupied a space on the bottom of the frame and had since been removed. Perhaps the young man had lived here at one time.

The signature of the artist in the right lower corner was barely discernible, only the beginning letters were clear. F..O..NI, no that was t. FONTE..N "Mon Dieu!" I exclaimed out loud. Fontenot! The same identical name as on the crypt in the cemetery!

A coincidence? What was this portrait doing here at Gerard's? This was too much of a coincidence to be a coincidence. If Fontenot was the artist, then who was this in the portrait?

Perhaps this was a picture of the scientist himself, the creator of that strange dungeon-like vault. The supposed reviver of dead corpses! Or maybe this was the creation himself? I looked closely at the hands. They might well have belonged to the man who had opened up the tomb and helped me escape that night. But I could not say for sure.

It just meant another mystery to solve, raised another question to answer; to join the many that I eagerly wanted to ask of Gerard. I strolled out onto the balcony and heard Gerard below, to the rear of the house. I climbed down the same staircase as last night, but I turned to the right in the direction of the voices. Beyond a small trellis, filled with blooming flowers, was a large, uncovered brick courtyard, with a small fountain in the center where a cupid was pouring water that trickled gently into a round pool of water lilies. Completely surrounded by beautiful, extremely tall and shady myrtles and blooming lavender, the courtyard was a little slice of heaven. At the far corner, under the shade of a grand old oak, sat Gerard at table, commanding a young black male in French. He nodded to Gerard before taking off to the other side of the house and disappeared inside a large cabin, unattached to the main building which I concluded to be the kitchen. Gerard waved for me to join him.

The table setting was immaculate. A white tablecloth covered an iron table. Delicate crystal glasses and china cups were filled with water, coffee and red wine (which I came to know as Gerard's drink of choice). Matching china plates were filled with scrambled eggs, grits and thin round, rare steaks. A thick spicy tomato sauce sat untouched.

"I enjoy the finer things in life," he admitted. "A cigar, wine, different foods."

"It doesn't repel you," I asked as I took a seat opposite from him, "or upset your stomach?" I unfolded my starched white linen napkin.

"No, I suppose I got used to it over time," he replied while cutting into his steak and eating heartily. "You will also," he paused, his full fork in mid-air, "especially if you live as long as I!" He laughed and I smiled not knowing how to reply; plus the fact that I was slightly uncomfortable, unused to what for me was luxury. I did wonder just how old he was.

"This evening," he replied to my thought. "This evening I will tell all about myself and my...uniqueness." He leaned over the table towards me, "Which is our uniqueness now, n'est-ce pas?" He knew what I was thinking and if I concentrated hard enough, I could read his mind- for the most part. "Yes," he continued, "there is a great telepathy, even an empathy, between us." Another pause while he finished chewing. "Because of our special... relationship." Again he laughed heartily and happily, before gulping down a whole glass of his special wine. "Eat, eat," he urged me.

I tried the different foods and they were quite good, especially if I slathered fresh butter over it. Actually, I started to eat a little of everything and my body felt little or no rejection to it at all. The coffee was good, dark and strong just the way I liked Selena to make it.

I did notice the utensils were made of simple pewter. There was absolutely no silver on the table. "No silver," he replied. "Of course, it does not burn me now, as it first did." A question took shape in my head, but he answered before my lips could form the words. "It simply...annoys me. Yes, that is the best way to describe it. It annoys me." He sipped his coffee. "You too, will get used to handling silver so that it does not cause the pain it once did." Here he leaned near me in his intimate manner, as if confiding a secret. "In fact, it is necessary that you learn to handle silver, so no one can use it against you." He returned to his plate of food. "I have many such survival tips." His short laugh was echoed by a mockingbird's call.

I was about to ask how this was possible, when the young servant returned, bearing a large, slightly cooked ham. Gerard motioned for him to slice it up and serve us. The boy was dressed all in white with a light linen jacket and I thought he must be very uncomfortable in such a formal looking costume. His features were large, yet well-proportioned; his complexion dark brown, common in this French colony of mixed breeds. Huge hazel eyes showed his emotions readily. He was mulatto; handsome in his own youthful right. I could tell by the way his clothes fit and his manner of carrying himself, that he possessed a strong and muscular frame. Gerard next spoke authoritatively. "This is Henri. You will treat him with the same deference as you do me." He paused to make sure the young man was listening. The boy nodded. "You are to consider him as another master of this house." He put particular stress on the word master. "Obey him for as long as he stays." At this point they both looked at me as if for a response. The boy's glance had a subtle, but distinct look of…jealousy?

I deliberately clouded my thoughts about my plans which was easy for I did not know myself. I merely nodded and replied, "Merci, Gerard."

"You must call me mon frere. After all we are going to become..close to one another."

The boy shot me a quick glance and this time it was unmistakably a glare of anger. "Bien sur," I replied. "Mon frere."

"Now you, get along and tend to your duties." The boy obligingly left. Gerard called out after him, "and be sure that everything is cleaned and polished for our special guest." He then turned back to his food and drink. We ate for a moment in silence, till he spoke. "That boy. He is handsome, non?" He looked at me carefully, searching for a particular response.

"Yes, yes, he is. Which reminds me. In my room there is a…"

"Portrait?"

"Yes, who is he?"

"You do not know? But haven't...surely you met him?" Gerard lowered his knife and fork for the first time since I sat down.

"No, should I have? I do not recall."

"Was it not he who rescued you from that mausoleum vault?"

"That was him?"

He returned to his bloody ham. "I presume so."

"How did you know..?" He held his hand up for my silence, while he finished a particularly large morsel of meat, before delicately wiping his lips with his napkin.

"That painting, I believe to be a self-portrait of Julian Fontenot. The so-called 'monster' that was revived from the dead through scientific means by a Dr. Francois Fontenot, whose own likeness, by the way, is hanging downstairs in the study. Whoever the artist is, his work is excellent, non?"

"How did you come by...?"

"I found them in a small second hand shop in the city. They sell all kinds of antiques and odds and ends. I will take you one day." He rested his knife and fork in his plate, apparently finished with breakfast and poured us both a full glass of his wine blend.

"So it was he in..?"

"It had to have been."

"So the tunnel and vault were built by this, Dr. Fontenot?"

"Yes." He gulped down his drink and made a sigh of satisfaction. "And I know what you are about to ask next. But it was not I who carved your name and date of death on that sarcophagus lid."

"Then who? One of the Fontenots?"

"I do not think so." His gaze turned far away towards some distant place and time, perhaps towards someone. I could not read his thought, but I sensed he had an idea who might have perpetrated such a cruel joke. Another player in this game of chess with my life and my loved ones at stake?

"Yes, it was very cruel," he responded to my thought.

"But..is my secret..safe? How many out there know about me? About you?"

"Danger is something you will have to learn to live with, mon frere. Just as I have. And not only danger from misguided humans, but from others- immortal beings who are jealous. Not to worry though, Henri, for I will teach you the ways of the werewolf. I have not survived all these many years for nothing." He patted my hand warmly and left it there.

"And now I must go," he said dismissing the subject. "I had hoped to show you my land and home myself, but I find that I have numerous duties which require my...personal attention. I will, directly, send you Toussaint, was born here. Rather an old man now, he is still a most reliable and faithful slave. I could not run this plantation without him. He is sort of my..foreman. I have instructed him, and all my slaves, to extend to you every courtesy and obey your every wish." He squeezed my hand, clasping it tight.

"Again, I am most happy you are here with me." He waved one arm about him. "Treat all I have as if it were your own." Releasing my hand, he started to rise but stopped. A single dark eyebrow arched as he looked at me closely, and said simply, "Gabriel."

"Who?"

"You were about to ask me what was that 'winged creature' which had rescued you from the mire, non?"

"You call it Gabriel?"

"That is the name I have given him, because he is… like a guardian angel. He watches over me and mine."

"What is it? Exactly?"

He rose from the table and patted me on the shoulder, much as Pierre had always done. "I will let

Toussaint introduce you. I assure you he is harmless. Think of him as an overgrown pet." He chuckled mysteriously. "Toussaint will be by shortly, so please sit for awhile, enjoy the rest of your breakfast and my special wine. Perhaps you can guess the special ingredient. But beware... it is very addicting!" He turned to leave, his hearty laugh echoing behind him. It was a friendly laugh, loud and boisterous- and catching. A laugh without worry, without care. "Exactly. Sans Souci." I heard him shout. I looked up from my wine. "Sans Souci." He was facing me, his arms outstretched. The house, the crepe flowers- the beauty of it all- was his background. I knew what he meant. He had read my mind- now I read his. And I understood.

This land, his home and plantation; his slaves and possessions; his view of life- and death. It was all 'sans souci'. I thought what a wonderful thing, a most glorious way to look at your life- your future, even your past.

And for the first time in a long time, as his figure faded in the distance, I felt worry lift itself away from me. For a grand moment, there in that beautiful spellbound spot, my curse seemed only a mild annoyance. Something that maybe I could live with, as Gerard seemed able to.

So I relaxed beneath that shady oak, drank more wine (which made me not in the least inebriated) and felt happy and carefree. And from that moment on, I tried to adopt that same motto, that same attitude. Embrace it as part of my life- no matter what comes. I raised my glass in a silent toast.

A Sans Souci!

4

Toussaint was a very dark, older man with a thick crop of curly gray hair. He still had an obvious strength in his frame, no doubt from hours of toil and meaningless labor as a slave. As I grew to know him, I found that the lines and deep furrows in his face, denoted not so much age as it did wisdom. In this, he reminded me very much of grandma-ma. His French was sharp and articulate, showing he had been well educated.

One day, I would come to regard him as my closest confidante.

We started the day with him showing me the land and fields which were extensive- acres and acres of sugarcane, cotton and rice patties. The plantation extended all the way to the great river's banks where a large bayou leisurely meandered its way into the deep waters. A pasture on higher, drier ground held over 100 head of cattle, and as many goats and sheep. There was even a large man-made pond filled with fresh-water fish. A huge pecan grove marked the most southern boundary to the plantation; a small vineyard denoted the north. I was in awe.

And all along the way, the slaves were hard at work. Occasionally we stopped and Toussaint would converse with one or two; or give orders to the different field hands. He sometimes used an African dialect with them of which I had no understanding. I did notice though, that most of the slaves seemed elderly or perhaps middle-aged. Many were women. Most notable was an obvious absence of young males. I also noticed the large whip Toussaint had with him. It looked well used.

We rode all that long, hot summer day. The horse provided me was old and slow; it acted drugged almost. Maybe it was the only way to keep him calm, while another creature, such as I, rode upon it. Toussaint had given me a straw hat with a wide brim to protect me from the relentless sunshine for clouds were sparse that day. He remarked that I looked very much the planter gentleman in my new clothes.

And I did feel quite relaxed and comfortable while

touring Gerard's small empire. But I had my questions. How had he come by all this? And whereas I had seen many slaves, there were just not enough of them for the amount of land owned. Which brought up another question in my mind.

Much of the fields lay uncultivated with only about half of the total fields being planted and harvested. The land was obviously not being used to its utmost. But when I brought any of these questions up to Toussaint, he merely shrugged and replied it was the master's way.

The land and sky grew a rose color and the sun fell low in the west, as we approached the slave's quarters before going back to the main house. The small cabins were some distance from Gerard's mansion and numbered about a dozen or so. The (mostly young) female slaves stared silently and long at us as we rode slowly by. They were doing chores- washing clothes or cooking in large cast iron pots over open fires. One was churning butter. I noticed more than a few were heavy with child. Several small children, all girls, squealed and scurried about. Some approached us and Toussaint greeted the little ones with affection. I remarked to myself that many of them were very light skinned.

I wanted very much to stop and look inside one of those tiny, wooden cabins and see just how these poor people lived their everyday lives, especially as compared to the luxuries of the plantation house. Behind their homes lay a tiny bayou, contributing mosquitoes and a foul stench, made worse by the stale, humid summer air. Toussaint insisted that we go on quickly to the house for he had many chores to do before it got dark. He said I could explore the rooms in the mansion on my own before dinner.

Leading up to the main entranceway was a magnificently grand oak alley with a small carriage road in the center that curved at the front entrance and ended at a covered carriageway at the kitchen side of the house. The oaks were huge- tall ancient sentinels, certainly to have been one, maybe two centuries in age, planted no doubt by some intrepid explorer long, long ago whose name and figure time has now forgotten. Immense trunks connected to writhing roots at the base of each; roots so large that a man could climb up on them and hide himself easily.

Amongst the trellised shadows, under the trees far-reaching heavy hanging, limbs, curtained thick with moss, were placed, randomly, here and there, many statues- some broken, some intact- all covered on their shadowed side by green/brown mold. There were nude female statues, cupids, a man on a rearing horse and a warrior god among others. Perhaps Gerard acquired them at that same shop where he found the portrait of Julian Fontenot.

Close nearer the house, one statue in particular loomed large. Curiously, it had no mold on it. It even looked new, fresh. It was of a winged gargoyle crouching with bended knee on a substantial plinth. It was the largest statue of the group and certainly the largest I had ever seen. If it had been standing, it would have reached to the second story of the house. The other gargoyles at the cemetery vault were miniscule in comparison. In fact...

It was then that I realized just what I was looking at. I stopped the horse but this time he was reluctant to obey me, showing some spirit for the first time that day. "Toussaint," I asked in wonder, "is this," I pointed to the statue. "Is this...Gabriel?" I looked Toussaint straight in the face. His reply was to grab the reins to my horse and gently guide us to the main stairway leading to the front door of the mansion.

"Answer me, Toussaint. Is that Gabriel?"

He did not look at me directly, but mysteriously replied that at night all things were possible in this land. "I must now take your leave, Master Henri. Master Gerard needs me. Please take your time and look through the house; make yourself comfortable. You should find café-au-lait, little cakes and wine in the study. The master usually suppers around nine in the evening, in the downstairs dining room. He appreciates promptness."

I dismounted. Then before he left he added, "It has been my sincerest pleasure to serve you today. I hope your stay with us will be a most pleasant one." With that he rode off in a flash, my horse trailing behind.

I turned towards the entrance. The house was built in a simple Creole manner, but with the addition of a second story and wide balcony above. Downstairs a small porch wrapped around the front of the building. The entire structure was built up on brick pilings in case of floods. The double staircase was dark red brick with wooden railings painted white. The main frame of the house was a pastel yellow with white trim on the square columns and banisters. The floor to ceiling shutters/doors were a dark, swamp water green.

It was not one of those columnar goliaths of later years, that sprung up with the burgeoning economy based on sugarcane and cotton. When Dixieland had more millionaires than anywhere else on the continent; built on the breaking backs of black slave labor. No, this was a simple, yet elegant house, a small mansion in its own way- a place easy to call home.

I walked up the stairs and strolled around to that side of the porch, where the rain cistern was which Gerard and I had bathed in last night. There was a young slave girl, dressed in gingham, with a white scarf about her head, sweeping. She looked up at the sound of my approach. "Oh, monsieur," she spoke with some relief. "I thought it may have been Master Gerard. You must be the new master." She curtsied politely, demurely. "I was told to show you inside and fetch whatever you may require or desire." Possibly- barely- sixteen years old, she was already demonstrating the blossoms of womanhood. Her speech was in a wonderful, lilting patois, a mixture of French and English, but I understood her none the less.

She passed by and showed me towards the front door. Opening it, she gestured for me to enter first. Her features were familiar, a little like old Toussaint. "Would you be Toussaint's daughter?"

She put her hand over her mouth and gave a small girlish giggle. "Oh no, Master Henri. He is my grandpa-pa."

"I thought I recognized a resemblance. How are you called?"

"My name is Juliette," she replied with downcast eyes.

"The name suits you." Her milk chocolate cheeks showed a slight blush.

She closed the door behind us. "The dining room is to the right and the front parlor to the left, and beyond that room is the study, where you will find hot coffee and milk waiting for you Monsieur. There is also wine. However," her soft voice dropped into a conspiratorial whisper, "if you prefer, there is some of master's rum kept locked in his cupboard. The skeleton key is in the right hand top drawer of the roll-top desk." Her tiny giggle surfaced again. "If you wish, Master Henri, allow me to pour for.."

"Non, ma cherie. I am sure I can manage. Thank you though, Juliette; I suspect you to be a real treasure."

The blush returned to her soft, round face again. "Bon, then I must finish my chores before tending to supper. If monsieur wants for anything just ring the hand bell that is on the tray- like Master Gerard does- and one of us will come running directly."

"Merci, Juliette." She curtsied, then disappeared down the hall towards the rear door. As I watched her small, graceful figure, I felt a yearning in my loins and thought of Selena. I was starting to miss her- I had to occupy my thoughts with something else.

I looked about. I was in a large foyer with highly

polished pine floors. A single steep staircase on my left, led upstairs. It was of a different wood, with an elegantly slim banister, probably all built of mahogany. The walls were papered in a light silver color, with raised designs of flowers and vines in a rich pattern befitting the entranceway to a plantation home.

A grand longcase clock commanded the room. It was not of French design as those at home. Instead, it was most likely an English or Scottish clock, with a finely polished brass dial. The solid wooden case of darkly stained mahogany was shaped with a bonnet, trunk and base. It was working steadily, his tick strong and healthy. Standing before it, it struck the hour of five for me, on a large bell that was loud enough to be heard, not only throughout the house, but outside as well- probably even in the kitchen. I wondered who had been keeping it in working order and I longed to take a look at the mechanism. But that could wait for another day. As I turned away I felt a deep chill which I thought was odd on such a hot day.

I ignored it and wandered into the front parlor. It was decorated mostly in white, the elegantly upholstered settee and chairs in pale greens with rose-tinted tiny pillows. A white marble fireplace mantel graced one wall. Atop it was another French clock, this one all in black onyx to contrast with the white room. A harpsichord was in the far corner; the floors were bare, polished pine. A soft breeze blew against the thin white drapes, which covered the floor to ceiling windows that were in every room. They were of the type that one could raise from the bottom, and treat it as a door, or lower it from the top as a window. They were all open this late afternoon, mostly from the top, enabling a breeze to circulate through the house with fresh, cool air.

I next went into the study. This room had a large, hand-woven imported rug, in a deep ruby color, that extended into every corner. Its only decoration was an unusual silver fleur-de-lis (a family crest?) in the center. The study walls were mostly covered in bookcases, with wooden panels surrounding the windows. Here was a darker, more somber atmosphere, especially in contrast to the parlor I had just left. The smell of old print and paper filled the room. Open books and old manuscripts were scattered about. A dark oak roll-top desk was against one wall, next to the locked cupboard which Juliette had mentioned, containing, I suppose, some choice expensive rum and perhaps other liquors. A delicate writing table was on the opposite side near a window. A round table next to a plush red settee welcomed me with a wooden tray carrying a pitcher of coffee and another of milk, with large, yet delicate china coffee cups. I helped myself by pouring equal portions of milk and coffee to make an inviting cup. Sugar was there, but no need; it tasted as flavorful as it smelled- dark, rich, strong.

Drinking my café-au-lait with savored pleasure, I decided to leisurely peruse the titles in Gerard's collection. Mostly French names, I recognized only a few. I was, myself, not a very well-read man. Working outdoors and trying to make a living, my schooling as a child was rather rudimentary; as a young boy even limited. I did recognize the name Shakespeare.

There were many foreign titles as well; Spanish and English names; German works which I found completely indecipherable. One thing they all had in common was they were worn and well-used. I took down a large leather volume from Britain. Of course, it was printed in English which I could not read. Perhaps Gerard would teach me.

Suddenly, I felt overwhelmingly inadequate. He must be a very intelligent, well-educated and extremely worldly man; a successful planter and businessman. I felt poor, unlearned and inferior in comparison. He was probably a very seasoned traveler, sophisticated; while I was just a rural boy, trying hard to make a living; trying hard to discover something about myself. I had never even been to our colonial capital. It might be best if I left soon and return to my simple life, with my simple ways, where I belonged.

My confused thoughts tired me. It had been a long day and I had seen many wonderfully new and different things. I decided to relax with a book. There was a French book already open on a table. Voltaire. This was as good a time as any to begin my education. I poured myself another cup and settled down in the comfortable settee with my book. And there on the side table were the little cakes as promised. I tried one- very sugary, but not too bad, especially when accompanied with the coffee. I had another for I realized I was hungry. Perhaps, as Gerard said, it was possible to become used to regular food again.

I began to read and must not have stopped for almost two hours straight. A heavily carved wooden clock hanging above the roll-top desk read seven o'clock. I closed the book, laid my head down and, removing my boots, propped my feet up. I had read almost the entire book, which was unusual for me. It was a play of comedies- a farce, I believe it is called. Very enjoyable and funny.

Perhaps, the curse had not only given me super strength and acute senses, but also helped my mental comprehension. I should try mathematics, since that had always been a weakness of mine. I vaguely wondered if there was an uncomplicated mathematics book in here, but instead of searching for one, I closed my eyes and day-dreamed.

I thought of my normal childhood days near the cold bay in the north. Then, truly was a carefree time. Who would have supposed- my family, my people- would be forceably separated and spread over a continent, including the West Indies. And who would have supposed I would end up here, as I was, trying to live with curses and witchcraft and gargoyles.

I remember in my slight slumber, hearing the clock in the hallway strike, but I must have fallen sound asleep for the next thing I remember, I was waking to the sound of the clock striking again. This time it was nine o'clock. And time to join Gerard in the dining room. I jumped up quickly, grabbed my boots and dashed for the door, in order to quickly go up to my room, change and make myself presentable for dinner. I smelled the food and already could hear his distance voice giving orders.

But I stopped at the door into the hallway. There on the wall was the portrait of the infamous Dr. Fontenot, which I had not noticed before. He had long gray hair, with a very thick mustache, also gray, which almost covered his entire mouth. Dressed elegantly, he was in the same pose as Julian's picture upstairs. I did not have time to study it carefully, however I looked at the eyes to see if there was a hint of madness or insanity. I saw no such thing. It seemed to be a normal portrait of a normal well-to-do gentleman. I turned to rush upstairs, yet something caught my eye. Yes, there in the lines around the mouth; in the tiny creases near the eyes. Most definitely- a strong sense of ...cruelty was present.

I raced upstairs, quickly and quietly as possible, changed shirts, shoes and socks, washed away the smells and dirt from the land and the hot humid day, slapped some French cologne on myself that was there by the basin and was back downstairs in only a matter of a few minutes.

As I passed by the longcase clock, I checked my pocketwatch against it. They were in perfect synchronization. I started into the dining room, but looked back towards the clock. I thought I had seen (or perhaps sensed) someone but no one was there that I could see. Yet, I had a feeling a presence was here. Reaching towards the clock, I immediately felt an extreme tangible coldness all around it. Odd, why would a spirit be haunting this place, this particular timepiece? Was it trying to communicate with me? Perhaps as a supernatural being, I was able to detect such things-such supernatural things? I'll have to ask Gerard.

I heard his voice calling for me and the cold promptly left- gone entirely in a second. I promptly forgot about it, attributing it to an overactive imagination. After all that has happened to me, it was little wonder that I didn't see a ghost around every corner.

He was seated at the head of a long dining table of highly polished mahogany. The service was immaculate and expensive as I knew it would be. There were settings for only us two. A large crystal chandelier above burned brightly. The windows were wide open, allowing a gentle evening breeze to bring in the distant scent of honeysuckle. A bouquet of gladiolas graced the center of the table. The wallpaper was a pleasing cameo color; large mirrors, in heavy gilt frames, graced each wall. It was a grand atmosphere conducive to the consumption of food and drink; a perfect place to enhance one's dining experience.

He stood up as I entered and motioned for me to sit to his left, where I would face the open windows. After we sat down, he patted my hand. "And now, mon frere, how did you enjoy your day? Was it everything you expected?"

"Even more so. It is..picturesque. Idyllic. This must be one of the largest plantations in the colony."

"Oh no. No, not at all. Sans Souci is rather small and quaint compared to some along the river. They are becoming ever larger and ever more grand with each passing decade. Trying to outdo one another." He said this with some disgust. I wondered just how many decades this home had seen. He poured us both some clean, cool water.

"Really, I had no idea. I would love to have my own

land one day. It is a dream of...ours." My voice grew to a murmur.

"I know mon frère, I know." He placed his hand over mine at the table. "Perhaps one day, we might share...." He stopped speaking as the double drawing room doors leading to a back parlor opened and the same young boy from this morning entered carrying a large covered tray of what smelled like fresh venison. I watched the young man; he noticed our hands together.

Gerard let our touch linger a moment longer. "Tonight we are having pheasant and boar with gravy, potatoes and biscuits. Rare of course. It is my fresh kill from today. You know how I love the hunt!" He laughed boisterously. "I am lucky. Sans Souci provides everything that we consume here. Self-sufficient we are." In rapid French he ordered the boy to slice the meat and serve us the food. The young slave was again wearing his starched white uniform. I wondered if this same scene played out every evening, whether there were guests or not.

Our conversation did not resume until after the boy had left. "And Toussaint?" Gerard asked while cutting his rare meat and pouring a deep red gravy over it. "What did you think of him?"

I replied between bites. "A most amazing man. He was the perfect guide and host. I look forward to getting to know him better. He seems very...wise." Gerard nodded while chewing. "He reminds me of someone dear to me." There was a loud moment of silence- an awkward silence. I continued. "He has been with you a long time, non?"

"Most certainly. He has been with me longer than anyone ever has- in my long, long life." He stopped eating and drinking and stared straight ahead at nothing. I tried to read his mind but could not at that moment. He collected himself and returned to his meal. "Yes, he is a most remarkable man, indeed. He helps me with everything here. In particular, handling the other slaves.

Keeping them in line and so forth."

He washed down his food with a large helping of wine. I wanted to ask him more about the slaves. It always seemed tragically odd to me- for one human to actually own another; to view them as property and not as another human.

He poured us both refills. "I will relate my history later after our meal. How I came by Toussaint. How I came to be...what I am today." He looked directly at me. "How I came by- this curse- as you refer to it."

I did not understand how he could think of it as anything else. I changed the subject. "I also met his granddaughter."

"Ah, the lovely (and young) Juliette." he exclaimed, leaning in towards me. "And what did you think of her?"

"Very pretty. Polite and well-mannered. For her station I mean."

He laughed his infectious laugh. "No doubt, she will turn many a man's head one day. Including the wealthy gentleman's." He raised his wine glass as if in a toast, took a large swallow and we went about finishing our supper.

"I've been wanting to ask you..?"

"Yes?" He appeared preoccupied with the last of his food, but he knew what I was about to ask. He just wanted me to formulate the question out loud. Or per-haps he was already mentally preparing an answer.

"It seems to me that much of your land lies fallow and unproductive." I paused. "Are there not enough slaves? Or..?"

His look stopped me in mid sentence. He had turned slowly towards me and was staring dead direct at me in silence. The warmth I had known in him since I'd been here had all but disappeared. Replacing it instead, was an icy glare which held a warning. An obvious coldness had descended over him. He had deliberately blocked his mind to me for I could not read any of his thoughts in the slightest.

And for the first time in his presence, I felt...frightened.

Then in another instant, the look was gone and he returned to his usual, warm charming self. "You are correct, mon frere. Yes, part of the land is deliberately not being put to full use, but not for lack of slaves or money. I could do much of the work myself. Why in one day, I can do the work it would take an ordinary man a week to accomplish. The fact is," he swirled the remaining wine in his glass, "there is no need. What is being farmed and produced is enough to sustain myself and my lifestyle. It supplies me with just the right amount of income to keep others- neighbors and officials- from prying, and sticking their inferior human noses where they do not belong." He stopped to take in a deep breath, then grinned at me mischievously. "No need to arouse anyone's...curiosity."

"I don't quite understand. How did you come by all of this? Sans Souci? Did you inherit wealth?"

"Henri! Are you so naïve?" At this he laughed again, but I did not join in. He stared at me with wide wolf eyes of cold blue, with arched eyebrows, as his grin slowly widened into a smile showing sharp wolves teeth. (How had he managed that without fully transforming?) His mind was open and I could read his thoughts. All of this- the land, the house, most all his possessions— came from his victims!

I did not know how to reply, what to say. Speechless and appalled, I was unable to form any coherent thought; there was only a feeling of horror. But he merely laughed again at my astonishment and rang a crystal bell for the boy. "Come, let us go into the study and I will tell you the long, yet interesting story of my life eternal."

The boy arrived to clear away the dishes as we rose to go into the study. Gerard put his arm around my shoulders, kissing me quite affectionately on the cheek. He grabbed the decanter of wine. "You and I will have a long, long talk. Enjoy the wine, some cigars, and..each other's company." I heard a loud sharp clatter of china and looked back at the boy. His head was down, busy with the dishes, but my sharp eyes detected a single tear streaming down his cheek. Then I knew. I should have guessed earlier. Perhaps I did know yet would not acknowledge it- in my naivete as Gerard said. So the boy was in love with Gerard. As for his feeling towards the boy, I could only guess.

"Have you seen the back parlor?" Gerard asked, paying the boy no mind. I shook my head no. We exited through the drawing room doors and entered the next room. It was a spacious parlor, easily the largest room in the house, designed for dances and balls. Done mainly in white similar to the front music parlor, this room had light blue trim and a small Italian pink marble fireplace mantel. On the ceiling, a carved cornice circled the room. The delicate chairs and settees were pushed against the walls exposing the highly polished wooden floor. Hanging above the mantel was an oil painting of Sans Souci displaying its simple grandeur and Creole majesty. I could easily imagine a magical party here, filled with splendid costumes, finery and gowns floating about the dance floor. Guests would spill out the large windows onto the surrounding porch and continue the dancing outside.

"Perhaps soon I will throw a small soiree, with you as my honored guest." He read my embarrassment and laughed. "A masquerade party would be most appro-priate, don't you think?" I could not help but laugh with him; his heartiness- his joie de vivre- was infectious.

He spoke to the boy as we went back through the dining room and proceeded down the hallway, his arm still about my shoulders, which I was (strangely), quite comfortable with. "Be sure to bring me Mercutio, after you finish your chores and before you retire." He explained to me that Mercutio was a small pet monkey that he had stolen off an organ grinder. "I saw him and just had to have him!" I could guess what became of the poor organ grinder.

Passing the clock this time, I noticed no presence nor felt any chill in the air. In the study, candles and oil lamps were already lit waiting for us. The tray of little cakes had been replenished and I smelled fresh coffee. He motioned for me to have a seat in the most comfortable chair in the room- a luxurious, brown leather piece, well-worn in all the right spots. He poured us both large goblets of wine, but paused: "Or would you prefer brandy at this time?"

"Perhaps later. With cigars?"

"Yes, of course. Bon. Good!" He handed me my glass. "You are learning to appreciate the finer things, mon ami." I, too, realized that and only hoped not to become too accustomed to all this.

He glanced at the book I had been reading. "I also see that you have been reading. An excellent choice- an author the French aristocrats should give closer attention to, eh? I expect a tremendous amount of blood being spilt over there- what a waste. Ha! You and I would have a veritable feast. Yes, mon frere? A veritable feast!" And with his boisterous laugh, he sat down opposite me, crossed his legs and took a sip of his wine, making himself comfortable.

"You will find in your hypersensitive state, it is easier for you to study and to absorb knowledge, to learn languages, etc. I have read most every book in here at least twice and I encourage you to make use of it as much as possible."

"I intend to." I was surprised at my confidence.

"Bon. Now where shall I start: when I was born a man or when I was born not as a man? Mais bien sur, it makes more sense to begin at the beginning, don't you think? It will do me good to reminisce." He refilled his wine. "You are in for a treat, mon frere. I have never spoken of this- about myself and my origins- to another living being all these many years." He looked at me directly. "You do understand, comprendre?" I nodded. "Then let us begin."

What I relate next is told in Gerard's own words, in his first person. What he told me on that long night, so long ago, as I sat eagerly in that comfortable chair, sipping my wine. Listening intently to every word, hanging on to each syllable, trying to capture each and every inflection. Discovering what made Gerard, the man- a man. And how he came to be- Gerard Mereaux, the wolf. Loup Garou.

GERARD'S STORY

5

My initial birth (as a human) occurred not on land, but on water- the sea. Aboard a French galleon slave ship. My parents were traveling to the New World for my father had been offered (and he accepted) a political post of some importance in the West Indies on Martinique or Guadeloupe or some such place. What particular post or position is not relevant. What is relevant was that he would not wait for a decent sailing vessel carrying people and supplies. He had to take the first ship sailing to that part of the world and subject my mother (heavy with child) to the foul stench and un-cleanliness of that damned vessel.

My mother was a beautiful woman with an ivory porcelain complexion and dark raven hair (there is a tiny portrait of her upstairs- I shall show it to you), but she was rather petite and delicate and not at all suited for a long sea voyage in her present state. There were complications during my birth, of which not the least was the ship struggling through the midst of one of those ferocious tropical summer storms which can occur suddenly and without warning in this part of the world. It was a most difficult birth and no doubt, I was a reluctant participant. To put it simply- she died giving birth. I was her only child- there are no siblings. I was immediately given over to one of the slave girls who happened to be full of milk. Apparently she had just lost her child in their filthy cargo hold. Ironically, we landed the very next day at our destination, along with blue sunny skies. The year was 1635.

And so I came into this world accompanied by death and he has been my faithful companion ever since.

We settled onto the island; my father's first task was finding a more suitable wet nurse and once I was turned over to her, he washed his hands of me and immediately absorbed himself into his work. I do not know if he mourned for my mother- perhaps he did in his own way. Perhaps he even loved her. But with me he never showed- even once- anything ever remotely resembling affection.

When I was a boy, I believed that he blamed me for my mother's death. However I have since come to the conclusion that was not the case, at least not entirely. He never loved anyone as far as I knew. I suppose he never had the capacity, or lost it a long time ago. Oh, I know that many men do not display affection readily, but a child can sense a lack of love and caring. Simple kindness even seemed beyond him. In fact, for whatever reason, he appeared to be full of anger, towards everyone and everything. I firmly believe the only thing he seriously cared for was his wealth and position in colonial society.

He beat our slaves at times. However, his pack of hunting dogs was especially vulnerable to his wrath. More than a few times, in the middle of the night, I would wake to their cries and howls of pain as he whipped them one after the other, particularly if he had been indulging in his favorite rum. Later, I would sneak out of the house and apply salve to their bleeding wounds. Not so much because I am tender-hearted (for I assure you I am not) but because it was an act of rebellious defiance against him. He found me out once and beat me so fiercely I was unable to walk for some days. I still bare the scars. After that, I vowed it would be the last time he would ever lay a hand on me. And I kept true to that promise. I avoided him and he avoided me.

As far as the nanny- well, she was simply a.. presence. Hardly an influence in my life- certainly not a motherly replacement- she was just there, a household slave who did her tasks. Even though a half-breed, she was very dark skinned. She fed me as an infant and clothed me as a child, but showed me no particular affection. Though we did have one thing in common- an intense hatred for my father. Whenever his back was turned, it burned in her eyes and I knew it reached deep down into her soul. I do not recall her discussing him with me, for she was very close-mouthed, but as a lad I did once overhear her say to another female slave (in her French-African Creole that she thought I did not understand), that one day there would be a great retribution and white slave owners such as my father would pay dearly for their sins and atrocities. Just what atrocities and sins she was referring to, I could only imagine, though later as a young man I would come to know of them first-hand.

Meanwhile, my father prospered very well (for no matter what type of man), he was an accomplished politician and trader and soon acquired a huge plantation, on a much larger island. The plantation was even larger in acreage than what you see here at Sans Souci. It was there I came to live and there I grew into my manhood. At the young age of seventeen, I became overseer of a full-fledged plantation and I ruled it with an iron glove. There was little interference from my father for he was busy with his post and business on the other island. I also found out later of another of his preoccupations- that of ravishing young slave girls below the age of ten.

So I busied myself with the plantation and fields of sugarcane, tobacco and mostly bananas. The house was a rambling grand shack of a mansion, having never been completely finished by its original owner. It was still, appropriately ostentatious enough for a French colonial official. We never bothered to really repair it to its original

plan of glory, but the acreage was immense, extending
from the sea into the plains and included, further inland,
forests and steep mountainous cliffs, which were already
in danger of becoming deforested because of the
demand for lumber. It was one of the largest plantations
on the island and I controlled every inch of it, including
approximately one-hundred African slaves.

Included with this newly acquired possession was a
slave named Toussaint. He is the forefather and
namesake of the Toussaint you know here at Sans
Souci. It was with his help that I turned a decrepit
plantation into a productive and prosperous enterprise.
He had a remarkable way of controlling and handling (or
perhaps coercing is a better term) the slaves into doing
their tasks and duties. He professed not to use voodoo,
though he definitely had knowledge of it and probably
practiced it in private. Of course at that time, voodoo was
widespread (on that island in particular) and, growing
more and more curious about it, I decided to learn its
ancient African practices and possible potent powers.

I read, studied and observed, venturing out late with
Toussaint to their pagan ceremonies, which were much
like the one that you attended not so very long ago. I
allowed my slaves to practice their voodoo which is a
religion to them. As long as it did not interfere with the
workings of the plantation. In fact, I feel many of them
worked harder for me, knowing I was a true believer.
There was one other important condition- that I learn all
they knew.

Toussaint, proving once again how invaluable he was
to me, introduced me to the local voodoo priestesses. We
traveled to nearby islands to meet others. Many were
free people of color. But from each and every one, I
gathered their secret methods, memorized their magic
potions and learned their erotic dances and strange
chants. I came to understand their worship of the snake;
became proficient with their abilities to cast spells and

place curses; learned how to hypnotize others easily, without having to use shiny baubles or tricks.

I started with simple, but important tasks- such as increasing the fertility of the land, making the rain to fall or the sun to shine and cause storms to change course. By giving my slaves certain herbs and teas, I raised the productivity and efficiency of their labor. It was after that, I decided to try for larger objectives and actually place spells on select people when it would be my advantage to do so- my need for experimentation coinciding with my strictly selfish purposes.

The first person I practiced my abilities on was a great landowner and lender on the island. A colonial French aristocrat, he was very rich and old- and very much disliked by the settlers and the slaves alike. My father and I owed him a great deal of money for a debt we had incurred when purchasing the plantation and for planting that first season. Perhaps out of forgetfulness, perhaps out of spite, I had missed our last payment of several thousand francs. He had sent a message stating that I must pay by the end of the week or he would start legal proceedings against us. I decided that this would be an excellent opportunity for the first test of what I had learned. If I failed, I would simply pay him, for I had the money. That wasn't the issue.

I arranged to arrive late one evening when he would be alone; his extremely handsome son and sole heir, having gone into the port city on one of his skirt-chasing episodes which he bragged about incessantly. (I will mention him later, for he also falls victim to my magic in a most memorable, yet tragic way.) Dismissing his servants, we got down to business. I poured us both brandies as he fumbled arthritically through the loan papers he was retrieving from his tiny overflowing safe. All I needed was for him to take one small sip from his doctored glass which he did as we sat down at his desk. I pretended that I was about to make my payment, when I noticed his labored breathing. Beads of sweat began forming on his forehead and there was an obvious lack of concentration. He had reacted much sooner than I had expected.

I calmly walked over to where he was sitting in his chair and gently placed my hand over his heart. He looked up at me and tried to speak but could not. I leaned down close to him, fixing my eyes on his. He was now in a trance, in my power. I told him to take my papers and sign them showing that they had been paid in full. He did as I requested. I also signed in the appropriate place as borrower, then pocketed my copy. I instructed him to remember nothing of this evening except for one thing: that the loan to the Mereaux's had been paid off. I cleaned up his brandy glass even though the potion I used was undetectable.

But before leaving, I decided to take a look in his safe. He was still in a trance for my power over him would diminish only after I left the area. I found several other loans such as ours. And then I came across a very interesting will. Apparently, upon his death, the father would leave virtually nothing to the son (the wife/mother being deceased). That was different than expected. Instead everything of value, including the notes, home and lands, went to some woman named Satine Des Villiers. I had heard that name before, but where? She must be some whore who somehow managed to get her claws into the old man and his money. How sad for the boy. I wondered if he knew that he was hardly mentioned in the will at all- receiving no money, no lands, nothing of any consequence.

I closed the safe and exited quietly. The old man would most likely recover with no ill effects and will never question the legality of the signed papers. It was on the ride back to the plantation, when I realized where I had heard that name before. It had been one of the voodoo priestesses mentioning a most powerful witch from one of the other French islands. She showed great awe (perhaps even fear) when speaking of her. And her name was Satine. I was positive it was the same woman.

Apparently I was not the only one casting spells. She had no doubt tricked the old man into signing that will naming her beneficiary and ignoring his son. I mentally made it one of my goals to meet this witch and learn what I could from her as I had the others. It was probably possible as long as she did not see me as a threat. Little did I know that meeting her would be one of the best things that ever happened to me and, at the same time, one of the worst, most dangerous acts I could possibly do.

However before I could pursue that objective, I had a visit from the young son I had mentioned earlier. It seems his father had died two weeks ago- the very night of my visit- of apparent heart failure. There was, of course, no doubt in my mind that my trance and potion contributed to his death. The poor boy was drunk and unshaven, looking like he had not slept in some time. It had come as a complete shock to him to find out he was completely disinherited. His question (or questions) to me were: What had transpired between his father and I? Had he appeared ill? And (the question most important to him) had I paid him in gold coins and if so, did I see where he may have secreted the money- for it was not in the safe. Some other hideaway perhaps?

I poured him a stiff drink (which he promptly swallowed in one gulp) and, after offering my condolences, replied that his father and I had conducted our business as usual and nothing seemed out of the ordinary. He perhaps did appear a little fatigued, now that I thought upon it, but otherwise he looked to be himself- in perfect health. As for the money, I did not see what he might have done with it. I assumed he placed it in the safe after I had left.

No, the son replied sourly. No money there, or

anywhere at all. He laughed sardonically and, being in his cups, began to talk. Apparently everything his father owned had been left to some strange woman, he had never even heard of before, and he, his only child, was left with nothing.

I poured him another drink and sat down close to him trying to display noticeable sympathy and surprise. Perhaps she will be generous, I suggested. She must have been important to his father for him to leave all to her.

He laughed again, and said that she was probably some prostitute who had somehow blackmailed or bewitched him. She had not even come forward as yet to claim his rightful inheritance. He then leaned in close to me and whispered that he suspected foul play.

His announcement did not alarm me. I knew if the authorities suspected someone it would not be me. I had no apparent motive; the potion I used was untraceable. In fact, at that moment I was more concerned with him. Even though he was disheveled and unkempt, I could not help noticing how his manly beauty still shined through. I understood fully how easily he could seduce any girl. His conquests of the fairer sex were legendary. And I was struck through with lust.

I had discovered at an early age, my proclivities towards my own gender. It never felt unnatural to me and certainly never left me with any guilt whatsoever. In fact, as you will come to know, guilt and remorse are uniquely foreign to me. But most of the males I had experimented with so far, up to that time, were young slaves- those either with the same tendencies as I- or those too timid or afraid to risk the wrath of a white man. Of course, I can mate with women- I have and still do. But that is merely for reproductive purposes only- to produce a male child. When it comes to passion- what you, Henri, might call love- only a man can satisfactorily suffice.

So on that evening, I decided to take advantage of

this young Frenchman's visit (and his condition) to try another potion- this time a love potion. I poured him another drink mixed with the potion I already had prepared and kept handy for just such an occasion. I was careful he did not notice me, even though he was oblivious to my actions. He held his head in his hands, whimpering almost to the point of sobbing, saying over and over again that he could not believe he was now penniless. Certainly I was a cad to take advantage of the poor boy's calamitous circumstance, but I was eager- to not only satisfy my ever mounting lust- but to test my magic. If such a handsome man, known for his love of women, would fall in love with me, another man, then my magic must indeed be potent. If I could make a man change his whole nature, then I could manipulate anyone.

He drank the doctored drink down as he had the others, then I made sure he looked directly into my eyes. A few moments passed as we stared at each other, our eyes locked. His gaze opened wide, at first startled, then the look of bewilderment filled his face. He looked away, then back at me again. He sprang to his feet, pacing back and forth in front of me, running his hands through his long light brown hair. He shook his head vigorously as if to literally throw out the thoughts that were flooding his mind. To dispel my magic. I sat there calmly, observing his reactions, taking satisfaction in my handiwork.

What is this? he exclaimed. What is happening to me? I have never even conceived of this idea before. He looked at me, his eyes pleading for answers. This feeling, This urge! Non, Non, Non, he repeated over and over again.

I rose and came up to him quietly and laid one hand on his shoulder. His thoughts were no longer upon his disinheritance. He looked at me helplessly, questioningly, not knowing what had come over him. These thoughts and feelings, these urges, were obviously very foreign to him. I drew my face close to his- I wanted him to take the first intimate touch. And he did.

His kiss was full of tremendous passion and skill. His embrace forceful and strong. And his masculinity sprang up against me powerful and needy. His naturally sexual aggressiveness had taken control- only this time with another man.

All that night, he gave his body over to me completely and with abandon. And I abused it, penetrating deeply and often. Again and again, he whispered how he loved me, that he could not live without me. And I felt supremely powerful.

The next morning he was groggy and incoherent- aftereffects of the potion and liquor. I dressed hurriedly to leave and go about my duties on the plantation. As I sent him on his way, I instructed him that he would be obliged to answer my summons at anytime day or night. He stumbled away and was barely able to set his horse.

That night I lit a red candle and called him to me. He arrived shortly thereafter- unclean, unshaven and still inebriated, yet eager for our lovemaking.

I exercised my control over him; I lorded my power over him. There was nothing he would not do to please me. And for hours, he did please me. So I knew, that I had changed him and his life forever. Never again would he be the same; never again would he be the ladies man. It was that fact that pleased me the most.

There was that night and one or two others, but after that I never summoned him again. I had had my conquest. Then, a few nights later- one cloudy and windy night that foretold the coming of a storm- he pounded on my door. I did not answer. He pleaded with me to let him in; he called out my name over and over again. He knew I was inside. He proclaimed an undying love for me; that he did not care what others thought.

The storm steadily worsened. The wind whipped itself into a frenzy and the rain started to fall. Still he knocked and still I did not answer. Then his tone changed. You demon! he screamed; shouting I must be the devil himself to do what I had done to him. How could I be so cruel? Then as the rain began to fall in sheets, he started to sob and moan. He said his love for me had become as a drug. He had to have me or he would surely die. He was not able to sleep or to eat, that only drink had sustained him, and not even that anymore. He needed me and if I was not going to receive him then I should set him free. Release him from the spell, reverse it. He pleaded with me for help, for compassion; for relief from this torment. And still I did not answer.

I quietly went around the house, snuffing out all the lights, except for the small hand-held candelabra which I carried with me as I slowly ascended the stairs. I could still hear him sniffling and begging at the door even with the din of the storm. I assumed he would eventually gather himself together and go home to his rum bottle.

It was the afternoon next, when I found out he was dead. Apparently, he had lost his way in the storm that night and fell off one of the various sheer cliffs that dotted the landscape. People wondered just what he was doing wandering about in the middle of a thunderstorm, but none doubted that he had been acting strange since his father's death and his having been disinherited. His notorious drinking binges were common knowledge. Our love affair was not.

And so, in the matter of a few weeks, I had managed (unintentionally, of course) to destroy one of the most prominent families on the island.

6

"I tell you of these things, my first experiments with

magic, to simply give you some idea of my nature. Long before I became a werewolf, I had what some would call (to put it mildly) a callous mentality. Perhaps it came from an unloving childhood, perhaps not. I apologize for nothing. As I said, I did not purposely hurt that father and son. I did not know of the old man's poor heart. As for the boy- his own nature killed him. He simply could not endure the fact of what he had become, of being treated the way he had treated so many girls and women, leaving them alone in their despair after they had given themselves over to him completely. The great manipulator had finally and forever, been undone.

"Mind you, do not think for one moment that I was performing from some deeper sense of justice. I was, most assuredly, acting out of pure selfishness. It is mostly innocents, those who just happen to cross my path, who have been my victims over the years. Your hunting party is an example. The fact is, simply put, I see myself as the predator and humans are the prey. It just happens to be, what happens to be. I have accepted it," he paused, "and so must you, Henri."

At this point Gerard took a break from his tale and he motioned for me to join him on the settee. He poured us both brandies as I sat down close to him. Pressing his knee firmly against mine, he put his arm on the back of the seat behind me. I did not move away from his nearness. We sipped our drinks for a moment in silence.

I studied his handsome face and figure. This youthful looking man was over one-hundred years old! I was amazed. His life, his experiences, was like a legend. And though I was most eager to hear more, to learn it all, so much of this was beyond belief. It was hard to realize that I was as he. Would I too live to be over one-hundred and retain my youth? Would we live even longer, centuries perhaps? Virtually immortal?

Sitting there, listening to the first of his tale, I felt a great deal of shock. Not at the fact that he sexually performed with men as well as women. Curiously, that did not disturb me in the least. What did disturb me was how cruel he had been. How cruel he must still be- even all his long life. How different from my own kind, sympathetic nature. Was that precisely why I felt so much guilt and he does not? The ever pervading question in my mind then was- would I too develop a callousness, as time wore on, an unfeeling for those hapless victims he called our prey?

I was observing him closely when he raised his head and looked at me. His deep-set blue eyes burned into my own. They seemed to be pleading for me to... to understand him. His thoughts were easy to read. He had opened up his mind to me. He wanted me to know all.

He had been so very lonely. Every day for all these years he suffered an unendurable loneliness. Forever it seemed, with no hope of finding another like himself. He had searched everywhere for one such as he; attempts to create another always resulted in their death. But now his world had changed- now I was here. And not only a handsome Frenchman with dark features like his own. I was another such as he- a werewolf. And more importantly: a werewolf of his making. I was his creation and the blood ties between us were undeniable, even irresistible. He leaned in close to me, his eyes searching for something more. His lips searching.

He halted with a knock to the door. His young slave promptly entered with a tray of some type of green liqueur and tiny crystal serving glasses. A monkey was sitting on his shoulder, chattering away.

Gerard stood up abruptly and addressed his servant in a dominating, commanding voice. "Now that we have a houseguest, you must wait after you knock for permission to come in. This is most important. Do you understand?" The boy nodded in answer. "This means any closed door." Gerard's words were emphatic.

"Yes, Master Gerard. I understand perfectly." His eyes

remained downcast and I thought that it might be good for me to talk with the youngster, get to know him and he me; to try and dispel any resentment he may hold towards me. He needed to see me not as his replacement. At least, not intentionally.

"Now hand me Mercutio, and you may go." Gerard took the tiny animal and it perched upon his shoulder, still chattering. Dressed in a little red uniform and hat with miniature trousers, it stopped chattering when Gerard gave him a large walnut, which he promptly gave his full attention to as he proceeded to break it open to get at the rich morsel inside.

"We will need nothing until tomorrow. And," he turned to look intently at the youngster, "remember what I just told you." He turned back to his pet, giving no more attention to the boy, who- I noticed- was slow at leaving and closing the door behind him. So now Gerard was tossing aside another, refusing him love after giving it so freely. Only this time he was a willing victim, the boy's love not a product of magic or voodoo.

Gerard brought the monkey over to me and we played a bit together. It scampered into my lap and I fed him a little cake. "Here we are." He had poured the green liqueur into the small glasses for us both. "Absinthe. Just what we need tonight as I relate the rest of my tale. A few thimblefuls of this and we shall see the world in a very different light." He laughed heartily and we drank down the liqueur. The wormwood left a bitterly strange sensation to my tongue and throat. The monkey got down and started to scamper about the room investigating every nook and cranny. "He is good. Does not break a thing. Perhaps he knows I would skin him alive if he did!" He chuckled under his breath as if at some private joke, poured us both more absinthe and then sat down across from me.

I looked out the window to catch a glance at thin clouds passing over the full moon. The trick of light made them appear like white wisps of cotton. I felt the moon's power tug at me, making me itch to transform. However Gerard obviously had command over me and neither of us transformed that night. Was it his master witchcraft or simply his willpower after so many, many years? I wondered as to the limits of his powers. A roll of distant thunder brought my attention back inside to this comfortable setting and Gerard's story. I was eager for him to continue.

"Now..," he stroked the facial hair on his chin in contemplation. "Yes, now about Satine." He lit a cigar and I followed his example. He smiled at me. "You know, mon ami. You are more like me than you care to admit." My eyebrows arched and the look that registered on my face must have been comical for his forceful laugh again rang through the mansion. I returned the laughter.

I leaned forward to hear more. "The witch, Satine- it was she who cursed- I mean, caused you to become..?

"In a moment, mon ami. In a moment." I relaxed back in my chair. He was relishing this- relating his complete story after all this time. He also relished having one such as I, as his attentive audience. "One thing at a time. First I must tell of how I met her and what happened between us. I will try to describe her objectively- just what sort of creature she was."

"Was she very powerful?"

"Very. Was and as far as I know, still is. She could fly, call upon the trees to buoy her. And she notoriously liked to raise- and command- the dead."

"Ghosts?" I asked incredulously.

He shrugged. "Zombies, mostly." He puffed on his cigar. "I would have killed her on that island if I had had the chance. As it is now, I know assuredly she will one day search me out, purposely to try and destroy me." He paused, "But I will be ready."

"Why does she hate you so?"

He waved his cigar in the air. "Because I could not

161

love her." He chuckled. "I do not know. Probably because I used her. You know, mon frere, what they say about a woman's scorn." He puffed on his cigar again before continuing, saying reflectively, "She was very capricious."

And so, with that said, I relaxed with my drink and cigar, while the monkey scampered about the room, searching for little nuts Gerard had hidden about. As my maker continued on with his story and the thunder rolled ominously closer.

7

As I mentioned previously, I had learned much from the voodoo priestesses on the different islands, but I wanted to know more- much more. I toured many of the smaller islands. Some Spanish and French colonies, others were Dutch or Portuguese. I learned more potions, spells; attended ceremonies. Witchcraft and the occult fascinated me and I became obsessed with my growing powers and psychic abilities. I especially wanted to find this particular witch- if she really existed. Whenever I mentioned her name, it provoked admiration or fear in those I questioned. Regardless, her name always, without fail, was accompanied by the most ominous warnings to stay away from her. That to search her out would not only mean the loss of everything I possessed, but would also end with my utter destruction. However I ignored their admonitions. I could not be frightened. In my arrogance and youth, I did not think of the danger and certainly their cautions did not apply to me for had I not already proved to myself, sufficiently, my prowess and powers? Yet I wanted more. I already knew more than those pitiful slaves from Africa. Their knowledge seemed limited and mostly superstitious. If there was a devil, I wanted to meet those who worshipped him; those who served him; they who could summon him. Little did I know how well my wishes would be granted.

However I did not have to search for her. It was she who found me. One wet sweltering summer afternoon, over a month since the lender's death which I accidentally helped to accelerate, she came to my door. I answered it myself as was my custom, for I had few household slaves and even fewer guests.

Before me stood a petite young girl and though the day was hot and humid, she wore a cloak about her shoulders. She seemed barely a mature woman, but with a closer look, she demonstrated a bosom of quality and quantity. Her dark-brown complexion told of a mixture of French-Spanish (or perhaps native Indian) heritage. She had on only the slightest facial powder- some rouge. Long straight raven black hair cascaded from beneath her hood down over her slight frame. Wide dark emerald eyes looked up at me and were large saucers compared to her otherwise delicate facial features. Except for the lips. Those were full, supple and tinged a natural red that contrasted against her brown complexion in an enticing way. I imagined she had large red nipples to match. There was a noticeable black mole on one side of her face near the left corner of her mouth. It gave her an added air of exotic beauty.

Her small size lent her a certain delicacy, but only at first glance. I knew from her posture and the way she presented herself before me on my veranda, that she was strong and determined. A willful girl out to get what she wanted from this world- a kindred spirit. I knew immediately she was the witch I had been seeking.

"Pardon-moi monsieur, for disturbing you. I am looking for Gerard Mereaux."

"You have found him mademoiselle."

She pushed back her hood to completely display her face and hair. I noticed even with those simple movements that she carried a great deal of grace and manner. "I am Satine Des Villiers and I have come here to say thank you."

"Won't you come in, s'il vous plait?" I opened the door wide and extended my arm beckoning her to enter. Once inside, I took her cloak and asked her to make herself comfortable. "I'll ring one of the servants for a cool beverage, if you would like."

"Merci, mais non, monsieur. I will not be staying long." She was dressed in black with white lace collars. I thought to myself that at least, she was properly displaying some sort of mourning. She sat upright, even somewhat rigid, with her hands crossed in her lap in a genteel manner. Like many women on the islands, particularly during the summer, she did not wear gloves. Inwardly however, I surmised that there was nothing really genteel or dainty about her true nature. She continued, "As I said, I have come here to say thank you."

I sat down across from her. "I am afraid I do not understand, mademoiselle. Thank me? For what?"

She gave me an all-knowing look and leaned forward slightly. "For helping me. For doing what I dare not."

"I am still at a loss here. I do not know what you could possibly be referring to."

"Did you not see him the night of his death?"

"Earlier that evening." I corrected her.

She nodded and smiled as if sharing a confidence. "Then I say again. Thank you." Her voice was barely a whisper.

"I still do not know what you mean, mademoiselle." I quickly changed the subject. "Pardon my absentmindedness and allow me to offer my condolences on your loss." She lowered her head and eyes appropriately. "Are you going to live on the plantation? It is very beautiful and perhaps the most profitable on the island. You are now a great heiress."

She ignored my last remark. "Yes, I plan to stay and," she hesitated. "And that brings us to the real reason I am here, monsieur."

"And that is?" I wished she would get to the point. Witch or no, I did not appreciate her earlier inference that I may have 'contributed' to her benefactor's death.

"I am here to ask you to come work for me."

"Work? For you?" I had not expected that.

"Yes. Manage my plantation. I myself have neither the knowledge- nor the inclination. So I must find someone. And I know that you are quite capable." She put particular emphasis on the last word. "I know that you have turned this plantation into quite a profitable enterprise. Much more so than it was before your father acquired it." She looked down at her delicate hands. "And one day it will be yours."

I observed her closely. Every sentence of hers seemed to be loaded with double-entendres. "But my time and hands are already full. I could not possibly take on more responsibility."

"You already manage a thousand acres, why not manage two thousand? You handle two hundred slaves, why not five hundred? Due to the notes I have inherited, I now have access to a great deal of money and am quite prepared to pay you a handsome figure."

I rose and paced the floor, my mind clicking. Perhaps this would be an excellent way for us to become acquainted, where I would eventually learn her witchcraft and, at the same time, take advantage of a great financial opportunity. To govern two of the largest money making plantations on the island was sorely tempting. Also, no one would question our time together and she could secretly teach me under the guise of conducting business.

I stopped pacing and looked at her. She had been observing me closely. I realized I had better be careful what I was thinking in her presence, for she was probably adept at reading minds and thoughts. Her expression had not changed. In fact, she always looked calm, unemotional- her face placid as a lake. I poured us both a drink and handed her a full glass, "Sherry?" She accepted it and I sat back down. "I thought perhaps- rather- others thought perhaps you were not going to claim your inheritance. Have you been, traveling abroad?"

A slight twinge around one side of her mouth broke her stone facade. Had I hit upon something? Had she been off somewhere practicing witchcraft with a coven- or perhaps communing with her master?

"Yes," she sipped her sherry. "I was away on one of the other islands and did not hear of his death until two weeks after the fact. And then a storm prevented my immediate return. But I am here now and have already met with the attorneys and am in complete control of the estate." She put down her glass, which was, to my surprise, empty, and rose up out of her chair. "In fact, I have another appointment to go to. What is your answer, Monsieur Mereaux?" she politely demanded.

I rose also. "Let me think on it and I will give you an answer in the morning." I hesitated, even though I knew I was going to accept her proposal. I helped her on with her cloak and offered her the door.

She turned back to me. "I will have the proper papers ready for you to sign in the morning. I will see you then."

Her youthfulness and small frame belied the prima donna female within. "You are very confident, mademoiselle."

"And you will be a very wealthy man Monsieur. Good day." She started down the steps. The heavy afternoon air was developing into an evening mist.

"One thing more I have to ask, Mademoiselle Satine." She turned at the bottom of the steps and looked up at me on the veranda. "How did you get him to do it?" Of course, I was referring to the old man willing all of his possessions over to her.

She smiled her enigmatic, all-knowing smile. She knew exactly what I was speaking of. "And you monsieur? How did you get his son to do it?" She paused to let the words sink in. "The thank you earlier was for eliminating the one obstacle that might prevent me from claiming this inheritance- the son. I believe he jumped because of a broken heart. It is the romantic in me." She shrugged and turned down the path towards the gate and road where her carriage waited. "It would seem we both have our secrets." Her voice was like the misty breeze slapping my face.

Touche, I thought. My tawdry attempt to embarrass her had backfired. I had to realize that this was one formidable female. She was probably wise to my casting of spells and voodoo practices. And most assuredly, she knew of my affair with the son. If I were to learn and eventually gain her powers, I must tread very carefully indeed or I might very well become a victim myself.

8

The very next day I signed the papers and assumed my duties as foreman of her plantation. It was close to our own, even one parcel was adjoining. Most everything was nearby and accessible on that island, until you reached those treacherous mountains. With a little effort, I was quite able to manage both lands. Of course, as for my own property, I became ever more reliant on Toussaint, for I might even be gone elsewhere a day or two at a time. But by now, he had become quite capable and trustworthy. I am sure he was aware of my ever-increasing dealings with voodoo and the black arts, and he may even have guessed as to my relationship with that boy, but of course he never referred to it. Which was as it should be, after all- he was still my slave- albeit a wise and loyal one.

As for my relationship with Satine, it was strictly a professional one- at first. I went about my tasks, working on her land and sometimes, for many days at a time, I would not see or need to speak with her at all. I would occasionally catch a glimpse of her having tea on her veranda or under one of the giant oaks surrounding the plantation home. Always in the late afternoon or early evening; I never saw her in the mornings and seldom ever at midday.

Her accounts and money affairs were handled by a banker from the city, whom I saw coming and going more often than I saw her. He was there almost daily and I suspected he was somewhat infatuated with her. Perhaps she did not even need to cast a spell on that one. I did hear the news however, that several of the loans and notes on various properties in the islands which she had inherited from the old man, had been called in, most all of them due in full. And that, she even had more than one family evicted from their lands and they had to sail back to France in poverty and disgrace. All this she apparently accomplished within her legal rights, though I could not help but suspect some sort of trickery being involved. Perhaps her expertise extended well beyond witchcraft and included the all too human talents of seduction and bribery. It would not be too difficult to accomplish on this corrupt isle. Who would be the wiser? I am sure the greedy governors and officials did not care, even if they did know or suspect. They may have been either in her pocket or her witch's palm. It certainly was not any of my concern. The more wealth she accumulated, the better for me.

What was my concern was now having to manage almost twice her original land holdings because of these foreclosures. And, what with the foremanship of my own land, my time was completely accounted for. That summer, I had practically no time to study and practice my witchcraft. But I contemplated for the wet season coming, when I would have more free time, and planned how to ingratiate myself with her and learn, or even steal, her knowledge and powers. She seemed to have no man in her life (other than the banker) and I knew how to use my charm to advantage. Of course, I would be dealing with deadly fire: and the thought of it excited me to no end.

And so I plotted my dangerous course carefully, thinking long and hard about how to achieve the ultimate goal. I knew I would have to stay several steps ahead of her in order to outwit the female, especially if she was as powerful as they say- which I had no doubt. Then one evening in late autumn I began the beginning of what I had come to foolishly think of as my conquest.

I had noticed while overseeing her slaves, that they were remarkably simple. Perhaps that is not the right word. They just seemed very different from my own (or any others) though many came from the same regions in Africa, maybe even the same tribes. Hers did their work yes, but were...docile, less alert, slow-moving.

The whip did not make them move any faster. They seemed to not even feel the sting of its lash. Toussaint even remarked about it: "Like sleepwalkers" was his observation. I concluded they were being drugged in the food and drink provided by their mistress. I needed to use them for an extensive irrigation system I had planned, pending her approval and so the first day that the weather gave a hint of the wet season (which for the islands meant it was still warm, but a lot wetter with shortening days), I paid her a visit.

She was upstairs on a tiny balcony overlooking her domain having her usual tea. She saw me approaching and motioned for me to come up. I had visited her house several times, but only for short periods to conduct immediate business and let her know of my plans and progress. She was always agreeable and trusting of my judgment, allowing me to have free rein. She obviously cared not for the details of running a huge plantation and only cared to concern herself with how to enjoy the financial returns. A female house slave in African dress, directed me upstairs and through Satine's bedchamber onto the balcony. I noticed she had few house slaves, as did myself- the better to have fewer prying eyes. I observed her room quickly, nonchalantly, as I went through.

It was furnished sparsely with a tiny dresser and mirror, a writing table, simple chairs, an armoire and little else. The bed however, was an extravagant centerpiece. A monstrous work of art, the dark wooden frame was carved to resemble an ancient Greek sailing vessel, with a huge looming female figure or goddess representing the bow at the foot of the bed. Thin, white whispers of drapes surrounded the bed, decorative but functioning as mosquito netting. How appropriate, I thought to myself. Cleopatra and her famous barge! Suddenly I had a passing thought. Could perhaps Satine be a reincarnation, a cat with many lives? I dismissed the silly thought as I walked outside onto the balcony.

Many women would not have allowed a man to pass through their bedroom, and though traditions and morals were more relaxed on the islands, I considered this a good sign. She was dressed in a pale apricot, light linen dress which complemented her dark brown skin beautifully. The cloth seemed to flow about her and with her, though there was not a hint of breeze on this side of the house. Her breasts showed firm and obvious through the thin fabric and seemed proportionately large with her tiny frame and cinched waist. We sat down and she poured us both some dark, aromatic tea. With my suspicious nature, I was hesitant to accept it at first, for who knew what sort of potion she could have added. But seeing that she poured us both from the same pitcher, I took the chance and sipped the tea with her. It was strong and well-brewed. Of course, she could have previously doctored my cup, even the saucer, but I knew her to be (if nothing else) a highly intelligent woman and it would not do to cast a zombie spell on her money making manager. At least not yet.

Ostensibly, I came to her to talk about diverting water from a creek on one side of her property for irrigation purposes. It was necessary, I said, plus with the harvest almost over, I need to find projects to keep her slave labor busy. We would also be doing repairs to barns, store houses, mills, stables and equipment. She agreed as always, with a nod of her head and her delicate smile. We sipped tea for a moment in silence. Then I put down my cup and thanking her, said that I was finished for the day and needed to leave for my presence was required at my own place.

"Please stay and have some more tea. Here," she refilled my cup. "You must not work so hard everyday. A man- such as yourself- also needs time for leisure."

"Yes, I suppose." I looked at her directly, but she had already turned her gaze, looking out towards the land. "It is beautiful, this time of day, n'est-ce pas?"

She shook herself to dispel her daydream and looked back at me. "Yes, it is. Very beautiful. The trees, the land, the wild flowers. And I have been meaning to thank you for all you have accomplished."

"De rien. It is my job." I shrugged and chuckled. "Believe me, I am thinking only of my percentage."

"For whatever reason, you do it well, Monsieur. And the accounts show it. Income is high, expenses are low. Your percentage- as we agreed upon-should total very much more than expected. By the end of this year we shall be- how do the English say- 'sitting pretty.' " We both laughed at that. Hers was a small chiming ring of a laugh, like the tinkling of a tiny crystal bell or how the wind can whistle through the leaves sometimes.

"You know, mademoiselle, I don't believe I have ever heard you laugh so."

She smiled wider this time demonstrating a perfectly even row of bright white teeth. "Please, it is time you addressed me by my first name."

"Very well- Satine. And you must call me Gerard." Her arm and hand were extended on the table, and I (in my audacity), put my hand tenderly over hers. She merely looked at me with a slight puzzlement on her face and then calmly, and just as tenderly, withdrew her hand and placed it in her lap. Her gaze returned to the landscape and the distant treetops.

That must be my cue. Yet I had made my intentions clear. I looked at her closely. Her profile was actually quite regal in appearance. Young, but regal. Sitting there seemingly demure, I could feel the fire inside her. Her highness, a youthful Cleopatra, was explosive, a bundle of dynamite- and I arrogantly thought I would be the one to light the fuse. I finished my tea and rose to go. "I must leave now."

She calmly turned back to face me. "I was thinking of hosting a small gala. Perhaps one evening this month. To meet our neighbors. Other plantation owners. To," she hesitated for the right words, "establish myself among the.. the.."

"'The Landed Gentry.' The bourgeoisie?"

Her tiny bell laughter rang again. "Yes. What do you think?"

"I think it is a lovely idea. Very wise. Most of the island will be beating the door down in order to attend."

And then, not totally to my surprise, for a brief moment her highness showed me the right side of her face, for her sharp tongue tore through the air like a bullwhip. "So they can come and gawk at the whore? See how a slut lives?" Her voice grew quiet again, becoming almost a whisper as her gaze returned to her land. "I am

well aware that some have even whispered 'murderess'
behind my back."

"Then this will be your chance to show all of them that
you are, just who you are: A young, beautiful and vibrant
woman with nothing to hide. Generous but not lavish.
And for what it is worth, I have never heard such
whispers." She stared back at me briefly, still with her
dark black look. Then in the next second, our laughter
rang through the trees.

We were still chuckling as she escorted me
downstairs, arm in arm, and to the door. I was relieved
that she was becoming more relaxed and comfortable
with me. "I would like to ask you one thing, Gerard. For
the party."

"Anything."

"Would you please be my escort for that evening?"

"Nothing would give me greater pleasure." I kissed
her softly on one cheek. She did not back away.

"Good. Then I will soon let you know of my plans for
the party."

"I look forward to it. Until soon, mademoiselle."

She grabbed my hand and held it gently, warmly for a
moment before letting me go. "Remember- it is Satine."

"Of course. Until soon then, Satine."

"Avoir, Gerard. Until soon."

I turned and left, feeling quite satisfied with the way
events were progressing. One thing did disturb me
though. I needed to find out just what was on her agenda.
What was she after here? I had believed that money and
possessions were important to her, but they are not her
top priority. What else was there? Power? Ambition and
control over others? Over men? Perhaps even love,
simple love was important to her. I had to get beyond the
placid exterior of the woman and uncover the seething
witch beneath.

Time passed by slowly and for awhile, I only saw Satine from a distance.

Harvesting was finished and I busied myself making improvements to both her lands and my own. There was always some work to be done or some slave issue to deal with, such as their medical problems, illnesses, pregnancies, etc. and of course, discipline. But actually, for the most part, I had very little trouble in that matter. Her people were obviously drugged and easy to control, but only productive to a certain extent. They needed almost no supervision for they worked like automatons. My slaves were, of course, the opposite. Active and alert, they would sing (oftentimes it sounded like a litany) as they toiled away to the beat of their African drums. Toussaint and I let them have some 'freedoms', certainly more than most plantation owners. I gave them the Lord's Day off to practice their religious voodoo, which no other master did on that island. Sometimes I would even be there observing and studying their ways, but never participating. Most all of the neighboring landholders criticized me, saying that I was setting a dangerous precedent; that it was not proper for a master to behave so and that it would lead to unrest among other plantations.

The island itself had been in terrible turmoil in the past and many masters feared the near future, anticipating a revolt of some size. Most ignored the warning signs, but in secret, the French colonial masters lived in constant fear of their slaves rising- as one- in revolt and massacring the entire European population in their sleep. However, I paid the other landowners no heed and did whatever I wanted. It was not out of any sympathy for the slaves and their pitiful plight. I did what I thought best and I still do with the slaves I own now.

So, for my part and my father's plantation, I ran it firmly but was quite judicious with the whip (or other punishment)- only using it when absolutely necessary. Perhaps to set an example or to punish the slow or insolent. Runaways on my land were rare. Toussaint and I knew many of them by their faces and names and we always kept a close eye on 'the bucks in the stable' (the larger, more muscular men), plus the older ones who showed some bit of intelligence or leadership abilities and who might cause others to revolt.

And with Toussaint: even as I came to depend on him more and more, I had to face reality and keep close watch over him. He would be the perfect leader to start unrest. An unusually learned Negro, he had been taught French at an early age and held (or seemed to hold) respect in the eyes of the other slaves. I kept him within my trust, giving him those responsibilities that did not require my constant supervision. When it came to discipline, I usually had him administer the punishment and wield the whip. He would do so, but I could sense his reluctance and distaste. Yet I purposely did this to allow the other slaves to see that Toussaint was not really one of them.

Only once was there an exception where he refused my order. One misty morning, I had a visit from an irate plantation owner from one of the smaller nearby islands. He was searching for a runaway of his who, word had it, had escaped to this island and was hiding, perhaps, at my plantation among my people. I was not too surprised, because this Dutchman had a notorious reputation for abusing his property and even beating some of his people to death, which I did not doubt. I quietly questioned Toussaint and yes ,he thought he might know where the runaway was. I had him bring the young male to us, his arms tied behind his shirtless back, his feet shackled. There, on the ground before us, as the owner and I stood on the veranda, the boy pleaded for my mercy and to not send him back with his previous owner. He cried for me to purchase him and in return he would always be faithful and never would run away again. His French was poor, his African accent heavy, but I understood him well enough. The scars on his young back, horrendously deep and numerous, spoke for him. I also noticed where he had been branded more than once.

The outraged owner promptly descended upon the poor boy with his riding crop, flailing him unmercifully as he groveled in the dirt. I saw Toussaint move to stop him, but I quickly and silently blocked him with my arm and he held himself in check. I calmly went down to the ugly dramatic scene and grabbed the man's arm in mid-flight. He let out a curse and demanded that I let him go, until I quietly pointed out to this obtuse man, that this was neither the time nor the place for the slave's punishment for many of my own slaves were gathered round observing. I directed him inside, and we left the young boy crying and bleeding on the ground. Toussaint followed us, unobtrusively, in silence.

I poured the Dutchman a potent drink and made him an offer for the boy/slave. He adamantly refused, saying he would not sale him at any price. That he had a special punishment planned for this one and he must be made an example of or they would all try to run away. I believe he mentioned something about castration and ants.

I knew that if I let the boy go, he would surely be slowly killed by this pompous man. But there was nothing I could do. I told Toussaint to escort the slave and the owner safely to the edge of our property. He would be on his own after that. Toussaint did not move to obey, but stood rigid as an Egyptian statue staring straight ahead.

Nothing could have surprised me more. Again, I gave him the order and again, he still did not move. The Dutchman stared from one of us back to the other anxiously, but also perhaps, somewhat enjoying the scene. He helped himself to another drink.

I walked over to Toussaint, more bewildered than angry. I started to whisper to him, but he interrupted and in a very small voice, so as to not be overheard, he asked to speak freely. I allowed it. He mentioned that this boy would surely die if we let him go and that he could be a very valuable piece of property. I shrugged, saying it was not my business, that the owner does not want to sell him. Make him, he replied forcefully. But why, Toussaint? Why this boy? We have plenty of labor, what was so special about this one? He looked me directly in the eyes and spoke frankly. He knew this boy well and the boy would be eternally grateful to me and make a great household slave, attendant upon my every wish. I still did not understand. I can have many servants if I want, I replied. He looked at the floor and then spoke slowly choosing his words carefully. Not like this boy, Master Gerard. He would serve you in ways no other could. He would serve you at night, in private, in.. I stopped him at that point. Now I understood. And I was intrigued- very much intrigued. I had already taken notice that he was an extremely attractive young man with mature ebony muscles that spoke of the sensuous manly powers he must possess. He could serve me pleasurably for many hours at a time. I whispered for Toussaint to wait outside.

I turned to the owner who was again helping himself to another drink. He again demanded that I get an escort together, this time to safely take him and his property all the way into town to the harbor where he had a small boat waiting. At that point, I made up my mind. Now don't misunderstand me, I was not acting out of sympathy, but strictly for my own selfish purposes only. And also, out of my total disdain for this annoying portly old Dutchman.

I quickly, deftly, grabbed him firmly by the throat. He gasped with surprise, the glass dropping with a crash to the floor. His eyes were wide in panic, he could not breath. I made him look directly into my eyes and in the next moment I had him hypnotized. I relaxed my grip and he collapsed into the nearest chair, staring blankly ahead of him. He was completely in my control. I then instructed him that he was to completely forget about the boy and this visit to my plantation; it never happened. I caused him to believe, forever convincingly, that the boy, trying to escape, had drowned in the sea. The Dutchman, and everyone else on his plantation, must know that the boy had died- he was dead. I made him repeat what I said, over and over again. The boy was dead. I made sure he would only fully wake from the trance when he arrived back home at his plantation.

Letting the fat man go, he awkwardly mounted his horse and rode off. And my spell worked, for we never saw nor heard from him again. Although I did find out, about a year later, that his slaves- having had enough of his tyranny- all revolted, en masse, and the poor old Dutchman met a particularly gruesome end. His slaves actually reverted back to their African roots of cannibalism! I truly relished that bit of news. How befitting.

I was quite proud of my handiwork. For the first time, I used no potion, no candle, no incantation. Only my psychic powers of persuasion. I was becoming stronger.

As for the youth, he became my personal household slave and served me faithfully both day and night until I left the island to come here. As for Toussaint, he promised never to refuse my orders for any reason and he kept that promise to his dying day. Of course, I warned him if he ever broke that promise, it would cost him dearly. What I never did understand though, was how he knew that particular boy/slave had the peculiar abilities and yearnings to please other men.

10

That is a microcosm of our lives on the island and the background behind which we ran our plantations. My father stayed mostly at his post on the other island and when he did visit the plantation, he would usually stay in his rooms in another area of the house and we would only see each other at dinnertime. He never interfered with my overseeing duties; he was happy as long as the plantation was profitable and gave him the extra prestige necessary for a man in his position (and help inflate his already overinflated ego).

Then a note arrived from Satine. She had selected a few possible dates for the party and wanted to know when would be the best for myself. She had also sent along a preliminary list of 'guests and notables' she thought to invite and wanted my opinion on it. Was there anyone she had left out who should be included? Were there any names that should be excluded for one reason or another? It was to be a masquerade party which was always popular among the gentry.

I made my notes, simply adding a few names she had missed, but otherwise making no major alterations. Almost half the names were from neighboring islands; it totaled around 250, but eventually grew to over 300. I did ask her to select one particular date- for my convenience, I said. And she did as I asked. But the real reason I asked her to choose that date was because I knew my father would be busy with his governmental duties during that time and hopefully would not be able to attend. It turned out in my favour and he had to send his regrets.

I remember the night of the gala well for that night my

life changed irrevocably. It was a beautiful and clear evening, with a full moon and cooler than normal temperatures for that time of year. The rainy season should have already begun, but so far all we had seen were a few mild showers. The French colonialists were all in the party mood. My costume, I must say, was impeccable. I went as a joker, a harlequin, which maybe was not the most original, but the different twist I created with the makeup was. It was particularly gruesome, with bloody tears over a white foundation and with black sunken hollows surrounding the eyes. My lips were curled into a permanent dark red smirkish grin of evil. I even stained my teeth a dirty yellow which enhanced the skeletal image. I added two large fangs. For the piece de resistance, about my neck, in thick makeup, was a large bloody scar made to look as if my throat had been cut. It was very macabre- just as my humor has always been.

The costume itself was somewhat typical, with a bell-cap and purples, greens and golds; trousers and vest. Only I did add a blood stain or two- one directly over my heart. A black cape and dark riding boots finished the ensemble.

As Satine's escort, I arrived early and was entranced by all her preparations. Everything was exquisite. The yard and house were lit with hundreds of candelabra. A sumptuous buffet was being prepared, outside by her slaves, who were dressed in fine livery and white gloves. They did their tasks in that same somnambulistic manner that I have noted before, which added a ghoulish element to the party's atmosphere. Tables, with white tablecloths, were set up all around, mostly outside. She had obviously spent a lot of time and expense on the oc-casion. Her people were pouring champagne into a huge three-tier silver centerpiece that began to bubble and flow like a fountain. How did she accomplish that I wondered?

I entered the long hallway to her home. To the right a large ballroom had been created; the room emptied out of most furniture, save for some small chairs lined against the walls. A ten-piece orchestra, crowded into the far end of the room, was rehearsing. Everything was bright and shiny, painted and polished- from the wooden floors to the large open plantation windows to the crystal chandelier hanging from the waxed plaster ceiling. All was spectacularly rich and extravagant- perfect for the type of guests she would be entertaining. Their tongues would be wagging for months later. I hoped that all the effort she had put into this evening would be worth her while.

I turned back and looked up the stairway. Our hostess appeared above on the landing and slowly began her descent down the stairs. It was she- Queen of the Nile, Cleopatra herself, in all her regalia! Perfection itself. I shall attempt my best to describe her that night, though words can hardly convey her overall effect.

She was- absolutely stunning. Her headdress was composed of golden and ebony snakes each with bright emerald eyes. They curled about each other in a writhing orgy. Her dark hair had been braided and hung down in rivulets over her shoulders, lightly caressing her bosom. She was wearing dark makeup which made her look almost Nubian. The eyes were particularly arresting. Surrounding her emerald orbs, were painted the designs of the Egyptian symbol of fertility in black charcoal. A slight tinge of rouge accented her cheeks and lips.

Her dress was simple- long, straight, black satin sheen. It looked to be one piece. Her shoulders were bare exposing her silky bronze skin. The dress clung tightly to her hips and thighs and was not like contemporary European clothing, with heavy female undergarments. It revealed more than just a hint of her full round breasts. A heavy, gold ancient-appearing necklace with a large emerald scarab amulet, dangled low- accenting abundant cleavage. Bracelets of gold snakes covered her wrists and arms. A gold scarab

181

brooch, also with green eyes, heightened the Egyptian effect. Black sandals gave added stature to her tiny frame.

She greeted me with a small kiss on the lips and I told her how magnificent she looked, like she had just arrived in Rome itself. She laughed her tiny laugh and asked if her costume was too scandalous. I replied- yes definitely- most definitely. She said good, that was what she had hoped to achieve, and we both laughed loudly and wholeheartedly. I liked the fact that though she professed to dislike all the talk behind her back, she still enjoyed causing a stir. Like myself, she wanted to shake the world up. But then again, most of the French (and especially French colonialists) were all decadent, and this particular French-settled island was the most decadent.

We moved towards the entrance where we would greet the guests, who would be arriving soon. She complemented me on my costume and make-up, saying I was a very good artist; that I was very frightening and 'tres bizarre'. I bared my teeth and growled- she feigned horror and we laughed again. As if on some unspoken, unseen cue, a slave was suddenly there beside us offering us champagne from a silver tray. We started to imbibe.

The guests began to arrive and I introduced her to the many that I knew. The men were delighted and admired their hostess' costume, while most of their wives would cast a disapproving look sideways- yet were burning inwardly- green with envy. Jealous hypocrites all. Those females would love to show their attributes if they had any to display. As for their costumes, they were the standard fare- nothing notable, none memorable. Nume-rous kings and countless queens flooded the house and floated about the grounds. Enormous blond wigs rode atop skinny, scrawny wrinkled necks that I thought would snap from the weight.

All were trying to bring alive the feeling of French

civilization and aristocracy to this humid, poor island in the middle of the sea. A colony ill-run and sorely managed by greedy politicians, governors and mayors; over-ran by crooked traders and covetous landowners. I knew this quite well, for my father was one of them and I was acquainted with his money-hungry cohorts. One day, it most likely will all explode in their faces and their blood shall run like rivers to the sea.

All the notables were there that last evening before the rains came. Even some Catholic ministers. The sea being so calm, many came from far-away islands. No one wanted to miss the opportunity to dine and drink in the house of this notorious woman. I was glad she had dressed the part. After tonight, her notoriety would be certain.

Most all of the guests were old boring pompous individuals, but there was one grand exception, from Venezuela, I believe. Maybe I say that because he was dressed as Don Juan (or perhaps it was Zorro) all in black with a black mask, but his good looks and muscular frame were very evident. He immediately aroused my attention, but he appeared to only have eyes for Satine, who herself was not impervious to his masculine charm and graciousness. He kissed her hand and asked if she would have a dance for him. She glanced briefly at me. His gaze followed her glance, then he nodded cordially at me and added, 'with monsieur's permission of course'. 'Of course monsieur, certainly', I replied. 'Until then', he said, as he kissed her hand once more before joining the others inside. Satine and I smiled and winked at each other, before resuming our duties at greeting more arrivals.

The orchestra started playing a waltz; the guests had begun to dance; champagne was flowing everywhere. She whispered into my ear that I could have him if I wished. 'I think he prefers you, ma cherie', I whispered back. 'Oh but, we both know you have, how shall we say-a certain means of persuasion.' I did not know quite how to respond to that, but she started to laugh and I joined in. 'Shall we dance?' she asked me.

And so we danced and then danced again and I entirely indulged myself in food and drink that night. At one point I left her with a not so boring couple who had just arrived from France and I wandered outside and sampled the fare- roast pig, shrimp, black beans and rice, plantains, creole okra, corn, native fruits (some had been shipped in) and many other interesting choices. She had certainly spared no expense; and the champagne fountain kept bubbling. Inside, rum, brandy and other spirits were offered for those guests who preferred them and she had even provided a quiet smoking room for the gentlemen to enjoy their cigars in comfort.

I came back inside and found Satine waltzing with one of the leading governors from the islands. An older, elegant gentleman, very wealthy, very widowed. Perhaps her next target? I spied Don Juan standing to one side by himself, sipping a cognac. He was intently watching Satine. I thought to do something clever, fun and risque and find out if he were the playful sort or not.

I walked over to him, bowed and asked him to dance. He did not react at all, pretending as if he hadn't heard me- perhaps thinking me a simpleton, a joker like my costume. He tried to ignore me, hoping I would go away. I asked him again, holding my hand out.

He looked at me impatiently, 'Certainly you are joking, monsieur?'

'I am a joker, yes monsieur, but I am quite serious about our dance. Now, shall we?' I still held my hand out.

'Ridiculous. I couldn't. You are not just a joker, but a fool. I..' He looked about, not nervously, just annoyed at my attention. Near us were two young and very beautiful ladies who had overheard us. They were giggling and whispering to one another and one of them waved her fan at him, encouraging him to go on and dance with me.

He looked back at me, 'Then again, it might prove to be amusing. Very well.' He sat down his drink and took my hand forcefully.

So we joined the others on the dance floor and at first, no one noticed the two tall men dancing together. Then gradually, people's eyes adjusted to the fact and they started to point and laugh. Satine noticed us right away and, smiling widely and brightly, waltzed with her partner over to the orchestra and told them to keep playing this particular tune. And so Don Juan and the ghoulish harlequin became the most popular couple on the dance floor.

At first we did not speak to each other, we merely enjoyed our audience. But as the waltz continued, we whispered to one another. I began. 'You are a remarkably skilled dancer, monsieur.' And this was no exaggeration. 'Where did you learn?'

'From my older sisters.' He continued without pause. 'Monsieur, may I ask you a frank personal question?'

'Is there any other kind?' I subtly squeezed his body tighter to me, bringing his large muscular chest against mine. He did not react, but allowed it.

'Madame Satine. She is for you? Tonight?'

'It is Mademoiselle Satine and she decides who she is for and when.'

'I thought she was widowed.'

'Non, it is a common misconception.' My sex was growing, pressing hard against his thigh. Still he showed no response. He had an amazing ability for self-control.

'Bon. Then I do not have to ask your permission to visit her tonight.'

I laughed. 'You are bold monsieur. As audacious a man as I.' I brought my face close to his. He did not attempt to move away.

'Yes, I can be very bold. In fact,' He paused for emphasis to make sure I understood his exact meaning. 'I can be many different things- to many different people.

To men as well as women.' Another pause. 'For instance, if I have to go though you to get to her- I will.'

Seldom speechless, I found myself so at this pronouncement, but only for a slight moment. I tried to look him in the eyes, yet he never would look directly at me. He was afraid of my hypnotic gaze, no doubt. 'What do you mean? Through me? A duel or..sex?'

'Call it whatever you wish. Only it would not take place with firearms, in a field with seconds. It would happen when we are alone together, in private. Our only weapons- our nude bodies.' For the first time he looked me dead direct in the eyes- his dark orbs shining at me behind his mask. 'At your place, monsieur, at your calling,....'

Precisely at that moment, unfortunately, the music stopped and we parted. Everyone clapped and applauded (especially the females), as we bowed, first to each other, then to our audience. Shortly, the music resumed and the dance floor again filled with people and when I looked about, he had disappeared. He may have gone outside for fresh air or perhaps to the gentlemen's cigar chamber, but I did not seek him out. I knew I would see him again and, though he may have been trifling with me, we would still have our 'duel', without using a magic potion. It was wonderfully engaging to find a man like myself- handsome, cavalier and not afraid of sexual experimentation. I did not even mind sharing him with Satine. But what I could not have possibly guessed was that the very next time I was to see him- I would be witness to his death.

Soon the night was coming to a close and there were very few guests left. Satine's slaves were carefully and methodically going through their paces cleaning up and putting the house and grounds back to normal. I vaguely wondered if they ever slept at all or perhaps they actually were asleep even as I saw them performing their duties.

I had noticed that Satine looked tired and fatigued as

the evening wore on and seemed even a bit impatient, perhaps for the party to end. I had glimpsed some gray hairs about her temples and a few facial wrinkles, deep underneath her eye makeup. Strange, I had never noticed that before. I would have guessed her much too young to show any signs of aging.

With only a two or three stragglers left, I ventured upstairs to look for her. I approached her bedroom cautiously. I called out her name, but there was no answer. I knocked and called again. Perhaps she was on the balcony. Surely she had not yet retired. In the back of my mind, I thought I should just leave, yet instead I slowly entered. The room was completely dark, save for a few candles lit here and there. Her balcony doors were wide open letting the night sea breeze blow the white curtains into ghostly shapes. Distant thunder rolled. I whispered her name. Hearing muffled sounds, I turned.

What I saw froze me stiff, as the blood in my veins turned to ice. For never in a million years, would I have ever in my wildest dreams imagined that scene.

There she was, naked, in that magnificent barge of a bed, Cleopatra, straddled atop our Don Juan. He was obviously inside of her and she was quickly riding him to climax. But what utterly stunned me was her- her appearance. At first, I thought it wasn't even she. For she had...changed.

Satine had become a very old woman. No much more than that. What I saw was a wrinkled, ancient old crone of a woman, scarcely human, with long gray thinning hair and loose skin falling about her in folds. Her once firm and pliant breasts, sagged down to her belly; her face barely recognizable. It was impossible to believe my own eyes! This was the same woman who only hours ago was one of the most beautiful, sensuous women on the island. A pure pleasure to the eyes was now this! Was this her true look, the other a mere facade? Did she actually physically change or was all her beauty an

187

illusion? And what I was witnessing- was it real or also an illusion?

A cloud moved aside and released the full moon's rays and I saw, more clearly, the man I had danced with earlier. His magnificent physique was bare and absolutely still, without any movement, his muscular arms outstretched. He was seemingly incapacitated and looked not to be alive; yet then- in a gleam of moonlight- I saw his eyes dart towards me. They were pleading with me- for help, for release. That was his sole movement, the only way I knew he was alive; save for, I suppose, his stiff sex.

I just stood there in a state of shock. This was not mere sex I was observing. She was performing some rite of magic, some sort of ancient witchcraft. I realized she was slowly killing him, making a...sacrifice of him. I told myself to leave quietly and quickly, trying not to disturb her; to leave and pretend I never saw this.

I backed out slowly knowing well that she was most probably aware of my presence. Unable to resist, I could not take my eyes off the macabre sight. I felt that I too was becoming part of a trance. My stomach began to turn. She was nearing climax. Or rather, I suppose, he was and so he would be spent. And what then?

I somehow found myself on the balcony in the fresh air, trying to breath steadily and deeply. I thought I might vomit. It occurred to me that might have been me back there. I could have just as easily been the sacrifice instead of him.

I started for the back stairs that led to the courtyard and patio, but her voice broke through the night air. 'Come in, Gerard.' The voice was flat and authoritative. I hesitated. 'Come in Gerard,' she repeated. It was a command.

I reentered her boudoir. She was as herself again, clothed in a thin flowing white dress, cinched tight around her restored figure. She said nothing as she serenely went about lighting more candles and then poured two goblets of brandy. Don Juan was still lying in the bed, eyes wide and vacant. He was obviously dead, even though his sex was still gigantically straight.

She brought over the brandy and handed me a glass. I stood like a statue. 'Do not be afraid Gerard. It is only brandy and nothing else. You are much too valuable to me- and my operations.'

I swallowed the drink; it helped me find my voice. 'Valuable? Any number of men could run your plantation. It is not that difficult.'

'It is not those operations to which I am referring. I am speaking of other special interests. My hobbies, if you will.'

'Your witchcraft?'

'Yes.' She turned towards me directly, her face still somewhat in the shadows. 'There is no sense in hiding it now, after what you have witnessed. Please, let us go outside and sit. I will pour you another brandy. It is a cool autumn night and there is still a few hours of moonlight left before the dawn. We have much to discuss.' The thunder rolled closer, in warning.

I saw her clearly in the candlelight as she passed by me. She had regained her beauty, yes- yet there was something more. Why- she was even younger than when I had first met her! She was like a girl of sixteen who had just reached puberty and the flower of womanhood. Her face was smooth and taut; hair shiny black and vibrant. Her skin clear, bronze and silky; breasts large, firm and obvious under the thin fabric. I tried not to stare in disbelief as I followed her onto the balcony and we sat where we had had tea not so very long ago. I felt lightheaded- I had drunk my brandy too fast.

Silence passed for a moment between us. She stared up at the moon. 'Once a month, or so, I must take a... victim. A male victim who will die in order that I may live. If possible, his seed should be within me.'

189

'A sacrifice in order to retain your youth?'

She turned to look at me. 'And my life.' She hesitated. 'I am very old, Gerard. It started in Egypt many centuries ago.' She waited for me to absorb the idea. The concept that I was looking at a thousand year old witch? I took a large gulp of brandy. She continued. 'It came about almost by accident, involving alchemy, the book of the dead and ancient gods of Egypt.'

'The devil?' I asked incredulously, stupefied. What have I stumbled upon?

She laughed. 'I made a pact. In exchange for my allegiance, they gave me powers beyond imagining-eternal life and everlasting youth.'

'And you give him...'

'Souls,' there was a brief pause. 'I stay young and alive as long as I keep supplying the ones from long ago with souls.'

I thought for a long moment. 'Are you what is known as a succubus?'

She laughed again. 'I have been called that. The fact is- I can choose the style of sacrifice. I have invented some very clever methods. My personal favorite is my gorgon-self.' She leaned over the table nearer to me. 'I can turn men into stone!'

I sat back in my chair, trying not to show my shock-and growing excitement. Thinking that this... this must be my fate. I had wanted to meet and learn from the ultimate witch and here she was across the table from me- the devil's evil mistress herself! All that had passed before in my life was leading me to this point. All before was mere fly specks. Yet I must be wary. 'How do I fit into this? You said I was important to your operations. Why me? Why anyone? I cannot imagine you needing any one for any thing.'

'True.' Her gaze grew distant but only for a moment. 'Even immortality has a price. One lifetime of loneliness is enough, but several?' She sighed softly. 'The fact is,

Gerard, I like you. We are the same you and I- driven, ambitious, controlling. And inquisitive. You do want to learn all you can of my art, yes, mon cher?'

'Perhaps.' I replied cautiously. 'But at what cost to myself? You did just mention the word price.'

She laughed loudly. 'Oh Gerard. You will do it at any cost. Do not deny it. Why you would fuck the very devil himself if it profited you!' Her language was not what shocked me, but the fact that she was correct. I would do exactly what she wanted if it were to my advantage. And why not? In the back of my mind was the thought that surely the devil would have male consorts as well as female. After all evil does what evil wants and can do anything to anyone he wants. And so could I.

I laughed also and relaxed even further into my chair, wishing I had more brandy. 'What do I have to do?'

She looked back at the moon which was now barely noticeable because of the ever increasing clouds. It was setting quickly to make way for the dawn. 'Obey me,' she said simply. 'Be my accomplice. Help procure victims.' She glanced towards the bedroom. 'Dispose of them…afterward. If you pledge allegiance to me, I will teach you what I have learned and perfected over the centuries. Much more than simple potions and spells. How to manipulate people miles away to do your bidding; how to raise a corpse or summon the ghost of one long dead- and control them. How to put magic into objects such as writing utensils or mirrors so that what you forge anyone's signature or you can see what is taking place elsewhere. You can manipulate the weather, the sea, the wind, the sun and the moon; to make a whole forest come to life and move its limbs like arms.' She looked directly at me, her youthful green eyes ablaze with the lust and talk of power. Her voice began to rise with the thrill of domination. 'The whole world and the people in it will be yours to command. Puppets on a string. You can have riches and live like royalty. Travel the world, enter into courts of kings and queens with ease; manipulate rulers and politicians to do your bidding. With only a small effort, any woman- or man- will succumb to your charms.' She sat back in her chair, intently observing me for any reaction.

This all seemed impossible for me to fathom. 'If you are so all-powerful, and can enter and leave the courts of royalty so easily- what are you doing here? Why bother with- all this?' I spread my arms out.

'It suits me.' She shrugged, 'Boredom, perhaps? The fact is, there are the winds of fate which even I cannot totally manipulate.' She looked back at the moon as it disappeared. The last ray of moonlight danced on her face, shined in her eyes. 'Also, it is better for someone like me to not stay in one place too long. Humans are meddlesome animals.'

'But why this particular place? This stench of an island?'

'It is just a place.' She gave a thoughtful pause, but I knew there was more to it than that. 'Actually, I was attracted to the practices here- the voodoo. The beliefs in zombies, werewolves and the supernatural.' She smiled brightly, 'I fit in nicely, non?'

Curiosity and questions abounded within me; they overflowed. 'Do you have enemies? Angels from heaven perhaps? From God? Or from his priests?'

The pleasant peal of her laughter again rang. 'Everyone has enemies, especially if they live as long as I have. But, for now, there are none to speak of- here on this island,' she added. I thought to myself- is that why she came here? To escape someone or something? She continued, 'I have never met an angel (or demon) personally, though I know them to exist. As far as priests are concerned- so called 'men of God'- I find they usually have their own agenda. You will see: every man has his price.' She paused for a long moment, choosing her words carefully. 'There were some who discovered my secret, but I destroyed them one way or another and moved on. From place to place; another country, another town, another victim.' She almost seemed weary with it all. Quite different than a moment ago. I realized one very real reason why she wanted me as her protege. She needed me to help relieve her boredom.

'Are there others such as yourself?'

'I believe there are- somewhere in the world. There must be, though I have never met them; and to do so may mean...my destruction. Or theirs.'

No room for competition, I thought, chuckling to myself, wisely not saying it out loud. How long before she would discard me- use me up like the other in her bedroom. I knew, even then, that she would never teach me all that she said she would. It was too risky for her and her position. 'And I will also enter into an agreement with your masters?' Whomever they might be.

'Non, that is only for me.' Her reply was flat and final.

Great flashes of lightning were now interrupting us every few minutes. The first rays of dawn could barely break through the clouds. I knew there was a lot more she was not revealing- it could wait for another time. I needed to be alone and ponder over all that had happened that night; all that I had learned about her. And plan my strategy. 'I assume you wish for me to dispose of our friend.' I wanted to get the nasty business over with.

She nodded. 'There is a deep bog over there.' She pointed towards it, but I knew where it was- a nearby pool of quicksand. I started to rise, but she had more to say. 'First, I have a request of you.' She leaned towards me and casually, gently, grabbed hold of my hand which was extended on the table. She slipped it beneath the neckline of her dress and placed it over one of her young breasts.

I began to grow excited. 'Why?' was all I could say. I withdrew my hand and put it safely in my lap- as if I were the innocent damsel.

'I want you to be not only my student, but my lover.'

'And end up like Don Juan!'

She laughed, 'Non, mon cher. I promise that will not happen.'

It was my turn to laugh. 'And how can I be certain of that?'

She came over and sat in my lap and kissed me softly on my clown lips. 'Of course, you can never be certain. However, I do not want to jeopardize what we might have together.' My hands caressed her young thighs, her hips; her centuries-old legs. She continued. 'Not only our working relationship on the plantation, but also as my..' (she kissed my hand, licking my fingers one by one between words), 'protege in the black arts, and now..', her tongue was inside my ear, wet and soft, 'as my consort.'

Why tonight? Have you not had enough?'

'That was more like a requirement, a necessity. You and I will be strictly pleasure.' Her hand rested on my stiff sex. 'Join me now on my barge for a voyage together.'

'I need to dispose of your handiwork first.' She was already leading me by the hand into her room.

'Oh no. He will remain there beside us while we make love.'

'What? Having sex next to a fresh corpse!' I should not have been surprised.

'Yes!' Her green eyes sparkled with decadence. 'A test.' She went around to the empty side of the bed, untied her dress and let it fall in a heap at her feet. She laid down, very close to the body; her youth inviting, her breasts full and firm, ripe and round with the bloom of maidenhood. 'And Gerard, you will be interested to know that once my body renews itself, it is as if I were a virgin again.'

I undressed, knowing full well the danger I was putting myself in by dealing with such a woman. And to tell the truth, the morbid bizarreness of making love beside a corpse appealed to my darker nature. It was doubly exciting for me.

So, in my evil ghoulish makeup, as the day became brighter; as the rain began, heralding the wet season; I made love with Satine for the first time. It was spirited and exhausting sex and all the while the corpse stared up at me with his vacant, dead eyes. His sex was remarkably still stiff as if he wanted to participate with us. I would, (not accidentally), touch him- feel his cold flesh against my perspiring warmth. And I would grow even more excited and redouble my efforts. It wasn't long into our lovemaking that we decided to include Don Juan, and Satine eagerly watched as I penetrated him. That was not my first menage-a-trois, but it was the first time to include necrophilia. I had passed my first test.

So that is the story of the beginning of both my sexual relationship with Satine and the start of my learning her witchcraft. I now knew her true nature and what drove her personally. For me- personally- it seemed that all my plans were falling into place. And one day I would take the advantage.

11

The wet stormy months sailed by as I immersed myself into the studies of magic and sorcery. She had a special way about her teaching where I was the conjurer and she was more or less an observer. I learned new, more powerful potions; strange incantations from some dead ancient language; more sophisticated, potent methods of casting spells and controlling subjects. She taught me how to identify the many various plants and herbs witches used- some for healing, others for teas, drugs, ointments, potions. And still other deadly concoctions used to bring life to an end or worse, put someone in a sort of stasis between life and death. I became proficient with all this and more. Familiar with the special fire that burns yet does not consume and is cold to the touch. I made my own voodoo dolls and other enchanted tools. She acquainted me with the legends of the undead and other demons. She showed me how, most times, I should add some of my own blood to the potion, in order to make a particular spell stronger and certain not to fail. In fact, cutting oneself is an artistic ritual among covens.

I was shown how to extract the venom from snakes, spiders and scorpions, in order to make a special brew which paralyzes a person so completely, their breathing and heartbeat become imperceptible and even a seasoned physician would pronounce them dead. A few days later the spell wears off and the hapless victim finds themselves buried alive.

I learned more about the different gods of the voodoo world and still others from the Egyptian underworld, though I never learned, positively, which ones supposedly helped her become the powerful, centuries old witch queen that she was today. We frequently held seances and contacted the dead.

Eventually it came time to test what I had learned and we eagerly turned our experiments on people, using mostly simpletons- slaves who were not of much importance to the plantations or who were sick. Some of our subjects were colonialists, but only those who were homeless or of not much consequence. She enjoyed torturing them- more tricks of the mind, than tortures of the body. Most importantly- I discovered that once a spell was cast it usually was nearly impossible to reverse.

On occasion, we visited a large cemetery far from where we lived, on another side of the island and there we disturbed the dead. I caused to rise from his freshly buried coffin, a zombie, and he followed me about- totally my servant- for a few days, but I disposed of him shortly thereafter because of his foul stench. I summoned the ghost of a small child who had also died recently. She spoke to us in her Creole patois, asking for her mother. We would use ghosts to haunt the living, mostly for no reason in particular other than to amuse ourselves, though sometimes we chose a person we felt was deserving of a haunting for one reason or another. They would eventually, inevitably, go out of their minds and then the ghost could return to its rest.

I was an apt pupil; learning and absorbing more with each passing week. About once a month, usually near the new moon, I took a break from plantation work and our witchcraft lessons, and we would seek out her next male victim. Sometimes we picked him up from one of the disreputable pubs we frequented near the wharves-usually choosing a strapping, strong seaman, in town for one night of pleasure; one who few would miss. His ship would simply sail out on the morrow without him.

Sometimes we selected a refined gentleman who had some how had the ill fortune to come within reach of one of our clutches. On more than one occasion, we had the excellent luck to encounter a handsome man who wanted to enjoy the company of both Satine and I. It was this style of man who stimulated me the most and in her huge bed we three would have many hours of prolonged and extended sex. Inevitably though, she would end up dominating the poor man, turning herself back into her true aged form and ride him to extinction.

I did finally have the unique occasion to actually witness her as a gorgon. Of course, I could only observe this by reflection. For if I were to directly cast my eyes on her as a medusa, I too would end up in stone. Upon the man's climax, as he watched in helpless horror, her long gray hair would come alive, wrap around her head and become a writhing nest of snakes. He would slowly become frozen forever in stone; to be added to her now extensive collection of nude male statuary scattered about her gardens and property.

Now concerning Satine and our personal relationship: She and I made love many times usually when she was at her youngest for that gave us both the most pleasure. She was insatiable, especially at such times. However my interest in her would wane each month, as she grew older and I, increasingly, would find myself longing to return home to the strong limbs of my young slave who would wait eagerly, patiently, for my return. He, and men like him, are what drive me to passion and fulfillment. Satine and women do not- they are merely a means to an end. Yet I had to be constantly on guard and careful, for she must never guess how much the boy meant to me; or rather, how little she meant in comparison. Of course, I was not in love with him either. He was after all, simply a slave. But I did not want him harmed and Satine would probably destroy him without a second thought. Her jealous possessiveness did surface from time to time.

My life continued very much in this manner for the better part of two years and there was little change during that time. Then near the beginning of the third year of lessons and working for Satine (and I had come to think of our love-making as work also), I came to the conclusion that I had very much learned all I could from her; or to be more specific- I had learned all that she was willing to teach me. She never spoke of her masters or her pact with 'the gods'; never mentioned us trying to communicate with them and I began to believe that her agreement (if there actually was one) might be near its expiration.

There were a few reasons I thought this. One was I sensed that as I grew in knowledge and in strength, she became less and less her strong confident self and more and more dependent, even vulnerable. Another reason was that she increasingly needed fresh sacrifices. What was once a month, even occasionally every other month, became twice a month and much of the time, we would have to choose her victim desperately quick. Yet I had to exercise great care. For though witchcraft and voodoo were well-known on the island, her perpetual youthfulness and lifestyle was the subject of much speculation. As the months passed, I tried my best to slowly distance myself from her (without incurring her anger!) and I was careful to only visit her bedchamber at night and only discuss plantation business during the day. Of course, her slaves were never the source of gossip, but they were certainly the subject of it. More than a few times I was questioned by their landowners as to their somnambulistic behavior. Perhaps they wanted to learn the secret in order to control their own people, I could not speculate; I would shrug them off and make some excuse or another- even suggested once that they had gotten hold of some cocoa beans. The words potion or voodoo were never mentioned, though I knew what they were thinking.

One other change which began to frequently occur with her which made me think she was losing her power, was her ever-increasing reliability upon me. More often she would become so weak, so quickly and age so fast that I had to be the one to procure the victim all on my own. Sometimes the immediacy was so urgent, I would have little time to choose. Of course, the younger, stronger and more virile the man the better, but I refused to sacrifice any of my best slaves. So I had to be clever and try to plan ahead- even travel across the island at times, where fewer knew who I was. This nonsense began to take up more and more of my time away from important duties on both plantations.

She was also becoming more dependent on me in another, very important way. I came to the conclusion that she was falling in love with me (in as much as a woman like her could fall in love). The changes began subtly and at first I thought it my imagination (some would suggest my ego). She would ask me to just spend the night and hold her tenderly. Increasingly, she did not even want to make love as much, which suited myself very well. Once, after our lovemaking, she pleaded for me not to leave and when that did not work, her tone changed. She ordered me to stay and insisted we lay there together, naked in each other's arms all night. It became increasingly much more of a chore to please her and I became determined that one day, whenever she seemed to be at her least powerful, I would leave her and this island behind.

Of course, I had to be financially secure in order to leave and, fortunately for me, that opportunity presented itself later that year and I took advantage of it. My father, as I mentioned earlier, normally visited the plantation only occasionally and stayed out of the business, but then suddenly, unexpectedly, he decided to resign his commission on the far island and retire permanently to the plantation. At first, he busied himself (or pretended to busy himself) with old leftover political affairs and such, but he increasingly had more spare time on his hands and began to meddle into my managing of the plantation. I caught him searching through accounts and private papers in my desk and when I asked him why, he brusquely replied that this was his house and his land and he intended to do as he saw fit with it. And- from now on I would follow his orders. Well this bit of news was most disconcerting for I had always had free rein and I intended to keep it that way. One way or another.

One day his interfering nuisances reached a climatic break when I overheard him giving Toussaint orders about how he wanted the slaves to be handled. And furthermore, Toussaint was to ignore any orders that I might give, and regard my father as the sole master of the plantation from now on! Well, this I could not tolerate and I resolved to put an end to his petty tyranny; plotting a most painful demise for him and this time I would not need to use witchcraft or potions. For his own lust and decadence would do him in.

He habitually imbibed most every evening until he was very drunk and then slept it off until noon the next day. Much of the time he was so incapacitated he was unable to walk upstairs to his own bed. It was to be on one of these nights (before he becomes completely intoxicated) when I planned to place the one thing within his grasp which I knew he would not be able to resist. Therefore, he brings about his own downfall- his destruction certain. I would simply and conveniently arrange it.

Already our slaves hated him immensely. He beat several every week with or without provocation. Even the merest suspicion of stolen bread or food, or of spilling or tasting his precious wine, would invite his wrath and he would make an example of them and cause the other slaves to watch as he lashed them to the wheel and whipped them to unconsciousness. Afterwards, they had to be doctored and cared for and were usually bedridden- therefore useless to me for many days, sometimes for weeks.

With that said, Toussaint came to me one morning in a very serious mood and asked to speak with me frankly and in private. I allowed it and he then cautiously mentioned that he has been observing an…unrest among our slaves and it was his thinking that my father's actions were the direct cause. It was also his belief that if my father continued with these public beatings there could be grave consequences. Already once, he had to persuade a group of angry men to disband and go back to work and he was positive others were hiding pitchforks, knives and homemade weapons secretly away. His worry was that one day they would all revolt and his life, mine, my father's and any slaves who did not join in, would be forfeit. We all could be murdered in our sleep like what had occurred on other plantations in the past. Knowing his fear to be genuine and his worries legitimate, I told him I already had a plan that not only would rid us of my father, but should appease our slaves at the same time. I did not know yet exactly when, though it would be soon. He left somewhat skeptical, but I immediately started to act. There was no time to spare. And when it was finished, I would be free of my troublesome father forever.

I had already selected the girl. She was a slave orphan and mostly helped with minor work about the house. She was a mute, never spoke as far as I knew, never gave any trouble and most believed she was a simpleton- her mental capacity somewhat retarded. A petite and innocent child, I saw how my father had his attention on her. She was the perfect age for his delights- eight I believe.

Eventually he would have had his way with her at his own choosing- in secret with no witnesses. What I planned was for him to be discovered in the very act of ravishing the poor girl. The slaves' fury would be immense, and I (in my disgust and appreciation for justice) would give my father over to them, in exchange for their loyalty and silence and they could do whatever they wished with him.

Of course, you must think me cold-hearted to use this small child in such a manner, and you would be right. It was despicable, yet it worked better than I could have dreamed. I had bought a brand new dress for her- bright and colorful to appeal to the child's senses- frivolously pretty and lacy enough to attract my father's eye. I had one of the women dress her up for the evening.

Father was in the main parlor drinking as usual. I had just left him there, the candles low and the room almost completely in the dark, telling him I was retiring early. I had already dismissed the household slaves save for two, a male and female which might provide additional witnesses. I walked into the back and called the little girl over. She was quite happy, with her pretty new dress on, dancing around the kitchen to some distant song in her empty little head. I saw her smiling- I think for the first time. It was a bright, wide silly grin; her missing teeth and red gums contrasting against her very dark complexion.

Earlier I had ordered the cooks to bake a special cake and now that evening, I instructed the girl to cut a few slices and go serve them to her master in the other room. She nodded that she understood and obediently went about her task of cutting out little cakes and putting them on a serving plate. She took great pains with each slice as only a simple child can do. I went out the back and strolled on the wrap-around porch towards the front where I could see my father sitting inside, smoking his cheap cigars and swilling his wine down like it was water. I hoped he was not too inebriated. Standing unobserved in the shadows, I had a front row view through the plantation doors. The stage was now set, all that was needed were for the characters to play their parts.

The child dutifully appeared bringing in the cake, sliced delicately into bite-size morsels. She left them on a tiny table next to my father's chair, curtsied politely to him and turned to go. My father predictably, grabbed her around the waist and set her roughly upon his lap. The girl did not struggle at first, most likely not understanding what he was about. His hands then reached under her dress to grope areas which even she, in her limited capacities, knew was inappropriate. She started to struggle against him, but he put a large hand around her tiny neck and her resistance ceased. From where I was, I could see her large eyes widen slowly in silent terror. She squirmed, but I could tell his grip on her throat was tight- and deadly. It would not be long before he would pull his sex out of his pants.

I had planned this evening carefully and now was the time to call Toussaint. I had spoken to him in secret earlier that day and told him to wait for my signal and to bring with him three male slaves, hand-picked by him, who were potential troublemakers- in other words, thirsty for revenge against my father. Of course, I did not tell him why, just to make sure these particular men had been previously subjected to my father's torturous wrath.

I gave our secret signal and from behind a large oak, Toussaint appeared with three others. They approached quietly, quickly, but not before my father had spread the poor girl's legs open and he had inserted himself. Her pain was obvious, yet even had the girl not been mute, she would not have been able to speak or scream for my father's grip was ever tightening around her throat. I thought perhaps she was choking to death, her eyes bulged; I heard a suffocating cough struggle from her tiny doll of a body.

In a moment they were beside me and observed the rape scene in shock. One of her arms flayed uncontrollably away, hitting the nearby delicate table hard, causing it to fall over and the plate of tiny cakes, along with my father's glass decanter of wine, dropped to the floor in a loud crash. Good, for now the household slaves would be alerted and could also serve as witnesses. The red wine had soiled the girl's brand new dress. You could barely tell where the wine stain ended and the girl's own bloody smear began. Toussaint and the others were impatient to go inside and stop my father's atrocity, but they hesitated, looking to me for permission. I held them back, one more second, then two, until the two house slaves entered the room and stood there a moment in disbelief watching my father still abusing the poor- now dead- girl. He was oblivious to all else.

I allowed the four to rush in and they forcefully grabbed him off of the girl. In his drunken daze, he shouted for them to take their filthy black slave hands off of him. How dare they! One of the house servants knelt down beside the girl and confirmed that yes, indeed, she was dead.

My father, looking up and seeing me, ordered me to command this dirty swine to unhand him. I serenely looked about me at the results of his carnage. One of the men holding him had been particularly mistreated to the extreme. My father had whipped him naked, in front of everyone and at one point the heavy sharp bullwhip had cut deep into his sex and testicles. Father had threatened him that he would finish the job if he ever caught him stealing again, when all he had done was secret away a cup of milk in their slave cabin to give to his sick baby daughter.

I had already- a long time ago- made up my mind what to do. He was still shouting nonsense when I came up to him and slapped him hard across the face. The look of astonishment on his face was worth a thousand pieces of gold. How dare his only child do this after all he had done for me. He began cursing me and called me a negro-loving sodomite. I slapped him again, harder this time. Out of his drunken stupor, realization dawned on him- I saw it in his eyes. He knew now, that I had staged this evening's play! But before he could say anything I tied a gag forcefully about his face. After tonight, he would never be able to hurt me with his words or actions again. I Instructed Toussaint, for him and the others to take father outside and wait for me, but to be quiet about it and let no one see them. For what I had planned next was particularly gruesome- painful and slow- and all would be able to join in.

As they exited, I held Toussaint back and quickly whispered that later I would give the three men (and their families if they had any) their freedom and will have the proper papers ready in the morning with gold coins for each, though they must never mention what had or will transpire this night. Of course, to do so would certainly result in everyone (including myself) being hanged by the authorities.

I then turned to the two household slaves, telling the male and female to clean up the room, leaving no evidence, and to please bury the poor child and pray over her soul; that tomorrow, they too, will have their freedom in exchange for their silence. I then went outside to join the others.

Around back near the kitchen, we had a few small sheds similar to the slave cabins, which we used for storage- food, grains, tools, sundries. It was to one of these where we took the old man. His attempts to struggle free from the strong grasps of the slaves was pathetic. However he knew, most assuredly, in his ever-sobering state, that tonight would be his last here on earth. He would die tonight and most likely, his death would be an extremely unpleasant one.

I had them tie him up- his arms wide, his legs spread- and he was then stripped of all his clothing. To think, this old man who had never shown his son (or anyone for that matter), any love or caring, who hurt and tortured others for pleasure, was now about to reap all that he had sown.

I produced a very keen and sharp hunting knife and gave it to the one slave whom I had described earlier. He should have the privilege of being the first.

The old man's muffled screams and futile struggles sent shivers of delight through me as, while Toussaint and I watched transfixed, each slave took his turn. Watching as they flayed my father alive-skinning him like an animal!

12

Here Gerard took in a deep breath and a long pause followed. Reliving his memories, and especially that particular night had obviously taken some emotional effort on his part. Emotions I am sure only I was permitted to see. He rose silently and stared vacantly into the dead coals in the fireplace. I firmly believed that if he stared at it long enough the fire would spring to life. Secretly, I wanted to see further demonstrations of his power.

Yet, it was hard for me to believe all he had told me- all that he had done. "Did you. . .participate?"

Gerard did not turn away from the mantel, but continued to stare at the non-existent fire. The clock struck one. "The bastard would not die. He kept slipping in and out of consciousness, yet his ungodly stubborn will kept him alive even after he had no skin left- save for his face, hands and feet. He had even been scalped." Gerard's voice groaned with anger as he turned to face me. "So I struck the final fatal blow and plunged the dagger deep into his heart!"

At this admission, I rose and walked over to the window and looked out at the full moon. The beautiful full moon that usually caused me so much distress, but at that moment I welcomed it like an old friend. I wanted to transform- for us both to transform- and we would play and romp like we did the night before. I wanted to return to a time before I knew all of this; to try and forget his morbid tale full of witchcraft and murder after grisly murder.

The last part of his tale was the hardest for me to fathom. That night of the poor girl's death, Gerard's planning and plotting his father's slow demise- all seemed too horrible- beyond my simple imagining. One thing that I did realize, now and completely, was that Gerard had truly been a callous murderer before he had become a werewolf.

"I know what you are thinking Henri."

"That was more than just cruel, Gerard. You knew that girl might die. You used her for your own purposes.

You killed that little girl just as much as your father did!"

Not caring for my accusatory tone, he threw his brandy glass into the fireplace with a sharp crash and turned to me, fury blackening his already stormy dark-blue eyes. I calmly returned his glare. He dare not raise his hand to me, at least not yet. For I too, was probably part of his plans. Someone for him to use- a tool suitable for some future diabolical purpose of his?

Calm and poise returned to him and he turned to the cakes and coffee and poured himself a cup. He called Mercutio over, who had been hiding and re-hiding his precious nuts all this time, and Gerard fed him a morsel of cake. The well-trained monkey then promptly curled upon a small pillow on the settee for a nap. "You know Henri- I am not a total monster. I can.. and do, love and care for others."

"Your story so far has not convinced me. Especially after such an unholy night as the one which you just now described."

"True. That night was one of the un-holiest of many unholy nights in my long life." He paced once around the room, then sat across from me and relit his cigar. "I assure you, I am not like my father. I do have a great capacity for love, and one day you will realize that. But what happened next was actually quite unexpected.

"I did fall in love and it was this love which caused my ultimate break with Satine and why she placed her jealous 'curse' upon me." He paused and when he continued his voice contained the hint of a small plea for understanding. "Perhaps you will not judge me so harshly once you know my complete story. Shall I continue?"

I poured my own cup of hot black coffee and thought of the shelter of my tiny warm, poorly furnished cabin, the soft body of my Selena, a drink with Pierre and the shared laughter with grandma-ma. But I had to hear it all- I had to know everything. Certainly, I was not one to judge. After all, I too was guilty of many things, including murder. I settled back down into that comfortable leather chair. "Continue."

As I said, remarkable as it may seem, I met someone who I came to care for dearly. And as it happened, we met the very day after I had gone into town to report my father's death. However my first task was to dispose of the body and it needed to be done that very night and without a trace. My first thought was to leave him in the murky quicksand on Satine's property where so many others had been disposed of. Yet I thought better of it. For if (in the unlikely event) those bodies were ever discovered, and my father's body dredged up with all the rest, it would automatically link me to their deaths. Satine just might try to convince the authorities, if it suited her, that I was a mass murderer. I put nothing beyond her capability. And of course, the actual truth would not possibly be believed.

No, I had to think of another way. And here Toussaint came through again for me with an excellent suggestion- however it was dangerous, especially at night- but we also would likely not be discovered. There was on the island, not very far from the plantation, a large and very uninhabitable swamp area, full of wild creatures- poisonous snakes, boars and crocodiles large enough to attack and eat a man. Occasionally, some of the more intrepid slaves (Toussaint included) would cautiously enter and hunt out there. Many runaway slaves had escaped into the swamp, knowing their white owners would likely not follow, but rather, just give them up for dead. Perhaps they managed to survive there or died- we never knew, for they were never to be seen or heard from again. Toussaint knew the exact area where the crocodiles slept and nested.

So he and I took my father's corpse out into the middle of that swamp that night. I insisted I go along because I had to make sure for myself that this one important thing was done correctly and completely without failure.

Careful not to be observed and by the light of one small lantern, we carried a canoe containing the covered and bleeding body to the swamp and quickly rowed to the area where the hungry large reptiles lived. Without hesitating, we threw the bloody thing over into the water and rowed away quickly, for their feeding began immediately and the water churned bloody with frenzy and we would have been overturned if we were not careful and quick. As we rowed away, I saw them fighting and turning in the swamp, tearing his limbs apart and devouring every scrape of flesh- and I felt an immense satisfaction flood my soul. The most difficult part of this episode was finished.

Now I had to obtain a death certificate from the local prefect, in order to legitimately take over my father's affairs and collect the inheritance. When Toussaint and I got back to the plantation, we rested until dawn, then we saddled up and rode to the nearest prefect's office.

I really did not know what to expect; how this scene would play itself out. It might be difficult to convince the official that we were night fishing in the middle of a deadly swamp and my drunken father had carelessly fallen in. I was prepared to use my magic and hypnotism to obtain the proper document. But as it was, fortunate favored the bold, for luck was on my side because this particular official knew my father from when they both worked on the other island in their different governmental capacities, and he knew well of my father's fondness for drink (and he probably knew of his other appetites also!) He just kept shaking his head, as he filled out the paper-work, saying what a horrible way to die. Of course, I played the part of a mournful and shocked son in an appropriate manner. He did not ask any questions, but simply handed me the stamped document, shook my hand and expressed his condolences.

Much of the time an investigation of sorts is conducted with a death, especially with no body, but at that time the officials on the island had their hands full with a slave uprising on a distant shore and what was one more man's accidental death when the devil had the islands by the throat.

Plus the fact that I worked for the youngest, wealthiest woman on the island, surely helped my matters for she had carte blanche with local government. Outside the office, I gave Toussaint the certificate and told him to de-liver it to our family's legal attorney along with a note I had written, requesting his presence that evening at my plantation home. Then in a few days, it would be mine- legally and in total and my plans were to sell it soon; take the money and proceeds and move here- to this even newer French settlement on the nearby continent, alongside the great river I had heard so much about; where land was abundantly available and affordable; where I could easily triple my fortune.

Back at home, I poured myself a satisfying drink, sat down at my desk and prepared the papers of freedom I had promised the night before. Toussaint arrived just as I was finishing and I had him take the papers, along with a few gold coins for each, and deliver them to the slaves involved. I was confident they would never alert the authorities.

After he left, I went up to my room, washed up, changed into fresh clothes and laid myself down for a well deserved sleep. Toussaint would take care of the plantations for one day.

I was at the dining table, finishing an early supper, when my attorney arrived. However, it was not the elderly man I had expected- the one whom my father and I had always dealt with before. This man was young, about my age (maybe a little younger) and well-dressed as befitting a professional man, but not in a 'dandy' manner which I detested, particularly here on the island. His short hair was blond, his eyes the lightest blue. He no doubt, was descended from French Normandy yet very tan and rugged to a healthy degree. I could tell immediately, even past his clothing, that he was most likely an active sports- and horseman. His day old beard attracted me.

We shook hands and he said he was from the legal offices of our attorney and I wondered out loud where the other gentleman was that I knew. His reply was that he was the youngest son, newly arrived from France and he was taking over the practice for his father who was retiring soon. He seemed slightly nervous- obviously new at this. Or perhaps it was because I might have stared too long at his beauty.

I welcomed him in and we sat down at the desk where he withdrew a packet of papers from his satchel and expressed his sympathy at my father's passing. He looked at me intently for a moment, perhaps searching for that pain and sorrow which usually accompanies the passing of a loved one. But seeing no more than my tired, fatigued look (which I am sure showed), he began leafing through the papers for me to read and sign.

I reached for his hand, 'And you are..?'

'Oh, Pardon-moi, monsieur. My name is Andre.'

'And I am Gerard.' I squeezed his hand and he squeezed back. It was a masculine rough hand; a hand more familiar to the reins of a horse than the paperwork of a solicitor. I looked directly into those clear blue eyes and my gaze was confidently returned, all his nervousness gone. We smiled brightly at one another, our hands slowly releasing their grip on each other and we both knew, without words, that we were interested in the same thing. And that was the beginning of our friendship which grew into romance.

I signed the papers to start the process of my receiving the inheritance. He said he would bring the documented copies by tomorrow after he had filed them with the proper office of records. I asked if he would like to come by tomorrow night and join me for a late supper. He readily accepted.

Our love affair was immediate and intense. We spent as much time together as possible. Any leisure time was consumed with one another. Whatever we were doing- hunting, drinking, playing cards, gambling- we were constant companions, pursuing pleasure as we pursued each other. And we were as equals.

I want you to understand Henri, I am quite capable of love and loving well. Unfortunately, my one regret with Andre was that it was necessary to keep secrets from him, which troubled me deeply. I never spoke of my dealings with witchcraft and the black arts nor of my relations with Satine and the victims we collected and sacrificed. And of course, I never mentioned my father or the truth of how he died.

I had already made up my mind to leave the island and Satine- now that I was with Andre, I was doubly determined. I would take him with me. However Satine must never know of my plans (or discover that I had given my love to another). I therefore had to plan my exit carefully.

Of course, she surmised that my father's death was no accident, but she could only guess as to what really happened. She was becoming ever more impatient and commanding with me. We no longer had sexual relations, even though she would occasionally make the casual gesture for me to stay the night. I always found an excuse or some reason to politely refuse her offer, though all the while feigning total devotion to her.

The months went by quickly and, as Andre and I grew closer, I was not so readily available for Satine as I once was. During the day I would see her, for I still worked managing her lands, but at night we seldom met or spoke and I almost never had dinner with her anymore. Now when she needed me to help with her sacrifices, she was, nearly always, forced to summon me.

She did pay a visit to my plantation once during this time- one late humid afternoon. That day I learned, she had indeed guessed that I had someone special in my life.

She looked very much the refined genteel plantation mistress that day, wearing a fine long dress (with high collar and crinoline) of white taffeta and lace, which made its distinct rustle as she roamed about the parlor, seemingly to admire my possessions and art. A large cameo on a long necklace accented her abundant bosom. Her ensemble was completed with a large bonnet and bow; she sported a delicate parasol. She was her youthful, beautiful self. 'So all this is yours now? Completely?' She waved her arm taking in the whole room and more.

'Yes. All mine. Completely.' She sat down and made herself comfortable. 'Would you like something to drink?' I asked her. 'Something cool perhaps?'

'A glass of sherry, would be nice. Thank you.' She was still gazing about at the furnishings, even though she had seen the parlor many times before. I poured us both a sherry, gave one to her and I sat down opposite her.

'And to what do I owe this visit? I was just at your plantation this morning. Are you here on business or do you require me for... some other service?'

Her soft laughter reminded me of when we had first met, when she held such mystery for me. 'Why so formal, Gerard? Cannot I pay a visit to an old friend and lover without it being for a particular reason?'

'I have never known you to act on anything without some reason or motive behind it.'

She looked at me directly for a moment in silence, her green cat eyes as mysterious and unreadable as ever.

'You misjudge me. I am hurt.' She feigned a look of
sorrow.

'I think not.'

She rose and glided over to the open plantation doors
and looked out; sipping her sherry in silence for a
moment before speaking. 'These last two or so years, I
have taught you much. Yes, mon cher?' She looked back
at me. 'You have become quite knowledgeable in the
black arts. Proficient even.' She started to walk about. I
wondered just what she was getting at. 'I would think, you
could be- one day- a formidable force.' She was now
standing exactly over the spot where the little girl had met
her untimely fate.

'I doubt that. You overestimate me.'

'I think not.' She laughed again, but stopped
suddenly, glancing down at the floor where she stood.
'How strange. I have a strong sensation that a horrible
tragedy occurred here. Right on this very spot. A child
was.. involved and...,' She paused and looked at me, her
feline eyes searching for the tinniest reaction in me. 'And
there was more, much more. Not so very long ago either.'
I said nothing, making sure I did not allow any surprise or
acknowledgement to register with me. I returned her look
with one of complete calmness. She began strolling
about the room again. 'You do not deny it?'

I had grown weary of her cat and mouse game. I
stood. 'Just what are you after Satine?'

'Does he know?'

'Does who know what?'

She avoided my direct gaze. 'Your paramour.' She
ran a white gloved finger over my desk. 'I believe his
name is Andre.' She then turned to me, the eyes showing
her true intent slowly rising to the surface. 'Have you told
him about your black magic practices or your father's
death? Does he know about...us?'

'What possible difference could it mean to you?'

'It doesn't.' She sat down at my desk facing me, her

voice taking on a deliberately meaningful tone.
'However..it should mean a great deal of difference..to
you.' I started to speak, but she continued. 'Discretion is
absolutely vital Gerard.'

'Have I not been discreet? Let me remind you, it is I
who has been hiding the dead handiwork you have been
leaving behind.'

'True.' She began thumbing through my papers on the
desk. I did not like that. In fact, I did not care for this
conversation and was eager for her to leave, yet I held
my tongue in check for the moment. She continued, 'But
we must also be discreet with love. Witches and warlocks
cannot fall in love for therein lies their detriment.'

'How so?'

'Simply put- we lose our powers and we
become..human, again.' Her gaze grew distant. 'I know,
for I loved once. Gods are jealous.'

'And you became human?'

Her next words were spoken in an evil hiss. 'I became
a centuries old creature and only the blood and seed of
the young man whom I loved could replenish me; and
now- this is my curse, to carry for all time. To replay that
horrid scene over and over again.' She walked over to
me and, softly cupping my chin with her gloved hand,
looked directly into my eyes. 'And I must never allow
myself to fall in love again, because this time it would be
the final end for me.'

I realized now why she had been getting weaker and
weaker; her craft having less and less potency. It was
just as I had supposed. She had been falling in love with
me! Settling in her seat again back at my desk, she
continued, 'And that is why you must not fall in love
either.'

'Nonsense. That could not possibly apply to me. I
made no pact with a god..or devil.'

'Every murderer has a pact with some devil,' she
replied bluntly. I sat back down, trying to think clearly.

Surely she was trying to trick me, but to what purpose? What she said could not possibly be true- she was just a constant and habitual liar. Jealous! 'Think about it Gerard. Have your powers been..waning?'

Perhaps, but I dismissed the thought. 'It is of no consequence. If need be, I will relinquish my powers absolutely and assume a normal, human life. With Andre... and without witchcraft.'

'If only it were that simple, mon cher. And even if it was, what if your precious found out what you were, what you have done. Would he love you still?'

I understood that as a threat. I stood up again, saying nothing; my physical stance told her this conversation was over. She had made her point and now it was time for her to leave.

Realizing my attitude, she rose without speaking, taking her delicate genteel manner with her to the door as I followed. Outside, on the veranda she turned back to me. 'Give him up Gerard. For his sake, if you truly love him, you must give him up. Both of us are governed by forces beyond our control.' She then quickly left, getting into her waiting carriage.

I knew she was delivering more than a mere warning. Whatever drove her- a pact with some devil or god, her so-called curse or her extreme desire for eternal youth, a necessity or perhaps just plain jealous scorn- whatever it was, I (and Andre) were in danger as long as we remained in these islands.

It would be easy enough for me to leave. My solicitors at Andre's firm could sell everything- the land, the home, the slaves- and send the proceeds to me, wherever I happen to be. I thought again of that French colony on the continent by a large river so wide and deep it is like a moving lake.

But it was different now, with my involvement with Andre. Would he be able to go with me? Would he want to? What believable reasons could I possibly give for this sudden move? I would think of something. After all, it could be most profitable for two enterprising French gentlemen with money to invest. The vast limitless land, marshes and bayous afforded an abundance of trade. Much different than from so confining an area as this island. Perhaps there, Andre and I could live and love freely.

One thing I knew for certain- we must go soon and it would be a permanent move. If I lost my powers, then so be it. If she followed or eventually searched us out, I would deal with her then. Perhaps I could prepare some type of careful defense in anticipation of her threatening us. Though I honestly believed she would not follow us- not immediately anyway and hopefully not for some time. She apparently had lived many lives, in many different places- wherever there was the scent of money and gullible old men. And of course, a steady supply of sailors, settlers and other adventurous young men such as are found in colonies like this island. Men without ties. One day (and I knew it to be inevitable), when Satine and I clash, I shall at least be able to choose the battleground.

As it turned out, all this was useless worry. For the furies or the devil- whoever ruled my fate- took matters into their own hands.

It happened only two nights after I had that last conversation with Satine. I had learned that a ship was sailing to a major port on the colonial coast in five or six days and that night, I was going to broach the subject of us leaving to Andre.

However, I never got the chance to speak to him about it. As it happens, we were in the midst of our passion, and because of that, we did not hear anyone come in and approach the bedchamber. If we had paid attention, we would have heard her shuffling slowly, struggling- even dragging her dying old withered and wrinkled body up the stairs. Two days ago she was vital and young! Usually her need for a sacrifice was predictable and most of the time corresponded with the new moon. But that night, with a full moon, was different and I will always regret not having been more on my guard.

Andre and I were lying together in our naked embrace, while the door slowly crept open. He had the extreme misfortune of being the first to glance over to see her kneeling there watching us. I saw a look of breathless bewilderment pass over his face and then absolute shock and knew what he must be gazing at- the dangerous witch searching for her sacrifice. But I knew not to look at her face.

Yet Andre did not know. I heard the hiss of the snakes and before I could utter a warning my poor, poor Andre- a love that I have never known since- turned to stone in my very arms! I felt his body grow heavy and rough. It cracked out loud, as he slowly and completely became a statue from head to toe.

My anger knew no hesitation. I jumped from the bed and grabbed the first object at hand that could serve as a weapon- a letter opener. Shielding my eyes, I flailed about, blindly lunging for her throat, but with the raise of one hand, she stayed me. I was completely blocked by some force, an invisible wall that prevented me from attacking her.

The gorgon was gone and she was Satine- dressed in the same Egyptian costume I had seen her in at the masquerade ball. Only this time it hung heavy upon her frail, decrepit body, in thick folds like drapes over a window. Her shriveled arms were but the bones of a skeleton. Then in a flash of red fiery lightning, she was her youthful self again- beautiful and glowing, enticing and powerful. She magically levitated into the air and floated above me.

Raising her head and arms to the ceiling, she summoned forth a wind- a whirlwind- suddenly there in my room. All my possessions and furniture began spinning about me, slamming into the walls, throwing themselves against me and crashing into each other, while her demented, evil laughter filled the room. Her wind's force was so strong, it caused the bed, carrying the heavy stone corpse of Andre, to slide across the room and slam into me. The impact fell me to my knees and I could only crawl on the floor, heading towards the balcony doors, as items buffeted me and broken shards of glass and other objects cut my naked body. Fortunately I came across some clothing as I struggled, cut and bleeding, outside. I glanced back at her. She was still floating high, her green eyes wide and frenzied with power, her dark hair flying wildly about her head as if it had a life of its own.

I managed to make it out onto the balcony where there was no wind; but there was smoke- and a lot of it. Mon Dieu! What else has she done! I heard all my things smashing about in the room, being broken, but I did not look back. Remarkably, I had a pair of trousers in my hand; putting them on, I then went down the backstairs. Once out on the patio, I stopped to look back up at my room, but it was downstairs where my attention was directed. The house was on fire and it was growing quickly and fiercely- flowing out the downstairs windows, traveling from room to room. I tried to approach the house, but the heat was already unbearable and increasing every second in intensity. The witch was deliberately burning down my plantation home!

I started towards the stables for escape. The witch's chaos had reached outside as well, with my people racing all about in panic, screaming in their African dialects- but I understood the universal language of fear. I ignored them all, for I had to find Toussaint and a horse.

As I neared the stables, it suddenly grew quiet. I could see my home was now totally engulfed in flames. It lit up the night sky like a thousand beacons. The eerie quietness was close, full and heavy with some near threat. I must be quick and saddle up; find Toussaint, ride to the port city and eventually escape from this island.

Then I heard it. It was soft at first, a slight breeze high overhead riding gently on the tops of the trees. She was coming! I tried to hurry, but in the next few seconds fury was all about me. The wind this time was accompanied by rain, torrents of stinging rain. Suddenly, I was in the very midst of a cyclone! I heard that loud laughter again, mingled with the howling winds and driving rains. Devil sounds surrounded me! In pain, I put my hands over my ears, but the laughter seemed to echo even louder in my mind. Her power and torments must have no bounds.

I tried to make it into the nearest stable, but could not. The winds and storm were too intense and all I could do was cling to a nearby tree. Through the rain streaming into my eyes, I could see in the distance that my mansion had been completely consumed. Over there, it seemed to be no storm raging. It was centered upon me! I managed to get down on all fours and struggled slowly, crawling towards shelter in the stable. Then as if by magic, it disappeared; all the stables had completely vanished, torn apart by the gales!

I had to make my way into town and I knew a short route, if only I could survive this storm's onslaught. Then I saw her. It was her face up above in the sky. Her face as large as a cloud, towering over me, coming fast at me! She appeared as some angry Olympian goddess, taking out her jealous wrath upon her poor subjects below. The face and eyes grew closer, ever larger, until it consumed the whole sky! I fell into the mud, lying on my back, closed my eyes and tried to shelter my face from her bewitching evil glare, thinking- all was lost!

Then again- all became quiet. Cautiously opening my eyes, I saw only the night sky- starry and cloudless. Her laughter and face were gone with the storm. The distant fire was diminishing. Had I passed out? Why had she not finished me? Had she overextended her powers? Or was there something other that she had planned for me?

I hurriedly got up and found the quicker path. It was through a nearby slave cemetery- the shortest route to town where clothes, safety and subsequent escape from her and this island, awaited. No one was about. I am sure all the slaves had by now run away into the mountains. But where was my Toussaint? Surely he would not have deserted me? Had she disposed of him as she had my other possessions?

Her power had completely overwhelmed me. I had never conceived that she could possibly be so strong. If I survived this, I would certainly never underestimate her again. I tried not to think of my Andre, now dead- nothing but a charred statue. I vowed to myself, there and then, to avenge his death; that I would destroy her one day- even if I had to sell my own soul to the devil in order to accomplish the task.

So barefoot and shirtless, I ventured through the dark, ghostly cemetery full of the unmarked graves of dead slaves, my only light that of the full moon. Only a few of the dead there had been buried with Christian ceremony. Most in a simple pine box, many in no coffin at all. I believe a great number to have been buried together in the same plot. Mass graves! Such was the horrendous condition of this French colony. It will be little wonder when that rebellion occurs which the white man fears so, inevitably resulting in their destruction.

I tried to hurry, but it was difficult to find my way among the crowded, unkempt graves; repeatedly falling in the mud and tripping over the dead limbs of fallen trees. At one point, I stopped to rest and sat atop a somewhat handsome engraved tombstone- one of the few in that cemetery. Some white owner obviously thought highly enough, or kindly enough, to recognize the poor dead black bastard. I thought of Toussaint. Where was he? Would I, too, have to lay my favorite slave to rest?

It was then I sensed that something was terribly wrong. I had guessed right- the she-devil had prepared a particularly ghoulish trick for me. Beneath my bare muddy feet, a rotten fleshed hand reached up from its earthly grave, clasping my ankle in a tight grip. I was so stunned, I could not move for a moment. Then as horror quickly filled my pounding heart, I watched as it raised itself out of the rocky earth. First an arm appeared, then its ghastly skeleton head peered at me with no eyes or lips, remnants of flesh hanging on its foul smelling corpse. The grasp it had on me was inhuman, strong and relentless, like a bear trap, far beyond normal human strength. I instinctively reached about for some sort of club or weapon and my hand found a heavy solid tree limb and I started to beat the living dead thing over the head with all the strength I had left, yet no matter how hard I bludgeoned it, its grip would not lessen. Finally, with its head bashed to a pulp, it stopped struggling- yet, half-in and half-out of its grave, the hand nonetheless gripped me like a vise! I forcefully brought the limb down upon the arm and it broke in two with a loud crack- and still the hand held on to my ankle! I tried to pry the fingers loose, but the only way to release myself was to snap each finger in two like a tough twig.

I tossed the rest of the hand away and ran towards where I knew the cemetery to end, the forest to begin and the road into town beyond that. Soon it would be daylight but I must hurry, for I knew she would raise more of these ghouls and one bite from any one of them and I would be as they- some type of deathless, senseless creature driven only by the need for human flesh and brains.

Just before I reached the edge of the cemetery, I was overcome by the sickening and stifling stench of the dead. They had risen! I stopped and glanced about. They were all around me! I counted two, four, ten, a dozen more, all stumbling slowly towards me; their arms outstretched, their hollow eye sockets not seeing- driven by the power of the ungodly witch.

I swung the thick branch (which I had miraculously kept with me) about, keeping them at bay, but I knew it would be only a matter of moments until they gathered themselves together and latched upon me with their skeleton hands. Some were just bones- walking skeletons- dead a long while. Others were freshly buried and still had on the rags they had been put to rest in. Some had no arms, some no feet or legs- crawling and creeping, pulling and propelling themselves along with their hands and bodies- all with a relentless hunger for my flesh. My only chance was to somehow run for it.

I noticed one was smaller than the rest, perhaps it had once been a child. Worms and maggots covered it, eating what little flesh remained. I smashed the limb hard into its chest and crushed the entire diaphragm, yet it still came at me. They were all getting dangerously near- almost within arms reach. I swung hard at its head and it lopped off like a ball. The corpse crumpled into a heap and I quickly jumped over it and ran for my life, past the others, swinging the branch wildly all the while.

At the forests edge, I turned to look back, expecting them to be following behind, progressing steadily forward in their cursed dead state. To my amazement, I saw no movement- the zombies were apparently gone! Had they been sent back to their graves? I stood quite still and listened intently. There was no sound of them either- just the noise of my heart beating furiously in my ears.

What was she planning now? What else was at her beck and call? Perhaps ghosts or some other type of undead demons. I quickly entered into the forest. Once daylight dawned and I was near town, I should be safe. Surely Toussaint would be searching for me. Hopefully her vengeful power had not reached out to touch him. Actually, I thought he was probably safe; she had one main objective this night and it was to destroy my life in some fashion or another. Right now, she was toying with me and I felt like a small mouse being tormented by a gigantic cat.

I made my way through the forest. The tall trees sent down ghostly shadows in the moonlight. I thought one of them moved, its limbs and trunk acting as a human would, and I stopped. But it must have been my overwrought imagination. I needed to get through these trees quickly, for I knew well that a witch's power was enhanced in deep dark forests. I also realized she was not done with me yet and something else was most likely waiting in ambush for me.

What was ahead for me was something even I would have never expected. I thought it to be just another tree among the many, straight ahead in my path, then suddenly it moved to block my way. It was a man, yet for some inexplicable reason, I could tell it was not one of those senseless creatures I had just encountered. Then the moon passed over the strange figure and I saw its face clearly.

Or rather what was left of the face, for the skin had been peeled away leaving only a bloody visage. In fact, the whole naked body had been skinned and I knew whom she had sent to undo me. It was my dead father!

This was impossible! For I had seen, first hand, his body ripped apart in the crocodile pond. It had to be an illusion. That despicable witch had conjured up his apparition to torment me!

The thing reached out its hand towards me and in an eerie, guttural voice called my name. I swung at him, but he vanished in an instant, only to reappear even closer behind me. He touched my shoulder and I instinctively jumped away; I heard a loud scream, but realized it was mine. I swung at him again and again, but he would simply disappear and then reappear in an instant some-where else. Moving frantically in circles, my head was becoming dizzy, my body increasingly tired with weariness. Then he was not there anymore and I was alone. Dropping down to my knees, I yelled out loud at the witch. Go ahead! I screamed. Finish it, Satine! Do your worst- kill me now and get it over with. I wanted to sob, but I would not give her the satisfaction.

Suddenly, my father's flayed figure was standing there before me. He grabbed my head with both of his bloody hands and I knew that this would be my end and I even imagined hearing my neck snap. Instead he spoke to me, in tortured speech like he was in great pain and from somewhere far distant. Why my son, why did you kill me? I loved you so, mon fils. Why?

You never loved me, I pitifully yelled back like a child. He then laughed showing teeth with no lips, showing wide eyes with no lids. Then, in the most bizarre macabre manner, his laughter changed into that of a woman's and Satine was again laughing at me. She spoke, using my father's ghost as her vessel, his mouth forming the words for her voice. His hands still held my head tight.

'You will not escape me, Gerard. You will not escape the curse I have planned for you. You are destined to be human, but not human. You will live among them, yet be none of them. My curse will be fulfilled.'

I yelled at her to kill me now or let me go. That tormenting me would not work, that I would not break- even though I thought to myself that I was already near the verge of insanity and if she continued, I would surely end up in the mad house.

My father's face grimaced wide with bloody teeth and Satine's sick laughter issued forth from it and then they were gone. Only the echo of that mischievous, evil-ridden laugh remained.

I wanted to collapse, faint dead away on the forest floor and let whatever it was she was sending have me. Take me without the benefit of a struggle. Ghosts, ghouls or flying beasts- I did not care anymore.

But the instinct for self-preservation is strong in me (as you well know), and I struggled to my feet and proceeded cautiously onward through the trees. I had made it thus far, perhaps I could make it all the way into town safely. Ahead was a clearing, bathed in full moonlight and I knew the road was just beyond.

Silently summoning the last bit of strength in me, I ran across the open field, hoping beyond hope, I would make it to the other side. Midway through, some thing made me stop and listen. I was able to see clearly in the night light and saw nothing, yet I thought I had heard something or someone moving about in the surrounding trees. I started to continue on, but stopped short- for this time I distinctly heard a noise, only I could not make out the source.

There it was again- louder this time and I recognized the sound as the deep growl of a wild animal. Most likely a wildcat or wolf and from the sound of it, a very large one.

I started to run again, hoping to reach the road and maybe some help on the way. There was a plantation close by, the owner of which I knew. I heard the beast burst through the brush and trees to chase after me. I had little hope of out running it and thought perhaps my one chance of escape was to scale a tree. If I only had the time.

I remember thinking that the creature must be very huge and heavy; it sounded like a galloping horse, though it was snarling and snapping; I dared not look back. It was drawing closer and closer with every step I ran. I leaped over dead trees, fumbling through the last of the woods. I imagined feeling its hot breath upon the back of my neck. Noticing a large oak near the edge of the forest, next to the dirt road, I sprinted for it.

But I did not make it. Just as I was about to take a leap for the tree, the monster reached out a giant paw and caught my foot. I tripped and fell and, immediately rolling over on my back, I started to raise the stick I had,

227

only to find my hand was empty- I had lost it somewhere in the woods! I felt a huge rock next to me, grabbed it and raised it with one hand, but it was slapped out of my grasp like a pebble! Then I saw the thing fully for the first time.

It was an enormous wolf, larger than a lion, more like the size of a bear. It had pounced on me- its strong thick limbs pinning my shoulders down to the ground. His eyes burned red and fierce, the fangs showing sharp and slick as it snarled down at me with foul breath. He put his large wet snout close to my neck, sniffing, taking in my scent; smelling the blood pulsing, coursing radically through my veins, bursting my heart. Was the wolf making sure it had the right victim?

Then he struck! Immense jaws clamped deep into my shoulder and chest almost completely engulfing that side of my torso. My blood spurted like a fountain as, with its monstrous strength, he picked my whole body up in his mouth and shook me fiercely about like a tiny plaything and then tossed me aside, slamming me hard against the oak that I had been running towards. My body hit it with a heavy thud and I slid helplessly to the ground. Before passing out from the unbearable pain and shock, I remember thinking that this time my world was over and I would be devoured by this creature, just as my father's body had been devoured before. Only I would still be alive when it happens! A fitting retribution only a witch like she could make possible in her twisted demonic way. I was to be food for this pet of Satine's!

When I woke, it was still night and the moon was bright and high. Was this the same night? It couldn't possibly be! It would be daylight by now. How long had I laid there? I even briefly thought that perhaps I had died and was now in limbo (or some such place) because hell would surely not be so earthly and peaceful. Yet the sharp stabbing pains throbbing through my body told me I was very much alive. I started myself up, frightened, looking for the beast. I did not see him. I listened- I did not hear him. He had gone! But why? Why did the wolf creature leave me alive? Something could have interrupted his attack and scared him away, but only the witch herself was capable of that. Why had she allowed me to live?

I looked cautiously about again. The beast was nowhere to be seen. Its huge paw prints though, were everywhere around me in the dirt beneath the oak showing the struggle, yet I did not observe any prints leading directly away from the scene. It was as if the wolf-creature had disappeared into thin air. But why bite me only once and disappear? Why had it not finished what it began and deliver a fatal blow?

Of course, in the back of my mind I knew the answer. The monster had accomplished what it had set out to do. It was not sent to destroy me, only to deliver Satine's curse. She had mentioned a curse and now it must be set to begin. That was no ordinary wolf- it was the hound from hell, called forth by her- and the curse was that of the loup garou!

Pulling my wounded and bloody body off the ground, I left the protected shadow of the oak and entered the wide road. The moon bathed me completely with its bright white light and suddenly- shockingly- I felt a strong powerful energy flood over and through my body, much more forceful and enduring than any witch's potion could possibly achieve. No more pain and weariness; the wounds utterly and completely gone. I gazed up at the moon and recognized that it was now a source of tremendous power for me! And, I want you to know

Henri- all during that first transformation into a werewolf, only one predominant thought was within me- that of the revenge I would ultimately wreak on Satine. I now possessed a superhuman power within me and that witch had just made the biggest mistake of her long and evil life!

That first transformation was the only one that ever caused me any pain or discomfort. It lasted for only a moment and was more similar to a giant thunderbolt than anything else. Or what I would imagine a lightning strike to feel like. That is the best description I can think of.

In a flash, I turned from a man into a man-wolf. I was not as distressed, as you might think; as others who have gone through this transformation would be. I do not know for I have never met another, only you- my Henri. You must have been very distressed, non, mon ami? It was painful for you because you resisted.

I took it as an adventure and I still do after all this time. Firstly, I was grateful to be alive (that was my main relief), however I slowly started to think she had actually done me a favor, with her so-called curse. I realized immediately, I had powers beyond that of a warlock, including the strength of twenty men. I felt all this surging within me, like a smoldering volcano. I could tear apart any man or beast; sunder a whole army into pieces! What great speed I had- all my senses super heightened- smell, sight, night vision. I was invincible and felt- immortal!

The one thing that did amaze me the most however, was my thoughts were still very much that of a man with logical reasoning. I was (inwardly) Gerard Mereaux, acting with purpose and forethought, yet outwardly, I had the appearance of a beast. And one of my first rational thoughts was I knew- as surely as I breathed- that the witch would no longer be able to control me and if I could get her within my grasp, I would be able to tear her centuries-old heart right out of her chest and she would be gone forever.

But my first need was bestial- I had to feed! Intense hunger gnawed at me; racking my brain and slowly dominating my primary thoughts. In this one respect, the beast controlled the man. Instead of following the road into town, I traveled back towards my burnt shell of a plantation. It took only a few minutes. The ruins were desolate; the heaping embers hot and still smoking; my sadness immeasurable. Satine had certainly been thorough- destroying in one night my home, my lover, my life. I kept to the shadows even though, strangely, no one was about- no authorities, no neighbors, no curious onlookers- all the slaves obviously having run away. I still believed that Toussaint would remain faithful and hoped tomorrow I should find him in town. Besides he had no where else to go.

I detected voices at a great distance; my newly acquired senses 'hearing' them miles away. I was upon them in minutes; but when close, I silently crept towards them. There were a dozen or so of them, slaves, (some of mine I had no doubt) and they were traveling together escaping into the hills. They carried their meager pitiful belongings with them. One strong young man took up the rear and hung slightly back behind the others. Their voices were many and varied, very confusing to me, until I realized I was hearing their thoughts as well as their speech!

My initial idea was to leap into the very midst of them, (literally frightening them to death), and slaughter them all like swine- men, women, and even the few children that accompanied their families. I could kill them all in mere minutes and still my ravenous hunger would probably be unsatisfied! But why do so? These people held no threat to me; they carried no weapons, except sticks and stones. My next thought was to spirit the young slave away without the others noticing- quickly and with stealth.

And that is precisely what I did! I snatched him from the road with lightning speed, (no one being the wiser), drug him into the forest and began to rip him apart- all before he could even utter a scream! Tearing off the limbs, I gnawed on them; my sharp claws cut open his torso and I fed on the intestines. For the tiniest moment, his fear had been tangible; I had felt it in the air; and I believe I fed on that too! It only served to increase my desire for flesh and blood.

After feeding, as I viewed the carnage, I did not feel pleased necessarily, but I did feel... supreme. Supreme over humankind! And I will tell you right now, Henri- I did not, I repeat- I did not feel evil. It just felt natural, like as if I were a lion and they were the antelope. I was simply a predator and they- the prey. And I have felt that same way about my victims ever since. I did learn, of course, to pick and choose the victim- if it were to my advantage or if it benefited me financially in some way. But much of the time my victims were simply just in the wrong place at the right time.

Now I could turn my complete attention to my most important task- revenge. But immediacy was important and I feared too much time had escaped! It was important to find Satine before the full moon set, so that its powers would be at my aid. This was perhaps the one and only chance I would have to take her unawares and defeat the witch now and forever. Bloody and determined, I set out for her plantation.

I approached the house in the open, under the moon's bright light, quite able to be seen. A monster wolf coming for the powerful witch. Only one room was lit- her bedroom upstairs. I silently, deftly, scaled up to her balcony and peered inside through the thin curtains. By the light of a single lantern, she was packing up her clothes and belongings into three very large trunks. She was obviously planning a long and extended stay somewhere. I saw a label on one trunk addressed to a villa in Italy.

She was in quite a rush, hurriedly and carelessly throwing things about. She knew she had little time before I would recover and seek her out. I always wondered how she had miscalculated the result of her curse. I imagine that, more than likely, in her jealous and egotistical need to exert her power and will over me, she had not thought of any real and subsequent danger to herself.

She paused in mid-step between two of the trunks and looked quickly about as if she had heard something, though I had made no sound. She started to return to her packing, but again stopped and looked out towards the balcony in my direction. She had sensed my presence and now was the time to make my move.

I moved out of the shadows and entered the room, standing clearly in the light where she could see the handiwork she had wrought. A distinct look of surprise crossed her face for a moment (was a little fear mixed with it?), but it was quickly replaced with her usual composure. She giggled, daintily, at my sight- trousers bloody and torn; my body covered in the thick hair of an animal; the large feet, hands and claws; my face slightly recognizable.

My how you have changed, Gerard. She had not spoken out loud, but I could hear her voice nonetheless, as she calmly turned back to her tasks. But you are still handsome- in a brutish sort of way. Her laugh that time was loud and slightly maniacal. I took a step towards her and she immediately got behind one of her trunks. Though she would not show it, my animal instinct sensed her mounting anxiety.

You ask me why, Gerard and I will tell you. She could read my mind, as I could read hers. Because you only used me to learn my secrets, to gain my power. You who knew only amateurish tricks and backwater voodoo! Yes, I taught you and I grew weaker while you grew stronger. Well, now I am no longer weak, Gerard. I am as the

Phoenix and will rise again and again and again!

Turning her attention back to her packing, she slammed one trunk shut and proceeded to rearrange another. And now you have power too- within a curse, of course. A curse not too unlike mine. You always wanted such grand and unique powers and now you have them- thanks to me! In combination with what I have taught you, you are now that significant force I once spoke of. She slammed another trunk shut and stared straight at me, with defiance and pride, with no regret for having destroyed my life and love.

But these powers do not come without a cost, Gerard. For your curse is not just that of a loup-garou. Your true curse is eternal loneliness. Now and forever. Forever Gerard, you will never know love or true happiness. You are the only one of your kind. For centuries, Gerard- for centuries- you will experience such loneliness that you will wish for merciful death, yet it will not come. Night after eternal night. You are the only one. The next words, she chose to speak out loud to spew forth her venomous hate. "Of course, no man or woman could possibly love you, for you are a freak. A freak of nature!"

Her mean laughter ceased, when I took a few more steps closer to her. She raised her hand to me and I immediately felt her witch's power. However, unlike the time previously- this time I could overcome her. For, just as she had said- I was not a mere human, not any longer- and the moon's power was with me!

"Do not come closer, Gerard. I am warning you."

It surprised both of us when I spoke. "You cannot stop me, Satine. You made an error in your calculations." My voice issued forth in a deep rolling growl, familiar yet unfamiliar. "You have no control over me now." I took another step forward.

She raised both her hands. Her power was palpable- an invisible wall between us. Still, I could break it! She laughed. "That voice! Coming from such a hideous façade. It is truly comical." I took her attempt to insult me as proof of her nervousness.

I edged forward. She moved slightly back, keeping her hands outstretched before her. I sensed her mounting fear- and shock that her witchcraft had scarcely any effect on me. Yet, I had one more question.

"Andre?" Her laugh this time was fully and unabashedly evil. "Please, Gerard! Do you really think I would ever- ever! play second to another. Especially to a man!"

She laughed again. At me she laughed. At Andre and myself she laughed. I would make sure it would be the last time she ever did so. I'd choke that laugh right out of her!

I leapt and she could do nothing to prevent me. I threw the heavy trunks aside like they were so much bags of feathers and managed to tear her dress, leaving a deep scratch on her shoulder. The witch bleeds! I was going to rip her heart out while she watched, helpless to stop me. I wanted her to see with her own eyes- for a few seconds- her very heart beating in my giant hand!

Then, expectedly, she summoned forth the wind, thunder and lightning again, there in her room and she herself became the whirlwind! She rose up into mid-air, spinning wildly like a top. I leapt again at her and succeeded at grabbing her feet and so we both went spinning around the room. Then, unexpectedly, she started to scream like a banshee and it pierced the night, extremely hurting my sensitive hearing. The lantern had fallen over and the place was catching on fire. Her wild wind fanned the flame.

Still her voice screeched and wailed, becoming ever louder and more painful; still I clung onto her with my sharp claws digging deep into her, crushing her ankles, causing her to bleed and scream more. If only I could drag her down, I would slit open her throat with my fangs- the very throat that I had once kissed in a mimic of passion.

Her screech reached an ultra-high pitched crescendo as my ears bled and felt as if they were rupturing. I wanted to cover them but dared not let go. However, eventually I had to, for they were bursting; I was howling with pain. As soon as I released my grasp, the balcony doors flew open and she spun out of the room. I rushed to catch her, but in seconds she was floating high over the treetops- her banshee wail and the gale following after her. She had escaped my revenge! Her house and possessions were in flames: She had lost those- as I had. Not much consolation; for I had so wanted more- her life, her blood- her death!

Watching her disappear into the horizon, I cried a tremendous unearthly howl into the ending night, at the vanishing moon. I howled and howled again after her- my pain, my anguish, my disappointment at not having succeeded- all poured forth from me. Anyone hearing me, would recognize the sound of deep pain in my long and lonesome howl. She had escaped my wrath! And I have never seen her since.

13

His tale having finished its climax, Gerard stopped to relight his cigar and pour himself a cup of coffee and lace it with brandy. But before he drank it, we both enjoyed another thimbleful of absinthe. We then sat in silence next to one another on the settee. Mercutio was curled up in a corner chair, snoring loudly.

"What did you do next?" I was eager to know.

"I made positive her plantation home was torched completely and watched it burn all the way down to the ground. She had left me with nothing and I made sure she was left with nothing." His eyes and voice grew distant. "It gave me only a small measure of satisfaction."

I had been totally engrossed all the while in his story, from beginning to end. I recognized his supernatural sensations of power and strength; knew the same never ending hunger he described; felt deeply his sorrow at the loss of his true love. I was thoroughly hoping his revenge against the witch would have been successful and she destroyed forever. I found it remarkable (why, I do not particularly know) that Gerard had become cursed as the result of a spell and not from the bite of another. I vaguely wondered just how many of us were out there. "And Toussaint? I suppose you found each other?"

"Yes, the very next day in town. We managed to 'procure' clothes and enough money for passage to the continent on the next ship." He rose and walked over to the clock on the mantel and checked the time with his pocketwatch. The sun would soon rise. We had spent all the night together- he relating for the first time to another living soul the extraordinary tale of his life and how he came to be- and I- listening with rapt attention and anxiousness. Like a protege paying homage to his mentor.

"On the very same ship that you had wanted to take with...?"

"The very same." He interrupted my question, but did not turn away from the mantel and mirror above. "The very same," he repeated, a grieving sorrow obvious in his voice and manner. Perhaps as supernatural beings, not only were our senses heightened, but also our emotions. I wanted to go to him, embrace him and comfort him in some way. Whatever wickedness he may have done in the past- or will do in the future- he still had loving feelings and, after all, was the one who had created me as I am. I would come to realize we were one in mind and spirit, and he would mold me further as my teacher. Yet something in me hesitated to approach him- that day.

"We arrived at the colonial capital on the banks of that mighty river, some days later and promptly made ourselves acquainted with the land and the many different peoples that arrived almost daily. The town and surrounding areas were teeming with settlers, who drained swamps and cleared the land. It was obviously more prosperous than the islands. I did not hesitate to use all my powers," he emphasized the word 'all', "to full advantage and began to acquire property." He turned to me and smiled. "I became quite adept at forging signatures, even complete documents, and took advantage of the lax laws and corrupt officials which can be so prevalent in frontier towns. I ingratiated myself into the wealthier classes of the French colonial society, using that most formidable weapon of mine- my charm- quite successfully." He laughed at that, the first time since relating the tragic end of his story. He sat down comfortably next to me and patted my knee.

"What about yourself?" I had to ask. "And adapting to being. . .to carrying her curse?"

He shrugged. "It did not take me long. Within a few months, I learned to change myself at will, simply and quickly, full moon or no. If I wish, I can limit the transformation to only certain parts of the body- my hands or face, for example. You will eventually learn that too, but it may take you somewhat longer. I believe I learned and adapted quickly because of the witchcraft I knew. I even became familiar with the feel of silver. It helps to be both warlock and werewolf!" He laughed and patted my leg again, and this time he did not remove his hand, but squeezed me. "And I will teach you my witchcraft- if you care to learn. It will help us grow even closer together." His eyes shined bright blue and spirited; his smile of perfect even white teeth was handsome. He was so very happy to have me there with him. I did not answer, though I had to admit I was happy (in some ways) to be there too. Happy to have some one like myself to talk with: some one who understood the loneliness, the isolation, the pain of being different. Another kindred spirit, another werewolf. Someone to teach me the ways of the loup garou.

The clock struck five o'clock. Dawn would break soon. I thought to myself that I should go up to my bedroom and get some sleep. His eyes were burning deep into mine. It did not take a mind reader to know his thoughts. Was he trying to hypnotize me? Only with a great effort, was I able to break away from his gaze. Perhaps he had even put a potion in my drink or glass, like he had done to others.

I gathered my thoughts together; there were many more questions still. "How did you acquire Sans Souci?"

Removing his hand off my leg, he rose and started to pace about the room- smoking his cigar, drinking his drink, blowing out a few candles here and there. "Yes. One more tale to end this long night of many tales." He paused. "The original owner was elderly- a planter of great means. And the first time I saw Sans Souci," he sighed heavily, "it reminded me of my old plantation home on the island, but more elegant and richly furnished. And," he shrugged, "when I set my sights on something," here he turned directly to me and I knew his inference. "It always becomes mine!"

He turned back to his pacing, a fresh drink and the last of his story.

Shortly after arriving in the colony, I became acquainted with this particular plantation owner- He was French. After visiting Sans Souci once, I gradually formulated a scheme to get the home and land. Like I said, he was old- and, fortunately- feeble in both mind and body.

Then lady luck again took me into her hands. He laughed to himself. I had been somewhat- careless- in disposing of my last few victims. Foolishly, in my haste, I had left pieces of their disemboweled bodies about and, to make matters worse, I had been glimpsed- in my transformed state- by some of the local populace.

And so there began to be a lot of rumors and speculation spread, of someone who walks among humans during the day, but turns into a demon/creature with the full moon. The words loup garou were being whispered on people's lips. Which necessitated me to set my plan in motion quickly, to achieve not only the goal of acquiring his possessions, but at the same time, to divert suspicion away from me.

It was easy enough to accomplish. The night I chose was when the moon was at its fullest. First I came here, to his home, very late, making sure no one saw me and silently crept up to the room upstairs. I had a potion ready and with me. He was in his bed asleep, snoring. Poor man, had never married nor had children and lived alone save for only a few house slaves. Maybe that was one reason he had a lot of wonderful art and furnishings, land and money.

Waking him suddenly, and before he could utter a breath of surprise, I blew the entire powdered potion into his face. He calmed down at once, coming into a trance and was now entirely in my power and susceptible to my suggestions. I sat him down at a desk and told him to stay still- that he would not remember anything of tonight or of my visit. He was to stay there, in that way, in the dark, until I came back with more instructions.

I then rummaged through his things and found what I needed: A gold pocketwatch with his family name engraved on it and a handkerchief with his initials sowed in. That would do to place near the scene. Next, I took a shirt and pair of trousers of his with me, which I intended to splatter with the victim's blood and bring back to the plantation and leave as incriminating evidence.

So you can gather what I was planning. It took me only an hour or so, to accomplish the deed, maybe less. I ran as fast and as unseen as the wind into town and luckily, found two homeless persons in a filthy alleyway. They were arguing over a piece of bread! Can you imagine? Well, I promptly ended their hunger and satisfied mine, then put the watch and kerchief into their cold, bloodless hands. I wiped the shirt and trousers with their blood and entrails and carefully ran back to the plantation. All this was done very quickly and unobserved by human eyes.

Back here, I found him as I had left him. I hid the bloody clothes away in another room, but not too well. They would be discovered easily by anyone searching for evidence. I instructed him to write out a new will, leaving all property and belongings of his to me- the son he never had. It was written down all very legally and formally, in his handwriting and with his signature. It would not be doubted by anyone. I had him make another copy, along with handwritten instructions, which I would later have delivered to his solicitor's offices. I asked him where any pre-existing will may be.

He went over to another cabinet and withdrew a folder containing the old will and several other papers, including the deed to Sans Souci. I told him to burn the original will, which he did- putting it into the fireplace, thoroughly soaking it with kerosene and lighting it with a candle. To further ensure my inheritance, I had him add my name to the deed. I signed alongside. Any copy of the deed at the solicitors, I would forge or modify later. Sans Souci would soon be mine.

Then I left, my work done. I had set the wheels in motion and now they would turn on their own. I instructed him to go to sleep and when he woke, he would remember nothing of my visit or this night. And if asked about the new will and the addition of my name to the deed- he would reply yes, he had those changed to include Gerard Mereaux, for he considered me as a son.

Soon the authorities came here to the plantation in order to search the premises, after finding his personal items on the bodies. Subsequently, the bloody clothes were found. In short, he was arrested and was awaiting trial; however, the village folk were on edge and mob mentality can rule, especially on the frontier. Some called him a witch, others claimed he was a loup-garou. As soon as he was arrested, the gruesome killings stopped, which only further fueled speculation. The evidence was not absolute proof, but to a populace frighteningly hungry for revenge and blood, it was all that was necessary to condemn the man. The idea that perhaps someone had framed him, did not seem to occur to anyone.

As for the poor old man, he was dumbfounded- most of his memories erased by my strong potion. It probably accelerated his approaching senility. He could not possibly explain the evidence and vainly proclaimed his innocence, futilely protesting his incarceration. I suppose he never really guessed what was happening to him until it was too late.

And it did not take long. A few nights after his arrest, he was found hung by the neck in his jail cell- some say with a silver-tipped arrow piercing his heart. Of course no one claimed responsibility and, as far as I know, local officials did not pursue the matter. I suspect they were as much to blame behind his demise as anyone. Officially, they proclaimed him to be a madman, dead by his own hand. Unofficially, the story goes that they cut off his head, burnt it and his headless corpse, then scattered the ashes about. I suppose to prevent his resurrection.

"And that is how I came to 'acquire' my Sans Souci!"

I did not speak for awhile, still absorbing all that he had told me that night. "You probably want to get a little sleep, Henri. It will be sunrise soon. As for myself," he poured himself the last of the hot dark coffee, "I stay awake- sometimes all night- particularly during a full moon. I have grown accustomed to it; it does not bother me. I prefer it, in fact."

"Yes," I spoke as I rose up from the chair. "I think I will try to rest some. Tell me, what became of..?"

"Toussaint?" I nodded. He had finished my question, still reading my mind. "He happily married one of the slave girls here on the plantation and produced the man you met this morning. He is very much like his father, both in looks and in manner and I have become quite fond of him- as I was his father. Toussaint worked hard for me, until the very end. And he never once judged me," Gerard waved his arm emphatically, "or cared what I had become. Then it came to be my turn to take care of him." He turned towards a window, the last rays of the moon dancing on his somber face. "He died peacefully in his sleep."

I walked over to the door leading to the hallway. Mercutio was stretching and rousing himself awake slowly, ready for a new day. I said goodnight and started to leave, but he spoke again.

"Henri," he called after me. I stopped and turned to him. He walked over and looked closely at me. His eyes were slightly moist and I could visibly tell what great pains it had taken him to relive his story so completely and honestly. Even Toussaint did not know so much of his life- only I was so privileged. Only I could come to know the real Gerard. Only, not yet, not at that moment anyway.

"Please, Henri, if you will. Think about what I have told you tonight and try not to judge me too harshly. But rather consider the man behind the actions. A man may do wicked things, but that does not necessarily mean he himself is evil, non?" He turned back to the window. "If anyone can understand, it will be you, mon frere."

There was a long pause, for I did not know quite how to respond. But before I could turn to go, he continued speaking. And what he had to say was very important for both our futures.

"Satine will return soon. She is just waiting for the right time to appear."

"How do you know? How can you tell for sure?" I was intrigued when I should have been frightened.

"I know. Small signs. Her tricks have already surfaced."

"For example?"

"Your name on the crypt. That was her doing. I am certain of it. She is making her presence known." He paused, "She is telling me that she knows about you."

"I thought maybe it was Dr. Fontenot's handiwork. A joke perhaps? It had to be Julian who I saw in the mausoleum and cemetery."

"Yes, but Julian would not have played a prank like that. Not on you." He paused to reflect. "Unless he was 'influenced' by the witch, but I doubt it. And the good doctor has not been heard of or seen in quite some time. He has vanished- to somewhere in Egypt, I believe.".

He turned to face me, the light from the last candelabra flickered mysterious shadows across his tan chiseled face. This time I showed no hesitation. I walked over to him and he embraced me warmly and I held him tightly in return. Slowly, he moved his head to look directly in my eyes, searching for the same desire that he felt. But I suppose he saw none, for he released our close embrace and walked back to the window, waiting and watching for the sunrise.

I walked into the hallway, my hand on the doorknob, yet there was one more question. "If she is here- somewhere- why now? Why has she come back now to taunt you?"

He answered without turning around. "That is simple, mon cher. It is for one reason only. She is back because now- I have you." With that said, I walked out and up to my room.

I laid awake most of that early morning pondering my situation and what I must do. Much of me wanted to escape from this nightmare, run back to what was familiar to me. Yet I knew reality would assert itself and I could not escape what I had become no matter where I was, no matter who I was with. No, I must stay and learn all that I can. I would start with Gerard's library. He was right- I was developing a thirst for knowledge and languages. I could also make myself useful around the plantation, learn its complete workings and perhaps, help it reach its fullest potential.

However, first and foremost, I must learn how to live with what I was. Human, but not human- this 'cursed thing' called a werewolf. I would use Gerard as an example. He had adapted quickly, but then, he already had a temperament for killing- I did not. He had a distaste for humanity- I did not. He did not seem to carry the human frailties of guilt and remorse- as I carried them. They were sometimes such a heavy burden upon my shoulders, upon my soul- that I thought I should surely die. And many times already, I had longed for the release that only death could bring.

Somehow I must take from Gerard those attributes I most admired: His strength and confidence; his sense of purpose and aggressiveness. Yet at the same time, I must be wary not to become as callous and unfeeling towards others as he is. I must find some way to preserve my own sense of humanity- though not human. Keep my compassion and respect for human life- though a murderer. I knew it would be nearly an impossible task, though in time I might succeed, especially if I were to live the many years that, apparently, these other immortals have lived. No, I must keep a part of my humanness intact or, for me, it would surely result in madness.

I did want to try and understand him. To realize his motivations and consider the man, Gerard- not the wolf within. True, he had done many despicable things-murder being not the worst of them. He had indulged in everything from necrophilia to patricide. He used others. He had no respect for human life. Was that not evil? But then I thought that I too had committed wicked acts-murder being only one of them. And yet, in my heart I did not feel evil.

As for his loving me- he was in love most definitely. Not only because I was his werewolf- created by him, blood brothers as it were- but also because he was at-tracted to what innocence and naivete I still carried with me. As for myself- was I in love with him? No, not at this time, yet I had to admit to myself that loving him was possible. For just as my innocence attracted him- his audacious, even brutal nature... drew me close. Actually, I had no doubt that I would have been in his bed with him that very night- but only one reason held me back. My fidelity. I was in love with another.

And what of his offer to teach me his witchcraft? Should I accept or decline? I quickly decided to learn all that I could. However, I refused to sell my soul- for surely one curse was enough! Knowledge about voodoo and witches would certainly help if I ever needed to defend myself. Not necessarily against humans, but from other supernatural creatures.

Which made my thoughts turn to Gerard's nemesis-the witch Satine. Was she really the evil succubus Gerard portrayed her to be? A Phoenix witch who, with the proper sacrifices, could live forever? I concluded that any understanding of supernatural beings and their ways, would benefit me tremendously. For if she was as evil-spirited as Gerard described, then I (like his previous lover, Andre) would probably be in great danger- if (or when?) she decided to make her appearance.

As all these thoughts crossed and criss-crossed in my mind, one question became foremost: How long should I stay? I missed Selena deeply and yearned to be back with my family. I had only been gone a few days, yet it seemed like an eternity.

The sun broke over the horizon and its first rays danced across the bedroom and brightened up the picture of Julian Fontenot. While I was growing drowsy, the plantation and its people were coming to life and I heard the first stirrings of a busy household and the surrounding fields. I closed my eyes and managed to get some slumber.

END OF PART TWO

Loup Garou

PART III
SANS SOUCI

1

That was probably one of the last times where I slept for a long period at any one time. After that, I was awake most every night reading in the library or privately in my room. And during the day, I was busy about the plantation with Gerard or Toussaint.

I learned everything I could about owning and operating a large plantation and Sans Souci was one of the first in the area. Even though Gerard never kept it working to full capacity, he (and Toussaint) were excellent teachers. Hi experiences on the island as manager of two profitable plantations, insured me of his expert advice and knowledge.

Purchasing and selling, accounting and bookkeeping, and slavery, especially, were all new to me. The physical labor I knew the experience of, but now with having slaves, that was not so longer necessary and it freed much of my time to learn about the plantation's workings from the inside mechanics as it were.

Except the issue of owning a human being seemed so unnatural and alien to me. I told myself, if I ever acquired my own property it would not include slaves and if it did then I would find a way to free them.

I absorbed all the masterful knowledge I could with hearty relish. Having many diverse crops and livestock saw to it that the plantation was busy every season throughout the year. Included in my schooling was also how to manage a fully functional household for Gerard counted that essential. He would say it separated us from the beasts! I came to the belief that his civilized daily routines (from a hearty breakfast at dawn to his late night bath after dinner) were purposefully meant to remind him of his humanness. It came to be my routine for the most part, also.

On rainy days (or times when Toussaint and Gerard were on a trip to town or at a slave auction) I would busy myself in the study or be repairing the clocks on the plantation. From his British colonial clocks, with their hardy durability, to the more delicate, yet precise French clocks, I learned about them all. He even provided a special well-lit workroom for me, furnished with custom made tools required for the trade.

The one clock which I did not clean or repair (until, as it happens, I had to much later) was the longcase clock in the hallway. I tended to it though, faithfully, winding it regularly and making sure it kept perfect time. Gerard was more than happy to allow me to care for it- one less task for him. He did mention that it was the only clock included with the plantation. He had personally selected all the other timepieces.

However, as I tended it, wound it and set the hands every day, I never again felt the presence which I had encountered that evening soon after my arrival. I never made mention of the occurrence to Gerard or Toussaint (who I soon came to speak very freely with as a friend). Eventually I forgot about it.

My clock workroom was not far from the kitchen and I could easily see the doings and business of this beautiful place. The chimney was constantly smoking, starting before dawn and ceasing only until close to midnight. Therefore, I saw Juliette often. She ran the household almost single-handedly; the young girl inheriting the task from her mother (who apparently had disappeared suddenly a few years ago). She would bring me a mid-day meal when I was in the workshop and we would chat for a moment about many things, including the various clocks I had disassembled on the tables. She possessed a very keen mind and if I had not been married, I would have entertained carnal thoughts about her, for she was extremely beautiful- and extremely young. Yet it was her natural charm that made her so attractive and I learned not only about the kitchen and household duties, but I discovered some interesting details about Master Gerard.

One detail in particular interested me. Or rather one person in particular.

According to Juliette, the boy that served Gerard was purchased only a year earlier, for the express purpose of being his master's personal servant. I took that to mean he was purchased to be Gerard's consort; though of course, Juliette in her girlish innocence did not know of such things. Her mind was easy enough to read, for her facial expressions and body gestures gave away her thoughts readily. Quite different than my Selena, who was less animated.

The boy, came and went predictably, serving coffee and breakfast, slicing meat at dinnertime, bringing cigars and pouring our wine in the evenings, as Gerard and I huddled over the books and compared ideas on the workings of the plantation. Every night my bed would be turned down, though I seldom ever slept. He spoke very little and when he did it was in a low murmur. I wondered just how educated he might be.

I wanted to speak with him alone, to let him know I could be his friend. That he need not resent my closeness with Gerard, for I had no intention of being his replacement in Gerard's bedroom. Juliette also confided to me that the servant boy's predecessor (who, she remarked, was also rather young and muscular) had been found dead one morning- the tragic victim of some strange wild beast! 'Torn to shreds' was one description given by those who had discovered the body. What made the death even more mysterious, was the fact that he was found only a few paces from the front steps of the house and no one had heard or seen a thing. No tracks were to be found; nor any visible signs of a struggle. Juliette whispered to me conspiratorially- 'Voodoo'- nodding her head knowingly. As she spoke, I thought of that winged creature of Gerard's.

It became obvious that this young boy of Gerard's was definitely avoiding being alone with me. He would never give me direct eye contact. So, reluctantly, I decided to take the liberty of entering his mind and reading his thoughts.

I have always considered mind-reading as an intrusion upon one's private realm- a violation of that person's sanctity. However, Gerard's argument was to consider it as a natural ability which serves an all important purpose: to detect those who would do you harm. Simply put, it was another defensive tool useful against our enemies, human or otherwise.

So, right or wrong, I entered the boy's thoughts. But all I could read from him was emotions- some jealousy towards me and my presence in the house; love (I supposed for Gerard); and a great deal of fear! I could not sense clearly just what his fear centered on, but it was- most definitely- his predominate feeling. Perhaps fear of being discarded by his master or even dispatched as the slave before him had been. Perhaps it was fear of Gerard's brutal temper which I would come to experience first-hand as my visit grew ever extended. It would actually be some time before the boy and I spoke together and he would confide in me. Unfortunately, by then it was too late.

As my time at Sans Souci progressed from days into weeks, there was one more all important pursuit in which I buried myself- the study of lycanthropy. I had to know all about myself, to separate the myths from the truths. To learn of our origins, if possible; and to discover if there were others such as us. Surely, Gerard and I were not the only ones.

Unfortunately, the more I studied and read (for Gerard had several titles on this subject, the occult and other supernatural phenomenon) the less I recognized myself in the pages. One legend tells that we began as the devil's own children, which even the dark lord, himself, could not control, so he therefore banished us from his underworld and set us out upon an unsuspecting human populace. Some books mentioned silver as being deadly to the werewolf; other works did not mention silver at all. Contrarily, fire was often regarded as the one particular method to bring about our destruction, as it was for witches and all other evil in-humans. 'The only way to cleanse evil away with permanence', was how one author described it. And of course, there was decapitation.

The pentagram was thought to be the sign of the werewolf appearing as a scar on his person. Other authors said that the symbol could be seen on his next victim. Reading this, I painfully recalled my own experience with that five pointed star. I began to think that grandma-ma and the voodoo priestess knew more about lycanthropy than these so-called experts.

There was one consistent line of thought, though, that kept rising from these different tomes- the power of the moon, a full moon, over the werewolf and his transformations. Gerard had, over the years, managed to control his changes, at will and at any time of the month, most probably with the aid of his own witchcraft. And now he was to teach me. It would be my first practice in the black arts. It would become a life-long affair.

It was also one of Gerard's theories that a stroke of lightning (if it did not kill the werewolf) would make him even stronger. Invincible. After all, he reasoned, if the tale is true, lightning was part of the formula used by the mad Dr. Fontenot to artificially create life from dead tissue. So therefore, with every lightning and thunderstorm that passed over Sans Souci, I would see Gerard outside in the pouring rain, half-naked, out in the open or sometimes near a particularly tall tree hoping to attract a bolt of energy. As far as I knew, he never was successful.

During that first long, hot summer at Sans Souci, Toussaint became my true confidante. He did not speak much, but the little he said was so full of wisdom and advice that he actually told me a great deal. He seemed to never waste a breath on small talk. I purposely tried not to read his mind, believing that even his thoughts were not spent on petty things. I doubt if I would have been able to anyway for Toussaint was one of those born with a strong will- and I am positive he knew his own share of voodoo also. So I was quiet and observant and asked only the most pertinent questions and took up only the most pressing topics.

He did tell me some information that Gerard failed to readily share at first. He taught me about familiars- those creatures (sometimes an object) sent to the man or woman practicing witchcraft. These familiars would appear suddenly (supposedly sent by the dark master) to serve and protect the witch or warlock. The familiar could range from an animal as simple as a housecat to a giant supernatural mythical being. "It could be the trees or a cloud. The type of familiar depends on the personality and character of the one practicing the craft and also..", here he paused for emphasis, "it depends upon the immediate and future needs of the witch. The familiar specifically will help battle and destroy his enemies. The more powerful and numerous the enemy, the more powerful the familiar must be." As he spoke these words, I realized just how important Gabriel was to Gerard. The gargoyle not only was protector of the plantation and its environs, it was also Gerard's first line of defense against the evil witch should she return.

"Will I too, acquire a familiar, Toussaint?"

"If you keep learning and practicing the craft and arts as Gerard knows them," was all he would say.

One day as Toussaint and I were riding around the plantation on our almost daily routine of overseeing the slaves in the fields (Gerard being busy on some 'personal business' in town), Toussaint started speaking frankly, even confidentially to me. I was surprised for in this one small conversation he shared more thoughts and words than he had during the entire previous weeks since my arrival.

It started with an innocent enough question, "Do you miss your wife?" "Immensely," I replied with some emotion. "I miss my whole family. My parents, brothers and sisters- my entire kin, save for my cousin, Pierre- were separated from me during the expulsion by the British." I spewed the last word out with venom.

"There are many from that tragic episode who have settled here." We turned and rode slowly down one of the paths to the sugarcane fields and he continued, looking at me directly. "Perhaps one day when we are in the colonial capital you might care to look at the citizen registry."

Perhaps, I thought; if they had survived. Pierre and I had registered at the port where we disembarked. I thought of my father- he could write very little and my mother and sisters could not write at all.

Before I could reply he began to speak again; now looking only ahead of him at the path, while I rode alongside. "The longer you stay the worse it will be."

"What do you mean- 'the worse it will be'?"

"The harder it will be for you to leave."

"Yes, Sans Souci is almost dream-like," I sighed, "but I will learn what I can and then return to my meager yet comfortable cabin."

"And so then, you are doing to Master Gerard what he had done to the witch back on the islands."

It wasn't a question and I was genuinely taken aback

by that statement. "No of course not," I argued. "It is not the same situation at all." I had never thought of myself as using anyone. I merely wanted to learn about-everything. The workings of a plantation, witchcraft and voodoo, but in particular- the ways of the loup garou. For that information only Gerard could provide me. Besides I was not sleeping with him, as he had been with Satine. But then, uncontrollably, my memory chose to take me back to my first night here at Sans Souci and the naked embrace Gerard and I shared in his bath.

Toussaint darted his head to me quickly, with a sharp look and then stared back straight ahead at the trail. Had he read that last thought of mine? "Master Gerard would like you to manage the plantation one day in the very near future. He believes you to be quite capable." He paused, "As do I."

"Merci. Yes, I would like that also..but," Toussaint interrupted me.

"There is an undeniable bond between the two of you. A mental and emotional connection." He spoke slowly, weighing his words carefully. "Because of what.. you both...are. You share an intimacy. A man must not deny his true nature."

I was surprised at his frankness on this subject. Was he actually encouraging me to embrace lycanthropy? And Gerard along with it? "I am married and very much in love with another- with a woman. Gerard knows this and that I will leave one day to return to my family."

"The longer you stay the harder it will be for you to leave," he repeated himself. I started to say something, but he continued, "The longer you stay at Sans Souci the stronger the ties and bonds between you and Gerard will grow."

"Of course, that is natural. As it should be."

"The two of you will become more and more as one. Inevitably alike."

"Now that I refuse to believe. No matter how many

centuries pass, I could never become as cruel and cold-hearted as he."

"Perhaps." Toussaint spoke doubtfully, still staring straight ahead. We were approaching a group of slaves chopping down and gathering sugar cane stalks. "Within every man lies a beast waiting to be born. The master is counting on that." At this point we stopped while he gave instructions in Creole to one of the older males.

He must be wrong. He had to be. Gerard and I were too opposite. No matter what happened in the future to me or what curse I carried, I would not be a heartless murderer. Then my mind flashed back to when I had attacked Pierre and I felt the extreme pain of remorse. I had to admit- yes, I could act as an animal- behave as a beast. What else was it Toussaint had said? 'In every man lies a beast.' I had heard words like those somewhere before. I searched my memory and found-

Mon Dieu! I remembered. I could hear her now as if she were beside me. It was grandma-ma with her distinctive speech, saying, 'Many men, my son, have a beast within that when certain conditions are met, the beast is released and the human side disappears.'

Suddenly, I needed to be alone and without explanation, I pulled my horse around and galloped full speed back to the mansion. Toussaint and I never discussed that conversation and he never brought up the subject of my special relationship with Gerard. We talked of many things- many secret subjects- but that one in particular, was never mentioned again.

I swore to myself that I would never be like Gerard. But soon there would be another full moon and we would undergo the transformation in unison, and I knew he wanted us to hunt- and kill- together. Perhaps I would be able to simply refuse human flesh, though deep inside myself, I knew that was not possible. I could control it, but not for very long. The hunger was always there; a constant, never-ending lust; day or night, full moon or no.

I would suppress it, hide it temporarily, yet time and time again, it always surfaced demanding my attention- no matter how hard I tried otherwise.

I brought up the subject though, to Gerard a few nights before the next full moon. We were in the study late one night, the household asleep. He was going over some books and figures, making notes, while I sat in my favorite chair reading some odd novel about some undead ghoul who slept in his coffin during the day and thirsted for human blood every night. The lights were dim for we did not require much light. Mercutio had crawled into my lap and was napping. "I want you to teach me how to control the transformations."

"You will learn gradually, mon ami," he replied without looking up from his addition. "You probably already have some control over it. We will find out in a few nights."

"With witchcraft, I can learn to control it even more quickly." He looked towards me. "True," was all he said and he went back to his papers. His mind was absorbed with his task. Still, I interrupted again.

"I want to be able to control the hunger. Possibly even eliminate it." Laughing, he put his pen down and stared intently at me. More and more on such evenings, we would simply read each other's thoughts, actual speech not being necessary.

C'est impossible, mon cher. The hunger will always be there.

But with the help of witchcraft, I might- he was shaking his head- be able to suppress it.

Non, it is not feasible.

How do you know? Have you tried?

I do not have to try it. I know it will not work.

You don't want to try it.

Ignoring me, he went back to his paperwork, dismissing my idea. His attitude was to be expected, however I was becoming more and more irritated with it. I tried to concentrate on my reading.

Unexpectedly he began speaking out loud. Mercutio stirred in his deep sleep. "We will go hunt in the city during the next full moon." He looked my way. "It will be a learning experience for you."

"Very well," was all I said without looking up. I heard him put down his papers and he walked over and sat in the settee opposite me. I looked up at him, curiosity getting the better of me. "What do you exactly do when you go into the city?"

"You have not guessed that yet?" He was giving me a mischievous look, inviting me to read his mind. Which I did- and knowledge set in.

"Sacre Dieu! You go there to carefully select your victims! You choose them, meet them, even befriend them sometimes. Then later- one night- you stalk and hunt them down." I shook my head. "Those poor unsuspecting souls. You are diabolical." I returned to my book. "Though I am not surprised. Satine must have taught you well."

I did not have to look up to sense the anger flaring within him like a volcano, at the mere mention of the witch's name. "You will eventually be doing the same."

"Never!"

"Oh my dear, dear Henri," he chuckled, patting my knee before he rose and walked over to the window and the waxing moon. Tonight it was hidden behind a cloudy sky. Distant thunder rolled across the earth. So distant only he and I could possibly hear it from so far away. Or did I just sense it? "Non mon cher. You will plot and scheme, maybe not quite like myself.."

"I should hope not!"

He continued, ignoring my interruption. "But you will. You will in your own way. After all," he turned to face me. I met his gaze. "You want to select those deserving of death: Murderers, cutthroats, rapists. Men and women who have no regard for life. Those who have cruelty and evil in their hearts, n'est-ce pas? Am I not right?"

I selected my words carefully. "If I am to be- what I am- and have to kill; then yes, I wish to only hunt those who are deliberately cruel and heartless." I was looking him directly in his eyes.

"Like myself?" He knew my meaning.

I did not reply right away, but pretended to turn back to my book. Mercutio, now fully awake, stretched himself and then leaped from my lap onto the back of the settee and chattered something at Gerard as if scolding him. He then, single- mindedly, set out to find his store of hidden treasures around the room. "I shall also select those people who long for death for one reason or another. The ones who are in deep pain with no hope."

"Like yourself?" I said nothing. He continued. "You could become some sort of dark avenging angel? In wolf's clothing!" Again, I did not respond. He walked over and putting his hand on the back of my chair, bent down close and whispered in my ear, "And so you fancy yourself judge, jury and executioner? A bearer of men's souls?"

"Yes!" I shouted. "I mean no- No!" I slammed the book shut, hastily rose from the chair and walked over to the mantel. I am confused, Gerard. Please help me.

He sat down at the chess table. "I understand."

"You do?" I was skeptical.

"More than you realize." He paused a long moment then gestured for me to join him across the table. "Set. Let us play a game of chess and forget this heavy conversation and simply enjoy our wine, cigars and each other's company." He smiled, suddenly being his charming self. "I do believe you owe me another match. I must regain my title. You are a quick learner, my friend." He arranged the pieces on the board as I refilled both our wine glasses and sat down to play. "If you acquire the skills of my witchcraft as easily, you will be a tremendous ally when we commence the battle!"

His words concerning the clash with Satine frightened

me for the first time. And I would be fighting on his side-
the side less evil. "I only want to learn what I need to
protect myself and mine."

"Believe me when I say that you will want to learn all
you possibly can. The witch is 'tres formidable'. She will
want to destroy you, me, Sans Souci- all that we hold
near and dear." He moved his queen forward for defense.
Or was it to attack? We had both agreed not to read each
other's thoughts when playing cards or chess. "Even your
beloved family would probably be in danger." His gaze
wandered as I thought of my humble cabin up the river.
"If only I knew how she will first appear."

Slowly our concentration returned to the game. "It is
your move. Be sure to make it cleverly. I intend to win
this time."

2

The next night Gerard went back into town,
supposedly to select victims for our 'excursion' tomorrow
night- the first night when the moon would be completely
full. Gazing up at it from the balcony outside my
bedroom, I felt again, its power and I found myself
wanting to change. For the first time since Gerard had bit
me, I actually longed to transform. To become the beast-
and feed! I turned away and stood in the shadows out of
the moonlight. I could control it tonight, but tomorrow I
doubted I would be able to resist.

Unexpectedly, I saw some quick movement in the
dark near the cistern where Gerard and I bath. It was
Toussaint. He was looking up toward the light from my
bedroom, searching. I stepped out of the shadows and
he motioned for me to come down and join him. I could
read from his thoughts that he wanted to show me

something and it had to be tonight, while Gerard was away. I went down the back stairs to join him.

"What is it?" I asked. He said nothing but simply gestured for me to follow. We turned and headed in the direction of the slave cabins passing the empty pedestal where the stone gargoyle sat during the day. Gabriel must be on some mission for Gerard, perhaps he was even spying secretly on us. But he did serve as protector over the property, and my mind searched for some sense of the gargoyle's presence nearby, yet I detected nothing. Of course being Gerard's familiar, it might be able to cloak itself from me.

Toussaint led me to a lone tiny cabin, barely lit, at the end of the long line of slave cabins, next to a tepid mosquito-filled pond. I knew without actually seeing inside, that here was a slave girl in labor and I instantly realized why Toussaint had brought me here. To witness the birth of one of Gerard's off-spring!

"Why does Gerard want an heir so badly? We are immortal after all."

"He wants to discover if a male produced by him will carry the curse." I must have presented a curious look for he explained further. "Legend states that werewolves' first born male-child will have the ability to shift shape. Supposedly it is only demonstrated after puberty." He shrugged, "And even though it is only a legend, none of the slaves will allow a man-child of the master's to live. I am here to assist if need be."

"To assist? If it is a male..?"

"And it lives?" He let out a deep breath, "Then the baby will be drowned in the bayou!"

Oh what a horror! Superstitious slaves resorting to infanticide. "But surely Toussaint, surely you cannot condone this! Even if you did.. believe in the legend."

"It does not matter whether I believe it or not, Master Henri, for the others do believe- firmly!" He paused, hesitating, "And it would be better if I were the one to commit...the unholy act, while we all pray over the poor child's soul."

He entered the cabin and I followed. The only light came from a small fire in a pit in the dirt floor at one corner of the one room building. The female giving birth looked to be only a child herself and she seemed to be having a difficult time of it. The midwives were encouraging the already exhausted girl to try again. One dabbed the poor girl's sweaty forehead and neck with a damp towel. A few of the older males stood about to witness the birth. They were there to make sure that, if indeed it were a male, the dastardly deed would be carried out with no hesitation; without the mother giving argument or even having the chance to hold the newborn.

The cabin was stifling hot and uncomfortable, even for me. Reeking of blood and urine, it was a terrible place to have to live; an even worse place to have a child. Eventually, after some agonizing moments for us all, the child was delivered. It was a boy. But this time Toussaint did not have to drown the infant. It did not cry or move- the poor thing was born dead- stillborn. All in all, a better fate for the little one. The young mother was crying and while I resisted reading her thoughts and those of the midwives, I got the distinct sense that the girl had been given some potion previously to actually achieve the result we had just witnessed.

Toussaint and I stayed briefly for the quick burial and joined in a group prayer for the child's soul. We left the small crowd that had formed as they continued with their rituals- a mixture of African voodoo and Christianity- sending the tiny innocent soul onward to heaven.

Walking back to the mansion I asked, "Why Toussaint? Why did you feel the need to show me this?"

"You must know everything about the legends of the loup garou." He looked hard at me, "Ideas that you might not have seen in print." He was right- I did not recall reading about the first-born male inheriting the curse. "And," he hesitated.

"And?" I encouraged him to continue.

"You must know all there is to know about Master Gerard. Things he may keep from you."

"I know he can be a monster."

"Sometimes yes. Sometimes no."

"But surely he knows what happens to the male children. He must know."

"He most probably does know. Fortunately, most of the males are stillborn- for reasons unknown, but he can produce again quickly. The gestation period is shortened by half that of humans. He impregnates the females and seems to forget about them. One day though I expect him to be present at a birth and when that happens- and it is a boy who breathes life- then the rest is up to heaven."

We walked the rest of the way in silence until we reached the stairway to my room. He had one more thing to say- a warning. "Please try to control your thoughts near Master Gerard. If you think upon tonight and events such as this, he may react violently. Not to you so much, but to his people. He does not use the whip often, but when he does it is most savage." He turned and started away.

"And you Toussaint? Has he ever beaten you?"

He answered without turning around. "No Master Henri, never. Not yet any way," he added, as he disappeared into the night.

3

The next day I busied myself in work about the mansion and on my clock repair, trying not to dwell on last night and another consequence of this curse which I must try and digest. I did not think much on the upcoming evening, but I had to admit to myself, I was quite eager to visit the teaming town I had heard so much of. To see it for the first time and experience all the flavors and sensations it had to offer; to mix with unique travelers and humans and then- give myself over to the power of the moon. I did not see Gerard that day, except briefly at our early morning breakfast of rare red ham and dark black coffee. I could not read his thoughts clearly, but there was certainly a tremendous amount on his mind and I knew he had a very special night planned for both of us. A type of demonstration of his powers and an experiment for me to practice and display what I have learned. I had decided now that these powers I must acquire as perfectly and completely as possible- if I were to survive this 'curse' with my sanity intact. So also, that my family (and I still intended to have children, including male children, regardless of some legend) would be able to live and thrive without experiencing punishment for my sins.

The day went by slowly for me, full of agitated anticipation, especially as the late afternoon became early evening and I began to feel the moon gaining strength. Finally, I could not concentrate any longer on my repairs and I went to take a calming lingering bath in the cool water of Gerard's cistern.

I was lounging nude in the soothing water, starting to relax when Juliette and another (much older) female slave walked by under the nearby veranda. Dressed in robes similar to those in the islands and in Africa, they carried baskets of laundry upon their heads and my thoughts went immediately to Selena. I waved at Juliette and even though she saw me, she demurely looked the other way. Of course, that was befitting considering her station and that I was master. She always was so very proper and I had no doubt she would one day become the perfect lady and make some husband (French or black) very proud. It was most unfortunate for a girl like her to be a slave. Thinking of all this, I became aroused.

In fact, I had noticed that as the moon grew every night in brightness, I became more sexually charged. The hunger increases, yes of course, but so also did my libido. And I was agonizingly tempted to make love to some female. Or even, I had considered- in order to satisfy the immediate craving- the act of joining my maker in his bed.

So while I was dressing back upstairs in my room, I tried not to think of sex or feasting or anything specific, other than getting ready for the night. Gerard wanted us to dress formally and all my attire had been laid out on the bed and bureau by the young boy. I had never worn such finery in my life. A tailcoat, vest, cravate, top hat, a silver cane and highly polished black boots. There was even a pair of clean white gloves. Remarkably it all fit- almost as if they had been tailored made just for myself! I thought again, as I glanced at Julian Fontenot's portrait- what man's clothing was I wearing?

As the sun crept below the horizon, my excitement about this evening mounted. Living this one month at Sans Souci had opened my eyes to new worlds. I am not only speaking of the supernatural, but of so much, much more. My family and I were part of the poorer classes, always struggling at hard work just to feed and clothe ourselves. We had never been favoured with such niceties as what I enjoyed around me here. Now, I knew what it was like to live and dress as one of the upper elite. Admittedly- I enjoyed it immensely, but I made a promise to myself that when it came time for me to leave, I should do so without regret or look back with longing and disappointment, at how comfortable life could have been.

Yes, one day I will undoubtedly miss Sans Souci. And Gerard, himself, I suppose. As for now, I would enjoy all he (and the plantation) had to offer.

I met him in his bedroom. It was a huge room, much larger than mine; only one room downstairs (the ballroom) being greater in size. Furnished in very masculine dark colors and woods, the room was sumptuously rich, even regal, though in a comfortable southern colonial manner. He was finishing dressing when I entered; his gigantic armoire, heavily carved in black walnut, was open displaying more clothes and boots than I had ever known any one man to own. A small framed portrait of a mature woman with a delicate oval porcelain face was on his mantel sitting gracefully next to a gilded clock held up by cherubs. The picture was of Gerard's mother, yet he did not have the same features, except in one striking respect: The deep set, deep blue eyes he had obviously inherited from this lovely woman.

He was putting on a ruffled white shirt like mine. My mother was a beautiful lady, non?

Mais oui, she is very beautiful.

How do those clothes fit?

They are yours?

Of course. I am not that much taller than yourself. I had them slightly altered for your size.

I should have known. We communicated almost exclusively by mind reading when the moon was full. This would make our evenings out (and our hunts) that much more intimate.

You have the potion?

Yes.

And you made the concoction yourself and did not seek the help of Toussaint or Juliette?

Non. I accomplished it all on my own.

Bon.

My task for the evening had been to mix a paralyzing potion for our victim to consume. I am still reluctant to use this.

You will not be when you come to know the selection

for tonight. He guided me over to the opposite wall and we stood in front of a worn antique oval mirror in a tarnished gilt frame. Standing close together, we gazed at our images. He affectionately, casually, placed an arm around my shoulders. I never realized how much we resembled each other.

His blue eyes burned intently as he spoke matter-of-factly, "True. We are like brothers. Maintenant, regardez." He waved his hand over the mirror and immediately, it fogged over showing no reflections. "Show me the one I am thinking of. Where is he?"

The mirror remained clouded for one moment more, as I stood there in awestruck silence, then slowly, it began to clear revealing a man's image. He was a rough, red-haired and heavily bearded fellow with large facial features and a thick muscular frame; an uneducated man who did hard labor for a living and who enjoyed fighting. More than one scar decorated his face where someone had severely cut him. He was in a tavern, at a table, gambling with three other men. He shuffled some cards.

"Amazing!" The word escaped from my lips in a breathless hush without my knowing.

"Yes- it is." Gerard stated simply. "Now, study him: Can you get any impressions?"

Impressions?

Try to read his thoughts.

But he is miles away.

That is of no consequence. Concentrate Henri. What sort of man is he?

I did as requested and summoning all my telepathic powers into focus, I delved into the man's inner thoughts. What was in his heart; what did he hold secret?

"He is a lumberjack and he- he hates women!" I turned to Gerard.

"Good, good. Keep looking at his image and concentrate ever harder. Tell me- what does he do to his women?"

268

With my utmost, I tried and tried to see the man's real self, and just as I was about to abandon the effort, in a flash, I saw his past. His most violent past!

"He rapes his women; he abuses them. Many have been beaten until they were near death." I paused to absorb more. "Some of them may even have died. He does not know because he leaves them alone- prone, hurting, in pain- and in tears."

"Excellent Henri, excellent. You are quite an apt pupil."

"Also," I continued, "He was abandoned by his mother at an early age and has never known love. He is a notorious thief, scoundrel and cheat and has murdered more than once. Many times in fact!"

"Yes, yes Henri. I am proud of your abilities." Do you not think he will make a deserving victim? Someone we could even toy with before devouring justly.

Yes, I suppose. I looked at Gerard and added mischievously, "Even now he is cheating at cards."

He glanced at the mirror, "Now that I missed!" We both laughed heartily and I had to admit to myself that I was ready for this night. Ready to use my powers, ready to feast.

With another wave of his hand, the mirror returned to normal, again showing our reflections. "Come. We must go. Toussaint waits with the carriage." He went about the room snuffing out the lights, but as we started out the door, a thought occurred to me and grabbing him by the arm, I pulled him back towards the mirror.

"Can this tell me where my parents are? My family?"

"It should be able to." He added with emphasis, "If I allow it."

"May we try, now? Quickly?"

"Perhaps another time, Henri. It is dusk and the moon will be rising .."

"Please." My voice, my grasp expressed my need to know.

"Very well, very quickly. But first- " he looked at me closely, "Are you sure, Henri? It might be better not to know."

I shook my head. "I must know."

"No matter how painful the image?"

"No matter how painful."

"Then concentrate on your father and mother." He waved his hand over the mirror and it again magically fogged over. I isolated my thoughts to be only that of my parent's images. He continued his command. "My servant, search and show us the ones that Henri wants to find. Where are his mother and father?"

The mirror slowly began to clear and, at first showed only a dark landscape, foggy and wet near some swamp or bayou. Then as it became clearer, I realized we were looking at a cemetery similar to the ones in this area with many sealed tombs above ground. The mirror led us through the graves as if we were following some floating spirit and then it stopped at a pair of pauper's graves. Carved upon the headstones were the names of my parents, Annette and Jacques LeBlanc. I turned away. The mirror instantly lost the image and returned to normal. I covered my face with my hands, wanting to cry, but I could not.

"I am sorry Henri. Truly sorry." He paused a moment, observing me carefully. My tears still would not flow. "Come we must go."

Downstairs, Toussaint (dressed in fine livery) was waiting to take us in a luxurious black carriage which I had never seen before. It was polished to a fine high gloss and was lined inside with black leather. Four huge dappled grey steeds (whom I also had never seen before) were restlessly harnessed to it.

We got in and Toussaint immediately drove off, while Gerard and I rode in silence most of the way. I was still thinking of my parents. So they had made it to this new land only to die here. At least they were reunited now. My only hope was that they had enjoyed some time together before their ending. The images from the mirror had given me an answer, but still left me with many questions. What had happened? Where were my siblings? The young ones? Were they together, alive-maybe living nearby?

Perhaps, sometime when Gerard was gone, I would ask the mirror myself. Never, for one moment, did I doubt what I saw and I accepted as fact that I would never see them alive again. A solitary tear trailed down my cheek. I could shed no more.

I glanced out the open window at the fast moving scenery. We were moving at an unearthly speed. I glanced at Gerard who was looking out the other side. Was he manipulating the horses and carriage? I could not gather his thoughts, which meant he was concentrating hard on some thing.

As we flew down the road, I imagined I saw an object in the woods moving along with us. It was best described as a white blur that would appear periodically between the trees. I tried to dismiss it as drifts of fog or perhaps my mind playing tricks, then it would reappear again and again as if following us, running parallel to our carriage. I glanced over at Gerard, who was still in deep contemplation and took no notice of me or what I thought I had seen. Turning back, I looked deep into the woods with my acute eyesight. There it was again keeping pace with our great speed. It was not my imagination and it wasn't Gabriel, for looking up I saw his silhouette against the full moon. He would be with us in town, hiding in the shadows, ready for Gerard's command to come to our aid aid help dispose of an unsightly corpse.

I leaned my head out the window so that the moon's bright and powerful light fell upon me. I gloried in its radiance and majesty, gathering its strength as my own. It called on me to transform, but I resisted the temptation. I could control it, for awhile, knowing that later we would both be feasting. And feasting well at that! On a strong, young male whose blood and body would infuse us with even more power and vigor. A power that I was beginning to adapt to and control; a might that set me above the normal human male; power that I could now- admittedly- appreciate.

In the distance ahead, I saw the horizon glow from the lights of the city. I turned to search the woods next to us. The white blur was no longer there. Had it been an apparition? Or perhaps the witch was back? I looked over at Gerard who was rousing himself as if from some deep trance. We started to slow to a canter. Surely if Satine was near, he- maybe even I- would be able to sense her. Unless, and this was a shuddering thought, she could somehow disguise herself or cloak her presence.

For now though, my mind was captivated with the coming night. I will always remember my first time in that city. Long before we were in the center square, I could hear and smell the teeming town with its many different peoples from across the world. A port city of no small importance, it brought to my senses strange smells of foods and wines I had yet to taste; sounds of different music I had never heard before; and piquantly arousing sights of humans engaged in dancing, drinking, fighting and gambling. Any vice of any invention was offered in this place. Sexual aberrations were normal.

On the very outskirts of the town, we passed a solitary brick building where several young boys stood outside, and I knew the place was occasionally frequented by Gerard. Next was a large park that contained many centuries old oak trees whose limbs were so heavy they touched the ground. This was where duels are held: some famous, many infamous. But here also, lynchings often occur. Most of which were unjustifiable hangings of luckless young male slaves. I could smell the blood, death and hate.

As we approached the city center and the streets

became more narrow and crowded, we drove by numerous vendors and French merchants hawking their wares. The town was thrillingly alive. Seeing this thriving atmosphere for the first time was exhilarating. Free African and West Indie ladies carried baskets loaded with fruits and vegetables on their heads. None to my surprise, I saw several wealthy Frenchmen (dressed as Gerard and I were) walking arm in arm with beautiful, young mulatto girls. Or perhaps they were quadroon. My sharp hearing detected many languages, but French and its various dialects dominated. Beggars and homeless children, hungry and in tattered soiled clothing, were another common sight. The two distant cousins, prosperity and poverty, were to be seen everywhere. The whole place was as busy as if it were the middle of the day.

I noticed numerous brothels and bordellos all along the way; the women hanging out of the windows, exposing cleavage- enticing customers; beckoning the sailors and seamen; standing under the lamp posts, whispering to finely clad businessmen; teasing shy virginal lads. It was altogether hard to control my excitement and desire.

Gerard looked over at me, raised an eyebrow and patted my leg with his hand, admitting he too was aroused. That every time he came to town it had the same effect on him- no matter how often or how little he traveled here.

He looked back out towards the shops and pubs, but did not release the firm pressure of his hand on my leg and though I tried to exercise control, I found myself growing even more excited.

So it was with a mixture of relief and anticipation, when we finally arrived at the entrance of the tavern we had seen in the mirror. Alighting from the coach, I first noticed the pervasive smell of urine and vomit. Here was a particularly dark, dank and dismal corner of the quarter and I felt certainly out of place in our fine wardrobes. However Gerard seemed to pay it no heed and we went inside, while Toussaint took the carriage to some nearby stable to rest and water the horses.

The tavern was a den of thick smoke and chatter. A solitary piano player in one corner provided some not too discordant music. Two women, not particularly pretty, but still voluptuous and desirable were the entertainment. They were on a tiny stage next to the piano player, dancing the can-can in their own lackadaisical fashion. The other girls either lounged around the bar and piano or were waiting on tables serving men their drinks. All showed a great deal of breast and leg with colorfully ruffled lace undergarments and garters. They were similar to the women I had known before Selena came into my life. Wooden stairs led to private rooms on the second floor which could be engaged for sex or private poker games.

Gerard and I sat at a table in the corner shadows. After we had entered, no one gave us second glances, so I gathered that the occasional gentleman patron was not uncommon. In fact, one other well-dressed male was present, who looked rather like a riverboat gambler. He was playing cards with the very man we had seen in the mirror and who Gerard had selected as this evening's victim.

After our red wine arrived, served by a plump seemingly tired waitress who smelled of her monthly menstrual cycle, Gerard asked me if I knew what to do.

Yes, I am to concentrate my thoughts on him and when I have his attention, I will make a telepathic suggestion that he join us with his drink. Which, once he sits down, I doctor with the elixir. Then after conversation and some time passes I am to make another mental suggestion that he ask the two of us to join him in a room upstairs for cards and drinks.

So, while sipping our inexpensive vinegar-tasting

wine, I focused all my thoughts towards the man at the far side of the room. The mirror had depicted him just as he was here before us- a sandy red-haired large muscular man with a frizzy thick beard. He looked to be dressed in his day-work clothes, appearing unkempt and dirty. Laughing loudly, he slammed down his card hand and (to the extreme dismay and surprise of the other players) grabbed the pot of money and pulled it to himself. With his laughter still echoing in the tavern, he suddenly started and looking up, took notice over in our direction, as if he had heard someone call his name.

He went back to his card game, but as I continued to focus my concentration further, he turned in his chair to face us. He had now, most definitely, heard my silent beckoning.

He obediently followed my instructions. Without hesitation, he gathered his money into his trouser pockets, grabbed his pewter mug full of some vile cheap brew and walked directly over to our table. He stood well over six feet tall; that and his large features, together with the extreme breadth of his shoulders, gave him a monstrous appearance, though I knew I could easily conquer him. He glared down at me with a drunken bewildered look.

"Do I know you monsieur?"

I was about to reply when Gerard interrupted with a wave of his hand across the table, getting the simpleton's attention. "We met one evening before, monsieur. Remember? I am Gerard Mereaux."

A light sparked in his dull brain as recognition. "Yes, you introduced yourself- and bought drinks." He tried to stand rigid, but it was easy to tell he was well inebriated. His deep bass voice was slurry and overly loud; his body swayed slightly as he towered over our table. Yet, he still wanted more drink.

"Join us. I will buy another round." Gerard was light-hearted for he was in his element. He and Satine must

275

have enjoyed their many nights hunting and befriending men for sacrifice. Collecting victims and freezing them as statues, like others collect art.

The man sat down heavily. I did not know exactly what Gerard had planned for this unwitting dupe, but I did hope the torture of this one would be long and befitting his crimes. Now that we were close in proximity, I recognized him as an unremorseful evildoer. He had killed; robbed and stolen from most everyone he met or knew. A rapist several times over, I sensed the fear and disgust from the women in the room. They tried to avoid him entirely. More than one had had the misfortune of being in his clutches and they carried the scars to prove it.

As we waited for our drinks, I introduced myself to him and shook his hand; sensing immediately an impression from him, one that again confirmed that he was a cruel and sadistic man. If he had half a brain, he would have been positively treacherous.

Our drinks came along with a bottle of absinthe, which would be for later upstairs. The uncouth man slapped the girl soundly on her oversized posterior. She returned him a wicked look and I knew she wanted to slap him but dare not. She was familiar with this cad and so ignored his drunken rudeness and went on about her job tending to the other tables.

It was while he was occupied with the waitress when, with a flash of superhuman swiftness, I poured the potion into his drink. I probably could have done it right in front of him, he was so blurry-eyed from alcohol. We did not make any real conversation- the man's speech becoming increasingly thick-tongued and incoherent. Gerard mentioned something about hiring him for a job- the perfect job for his thieving hands! The prospect of making money appealed to his clouded senses and he became somewhat alert- for the moment. I silently told Gerard it was time to take him upstairs.

Yes, he replied. "Let us three go upstairs and we can discuss this matter more thoroughly in private over a bottle and a deck of cards."

The man rose clumsily from his chair which fell over with a crash. I picked it up and looked around. Hardly no one had noticed and those that did, did not care. As the three of us climbed the stairs, I read some of their thoughts. The men assumed we were just two gentlemen who wanted to gamble for high stakes and I could read they hoped the lumberjack would lose. The women were a bit more speculative, but no one cared if they ever saw the man again. In fact, they wished he would disappear completely and never darken the doorway to the saloon again. Gerard had planned this evening well and little did the tavern folk know- Tonight their wish would be fulfilled!

The room was simple and smelled of sour linens. It contained one small dirty, fragile looking bed, a round table like the ones downstairs and two wooden chairs- also fragile looking. One window, undraped, let in the full moonlight. I cautiously tried to relax in a chair and poured us each a glass of absinthe while Gerard started to make us both comfortable- taking our jackets, hats, and vests, etc., and putting them in a corner out of the way. I gave each his glass (I rose for they remained standing) and we raised our drinks for a toast.

"What shall we toast to, Henri?"

"Perhaps .. 'to long life'?"

Gerard laughed and slapped me on the back. "Perfect. How very keen. Well then -'to long life'. "

"To long life," we echoed and downed our drinks. I poured the giant another, which he swilled even faster than the first. I sat back down, loosening my ruffled shirt and wondered when the potion would take effect. Had I made it too weak for such a large strong man? I poured more drinks for us all and settled back as leisurely as possible in my rickety chair ready to view a spectacle. I vaguely thought this must be how the ancient Romans felt when witnessing their barbaric games.

The man was becoming noticeably disoriented. The thoughts I read were jumbled and incoherent. The combination of the drug with the absinthe was now gradually taking its effect. He started towards the other chair, but Gerard swiftly moved to block his way. His drugged eyes showed bewilderment and he grabbed Gerard by the shoulder, trying to shove him aside. But Gerard, strong and stiff as a statue, was not to be moved. The man tried again to shove him, yet Gerard stood still. Then with a gentle soft push, Gerard caused the lumberjack to fall onto the bed. The man's bewilderment grew into astonishment and he stood back up quickly only to be shoved back down again- this time with some force. Now his astonishment turned to anger, but this time when he rose, Gerard landed a powerful backhand slap to his face which sent the man sprawling across the bed, face down- his head hitting a flimsy bedpost.

Next, Gerard transformed his hands into giant wolfs paws and he began shredding and tearing the clothes off the man and I suppose it was then, when the poison took total effect, for the giant was now unable to move. Gerard deftly turned him face up. Complete paralysis- only the man's eyes could move. Full of anger they were, but increasingly, that was replaced with fear. I could smell the fear in him and it was likely a new sensation for him. Tonight he would experience other new sensations which his limited imagination could never have guessed at. I finished my absinthe in one gulp and pouring myself another, leaned forward in my chair, hungry with antici-pation.

As I watched Gerard rape this man, I felt absolutely no remorse or pity for our victim's plight and offered no assistance. I would not have stopped Gerard even if I had the ability. I did hope he would be quick about it though.

Gerard slapped him repeatedly and roughly while penetrating him. His scarred face was becoming bloody and bruised. His wide eyes, the only signs of life within him, darted back and forth pleading for me to intervene and rescue him from this degradation. However, I remained seated and unmoved.

Then Gerard fully transformed himself and the man managed to utter a desperate gasp of horror at this demon. As the wolf's large barbed penis cut into his bleeding rectum, he started to gurgle and cough. I rose and shoved a handkerchief in his mouth. His eyes registered the fact that now all hope was lost. I was not going to help him and he realized he was going to die this very night.

I sat back down and watched a few more minutes, but the hunger within me was becoming increasingly uncontrollable. A passing cloud released rays of moonlight which streamed into the room and flooded its light upon the grisly scene. The smell of blood was intoxicating me and I could not control it any longer- I allowed myself to transform.

Rising, I bent over close to the man's face, smelling his sweat and fear. His eyes grew large with terror as I showed my fangs to him, dripping saliva on his neck. I heard Gerard pumping and thumping, almost shaking the whole room, as he came close to his climax. The man closed his eyes ready to accept his fate.

Gerard growled out, "Now!" and I gave no hesitation. Leaning down upon his thick throat, I bit him so deep it severed the spinal cord. Blood gushed into my mouth like a fountain and my ecstasy was immediate. Powerfully exhilarating, I drank and ate upon this stranger as if I were addicted. I freely and willingly permitted my predacious nature to take over.

The smell of his intestines filled my nostrils as Gerard buried his face in the man's midsection and I heard the ripping of organs and bones. Our feeding frenzy came to be an exciting orgy of blood as we devoured the victim together.

Slowly a feeling of satiation set in me. Actually that is not the entire truth, for with this curse we are never completely free from the hunger. Actually, what I was feeling was more like a sense of fulfillment and completeness. This sensation had only occurred to me before as a human male in sexual situations- mostly when I was with Selena.

How shocking to my soul that I should compare these two 'happenings'- the one lovely and creative, the other bloody and destructive! My dark nature had surfaced and was not to be ignored. As Toussaint (and grandma-ma before him) had told me- 'A man must not deny his true self'. I was a partial beast and I had to face the fact that I not only required the taste of human flesh, I lusted after it.

I was ready to clean up this mess and leave, but Gerard wanted to show me one more thing. He pointed a sharp claw at the man's bloody pulp of a head. "Crack it," he snarled. "Break open his skull." I complied with a sharp chop, splitting the cranium in two and exposed the brain. I remember remarking to myself that it seemed rather large for such a small-minded person. "A delicacy." I tore it from its resting place, broke it into halves like it was a loaf of bread and we shared a final treat.

What do we do with the remains? And all this blood?

We mop it up, bundle it all, including the mattress, climb the rooftops and give it to Gabriel who will be waiting. He will dispose of it all in an appropriate fashion. But we must be quick about it and not be seen.

Still in our transformed state, we used the sheets to clean up as much blood as possible, gathered them, the mattress and his ripped and torn corpse, and proceeded out the window. Left behind was only a tiny spattering of blood on the floor. People might guess some great gruesome tragedy occurred here, however they would never be able to say exactly what. There might be a mystery, yet there was no evidence of a true crime and the man's disappearance would soon be forgotten.

We easily carried the bloody bundles (and one clean bundle with our clothes in it) out the window and in a flash, fled over the rooftops. If anyone should happen to glance up they would only sense a blur and see nothing specific. Gabriel met us only a few houses away. Swooping down like a large supernatural bat, it grabbed the bloody items in its huge claws and in another second was gone in the distant moonlight. I followed Gerard, jumping and climbing over the roofs, until we came to the stables where Toussaint and the carriage awaited.

In the shadow of a large chimney, we changed back to our human form, clothed ourselves, jumped lightly to the ground and approached the stable with the air of two simple ordinary gentlemen who had just come from a wild night in the town gambling, drinking and enjoying sex. I seriously doubted the wisdom in all this, yet Gerard reviled in such risky behavior.

We did not speak for a long time on the road. The carriage moved at a normal un-supernatural pace; Gerard seemed to be napping next to me. I had never known him to sleep- ever- at all. As for myself, my exhilaration would not subside. I felt like I had taken a powerful drug. This evening had opened my eyes to the wonder of my being! It made me come to realize that what I was- what I had become- was not so terrible after all. I no longer thought of myself as evil or as a product of something evil. Now, with Gerard's help and teaching, I would be able to control my transformations and feast only once a month or so. Most importantly, I could carefully choose a victim beforehand.

Gerard's thoughts interrupted my own. How do you feel mon ami?

Very well, excellent in fact. Like I.. like..

Like you had just tasted an extraordinarily fine wine..

or experienced unusually good intercourse?

I sighed, Yes, exactly. I agreed.

Bon, my friend. Moi aussi. You are becoming accustomed to your new skin. He turned to look out the carriage window and I felt his concentration turn toward driving us back to Sans Souci at a rapid pace.

I looked out my side of the coach at the setting moon. Its dusty glow was so beautiful over the tall treetops of giant cypress. The scent of the swamp filled my soul and my thoughts again turned to how much this land, this new country, meant to me. Half-earth, half-water; unique unto itself. Still, a wilderness to be explored; still, a land yet to be settled. It offered with outstretched limbs all those opportunities that young, eager men such as Gerard, Pierre and I looked for in the latter half of the eighteenth century.

Yet framed within that same thought, I had to realize, Gerard was much older than myself. He appeared to be the same age, in his early twenties, and that would never change. Not only immortality, but eternal youth was his to enjoy- for me also.

And of all the many changes I have had to come to terms with- immortality, my ability to shift shape into a wolf-man, my supernatural powers as a werewolf and warlock, and of course, my need for human flesh; after all that, perhaps it was the idea of eternal youth which was the hardest for me to grasp- to believe.

To think! I will never age, but remain young forever! And for the first time, during that carriage ride back to Sans Souci, I thought perhaps. . . just maybe. .there were a few blessings hidden among what I had considered a curse. Like Gerard, it depended on my frame of mind and how I looked at it.

Perhaps also, with my ever increasing control over my transformations and subsequent feeding, I might be able to live a somewhat normal life with a wife and family. After all, my appearance to the outside world is as a natural human husband. Then for that week or so every month, I could return to the plantation- and Gerard.

However I made a promise to myself that very night: Selena and our children must never come under the influence of Gerard's bad side. His callous, careless view of human life was not acceptable to me. Then my memory turned to the nightmarish evening he and I had just shared and I realized that I too, must be careful of his influence. I can try to convince myself over and over again how much I valued human life, but the fact was- I am no longer one of them and some of their lives are forfeit. I must kill! Through a freak of fate, their deaths give me life; their blood and hearts endow me with superhuman strength. But I could- I must! - Chose them with discretion.

Lost in my thoughts, I did not notice the white shadow haunting us. Not until we passed through a low thicket of palmetto, did I see again the white blur and this time it definitely was following- not us- but me! It disappeared behind a thick grove of trees and when it reappeared, I got a better glimpse of the mysterious ghostly figure.

It was an immensely large white horse and it was easily keeping pace with our unearthly speed. Why, it practically looked like it was flying low over the ground! I tried to see if his hooves were actually touching the earth or detect dust rising from the path, but I could not. Then, as we skirted around a rather large basin of water on my side of the road, the ghostly steed leaped and seemed to actually float in mid-air above the marshy landscape. Astonishing! What was this creature actually? What could it mean? Was this an enemy or a friend? Perhaps it was another creature of Gerard's from his stable of surprises.

Gerard stirred. Glancing his way, I decided not to tell him what I had seen, although why I should keep this from him, I did not really know. It just seemed the prudent thing to do and my instinct told me not to alert him about the animal. When I looked back outside, it was gone. The horse- if indeed that was what it was- had appeared twice just for me to see. Following the carriage so as not to be seen by others. But why?

I leaned back in the luxurious seat and relaxed. I felt contentment: about my life, about my future. A feeling I believed I would never experience again. Soon it would be dawn. I thought of luxuriating in Gerard's bath or lying down with an interesting book; my body might require some sleep. Our usual breakfast will be foregone, I am sure. I gave no thought of tomorrow night and our coming hunt. However, I did close my eyes and dreamt of the city and visiting it again, soon. In the daylight- as a human, as an ordinary man.

4

The next day I rose not long after dawn and looked outside. The horizon was red with warning. What few clouds there were, were dark with moisture and beauty; the air heavy, hot and still; thick with dampness. Tonight's hunt would be wet.

Gerard was out chopping wood which he often did after a night of feasting. I too felt a tremendous energy inside of me and was ready for a full day of productive and perspiring hard work. The corn fields in the northern section of Sans Souci needed working and so I rode out with a group of elderly male slaves, whom Toussaint brought along in an uncovered wagon.

An occasional shower would pass over, teasing us with a foretaste of what was to come. There was little breeze in the fields and it was so hot and humid, I wondered how the old slaves managed. They had to be uncomfortable and I thought it likely they would collapse from heat exhaustion. Though none did- and we continued to work through the whole day- burning overgrown brush, digging irrigation ditches and chopping back dead stalks. In the cool of the day, if it could be called that, I had Toussaint take them back home and told him to make sure everything on the plantation grounds was secure, for we all knew a big blow was probable tonight. I rode back alone on a trail that skirted the plantation to the northeast. The day was long and still so sultry, I thought I would take my time riding back. I remembered a nice, flowing stream along the way that offered a clean bath for a working man drenched in sweat.

In the late summer, as it was, the stream had become not more than a mere trickle, but it emptied into a nice pond of fresh water. I tied the old mare under a shady sycamore and proceeded down the small bank to the pond, when my acute senses alerted me to a single human presence- A female actually. I heard a splash and then another. Curious, I crawled silently towards the edge of the pond. Peering from behind a thick tangle of marsh reeds, I recognized Toussaint 's granddaughter, Juliette, bathing herself in the middle of the small pond, the remainder of the late-afternoon sunlight softly caressing her brown skin. This must be her own special place to be by herself. I felt like I was intruding upon some special sacred scene, yet I could not turn my eyes away.

Her beautifully soft cocoa-colored flesh glistened from a single sunray that seemed to be beaming down directly for her from an ever-increasingly cloudy sky. She rubbed a cloth across her back and shoulders. Sensuous shoulders that appeared to be delicate, but I knew were strong for her size. I kept observing her as she turned to face this side of the pond where I lay hidden. Her young breasts exposed themselves to the sunlight, dripping with fresh water. The wet towel caressed them. They were substantial for her age- firm, soft and succulent- I longed to bury my face between them.

Moment to moment, my excitement grew in intensity and I had the need for immediate satisfaction. The full moon's power was taking my sexual appetite to a peak as ferocious as my hunger for flesh. I had to quit the scene before I gave into my weakness and commit some act I would be very sorry for.

Silently, I ran back to my tethered horse, jumped on her and rode back to Sans Souci at breakneck speed. The old mare could hardly keep up with my whip and I probably could have ran the distance in half the time. I do not remember what my exact intentions were, or if I had any at all. Perhaps find a slave woman and have my way with her (which I could easily demand as one of the masters of the plantation). All I knew was I had to be far away from Juliette for desire had seized my brain and there was no letting go until I found full release. Of course, sex with her was not an option- mostly because I could not betray Toussaint's friendship and take advantage of his young granddaughter. No, I must satisfy this craving in some other way.

What did transpire was entirely unplanned and completely unexpected. I rode to the back of the mansion, leaving the horse un-tethered and entered through the rear. Remarkably, no one was about. Usually there was some activity, but the house was already shuttered, so the slaves must have been busy elsewhere, getting ready for the impending storm.

When I came round to the front stairs, I sensed someone. Looking up, I saw Gerard on the landing. He had just finished some sweaty chores and was about to go to his room for a change of clothes. "Gerard," I exclaimed. He stopped and turned towards me as I bounded up the stairs in giant leaps. His open shirt ex- posed his perspiring muscular chest.

Instantly, he knew. Instinctively, we both knew. We did not have to read each other's thoughts to know that it was time. Time to consummate our brotherhood. I approached him, his arms outstretched to receive me. Within our tight embrace, I felt his relief at finally enjoying what had been a previously unrequited love. Our sexual aggressions were at their peak and I would be able to make love easily. Standing together there on the landing, our eyes lingered upon each other for a moment, before they closed as our lips pressed together. Our tongues..

Our interruption was sudden and immediate, for all at once the most unearthly bell began to toll! It was the sound of a large tower clock bell and to our sensitive hearing, we seemed to be right under it. We were instantly and helplessly racked with pain. I fell to my knees, covering my ears, but that did not give me any relief from the torturous ringing. It seemed to be coming from inside my head and was rising in crescendo with each strike. As my ears began to bleed, Gerard let out a huge howl of anguish and transformed into his wolf-self. I could not for I was in too much pain.

The tolling of the bell would not cease- twelve, thirteen, fourteen strikes and still it continued. The pain ran deep into my bones; its echoes stabbed through to my very soul; still it would not stop! It was a supernatural ringing and finally I realized where the source was- it was emanating from the haunted grandfather clock below in the entranceway! Only it was not the normal sound the clock makes. The ghostly ringing resounded throughout the house, seemingly rocking its very foundation. It was loud enough to be heard for miles away.

Gerard jumped over the landing to the floor below. "No!" was all I could manage to yell after him, for I knew what he was going to do. Yet I could not stop him for the painful haunting of the bell had left me prostrate on the floor. The clock crashed apart as he shoved it over onto its face. Still the sound would not cease! I peered through the banisters at him, as he howled and howled again in anguished pain. He wrenched the brass mechanism from the hood of the clock and taking it outside, bashed it soundly on the brick entranceway. It broke into a hundred pieces and only then did the tolling of the bell come to an end.

As I struggled to my feet, Gerard issued out one long last, eternally mournful howl, expressing his untold suffering from decades of disappointed loneliness, and I watched his lone wolf's figure bound quickly away into the trees surrounding the mansion.

Dusk was descending. I limped slowly down the stairs, my body hobbled and still shaken, and I examined the destruction. Yes, the clock might be able to be repaired, but not without a great deal of difficulty and time. Picking up a large plate of the brass mechanism and holding it near my heart, I could feel that the haunting presence was no longer there. Whatever had possessed the clock was now gone forever.

So ghosts can inhabit the earth in some form or another! With unique powers, different from that of a werewolf or witch!

And this one, whoever it might have been, had successfully prevented Gerard and myself from becoming intimate that day. Perhaps I should thank the spirit world; then again, perhaps not. The extreme sexual desire I had felt earlier had disappeared, though I could still feel Gerard's anger in the air around me. His madness at failing to satisfy and fulfill a century-old fantasy, had to be most profound. This night I would be hunting alone.

I proceeded to pick up the broken pieces and take them across the way to my workshop. Remarkably, I still saw no one- none of the usual household slaves were to be seen. Had the sound of the bell scared them away? I went into the kitchen and there were two females preparing dinner. They bowed their heads towards me in obeisance as I entered, but there was no other reaction from them. They acted quite calm and busy about their business. How could they not have heard that sound? It had been louder than cannon fire! I helped myself to a cool drink from the barrel.

As I was leaving, I met Juliette returning from her bath. I felt only the merest twinge of desire; certainly nothing as overwhelming as before. She had noticed the large pile of broken clock pieces just inside my workshop and asked what had happened. I replied simply that it had accidentally fallen over.

"Strange. What a pity," she appeared thoughtful for a moment then shrugged and started to go about her tasks. "Can it be repaired?"

"Yes, but not without great difficulty," was all I could say.

She put on her cooking apron and spread some flour on a table. "But, you are accomplished at that, are you not, Master Henri?" She looked up from her work.

I nodded, but I had to ask, "Juliette-"

"Yes, Master Henri?" She watched me closely, waiting, anticipating.

"Did you hear anything- unusual, a few moments ago? Earlier? Like.." I hesitated.

She began to lay out the dough for tomorrow's beignets. "Like what?"

"Like a large tower clock bell sounding out loudly?"

She stopped her work and pondered my question. "No, Monsieur Henri. I heard nothing like that at all. Certainly nothing out of the ordinary." She went back to kneading her dough. "There is no clock tower near here, not for many, many miles. You could not possibly have heard that one. It is too far away." She looked back up at me. "You must have been mistaken. Perhaps you heard something else? There has been a lot of distant thunder." She shrugged again- and resumed her work. "Tonight should bring a big storm to Sans Souci."

"Yes, that must have been what I heard." I started to leave, but turned back. "Do not bother with dinner tonight, Juliette. Master Gerard has left and will not be back until morning. And ... I am not hungry."

"Yes, of course. If you are sure, Master Henri." She curtsied as I left.

Juliette was always so polite, so well-mannered and spoken, a real wonder- especially when considering her station. I decided on buying her one day from Gerard and giving her her freedom. She was much too intelligent and accomplished to be a slave. Her delicate mulatto beauty would easily attract some wealthy Frenchman.

After making sure the workshop was shuttered from the coming wind and rain, I casually walked out into the woods. Night was falling rapidly as dark storm clouds started to mass themselves dramatically. A pendulous sight. Distant thunder rolled ominously towards Sans Souci. It was, no doubt, one of those great storms from the warm gulf waters and flooding was common in these occurrences. Of course, inclement weather would never prevent Gerard or I from the hunt. I came to rather enjoy it that way for it made the hunt that much more interesting. We could stalk and kill in the most torrential rains, irregardless and heedless of severe floods- the most extreme heat or cold never bothering us. Maybe we would cross paths while hunting.

It was on nights like this when I would never know what the moon held for me. What sort of human I might encounter. Trappers and hunters (like I used to be) and late-night travelers were not unusual in this newly settled country of swamps and marsh.

There were many gangs of thieves about the area which held up carriages and robbed passengers at gunpoint. A lawless land, human life was carelessly for-feit. The perfect scenario for beings such as Gerard and I. If I was lucky, I might come across such a group tonight and destroy them all.

I was deep into a swampy area, well away from the plantation, when I transformed at will. The light of the moon was obscured by the heavy clouds, and occasional raindrops heralded the storm's approach, yet I felt the lunar power nonetheless. As I prowled through the wilderness, I reflected on last night and found myself longing for another adventure like that one. Gerard had planned it to the minutest detail and we had executed it to perfection. As for myself, I harbored no guilt for my part in it and even thought so sure of myself, that I fancied I should be the one to choose the next victim.

Lost in my thoughts and full of confidence, I was not aware I was being followed until the human was almost upon me. I turned sensing someone, yet no one was there. I listened carefully: he was slowly advancing, but still, I could not see him- and he made absolutely no sound! Obviously an expert tracker and hunter, it had to be one of the natives from the area. And, remarkably, he knew what he was hunting! He was stalking the supreme predator- myself. He was purposely after a werewolf!

How had I let someone slip up on me so closely, so easily, so unawares? Crouching down, I advanced slowly towards the brave foolish man, lightning now beginning to flash regularly. I knew he would be armed with a silver weapon of some sort, yet I felt no fear. A loup garou fears no mortal man, no matter how stealth a hunter he is.

In one particularly prolonged and bright display of light, we spied each other. Giving the human the advantage, his bow at the ready, I still made the most of it, bearing fangs and claws, looking my most ferocious. Yet the brave exhibited no fear and held his silver-tipped arrow steady, aimed directly at my chest. I ran straight for him, as quick and fleet-footed as the messenger god himself..

Agilely dodging aside, the arrow missed its intended target, but did lodge in my right shoulder. The searing pain was immediate and unnatural as the silver burned into my bloodstream. Pulling it out quickly, I had to thank Gerard again for preparing me for just such an event. By gradually feeding me thimblefuls of liquid silver in his special wine, I had built up an immunity. Only that was what saved me, however, if he had hit my heart- I still cannot say what might have happened.

With no time to lose, I reacted for he had another silver arrow drawn and at the ready. Howling fiercely from pain or anger or even from my own carelessness, I made one gigantic leap, pouncing on him and knocking him to the ground. The arrow had whizzed by my head missing me by only an inch or less. My giant paws had his strong shoulders pinned, my weight upon him holding him down. He ceased to struggle. The brave warrior was mine!

Looking down at him, even in the dark, I recognized this man, but from where? Then in another second, I knew. Snarling, I showed my fangs, close near his neck and I was impressed that he still showed not the slightest hint of fear. It was the same strong warrior from my sick room! In that tiny native village where I recovered after Gerard's attack. Where I had first met Selena and grandma-ma. He was that very one who argued that I should be destroyed!

I briefly read his thoughts and my admiration turned to astonishment. He wanted something from me. He was asking to become as I was! To be loup garou and live many lifetimes. He desired immortality!

'With just one bite, you can grant me eternal youth and superhuman strength,' his mind read. 'I will join you in the hunt and be forever your loyal servant!'

I had to decide in a matter of seconds. As it was- there were three choices left to me: Bite him and if he survived, then he would become as Gerard and I. I was seriously tempted- he might prove a better companion than Gerard. Secondly, I could just let him go; but of course, he would then simply try to hunt me down again, now or later; and eventually, Gerard or I would have to kill him. And finally, the third choice: kill him now and be done with it.

Before I could act on my decision, another long flash

of lightning occurred, and a distinct blur flew across my vision from left to right. It traveled by so fast it left a whistling in my ears mixed with a loud clap of thunder.

I did not have to see him to know what it was. Gerard was here! I looked down at my warrior, who I still had pinned to the ground. Dark blood was gushing out of the throat that Gerard had silently slit from ear to ear. It pulsed out with each pump of his slowing heartbeat. Gerard had made my choice for me!

Gerard's wolf-self strode casually over to us and he bent down close to the poor man's bleeding throat, breathing in the scent of blood and impending death. He looked up at me, with his snarling snout slowly forming into a hideous wide grin of dripping wet fangs. Thunder rolled and the rain came in a sudden downpour, drenching this dishonorable scene.

The anger within me was uncontrollable; I could contain it no longer. With all my might, summoned from all the pain and anguish I had experienced since he first bit me, I slapped that evil grin right off his furry face! The strength of my blow surprised us both. It sent him sailing directly into the nearest tree, which cracked in two from the impact and fell in a thunderous crash.

Again, thunder rolled and lightning flashed and the wind picked up blowing sheets of rain across this supernatural clash. Gerard visibly shook off the shock of having been hit by his protege. He stood and, with deliberation, walked over to me and what I now considered my prey. His blue eyes burned with intent.

Never hesitate. Humans are too unpredictable, especially a strong determined warrior such as this. Now-let us feast!

No! My backhand landed solidly on his face. He remained standing this time, but the slap sent some teeth spewing from his mouth. He turned to face me. Blood, mingled with spit and rain, dribbled from his mouth. I warned Gerard to stay away.

You should not have done this! He was mine. He still is mine; for me only. You shan't have him!

The blue eyes turned red, filling with anger and blood. How dare I defy him! He leapt upon me and we rolled in the mud scuffling and biting and clawing, inflicting numerous bloody wounds on each other. I knew he was the stronger, but I was not going to let him command me anymore. He dealt me a particularly strong strike and I flew far into a nearby swampy pool. He jumped in after me, giving me no time to recover.

The storm raged about us and grew in intensity as we bled and fought one another; our conflict seemed to increase with the typhoon's power. Summoning all the beast that was possible within me, I managed to inflict a severe wound upon his throat; my jaws clamping into him and not letting go. His gurgled howl of pain was masked by a particularly fierce crack of thunder, yet he fought free by inflicting his own severe wound upon me.

He broke my arm, I cracked his ribs as we wrestled; us knowing neither could die; knowing this clash could last forever if we allowed it. For even though we inflicted pain and great wounds upon each other, we healed as rapidly. Still our rage continued. In the midst of ever-increasing gales and whirlwinds, we fought; while my warrior lay dying, drowning in his own pool of muddy blood.

Gerard threw me aside like I was a sack of cotton and, as I landed against a specifically sharp outcropping of rock- the wind severely knocked out of me- I helplessly transformed back into my human self! I was tiring, but stubbornly determined to fight on and not let him have my rightful prey. Not let him take from me again, as he had taken everything else from my life and given me in return this blessed curse.

I transformed back quickly and leapt for him; again trying for his jugular. But he was ready and stepping aside, he tossed me across the clearing. The shock of my severe landing, once more caused me to become human. I heard his growl of mean laughter echo in the winds.

Too weak to transform this time, I ran for him and, quickly picking him up and with surprising strength, threw him into the largest oak nearby. I heard his back break (or was it thunder?) and this time he too turned to human form from the forceful impact. He was tiring also, yet my intractable anger would not allow me to surrender and he knew that.

We ran for each other and embraced in a death grip. There we were, two male immortals fighting in the midst of a sea of wind and rain over what was becoming less and less important. It was now the fight itself which mattered: my pent-up resentment, his lack of gratification; and neither one of us willing to admit defeat. However, I was wise enough to know he was too strong for me to conquer- the best I could hope for was a stalemate.

He flung me forceably to the ground near the brave. I smelled the blood and heard the man's last gasp. I wanted to drink and gain strength from his blood, for I could barely stand upright on my feet. Gerard was on his knees, breathing heavily, tired of this fruitless fight."Go on," he shouted above the tempest. "Go on and take your precious warrior! He is yours. I do not want him at any rate." He stood up and, grabbing me by the scruff of my neck, spoke with finality, "Nor do I want you either!" With that said, I was thrown roughly back down into the mud, my face falling upon the brave's bare chest.

When I looked up, Gerard had left. Turning back to the poor warrior, I straddled his lifeless body and (still in my human form) I plunged my fist into his chest, removing the barely beating heart and devoured it hungrily. A moment afterward, I felt my weakness and tiredness leave. Then uncontrollably, I began to cry. As I lapped up his blood, as the torrential rain pounded down upon us, as I gained in strength- I cried. Rivers of blood, I cried. For him, for me, for this new 'other-world' and all I had become. I cried for lost innocence, for my lost soul. For this thing which had a hold on me and I tried to regard as 'my blessed curse.'

I do not recall just how long I remained there over the body, but I eventually gathered myself up and proceeded to bury him in a muddy, deep wet grave. I took his trousers, for mine had been torn to shreds and were useless. The storm did not let up in intensity as I staggered back to Sans Souci. In fact, it seemed to be gaining in ferocity. On the way back, I remember hoping lightning would strike me and then (if I lived) perhaps I would be the one who dominated and commanded.

As I approached home, I knew Gerard was not near- I would have sensed his presence. The mansion was safe and secure from the storm and no one was about. Silently, I went upstairs to my room and cleaned myself off. I laid down on the bed- mental and emotional exhaustion overtaking me. And though not actually sleepy, I closed my eyes, trying to take some needed quiet rest; dozing fitfully with all the decisions I now had to consider, as the storm's winds buffeted loudly against the protective shutters. The turmoil with out, echoing my turmoil within.

5

I rose long after dawn, my body and mind awake and fully recovered, dreading having to face Gerard. Yet it had to be done. Over the night, I had decided to pack my few things and leave to go back to my simple life of hard work and small wages: To go back to the arms of my wife. I had deliberately missed the usual breakfast, but would inform Gerard of my decision as soon as I saw him. However, I did not have to wait long, for as I opened up the shutters and walked out onto the balcony to view the destruction from the night's fury, Gerard was ascending the back stairs and he joined me at the railing.

The morning seemed exceptionally bright and clear without a cloud in the sky. An extreme heavy humidity was in the air with all manner of insects buzzing annoyingly about. I noticed beads of sweat circling Gerard's forehead. At first, we said nothing, thought nothing, as we both stared out upon the grounds, watching Toussaint direct the slaves at their tasks of clearing away the debris of fallen limbs and uprooted trees from swollen bayous.

I hope the fields did not experience too much damage; he directed his thoughts into conversation. I did not reply, but kept my mind as blank as possible. We should go survey the damage later; he continued his train of thought. We need to build a levee there- here he pointed a finger in an arc to my left towards the river. For one day it will rise and carry its floodwaters all the way to us and threaten Sans Souci. Your engineering expertise can be put to good use.

"Yes, a great flood is likely." I spoke out loud. For now I was going to hold my tongue (and thoughts as well). Let him do the speaking.

After an awkward pause, he began to verbalize his thoughts. "I want to apologize for last night. I was wrong and- hasty."

I turned to face him. He was looking straight at me, his hair waving in a soft breeze that had picked up, partially dispelling the thick air. I did not reply, but quickly searched his mind for whether he was sincere or not. It seemed so, then again he could easily trick me for he knew when I was reading his mind. He continued, "I was concerned he would harm you."

"I had the situation under control," was all I said.

"I know that now. Again, I apologize."

Saying nothing more, I turned to face the yard again. He did likewise. "And your shoulder- where the silver arrow pierced your skin?"

I replied curtly, "It is merely a little sore. Still. That is all."

"Bon." There was another awkward pause. "You know, Henri- I have been giving a great deal of thought to what you have said about us- you and I- being a product of the devil." Yes, what was he getting at? "Well, I have come to the conclusion that idea is probably not true at all. In fact, it is highly more likely that we are of God's creation, like everything else in the universe!" I snorted loudly at his nonsense. "Why not, Henri? Before you became an immortal, you were God's creation, weren't you? Well then, why are you not still his creation?" He looked at me closely for any reaction.

"I thought I was your creation!" My tongue was sharp.

At that retort, he turned back to view the slaves still at work. He was silent for a moment. "Besides, I do not even know if there are such things as devils and gods."

That brought a quick response from me. "Where did Satine get her powers and abilities from then?"

"I do not exactly know. She always referred to her 'gods' as bestowing some legacy on her."

"Gods?"

He nodded. "Egyptian, I suppose. Or those even older."

"That does not mean we are God's creation."

He sighed. "Well, I for one believe I am. And I also think, Henri," Gerard made sure he had my full attention before continuing, "God must have had his reasons for making some of us human and some of us not human. Reasons that you and I could hardly even guess at."

"We are freaks!" I spoke with true self-disgust.

"Freaks? Come now! Do not be so hard on yourself- on us. We are what we are. It is fate! As simple as that and we must learn to live with what we are dealt. Freaks!

Non, mon ami, I do not think so. We are quite normal, in fact."

We stared at each other in wonder at his conclusion. He began to laugh; I smiled. I had to admit, his laughter was engaging and I was glad to hear it return, however,..

"Gerard, I have something to tell you. I have decided..."

He hastily interrupted me, "Hold that thought, mon ami. First, I have something I've been meaning to show you. C'est tres important! Come." He grabbed my hand authoritatively and I let him lead me into the bedroom opposite my own. Much cooler than the other side of the house, here was a large dark and dusty room used for storage and little else. Gerard went to one of the windows to let in some fresh air; clouds of dust billowed from the drapes, captured, floating in the rays of light.

Walking over to the brick fireplace that was along the far wall to the left, he turned one of the two scones above the mantle to a ninety degree angle and then obediently, the complete fireplace, from floor to ceiling, also revolved ninety degrees and opened into another room! It was a tiny room(more like a large closet) full of dusty books and printed matter, including manuscripts and what looked like hand-written scrolls.

"From ancient times, my dear friend! All this is from ancient times." He lit a lantern, so we could see easier, as I started to look about, fascinated. "I should have told you about this room earlier, but.." he sounded apologetic, "but, I had to make sure you were willing to stay and learn all my witchcraft."

"All of this- concerns the occult and the black arts?" I could not disguise my wonder.

"Yes, and more. What you see is the fruit of my searches for over a century. From the far reaches of the world; from the four points of the compass. Most of it is older than our enemy witch herself!"

I marveled at the private library. It smelled of aged

and yellowed papers; it spoke of antiquities and far-reaching, long-dead civilizations. I took a book from a shelf- nothing in particular, just a book. It was written in some ancient language I could not read, yet I knew it was full of recipes for deadly potions and incantations for spells. I said nothing aloud, but he knew my curiosity was peaked.

"Come, regardez." He pointed me to one certain book which seemed to have a regal spot all its own. It lay open on a small podium. "It is said this was written in human blood and bound with human flesh! Most likely it hails from ancient Sumeria."

"The Book of the Dead!" I whispered with incredulity, as I lightly caressed the binding and pages with reverence. It may have been my imagination, but I could have sworn I felt a surge of power emanating from the work.

"Very good, Henri, you feel its power also. You impress me more every day." He came over closer with the lantern so I would better see the ancient script. "If there is only one book you have time to study, be sure to make it this one."

I turned the pages gently. They were surprisingly not brittle nor torn with age, but intact; it had been remarkably preserved. "But what sort of language is this? I cannot read this, Gerard!"

"I do not know what original language that is. But I am sure it is long dead."

"Then how can we possibly study from this and learn from it?"

"The book will allow it."

I tried to read his thoughts. "I still do not understand." Exasperation played in my voice.

"It will allow- certain ones- to understand its words. It allowed me only after a time."

"What do you mean allow?"

"As you look at it, and study it, one day the letters and

symbols will suddenly and profoundly change into a language that you are most familiar with. In our case the French language. However, this is only when the book feels you are ready- or worthy- of absorbing its knowledge." He had emphasized the word worthy.

"It is magical then?"

"A simple description, but befitting. Yes, the book has its own special power- and uses," he added. "It is from somewhere within this work that we will find the secret formula or weapon that will destroy Satine, once and for all. Forever!"

"I can take this volume- any of them- to my room to study?"

"Mais bien sur, mon cher. I encourage you to do so. All I ask is that you place them back here when you finish. Remember, none of the household slaves know of this secret room. And we must keep it that way."

"And Toussaint?"

"We must never take the chance of losing these books and manuscripts. And so, unfortunately, my loyal Toussaint does not know. Bear in mind, the witch is very tricky and can persuade even the most loyal to betray their master- or friend. Only you and I know of this room and its contents."

He blew out the lantern and I followed him back into the storage room. "Now let us go survey the plantation and see what damage occurred last night, shall we?"

So, that was how I stayed on at Sans Souci. I had firmly made up my mind to leave, but now.. I could not! not yet. It was as if he had purposely held back this information for just the right moment and used it in order to keep me here awhile longer. Which made me ask myself- What else did Gerard have secreted on the plantation?

I did not let it annoy me, for I now had an extraordinary and immense task ahead of me. Even more to learn! Already, I knew more than Selena and grandmama combined. I thought of the voodoo priestess and how she must know a substantial amount concerning the supernatural. About werewolves and zombies also.

That night, Gerard and I did not have dinner together. The day had been most productive and we discovered that little severe damage had occurred from the hurricane. The pecan grove suffered the most. With a few uprooted trees, the immense acreage was everywhere littered with brittle broken limbs, though it looked worse than it actually was. The sugar cane fields had flooded as did the rice patties, but they grew near the bayous and swampy areas and on occasions such as this, flooding was expected and not entirely unwelcome depending on the amount of water. It provided a sort-of natural irrigation. The other crops on higher ground also suffered, though not from the rain, but from the winds and we definitely had quite a bit of replanting to do. But it was not of any great economic impact to the plantation.

At this point of my story, I must interject some notion about my feelings at that time towards Sans Souci. Not only was I becoming extremely attached to the place and happy working the plantation, but I believed Gerard and Toussaint (both) were becoming rather dependent upon me. And to be quite honest, I had even, (on occasion), fancied myself as the future foreman of the land! This is a most important point for it helps give purpose for my actions in the future.

That evening, I did not even once consider hunting or transforming. Gerard had gone off to town; perhaps to hunt, perhaps not. I was eager to start studying the works upstairs. Even my hunger seemed diminished though the moon shined bright.

Quietly and unseen, I went upstairs, unlocked the

secret panel and chose a book at random. I glanced at the open Book of the Dead and saw only the jibberish I had seen earlier, so I left it for another time. Perhaps, one day the book itself would try to communicate with me.

I returned to the library downstairs with my selection and as I settled into my favorite chair, lighting a cigar, the boy entered bearing the usual late night coffee and brandy. Mercutio was on his shoulder and when the monkey saw me, he jumped quickly into my lap, chattering all the while having something important to tell me. I gave him some large pecans I had picked up from the grove and saved just for him, which he promptly scampered away with to hide with his other treasures around the room.

I briefly considered taking advantage of Gerard's absence and engage the youngster in conversation, but it would have to wait for another time. I was interested in only one thing that night and for many, many evenings thereafter. And that one thing was witchcraft!

On those many nights, I not only studied the art and craft, but I practiced it; sometimes with Gerard's aid and advice, sometimes on my own. But that first night, alone with the ancient writings, was the most memorable for me, because it was on that night when I finally came into contact with my familiar.

I had completely forgotten about that white blur of a horse I saw from the carriage the other evening; what with learning of the secret room and its contents and the fierce fight between Gerard and myself yesterday night. Not to mention coming face to face with the native warrior who had actually been hunting and tracking me down! (And of course, his subsequent death). So what happened that evening came as an absolute surprise.

Firstly, I thought I heard my name being called. It was more a thought than a voice, with no particular gender; just a neutral voice that interrupted my deep concentration, asking me to come outside. Stopping in the midst of my studies, my first fearful thought was the witch was here and she is trying to lure me away, perhaps to my destruction. The voice was definitely not from my imagination.

It was near midnight when I gave in to my curiosity, put the book down and looked out the window. There, with a sudden flash between the distant trees, I saw the same white horse from the other evening! It would disappear and then reappear like streaks of lightning- and as fast as a comet. I proceeded cautiously out the back of the house and peered around the corner. With some relief, I saw Toussaint crouching in the shadow of the cistern bath, watching for the same apparition that I had seen. He glanced my way as if on cue and gestured for me to join him.

I knelt down beside him, our eyes searching between the thick tall trees where we had last seen the ghostly steed. "What is it Toussaint?" I whispered. "What sort of animal can float above the ground like that?"

"I do not know, Master Henri, but I do know it is for you!" He did not move his eyes away from the woods.

"My familiar?" It was more a statement than a question- a statement of pure wonder. Toussaint nodded. "So it is true. I suspected as much." I thought for a moment, my excitement and eagerness mounting. "We must catch it Toussaint, you and I. Catch it and keep it somewhere away from Gerard and others. No one but you and I need know about this."

"That part is true." He turned to look seriously at me. "But you must not try to keep it penned. It should roam freely. He will be there when you need him." His voice, as always spoke with wisdom.

My eyes kept searching. "Yes. Yes, of course. You are correct." I looked at Toussaint. "Do you believe he will come to me, if I approach him? Or do you think he is wild, untamed? Unbridled?"

"I think that," he paused, "yes, he will not run from you. He is here to serve you after all. And remember, he is a reflection of you- your witchcraft, your needs- your inner character."

I thought upon this for a moment before rising. "Come join me. He is just beyond that grove there." I pointed. "I can feel him."

"I will go behind you and remain a few paces back. He is to be yours and only yours."

As we approached the nearby line of trees, I saw the flash again, yet heard no sound. The horse was able to move freely within the thickest woods and brush and make not the slightest noise. It stopped still, in the open, and turned to face me. I was only a few paces away and finally able to see him up close and clearly.

He was a very large white steed, considerably larger than the dapple-gray carriage horses of Gerard's. And as much as I loved and had worked with horses over the years, he was most positively the most massive and giant I had ever seen. Yet oh, so beautiful at the same time. His thick shimmering mane cascaded down, long on one side of his neck. He was solid white, a bright silvery white- like the moon- save for one dark grayish spot on his left haunch. I discerned it quickly even from that distance, as a star- a five pointed star- a pentagram. He was for me! And for me only.

He neighed and snorted, pawing the ground with one hoof and raising his mighty head up and down. I could read his thoughts. He danced and pranced, showing himself to the advantage. He was welcoming me. Just as I thought how lovely it would be if I had some oats or sugar to give him, Toussaint appeared silently next to me. Reaching into his leather satchel, he gave me a handful of corn kernels. How had he known?

I approached the well-spirited stallion slowly, cautiously, a step at a time, making no sudden moves. He did not move back or retreat, but remained still and unafraid. Holding my arm outstretched, I opened up my hand to show the treats for him to enjoy. Stopping a few paces away, I silently called him to come to me. He shook his head and magnificent mane once more and then came up to me without hesitation; with no faltering or pause, he ate right out of my palm.

He allowed me to caress his neck and back; my touch conveying trust and love; his willingness let me know he was comfortable with me. So tall and muscular, my arms could barely encircle his neck.

It was time to ride and, surprisingly, as if in response to my thought, the horse bent down onto his front knees, and bowing his head, offered me to mount. I was instantly upon his back; he rose and I waved at Toussaint as we galloped away.

However we were not on the ground for long, because this majestic familiar could leap so far and so fast in the air, over the treetops, it was as if we were flying! In one jump, we could cover a mile or more. So now I had the means to travel anywhere, anytime and be there in a matter of minutes. Most likely, travel between Sans Souci and my own small cozy cabin could be accomplished in half-a-day, or even less. This was my familiar- granted to me by what supreme power, I could not even conceive. Yet, holding on tight to his mane as we flew and rode across that watery landscape, I gave thanks. He was mine: my servant, obedient not only to my wishes, but devoted entirely to my protection and survival. Like Gabriel was to Gerard, though more like a pet. My alter ego.

Just as that thought escaped my mind, we flew high over the wide river and then he descended suddenly into a particularly swampy area and silently crept beneath an extremely thick canopy of cypress. We were hiding from someone- or some thing.

My senses detected movement from above. I heard the same swish of wing and flight that told me Gabriel was near. Looking up I saw, through a break in the trees, the familiar flying figure against the starry sky. He had not seen us and was most probably on some mission for Gerard. In fact, I barely could discern it- but, yes- he was carrying what looked to be a large bundle in his sharp talons. No doubt, the remains of another victim of Gerard's the gargoyle was to dispose of. That was one of his purposes as Gerard's familiar. However, mine would be used for other tasks. Just what, at that time, I could not guess, though he would not be used for discarding the results of my monthly hunts.

I realized also, not only was my flying steed's senses even more acute than my own, but he substantially understood his existence must be kept secret from Gerard and Gabriel. It was better, for now, that they not know I now had my own familiar.

As soon as it was safe, he leaped into the air again, silently crashing through the treetops and we soared like an eagle over the bayous and swamps.

I learned to guide him and he grew accustomed to my touch and thoughts. The freedom of flight was exhilarating and the different perspective of seeing this unique watery land from above brought back to me how much I loved this area of the world. I glimpsed Sans Souci in the moonlight- full of grandeur and resplendent with French colonial charm. I thought of riding over to Selena and home, but it would only make me sick with longing. However, I knew I could not wait much longer and most likely, after the next full moon, I would leave for my modest little cabin.

We leapt and flew, then descended only to leap up and fly again and we did this for hours until the moon had all but disappeared and the first signs of day rose in the east. Finally, at the house, we alighted into the shadows, unseen by the household, quite near where I had first been introduced to him. I dismounted and noticed Toussaint asleep, waiting, propped against an oak near the clearing. I walked over to him and gently roused him from his slumber. When I turned around though, my familiar had gone. But I knew he would always be in the near distance waiting for my beckoning. Like a fiercely loyal pet.

Toussaint and I walked slowly back to the mansion, which was already stirring with morning life. Our voices stayed low. "Unbelievable Toussaint! It is as though he could fly."

"I saw, Master Henri. It must have been a great adventure."

"It was indescribable. Absolutely thrilling!"

"You are now a fully empowered warlock." We stopped and he looked directly at me. "If you keep up your practice of the craft, you will be quite a valuable friend," his pause was only for a heartbeat, "or a worthy foe."

"Foe? To whom?" Did he mean the witch or Gerard? I could not read his meaning.

"To whomever presents a danger to you. Or to those dear to you." We resumed our slow walk to the house. As we neared the back patio and were about to part, I thanked him for his trustworthy support and wisdom. "Mais bien sur, Master Henri." Before I turned to go inside, he put his hand on my arm. "What is the stallion's name?"

"Name?"

"How is he called?"

I had not given it any thought, but just then, in the faint distance, I heard what I thought to be the neigh of a horse. At first, I believed it to be my imagination for Toussaint did not look towards the sound- he had not heard it. But it was my familiar speaking to me.

"His name is- Montesquieu."

So now Toussaint and I had another secret to share! I
had to be increasingly diligent, whenever Gerard was
near, to disguise my thoughts and focus them in a certain
direction, so he would not read all I knew.

Therefore, as the moon waned, I threw myself into
managing (with Toussaint's help) the entire plantation,
never bothering Gerard with minor details. Sans Souci
began plans for doubling its production and all of us
began anew in a great (and profitable) working
relationship. Gerard even became more like the
plantation owner of his youth when he was human. Even
I pondered on the idea: now that I had Montesquieu, I
could stay at Sans Souci more or less permanently and
still be able to visit my family every four or five days at
regular intervals. At that time, it never entered my mind
for them to move here.

I visited with Montesquieu once or twice a week when
I knew we would be alone and isolated; usually very late
at night, near dawn. Sometimes there was only time
enough to feed him some sweet treats and brush him
down. He was actually very affectionate, however with
his large hoofs, strong legs and haunches, he would
make a formidable fierce fighter in any struggle.

On quiet rainy days (which occurred more often as
autumn approached), I worked on the longcase clock
destroyed by Gerard. It made a great challenge for myself, but I had no doubt I could repair it, given the right
materials. Otherwise, I always had my head in the
manuscripts upstairs in the secret room or in the study
making notes on one thing or another. From ancient
times until the present, I uncovered the sacred secrets of
witches and covens. Knowledge not accessible (and
certainly not easily understood) by ordinary men. I could
not imagine a more complete, definitive library on the

subject of the supernatural and the occult. I made a point to ask Gerard if Satine might have had such a library once.

If she did, she did not share it with me.

When I first meet her, I must be ready- instantly- to make battle? I asked silently and with a certain amount of trepidation.

Not necessarily. If I know her- and I think that I do, he puffed on his cigar for a moment- I believe she will somehow make her presence known to us. She may even knock on the front door and introduce herself. He leaned towards me. Or she might disguise herself and insinuate herself into our household. Be very careful Henri, for she will try and turn you against me.

What makes you so positive?

Because you are no longer mortal. She will try to join your powers to hers. Promise me you will be diligent. I did not readily reply either by word, thought or deed. "Promise me," he commanded out loud.

His seriousness was unsettling, but he made sense. "Yes, Gerard. I promise to remain diligent."

"Bon. Maintenant," he settled down in the settee, laying on his back and propping his stocking feet up. "We must plan our masquerade party. We have less than a month."

"Are you sure you wish to do this? Don't do it on my account."

"Nonsense. The party is for all of us, not just to introduce you as my.." he waved his hand around still holding the smoking cigar,"..well, just to introduce you to some of the local dignitaries and landowners. You will need to meet them, since your plans are to continue working on here at Sans Souci." So he had guessed that. "And it will be necessary to use these people (or even to control them) if not through potions and hypnotism, then through the most common of all means of persuasion."

"And what is that?"

310

"Why, with money, my dear Henri. Money is the
ultimate tool available- even for witchs!" We laughed
together like we had when we first met. "Besides, you
need to make business contacts and intermingle for,
unfortunately, you and I still need- require- humans. For
one reason, we grow older, yet do not apparently age."
Here he tapped the floor calling Mercutio over, who
promptly scampered over and jumped up onto his chest
and laid himself down, comfortable against Gerard's
strong heartbeat. "The more officials you know and
control- or have sway over- the better. Then the fewer
are the questions asked by those interminable gossips!"
He let out a long sigh. "Humans are such a pain. It is a
pity that we cannot live without their occasional help." He
started to rise. "I must make out the guest list."

I laid my hand upon his shoulder. Do not disturb
yourself or the little one. I will write the names down, as
you call them out to me.

Thank you, Henri. I proceeded over to the desk,
pulled out ink, quill and paper, and we made our plans for
the upcoming party which would end up being much
more than just a party for both of us. It would lead me to
a new beginning, for that night I would have my first
introduction to the powers of our ultimate nemesis.

The entire plantation and household were involved in
arrangements for the upcoming event and in three
weeks, we were ready for a full fledged extravaganza.
Juliette oversaw all the kitchen details, menu and food
preparations; Toussaint and the boy were responsible for
the decorations, lighting and table settings. Tents were
erected for lavish buffets and drinks. I selected the wines.
Gerard oversaw every thing; he covered the minutest
detail. He never was much for displaying excitement, but

I felt it within him every time he came near. The entire downstairs and grounds were to be open to the guests.

The dining table was enlarged to the utmost capacity. Other tables were assembled outdoors. All was highly polished: the glass chandeliers, the wooden floors and furniture, silver utensils. Silver still annoyed me whenever I touched it or even heard its clink. It always reminded me of my painful wound from that silver-tipped arrow and my close brush with true danger. But I handled the silver like a human, with no pain or discomfiture, no matter how much it grated on my nerves.

As time neared for the masquerade ball, I worked daily around the house or in my clock workshop; studying every night and taking secret rides with Montesquieu a few times a week. Upon his back, high in the sky, overlooking the land and fields and swamps, I felt so free, so alive and privileged to be able to view all this from above and achieve a different perspective not available to ordinary men. This wilderness held so much potential with its wide variety of species; a virtually untapped and seemingly inexhaustible supply of raw materials. Able to see miles away, my heart filled with wonder every time we rode.

Time went along in this busy manner for those quickly passing weeks, when, almost upon the very eve of the gathering, I realized with a start, I had not chosen a costume. I ran outside to interrupt Gerard's bath, the waxing moon almost full.

Good, good, you have come to join me.

Not exactly. I was wondering..

Join me anyway, Henri. We have not bathed together in awhile. I did as requested, undressing and slipping into the cool, refreshing cistern water and we proceeded to sponge each other down. By this time, I felt completely comfortable being naked and alone with him.

I was wondering..

What sort of costume you should wear?

Exactly. What are you going as? I do not have anything chosen yet. He turned his back to me so I would massage his neck and shoulders. I knew how much he enjoyed that.

Why, we do not need costumes, Henri. They have been provided for us. My bewildered thought made him laugh. Mon cher, we will simply transform ourselves and the guests will not have a clue that we are actual loup garou.

But could that not be dangerous? I mean for us. If someone should happen to discover the truth.

We shall be careful. He turned to face me and started rubbing my chest with his sponge. He knew how much I enjoyed that. No one will know. We will only transform our faces and hands and be in ordinary dress like the plantation gentry that we are.

How clever, I had to admit. Perfect- except- I am not sure I can control it as well as you.

Yes, you can Henri. Try it now. He stopped massaging me. Transform only one part of your body. Your right hand for instance. I hesitated. Go on, summon the moon's power and concentrate. Try, he encouraged me.

It took me almost a complete minute, allowing the moon to take over just my hand. And I was successful- only my whole right arm changed into the wolf! I closed my eyes and concentrated again. This time my arm changed back to normal, however the hand did also, save for five sharp talons where my fingernails would have been! He laughed heartily at my predicament.

Keep practicing and you will be successful. Remember you are not only a werewolf but a warlock now. One who can exercise great control over a great many things. He looked deep into my eyes- searching for..? You are coming into your own, Henri, and becoming powerful. He paused before speaking out loud. "It is refreshing to see it. You are just the type of companion I always hoped would one day join me here at Sans Souci and end my endless days of boredom and cease my ceaseless nights of solitude."

I turned my back to him and changed the subject, "About the Book of the Dead?"

Yes? It was his turn to rub my neck and shoulders.

You have personally witnessed its power?

Yes, once and only once. A bright green light emanated from it shining towards the ceiling like a beacon.

After that you were able to read- I mean, interpret- the book?

Yes.

Then read it to me.

He stopped massaging me and leaned himself back against the cistern wall. "Your hunger for knowledge is commendable. But it cannot be accomplished in that manner."

"Why not?"

"It will not allow me to. I have tried it before."

My interest was piqued. "With whom?" I asked, probably a little too demanding.

"Why Henri! I do believe you are jealous." He laughed and then it was his turn to neatly change the subject. "We can try to read it together, but have patience, mon cher. It will demonstrate itself to you, and only you, when and only when, it believes you to be ready." He sighed heavily. "I do hope it will not be too long a wait, for I believe the witch to be near."

"I feel her too." He gave me an inquisitive look. I placed a hand on his shoulder.

"That is why I must found out what that book says. Then I can be of greater assistance."

He laid his hand over my own. "I know. You are already a tremendous help." He splashed some water on me playfully. "Now go. I sense that you want to finish some book or other treatise upstairs in your bedroom;

what is this one about? Ah yes- invisibility. Very good, Henri."

"Yes," I replied eagerly.

"When you are ready to attempt it, come and get me." He started to climb out of the bath. I followed. "The party is already two nights away."

"Of course. One question, Gerard- The guests invited- Are they..?"

"From all walks of life mon ami. From governmental officials to the local baker. Some are Sans Souci business acquaintances who you will need to meet. I will introduce you." He sighed while dressing, "I do hope they have some clever costumes this time and not just all wigs and cleavage!" He chuckled and slapped me on the back, "However I have made sure to invite some very handsome youths for our pleasures. They are quite easy upon the eyes." The gleam in his eye, along with his sly sensuous grin, told me I would need to be ready for experimentation come that evening.

I laughed at his thoughts (perhaps a little nervously) and we told each other goodnight. Going upstairs, I amazingly realized that at one point in our conversation, I almost thanked him. Thank him! The very man who set a curse upon me! This was a surprising twist of thought for now I was becoming actually grateful for some of the things he had done. Because of Gerard I had become much more educated and well read; I learned many languages, including ancient Greek; I studied the words of philosophers and scientists; sharpened and honed my mathematic skills; geography and history beckoned me as favorite subjects. Even without considering all the supernatural education I had received, my 'earthly education' had been substantially increased. Not to mention the workshop and tools he provided for me to work on timepieces. And with the knowledge of plantation management I could work anywhere. More importantly, he taught me the ways of the loup garou and how to survive.

Yet I knew I would never leave this area. Even that very night in my bedroom with the balcony doors open wide to catch the slightest late-summer night breeze, I remarked how much I loved this land. The scent of late magnolia blossoms; ouisatch and oleander; the curtains of moss cascading from giant cypress and oak; the sound of the night owl seeking his prey (or mate); the soothing patter of rain and the thunderous roll of an approaching storm- all this I loved- all this was my home.

7

For the next two days the entire plantation was buzzing about with exciting preparations. The landscaping was done to perfection: Weeds were pulled, hedges and grass trimmed; the huge oak alley was cleared of trash, dead fallen limbs and horse manure; any muddy holes in the carriage drive were filled in. The ballroom was immaculate; the wooden floors were polished to a high gleam; inviting- waiting for the dance to begin. Gerard and I made sure that every slave had their hands busy. A few of the females were sewing Gerard's and my fine clothes for tonight.

On the day of the party, I was mostly in my workshop finishing the repair on the longcase clock Gerard had failed to completely destroy. After manufacturing more than a few metal pieces on the forge, I finished work on it that very afternoon and thanks to my superfine eyesight and quick dexterity, I had it set up in the foyer again with its old familiar soothing tick. Setting the time to my pocketwatch, I realized it was time to get ready for the evening,s festivities. As for the longcase I did not care whether Gerard minded or not. It felt good to have my old friend back.

"What is that monstrosity doing back here?" He yelled. "Henri!"

I met him coming down the stairs. "Yes, Gerard, I repaired it. Please, do not do anything rash." I put a hand on his chest. "You will sense that the spirit is gone. It will no longer trouble us. This is only a clock, now."

"It is strange, but I never had the sense that the damned thing was haunted, until that bell from hell began to ring!" He looked closely at me, scrutinizing my thoughts. "Did you know about the ghost before then? You did didn't you?"

"Yes, from my first night in the house."

"Strange I never felt it."

"It just did not make its presence known to you, that's all. Now let us go upstairs and get ready. It will be dark soon."

"From the first night, you say?" For the first time, I saw Gerard exhibit bewilderment. "Why you? Why not me?"

"Never mind. Come." I grabbed his hand to lead him upstairs. It was just as well that he not observe the clock too closely for now, even though I was confident the spirit had fled. Still to this day, I wonder what previous incarnation had possessed the clock. Some one who obviously had a resentment or anger towards Gerard-such as the original owner of Sans Souci.

Our clothes were laid out on each other's respective beds. French finery for a lavish party of colonial gentry. Lace cuffs, well-tailored vests, polished black shoes with silver buckles (which made my feet ache at first). Our 'costumes' were matching and with our faces and hands transformed, no one (except the most perceptive) would be able to distinguish us apart.

The downstairs had been completely transformed for a gala befitting a plantation twice Sans Souci's size. The house was lit like daylight with crystal chandeliers in every room and silver candlesticks on every table next to offerings of meats and savories, cakes and candies. Gerard had his young boy dressed in a tuxedo, pouring champagne, coffee and beverages all night behind a sumptuous buffet in the dining room. Juliette, dressed in a traditional African robe of reds and greens with a matching headdress, strolled among the guests serving canopies and finger foods. Her demeanor was so elegant and calm, almost regal for such a young girl born a slave. She reminded me again of my Selena.

And, that night, she was even more beautiful than usual. Her complexion, glowing soft and dark, was free of blemish; her large black eyes shined with innocence, yet with knowing. She still had a small amount of that facial fullness which young girls have and later lose as a woman. Yet her young figure showed every curve of a developed woman. However, she was an inexperienced virgin, and whenever I saw her I could not help but think of that day when I saw her bathing and how delightful her untouched body must feel, and ..I grow excited.

The guests began arriving at twilight. It became a beautifully clear summer night, balmy and sultry; the moon rose, full and near, on the horizon. Earlier in the day dark storm clouds had gathered and thunder threatened, so Gerard concocted a spell to change the course of the storm which supposedly worked. All I knew for certain was we would have no rain tonight. Only moonlight- and the power it gives.

The costumes that evening were certainly not of the common or usual sort. These colonial folk, whether poor or rich, knew how to dress in masquerade! I saw clowns, animals and beasts, catwomen, feathers and sequins everywhere. There were those with small masks that covered only their eyes and then others had huge feathered headdresses or wigs and some sported large heads of plaster characters that looked wickedly unwieldy, yet they bore them expertly on their neck and shoulders. Goblins and hobgoblins, ingenious creations all- and I was able to see each and every one for Gerard and I, defying convention, greeted the guests together, at the front door as they alighted from their carriages. Our so-called costumes were quite popular and we were complemented many times on their realism. I could not resist following Gerard's lead, occasionally displaying wet fangs to the delightful squeals of young impressed ladies who had tried to feel my furry face..

Outside was not only decorated for the ball with stringed lanterns and torches, but there Gerard provided unique entertainment. He had a space cleared on the back brick patio (where he and I had our first real conversation) for a group of scantily clad male trapeze artists, performing difficult acrobatics of strength, skill and dexterity. Bowling and horseshoes were played on one side of our lawn near the kitchen and my workshop. On the other side, by the bath, a large table had been provided for a fortune teller to give readings. At first I thought the girl was Marie- that voodoo priestess who seemed to always slip back into my life- doing the fortunes and reading the tarot. But this was just for entertainment and not meant to be taken serious. Marie was above such a tawdry display. For mere amusement, I had the dark-complexioned native woman tell my fortune. I mistook her for a mere charlatan.

However, after I cut the tarot cards, she made an interesting observation. "Death. Death is all around you." She gave me a worried look and turned over another card. I saw her hesitate.

"Yes? What does it say?"

She looked up at my wolf's face. "It would seem that the family you left behind is in danger of some sort."

"From what? From whom?" I growled and snapped.

She shook her head. "I am not sure." She turned over another card.

"From a man or a woman?"

She would not look at me directly, but replied simply,

"From- you!" She then turned over the last card, but I had had enough and started to leave. "Wait monsieur!" she called me back. "The cards have one more message, which I cannot interpret nor understand. Something about a mirror." She looked at me with curiosity. "They are saying for you to 'look in the mirror'. Perhaps you know the meaning?" She gathered the cards together for the next person in line.

I left abruptly. Yes, I knew the meaning and I started to go upstairs right away and summon the magical mirror awake, however I thought I would wait until the right moment later in the night when Gerard would be preoccupied with guests and the party, then I could sneak upstairs.

It was uncanny that she knew about me leaving my family. And then there was her statement about death. Maybe she did have fortune telling abilities. But where had Gerard found her? Perhaps she was a student of Marie's. I dismissed the episode temporarily and joined the party in the ballroom.

Gerard had hired a five-piece orchestra to play for the evening and the large room was already crowded with people dancing- their colorful costumes swirling to waltzes, minuets and local folk dances. Gerard, in his wolf's costume, was in the very midst of it. He was enjoying a waltz with a rather tall girl who had arrived dressed as a boy.

I had already met her (and her two companions) at the door when they arrived. She was apparently a friend of Gerard's (the only 'friend' I knew him to have) and she lived in the colonial capital. I do not recall all their names, but I most assuredly remember their costumes, for all three had definitely defied convention.

The girlfriend of Gerard's had brought another female and a male along with her. They were all dressed in the gender of their opposite sex. The two girls wore tuxedos, had their short hair combed back and, to most of the

guests I am sure, they were two young males, however
effete. Reading their thoughts, I knew they were sexually
involved with each other, but the one who knew Gerard
had another, great deep secret, that I could not unravel.
She obviously had strong willpower over her thoughts
and actions, much like Gerard and myself. Perhaps she
was a witch.

The young man dressed as a woman, fooled most all
of the guests, including the ladies! He had on a gown of
satin red, decollete, matching gloves, shoes and jewelry.
The 'wig' was his own natural shoulder length black
raven hair. His black mask sprouted red hawk feathers.
Dark red lipstick and rouge completed the facade and I
know he turned many men's heads, who had no earthly
idea they were lusting after another male.

Gerard desired the young man also and I knew
immediately, that the female friend of his had brought
along the man just for him. At the time, I supposed it was
for sensual pleasures, though I should have known
differently. Practically all the dances were led by Gerard
and 'the woman in red'.

He did save one dance for us- a tango. We were very
celebrated in our 'wolf's clothing', dancing together in a
tight embrace. Though I had never danced a tango
before, I instinctively followed his lead easily, seeing in
his mind the next step beforehand. We moved as one
and my mind began to wonder if lovemaking with him
would be as naturally smooth as this.

There was one other costumed guest who attracted
my curious attention, in particular. A diminutive figure
(most likely a woman) it was cloaked only in a dead
man's shroud. I could see no face, but if it had a scythe, it
would have resembled death itself come to call. She was
completely cloaked; showed no hands, face or any flesh.
I also received no thoughts or even simple feelings from
the character which made me that much more curious.
As far as I could tell, it merely floated around the house

and grounds, consuming neither food nor drink and not speaking to or acknowledging any person. I remarked about the deathly figure to Gerard when I finally managed a moment alone with him.

Did you notice the guest dressed as death?

Yes, strange. What do you make of it?

I cannot guess. I believe it to be female, but the thoughts are blocked to me. I cannot read her mind.

Neither can I. Most remarkable. That means one of two things. Either she is a witch or some sort of voodoo priestess (of which there are more than a few in this land) or. .

Or it is death itself paying us a visit!

Gerard laughed at my idea and then placed his furry face close to mine and whispered his thought in my ear. "Later, towards the end of the night, I will unmask the thing and I want you there to witness what sort of creature it might actually be."

I started to make a suggestion as to whom I thought it may be, but we were interrupted by a group of rowdy guests and we parted. Moments later, Gerard had been joined once again by his male/female date for a dance.

The party and dancing went on into the early hours of the morning, but it was at midnight (I was in the foyer when the clock struck twelve) when I realized Gerard and his date had disappeared for an extended length of time. Perhaps they had gone upstairs, perhaps they went for a walk under the lighted oak canopy. Now might be an opportune time to gaze into Gerard's magic mirror and ask about Selena, Pierre and grandma-ma, even though I put very little faith on what that amateur fortune teller had told me.

I bounded up the stairs, but at his bedroom doorway I promptly forgot about my reason for coming upstairs. I sensed that someone was in the storage room. It was Gerard and his companion- and I smelled.. blood. Gerard was feasting!

Hunger possessed me immediately and passionately, but I refused it and turned to leave. However, Gerard's voice called to me from inside the locked room. "Come in, Henri." And I could not resist.

Unlocking the door with my witch's power, I slowly entered not quite knowing what to expect. What I saw was nothing near what would have entered into my imagination.

Gerard was in one corner, lying naked on a pile of blankets, in human form with the young man he had danced with all night, lying beside him also unclothed, his throat bit in two and his midsection tore open from sternum to navel! Gerard raised his face to me, his mouth and chest covered in the poor boy's blood.

Yet what happened next was extremely startling even for me. Behind me, I heard a low, unfamiliar growl from the other side of the room- the growl of a wild animal, but not that of a wolf! Turning slowly I saw, on a dusty, torn settee, a huge black panther devouring a girl's nude body! I recognized the dead girl as the 'boy' that had been brought to the party by Gerard's friend. Then the large cat, itself, must actually be the other girl- Gerard's tall friend who had supplied the victims for the night!

So she was another shape-shifter- though of a different sort, not ruled by the moon like us. Mon Dieu! A true catwoman! And that was the black secret within her! She snarled nastily at me and my interruption then, clutching her victim in powerful jaws, the cat (as silent as the grave) took one gigantic bound and disappeared out the balcony doors leaving behind a thin trail of blood. It leapt to the ground and was in the woods in a matter of seconds. No one would have believed their own eyes! As it was, none of the guests apparently saw the black shadow, it had moved so swiftly, like my Montesquieu.

"Come join me." Gerard beckoned. I wanted to leave, but could not turn away. "I know you are hungry, Henri. Please- feast." Still I hesitated. He walked over to me and held out his bloody hand. I transformed into my human form, but still, I did not move. He took one dripping finger and, touching my lips, smeared thick fresh blood over them. I licked it off, sensually and slowly, then I sucked the blood off each of his fingers one at a time. No longer able to resist, I undressed and joined him in his midnight feast.

After we had our fill, I had to ask him why he never told me there were others similar to us."Well, when I met her she was human." We cleaned ourselves and the room quickly while we talked. "She was my intended victim, but her thoughts showed that she desired to be like me, an immortal." He paused while wrapping up the dismembered corpse in a tarp which he probably kept hidden just for such a purpose. Looking at me he spoke, "Much like your native warrior, she wanted me to bite her, but not fatally. Though even a superficial scratch usually results in the human's death. "

"But I do not understand. Shouldn't she be a wolf?" I had piled all the bloody sheets and clothes into a bundle.

"Perhaps if I had bitten her and fate allowed her to live. I do not know if there is such a thing as a she-wolf," he pondered. "Instead I used witchcraft."

My breath drew in audibly and it was my turn to pause amidst our bloody labors. "So, basically, you did to her what Satine had done to you?"

"Not at all!" he snapped back. "She was a willing victim. I was not!" We resumed our work in silence for a few minutes while he calmed down. "Gabriel will throw the corpse and clothes in the bog after the guests have left."

We finished cleaning up, changed into fresh clothes and started back to rejoin the others. He stopped me on the landing.

Let me explain one thing.

There is no need. But he continued.

I put the spell on her mostly just to see if it would

succeed.

Well, it did.

I also did it for her. She hated her human life.

Because like you, she was a lover of her own gender?

Yes. Exactly. He glanced my way with amusement. You are most perceptive, Henri.

Sometimes I wish I was not so perceptive and was still the naive Frenchman who first came to this land.

He chuckled at me. We then transformed our faces and hands back, descended the stairs and in an instant were among our guests with the party still in full swing, most everyone becoming well inebriated. At the bottom of the stairs, I stopped him. I had to ask, "Do you see her often?"

"Occasionally."

"Does she ever have- regrets? About her decision?"

"Of course not," was his tart reply as he wandered off into the music room greeting some tiny mayor of some tiny nearby village and his portly wife.

I wondered just how true his last statement was and- more importantly- I also wondered how long I would carry my own regrets with me.

The party ended with the rising sun, but just before dawn, I had the most profound and sudden sense that Gerard required my presence. I was in the music room at the front of the house, listening to an excellent classical tune being played expertly on the harpsichord, when I knew I needed to seek him out and quickly. Following my intuitions, I found him in the study alone with the small guest dressed as Death. I closed and bolted the door behind me. Gerard (now in his human form) was demanding the figure to show him or herself. I carelessly transformed back to Henri, not thinking it would matter to the cloaked individual.

"Who are you? Show yourself! Remove your hood."
The figure made no attempt to comply, but merely stood
there silently, demonstrating no movement, showing not
even a sign of life.

"I repeat- Who are you?" Gerard's anger was
mounting. I drew in closer to them. "You are uninvited
and I demand that you show yourself!" Still there was no
response or movement and Gerard could contain himself
no longer. He grabbed the little figure by the shoulders
and shook it with extreme violence. I was about to
intervene when the hood fell off the figure and its true self
was revealed to us.

Both of us were in disbelief. It was a death head
staring at us, a skull. The figure was a walking skeleton!
Gerard let go of the thing and instinctively, we drew back
away from it. As we gazed in shock upon it, the fleshless
jaw dropped, remaining open, and a hollow voice
seemed to issue from it.

Sounding as if it were traveling over a great distance,
it was a deep male voice, perhaps originating as far away
as hell itself. "Beware, Gerard Mereaux! Your demise is
at hand. Death is nigh. For you and those you love.
Beware!"

"No!" Gerard raised his hand and punched the
monstrous thing with all his strength and fury. But his fist
hit only air! The cloak fell to the ground, empty, before
Gerard could connect. The living skeleton had simply
vanished into thin air! Even Gerard was astounded by it
all. He grabbed the fallen garment in frustration.

I could not help but voice my bewilderment. "Could
that actually have been Death itself?"

"I do not know, mon ami. But it was certainly here to
give me a warning. I do not know what sort of
supernatural messenger that- entity- was, however, I do
know who sent it. Which means..", his voice trailed off.
He threw the garment roughly into the fireplace and

proceeded to light it, while I finished his thought.

"It means the witch is quite near and knows all about us and- our homes!"

"Yes," was his only reply. He watched the clothing start to catch ablaze.

"We must prepare ourselves."

"Yes. " He did not look up, but stood staring intently into the increasing fire.

"I will go into that secret room and demand the book reveal itself to me. And I will not leave the room until it does!" I declared boldly. Then I paused hoping my next question did not sound pathetically helpless. "What else can we do?"

I could tell he was in deep thought as he walked over to me. "Yes, we need a plan of action. And the first thing to do is enlist the aid of an old friend and through her second sight we will know how to proceed."

Right away, I knew who he meant- The voodoo priestess, Marie. The same one from the ceremony. A friend of grandma-ma's. "An old friend of yours?" I threw an accusatory glance at him. "I am learning quite a bit about you and your 'old friends' tonight, eh, Gerard?"

He paid my remark no mind, continuing, "Let us say, she is an old- acquaintance. Though she will help us if I ask."

"Why? Why would she want to help you? Us? Does she not think of the loup garou as demons? An evil travesty of nature?"

"Non, non, mon ami. She realizes we are as natural as the clouds and rain. After all, it is the heart that is evil or good, not the man. Besides," he lowers his voice to a conspiratorial whisper, "she herself, has many great powers. She is quite possibly the strongest psychic I have ever encountered in my long life."

"Besides all that," I tried not to let my reluctance to bring her into our affairs show too much, but I feared I was failing, "is the book not enough? Whatever it says.

You have read it. Don't you know?"

"I am not totally convinced it is enough. I want to be prepared in every way. I want to be stronger; I want you stronger too. I cannot help but feel there is some element missing. Just what- I do not know, however a séance will tell us."

"Séance!" I should have expected that.

"Yes, a séance." He nodded. "Why not? We have done it ourselves, you and I, remember?"

"And we were successful, non?" He nodded again. I could tell he was ready to leave the study and join the lingering guests. The garment was almost completely consumed by now. "Then why don't you and I perform the séance ourselves?" He started shaking his head. "But.." I wanted to continue arguing, except he interrupted me.

"Non, non, mon cher. When it becomes very personal (like this is), it is best for an objective personality to make the spiritual connection. Besides she has great experience at contacting the other side. Comprendre?" I nodded, reluctantly acknowledging his sound reasoning. "Bon, it is settled then. I will send her a note requesting she visit Sans Souci as soon as possible!" He patted me on the shoulder. "Come, let us join the stragglers left. We may have to burn the place down to get them to leave!" He laughed loudly, his good humor having returned. It was not so easy for me. "Perhaps there is more of that excellent champagne still left. It is good, n'est-ce pas?"

"Yes," I agreed and smiled as we strolled out the door, his arm about my shoulders- doubts still circling in my head. "Yes, it is very good, indeed."

The morning after the wild festivities, the plantation hands were again busy. All day long- cleaning, washing, mopping and picking up after all the many guests; arranging the rooms and furniture back to their usual state. I calculated there must have been at least two hundred people to visit Sans Souci last night.

Other than that, we observed an ordinary day on the plantation. However, it was to be that night which would change the course of our lives and lay the foundation for combating the witch.

Marie arrived as the sun was setting, the very evening after the ball. It was almost as if she had known of Gerard's beckoning even before our decision to contact her! She wore a fine Caribbean robe of solid dark green leaving her shoulders bare. Her rusty-red curly hair was tied up in a crimson sash. It was Toussaint who first observed her in the oak alley approaching the house on foot. I watched in wonder as her tall and stately figure slowly strolled beneath the majestic oaks in the fading light and I was again reminded of Selena. The voodoo queen was alone and in island sandals.

Curiosity getting the best of me, I tried to read her mind, but she allowed me to gain only a few thoughts. The main fact I gathered, and which I wanted to know, was she felt no fear. In fact, she was perfectly calm- even pleased to be here and to help if she could. I was not able to tell just how she had been able to travel here so quickly, but logic told me she could not possibly have walked the complete distance.

To my mild surprise, she and Gerard did greet each other almost as if they truly were old friends, kissing each other on the cheeks as was the custom. I knew they were communicating with each other in silent thoughts, so I did not intrude by trying to read their conversation. I doubt they would have permitted me the privilege at any rate. She wore no jewelry, save for some long emerald earrings and one tiny ring of emerald and gold. I made notice that there was no pentagram or talisman around her neck or close to her heart which would protect her from evil demons, witches or loup garou. She obviously felt safe with us for she appeared to have no silver on her person at all.

"And this, Marie," Gerard proudly introduced me, "C'est mon ami- Henri LeBlanc."

"Mademoiselle," I bowed and kissed her hand.

She looked at Gerard. "So this is the handsome companion you spoke of. I agree, tres beau." She turned back to me. "It is a pleasure to see you again Monsieur."

So she did remember me from the ceremony! I tried not to blush from her scrutinizing look, as I wondered just where and when they had spoken to each other about me. "Please, call me Henri." She took back her hand gracefully and we three turned and went arm in arm up the stairs to the front door and yet. . .I felt so strange. (Of course, I could not dwell upon it for they would read my nervousness). The last (and first) time I saw Marie, she was officiating the voodoo ceremony where I became so violently sick before transforming for the first time. It was also the night I first saw Gerard in his human form. And also when my prize horses were slaughtered by....I drew in a deep breath.

Since that time, I had become almost a different person and I wondered how I must appear to her, yet I did not receive any reaction from her. They were deep in their own private, silent conversation. Her demeanor was cool and collected; her mind very disciplined. I knew well- she let me discern only that which she allowed.

She, however, had not changed at all- her carriage and regal manner were just the same. Actually, she was even more impressive today, for we were close to one another, friendly and cordial. She still had the dignified and elegant bearing of Selena, combined with the intellect and regality of grandma-ma. I felt like I was in the presence of actual royalty...and I suppose I was.

'It is good to see an old friend's familiar face once more.'

"It is good to see you again, aussi, Marie. I am honored that you came so quickly.'

'I had to, especially upon the strength of your note.' Marie looked about the house as we entered. 'The witch- she will make her appearance soon- I believe.'

'Yes, and Henri and I must be prepared. You can- advise us?'

'I will do what I can. Tonight, the stars are auspicious. However, as you are well aware, contacting the other side can sometimes yield knowledge- sometimes it can yield only disappointment.'

He nodded. 'We understand. Come let us go upstairs. I have a room and table arranged where we will not be disturbed.'

Gerard led us up to the storage room which, at one time or another, he must have had the house slaves clean up, dust and prepare just for this occasion. The room was empty save for a table and three chairs. The curtains were closed and I lit the solitary candle on the table to provide our only light in the dark room. Gerard closed the door behind us.

Before Marie took her seat at the table, she walked over to the mock fireplace and put a hand gently on the wall of the secret panel. She said nothing, but we knew, that she knew a room was behind the panel.

"Shall we proceed?" She positioned herself comfortably at one end of the table and held her hands out for each of us to hold so we would form an unbroken circle. We sat down and complied.

She closed her eyes and began the ceremony. Calling upon her spiritual contact, she began to sway ever so slightly and her voice became poetic, almost as if she were singing. Only a few minutes had passed before I felt the presence in the room with us, yet I could see no apparition. I thought perhaps the entity would deign to speak through Gerard or myself, but at first, the only voice we heard was that of Marie's sing-song supplication.

"We are honored by your presence, my Lord, and we pardon disturbing your peaceful rest. However, we urgently seek your guidance for these two are under a heavy curse and we need to know, my Lord. We need to know how to successfully combat a most powerful witch- a witch known through the ages in various forms, by various names- the ancient one who calls herself- 'Satine'." At the mention of the name, the candle flickered noticeably as a wave of sharp coldness descended upon us. "She has sworn to destroy these two and all that they care for!"

She began swaying even more, her body rocking to and fro. Her eyes staying closed, she started mumbling in Latin, her voice changing until it was no longer Marie who we heard, but rather, the deep bass voice of a man, an elderly man. The words slowly became clear and distinct in the French we were accustomed to. A long moan emanated from deep within her. Gerard and I dared not move a muscle. Suddenly, she stopped swaying and sat straight and rigid, not moving even a single eyelash.

"The one of whom you speak is a most powerful sorceress. She is legend! The mighty witch has lived for many centuries and is known by different names in different parts of the world- an Egyptian succubus, the gorgon from Greece. She is a servant of the ancient dark gods, protected by the sun god and is a creature of fire. The Phoenix- the one witch that fire cannot destroy! To be true she can never be completely destroyed, but will rise again from her own ashes."

"But there must be a way!" Gerard spoke to the entity within Marie. "A way to perhaps capture her or send her back to oblivion where she will be unable to harm us."

Marie turned her head, her closed eyes staring at Gerard. "There is a way- only one way- and it will be a most dangerous task for all of you. She can kill with a single thought! If you fail in this endeavor, it will mean the end of you and yours."

"If I am to die, I would rather die fighting. So pray, old wise one, tell us how to combat this evil."

"It requires three. A trinity of powers. Only then can this great witch be conquered. But it must be orchestrated with precise timing and quickness in order to be decisive." The voice paused.

Gerard and I looked at each other in bewilderment. "What three? Are you speaking of witchcraft or..?"

The voice suddenly continued, interrupting Gerard. "The first that I speak of is at this table. The wolf who walks as a man! It is he who will commence and end the battle."

"Good, for there are two of us and.."

The voice interrupted Gerard again. "There will be only one loup garou at this battle." Gerard shrugged at me, but we let the old voice continue. "The second is the spirit of the one who has the most reason to hate the witch. An enemy ghost is the one power the witch cannot destroy or control. The one entity this witch will fear!"

"But I am the one who hates her the most and I am very much.."

"It must be a ghost- a spirit which she cannot control- the ghost that can destroy witches!"

"A witch hunter?" Gerard whispered.

"I am not able to see what the incarnation called itself when it walked upon the earth, though it is the second being necessary to destroy her." Gerard started to speak, but the voice continued, Marie's closed eyes now turning to me. "You will know when to contact the spirit, just as you did tonight to contact me."

"But who?" This time it was I who whispered an

interruption.

"You will know when the time comes," was all it said. "You will know!" Marie's body started rocking to and fro in an ever increasing manner, faster and faster, almost violently. Gerard and I looked with concern at her. The voice was now moaning louder, more insistent and when it finally resumed speaking it was tinged with mounting anxiety.

"The third!" The old man's voice was a hiss. "The third is a creature I have never seen the likes of before. Buried deep in the earth for many centuries it is stronger than ten loup garou. I do not quite understand the nature of this monster,(perhaps a god who fell from grace), but it is a fearful sight. And when it is awakened there will be nothing on earth or in heaven that can stop it. It is most powerful! It is relentless!" The excited voice rose ever higher in pitch, full of anxiety and awe. "Its enemies will all be hunted down and destroyed, even if it takes an eternity. It is implacable! Only the one who awakened it can control it. Beware though- Be on guard! Lest you lose that control."

Gerard and I were mystified, but the voice continued, slightly softer, slightly calmer. "Rising from its long slumber, all others will bow before it. Even the spirit world fears it." There was a hesitation. "I see it clearly- it is cloaked only in the musty, moldouring wrappings he was buried in!" The voice began to rise, insistent again; it grew to a shout that I feared the whole household would be able to hear. "It will seek out its revenge! It will seek out the witch! The only creature which can contain her and her powers; the only one able to take her back to the inferno. Slow moving, deadly- it smells of the crypt- of centuries of death. I cannot look upon it, do not force me to look!" There was a pause then Marie issued a shrill shriek of fear and her eyes opened wide. The spirit's voice was full of alarm. "Its eyes are ageless- red as ox blood; they can see across the oceans and the centuries.

They see me! They see us! Do not look on them or you are his slave! Yet I cannot turn away." Another terrified shriek and then Marie closed her eyes and began swaying and circling in such an agitated manner that I could barely keep hold of her hand. "A face, a monster most foul, it feeds upon fear itself!" The voice stopped suddenly and the room was filled with dark silence.

Marie's body slowly halted rocking and swaying and she became quite still. Gerard and I sat dumbfounded and perplexed with so many questions we did not know where to begin. In fact, there were more questions now than when we began the séance. The voice spoke once more, as if from some great distance, sounding like an echo. It was returning to its netherworld.

"Look to the book. The book of life and death. There lies the incantation necessary to revive the monster!" The voice was fading fast. "Be very careful- Look..to the.. book." and then it was quiet. Marie slumped gently forward and we knew the presence had left. We all remained silent and still for a moment, with our hands remaining clasped together.

Taking in a deep breath, she slowly raised her head, opened her eyes and looked about the table at our stunned faces. And though she regained her stately and composed figure quickly, I was still able to see that the seance had drained her physically. Gerard was the first to speak.

"You are alright, Marie?" She nodded, but did not speak. "Shall I get you a glass of wine?" She nodded again. He rose, "I will get us each a glass."

As soon as he left the room, she turned to me. "You should return soon to your home. The witch will most probably come to you first to try and turn you against Gerard. Remember, no matter how she appears, she is a threat to you and your family."

Yes, I silently agreed. I needed to go back and make sure they were safe and relate all that has happened. To see them once more before making battle. I found myself completely committed to destroying the witch because I felt I had a vital stake in the plantation and the welfare of Sans Souci. I wanted to see it survive! Besides anyone who is close to Gerard, as I was, would feel her wrath.

He entered carrying a tiny tray with a small decanter of his wine and three full glasses. We each took a sip before speaking. "Do you know what just happened, Marie? Do you remember any part of the séance?"

She shook her head. "I remember very little and understand even less." She continued on answering Gerard's next question even before he was able to voice it. "For some reason I only recall the number three. That the number three is important in some way in order to defeat her. And," she hesitated, "I felt that my spiritual contact was most disturbed by some... thing? in his vision." She sipped her wine, obviously becoming more relaxed. "What or whom, I could not gather. I suppose the witch." Her last statement was posed more like a question, as she looked earnestly, first at Gerard, then at us both. We gave no immediate reply, so she continued. "I do hope this night has been of some help."

"Yes, of course. We are so grateful that you came." I bowed my head in agreement. "Tell me," he leaned forward, closer to Marie, "have you ever heard of this witch who threatens us? Or her name- Satine?"

"I have never seen or met her, yet do know of her. I particularly, have heard that her powers, over time, have become immeasurable, virtually unlimited." Finishing her wine, she stood up to leave. "Make sure you follow whatever instructions you were given, Gerard. None of you will survive if you do not. You have chosen a most dangerous adversary."

"Unfortunately, it has been chosen for us." We escorted her downstairs and outside to the front steps. A thick fog was rolling in which I thought was a bit unusual for this time of night, particularly since it was still late summer. It occurred to me that it was almost like a living thing, moving purposely towards us.

At the bottom of the steps, she turned, kissed us both on the cheek and said, "Adieux, mes vieux. Et bonne chance!" She then raised her arms, majestically, as if beckoning someone forward. The fog obediently rushed in, engulfing her in a thick swirl. She walked a short way and then her figure disappeared completely into the encircling cloud and it quickly moved away from the house and down the oak alley, taking her with it.

Gerard spoke in answer to my questioning mind. "Even Marie must protect herself from the witch and cloak her person in a dense cloud so as not to be followed." He glanced about. "She is watching from afar. Waiting. Satine has the unique ability to be everywhere at once. A truly ubiquitous being."

"Whatever we are to do, we must do quickly." I added a question as an afterthought. "It was my understanding that Marie did not like loup garou."

He looked at me and chuckled. "To a degree, I suppose, however she hates this witch even more and realizes that her evil, if it takes hold in this land, will lay waste to Sans Souci and then other plantations, eventually devouring the countryside parish by parish."

"So the fog- It is her..?"

"Yes, it serves as Marie's familiar. Some have cats or animals," he stared intently at me, searching my mind, "others a gargoyle or some such mythological creature as their familiar." He paused while I tried not to think about familiars, especially my own. "You are keeping a secret from me," he spoke flatly without emotion, but then he shrugged.

"Well it is of no consequence. Though I will say it is good how you are now able to control your thoughts and block them from those who would intrude inside your mind. That ability will be most helpful against the witch!" He slapped the banister soundly, "Now let us go inside, have our usual brandy and cigars and try to make some sense out of what we learned this night."

I followed him into the study, doubting that I would be of much help in discerning the meanings of what was spoken during the séance. The usual tray of brandy, café-au-lait and cookies was waiting and so was Mercutio. The boy had left the monkey in the room alone, but Mercutio was at his usual perch on the back of my favorite armchair. His chattering started as soon as we entered and scampering over to Gerard, he climbed up his leg and shirt, and crouched himself upon his shoulder to ask for a treat.

Gerard gave him a piece of cookie."I have told him repeatedly not to leave the animal alone in here, stupid boy!" Gerard always spoke his mind when he was angry and I knew from experience that he could turn violent at a spur of the moment. It was also my impression that, on occasion, he slapped the young man. Gerard could be a sexual sadist and the poor boy probably had the scars to prove it. They were most likely even violent in their lovemaking.

We sat and sipped our hot coffee. "How civilized we are," I remarked, "sitting here enjoying these fine things; soon we might be fearing for our lives."

"Not fearing," he corrected me. "Fighting! Fighting for these very things we enjoy now so casually."

"Which means the utter destruction of another immortal."

"She will not have it any other way. And even if she did- I would not. Not after what she did to Andre." His pause was only for the tiniest moment, but I could feel that his pain was, nonetheless, profoundly deep. Let us not speak aloud mon ami. The walls have ears. She is the closest being I know of that can truly be described as omnipotent. So..

So that is why it requires three different immortals to defeat her.

Exactly. The three- he echoed the words in his mind- the three. A werewolf-

A phantom and the third? Some sort of zombie?

No, not a zombie, exactly. He shook his head. I do not know positively, though I have an idea what the presence was referring to. Let us discuss that creature last. Now, he clapped his hands together and began strolling about the room, carrying his cup and saucer, occasionally sipping from it. I remained seated, excited but serious over this mystery, trying to remain calm. After all, what we were discussing could easily end as death for me. For my family; for Gerard; for any of us. For Juliette and Toussaint; for all of us. He continued our analysis of the séance.

One werewolf. Then the question is- who? You or I?

But we must conquer the witch together.

Yes, that is a given. Which means the other of us is..

The other of us is the phantom.

Yes, the spirit. The second enemy of the witch.

Which means that..

One of us must die!

The thought only then, hit me like a powerful blow to the stomach- I literally became ill and had to prevent myself from vomiting. I tried to remain composed. But we do not know that for certain?

She said- he had to correct himself- the voice said we must use the spirit of the one who hates her the most. That would be myself.

I am sure Satine has many enemies we could summon. It is the powers of the ghost that we need. The power to move objects- to create wind, fire and whatever else. I have read and studied all about the spirit world. I think, like you mentioned at the séance, a ghost of a witch hunter should do. Perhaps he would have heaven on his side.

Perhaps. He sat back down and pondered my thoughts while stroking his goatee absent- mindedly, until he seemed to reach some decision. But I still think not. It is best that you and I combat the witch together.

But…

But if we call up a long ago enemy of hers or some witch hunter long dead, we will not have as much control over him and the situation.

If we are the ones who summon the spirit, then it must obey us and return to the grave when we command it to.

In theory. And what if he is so powerful, and wishes to live again- inside someone. It will then possess that individual. He could even possess you and Henri LeBlanc would be no more.

I shrugged. There is always an exorcism.

Which sometimes works and sometimes they are a complete failure. Non, mon ami, it is too risky. He paused in contemplative thought again, taking a long sip of coffee. Besides, and think hard on this, if it is I who returns, I will be the ghost of a loup garou. I shall still have my powers as a werewolf and as a warlock!

Plus new powers as a spirit?

Yes, yes. Exactly. His thoughts were becoming full of excitement as he rose and poured us both a brandy. That must be it! He handed me my glass. Do you realize, my powers would be immense. And that bitch will know true fear!

I could neither make sense nor argue with his reasoning. I, myself, felt true fear as we discussed death in such a cold, clinical manner. He seemed almost cheerful about it! The truth was it was impossible for me to imagine him not being in my life in some way. My, how I have changed in the last few months! Still, I had to voice my increasing concern out loud. "And afterwards? What about afterwards? You would have to return to the grave!"

Henri, mon cher! Do not be so negative! After her defeat, there can be an infinite number of possibilities for me. You know how intriguing the spirit world is- to you, to me. Ever since that clock. ...

You could possess someone?

Yes. He paused, sipping brandy, his mind wandering- I could not follow its direction. Yes, and I think I know just the perfect subject. What did he mean by that? Who did he have in mind? I tried to read that thought, but his mind hurriedly switched over to the next subject- Who then is the third party? What sort of creature?

You said you had an idea?

I remember, Satine once mentioning a love from long ago. In Egypt, where she first achieved her powers centuries ago. She denied his love in order to keep her powers and live forever.

And the lover? What happened to him?

I do not recall if she said. He must have died a horrible death, I am sure, if he was involved with her. I believe she betrayed him. Therefore, I have the notion that- this thing, if it is her old love- will seek revenge and take her back with him.

Yes, I remember. The voice said something about an implacable seeker of revenge. It will take her to the grave?

Or some such place, an oblivion where she can do no more harm against us, her powers neutralized. And so, he must be the only creature strong enough to capture her and bind her powers. I suspect our main mission- yours and mine- will be to tire her. Then when she is in a weakened state, we lure her into his eternal grasp. The creature will do the rest!

But where do we locate this monster? Egypt is far Gerard; we have no time! Besides it must be mere dust and ashes after all this time. And...

Try to recall Henri, the description the voice gave. Think of old Egypt- musty wrappings, eyes of ox-blood red, strong as ten of us, the smell of...

Realization hit. "A living mummy!" He nodded. I could not help but exclaim, " Mon Dieu!" as I slumped back in my chair, feeling the (now unusual) sensation of tiredness. Gerard rose and taking a bottle of absinthe from his cabinet, poured us both a generous portion. He brought over my glass to me and I drank it in one gulp. He sat down opposite me and lit a cigar. I could not exactly read what he was thinking. He had again, closed his mind to me for the moment, permitting me to know only what he wished me to know and nothing more.

"I know," he spoke slowly and deliberately, "some one in Alexandria."

"Egypt?" He nodded. "Who?"

"Dr. Francois Fontenot."

"What?" My boisterous exclamation startled Mercutio from his snoring slumber. I even startled myself. It would seem that Gerard was an endless source of surprises!

"He corresponded with me recently."

Unbelievable! "You have been in correspondence with that mad man?"

"Mad... perhaps. Brilliant, there is no denying." I shook my head. "After all Henri, he discovered the secret to life through scientific means. Mysteries the Gods are so jealous of."

"And you believe that?"

He hesitated, then replied very seriously, "Yes. Yes I do."

"Well, I do not!" was my thoughtless hasty retort. "I, I. . ." Then my mind went back to that figure in the cemetery; to the secret chamber and tunnel, the chains; the portrait in my room; to that strong hand pushing open the tomb. "Yes, I suppose that.. Yes, I believe!" I put my head in my hands feeling helpless. So much has happened; so much is still happening! And all of it so hard to contemplate, so difficult to grasp with all its ramifications. Ghosts and gods; mummies and monsters!

"You are tired, Henri. Perhaps we should continue this discussion over breakfast."

I regained my composure. "No, that is not necessary."

I drew in a deep breath. "If this man-made creature named Julian is real, then where is he? Does the good Doctor know?"

"No, he does not and I do not know the story behind the experiment at all. Julian must be nearby, but he does not want to be located- apparently. I cannot read or gather his distant thoughts. I have even tried to locate him using the enchanted mirror, but to no avail. It would seem that he is a normal man in appearance, but some thing is missing."

"What?"

He replied without hesitation or emotion. "He has no soul!" I was visibly appalled at that statement, but Gerard calmly continued, "You see Henri, Dr. Fontenot can revive the dead, yet he cannot revive, or create, a soul. Only a god can do that. I suppose," he added with a shrug.

I sat still for a minute trying to comprehend it all. His words seemed to make sense- If any of this supernatural world made sense. Then another light shone in my naive, dull and tired brain. "And so it is Julian whom you will seek out and possess once you become a body-less spirit."

He rose to pour himself a thimbleful of absinthe. "Precisely! You are most astute, Henri. More than you realize. But think on it- it is only logical. I will not be invading someone's own inherent sacred domain. Julian is an open receptacle. And.. I would still be in an immortal body!"

"If you can locate him."

"It might be a long search, but one I am willing to undertake." He looked out the window at the moon. "I really have no other choice, now do I." I never heard him sound so fatalistic before. He had always emphasized looking for options.

"Perhaps we should hunt. We still have a few more hours of night."

"Not tonight, Henri." Gerard had never before refused the offer to hunt. I understood- he had much on his mind; after all, he had more at stake then any of us.

I too needed answers to more questions for I certainly had my doubts about this plan of action. Mercutio was pulling on Gerard's pants leg, trying to get some attention. He shook the little monkey off and we paid him and his chatter no further mind. "Exactly what is the doctor doing in Egypt?"

He turned to me. "Still endeavoring to unravel the mysteries of life and death. He is on an expedition now." There was a long pause- "You know, Henri, I have been contemplating this battle of titans for some time and I believe the doctor can help us. As an excavator, he should be able to find the original sarcophagus containing the one whom Satine had once loved. The very tomb, may give us some answers. Any bit of knowledge about her past and origins will only help us in the end."

"And you trust the doctor?"

"Of course not, mon cher. However, he is quite in need of money in order to continue his research and experiments." Gerard's large smile showed his satisfaction with his own cleverness. "Once the proper sarcophagus and mummy are in our possession, he will be well rewarded."

"Do you think Satine's lover was a king or pharaoh?"

"I seriously doubt he was a leader of the people. More than likely he served in the pharaoh's court as a high priest or some such personage. It is my guess he fell in love with her, but it was forbidden for a priest to have-relations. So," he sat back down and looked at me intently. "As we both know from our studies, his punishment would have been.."

"To be buried alive as a mummy!" I finished his sentence with a sharp, breathless exclamatory sigh, my brain churning to find logic out of all this. Fortunately,

Gerard's mind was now open to me again and I could read his thoughts.

This will all take too much time, Gerard. It may take the doctor months to find and excavate the correct tomb. And even if he does find it, there will be another delay in shipping it here. We must have it here before the witch attacks.

He puffed thoughtfully on his cigar. I will have to send Gabriel.

To fly across the ocean? Into the rising sun? He will never accomplish it.

He will need to go the long way around the globe so as to stay in darkness.

Can he perform such a task? And bring the heavy sarcophagus back?

I do not know, but he will do as I ask. And he will either succeed or die trying.

Knowing all this, I did not hold out much hope for our victory. There were too many possibilities for failure. Please be more positive, Henri. I need for you to be confident.

And if Satine finds this information out?

Which is exactly why I have been warning you to be cautious and diligent about what we say, do or think. He sighed heavily and leaned back into his chair. It is also why I sometimes do not divulge so much information to you.

I can control my thoughts very well now. You just said so.

I know, I know. But she can be truly tricky. Mercutio was still scampering about, chattering loudly at both of us; however we chose to ignore him, so deeply involved were we in our conversation.

So then- my thoughts were finally coming full circle- the book will give..

Gerard spoke out loud. "It will give us the sacred formula and incantation which will make the mummy rise.

The book.." Gerard could not finish, for at the mention of the book, his tiny monkey started howling and leaping about on the furniture, like a wild deranged animal, eventually jumping up onto the mantelpiece and throwing pecans at us both.

Gerard jumped up, shouting, "Mercutio! Behave! What on earth has gotten into you." He started to grab the little primate, then stopped and turned. We both stared at each other with our mouths agape. "The book!" we shouted in unison.

We bolted up the stairs together to the secret room. The panel was closed, but a strange light emanated from behind the secret door. "It is awake and ready for you!" Gerard's excitement was palpable. I, too, was eager to read the book and fulfill my destiny. The hunger for knowledge was even more insatiable to me than my hunger for human flesh (if that were possible!). Of course, I can learn all I want with no sense of guilt.

I lit one of the lanterns as Gerard hurriedly opened the panel. There the book was on its podium, open to the very page we needed; a beacon of light shooting from the pages upwards to the ceiling; and, in a supreme illusion or trick of the eye (trompe d'oeil) it seemed to go on limitlessly out of the house and into the sky and heavens.

Gerard rushed to it first. "Can you read it, Henri? Can you interpret it?"

I picked up the book and holding it, the beam slowly diminished into the pages, until the only light produced was a soft greenish glow- a light by which I could read the once indecipherable words. The ancient foreign tongue was now gone and had been replaced with my own native language. "I can read it, Gerard! I can read it," I looked him in the eye, "and understand it!"

"Bon, bon! What does it say? Does it give the formula for the incense of revivification? Along with the spell?"

"Yes," I turned the pages. "The entire book is in French."

"You must commit it to memory, Henri. Write it down and memorize it. Now, immediately."

"Of course I will, but why hurry? The book is completely transcribable now. I can read it at leisure."

"Non, non, mon ami. It can change back upon you at any time! You must study it now and you must be exact. Any mistake may cost us dearly."

"Of course, Gerard." I replied calmly. "I will study it right away- all night and day if I must." I stared at him sharply, my mind growing accustomed to his methods. And to his lies. "Tell me, Gerard. Why must I be the one that interprets it? I thought the book had opened itself up to you previously, and you were able to read it."

He said nothing in reply, but stared back at me, finally defying me with the truth. "You lied to me Gerard! You never have been able to transcribe this. Not even a single page, for even a single moment. You lied to me." He still said nothing. "You are using me. You needed me all along, just for this task. Just for this one purpose!" I had to ask the all important question. "Was this your plan all along? To make me as you, so I would come here to Sans Souci searching for you and then be convinced to help you be rid of your sworn enemy?" Again, I got no answer from him, silently or verbally. I asked once more, "Did you change me to a werewolf deliberately, Gerard?"

"Non, mon cher." Gerard's tone was soft- sincere and loving. "It is as I told you our first night together." I let my mind travel deep into his subconscious, and he allowed it. There I discovered- that, yes- in this one thing he was being honest. My becoming a werewolf had not been planned. The schooling of me at witchcraft though, had been very deliberate. "In fact Henri, even a superficial bite from me results in death for a human. Fate or the universe- something- decided differently for you!"

He approached me slowly, the text still glowing in my hands. "I love you, Henri." He hesitated, "And I know, even without reading your mind, that you do care-something for me- a little also."

That was true, but I did not care to discuss our personal relationship at that moment. I turned to take the book into my room and study it, thinking I could probably finish the complete tome within twenty-four hours. Just then, the one lantern we had lighted was snuffed suddenly and mysteriously out. We could still see in the dark, with our wolf's eyes, the only light coming from the dim glow in the book. Gerard and I looked at each other in wonderment for a moment before the breeze began. A breeze that became a wind from nowhere; which soon surrounded us completely in a whirl. An impossible wind that should not have existed in that tiny airless, windowless room. It increased steadily in velocity, whipping papers and books about. The whirlwind was for Gerard and I. It was the witch!

"She is searching for us!" Gerard had to shout above the increasing din. "Quick, Henri. The invisibility spell. We must use it now. Did you perfect it?"

"Yes, and one better." I handed him the book to hold, while I bent down behind one of the shelves and pulled out a large thin white linen cloak. A gust of wind buffeted me, almost blowing the cloth out of my grasp.

"What is this?"

"Hurry, stand close to me." I covered us both completely and a moment later, enwrapped in my magical cloak, we stepped out of the secret room without being detected. The wind remained behind in that tiny space whirling about searching, while we stood there for some minutes, together under the invisibility cloak which I had created just for such a purpose. We listened to the wind die slowly down, quieting itself, until finally, nothing was left but the rustling of papers as they settled to the floor. She was gone.

"Amazing!" was all I could say. We entered into the upstairs hallway before removing our protective garb.

"What I am most amazed about is you, Henri."

"What do you mean?" I asked modestly.

"You. You are so seemingly always prepared for the unexpected. How clever to invent this magical cloth."

"It was simple. I merely put the spell on the cloak rather than myself and made it permanent. Some would call it a cursed item."

"I call it a miracle. Thank you my friend."

"The true miracle was that I had left it in that room."

He chuckled and, putting his hand on my shoulder, we strolled over to our rooms. "There is no time for us to lose, with her so close. I must send Gabriel away this very night." I cast a worried glance at him. "Do not fear. He will succeed and bring back the creature with him. You will see. And tomorrow I will go into town and send word to our Dr. Fontenot about what is afoot and why we need his help. And of course, what he can expect for recompense." We stopped outside his bedroom door and he handed me the still slightly glowing book.. "Now, I am going to change and take a bath and you.."

"I am going to start studying and will write down and memorize all that I feel is pertinent."

"Bon. Come and get me if you find some thing…truly enlightening."

"Gerard," I had one more question before saying goodnight. "How or..when do you plan on," I could not bring myself to say the words, "entering the spirit world?"

He caressed my cheek with his hand. "Do not concern yourself with that minute detail. Destiny will take the hand when it decides it is time. Now go- mon cher."

I embraced him briefly and then turned to go to my room, not looking back, though I did say, "Bonne nuit."

"Bonne nuit," he called after me.

Inside my room I made myself comfortable on the bed and concentrated on my task at hand. It would eventually take me two full nights and days to study the book of the dead which still emanated with power. I would read and reread, making notes and cross references; studying it cover to cover and over and over. And I tried my best not to think about anything else.

9

The next morning I breakfasted alone, Gerard having already saddled up and gone into the big city before dawn. He would not be back until the next day. Part of me wanted to go with him, for my having been there only once simply whetted my appetite, and I wanted to return to see and do more (and not just as a man during the day). But I knew this was the best opportunity to complete my research while Gerard was gone and tonight I could fly with Montesquieu without any worry of discovery.

"Be careful of the witch. She may be lurking about. Montesquieu will most likely be able to sense her presence before you do," was the only warning from Toussaint.

The young boy served me that morning, wearing his usual dignified attire. He was- noticeably- becoming less and less close-mouthed around me and much more solicitous. "Would you like anything else, Master Henri? Before I begin my other tasks?" he asked while pouring me a strong cup of chicory.

"No, I do not believe so." He started away. "But wait. I do not see any of Juliette's special sweet potato cakes. Could you please ask her for some? For me?" I added.

"I am sorry master Henri, but Juliette is sick this morning and is lying down for an early nap." He paused before leaving- the perceptive boy knowing of my affection for her: "But it is nothing serious according to her and most likely she will be back at her duties later in the day. Perhaps I could get one of the other cooks to make you the dish?"

"No, merci," for it would not be the same and I went back to my food and notes. "I will look in on her later today. Let me know if she starts to feel worse. That is all." Perhaps tomorrow morning or later this evening I might have a nice long chat with the boy (if he permits it) and find out more about him. I shouted out an afterthought to him. "Oh, when Gerard's away you needn't dress up so formally for just me. Especially on such hot balmy days as this one." I crunched into a flaky biscuit smothered with strawberry jam..

He turned to me, speaking most earnestly, "Oh no, Monsieur Henri, I could not possibly do that, for if Master Gerard ever found out he would beat me within an inch of my life!" He quickly disappeared around the side of the house heading towards the kitchen.

I could feel his fear from here. He loved Gerard, but was also terribly afraid of him. I briefly thought, fancifully, that I should serve as his protector, then wisely realized that would probably make matters worse and Gerard would then take his anger out on both of us.

I left the care of the plantation to Toussaint that day, staying mostly indoors studying that heavy book while I was still able to transcribe it. Occasionally I would stop and relax to play with Mercutio or take a walk around the grounds. I noticed that the statue Gabriel was not on his plinth as usual and hoped for all our sakes he would be successful at his life-or-death endeavor. Before I knew it, night was quickly approaching. I summoned Montesquieu and we rode and flew to the four corners of Sans Souci searching high and low for any sign of the witch, but found none. Of course, I did not know exactly what to look for.

Even though Gerard was gone, Montesquieu and I kept mostly in the shadows, never knowing if he might arrive home earlier than expected. I realized Gerard was most likely already wise to the fact of the existence of my familiar. He just never let me read that particular thought.

I also had to face the fact, that Montesquieu (and Gabriel) would be needed in the upcoming battle. Both will have to be used strategically on the front line of battle, yet the thought of putting Montesquieu in harm's way hurt me deeply. I had been fond of him since I first laid eyes on him and that fondness has only grown with time.

He was more to me than a familiar; more than just a pet. He was my companion- my friend- and I was eager to show the fiery white steed to Selena, Pierre and grandma-ma. They will be so impressed with all the knowledge of witchcraft I have acquired. I hoped they would understand and not be fearful or skeptical. I will use it only for our good. After all, it was necessary, not just for my protection, but for theirs also. Their own knowledge of voodoo, medicine, enchantments and psychic abilities were miniscule compared to what I could now accomplish. I had changed in so many ways, yet deep down I was the same Henri LeBlanc they had first met not so long ago, but which seems like an eternity past.

Thinking of Selena and my family reminded me of Gerard's magical mirror and how tonight would be the perfect time for me to try my own hand at summoning its secrets. Perhaps after more work on the book and a nice cool bath.

However, as I alighted from Montesquieu and he flew off (after some large nibbles of sugar I had saved for him), I saw Toussaint hurrying towards me and I knew the book, my bath and what revelations the mirror held for me would have to wait. His concern was over his granddaughter.

Juliette had not been seen all day and I meant to ask after her earlier, but I had been too absorbed in my book work and I forgot. Apparently, she had been bedridden all day, her fever having steadily worsened and then suddenly, and surprisingly, as dusk descended, the fever lowered as well and she got up (against her grandfather's advice) and went back to work in the kitchen. Only now no one could find her- she had disappeared! Toussaint needed my help in finding her.

"I believe the fever returned and she must have wandered off in a delirium. That is the only explanation I can think of." He started to ask if Montesquieu and I would help look for her, but I had already read his request and had whistled for my companion who appeared by my side in less than a minute.

"Of course, Toussaint- rest easy." I tried to appear calm and confident that she would be found soon- safe and well. "You may ride with us if you wish."

"No, Master Henri, I want to search the bayous near the cabins. They are already searching for her. I fear.." He could not continue his sentence, but I knew the thought any way.

"Do not fear, my friend. She is not drowned- that much I know. I do not actually know- how I know- but she is still alive!" I hope I sounded assured. "We will find her safe and sound!"

We parted; Montesquieu and I riding- flying with the wind- and I immediately knew where he was taking us. It was, of course, to Juliette's special private bathing pool. It took us only a few minutes to get there.

He landed as easily as a bird, his hoofs finding firm ground near the fresh water pond. I looked at my pocketwatch. It was just after midnight- the supposed hour of the witch when evil is at its most powerful.

Seconds later I found her- her young body lying naked, face up in the reeds. It was a blessing that Toussaint was not with me, for she was extremely cold to the touch, her heart barely beating. Somehow or another, she had lost a lot of blood. I took off my shirt and wrapped her limp body in it. Fortunately the psychic impressions I received from her as I cradled her in my arms- carrying her back to Montesquieu and on to safety- I could tell she had not been sexually molested. Her full breasts were now close to my face, my fantasy so close to fulfillment, but I put such things out of my mind. The poor girl had no wounds, save for two large puncture marks on her neck that were dripping rivers of blood down to her shoulders. She must have become the hapless victim of a voodoo curse. The witch was making herself known, little by little, choosing her innocent prey carefully!

I was about to leap carefully on the horse's back, but he reared suddenly, his large hoofs pawing the earth. He sensed the witch! In the next moment, the tops of the surrounding pines whipped in a strong and sudden breeze coming out of no place. It circled round the pond blowing towards us. I thought I heard a whisper in the trees calling my name.

"Steady Montesquieu!" I commanded him. "We must leave with as much speed as possible." He knelt in understanding and I carefully mounted disturbing Juliette as little as possible. I knew just what herbal remedy to put on her wounds- however it had to be done quickly- for unfortunately she was dying.

When we returned, I raced into the mansion, carrying my precious cargo as gently as possible. I met some slave girl along the way who gasped and put her hand to her mouth in shock at seeing Juliette's limp and semi-nude body. But she was intelligent for her station and ran to get a gown without me having to tell her. I laid Juliette down in the comfortable settee in the study and tried to get a teaspoon of brandy in her. The slave girl appeared quickly with a housecoat and a blanket.

"Cloth her and keep her warm. I will return with some medicine." It did not take me long- upstairs in my room- to make a concoction to heal her wounds and stop the bleeding. I had collected many plants and specimens over the last few weeks and, with my new found knowledge from the book of life and death, I understood exactly what to mix. I also, hurriedly, made a drink to help build her blood back up and give her strength. If this succeeded, then it meant that book had already proven itself a blessing.

Back downstairs, Juliette was alone- the slave girl having disappeared, no doubt, to alert the others and find Toussaint. My poor patient was clothed and wrapped tightly in a warm blanket.

"This will stop the bleeding." I spoke to no one in particular, as I applied the oily dark green salve to the two deep fang marks on her neck. "You will be alright, I promise." She made no noise nor showed any motion, but remained still and lifeless. Her lips barely accepted the drink I had made, now mixed with brandy. I sat down by her side and waited.

The entire plantation seemed to be awake and our African/ West Indian slaves were wary enough to gather just what was responsible for Juliette's condition. Voodoo was being practiced here at Sans Souci!

Toussaint appeared (the small crowd making way for him) and he knelt beside his prone and dying granddaughter. He did not speak, but I could tell he was having a hard time holding back the tears.

Rising, I rested my hand on his shoulder and spoke gently. "Toussaint. Toussaint." He could not turn away from the girl. "I need your help. I have stopped the bleeding, but we need.." I paused. He rose and faced me- my voice dropped to a whisper- "You must take me to her room. Most likely what we need to find will be there."

"Yes, yes, Master Henri." He started to regain some composure and we quickly left the girl in the care of a couple of the older slave women. "The rest of you go back to your cabins." I sensed their fear. They knew that something wicked was near and that any one of them might end up as Juliette was now. I believed that none would run away though, for whereas they feared Gerard's wrath, Sans Souci and he have served as protectors for them as well (especially when compared to other non-French plantations) and I knew they would be performing some voodoo ritual on the bayou immediately, in order to rid us of the evil presence.

Once we were in Juliette's small closet of a room, Toussaint spoke: "What are we looking for Master Henri?"

"I do not know exactly, my old friend. However, I will recognize it when I see it." Some intuition led me to a collection of small dolls and figurines in a corner etagere. They had to be a great source of pleasure for the young girl, as they were all arranged orderly and were neatly free of dust. "Or perhaps I will sense it", I spoke while looking carefully at each one. Finally, I found what had been used to harm the girl. There was a roughly made voodoo doll (obviously not part of her collection) wearing a piece of Juliette's clothing with a strand of hair tied to it. Two large sewing pins were firmly stuck in the tiny doll's neck.

"Regardez, Toussaint. Look here." I showed him the doll. He moved to grab it, but I stopped him. "Non, I must!" He nodded. I ever so gently picked up the makeshift burlap, cotton-stuffed doll and smoothly removed the lethal pins.

"Come we must return now." Toussaint was eager to be back with his granddaughter.

As we left, I happened to glance back into the room towards the doll collection and was shocked when I saw the transparent apparition of a man. To be more exact, what actually shocked me was that the figure looked like Gerard, with his evil mocking grin! Suddenly it was gone. I looked for Toussaint to ask if he had also seen it, but he was already out the door. I quickly joined up with him bringing the evil doll with me.

Back in the study, Toussaint bent over Juliette. "She

is still unconscious." His voice carried his desperation.

"Did she move or make any sound?" I asked the slave women.

"She murmured something, Master Henri, once, then turned in her sleep, but went right back to the way you see her now."

I gently moved Toussaint aside and sitting down on the edge of the settee, leaned in close to Juliette. I let the empathic touch of my hand softly caress her beautiful bloodless young cheek and a moment later, she slowly opened her eyes from her death sleep. She looked alert, though I knew she was extremely weak and tired for she had been drained of much blood.

The first thing she saw was my concerned face peering down close to hers and her lips widened into a weak but bright smile and at that moment I would have liked to kiss her deeply, save for the presence of her grandpa-pa. I allowed myself to read her mind. She remembered nothing of the last twenty-four hours, except for having to lay down from feeling sick and weak. What surprised me was another thought in her mind: she wanted me to kiss her! And that was how I found out she was attracted to me as much as I was attracted to her.

Her eyes slowly shifted to the worried look on Toussaint's face and she tried to rouse herself. "What happened? Why am I in here?" She strived to look around at all our anxious faces. "Did I faint?" Her voice was full of fatigue.

I rose, allowing Toussaint to have my place by her side. "Oh my dear petite chou." He hugged her tight to himself. "My dear, dear baby!"

"But what happened? I feel so very tired like I could sleep forever."

"Oh my dear, dear girl," was all he could say while rocking her in his arms. "My little one, my baby."

I brought over the glass of brandy mixed with the potion to help build her blood which I had tried to get her to swallow earlier. "Here Juliette, drink this and then you can just lie here tonight and sleep as long as you need. We will speak tomorrow about what happened, whenever you have regained some of your strength. I will bring you more medicine, early in the morning." I paused before continuing. "Remember, we all love you very much." Her dark eyes met mine for a moment and then she closed them in weariness. Toussaint had her drink down almost all of the glass.

I left them to run upstairs to Gerard's bedroom. We could all discuss what had happened to Juliette, but I knew it would do no good to question her. She remembered nothing; her mind blank. The events conveniently erased by the voodoo curse.

But who had cast the spell? Who had made this doll which I still carried in my pocket and placed those pins in the neck to resemble the attack of some blood thirsty nosferatu? And was that apparition I saw actually Gerard? Through astral projection perhaps he could visit Sans Souci! I knew he had much power still as yet undisclosed to me. But what would be his motive? Could he be that jealous of my feelings for Juliette? Or was all this traumatic confusion caused by the witch? I wanted some answers and I knew where I might find them. I only hoped I would be able to work the proper magic.

I practically threw open the door to the room and turned to where the mirror had been on the wall. It was no longer there! In its place was a portrait I had never seen before of some young woman in Elizabethan costume. Odd that, but I did not dwell on it. In my panic I looked about. There the mirror was on another wall. Perhaps he had moved it or I had been mistaken. No matter- it looked to be the same.

Standing in front of the mirror, I cleared my mind completely. For my first request, I wanted to see just exactly where Gerard was. Was he in the town as he said he would be? I waved my hand before it, summoning its magic and mentally called upon it to show me Gerard.

The fog appeared over the mirror as before, which slowly cleared and yes, it revealed Gerard to me. He was at some small table, dining elegantly by candlelight. Yet something seemed not quite right to me. The place perhaps? It was dark all around him and I could not tell if he was at an inn or even with some one else. Looking up from his wine and food, he stared directly at me. I could see his face clearly for the mirror focused nearer, showing his visage close up. He became angry and barred his fangs. Angry because he knew I was spying on him! He waved his arm, the image disappeared and the mirror returned to normal.

It was of no consequence to me. I was no longer afraid of Gerard, though I must find out the truth. I wondered if the mirror was able to demonstrate the past as well as the present. I concentrated all my mental powers, asking it to show me the culprit who stabbed the doll I presently held in my hand. It did not react for what seemed a long time and just when I was about to repeat the request, it fogged over and then, presently, showed me the same doll I held. It was being picked up by a man's hands- a white man's hands, elegant and manicured like a French gentry land owner, similar to Julian Fontenot's in his portrait. They perhaps- could have been- Gerard's hands. As I watched, one hand held the doll steady and then with the other hand, the man stabbed the pins deep into the doll's neck. Then the mirror fogged over again, returning to normal, never showing me a face.

So according to the mirror, it was a man who performed the voodoo curse! Not Satine. Gerard could have been the man responsible. But even if he was jealous of Juliette, it made no sense. He knew I had feelings and affection for him also. If he were to harm Juliette, it would only help destroy what relationship he and I had. Unless- much of what he has been telling me were lies. Like him being able to read the book of the dead. He could have even lied about what happened in the West Indies; about the history between him and Satine.

I had one more request from the mirror. I wanted to see Selena, my family and my small familiar cabin. It obeyed my command readily. Of course, they would probably be asleep, this being the middle of the night, but surprisingly, there she appeared- my beloved, heating what looked to be a pot of milk over the open fire, and.. And I saw immediately that..She was with child!

It was remarkable and wonderful. I felt an all consuming joy! She was carrying my child! Oh, blessed day! I did not stop to think at the time that it strange that her figure be so swollen and noticeable in so short a period of time. Perhaps I just did not care, for I could barely contain my joy!

I kept watching her actions in the mirror. She carried a cup of milk into grandma-ma's room, the one Pierre and I had added on to the house. The room was so dimly lit, I could barely distinguish grandma-ma lying down in bed; however, in obvious discomfort; sick, with a wet towel over her feverish forehead. Selena's sweaty brow was furrowed with fatigue and worry. How strange to see grandma-ma sick, for I never thought her to have been sick a day in her life. She seemed to have aged noticeably. How horrible! I needed to get back home to them in the next few days. Gerard and his witch-hunt would have to wait.

I waved the mirror silent and turned, thinking it would go clear and return to its normal state. But, happening to glance back, I saw the scene had switched and I was now looking at mountains- rolling and heavily forested with tall pines; grey-blue mountains far from here; probably somewhere east on this large continent. Why was the mirror showing me this? I had not requested or commanded anything more from it.

It then showed a small log cabin, with a smoking chimney- its inhabitants just waking up for the day's labors. The scene shifted to the inside of the home, and what I saw took me completely by surprise. I saw my mother- my dear, precious mother- cooking over a kitchen fireplace! Then, as I stood there in Gerard's room dumbfounded, I saw my father drag himself into the room, still half-asleep and he kisses the busy woman on the cheek. They were alive! My parents were still alive! And what was really blessed- they were together again. Were the children there? My brothers and sisters? But the mirror would not answer me that. It grew foggy, then cleared, to reveal only my reflection and that of the room about me.

My anger knew no bounds. He had lied to me about my parents. Another lie! To keep me with him here, no doubt. That cursed beast! That unmitigated liar! If he had been nearby, I would have attacked him on the spot with all my might. I felt so manipulated, so used! He said I was gullible and I suppose he was right. As soon as he returns, I will confront him and demand from him the truth. His mind must be trained so well that I could not distinguish his lies from the truth; nor he himself.

I left his room in a rage. So he not only lied about being able to read the ancient book of the dead (which he at least admitted), he lied about my family. Making me think they were dead! That scoundrel! What else might he have lied about? Or omitted telling me? The cat-woman came to mind. He said previously he had never made another beast- that I was the only one. Perhaps there was a whole pack of wolf-men out there, somewhere, which he had created. Well, he can get one of them to help him against the witch!

And that leads to one other thought I must consider. All his long story about Satine- could that have been a fabrication? Was she the so-called evil sorceress he had portrayed her as? Marie seemed to believe so. Or perhaps Satine was the one wronged; the one manipulated and then discarded. He may even be much older than he declared. Or younger. I was furious. Part of me wanted to pack the few things I came with and leave that very night, but I calmed down somewhat after helping myself to his expensive liquor downstairs in the study.

I was careful so as not to disturb the sleeping Juliette who was wrapped up tight in her blanket on the settee. She already had regained some of her colour back in her cheeks. Her protective grandfather was asleep in a corner chair, but I was quieter than a mouse. Looking down at Juliette, she reminded me of an African princess- in carefree, worriless slumber- her brow young and un-furrowed- sans souci. A Cleopatra. Wait- was that not who Gerard had compared Satine to? Could there be some connection?

'Oh, stop it, Henri! Nonsense!' I told myself. There cannot be a skeleton behind every door. I downed another large stein of dark, sweet rum. You are thinking too hard, in too many directions; and there are no answers. At least not as of yet! Only speculation. I took the bottle outside with me, removed my clothing and cooled myself in the cistern waters, allowing them to wash away my anger- my pain- on another extremely humid and sultry night.

And I succeeded at keeping those draining emotions at bay and managed to relax, concentrating on more pleasant feelings. Feelings of joy and delight. My parents were alive and well! Selena was going to have my child! I was not concerned the least damn bit about the legends. I wanted children and they would be nurtured and raised as normal, mortal beings. No lycanthropes- no witchcraft for them- no shape-shifters. I was sure they would be the usual typical off-spring- taking only the best of myself and my wonderful beloved wife. For some reason, I particularly imagined a baby girl in Selena's image.

My thoughts turned to Selena's soft body; her mature breasts rubbing against my chest, as I inserted myself. With my erotic thoughts, the warm rum and the cool waters, I dozed off for a brief period. I must have needed a bit of sleep and reprieve from the anxiety of the evening. Emotions are stronger in immortals, after all.

Then so, I dreamed a dream so bizarre yet real, that even today, I can recall it as vividly as if it happened only last night. I was sitting in the tub, relaxing and Selena climbed over to join me. She came close, pressing her naked breasts against my body as my sex stiffened. She disappeared beneath the water and I felt her mouth on me. Her lips and tongue performed acts I did not know she was capable of.

But in the dream, suddenly, somehow, I knew it was not Selena. It was the young Juliette, beneath those dark waters, accomplishing skillful fellatio. But then how could it be her? a girl I have known as an innocent- a virgin! No, the mouth was too large and accommodating to be hers; the tongue too big, with great ability and much experience. In my dream, I realized it could not possibly be Juliette. It was Gerard's servant boy here with me! And Gerard had taught him well!

I tried not to climax; I tried to resist the enjoyment. But I could not! Then afterwards, as his head slowly rose from the still night water, it was no longer the young slave surfacing.

The sudden shock that then entered my system was paralyzing. I tried to move, but my body could not. I was bewitched! The face peering at me, the one who had actually pleased me, was the old crone of Gerard's description! Satine as her real self. Her long hair hung lifelessly down- wet, brittle and gray. Her wrinkled face showed centuries of age; the skin sagged and drooped. It was the succubus and she was here for one purpose only: To take my breath, my life. My very soul!

A shrill cackle issued from a wide toothless grin. It

seemed to come from some deep cavern- echoing painfully through my head. Still I could not move, as she brought her withered face closer and closer to my own, intending to suck the life out of me and restore her vital youth!

Suddenly I woke- startled, disoriented and, I must confess, extremely frightened. My heart was racing. It had seemed too real, too perfectly true. I realized my sex was stiff and, yes- there was the evidence of my climax in the water. Could the witch have actually been here? Has she been playing with my mind all this evening?

I lumbered clumsily out of the cistern and dressed myself slowly. I could not move any faster. My body, my mind- felt drained. The usual night energy I had come to enjoy was gone. If she had been here, (or at least been in my mind), she must be a strong sorceress indeed. And for the first time, I realized exactly what sort of powerful entity I would be encountering.

I wandered inside the plantation house, my wolf's quickness and power gradually coming back to me. I wanted to study, to read more from the book of the dead. To know everything possible in order to arm myself against this evil. I had to in order to survive.

My room seemed extremely warm though there was a slight night breeze from the balcony doors. Had I left those open? Probably the boy had opened them when he brought the fresh flowers to the room. They smelled so heavily, it was almost like a perfume. Yet looking around I saw no flowers and the bed was not turned down as usual. It was most strange, but I dismissed it as I went over to the small table beside the bed where I had left the book. It was not there! I felt certain I had put it there. I searched all around, yet it was not be found. Then remarkably, just before panic set in, I found the book inside the armoire, over by Julian's portrait. However, I seem to distinctly remember leaving it by the bed. Or had I? Why would I hide it here, inside a drawer, closeted

Loup Garou

away? Surely I would recall such an act.

I laid down on the bed to study (the book still permitting me) and I thought that it would actually be a welcome relief once Gerard is back home. Of course, I planned to still confront him about the doll and what I saw in the mirror. However, I had to admit to myself, that I had begun to doubt my very own senses. It was as if my mind was playing tricks upon itself. And was that not the way Gerard described her tactics- tricks of the mind? I must be careful and keep my wits clear and sharp like the tools in my workshop. I must not allow Satine nor Gerard nor any one or any thing else to play havoc with my thoughts and abilities. I will not relinquish control! I would remain steadfast and keep my mind and acts in check. I swore to survive and make sure my family and children thrive.

10

The rest of that night went by uneventfully and the next day, life at Sans Souci seemed almost normal. Juliette was slowly gaining her strength back, becoming her beautiful and energetic self. I gave her a special tonic to take every day for two weeks and she was so appreciative that that very morning I was privileged to enjoy her special pancakes before riding out to the fields with Toussaint. It was as if that night of danger and perplexity had never happened.

Gerard came back a day early. That very next night in fact. We met at table for supper. "Do not eat too much, Henri," he laughed, "for we are going hunting tonight."

It is not even a full moon, I thought as the boy served and poured for us both. I read the servant's mind. He was very pleased Gerard was back. I felt for the poor boy- to be so enthralled with a man who did not reciprocate.

"No matter about the moon. It is necessary. We must be at a certain place at a certain time. Near midnight."

I read it in his mind. There was a stagecoach with a great deal of gold and gems that was to be targeted by a gang of cutthroats. I did not have to guess, to know how he had come across this information. "And we will ambush the ambushers."

"Exactly."

"Pourquoi? You have plenty of money." We were eating bloody rare roast beef. I heard the servant's stomach turn as he watched us eat and lap up the blood with our bread. Gerard dismissed him with a wave of his hand.

I can always use more money. He paused in thought. We can use more.

I was not concerned about it. I wanted to discuss what had happened on the plantation. But first I asked about the success of his trip.

"I have good news. Very good news, indeed. The sarcophagus and other relics necessary for the ceremony to bring him to life should be here in another month or less. Gabriel is already there." My raised eyebrows showed the total surprise I felt. "Yes," he continued, "Dr. Fontenot believes he knows just where the 'cursed' tomb lies which we are searching for. The doctor knows Egypt like the back of his own hand!"

He resumed eating, but such a simple explanation was not satisfactory for me. I spoke out loud. "And how were you able to communicate with someone thousands of miles away overnight? Did you use a crystal ball or hold a seance or both?"

He chose to ignore my 'sardonique' attitude. "Actually, I used the mirror." I wanted to let out a gasp. "I took it with me." He looked at me with curiosity.

I put down my fork, trying to remain calm and not let him read my confusion. I gulped some wine before speaking. "But. .but how did he communicate in return? I do not understand."

"He has an enchanted mirror on his side of the world."

I did gasp at that bit of knowledge. "So the doctor knows witchcraft?"

Gerard concentrated on chewing and swallowing a particularly large succulent slice of meat before replying. "Well, let us say he knows some magic. After all, a man who can restore life to the dead must know some sort of wizardry." My confusion remained, but he chose not to read it. He raised his glass and seemed to ponder over it in deep thought before taking a sip. He turned to look at me directly. "There will be a total lunar eclipse soon- two full moons from now to be exact. I believe that will be when she attacks."

"Precisely when she thinks you are at your weakest."

"When she believes we will be at our weakest." He corrected me. His brow creased in deep lines. "What is on your mind, Henri? You are not as open as usual."

"But why did you have to go into town and take the mirror? Could you not communicate with the doctor right here at..."

His fist slamming on the dining table shook the crystal and china almost spilling our wine. "Do I have to explain my every move?" he howled.

"Non, but do explain this!" I growled back as I slammed the doll used to hurt Juliette upon the table and this time my wine did spill, the red liquid spreading like a pool of blood across his neat white tablecloth. His anger did not surprise me, but my anger did.

His calm demeanor returned instantly. "What is this? Has someone been playing with voodoo?" He drank down his glass of wine and poured himself some more, ignoring the mess I made. "You perhaps?"

"Non," was my simple reply, but I allowed him to read my mind and told him telepathically all of what had happened to Juliette.

His face hardened and he looked straight ahead at

nothing in particular. "So the witch made her presence felt in my absence. I thought she might." He went back to his last morsel of meat. "Juliette is well now, though, yes? Your medicine helped her?" He dabbed his lips and moustache fastidiously with his clean white napkin.

"Yes," I paused. "But I saw you?"

"What do you mean you saw me?"

"In her room. I saw you as a thin apparition." I then accused him. "You projected yourself here. You deliberately hurt Juliette!"

"Now why would I do such a thing?" He gathered my thoughts for a moment and then laughed. "Oh yes, because you think I am jealous of that little girl. Ridiculous!" He picked up one of the little cakes the boy had left us for dessert.

"Yes Henri, I am well aware of your attraction to her." He put his hand over mine. "And of her attraction to you, as well. But that is of no matter to me." He removed his hand and grinned mischievously at me. "Actually, I think you should take a mistress- and a male lover, also. It would do you good." I was speechless. He laughed. "You can be such the prude, Henri. Besides it is your wife who should be jealous- if ...she were to discover the truth." He finished his last bit of cake. "Furthermore, I am very fond of Toussaint's granddaughter and I would never harm her."

I searched deep in his mind and as far as I could detect he was telling the truth. He continued, "Besides, I would not need to resort to petty voodoo if I were to destroy someone, correct? You know me. . . and my powers."

"Do I?" Then, "Why would Satine do this?"

"To confuse you. To disrupt our lives." He patted my hand again. "To cause you to doubt me." I withdrew my hand from his, putting it in my lap. He smiled at me. "Now what is the other matter that is disturbing you? There is something else, n'est-ce pas?"

"Yes, another question of mine."

"You mean another accusation, don't you?" He read my anger.

"The mirror."

"What of it?"

"You lied to me."

"About .."

"My parents."

"I only showed you what has come to pass."

"They are still alive."

"Nonsense." He dismissed the idea with a wave of his hand. "We both saw their graves. Now- we just have time enough for our coffee before we go."

"I saw them. They are still alive. You lied to me." I repeated myself.

He seemed genuinely confused. "I do not know what you are speaking of, Henri, nor do I know what you think you saw. The fact is the mirror was with me. And besides, I cannot manipulate the past or cause the mirror to lie about it. My ability, unfortunately, is limited to only summoning the mirror to answer my questions- truthfully."

"Now who is speaking nonsense. I will show you."

"Please do." He rose, pushing his chair back impatiently and I led the way upstairs to his room. Once inside though, it was I who was confused, for the mirror was back in its original place on the wall!

He registered my surprise. "What is it, Henri?"

"The mirror."

"Yes?"

"Last night, it was on the other wall. Over there." I pointed to the opposite wall where a framed map of Sans Souci now hung.

"Are you sure?"

"Of course. And I also located you, in town dining at some inn by candlelight."

"Spying on me, Henri? That is not like you. I assure

you the only meal I enjoyed last night was not so traditional. Actually," he seemed amused with himself, "after I spoke with the doctor, I spent the entire night in the arms of a very young- and well endowed- male on the outskirts of town."

Now that I did believe. I scratched my head."'Then what does this mean?"

"It means, she has manipulated you yet again." He started to pace the room. "And it means she is very close. In my house- in my very room! We must be on our guard to the extreme."

"But..", I turned to the mirror.

"Go ahead, ask it yourself." He coaxed me.

Which I did, and the mirror proceeded to fog over and then answer my question as to the whereabouts of my parents. It again showed me the same graves as before. "That bitch!"

"Good, you are angry. Good!" He continued his pacing. "Tell me, Henri. If the mirror was over there- what was here in its place where it is now?"

"A portrait. I had never seen it before."

"Of..?"

"Some young female. I paid it little attention."

"Try to describe it. Use your mind's eye."

I closed my eyes and concentrated. "She is dressed in what appears to be old Elizabethan clothing. She is young with petite features; has long dark lustrous hair and bright emerald eyes. Her complexion .." I started to understand the implication.

"Was tan, almost bronze." He finished my sentence. "And there was a mole on.."

"It was she!" My words were uttered in a hiss of hatred. "She was here- watching me!" He paused in his pacing and we stared at each other- thinking the same thing. "The book!"

We ran into my room. The book was were I had left it on my nightstand. "Thank goodness," was all he said.

I thought of last night. "But

"Yes?" His right eyebrow ar

usual.

"Last night, I thought I had r

not where I remember leaving i

He grabbed both my should

nodded. "Was anything else ou

head. "Did you sense any prese

smell of flowers.

"Lilacs." He let go of me and

smelled the strong scent of lilac

flowers of any kind in the room."

"Quick, look through the book. Are there any pages missing?"

Picking up the book, I thumbed through it. "None that I can see. Perhaps I had interrupted her as she was searching for this." I turned each page separately, carefully examining each one. "Or, I would imagine, the book would not allow such a one to transcribe its contents. It might even have secreted itself away from her."

"True, we actually do not know all the abilities and powers the book holds." He stopped pacing and turned to me, looking severe in his dark clothes and finely trimmed goatee. "Mon Dieu! If she knows what we are about then... We are undone!" He sat down heavily on my bed and, for the first time since I had met him that fateful night when Gabriel had fished me out of the bog, he appeared fatigued. He sighed slowly, "And though we have the information and means, we may now lack the element of surprise."

"Perhaps not." I suddenly had a bright realization. I was the one who was pacing now. "What if the true surprise is not the mummy."

"Then what?"

"Why the other entity. The ghost!"

"Of course!" He slapped his hands together and

371

...ld not possibly expect my battling her ...clenched his fists tightly, his face turning ...ger, "She will pay!" The words were spit in a ...sheer hatred. He turned quiet and still- his ...s and feelings far away in some other time past. I ...ot intrude upon his mind, but I knew who he was ...inking of.

In a moment he came round, jumped off the bed and did a jig. He was back to his old self. "Mon ami." He embraced me, kissing me on the cheek. "You are brilliant. I taught you well. And we must plan our attack- and defense- as carefully as possible. But tonight," he rubbed his hands together in hungry delight, "Tonight we hunt. Tomorrow and the days after that will be for planning. Come or we will be late."

I wrapped the book and my notes and papers in another invisible cloth I had created and placed the unseen bundle under the bed. "They will be safe from prying eyes now."

I closed the door behind us. Gerard had already leaped over the banister and was heading out the door. I followed closely behind. We were wolves again, hunting together, out for the righteous kill. And I felt gloriously alive with anticipation.

Along the way, I sent him a thoughtful question. Where do you think she is now? What is she planning?

I do not know, but I only hope she is not in Egypt causing havoc with the doctor and his excavation.

My thoughts turned to my family and the horrible idea that Satine may be involving herself somehow in their lives and toying with them as she had with me. I still hoped the mirror had been true about Selena's pregnancy.

Within minutes we were approaching our destination- a not-so-well traveled road, skirting an especially deep and large swamp, far from any village. The bandits could be heard ahead; they had already commandeered the coach. We hid, as our human selves, behind thick palmettos and observed the scene. We are late, I heard Gerard think silently. The driver and the rifleman who rode alongside, were both lying on the ground beneath nervous horses hoofs, already shot and killed. A rotund man, and apparently his wife and small son, stood outside the coach, held at gunpoint by two armed men, while two others were taking down a large trunk from the top of the carriage. From their struggles and heavy heaves, it had to be quite weighty.

"But messieurs, that is all we have. All that we possess in the world." The man pleaded to no avail. He was a well-dressed French gentleman and, both he and his wife, foolishly displayed their obvious wealth. Idiots, Gerard thought, to not even try to conceal their riches. One of the men, painfully, snatched the ruby and diamond necklace off the lady's full bosom.

I looked directly at Gerard. They are going to kill them all, I can sense it.

Yes.

But we must move now.

Wait, wait one moment longer. He held me back.

The trunk was opened with little difficulty and the men gazed with stupour upon the plunder. Gold coins, household silver, gems and jewelry, mixed with some paper money, filled the coffer. "It must be worth thousands," one thief exclaimed in greed.

"One- hundred thousand francs to be exact," the owner cried, "and you may have it all. Please, just let us go free and unharmed. I am begging you."

Though the passengers fear was strong, the scent of the robbers sadistic avarice was even more prevalent. The poor little boy shivered and whimpered, holding tightly to his mother's skirt, trying, unsuccessfully, not to urinate on himself.

Now Gerard, Now. I insisted. We must save their-

One moment longer.

A shot rang out and the man fell face down- dead. I could stay still no longer. I had to save them and I leapt out from our hiding place, snarling and snapping as a wolf man. However, unfortunately in that very same particle of a second, more shots were fired and the mother and child were killed before I was able to intervene.

I felt the sting of the bullets as they all fired their weapons. They were not much more than pin pricks to me. Ignoring their screams, I slashed and ripped their flesh and two of them lay dead in the matter of a moment, their throats and viscera tore out. For a few seconds, they were able to see their own intestines flow freely from their bodies, before death mercifully enveloped them.

Gerard was directly behind me. Not bothering to transform, he twisted the third man's neck a complete 360 degrees. Which left one- the leader. His frightened, sweaty bewilderment was comical to me. Glancing quickly back and forth at the two of us, in his desperate confusion (and now out of ammunition) he drew a large knife. Gerard's laugh sounded like a howl. We both decided to have a little fun with this one. In a flash, I transformed back into my human self.

His shock was total- madness crept into his consciousness. He dropped to his knees, the knife discarded on the ground. Cupping his hands together, he pleaded for mercy. "Demons or gods, please spare my life! Please!!" he screamed. We walked towards him, savoring his terror and the man's own dreaded hope that death would not be slow and painful. He shut his eyes, "Please help me God!"

I could not help but reply. "God cannot help you now, monsieur. You showed that poor family no mercy and so now it will be your turn to be treated likewise."

I picked him up by the throat, applying just enough pressure so that he would be able to utter only the most painful speech. Gerard was right beside me. "Forgive me, almighty ones." His voice rasped with agony. "You can have the gold and riches. Have it all!" He shivered uncontrollably in my powerful grasp and we could smell the feces and urine as he could no longer control his bowels. Like the poor, poor child, whom he had killed in cold blood only minutes earlier.

I applied pressure slowly and steadily, crushing his larynx little by little, until his throat was mangled and his shallow breaths full of blood. I released him and he crumpled in a heap on the ground. "You may have the honors, mon ami."

Gerard stepped forward, "With pleasure." He bent down close to the man's face, whose eyes were literally bulging from fright and pain. Gerard raised his hand high and, one by one, changed each finger into a gigantic talon. The man watched helplessly, as Gerard leisurely and methodically sliced open, first his shirt, then his stomach. His silent screams received no pity and, much to our dismay, he died shortly thereafter. But not before he witnessed with his own eyes, two wolf-men feasting on his own body's organs.

We slowly walked back to Sans Souci carrying the trunk full of riches between us. We had not bothered hiding the carnage behind us, leaving it for the wild animals, vultures and alligators to fight over.

"You should have let me stop those men earlier. The family might still then be alive."

"To run into town and tell the populace about the werewolf that attacked them?"

"We could have caught them and hypnotized each one. Cause them to forget. You have done it before." I cast him an accusatory glance. "I could have done it."

"What is done, is done." He was not sorry; his callous nature seemed to always prevail over any empathic feelings he might have.

"You do not even need this treasure."

"No, but you will." He looked at me and smiled. "Especially with a child on the way."

I stopped in my tracks. "You know? Then the mirror was true in that one respect."

"Yes, and the fact that your wife's grandmother is sick. I confess- I have occasionally observed your family in the mirror." We continued walking, almost casually, though faster than ordinary humans. "And I know you need to go see them. But," he hesitated, "I would like you back here- to stay- permanently. Here with me at Sans Souci. To oversee the plantation. You have proven your capability and the slaves mind you well."

I started to speak, but he continued, "And soon, you should bring your family here to live. Even Pierre." We looked at each other, continuing our stroll, carrying my new wealth. "I have given it a great deal of thought and.. We can build another house at the other end of the plantation. Near the vineyards would be nice."

"On the small rise by the pond?" I knew exactly where he was talking about and pictured the beauty of it in his mind; envisioning a smaller, simpler version of Sans Souci. Would this be possible? Could this plan work out? However, as I had vowed to myself before, I did not want his anger and violent nature too close to Selena and my child.

"Do not worry about that, Henri. I treat well those I care about and you know," he spoke in a shy manner, "I care about you."

As for myself, I was beginning to care deeply for Gerard- one might even call it love. "But we have one other obstacle- the witch. I do not want to put them in any danger."

"I understand. But the truth is, they are in danger any

where from her. Simply by association with me- and now, with you. I am truly sorry for that situation." His smile tried to reassure me. "They are safer here at Sans Souci where they can be looked after. Though I must make this one confession to you, Henri." His azure blue eyes demonstrated tenderness. "I am selfishly happy that you are in my life."

We continued on in silence for a time, nearing the house. Day would dawn in a few hours. I sensed my Montesquieu not far away, staying a discreet distance behind us, deep in the swamp. Like Gabriel was to Gerard, Montesquieu was my guardian- my protector.

As we came up to the front steps, I had one more thought to share out loud, but Gerard spoke it first. "Of course, we must defeat the witch utterly. It is imperative that no trace of Satine or her evil influence be permitted at Sans Souci." That was my thinking also, exactly.

We placed the trunk of jewels, gold coins and other rich delights in the secret room upstairs and then we both retired to our own rooms. I had much to ponder and strangely- I felt tired- or more precisely, my mind felt tired; most likely because my emotions had been wrought over the last few days. Would it be possible for us all to live here? To prosper together at Sans Souci? This plantation was my dream come true. I already planned to start raising horses in the northern pastures. And- I might even be able to fulfill my other fantasies- which, more and more often, included Gerard.

Little did I know that the very next night that one particular fantasy would be fulfilled; but also, in that same night, I would leave Sans Souci; unexpectedly and unceremoniously, full of pain and anguish in my heart.

For the remainder of that night (our last hunt together), I read and studied, but mostly I mused about my newfound wealth (Gerard had promised it to me!) and what it might mean for Selena and me. The possibility of a joyful and fulfilling life here on this beautifully pastoral plantation was now closer to a reality. There was more than enough acreage for our own home a proper distance away from the main house. Selena would positively refuse to own household slaves; so, I thought I would buy Juliette, free her and pay her a wage. I would have all my loved ones surrounding me (including Gerard) and my child will grow up in this wonderful idyllic setting.

Then, intently, the idea struck me again, as it had several times before, about how sad an immortal's life must become. For he never dies nor ages, yet all the while, year after inexorable year, all those around him- his human loves, friends and family members- one by one, age- grow sick- and die.

"How do you cope with that?" I had once asked Gerard while riding our rounds on the plantation.

"I have not had to!" He looked at me harshly. "I have had no 'lover' for all these years. Nor do I know any humans whom I can refer to as 'friend'.

"That is very hard to believe, given all the time gone by. How lonely and sad you must have been." His proud anger surfaced visibly (for he hated the show of pity), but he stayed under control. I cautiously ventured another personal question. "What about your houseboy?"

"He is simply a...release for me. Just like all the others." He stared straight ahead at the well-worn path. "Immortals can lead a very lonely life. They must not fall in love with their human counterparts, but learn to stand alone. However-" he turned to face me, his look becoming soft; his voice sincere with emotion; the eyes seemed slightly moist; or, was a glint of sunlight playing a trick on me? "However, I do believe each immortal can find- with time- another of his kind. They might choose to love each other and the two become one for . . "

"For true eternity." I finished his thought.

I have often since reflected on that short, yet revealing conversation and the enigma known as Gerard. One side of him was cruel- even inhuman, but I had come to personally experience his other side- the side quite capable of great and expansive love. I also knew he would give up his own immortal life- if necessary- in order to save someone he loved. In order to save me!

In fact, that is exactly what did happen.

Dawn was quickly asserting herself through a cloudless sky, signaling another muggy day ahead for us, as I turned my thoughts back to my studies. When suddenly, the entire plantation seemed to be in an uproar and I knew Gerard was dispensing punishment to one of his slaves. He seldom whipped his people, wisely choosing any of a number of other recourses available to a hypnotic werewolf/master. Usually the whip was regarded as an inefficient tool for achieving cooperation. If he did decide that punishment should be meted out, he usually saved that 'honor' for Toussaint. Which, when the necessary evil was being done, I noticed Toussaint was light and few with the lashings. Gerard knew not to ask me to dispense punishment, for I would adamantly refuse.

But this morning, it was Gerard beating some poor soul fiercely. I walked out onto the balcony and there they were, by the cistern, surrounded by Toussaint and a few of the other household slaves- who were looking on with anguished and pained faces.

The recipient of his wrath this time greatly surprised me, for it was his young man- Gerard's servant and companion! He was cowering on the ground in the shadow of the cistern wall, his master flogging him over and over again with a sharp riding crop. The boy had multiple cuts- bleeding all along his naked torso and even his beautifully handsome face displayed the master's madness. The youngster's cries were not only filled with physical pain; I could sense his emotional pain- to think that Gerard would treat him so.

I rushed down the back stairs determined to stop this, knowing it might even mean another useless fight between Gerard and I. However, I thought he would not fight me in front of his people. I would simply have to intervene- the boy's screams becoming unbearable to my sensitive heart- and try to do so without seeming to challenge Gerard's authority.

"Gerard, enough," I shouted as I approached, hoping I expressed calm reason. I grabbed the crop in mid-air as it was sailing down once more upon the hapless boy and, it may have been my imagination, but I believed there was an audible, collective intake of breath from Toussaint and the other observers. Gerard eyed me fiercely, his blue eyes dark with fury. "For god's sake, what has the boy done?" I tried to remain coolly unemotional. However, I could read nothing from him other than uncontrollable anger. From the boy, I could only sense pain- in body and spirit.

I stood between them and for one tiny instant, we all thought that Gerard was about to turn his frenzied rage upon me. He released the bloody crop, letting it fall to the ground.

"Very well, perhaps he has learned his lesson." He glanced at the crouching and bleeding boy, who was trying to control his hysterical sobbing, and then Gerard looked back at me. "He is yours now, Henri; you can have him!" He bowed at the waist in mock reverence, gesturing with his arm. "I give him to you." He looked towards the small group, but they knowingly and wisely were already leaving to go about their business and morning duties.

I did not know what to say. Gerard drew in a deep breath, visibly regaining his composure and he spoke calmly: "Take him to Juliette. Between the two of you, you ought to be able to doctor the wounds properly."

"Yes, I know what to do." I sensed a small twinge of sorrow within him for what had happened. As he turned to leave, I placed a hand on his shoulder. He refused to meet my gaze; instead, he just stared straight ahead at the rising sun. He hesitated, about to say something, (for he would not let me enter his thoughts), then he simply turned and walked away quietly.

I gathered the boy up in my arms, trying not to agonize his wounds further and rushed him to Juliette. She had heard the commotion and (knowing her master) was already preparing a healing herbal salve. We gently washed his wounds and wiped the blood off him and then carefully, applied the medicine, covering all the cuts as best we could. "He will have scars, no doubt," was all she said. The boy had stopped his moaning, and became quiet, his countenance hard and resolute, determined not to show any pain- or sorrow- at his lover and master turning on him. However we both knew he was in great pain. I could sense that (and his wounded feelings), yet his mind was locked from me as to what had caused Gerard's outburst. Maybe he did not even know what he had done wrong.

It really was of no matter what actually happened and to this day, I still cannot recollect the cause of the beating, though I do remember well, carrying him up to my room, laying him face down on the bed and tending to him the rest of that day. And, after a time, he spoke and said many things; far more than he had ever said before during my entire stay at Sans Souci.

"What caused your master to be in such an uproar?" I inquired as I placed a wet cloth around his neck. He did not reply. I sat down beside him and tenderly massaged his shoulders and muscular arms, places unharmed by the sharp crop. I wanted him to know he could trust me and not fear me- for I was quite different from Gerard. And because now, I supposed, for all intents and purposes, he was my property. I was his owner- his new master!

I still could not read his locked mind and, after encouraging him to drink a little brandy mixed with a healing potion, he eventually fell asleep. So, going back to my studies, I watched over him that morning. I wanted to enter his dreams, but thought better of it. He would tell me if he wanted me to know what happened between Gerard and himself. Around mid-day, I went out and found Toussaint just as he was going out to the fields. He did not need me that day, so I stayed close to the house. Neither of us could guess where Gerard had gone off to.

Then as the sun passed its zenith and began its lazy summer retreat, the boy stirred and slowly, trying hard not to wince from the pain, he sat up in the bed. He reminded me of that proud strong native warrior whose brave heart I had recently (and reluctantly) devoured. Juliette had brought up a bowl of soothing hot broth which I gave him along with a glass of fresh cool milk. He moved agonizingly slow, but hunger made its demand and he began to sup hurriedly. I moved my chair near to the bed. He gazed up at me and asked, in a grateful, sad tone, "Am I yours now, Master Henri?"

"Yes, it would seem so." Part of me was happy because now I could protect and educate him. Then set him free. "Tell me about yourself, where are you from?" was all I asked and for the first time since I had arrived, he spoke freely to me and I pictured his story vividly from his mind.

He did not remember having a true mother or father nor any brothers or sisters. But the slaves who raised him, knew French and taught him the rudiments of the language. He did remember a tiny crowded, foul-smelling log cabin near a salty foul-smelling marsh; however, one-by-one any familiar black face left him- supposedly to be auctioned off. One face though remained a constant: the face of a mean-eyed older white man with red hair and a scraggily reddish beard who had a funny sounding accent- much different from the smoothly eloquent French of Gerard's. (I assumed he was speaking of a slave trader, most likely Irish.) He always carried a short whip with him and smelled heavily of alcohol and sweat; his clothes ragged and torn, demonstrated a lack of riches.

A mean-spirited taskmaster, who whipped everyone in his way without discretion or provocation, he put the boy to work as soon as he could walk. At first, he washed dishes; later he learned to shovel and clean out the stables; then, as he grew more into a man, he was put into the cotton fields as were most of the slaves. Then one day, he found himself on display for auction in the French Market, the old Irishman displaying the boy's shy nakedness- openly- and making suggestions that the youngster was proficient at certain acts of a sexual nature. At this point of his story, the boy stopped for a moment, and I grasped the truth, without reading his thoughts, that the young man had been molested by the filthy slave owner, not once but many times. The boy was hanging his head, ashamed to look up at me. "And then Master Gerard bought me that very day and..", he could not continue. There was no need for I knew the rest of the story. The boy wanted to cry, but his pride would not permit it.

I stood up and gently lifted his head by the chin. His eyes were moist. Suddenly and surprisingly, (though I should have expected it) he flew off the bed and went

down on his knees, squeezing me about the waist in a
bear hug. Then, with the deft swiftness of a cat, he
loosened my trousers and reached inside and grabbed
my sex in his hand. Taken aback, even startled, my dull
brain did not react at first. Gerard would have called it my
'naivete', and I suppose it was. Before I realized it, he
had his mouth around me.

With gentle force, I grabbed the young man's head
and pushed him back, saying, "Now then, there will never
again be a need for that. Not with this master." I rear-
ranged myself back into my trousers.

"I must service you and please you, master." I shook
my head no. "Doesn't all white masters want the same
thing?" Again, I shook my head. He slumped down on the
floor thinking I was displeased. "I am told, Master Henri, it
is what I do best. That it is all I am good for."

"Nonsense, I know for a fact you are a hard worker
and there are plenty of other tasks you are accomplished
at. Those not of a sexual nature."

"But," he hesitated, still looking down at the floor,
"Master Henri- it is also what I like. What I want." I could
tell his confession did not come easy, though it did mean
that he now trusted me explicitly.

So with that admission, I gently took him by the
shoulders and had him stand up. "Look at me," I spoke to
him softly, kindly (not as a master to his slave, but more
as a father to his son). He slowly raised his head and met
my gaze. "You need never be ashamed for preferring
your own gender, comprendre?" He nodded. "So then, if
that is the case, one day- uh, you may find-" I didn't
know quite how to continue- "a companion- someone
who- feels as you do- an equal."

"An equal?" His sad look turned to one of
astonishment.

"Yes, as an equal. You will no longer have a master. I
intend to give you your freedom as soon as possible."

The astonishment changed to happiness, yet only

briefly, for a great deal of apprehension settled over the boy. "But what would I do? Where would I go?" He looked down at the floor again. "I would not know- how to survive on my own." His voice trailed off- his fear of the unknown was understandable. A fear, I myself, was no stranger to.

"Non, non, my young man, I will take care of you until such time, and there will come a time, when you can survive on your own. You will leave tonight!" His astonishment returned as he looked up. "I will send you to my old home. To my family and wife. Up the river and northwest. There you may live and be accepted as family."

His winning smile returned. "Are you leaving also, Master Henri?" I shook my head and his doubt rose again. "How will I find it by myself? I dare not!" He drew a sharp intake of breath. "What if some white trade-master finds me alone, unaccompanied.." His voice rose in pitch; his eyes wide with terrible possibilities. He had not really seen any of this wonderful country; he had not even seen much of the surrounding plantation.

"I have a special horse for you." He shook his head and started to object, but I hastily assured him. "You will be alright. Not to worry, he knows the way and you will not be seen. I will prepare the proper papers of travel with my signature, stating your purpose and destination- though, I promise you, they will not be necessary. Trust in me and I will see that no harm comes to you again."

"I believe you master, but.."

"My horse is called Montesquieu and he will take you to my old home safely by the back trails and so quickly that you will feel like you are riding on the wind!" I placed a hand confidently on his bandaged shoulder. "It will be a great adventure for you."

"Truly, Master Henri? Truly? I can be free and live with you and your family?" The concept of freedom (and family) was almost unfathomable to the boy.

"Mais bien sur, but of course!" I knew he wanted to embrace me, but owing to our relationship of master to slave, he could not. So instead, I embraced him, briefly yet strongly, and told him to gather his possessions together.

"I have very little, master."

"I know," I replied, thinking of myself arriving at Sans Souci with my own 'very little'. I looked outside; dusk was rapidly settling. Where had the day gone! "Now go and be quick about it. Meet me at the edge of the woods in the rear of the house. I will be waiting with Montesquieu." I pulled out my pocketwatch from my vest pocket and flicked it open. Its tiny music filled the room with delicate beauty. "Fifteen minutes. Can you be ready in fifteen minutes?"

"Yes, Master Henri, but..."

"You can..tell time, I assume?"

He responded proudly, "Why yes, master. I can tell time, but.."

"What is it?" My tone expressed a wolf's impatience. Besides I knew what he was going to say. "About Master Gerard. Correct?" I poured myself a cold drink of water, wishing it was wine or even whiskey. Would I, one day also, be able to change water into wine?

"I think," he shuddered, recalling his beating only hours ago, "he will be most angry to discover I have left."

"He might," I gulped down the water. "Still, he gave you to me."

"But I know," he began again, "that.." then his words rushed out unimpeded, "Even though I am yours now, he would want me to stay here at Sans Souci."

"You can always return. But just realize, it would be on your terms as a free man!" Eventually Gerard would probably change his mind and take him back. The possibility of freedom was still hard for the boy to comprehend. "You do understand that it is best for you to leave Sans Souci. That your relationship with Gerard is over, or at least it will be very different." He nodded in sad acknowledgement.

I continued. "Do not worry about your ex-master. Leave him to me. I know a way- and I believe it is the only way- to dissuade him." The boy's wide eyes narrowed at me. Had he guessed what I was speaking of? I approached him closely. "I am quite capable of taking care of Gerard, so do not fret, young one. We will succeed in this and you will do well. I will follow in a week or so. Now go." I looked again at the time on my pocketwatch. "Fifteen minutes."

"I have no watch or clock."

"Here then take this." I carefully handed over my most prized possession. "Be careful with it. It is very dear to me. Tres cher!"

He looked at the precious gold watch with awe and admiration, holding it as if it would break from the slightest pressure. "Go ahead and open it in order to see the dial. Like this." He followed my instructions carefully and I knew he would be cautious with it; probably protect it with his life. It was undoubtedly, to him, the finest object he had ever held in his hands. "Merci, Master. God Bless You." He then left the room with no more words.

At our appointed rendezvous, I introduced him to Montesquieu and instructed the familiar to take the boy, straight away and with all haste, to my home- to Selena. I gave the boy a packet containing papers and a letter for Selena and instructed him to give it to my wife upon his arrival. The note read of how much I missed her and her warm, tender embrace; that I would be home shortly and to please, accept this young slave boy into our household until I could achieve his freedom; that he was trustworthy, hardworking, reliable; and to also, please, tend to his wounds.

The boy was visibly taken aback by the size of Montesquieu. I had to help him mount the large horse. "Merci Master Henri," and he handed me the pocketwatch. Then, at first hesitating, I gave it back to him. "Give this to your new mistress, my wife, Selena. She will then know, without a doubt, about your credibility and will welcome you and take you in."

There was one more important item for him to have. "Here wear this. Make sure it covers you entirely. It will protect you." I had him put a large, heavy cloak on.

"But master, it is a clear night. No rain- and hot," he complained. Montesquieu was eager to leave. I had to hold his mane tight, while the boy struggled putting the cloak around his shoulders.

"Wear it and do not remove it," I ordered him. "It is dark enough you will not be seen. You will be practically invisible. Promise me not to take it off until you arrive at my home."

He promised though he did not understand.

"Bon. There must not be any more delay. Hold on tight." I warned him, as I gently swatted Montesquieu on the flank. He took off like a torrent, and I could feel the boy's excitement. With each leap of the horse, so did his heart leap, filling him with the hope of a new life and the promise of freedom. He had practically forgotten about the painful beating earlier. "Cover your head with the cloak's hood." I yelled loudly after them, for they were disappearing fast and I remember thinking, as the last tiny speck of white vanished from my wolf's sight: Thank God Gabriel was not here.

I turned back to the plantation. Beautiful Sans Souci. How I hoped I would be able to come back to live and work here. Build another home for my family- a larger, better home than some simple three-room log cabin with dirty pine floors. To live in comfort; to live in peace. If we all survive the approaching battle of annihilation, which I had no doubt would occur soon. The witch had already tricked me (embarrassingly easy), even had entered into my mind's world and I could feel her eternal evil nearby, closer and closer. The memory of that erotic, frightening dream made me tremble.

But I had other things to think about that night; in particular, I had to concentrate on Gerard. I went into the study, unlocked the cabinet filled with his most precious spirits and chose an especially full bottle of very old and very strong whiskey. I took, for myself, a large shot of it (slowly savouring the burning sensation, the aged flavor, the heady aroma) before proceeding upstairs to Gerard's bedroom.

After lighting a couple of lamps and turning them low, (for ambiance I suppose), I poured two glasses of whiskey for us both and placing them on a small table beside the bed, I made myself comfortable in an over-stuffed leather chair next to the table. I loosened my shirt.

Sitting there with my eyes closed, I sensed him not near, yet not far. He will be here soon. This would be easy enough for me, for admittedly, I was attracted to him. Strangely enough though, I did not feel that way for other men- in general. Him alone. Perhaps it was something beyond my control- for he was my maker, my maestro. Since his bite, I have had many experiences against my original nature; this was just another one of them. I actually looked forward to it- anticipating the new sensations- and I believed tonight would unfold quite naturally. He was an immortal, as I, and that alone was an exciting and powerful aphrodisiac.

He was closer now; walking up the oak alley towards the house.

What will not be as easy, or at least I would have to be cautious of, is that he must not discover- yet- that the boy has left Sans Souci. Afterwards, I will tell him what I have done, when- hopefully- he will be calm and pleasant; full of understanding and satisfaction. While he and I are together, I must not think about the slave; not entertain the slightest thought of him. The smallest inkling- the tiniest fragment- of this knowledge might seem as a betrayal to Gerard, and our night together could change into something far from desire. I must concentrate all my thoughts only upon our mutual adventure.

He was coming up the walkway to the front stairs and I knew he sensed me. He was completely aware I was in his room waiting for him. If he would have me; which— I was positive- he would.

He bounded up the stairs in one leap, eager to finally fulfill our fantasy. At the door he stopped for a moment, then slowly entered. That night we never spoke a word out loud to each other until the dawn. Our minds were one as well as our bodies.

He closed the door behind him and bolted it shut.

Well, what is this? Now you want us to become closer? Maintenant? He began removing his shirt.

Yes, why not? It is past time. I almost said I was sorry. Instead, I stood, and held out my hand, hoping my nervousness did not show.

That is certainly true, mon cher. Yet, I am curious. He walked over to me and sat on the bed, ignoring my outstretched hand. What brought this decision about? I know you did not come by it lightly. I sat down next to him and we leaned in close to one another. Have you been secretly watching Juliette at her bath again?

The mere mention of that scene contributed to my arousal. I am ready. That is all.

I could tell that was so even without reading your mind. He boldly, decisively, put his hand inside my trousers and stroked me. His hand was strong and experienced and I grew every second under his expert touch. Groaning with pleasure, I closed my eyes, and leaned in towards him, savoring the moment. His face grazed mine and we kissed- a deep and long kiss. I noticed his mouth and lips were larger, firmer, than a female's. Our tongues found each other effortlessly, obligingly. His hand still kept stroking me.

In the next moment, I found myself lying on the bed shirtless with him on top of me; our hairy chests flexing against one another; our muscles straining together; our hands exploring. His strong manly heart, beat fast and forcefully, seeming to make mine beat in unison. Our tongues refused to surrender their aggressive hold on each other.

Never in any of my wildest imaginations or fantasies, would I have believed the ecstasy attained from two men massaging themselves together. Yet it was achieved by us that night- over and over again. And in these ecstasies, I experienced what I would later come to call an awakening.

We would finish, simultaneously, then lay beside one another for long satisfied moments, thinking of nothing but the mutual pleasure we just enjoyed. Then one of us would lean into the other, we would kiss and it would begin all over again. The ardour between us was assertive and forceful; stimulating each other with energy and vigor- as only two wolf-men could. Such pinnacles of passion! We also fulfilled our fantasies with mutual declarations of love.

Yet did I actually love Gerard? Yes, regardless of his cruel nature. I did love him. Was I in love with him? No, at least not in the traditional sense. I had that love with only one person, Selena. However, I was not going to bury my feelings (or lust) for Gerard- I cared for him too deeply. He was after all, my maker, my mentor and we were as one, especially that night- a oneness I never knew before nor have ever experienced since.

Towards dawn, which was scarlet with the promise of a storm, I must have fallen asleep for a brief time- from contentment I suppose. And therein lied my undoing!

A loud crash woke me and peering out through blurry eyes (I was nude, lying on my stomach)I saw on the bedside table- my pocketwatch! Viewing my precious timepiece- mangled and broken, the porcelain dial and workings in pieces- I knew my plan had not succeeded.

"You should not have fallen asleep, Henri. Even werewolves dream!"

"Well then, let me explain, Gerard- since you entered my mind without my consent! It is not as it would seem. Let me go." He was on top of me, pinning me down with his strength and weight. He was still the more powerful one of us. "If you let me up, I will explain."

"To deceive me more!" His full weight on top of me, he whispered in my ear: "All this night, all of our lovemaking, did that mean nothing to you?"

"Non, non mon cher! It meant everything to me- everything! I enjoyed it every bit as you did and I want us to remain close like this always. Please let me up." I fought against him, but he had the advantage, and was not going to free me. "The boy was simply afraid and I sent him to Selena. Please, do not punish him for it was all my idea." His sex was stiff and I knew what to expect next.

"Don't Gerard. You mustn't." He wasn't going to stop. "I am not one of your slaves or human victims! Gerard, don't! I am warning you."

"Or what? You have already decided to leave me and Sans Souci." The pain was immediate; dry and sharp, yet blunt; a pain unlike any other I had known before. "After all I have done for you; after all I have taught you!" He was thrusting himself more and more vigorously, until the act became violent. I was hurting not only physically, but psychologically. "You used me, you used me," he repeated in a shout, "you make love with me and then plan to leave me the very next day!"

I struggled against him, but it was no use. It only made the pain worse. I tried to relax, but each thrust was agonizing. "It is not like that at all! For God's sake, it was just a dream!" I howled in distress.

"Good! Good!" he shouted back. He enjoyed watching me suffer beneath him. Inflicting pain was an aphrodisiac for him. I was torn and bleeding and I howled again. His momentum increased until finally, I knew, with some relief, that he was reaching his climax.

Finished, he quickly got off of me. Covered in his sweat and sperm, I just lied there, not moving. He looked at my pillow. "Excellent! Even better- Tears! I made you bleed from one end and cry from the other. Excellent! You will always remember this. Yes, always!"

Grabbing his clothes, he stormed out, but not without saying first, ""And to think, I was going to invite your family here. Even build you your own plantation house." He threw my trousers at me, "Now leave. Get Out!!" His last words were shouted so loud, it disturbed a flock of great blackbirds in the distant trees. Thunder rolled as if in answer. I was sure the entire household had heard his roar.

In my room, I cleaned off the evidence of my violation and hastily dressed. I did not pack up anything to take with me. I had come here with nothing and I would leave the same way. I did bundle up carefully all the pieces to my watch and I left the ancient book of the dead upstairs in the secret room. As I went outside, with the clouds gathering ominously, I vowed that episode would be the last time I would ever cry. Except perhaps from happiness. And I have kept that vow all these many, many years.

I found Montesquieu near the large bog where I had once been swallowed up. That seemed an eon ago. He was unharmed except I noticed four large bloody claw marks on his one side. Gabriel! The gargoyle must be back and it had intercepted them. Or had he ever left? The statue was still missing from its usual place. Though it could hide itself anywhere, during the day. More lies, more deception of Gerard's? I wondered where the boy was. Probably huddled in some dark, dank cabin, chained and waiting to be dealt his harsh punishment. I hoped it would not be as humiliating as my 'punishment' had been. But I could not worry about him now. In my anger and shame, all I thought of was leaving and rejoining my beloved family.

I told myself I would never return. The witch can destroy him and have it all. I did not care. Toussaint, Juliette and the boy would have to survive on their own. I would truly miss them.

Poor Montesquieu. He would heal soon enough, yet he seemed disoriented and no matter how I tried to lead him towards home, he- stubbornly- took us round the bog and entered into a large grove of oaks. He seemed to want to show me something.

It was quite dark and shadowy, under the large boughs and towering black clouds. Raindrops started to patter a little at a time and I told Montesquieu that this could wait, that we must go and race ahead of the storm, for I was eager to be home. And then, as he followed his own dictates, I saw, in a particularly bright flash of light, what it was that he wanted me to see.

Horrified, I jumped off Montesquieu and ran to the largest oak in the grove. There, dripping blood, with deep deadly slashes encircling his whole body and throat, was the boy I had tried to help. He was nailed and pinned to the oak with sharp wire, his arms spread, his feet together. Crucified! I looked up into his once beautiful face. His eyes were bloody pools, for the birds had already been feasting on him. The macabre sight was made more so by the increasing raindrops, for as they fell on us, it appeared as if the poor soul was crying- crying tears from empty eyes.

I could not leave him there like that. So with thunder and lightning raging around us, I gently lowered him down and buried him, digging the grave with my bare hands. This ghastly act seemed too heinous even for Gerard. Could his anger really be that vengeful?

Soaked through with blood, mud and rain- and after saying a short prayer over the grave- I then mounted and we virtually flew all the way home. Home to a small but warm cabin where my family and my dear Selena (soon-to-be mother of my child) waited. I did not even think to look for the magic cloak I had given the boy.

Though it actually took us very little time, it seemed an eternity to me. The storm was buffeting us all the while, with fierce gales and hail stones. The god of lightning was working his powers to excess that morning.

Through the sheets of rain, I saw the small village in the near distance and our tiny cabin on the western edge. I alighted off Montesquieu even before his hoofs touched the ground. We were some paces away from the house under the large trysting oak where Selena and I would make love. I would introduce the familiar later in due time after I told them of all that has happened and of all I have learned at witchcraft and explain my ability to control my transformations. I patted Montesquieu farewell and he took off for his own shelter somewhere, as I turned to my old home. I could barely see it as another downpour started to exert itself. The cabin was lit well and I could make out a tiny trail of smoke coming from the chimney, showing that life was normal and active for another early morning. The nearby pens were still full of restless horses and livestock. I thought I saw Porthos and her colt.

I started to run out into the rain, then suddenly, strikingly, the hair on my neck and arms stood straight up. I managed one glance upwards to the top of the tree, to the dimly lit sky and it happened in one blinding stroke. I saw the fire and sparks first, then heard the crash as the great oak was rent in two all the way to its roots. I fell hard and heavily to the ground- unable to breath, barely able to think. Though I do remember distinctly, before losing consciousness, how my wet chest burned fiercely as if it was on fire and I distinctly smelled burning flesh.

How ironic that for all of Gerard's dancing around in the thunderstorms hoping to be struck, it was I (unplanned, even unsought for) who would end up being the one hit by lightning. And, the one, supposedly, to come into more power.

For a long time, it seemed, I laid there, in the mud and rain, unable to move.

My mind slowly shut down; my heart gradually ceased beating; and I knew- again- what it was like to die.

END OF PART THREE

PART IV
MARGUERITE

1

At first there was only the free sensation of lightness, which steadily increased to become so overwhelming that suddenly I found myself flying above the treetops, observing the marsh lands and bayous below. Tall beautiful cypresses reached upwards out of the waters trying to touch me, hold onto me. It was a clear day full of sunlight and I could see for miles and miles into the distance until the earth's curvature allowed me to see no more. I was traveling alone, wondering where my Montesquieu had gone; wondering, vaguely, how it was possible for me to achieve this bird's eye view. Yet I knew I had some purpose- I was searching intently for a place or for some one, though I could not say for whom or what. All I felt was a deep importance that I find whatever it was for whatever reason.

Then in a flash, the scene changed and I was back upon the earth, walking down the oak alley leading to Sans Souci. However, as I approached closer, I saw only charred remains and dying embers; fallen brick and collapsed columns, where once the proud and majestic plantation house had stood.

The wooden two-story structure which I was so fond of was completely destroyed and I was conscious of the most profound sense of loss and sadness. Soon the earth and weeds would reclaim what had once been my home for a brief yet lasting interlude.

"Would you care for some tea?" I heard Selena's voice behind me and turning, I saw in the near distance (under one of the more massive oaks, with its twisting roots spreading above-ground like giant writhing pythons) a petite lady, who was definitely not Selena, sitting at a white cast iron table. Dressed all in white, she was pouring tea for two and I realized immediately who she was.

I approached the witch without trepidation. In fact, I had a quiet confidence in my wolf's power and I also felt some extra strength coming from the clouds where I had been flying, which made me believe I could conquer any-thing, including her.

"Bonjour, Henri," she spoke calmly, even pleasantly. "I am glad to finally meet you."

"The pleasure is mine, mademoiselle." I lied in kind as I sat down across from her and accepted a full cup of tea served from her delicate white china. The hot tea possessed a strong, rich fragrance and as I took a sip of the brew, I knew full well that it may be poison. The taste was slightly bitter, but refreshingly flavorful. Delicious in fact. I irresistibly took several deep sips, thinking this must have been how Gerard felt when having tea with her in the past on the island.

Satine was very beautiful and she did not seem to mind that I was observing her intently. Long silky raven-black hair hung straight down reaching to her diminutive waist. Her petite facial features were a dark gold-like bronze (just like the portrait I had seen once in Gerard's bedroom). The beauty mark she bore added noticeably to her mysterious beauty and allure. Teeth, bright white and evenly spaced, smiled at me from across the table- a smile that reminded me of a cat that has been into the cream. I finished the tasty brew and she poured me more. Her eyes were shiny emeralds, lucid and alert-

presumably innocent- yet anyone perceptive enough would be able to glimpse the cleverness and cool calculation behind them.

"Where is Gerard?"

"Why should you care?" Her cat eyes stared deep into my mind. "After what he did to you!" I tried not to flush in shame at her knowledge of what had passed between Gerard and myself.

"Where is Gerard?" I repeated.

She relaxed back in her chair, sipping her tea. "Gone," she shrugged in simple reply.

"Gone where?" Even in my dreams I possessed a naivete.

"Wherever dead werewolves go, mon cher." She reached across the table and placed her soft hand upon my arm in mock consolation. "He lost!"

"Then I must exact revenge on his behalf," was my brave, fool-hearty rejoinder.

I thought I heard the ringing of a bell, but it was her chiming laughter. However, when next she spoke, she adopted a more serious tone. "The Gods have favored you, Henri. You are most powerful now. Stronger ever than Gerard.. . was." I tried not to demonstrate my surprise. "You now have the power of fire within you. Similar to my own- to a smaller degree, of course," she added.

Yes, that was what I felt. She was right. The power of the lightning was within me! She continued, "I can help you tame the fire and teach you how to use it to your best advantage. Much like Gerard taught you the ways of the loup garou." She rose and came over to my side of the table. "It can be difficult to control at first." She bent down close to me, her cleavage near my face; an emerald and diamond necklace dangled low between her breasts and desire uncontrollably filled me.

I refused to be seduced though and stood up hastily. Immediately, I began to swoon and the earth beneath me started to spin. I fell heavily upon my back, near the base of the gigantic oak, my head hitting hard against the large protruding roots. She had doctored the tea!

"I will ask you only once more, Henri." She looked down at me; her voice sounding like the hiss of a snake; a voice full of evil ambition.

"To procure your victims and then dispose of them for you later?" There was that hiss again. "Non, I will not cooperate. I refuse." I tried to speak with courage, though I felt my powers slowly slipping away.

"Join me and together we can conquer worlds!"

"I would rather die."

"As you wish Henri, but not before you provide a service for me."

"I refuse." I tried to clear my head in order to stand up.

"You have no choice in the matter." Then before I could rise upon my shaky legs, something grabbed hold of each of my limbs and my neck, holding me tight to the ground. The tree had come alive at her beckoning and I was trapped! Vainly, did I struggle to gain release, but the supernatural strength of her familiar had me pinned helplessly. I was now at her disposal.

The following sex act was finished in such a short time, that I thought at first, I had not climaxed. I was losing feeling in my extremities and had become almost totally paralyzed- save for that one part of my anatomy which she demanded performance from- and I did perform- even though in my mind, I tried not to participate.

Then, when she had finished (or I had finished rather)- in an instant- she disappeared. I had anticipated my doom, yet instead of taking my life and very soul with her succubus self, she had only wanted my sperm. However, I still could not gain release from the mighty tree.

Straight away, as I wrestled fruitlessly against the oak's unbreakable force, the breeze whispered my name and, looking upward, I saw what appeared to be a ghostly figure moving above the tree tops. It swirled and circled down towards me and my wooden captor. Then I distinctly heard Gerard's voice. The spirit was he! And knowing this- realizing he was gone from my living world- brought heavily upon my heart the most profound sorrow.

The intangible figure spoke to me, directing me to look deep inside myself for I now had the power of fire; yet, unlike Satine's, mine was white hot- bolts from the skies- pure as the full moon. 'Now, within you, Henri, burns an eternal blaze. Summon it!' Gerard commanded me. 'Break those wooden chains. You are now the strong one. Perhaps the strongest loup garou known to exist. Summon it now, Henri; bring forth the white fire and burst free! Fulfill your fate.'

His presence filling me with confidence, I did as ordered- I called upon all my wolf's strength, along with the lightning force now contained within every cell of my body. Invoking without, those powers within, white flames streamed forth (without warning) from my hands scorching the tree and earth. I managed to release one arm and (before the herculean oak had time to respond) aimed a lightning bolt at the center of its trunk, splitting the centuries-old tree in half. I was released!

Standing there strong and proud, (full of invincibility), my whole being glowed with a brilliant light, charged with current. Yet in another instant (caught unawares) tree branches, reaching from beneath the earth, grabbed me suddenly and I was snatched down into the ground.

But then- The scene abruptly changed again and with my next breath, I found myself in an underground room carved out of the earth. I had a suspicion I had been in that chamber before.

I found myself on my knees in the middle of a dirt floor. Two torches from opposite walls lit the shadowy room; strange incense burned from one corner; a dark statue of an Egyptian God, imposingly stood in the other corner. Behind me, an open door led to what looked to be a tunnel or hallway of sorts. Yet what took all my attention was directly in front of me. There, against the wall, was the most magnificent artifact I had ever gazed upon- beauty so exquisite, my breath was literally taken away. Bejeweled in lustrous pearls and dazzling emeralds, rubies and gems; painted in vivid colors- it was carved in immaculate detail with the visage of a pharaoh. Before me stood an ancient Egyptian sarcophagus of gold made, apparently, for a very important personage, indeed.

"Have some more tea, Henri." Satine's voice echoed through the chamber and beyond. Glancing to that corner near the doorway, (which had been empty only a moment ago), I saw her at the same table, in the same white dress, serving tea from the same china as before.

"He is for you." I smiled with wicked delight at her, imagining that Gerard's plan would finally work and she will be taken by the mummy to purgatory. The only regret was Gerard was not able to witness his victory- her final ending!

"Au contraire, Henri." She bent down to whisper in my ear, for I was still on my knees. Again, I heard that long venomous hiss. "He does not want me any longer. He wants the power you have. He comes not for me, Henri.. He comes for you!" The hiss turned into the shrill cackle of an old crone.

With that shocking utterance, an unseen clock began to strike and the earth trembled in response and, looking towards the sarcophagus, I watched it as it cracked open and the dusty, moldy atmosphere of Egypt, encapsulated for a thousand years, escaped into the room. It whirled briefly above like a living thing, while Satine's maniacal laughter, ceaselessly filled the room- though both she and the table were gone. I covered my ears from the painful noise. And then.. there was only an eerie dreadful silence. A profound silence, it pervaded the entire chamber with its grave-like presence; a calm forecasting the storm.

All at once, the torches were snuffed out and it was now dark (I could still discern the scent of burning incense). There was only one tiny light. A peculiar light, it shone down from above like a beacon, its source unknown, displaying the sarcophagus. It was fully open! And in the coffin- in shadow hidden from the light- the creature lay waiting. For me! I thought I detected movement from inside it. The incantation to raise the mummy was in my memory, but I dare not think upon it; not after Satine's cryptic revelation. The shuffling sound came again from the ancient coffin.

I must escape, leave before he becomes fully alive. I tried to rise, but failed; my knees, my legs were completely numb, unable to make the slightest motion. I was paralyzed from the waist down! And I experienced- perhaps for the first time- true horror. My wolf's strength, my fire power- seemed to have all deserted me. I was being held captive by some invisible force. I could not even crawl away, being frozen to that spot on the floor. What Satine had said was true- I was to be his victim! The mummy wanted my powers now.

He was out of the sarcophagus; shuffling, creeping towards me. Inexorable. Glacial. I dare not look up or gaze upon the unholy figure. In a moment it will have me and I would be in purgatory forever; never to see Selena again- never to know my unborn child.

Then it stopped in front of me within arm's reach. I glimpsed monstrous feet, bound in musty mildewed wrappings. He reeked of death and decomposition; a rotten stench of decayed organs, skin and bones; the stifling dust of centuries of entombment permeated the already thin air. I could barely breathe,

I felt frozen ice on the back of my neck, as the touch of his cold skeletal fingers lingered on me. I started shivering violently. Suddenly it reached down, grabbing my head between both of his cadaverous, yet immensely powerful hands and he compelled me to look up at him. Forcing me to gaze straight into his eyes.

Unlike the rest of him, the eyes were the only body part with a semblance of life. However, they were eyes meant to terrify; meant to mesmerize with menace; to hypnotize with horror. From behind moldering bandages, peered the eyes of a cold-blooded animal; a reptile- a snake or alligator- the eyes of a soul-less predator!

Non! I tried to turn away, but his grip was so firm I thought he would crush my skull. Immediately hypnotized, I had never felt such power. This being, who held centuries of ancient mastery and might within him, had to be the strongest supernatural creature ever to walk the earth. Even the combined efforts of Gerard and Satine could probably not defeat this monster. Perhaps only Dr. Fontenot's creation possessed enough power to rival him. And now, the mummy would be even stronger after absorbing my own force.

A wind began to rise, encircling us; he and I within the center. It steadily gained in size and velocity, gathering up earth and grave-dust: we were in a twister of sand! He picked me up by my head, straining my neck; his eyes burned into my mind, my soul; my body was completely limp- unable to struggle against the painful grip. The dizzying duststorm whirled faster, closing in and the chamber started filling up with sand. My fate was to be buried alive! Deep in the earth, perhaps I would die, most likely not- I would be forever interred! And he would be with me, my eternal guardian, assuring that no unsuspecting soul (accidently or purposefully) allows me to escape back to the real world. I was now where Gerard and I had plotted for Satine to have been- buried deep in the eternal sands of oblivion!

It was at that point (oddly on the brink of my demise) when I realized where I remembered this place from. It was the very tunnel under the cemetery built by Dr.

Fontenot. There must be a hidden room that Pierre and I had overlooked. But there was no Julian here now to help me escape as he did once.

The room was filling quickly like an hour glass- my time was running out. Sand up to my neck, it was starting to spill into my mouth, choking me. Yet, I still could not remove my eyes from his ghastly countenance- overpowering, numbing- I was held by an illimitable evil strength. His shriveled face- bound for such a long time- the cloth was peeling off like skin.

What a horrible sight to be my last for eternity! To haunt my mind's eye for all time. What did I do to deserve such an ending? I was the kind one, the one with a heart- It was I with a conscience still.

Mais non, non! He released his grip as we both were helplessly, and completely, covered with earth. The room, now full to the ceiling, had become my tomb!

"Wake up, Henri." I heard a voice in the sand with me. I tried to move towards it. "Be still, mon amour, it's me, Selena. Wake up, Henri."

The sand was no longer suffocating me; no longer did I feel the earth pressing upon me. Instead- I timorously opened an eye- Selena had a hold of me. "My beloved. It was a dream, all a feverish dream. Quiet yourself, you are alright, Henri. You are back home, safe."

Her beauty shone down at me; her voice soothed me- calmed my heart. It seemed she was always nursing me back to health. A perfectly sublime manner in which to wake up, I admit. Especially after such a nightmare, which dissipated from my memory as most dreams do upon awakening- Save for one lingering memory I couldn't grasp.

Irregardless, it was a comforting pleasure to be home.

We kissed. After our lips unwillingly relinquished their reunion, I took a silent moment to look deeply into her face. Gently putting a finger up to those full, feminine lips, I thought to myself:

Yes, it is true. Her kiss is always like our first.

2

"Are you positive this will be safe?" She nodded yes while snuggling beneath me, positioning herself, positioning me. "I won't hurt you or the baby?"

"Non, of course not Henri. As long as we are both careful."

Selena had become so very...huge. I caressed her swollen belly, laying my head upon her, kissing it. This was my child inside her growing! My seed- my wolf's seed. She would be giving birth remarkably soon. Her pregnant body actually aroused me much more substantially than usual and we made wonderful love- gently, yet passionately. Our heartfelt reunion was intensely intimate as we gradually- tenderly- reached climax.

But all during the act I was still concerned for her well-being and that of the child's and any discomfort (or comfort) she might endure. "Are you sure we are doing no harm?" I repeatedly asked too often. "Am I too..deep?"

"Non, mon cher, I assure you. It is safe for me, for us." She reflected for a moment. "In fact, Henri, you are being quite skillful." So after this long interlude of satisfying sex, as our union was about to attain its apex, Selena's head rolled back, her flushed body arched beneath my grasp and for the first time (that I was aware of) she reached multiple orgasms. I followed afterwards.

We lay there for some time, just holding each other, saying nothing. I could read contentment, even fulfillment in her, but mostly- she felt just pure happiness at having me back home. It was good to be back.

After a time, she brought us tea in bed and we stayed naked under the covers for the remainder of the day. I reached for a cup. "Oh no Henri, this is your tea."

She handed me a different cup. "My tea?" I had a strong feeling of deja vu, though I had succeeded at forgetting all but part of that dream. Later, I would gradually recall all of it, but it would be- by then- tragically, too late.

"Yes, this tea here," she raised her cup, "is brewed especially for my condition, and" she added with significance, "for our babies."

"Babies?" I was too stunned to even register my surprise.

"Oui, mon cher. I feel- I mean, I know- we are having twin boys." She sipped her tea slowly, relishing my stupefaction at her statement. I placed both my hands upon her stomach and tried to see with my mind's eye and witch's sense whether what she said was true. For some reason I could not be definite, yet I did seem to detect two heartbeats! Though again, it might have been wishful thinking on my part. I sipped my tea slowly- it was strong, slightly bitter- as I pondered on the idea of us having twins. That would most certainly be a life-changing event.

"One or two, I hope we have girls, so I can enjoy miniatures of you running about playing."

She laughed. "What a lovely thought, Henri. Oh, how I do love you so."

"And I you." We kissed warmly, yet in the back of my mind was also the thought, (if they were girls), then that would avoid the legends of male children inheriting my condition.

Sitting her cup down, she was clearly concerned

about something. All that day, I did not enter her mind to read her thoughts. I knew her instinctively, as she did me. "I have to say Henri, that, since I became pregnant, I cannot read other people's thoughts as well. In fact, all my telepathic skills have disappeared." She paused, picking her tea back up again. "It is the strangest feeling to lose that ability. I have had it since I was a little girl."

Secretly, I thought that this might be a blessing in disguise, for myself anyway. Now I would not have to bury deep within my conscience different events and acts that occurred at Sans Souci, such as the hunting and subsequent killing I participated in. Especially, I did not want her to discover- ever- what happened between Gerard and myself. "It will most likely return to you once you have the baby."

"Babies." She corrected me.

"Babies." We smiled at each other, enjoying the simple comfort of being together again. A soft warm rain shower began its soothing patter. The hot tea was relax-ing me, giving satisfaction. Strange, but I could not recall Selena (or her grandmother) ever preparing tea. Coffee had always been the beverage of choice, night or day, at mealtimes or not. "Now tell me what happened to grandma-ma. Is she getting better?"

Her frown and downcast eyes told me the prognosis was negative. "We believe it was a hemorrhage in the brain." She looked up at me, trying to express hope. "She may yet get better. I will tell you more later." She snuggled close to me under the soft quilt given to us on our wedding day from Pierre. "First, you must tell me all about your adventure and meeting your ..?" She searched to find the right word.

"My Maker." She nodded and holding me tight, laid her head on my chest, while I related most all that had happened over the last few full moons. "His name is Gerard Mereaux and he is close to one-hundred and fifty years old." She listened intently, almost with rapture, her eyes occasionally filling with wonder and awe, as I told of Gerard's story and all that I learned about myself and lycanthropy.

I informed her of my ability now to control my transformations. Of how I could subdue, (I did not say abolish), my frenzy for human flesh. I gave my assurance, they- meaning Pierre, Selena and all my loved ones- were safe from me. "That would not happen ever again. I have a great deal of conscience, deliberate control, even when I am a wolf; whether the moon is full or not." I was, of course, referring to when I had attacked Pierre.

"And so the witchcraft- it helps your control?"

"That is our belief. Regardez," I demonstrated my ability by growing a long talon from one finger. I could tell she did not know whether to be frightened or impressed. I suppose she was both. "I also now have telepathic abilities, even more acute than you (and grandma-ma) previously possessed." With this news she was noticeably impressed.

I described for her Sans Souci- the plantation grounds and mansion- (trying not to dwell on the luxuries I had enjoyed there); told her of the masquerade party (though I did not speak of the mysterious figure of death); and mentioned my meeting Marie- the same voodoo priestess she and grandma-ma knew.

I left out mention of the seance, as I dutifully failed to speak of my experiences with the witch and specifically, I neglected to talk of the supposed upcoming battle and- what was now certain- my lack of participation in it. I recounted rather innocent tales of magic and potions; of enchanted mirrors and other objects. I tried not to brag (But failed miserably!) about how readily I could learn languages, mathematics and other subjects; of not only how my intellectual capabilities have peaked, but all my other senses as well.

"So I now have the knowledge and ability to run and

manage a complete working plantation- including the slaves."

"Oh but, Henri- we won't own any, will we?" She sat straight up, expressing anxiety at the thought, just as I knew she would.

"Mais non, my love. Jamais. Never." I sat up in bed myself, desiring another cup of tea. "And one day, when we have the financial ability, we can have our own land and property." I added: "And build our own special mansion for us."

I leaned in to kiss her. "But Henri," she exclaimed, "we already have that ability." I read her mind quickly- she was referring to the trunk of riches which Gerard and I had seized! "It arrived only a few days ago. Don't you remember sending it?"

"What?" I sat further upright. "How long was I sick?"

"Five days and just as many nights. The treasure arrived during that time, so you must have had it shipped just before you left Sans Souci." That was impossible, I told myself.

"It doesn't matter if you can't remember, Henri. After what you have been through, it is little wonder! Oh yes, there was a note- a note from you." She rose from the comfortable warmth of our bed and going to her dressing cabinet, produced a paper with- most definitely- 'my handwriting'! I could tell immediately, whoever had composed this had gotten access to the notes I had given the poor sacrificed boy- and that same someone was a murderer. Of course, it was from Gerard- the master at forgery.

I stood up, pointedly and put my trousers on. "We must send it back!"

"But why? I do not understand."

"Ill gotten gains," was my excuse. When really I just wanted nothing more to do with Gerard. Certainly not to be indebted to him. "Where is it?"

"Pierre has it. For safekeeping," she added for

explanation. Sitting on the bed, she extended her arm to me. I sat beside her. "I still don't understand. It does not matter to me how you came by it, Henri. Really it doesn't matter."

"You surprise me, Selena. Are you certain? It was intended to be for you and I- and our new family."

"Then it is now at its rightful place. After all, money is money."

"I still believe I should return it." I started to stand up.

She placed her hand firmly on my shoulder. "Think twice, Henri," her voice had changed from her usual soft sweetness, to a stern siren. "We could live a lifetime- two lifetimes- on this." She kissed me on the cheek, her gentleness returning. "Besides in your capable hands, I am sure we could multiply that money many times over. And neediness and hardship will no longer be a problem for us." I did not know quite what to say to her new found 'authority'. I rather found it amusing, actually.

"All right then, as you wish." I relented, not too reluctantly. Secretly, I was pleased, but I questioned Gerard's motive. What was he planning now that I was no longer his partner against the witch? No longer one of the three necessary warriors?

Selena slipped on a simple, plain robe. I remember how she used to dress and groom herself impeccably. She must be very tired from carrying our child- children? "Let us make more tea," she suggested, "and look in on grand-ma-ma. It is time for her medicine."

As she went about preparing our tea, I noticed how the kitchen area was not as clean as she used to keep it. In fact, the whole house was in disarray, with everything dusty and cluttered. The pine floors looked like they had not been swept since I had left. The pregnancy and taking care of her grandmother must be exhausting for her.

"Each of us has a different tea, especially prepared for that individual. Even Pierre has his particular brew."

"I thought he didn't drink tea. All he needed was his flask." We both laughed as she steeped the herbs. It was so good to be home. "Are these recipes yours and grandma-ma's? I find it so hard to believe she is not getting better. She is such a great healer."

"Perhaps the hardest patient to heal is the healer herself. I also cannot understand why she shows no improvement. She is not getting any worse, though. Marguerite says it is just a matter of time, then one day, suddenly," Selena shrugged, "she will be back to herself."

"Who is Marguerite?"

She covered her mouth in embarrassment. Apparently forgetfulness was another new trait of hers. Of course, part of that might be my fault, for I have kept her occupied all day. I went round behind her and reaching around caressed her belly. The tea was almost ready to pour. "I cannot believe I forgot to tell you. She is my mid-wife from the village north. She came highly recommended and is certainly a god-send to me. To us all! Pierre found her."

Then she must be beautiful, I thought to myself. "Grandma-ma knows her?"

"Oh, I do not think so," Selena started pouring three different teas into three different cups. "Grandma-ma had her attack about two weeks before Pierre brought Marguerite by the house." She stopped pouring and reflected, "It was the strangest thing, Henri, the way we found her."

"Marguerite?" I kissed on Selena's neck.

"No, silly- Grandma-ma. We found her outside by the tree- you know the one." She kissed me knowingly. Yes, the one now destroyed, I thought. "Well, she had the oddest expression on her face, like something had frightened her. And do not say it was just the seizure that caused that. Non! She looked literally sacred to death. Only her strong will kept her from dying."

Mon Dieu! Could the witch be nearby? Marie had

warned me....

"So, back to Marguerite," Selena arranged the teas on a silver tray, which probably came from the trunk of riches. "She had heard I may need help- not only with the pregnancy and birth, but with poor grandma-ma. Come," she picked up the tea tray, "we can visit with her, to a degree. I believe she can hear and understand us."

I took the silver tray from her. "Henri, don't, it is..But the silver." Her astonished eyes drifted from the tray, to my mischievous smile, back to the tray again. "You can control this also! That is good, but.." her tone became serious. "Does this mean silver no longer harms you?"

"Unfortunately, yes it can. If enough of it enters into my blood system at once. Through the heart or the brain; by bullets or arrows or poison or.."

She stopped my morbid rambling with a finger to my lips. "Let us not speak of such things. At least, not today." She took my arm and led me into her grandmother's room.

I followed beside her, dutifully, hoping I would not be too affected by seeing what had once been a very strong determined and healthy, even vibrant, elderly woman now, for all practical purposes, semi-conscious and barely able to respond. Selena managed to set her upright for us and began putting the tea cup to her lips. Grandma-ma was able to sip a little at a time, yet there was no acknowledgement of our presence.

"Grandma-ma, it is me, Henri. I have returned." There was not even the barest flicker of recognition in her face or in her eyes. She just stared straight ahead at nothingness with a blank, forgetful gaze. "Grandma-ma, can you hear me? It is Henri, your son. I have come back to you. Nod or show some sign if you understand." There was no response, but she would sip ever so slightly her tea each time Selena held the cup up to her lips.

"I have to feed her in much the same manner. But she does seem to enjoy her medicinal tea."

"I wonder why she is not showing any progress then." I sipped on my own blend of strong savory tea, then put it aside for the moment. I picked up the old one's left hand, pressing it. "Squeeze my hand if you recognize my voice, Grandma-ma. It is Henri..your son." There was still no response. I held her hand a bit longer in order to try and feel some impression from her. I sensed nothing, but did hear a faint voice. It was simply two words over and over again. I could barely distinguish them, but it sounded like she was saying, 'Bad woman. Bad woman.'

That must have been her last coherent thought before the stroke. Or was it a warning? However, I could not get a mental picture of who she was speaking of. Satine must have been here, making herself known, playing tricks with people's minds as she had done with me at Sans Souci. I would stake my life on it!

I relaxed back in the rocking chair next to grandma's bed and enjoyed the rest of my tea. It struck me as very soothing, making me- not sleepy, but comfortable, content, complete- like I had not a concern in the world. Perhaps there was some drug/herb in it I was not familiar with.

Yet I was concerned about Selena's grandmother. She was obviously ill- her body and face looked thin and tired. Heaven forbid- I had to admit she looked much older than when I left not so long ago. She appeared to have aged twenty years in just a few months- her hair thinning; facial skin no longer taut; a body gradually losing the ability to care for itself.

Selena and I sat there for awhile making conversation- hoping that perhaps grandma-ma might be stimulated by the sound of our voices. "I still believe she will come out of this." Selena sat her cup down and turned to me with a curious look. "Henri, I must ask you. How does a one-hundred and fifty year old werewolf look? Did he age? Will you age?"

I stared dully down into my empty cup at the tea

leaves left on the bottom, wishing for more of the delicious brew. "Ma cherie, I must confess." I took her hand in mine and spoke frankly. "I will never age. Eternal life and eternal youth are mine."

Selena gazed out the window considering the ramifications of this pronouncement. As she becomes older and ages, as our children grow up and mature, "You will always remain looking as you do now, then. A twenty-one year old, handsome beautiful man. While everyone around you ages- and When," her voice trailed off into a murmur, then silence. Her shoulders slumped slightly as if some weight might be upon them; and then suddenly, as if waking up from a trance, she rises and coming over to me, sits in my lap and kisses me fully and deeply, creating another arousal. "But for now we are both young and attractive, energetic and. . ."

"Sexual," I added my own adjective to her words.

She laughed as she rose, still holding my hand. "Shall we go back to our warm, comfortable bed and make love again- this late afternoon?" The rain was still tapping lightly and lazily on the roof.

I jumped up out of my chair like I was a frisky boy again, eager and ready to be- friend, husband, lover. Admittedly, I felt more accomplished and skillful at my lovemaking for having been intimate with Gerard. "Yes, my heart's desire, I want to join you very much."

We exited the sick room, walking hand in hand and were about to enter our bedroom when, "Allo, Henri. Mon ami! You are finally out of bed." It was Pierre at the front doorway. "And I see you are fit as a fiddle and ready for love!" He could still produce that mischievous all-knowing look along with clever well-turned phrases. Yet the rest of him had been altered- dramatically- like the others around me. My whole family.

I embraced him. "Mon vieux, it is so good to see you. Ca va?" His body was thin, even gaunt. My bear hug felt his sharp shoulders and spine, which seemed inadequate to hold up his baggy, ill-fitting clothes. He had always been one of the largest in our family- now he was even smaller than I- thin as a rail.

"Ca va bien!" His voice was still robust. "And you Henri- how was it? Your time away. Inspiring? Dangerous? Are you still..?"

"Why don't the two of you go outside and get reacquainted while I take a nap. You can both talk and catch up on all that has happened." She paused at the bedroom door, "Oh and Henri- I will be waiting."

"Bon!" Pierre slapped me on the back, as we walked outside, just like old times.

"Yes, Pierre. Show me around. Have you done much with the livestock? The horses and corral? Whose land are you working currently?"

He did not respond right away so I read a few of his thoughts. They came across as disorganized, even somewhat incoherent. It seems he had already been imbibing at mid-day. Strange that. "Actually Henri..for now..I am not working. No time for that," he added flippantly. "I have been busy though."

"Let me guess- with the girls, correct?"

"With one girl in particular."

"And who is that?" We were approaching the corral. I held my hand out to pet Porthos who remembered me. Her new colt stayed close to his mother's side, eyeing the newcomer suspiciously. The corral looked unkempt; it stunk of weeks of manure. Posts were missing, falling apart- it was a wonder the horses had not ran away.

"Marguerite."

"What about her?" I could not believe how my horses- our horses— had been so neglected; un-groomed, hoofs untrimmed; one looked sick, maybe even malnourished.

"She is the one I can finally say I am in love with."

"Selena's mid-wife?" Now he thoroughly had my attention. "Well, mon ami! I guess it had to happen some time." I laughed while patting him on his protruding shoulder blade. "I just thought that it would be years from now before you would consider settling down." His laugh was hearty, boisterous, like before, but then it was followed by a deep and prolonged cough. Oh no, my poor life-long friend was ill- just how badly I later would find out. "This Marguerite- she must be a special type of girl to ensnare someone like you! Selena seems to trust her explicitly."

"Henri, she is the most beautiful creature." He laughed again, this time without the accompanying cough, "and I have known a few! She is dazzling; and what is more- she's a highly intelligent and accomplished girl, especially considering her age. She is very young."

"Pierre!" I scowled at him. Leaning over close to my ear, he whispered her age. "Pierre!" This was truly surprising for I thought he always desired the more mature woman.

"Come let us go have a toast inside to honor your homecoming. We were quite worried that you might not return in one piece." He patted his side. "I have an excellent aged whiskey here beneath my shirt."

It was good that some things had not changed. "Yes, I see the outline of your flask," I joked as we went inside to rejoice in our reunion.

Selena, anticipating our needs, (and apparently deciding to forego her nap), had already set the table with tea service for three. Each of us had their own single tiny china pot and cup filled with a special tea brewed especially for them. "I laid down but couldn't sleep." She smiled wide at me. "I am too happy." She took a sip from her steaming cup. "You know Henri, Marguerite is a wonder in the kitchen," Selena boasted.

I lovingly took her hand. "I seriously doubt she could be a better cook than you, my cherie."

Pierre poured a healthy shot of whiskey for the two of us and, giving Selena a small amount, we three toasted to our being together again. "I like to put a little whiskey in my tea." And he did just that. "Mine is specifically formulated to give me more stamina. Particularly in the bedroom." He winked, obviously thinking his remark was funny, though I could never remember Pierre being so crass in front of a lady. However, Selena did not seem to mind and was laughing lightly at my ill friend. Well I hoped the tea helps him, because to me, he looked pale and unhealthy with large dark circles under his eyes. And also, I would have never thought Pierre needed some 'stimulant' for sex, for he seemed the natural stallion among the mares.

"What is my tea for then? What purpose? For the healing after the lightning strike?" The answer came silently to me in my mind. I recognized a faint female voice- coming from some unknown place- speaking only to me: 'Why, its purpose is to give you a choice, Henri. To allow you to have what you said you always wanted.' I turned- we all turned- towards the open door. There stood a tall female figure in the shadows.

"Marguerite!" Pierre exclaimed. I was almost embarrassed for him by his love struck boyishness.

She entered the room slowly, a little hesitant, realizing all eyes were on her. I agreed that yes, she was beautiful in her way, looking much more mature than her teenage years. Marguerite was quite a tall girl, like many French Normans; her hair typically blond, the color of corn silk; her face fair, angular, with features resembling carved ivory. Even with a sharp aquiline nose and large prominent lips, her visage- taken as a whole- was attractive enough. I suppose, I could understand Pierre thinking of her as some young goddess of the earth, reaping and sowing, growing and cultivating plants, flowers and herbs. She had a small basket of freshly picked flowers with her even now.

Her figure, to my mind, was only somewhat appealing. She wore a loose fitting, 'peasant dress';

rather unattractive clothing, to be sure, which hid any attributes she might have. Perhaps she, purposefully, disguised her qualities from men's prying eyes. Overall, my first impression described her as- homely; not at all Pierre's style.

"Allo Monsieur LeBlanc," she curtsied politely, perfectly, reminding me of Juliette, yet lacking some vital trait Juliette possessed. A certain charm, perhaps? "I am so pleased to finally meet you." I stood and we shook hands softly. Her touch was as bland as her look. "These two have been most anxious for your return."

Pierre was immediately at her side, doting upon her like a love starved puppy- yet I believe I understood why. Though plain and simple in her dress and manner, she had a definite allure; her behavior (one could characterize her as aloof and reserved) was still interesting; certainly some men would find it enticing. Her voice- strangely delicate and soft for such a tall girl- gave the impression of a self-educated, self-assured lady of maturity- not like Pierre's description at all. Nevertheless, after seeing her for the first time, she held a certain fascination for me. "I am very pleased to meet you also, mademoiselle."

"Please, call me Marguerite."

"Bien sur, as you wish- Marguerite." Selena came over to her and they kissed each other softly on the cheek; then, taking Marguerite over to the kitchen, they began making plans for dinner and deciding what chores needed to be done. After a few moments, they went to look in on Selena's grandmother. Fresh tea for all of us was already simmering over the fire.

Pierre and I sat back down to finish our first cup and pour us another. I stirred a little of his whiskey in. "She is quite charming. Normandese, I suppose?" Pierre nodded. "Yet her name conjures up thoughts of the West Indies." I took a large sip- the whiskey was strong. "Where did you- come across her?"

"In the neighboring village. She came highly recommended by our mayor here. Selena and I are allowing her to stay at grandma-ma's old cabin for now." He slurped his tea like it was soup. "I love her, Henri. Very much."

"I can see that. You know Pierre, I only hope for your happiness. You do realize that don't you?" I asked pointedly. He nodded. I paused, searching to find the correct way to word my next question. "Have you been ill, mon ami? Are you feeling poorly?"

"Non, non Henri. It is a miracle- the weight just fell off. I have never felt better in my life. And it is all due to Marguerite." He paused for another loud sip of tea and whiskey. "I think, we shall marry very soon. After your baby is born."

"You have asked for her hand in marriage?"

"Yes, and she has agreed. Then Mademoiselle Des Villiers will become Madame Boudreaux."

"Congratulations!" We toasted to his happiness. The name he mentioned gave me pause for it seemed familiar. I tried to recall a memory from far back. But where had I heard that name before? I helped myself to more of the hot freshly brewed tea and promptly forgot about the mysterious name and my weakening memory.

As soon as we were alone, Selena and I crawled back under our comfortable sheets, on our busy bed, staying there the rest of the day and night. We did not even stop for supper.

"Why is our clock not wound?" It was the second (or third?) morning after my recovery. I surprised myself- I normally would have noticed if it had stopped. Selena and I had just finished another night and morning of love making. Her swollen figure (or perhaps the idea she carried my child) seemed to make me that much more sexually charged. In fact, both our sexual appetites seemed to be at a peak. I suggested to myself it must be because I had missed my (almost newlywed) wife for so long. She was steeping our morning teas. Seldom did she make coffee anymore. What was very different, was that I did not miss it.

"Oh, I am so sorry, Henri. I have been negligent and I know how important the clock is to you. Do forgive me." She kissed me on the cheek in recompense. Well yes- I thought to myself- it should be important to both of us. Then again, there was my pocketwatch: I had been intending, yesterday, to try and repair it, but something always managed to distract me even though Pierre and I were not looking for work. We could all easily survive on the coins and silver from Gerard's and my trunk. However, we did not spend much, or even make large meals. Even my hunger for human flesh seemed to be diminished. It was almost as if tea was our main sustenance.

Strange also, that Selena never asked about my pocketwatch, her wedding gift to me. But I suppose, she was distracted with her expectancy. Frankly, I was relieved she did not mention it.

One more thing that it is better she not know; One thing more to keep secret from her. Yet she was aware I had my private secrets about different occurrences at Sans Souci. However, she would never have imagined in her wildest dreams, what actually did happen. The previous evening the four of us had a most pleasant (albeit small) meal together. Selena and Marguerite had prepared a venison stew with potatoes and I was happy to get back to my peasant roots. Surprisingly, I had not much missed the creature comforts of Sans Souci, like I feared I might. Perhaps it was because of my dramatic exit. Yet overall, when reminiscing, I always had fond memories of my too short a time there. And even though my parting with Gerard was unpleasant, I hoped to God, he would survive his 'encounter' with Satine. I could no longer harbor him any ill-will.

Our conversation over the meal was also pleasant. Marguerite was quite intelligent, even a little worldly- for such a young, plain girl. Unlike Juliette, who as a slave was taught by her grandfather, Marguerite apparently had to learn everything on her own for her folks died when she was but a toddler. As far back as she could remember, she had always been an orphan: moved about from one orphanage to another, from place to place, always alone. Then, when about twelve years old, she ventured out on her own. Of course, that was unheard of for a female in that place and time. She traveled, living by her feminine wits (and wiles, I supposed) and became quite learned in medicines and midwifery. ("I would say she even knows more than grandma-ma," Selena admitted in whisper to me once, though I found that hard to believe.) So Marguerite became a rather capable and accomplished girl, especially considering her obstacles and I admired her self-reliance and maturity. She was now part of our household- Pierre's fiancé.

It was true that her knowledge of herbs and plants was formidable. The teas she created for each of us though, I was unfamiliar with and I wanted, one day, to deconstruct them and analyze the ingredients. If only I had access to Gerard's books. It seemed like I was slowly forgetting some of my own spells and potions. I did not want to admit to myself, but for some odd reason, my powers were dwindling; diminishing a tiny bit more each day.

"How much are we paying for her services?" I asked Selena one morning over tea.

"Nothing as of yet." My curious look caused her to explain. "Marguerite said she would collect after the birth."

"And how much is that?"

"I do not recall us discussing an exact amount. Strange that." She sipped her tea slowly trying to remember and then shrugged her shoulders. "I am sure it will be reasonable. Pierre will remember discussing it. She has been a God-send to me." She had referred to Marguerite in that way before. I looked about at the dusty house and dirty kitchen and thought she was not that much of a god-send. And what with grandma-ma still sick. "I trust her explicitly and hope she and Pierre will be very happy together." Selena poured us more tea.

"I am sure they will." then I paused in mid-sip, the word 'explicitly' hitting a nerve. "Does Marguerite know of the treasure?"

"Oh no, I doubt that!" She was quick to reply; then, scratching her temple as if it helped her to think, "Unless Pierre.."

"Unless Pierre told her. What do you do when you need money?"

"Oh yes, I forgot to tell you. My memory seems to be slipping. There is a large canister on the shelf over there," she pointed to a side cupboard, "full of coins and gold and we just use that for our supplies. Pierre periodically fills it up from the trunk." I spotted the tin can on the cluttered shelf. It was among the other canisters which most likely were filled with Marguerite's herbs and teas. Anyone could discover the money without effort and most likely Marguerite had already done so.

"Does she know about..?" I hesitated, for Selena had

always read my mind and finished my sentences. But then again, my own telepathic ability had been weakening lately, ever since leaving Sans Souci. Could that place be a source of power?

"About?" She could not finish my question. The intimate telepathy between us was no more.

"Myself. And my 'blessed curse'?"

"Oh," she laughed softly, saying, "What a perfectly curious phrase! Yes..I mean, no, of course not. Before accepting her, Pierre and I both discussed with each other the absolute need for secrecy about your 'blessed curse'." She paused in her thoughts, her mind wandering, distracted; unlike the sharp-minded Selena I had left behind. "I need to go into town and get some supplies." She spoke almost wistfully.

"I need to go work on the corral fence." I did speak wistfully.

"Or..", putting down her tea cup, she rose and grabbing my hand in hers, started to lead me into the bedroom.

"But ma cherie," I mildly protested, "should we not refrain- somewhat. Aren't you close to giving birth?"

"Marguerite believes I have approximately two weeks,"

When there next would be a full moon, I thought. "Does she realize the gestation period is supernaturally short? Has she raised questions?"

"Never. Not even once. Perhaps she has not noticed. She has been here only a month- or two. Of course, I never told her the true date of my conception." Selena leaned into me whispering as we disrobed. "Sometimes she seems ... simple." My questioning look caused her to explain. "By that I mean she is modest and unassuming- not a suspicious person. However, I know she is not near as young as Pierre would like to think she is."

"What? She seems rather young to me." I left my clothes in a pile on the floor.

"Oh you men are all the same. Perhaps as a female, I notice the little wrinkles, her premature grey hair and crow's feet."

It was almost as if she was describing someone else. "I never noticed that- I will have to look closer."

She shrugged, "As they say, 'Beauty is in the eye of the beholder'." She playfully pushed against my chest, and so, playfully, I fell back upon the bed. "This time Henri," she commanded, "it will be your turn to lie on your back."

Two hours later, Marguerite knocked lightly on the front door before entering the cabin, as Selena and I hastily dressed. Selena was the first to go out and greet her; I followed after, somewhat sheepishly, half-dressed, looking for a clean shirt. However, Marguerite seemed to pay us no mind, going on about her duties- bringing in supplies and herbs; preparing grandma's medicines for the day; etc. "We need to change her linens and give her a bath today."

Overhearing them, I realized, I too definitely needed a bath, for I had not bathed my whole person at once since I had returned home. Strange- living as a wolf-man at Sans Souci, I was more groomed and clean than living here in my cabin as a normal human male. I was becoming lazy like Pierre. So later in the afternoon I went out for a swim and bath, while the girls did their chores and shopping for the day.

That evening, Selena and I took a walk after dinner, as the sun was setting. Pierre had, as usual, gone off with Marguerite to find their own trysting spot.

We walked by our own old romantic spot. What was once a majestic and magical oak, under which we had made love so many times, was now split in two, all the way to the ground; burnt into crumbling pieces, with a large blackened hollow spot 'carved' out of the immense dead trunk. The trees large and heavy limbs had crashed to the ground- dead and obstructing the pathways. We stood for some time in silent sad contemplation at the scene. "I guess I shall have to chop this up for firewood soon."

"You could use some of it for the corral fence and the other pens."

"Yes, true." I kicked one particularly huge branch loose; it fell with a loud lonely crash. Suddenly I sensed Montesquieu.

I had not thought of him very often during the last few days; perhaps, I had not thought of him at all- I could not recall- my memory at that time being very hazy. However now, it was time to introduce him to Selena.

We strolled hand in hand down a path that lead into the thick woods. "Do you know what a 'familiar' is, Selena?" I noticed her look of confusion. "I mean a familiar for a witch?"

"Oh yes! Yes," she nodded, "I recognize the term. I have heard grandma-ma speak of household cats being sent to become a companion or pet for the witch. I do not recall her mentioning any particular purpose that they actually served though."

"They serve the witch (or warlock) in any capacity necessary; sometimes acting as a protector. However, the familiar is not always a cat or pet- it can be trees, other objects, a statue come to life and so on. The familiar given is particularly suited for the conjurer's needs."

"And you were assigned one?" I nodded. "By whom?" She hesitated, her voice becoming a whisper: "Do they come from the dark side?"

"I cannot say where they come from or how they are created. Though I will say- neither Gerard nor I have ever met the devil- we do not even know if any exists. Angels and demons are another matter, however." She started to ask another question, but decided to let me continue. "And my familiar is here especially for my express purposes only." We stopped walking (we were deep into the shadows) and I turned to face her- my voice becoming filled with enthusiasm again.

"My familiar is a magnificent steed, larger than any other I have ever seen, who is as fast as the wind and can travel great distances in a matter of minutes. Leaping over treetops and buildings, he can practically fly. He brought me here, through the storm, in practically no time at all."

"He has wings? Like in the story of Pegasus?"' Her voice still a whisper, she demonstrated some surprise and awe, as we held each other close and started to walk further into the shadows. There was a cool change in the evening air; signaling that the long summer in this southern land was slowly coming to a close to make way for shorter days- and longer nights of hunting.

"Non, ma cherie, he does not have wings. But he is the strongest, tallest horse ever to exist on this land, no doubt. There, in the distance," I pointed to a white shape behind a stand of small pine trees. I called his name out silently and Selena let out a small gasp of wonder as Montesquieu stepped out from the shadows and into the open.

He snorted once at us, but made no move to come closer. I held out my empty hand as we moved cautiously closer to him, yet some thing seemed different about him and our connection. I was not able to telepathically communicate with him; my mind and thoughts were not focusing as well as before. It became obvious he did not recognize me! Was I really so different now? So changed, even my familiar no longer knew me?

I called out his name and only then did he decide who I was and so- he carefully, watchfully, approached us- my arm still extended. He sniffed my open hand, (knowing I had no sugars or treats for him), yet he needed to make sure I was the master he had come to love and serve. Only then, satisfied that I was the Henri he used to know, did he allow us both to touch and pet him.

"What a magnificent creature!" she exclaimed. "Henri, he is gigantic. So tall and. . .beautiful. Why, I can barely reach his back!" Selena admired him: petting on him, caressing his long silver mane, hugging his substantial neck. Montesquieu permitted it- but whereas, usually he would start prancing about and showing himself off to his human admirers- he was instead exceptionally alert, motionless and aloof, still hesitant with us- with me. Perhaps he sensed some evil nearby, maybe danger approaching.

Suddenly, Montesquieu silently started- seconds before we heard the crack of a twig beneath someone's foot; My own once sensitive hearing had failed on me. Selena let the horse go and he vanished in a flash, like lightning. "Miss Selena, is that you?" It was Marguerite's soft, mousey voice. I heard Pierre's heavy trudge following her.

"Yes, I am over here with Henri." I put a finger to my lips. It was best that no one (save Selena), know of my familiar. Even Pierre needed to be excluded from this knowledge. Especially since he was so enamoured and, consequently, most probably careless with what he discloses. Also, I somehow felt Marguerite knew all about me- my werewolfism, my witch's power. She might even be capable of reading minds or tell everything about someone with just a touch or a brush of their clothing.

"I hope we do not disturb you. Pierre was just walking me back to my cabin." Her cabin, huh! I growled to myself. Marguerite's usual pale complexion was flushed- obvious even in the shadowy starlight. Pierre's eyes flashed at me with shared acknowledgement. But then strangely, quickly, he cast his eyes sharply downward in shame; or more specifically- as if he had just been chastised or rebuked for revealing a secret. It was evident, they had been making love in the early fall heather. I imagined Marguerite cared little whether we knew or not.

I deliberately tried to read her thoughts, however, I could not grasp even a single feeling- almost as if she were not there- but was, rather, an apparition, an image not alive. Pierre's thoughts were clearly written on his face- he was flustered and- strangely nervous. Usually he handled his women and moments like this with a care-lessness, which I often lectured him about, however this was to the other extreme. He was not only smitten by Marguerite; she had a great deal of sway- no, control-over him. That was quite different for Pierre.

"Au demain, Selena." "Until tomorrow," my wife replied. Pierre passed by me, slapping me on the back. I had missed that comraderie. He had turned, instantan-eously, into his old self again- nodding at me knowingly; they had just made love and he was ready for more. The tea made for that particular type of stamina must be working for him- but then- why is he so unhealthy in appearance? I noticed, as he half-ran to catch up with the tall fast-paced Marguerite, that he had a pronounced limp on his right side.

On our stroll back to the cabin, I gave some thought to what had been happening to me for the last few days since I had been back. My 'condition' was worsening. Not only was I losing my bewitching powers, but the strength, energy and acute senses of the werewolf were also diminished, almost becoming non-existent. The telepathy I once enjoyed, was severely crippled and getting worse. Was I turning back into a human? We entered the cabin and Selena immediately went to the fire to heat up our teas for the last cup of the night before retiring. Retiring, most likely, for sex and then- sleep.

Sitting there by the fire, (there was an early chill in the air), rocking in grandma-ma's old chair, I had to ask myself: Do I want to be human again? To get sick, grow old and eventually- painfully- die? To experience the boredom of everyday living? I would not only lose my powers, but my learning abilities would return to that of an ordinary man. Was that such a bad thing to happen?

One advantage to being human: I would age normally with my Selena and our children. And-

There would be no more killing. No longer the threat of discovery. No risk of suffering that centuries-old loneliness which Gerard has had to endure.

I took another sip of my tea; drew in a deep breath, exhaling it slowly; and relaxed myself. Selena was calling me from the bedroom. I will just think upon these questions tomorrow. Tomorrow I may be thinking more clearly. Perhaps without the tea. Yes, most definitely without the tea.

I rose to join Selena. And there was one more question I would have to answer tomorrow and this question was perhaps the most important.

Was I a better man for having been loup garou? For having learned the 'craft' of witches? Could I possibly become an even better man? With or without these powers?

I would sleep on it, after..Selena. I would sleep on it then.

4

The next morning, I rose before dawn to make myself a large pot of dark, strong coffee (like I previously always enjoyed, day or night), instead of having Marguerite's tea as usual. I immediately felt more alert and energetic; however, fighting the addiction was not easy. In fact, it was one of the most difficult tasks I ever set to do for myself. All that day, I constantly dwelt upon the tea's pleasurable, enervating effects and came very close to losing the battle. At one point, I even had boiled the water- the cup and saucer ready on the table. I imagined it more addicting than alcohol could ever be- at least, my tea recipe was- similar to a heavy drug. I had to keep my mind on other things- and not sex either.

So, early that morning, before life began stirring (all of us sleeping in later and later), I made the coffee and going outside with my full mug, I surveyed all the work that needed to be done. And there was a lot to do. Pierre's and Selena's neglect was evident everywhere. I would start with mending the fences to the corral and grooming the horses.

Doing hard, laborious work was the perfect antidote and- trying to concentrate only upon the task at hand- in a few hours, I began to feel some of my strength returning. Then, as each successive hour passed (without consuming the tea) I felt within me the power which I had come to appreciate. My wolf's power, in particular- the acute senses, the sharp intellect and instinct, the absolute strength and, (without fail), the familiar hunger- relentless still.

Only a week or so, from the autumnal equinox and a full moon, the day was cloudless and still; hot and sultry, more like the height of summer. As I chopped wood, tended fences and cleaned the pens of manure, my mind cleared itself from the drug's effects. My thoughts became less muddled and they inevitably, turned to Sans Souci; to Toussaint, his lovely granddaughter and, of course, to Gerard.

I harbored my mentor no hatred or ill-will for what had transpired between us, and I knew he was most likely remorseful for his actions. As remorseful as someone like Gerard could be. However, what was most important- I had, consciously and purposefully, stopped thinking of myself as a victim. I was not going to visit Sans Souci or find out if he had success in the endeavor to retrieve the mummy from Egypt. Of course, with me out of the scene, there could be no unholy three which, according to Marie and her correspondent, was required in order to destroy Satine. I was no longer going to help him- As long as the witch did not interfere with me and mine.

Oh, but how I did miss Sans Souci, though! Not the luxurious comfort and niceties, but the atmosphere, the land, the beauty and fields. I missed working and managing the plantation. However, there was the treasure and now Selena and I could buy our own land and build on it. It would seem that all might work out well.

Nor did I feel the least obligated to Gerard for sending us that trunk of riches. I had paid my dues and I would always have some emotional scar to show for it.

Non, Gerard was on his own.

It took all morning and well into mid-day before I had adequately finished all the work in need of immediate repair concerning the horses. Tomorrow, I would work on the hen house and pig pens and stockpile more chopped wood. I decided to set aside this evening to work on my pocketwatch. Selena had just left for market to get supplies and food- she had put off her shopping for some time now. I was instructed to make sure grandma-ma takes her medicine and tea later that afternoon, or 'She will start babbling nonsense and will not stop.' Yes, I missed painfully, those wonderful enlightening conversations with grandma-ma.

After washing off the mud, sweat and manure, (which I was covered in from head to toe), I proceeded to give Porthos a quick grooming. She needed brushing and bathing; her coat was caked with mud; her mane had knots running all through it. I led her from the pen and she stood still and well-behaved, beneath a shady pecan tree while I allowed her quickly growing (and ever frisky) colt, out to prance and dance playfully around us- yet, never did he drift far from his mother's side. A slight late summer afternoon breeze began to rise, carrying with it the faint fragrance of wildflowers and I thought again how happy I was to call this land home and country. How happy I was with my little cozy cabin and to be engaged again in strenuous physical labor.

Already I felt tremendously better for the first time since coming home; my body and mind were restoring themselves, responding quickly now that the drug's effects were diminishing. Also, I 'd lost all sense of time. I thought I had been back a week- only to find out that three whole weeks had passed! Yet every hour that passed I was improving- not only in my strength as a wolf, but also my witch's mind was becoming more in control of itself and I was remembering, (slowly at first), some of my potions, formulas and spells I had memorized. The languages I had learned and other facts and figures; the literature I had read- it was all coming back to me. I made a mental note to myself to check on the teas and their composition (later tonight) after Marguerite leaves for the day.

She should be here at any moment. Selena said the young girl would be arriving about this time of day. And then all at once-

She silently appeared as if conjured from the heavy air around us, stepping out from behind a tree like a wood nymph. Strangely, at first, with the sun in my eyes, I thought it to be a much smaller petite woman. With her long blonde hair and natural 'homespun' look, she appeared to be an angel, with the sun providing her halo as she approached. Pierre was not with her, but I gathered he was not far away and would be present soon. Wherever she goes, he goes.

"Bonjour, Monsieur Henri." She was carrying her wicker basket containing, as usual, herbs and what looked like slices of bark and weeds. I could only suppose she was replenishing our 'stock' of teas.

"Bonjour, Marguerite. Ca va?" The young girl was dressed even more 'dowdy' than usual that morning, but I knew the outer cover belied a sultry maturing body beneath. I wanted to touch her (now that my powers were returning) so as to get an impression from her- Just what are her intentions?

"Ca va bien, merci." she replied. "I see you are doing some much needed work. Bon, I am glad you are feeling yourself again." She started inside the cabin. "Oh Monsieur, shall I prepare you a late lunch?" She stopped, focusing her eyes on me directly, and I felt a twinge (or chill?) of something. A mental suggestion? "Or would you rather have some tea- Henri?" For the first time, Marguerite addressed me solely by my first name and suddenly, I was transported back to the oak alley and I was having tea with.. But that was a dream! Then why did it feel so real, as vivid a memory as an actual event.

I approached Selena's mid-wife, pointing to the basket she still carried, "Is that for our teas?"

"Yes, Monsieur. Have you been enjoying the brew I blended especially for you?"

"Too much so, I am afraid to say. It is almost inebriating."

"I am so sorry, Henri. I cam make it weaker." She took a step closer to me and then unexpectedly, we were very close to one another. She was even taller than Selena. I felt the fresh brush of her breath on my cheek. "Much of the time I must make due with what herbs and plants are available locally."

"I understand completely. I too know some things about herbs, teas- and potions."

"Excellent, then we should share notes and recipes. I would be glad to list the ingredients for you."

434

"My tea was meant.."

She finished my sentence for me. "…to heal you after the lightning strike." Her pause after, was barely perceptible, yet meaningful. She leaned in closer to me and I sensed her sweat- still sweet from youth. "The tea was specifically meant to restore you to your original condition."

A strange choice of words, I thought later, yet at the time I shrugged it off. She turned to go inside. "I wanted to ask you about Selena's grandmother. If she is not getting any better, perhaps we should change her medicines? Or consult someone else?"

"I am so sorry for your family, Monsieur Henri," she was back to her polite demeanor (while politely avoiding my questions). "I know how much grandma-ma means to you."

She touched my arm, warmly, compassionately, for just an instant; But in that one second, I received a strange sensation from her. A coldness? Yet her hands were warm. A chill? Yet the day was hot. The late-summer breeze was starting up again, stirring the tree tops.

I started to say something, however she spoke up first- her tone very 'matter-of-fact'. "Your grandmother has had a very severe stroke. Though I believe- given time- she will slowly recover and be almost herself again." She took a step closer to me (a large stride for this tall girl), so that I was able to see into her green eyes. "As long as she does not have a setback." Her voice inflection was flat- stern almost. Was she giving a warning? Then why did it sound like a threat?

"Yes I suppose, we can wait and see; I miss her so. She is such a wise woman-and has had a strong influence over me."

"Grandma-ma cares a great deal for you, also; she thinks of you as her son." I nodded. "It must be very comforting to have such a loving family." She spoke pensively, a hint of her own sadness and loneliness uncomfortably emerging. She turned aside to go in.

Yet again, I spoke; stopping her in mid-step. "Mentioning family. . .uh," She stared back at me, those feline eyes shining down just at me. Flecked with gold, they were sensuous, beckoning- summoning me to... Again, I experienced deja-vu- for I had seen those same eyes gazing upon me- somewhere different, on someone else. A memory tried to surface and then it was gone with the steadily increasing wind.

"Do you think Selena is having twins as she believes?" I had to ask for Marguerite's expert judgment as a mid-wife. The colt had been strangely shy and still all this time, staying by his mother's side, who was- herself- becoming restless. It was time for me to pen them back up.

This time, she planted her hand firmly on my bare chest and there she left it. A casual move- then again... Without a doubt, I sensed a 'strength' emanating from her. I might not call it a power, though she was- most definitely- some type of sorceress or voodoo princess. Yet her touch held something more. She was a seductress! Her touch sent me a shock; a message of desire- making me feel desire; commanding my appetites to come to the forefront of my thoughts.

Keeping her hand upon me, (myself wishing she would remove it), she spoke: "I believe she carries only one child." She paused, while I was becoming more and more uncomfortable. "The good news is that it is likely to be a boy! Of course- I may be mistaken- Henri," she again used only my first name, becoming familiar once more.

She withdrew her hand slowly, letting it linger against my hairy chest; allowing it to trail down my naked torso, stimulating me that much more. "I am sorry monsieur, if my opinion is disappointing to you." She returned to her demure, aloof self. "But as I said, I feel sure it is a boy."

My perception had always been that there was only one child. She merely confirmed my layman's opinion. I made some forgettable, unemotional reply.

As we both turned away to go about our respective duties, she called back to me with her gentle soft speech. "Do you hear them, Henri?"

"Hear what, mademoiselle?" I could not even guess what she was referring to.

"The drums."

"The drums?" I echoed.

"In the distance." Standing quite still and silent for a long moment, I listened intently, and finally- yes, there was the faint rumble and beat of drums. Voodoo drums! Not steady, more flowing; sporadic with little or no intensity; they sounded quite a great distance from here- somewhere deep, deep in the swamps. Those with ordinary human hearing should not be able to detect the drums at that volume and distance. And she had noticed them before me!

"What does it mean?" I asked.

"They are speaking of a war approaching. A battle supreme; a war among the gods." She walked up the small steps to the front door. "And soon to happen. Do you know what on earth they may be referring to?" She deliberately looked hard at me- anticipating- waiting for an answer.

"Non." I appeared disinterested and turned back to my horses. I was becoming tired and feeling withdrawals from the tea. 'You must decide Henri- and soon- if you wish to be among the gods on that day.'

I jerked my head back in her direction, but she had already disappeared inside. Who had spoken? I had heard someone's voice: distinct and real, yet, it was unrecognizable. It could have been male or female; surely, it was not my imagination- my own thoughts perhaps? However, I had to face the decision- the words were true enough; and now, with the drums signaling the battle- it was time to make my choice.

After locking the corral up, I went inside to change clothes, staying in the bedroom, my door closed, while Marguerite prepared late lunches for us and tended to her other duties. Actually, I was avoiding her- that look, her touch. However, she soon left to take Pierre his meal, for today (surprisingly!) he was working with a group of others on building a new cabin for a local family.

I went into the kitchen area. A sandwich of rare beef had been left for me on the table. Obviously, she knew of my appetite for bloody meat. I cleared the rest of the table off and taking my misarranged and broken pocketwatch out of a drawer, sat down to try and accomplish some semblance of repair out of this broken puzzle. The poor watch was in pieces, but it could be salvaged. If only I had my tools back at Sans Souci.

I did quite a bit of the fine delicate work necessary and placed different pieces together to discover exactly what might need to be done further. However my thoughts kept drifting back to Marguerite and the drums. They were still playing, if ever so faint; I probably would never have noticed them if she had not mentioned it. The drums meant Gerard would soon be fighting for his survival (and that of his plantation).

Was Marguerite the one Marie had warned me about? Could she actually be Satine in disguise? Whether or not she is Satine (or working with her), she surely knows much more than just herbs and medicines. There was a definite mystery about her, yet was she here to help or do harm? Selena and Pierre trusted her, but then they were obviously under her influence. If only grandma-ma would come back to our world. She would know instinctively.

As I was trying to manipulate the tiny coiled hairspring back into its original form, I absentmindedly took a bite of the sandwich she had left for me and instantly, profoundly, I was overwhelmed with nausea; my thoughts became confused, muddled, worse than any drunken state I had ever experienced. I had to put my tools down and grab hold of the table with both hands, for my head started to swim and I imagined I would fall out of my chair. She had doctored the food with some potion! And all I could think of was having more of that tea- that evil brew of her making.

I wanted the tea; I had to have that tea! It seemed absolutely necessary for my survival and if I did not have at least a sip of the beverage, right away, I would surely collapse right there on the floor and become a silent patient like Selena's grandmother, with my mind somewhere in a netherworld.

Rising ever so slowly, I stood upon wobbly legs and cautiously, unsteadily walked over to the kitchen fireplace and filled a pot with water from the fresh barrel she had just replenished. It was as if someone was commanding me, forcing me to do something against my will. I imagined in my mind, the witch taking a voodoo doll representing myself and manipulating my actions. I was obviously not in control; my movements followed someone else's dictates. So I brewed the tea, poured myself a large cup and sat back down at the table: the full cup in front of me- beckoning me, challenging me, insisting that this was the only way- the best way- for me to find peace finally and forever.

I reached for the cup knowing that I mustn't; knowing it would mean my doom. I had to fight back the urge- tremendous as it was; summon what will I had left- summon the power I once had- power that had just now started to surface again. I called up all my strength; mustered what little willpower I had left- and I did the next to impossible and threw the hot cup of tea upon the dirty pine floor, breaking Selena's delicate china into pieces- the tea spread below my feet like a living thing. I could not even allow it to touch me; I bolted out the door, going in no particular direction.

Running out into the woods- with each step on the

bare ground, with each breath of the humid, yet fresh outdoor air- I grew in strength. Gradually, consciously, I overcame the confused mindlessness that had been possessing me since my return. I ran until I was deep into the cypress swamp near where we had buried the horses that day. The day which seemed so long ago, yet was actually only a few months past. My whole life had changed since then, including my outlook on that life. Now- unquestionably- I knew I wanted my wolf's power and witch's abilities back. I decided to live and thrive with my 'blessed curse'. The task at hand was to solely concentrate on combating the evil in my family's midst.

I stopped beside a large brackish lake which was a favorite swimming spot for many of the villagers. Catching my breath, slowly inhaling and exhaling, I gathered the potent forces within me. Fortitude and resilience; spirit and courage; I was not going to be defeated so easily.

My sensitive hearing, (not having returned completely to me), I sensed, rather than heard, a presence. "Montesquieu?" I whispered, believing he was close. But it was not him. I stepped away from the shadow of a particularly large cypress and viewed a man and woman in the pool who were, clearly and openly- without regard for probity- having extraordinarily raucous intercourse.

I began to silently withdraw, hoping not to disturb them, but they were so intently involved in their copulation that even a thunderous rainstorm would probably not interrupt them. However, I halted in recognition. It was Pierre and Marguerite! Obviously, she was the one in complete control.

Admittedly, I have voyeuristic tendencies (my spying on Juliette's bath; my witnessing Gerard's rape of his victims), but this time I wanted to achieve a closer view for a more practical purpose. I needed to find out: was Marguerite actually the witch in disguise?

What I saw convinced me that all of us had been

duped. Her lily-white porcelain body was incredibly voluptuous and mature; it was not the figure of the young girl I had supposed her to be. Her ill-fitting, loose and unattractive clothing had purposely concealed the true female beneath. No, this was the remarkably beautiful body of a fully developed woman. Glistening in the bright sunlight, her long wet blonde hair clung against them both as she played the dominant role, with Pierre lying against the bank of the lake surrounded by the large roots of a cypress, enjoying the slow and expert handling of his male anatomy.

Then, after a moment more of observation, I concluded I was wrong. Something in their sexual act was bizarre. She was full of energy, while he just laid there completely still- not even caressing or fondling her breasts or body. She groaned loudly in coming ecstasy; he was silent. She had a healthy appearance; he was grey and sickly looking. Pierre stared blankly into space, his body now so thin, his skin seemed to be no more than a thin sheath, stretching over his skeleton. All the weight and musculature was gone; all the energy and robustness which I had known all our lives was a thing of the past. Did he even know where he was or what was happening to him?

She was a succubus! Like the one Gerard had described in detail my first night at Sans Souci. Marguerite was either Satine in disguise or was some sort of similar creature. The drums started sounding again from deep in the swamp (or had they never stopped?)

I had the brief notion to interrupt the pair and save poor Pierre, but I did not act. Granted he was slowly dying, yet I knew well enough- she was not quite ready to dispose of him entirely. She had some plan for him. For all of us. We had a few more days left and that would give me time to plan my strategy. I had to find out more about this witch that we were dealing with and I decided without hesitation what my first task would be.

Silently, I backed away, leaving the scene and moved with lightning speed to grandma-ma's old cabin. This was the perfect time to investigate Marguerite's rooms while she was so- obviously occupied. I hoped to find some evidence (what- I could not even hazard a guess) linking her- or not- to Satine. Were they one and the same?

If Marguerite was not Satine, then what was she doing here, toying with us? Satine practiced her witchcraft alone- excepting for her male cohorts. She would never include another female in her plans. According to Gerard, she could never abide competition. However, Marguerite clearly was no ordinary female. The question then is: what sort of creature was she?

Entering the cabin, I was flooded with wonderful memories: Of the time when first meeting Selena and her grandmother; of coming to this village, marrying and trying to make a life together. And there was grandma-ma's wonderful tall case clock which inspired me to first work on timepieces. Odd, it was running and keeping accurate time. Someone around here was attentive and dutiful. But I had no time to reminisce; the cabin had to be searched thoroughly and quickly. Surely there would be some item to prove just who I was dealing with. However, it took hardly no time before finding that one certain object which gave me the undeniable proof I needed.

Located in the back room- used for storage now- was a large armoire and, hidden from sight behind linens and sheets and blankets, was a framed portrait. As I pulled it out, surprise traveled through my system, literally, like a shock, for I had completely forgotten about the picture. I had only seen it once, and for a brief period at that, never imagining I would see it again.

It was the portrait of Satine in her Elizabethan dress; the same portrait that had been hanging in Gerard's bedroom, when he had gone into town; when the witch played tricks on me while I was at Sans Souci alone. This told me what I needed to know- it answered my question.

The eyes! The eyes in the picture staring at me- wide, green and.. with menace?- were the same as those which looked so piercingly at me earlier in the day. It was her eyes that... if I was not mistaken.. .were emitting a glow from the portrait. Glowering at me even now. She was watching! I hastily hid the picture back in the darkness of the armoire, hoping I had not been discovered.

There was now no doubt in my mind. It was unmistakable! Now, I had to admit that I was dealing directly (and by myself) with the most powerful witch- who had assumed a place in our household as Selena's midwife. I needed to rush back, but first I wanted to search the cabin some more to find what else might connect Marguerite with the witch.

And lo, there on the dresser of the bedroom was a scattered selection of jewels, gems, cupfuls of coins and paper money. I recognized the goods as that confiscated from the gang of robbers.

So apparently, Marguerite knows of that supposed secret also! Pierre was really not so clever. If only I could find the trunk itself; I would hide it, bury it. It would take only a few minutes, but it was most likely not in the cabin. For right now, the riches would have to wait. I must get back to the cabin and plan my next move. Decide on whether to enlist the help of Marie or even, Gerard. If only grandma-ma would awaken; she would know what to do. And those drums! Though in the very far distance swamps, they still persisted. Or were they in my mind alone, with no one else able to hear them?

I thought, briefly, of torching the portrait and thereby, perhaps, destroying the witch, here and now- or at least, be rid of her for the time being. Yet, I remembered that would not likely work, for she was already a creature of fire- a phoenix- the one witch for whom fire was an ally. I decided to take the picture with me, secret it away, until I discovered a way to destroy it- and possibly Satine along with it. It obviously held some importance to her and I would- sooner or later- ascertain just what that importance was.

I had to find something appropriate to cover the portrait and those 'all-seeing eyes'. Glancing around I noticed clothes were strewn everywhere; a basket of what looked to be dirty linens sat next to a large open armoire full of her drab, oversized clothes. My heart stopped for a moment in astonishment, for there, hanging for all the world to see, was my cloak- my invisibility cloak! The very same one that I had given that poor innocent boy for protection, the last night I was at Sans Souci.

Oh Mon Dieu! For Shame! The pain struck me as much as a powerful blow to the stomach.

As I picked up the cloak, the most tremendous sorrow and regret flooded over my soul. The horror! Regrets for that sad young man- to whom I had promised protection, safety and a new life- and then I had failed him. Regrets for believing Gerard was responsible for his death. He may have intercepted the boy and retrieved my pocket watch, but I knew now positively, that it had been Satine who actually had crucified him unmercifully. Only the most evil, vile witch could perpetrate such a heinous act. In the back of my mind, I had always suspected that the crucifixion was quite beyond Gerard's anger. Not beyond his capabilities, but beyond the anger he could hold for such an innocent young man whom he had once loved.

Vengeance filled my heart; wrath consumed my spirit. I was not going to let his death go unpunished. She will pay dearly- with her life- for all eternity. Now, I was willing (and eager) to do whatever was necessary to destroy her. I will go back to Sans Souci, although first I must take Selena and her grandmother away, for we were all in mortal danger, especially now that I knew her secret. I will enlist Marie's help if necessary. How could I have been so blind! All of us!

And Pierre! Saving him, before she sucks him dry, will prove to be a very hard task to accomplish, indeed, but I must not allow any more of these games to continue.

Hastily, I gathered the cloak over the picture and it automatically became invisible. I would hide it away and well, in order that she would not even be able to sense it-for it was obvious the witch knew the purpose of the cloak. Running all the way back to our cabin, I decided to destroy what teas remained, then pack up a few of their things and take grandma-ma and Selena away from there. Sans Souci would probably not be safe, for it will surely become the battlefield. I will take them to Marie's; they all knew each other well and the voodoo queen's magical fog would protect them from the witch's searching eyes. I would have to come back for Pierre later, knowing that to do so meant confronting Marguerite.

Reaching the house, I called out for Selena, but she was not home yet. I hid the portrait, still wrapped in the cloak, making sure it was safe, secure and not to be found. I then started to gather up all the tea- mine, Selena's, especially Pierre's and was in the process of pouring them all together into one container (I was going to discard them in the swamp) when, from her sick bed, I heard grandma-ma mumbling and talking to herself.

Oh madre! I had completely forgotten to give her her medicine; but maybe, perhaps, that was for the best. I would formulate my own remedy for her- one that was trustworthy and effective.

As I walked into her room, she was semi-propped up on her pillows as usual, and she kept babbling over and over, the same few words. At first, I could not com-prehend what she was saying; then, I realized it was a warning.

"Bad woman! Bad woman. There is evil in the house.

A bad woman is in the house!"

I lit a bedside lamp, for the day was swiftly disappearing and, sitting gently down beside her on the bed, I took her hand in my own. "evil, bad.." she repeated. I reached up to her face with my healing touch- much of my telepathic and empathic abilities were now back. Soon I would be able to call upon all my powers; and now, I felt too, the power of lightning growing within me. Later, I would be able to return- in force- and the witch will have to contend with me. Yet now, I had little time.

"Grandma-ma, can you hear me? It is Henri. Quiet now, shh..h..h. I am going to take care of you from now on. We are going to leave here in fact. Can you hear me? Do you understand? It is your son- Henri." I paused, the emotion swelling in my throat. "Please grandma-ma, come back to me. Please, please grandma."

As I softly spoke to her, she slowly ceased her murmuring, then very weakly, she reached with her other hand up to my face, feeling my facial features, trying to recognize me.

After a very long moment, her blind eyes began to moist over and I knew she was returning to our world. She spoke with tired relief and emotion, "My son, my son. It is you. You have come back whole. Oh, Henri, my son, my son." Her breathing was labored as if she had been walking uphill.

"Yes, yes it is me, grandma-ma. It is your son." I hugged her to me, grasping her tight as she started to cry. It was more than just a pity such a strong woman as she had become so dependent on others. Well, I would remedy that and restore her to that original vitality we all recognized.

We stayed like that for some time; grateful and happy, relishing our reunion and her awakening; then we slowly separated and I placed her gently back upon her comfortable pillows and, taking a nearby napkin, wiped away her tears.

Suddenly, she straightened herself up, turning her head towards the back corner, over my shoulder, as if her blind eyes could see something. Yet there was nothing there. She managed to raise her arm and point weakly- again over my shoulder. "Bad woman.. evil is in the house." She let out a tiny, yet deep and serious, sigh of pain and exhaustion, and fell back onto her bed. Her eyes remained open, though she seemed to have passed out.

"Grandma-ma, grandma- are you all right?" It frightened me, for it appeared as if she had had a relapse. I felt her pulse and, fortunately, that was strong. I presumed the excitement of 'seeing' me again must have tired her. I started to rise to get her a glass of water, when I stopped. There was definitely the strong scent of lilacs in the room. It could only be..

"Allo, Henri." The voice behind me caused me to jump off the bed like a frightened cat. From the corner shadows, where grandma-ma had pointed, emerged the figure of Marguerite, yet the voice was not hers. I was ashamed I had not sensed her presence.

"I know who and what you are Marguerite."

"And what is that, Henri?" Her voice sounded like tiny chiming bells.

"You are the witch- Satine!"

She stepped further out into the light. Striking her ivory-pale skin just so, the light gave the impression she was made of chiseled marble- hard and cold. "You will be our slaves."

"Non, jamais. Never."

"You will do as we request or- you will all die." Her body slowly ascended into the air, floating like a spirit, her long blonde hair twisting and writhing behind her head like a living thing. I turned my eyes away, instinctively, knowing that if I looked upon the Medusa, I would become stone and lose the war before it begins.

"Do not worry, Henri. We have something else planned for you."

At that precise moment, in that particular instant, the voodoo drums became louder- loud enough that anyone, any mortal could hear them. She turned her head in their direction. "Gerard!" I exclaimed.

She looked back at me, her green eyes glowing with hate and superiority. "Yes, he will be defeated." The hiss in her voice sounded familiar. "He will die tonight!" A crazed demonic laugh issued from that stone cold emotionless face. A laugh I had heard somewhere before. From what place? From what dream?

"I will not allow it. I will join him and together we will destroy you." My courage was great, even if my powers were not- as of yet.

"Not this time, Henri. It is too late for that." She floated closer to us. "As we said, there is something special planned just for you."

"Non. Non!"

Ignoring me, she drifted silently over to grandma-ma. The old ladies eyes looked upwards at Marguerite, seeing nothing, but they still exhibited fear, registered her fright. "Poor, poor grandma-ma." She reached out her arm, extending a hand over the old one's eyes. They promptly closed and the sick lady slumped back on the pillows- immobile, no sign of breath or life, as if dead.

"Stop!" I shouted and with my wolf's swiftness, grabbed Marguerite's wrist and instantly, painfully, I felt a searing burn stronger than any ordinary fire- it was unnatural- a fire from hell. Reluctantly, I had to release her. "You forget what we are, Henri." Her laughter was full of ridicule and derision.

If only I had all of my wolf's powers back. I tried to transform myself, to be able to fight her, but I was unable to do so. It had been sometime in fact, since I had had any sort of transformation. If only I could.

"You can transform, and you shall, Henri. Forever."

She was taunting me, confusing me, reading my mind. "You want to be loup garou? You want your wolf powers to return?" Her voice rose to a shriek, a high-pitched crescendo. "Then you shall have them- And In Abundance!" She pointed to a prepared cup and saucer which had mysteriously appeared on the bedside table. "Drink!" She commanded.

Without hesitation, uncontrollably, my arm reached for the tea; my hand clutched the cup and I raised it to my lips. I had no will power; not even the slightest control over myself. "This time you cannot refuse us." Yet, I did try to resist with all my might; tried to fight her power with all my will; knowing this drink was unlike all else- and would be my end. Yet I could not stop myself; my actions were those of someone else with no control or resolve of my own. I was her puppet.

And I took the drink I did not want to take.

Immediately, and intensely, I felt the agony. By far, more severe than any torment I had ever experienced (and that included my times in the pentagram), I slowly changed. Metamorphosing gradually, excruciatingly, bit by torturous bit. One part of my anatomy at a time changed, until after many minutes of raging, racking pain, I was completely transfigured into a werewolf.

She watched my suffering and misery with delightful patience; her green cat eyes shined down at me with glee, as I was groveling upon the floor. She laughed again at me. I lunged for her throat, but only threw myself against the back wall. She had simply vanished, just as suddenly as she had appeared.

So, now I have my wish fulfilled. She has given me back my wolf's powers. Only this time it is not a 'blessed curse', but rather an 'extraordinary curse'; One only a crafty witch such as she could devise. A werewolf curse I will absolutely have no control over. I am condemned to a lifetime of wandering and forever feasting on humans. The hunger is there, deep inside; even now it is all consuming. I will never know love again or any human contact or touch- other than that which ends in bloody death. Never to see my loved ones; never breathing or feeling or thinking as a human man. I will never be Henri again.

I am, night or day, full moon or no, unable to transform back into human form. I am now, permanently and irrevocably, LOUP GAROU!

5

I ran out into the setting sun. I could not even stop to see if grandma-ma had recovered from the shock of the witch. It was imperative that I be away from any human contact whatsoever. Selena should be arriving any moment. Absolutely no one must see me like this.

The hunger increased minute by minute as I plunged deep and deeper into the swamp basin, further than I had ever gone before- where there was more water than land (and less and less people). The curse she had laid upon me was that of a true animal; my only thoughts, eventually, becoming those for food- a frenzy for human flesh. Any animal I came across I killed and devoured, but it only served to increase the desire for man.

After I had traveled some distance, and time had passed, my mind started to function less and less as a human; my thoughts were becoming incoherent, abstract, distorted. Eventually, I would have no humanistic faculties at all and that fact frightened me more than anything else. To live and feed and die like a dumb animal! My creative, loving and productive self- the man known as Henri LeBlanc- would never exist again.

Even the great powers I had once known as a loup garou were not the same. I had the same acute senses- made for a predator- but I had not the supernatural strength as before. Much of my quickness- my speed and alertness- was depleted. Marguerite knew just what would hurt me the most.

My only hope was to find Marie; however, my thought processes were failing fast with each passing hour. The night turned into day, then night again. I do not know how long I was lost in the wilderness- two, maybe three days, perhaps longer. Howling and snarling- human speech was beyond me.

Mon Dieu, let me die! I cannot bear to live the rest of my life like this. Perhaps Gerard will survive the witch's onslaught and he could then take care of Selena and my unborn child. But most likely he would fail also. Marguerite/Satine was much too powerful for any of us alone to combat.

Drums- the drums kept playing. They were more pronounced here in the wilderness, but every time I thought I was coming close to them, their source seemed to switch and suddenly, frustratingly, they would be sounding far behind me or way across some large lake or another swamp. Maybe there was more than one group of them.

The wetland contained a sweet soft mist far out here, but my mind was becoming foggy in its own right, muddled. I was holding on to my humanness by a mere shred. Then! there was no mistaking the sound- Hounds! An animal panic filled my being and I started running; running anywhere, to any place. The hunters had released the dogs and they would soon be snapping at my heels.

I ran, hid and ran again, like any hunted wild animal. For the first time I was now the prey- so unlike those hunting excursions which Gerard and I shared far back in some vague memory. Suddenly, they were upon me! A pack of hound dogs, ten or a dozen more, jumped on me all at once, biting and snarling, ripping my skin, trying to tear for my throat. I broke a few of their necks, yet the others kept coming at me; clamping their sharp hound's teeth deep into my legs and arms as I swung about. Once they had seized me they were not letting go. I flung a few into the trees, hearing their bones and backs break from solid impacts. The only way to escape was to run; to try and summon what was left of my speed.

Perhaps I should just stay and die. Let the hunters riddle my heart and body with their silver bullets. I wondered- once dead- would I transform back to my human self? What a mystery that would be for those men! That was one of my last coherent human thoughts - morbidly humorous.

I ran; I could not reason properly; was not able to think clearly. I was in fog, then suddenly, something pulled at my feet and I found myself ensnared in a rope- a trap! Strung up by one foot- dangling, swinging from a tall tree upside down. Panicking, I growled, gnashed and snapped, thrashing about trying to break free. The hounds were soon below me yapping, barking for the hunters to follow, to hurry. Waiting for me to fall; wanting to tear me apart as I have torn others before- limb by limb. Relentlessly, unmercifully. Now it would be my turn. Was this retribution? Punishment for the evil I had done?

The rope snapped (or was it the tree branch?). The large hounds leaped on me, wanting my blood, my flesh. I no longer had any human thoughts- run, escape, hide, swim away.

I must have escaped them, for I remember swimming far into deep and dark brackish waters. It was not the large river though, which I knew so well. All I could think of was to keep swimming and they would lose my trail, my scent. The scent of the wolf that walks upright.

The cloud over the water was thick with little visibility, but the lake itself (or basin) also seemed to become more dense as I became too tired to continue any longer. I floated ready to sink; no longer immortal- ready to drown. I relinquished all the panic, all the hurt and pain; and so, in letting go, I drifted- ready to die. I approached a darkness so profound it had to have been a cavern. Hadn't I experienced something like this before? Where was Gabriel? He should have never set me free in the beginning. I do not care any longer. Let the lord or the devil take me- either one- I will accept my fate. I managed one last human reflection. Through my mind's foggy haze a mental picture of Selena gathered before me and then it dissipated. After that, I gave myself up to the dead- again.

Then, just upon the point of no return, I saw a clear light though I was in the darkness; I felt a lightness yet I was in the water; a buoyancy but I had been sinking. Was I actually living a previous dream? I could still hear the drums- or was it the throbbing in my head? Were they in heaven with me?

Eventually, the darkness of the water made way for a bright whiteness all about me, thick yet insubstantial. Is this what they call heaven? On a cloud? My eyes opened. There was no mistake- I definitely felt the lightness, the buoyancy. Prone on my back, I understood I was actually being carried in the air- floating in fact, but I could not distinguish a thing- the fog was still so thick. An angel must obviously be taking me to be judged by Peter or some other guardian at heaven's gate. I was too tired physically to think; too tired emotionally to care. Let us be done with it.

I felt solid earth beneath me as I was laid gently down. Gabriel? Is that you? 'Drink.' I was commanded. 'Non,' I refused, no more tea. No Marguerite, you came to gloat over my death- you have won. Now please leave me to a peaceful death. If you have any humanity left in you- Leave me. 'Drink' I was commanded again. I felt the tea upon my wolf's mouth; I felt the liquid upon my tongue as it soothingly slipped down my throat.

Only seconds passed before I sat up- alert. The thick fog was slowly drifting away over the dark waters which had held me captive. Yet how have I survived? I looked down- my hands, my legs, my body- I was human! Alive and a man again! I felt my face- I was Henri again. But was this a dream? Was this experience real? My world had become so much more dream-like and my dreams much more life-like.

Sunlight broke through low clouds; it was the beginning of a new day. In the distance, the fog whirled and swirled, as if- yes, as if it were alive! And it had carried me free of the boggy lake. Marie had been here and she must have been the one to make me drink a restorative remedy. She had saved my life and- in so doing- she, hopefully, has saved many lives.

The power and quick action of her potion was remarkable- stronger than any tea of Marguerite's; more potent than any remedy Gerard and I could concoct. To reverse a curse is difficult. Marie has again proven herself to be quite an ally. Perhaps also, she was much more than a voodoo high priestess- much more indeed. She might even be as ageless as Satine. I must go thank her and solicit her advice for Gerard and I in our upcoming battle. She once told me I would know when it was time to contact her.

With this potion I reclaimed all my previous strength and agility. Power was coursing and flowing through my blood again; I could feel it growing, hardening the muscles. My entire person was back; the mind becoming sharp again; telepathic abilities gradually being an instinctive part of me once more. What is more- I could recall all that I had learned at Sans Souci. I had been renewed! It was as if Marguerite/Satine's confusing evil tricks and concoctions had never occurred.

The fog (with Marie) was fastly disappearing from my keen sight. I started to hurriedly follow. 'Non, Henri'. Was that her voice? It repeated itself- 'Non, Henri'. The voice emanated from the far distant fog, yet the sound seemed to my ears as being close by. Whispering to me exclusively.

The voice continued. 'You must go home. Selena needs you. Beware though, the witch is present.' (Her voice was fading along with the living cloud.) 'Selena is having your children.' Then Marie's voice and the fog were gone.

Mon Dieu! Damn! I realized now what Marguerite/Satine had done. She had purposefully taken me away from Selena, (if I died so much the better), but the point was for me to be away and not witness the birth. To what purpose?

Selena had mentioned that Marguerite would take payment after the birth. The realization of her true evil ways hit me like a falling rock. She wanted my boy! A werewolf's firstborn male might have special powers- like Toussaint and the superstitious slaves believed.

I started to race back, for I had a very long way to travel and little time to do it in. I could make the distance far faster if I had my.. and before I had even finished the thought, there before me he was- my majestic Montesquieu! Standing grandly, neighing and rearing up on his hind legs; shaking his head and mane, pawing the ground. He had appeared like an apparition at the barest thought of him; as if my mind had conjured him. And he was as ready for action as I was. In one swift movement, I mounted and we were off- together again- and I was feeling like myself- after what seemed a long time. I was now the Henri whom fate had intended me to be. If only my lightning power would surface. And all this time, the drums had continued playing, their intensity steadily increasing.

We rode as one with the wind and in a matter of

minutes, we were back at the cabin. Before entering, I heard a woman's uncontrolled weeping- Selena's weeping-coming from inside. Entering cautiously into our room, I discovered her sitting in our bed cradling our newborn- my baby boy. Yet I could not grasp from her thoughts- they were so jumbled- just why she was so disturbed, even bordering on hysteria.

"Henri, Henri," she cried repeatedly at my appearance. "You are alive. Thank God. I did not know what to believe." Her sad tears turned to joyful ones. "I thought you might even have- left us."

I softly sat by her on the bed and dried her tears with my handkerchief, "Never, ma cherie. Jamais, jamais." She smiled and stopped her crying (if only for the moment) to show me our child- Marcel.

"He looks like you, Henri."

"Of course, proud parents always say that," I replied. Yet, he did have large bright coal-black eyes and a full head of dark hair like his papa. All the pain of the last few weeks was forgotten for the time being. I could barely contain my delight. My heart felt as if it would burst from sheer joy. He looked to be a healthy normal human boy. Taking the baby gently from her, I slyly and silently inspected the boy for any signs of loup garou and (though I did not know what to look for in particular) there were no unusual birthmarks or signs on him anywhere. No sign of the pentagram. He was a heavy child who soon started whimpering for more of his mother's milk. "He must take after Pierre's side of the family, for they were always heavy.." I stopped in mid-sentence for her crying resumed, albeit a little softer than before. "Quiet, shush. What is it my darling?" I put an arm around her, trying to comfort her and find out what could be upsetting her so.

She grabbed Marcel from me, almost in a panic. "She took him, she took my baby. My baby boy."

"Calm down, ma cherie. What do you mean, Selena?"

I caressed her head and neck. "Our baby boy is here, unharmed. Marguerite did not take payment."

"Selena believes she did." I heard grandmother's strong voice and the steady click-click of her cane as she appeared in the doorway.

"Grandma-ma," I shouted as I jumped up, beaming with a childish energy and smile that I am sure the old one could notice even without the use of her eyes. "You are well, I was so worried." We embraced and she affectionately rubbed my thick crop of black hair.

"My son, my son." We cried for a tiny bit together in our embrace, then I sat her down in the kitchen, in order to speak in hushed tones while Selena cradled a suckling Marcel, her sobbing slowly becoming intermittent.

"What happened Grandma-ma? Did we have twin boys?"

"I was not present at the birth, Henri. I only recovered after the witch had left."

"Tea, Henri! Could you make me some tea?" Selena called desperately from the bedroom. Grandma-ma patted my arm and shook her head- no- at me. I concurred silently.

"In a moment, my darling." I called back, "In a moment."

"I do not know for sure, Henri, but she believes she had twins."

"I must find out. At the plantation.."

"Where you have spent the last few months?" I replied yes. "It is called..?"

"Sans Souci."

"A lovely name." Her head turned upwards; she was listening at.. "The drums are telling a story my son. According to them there is not much time," She made a very significant pause before continuing. "..if you intend to save your, friend."

"I intend to and I will save my cousin also."

"Yes, Pierre was completely under her spell. She is

ageless, that one. I have never felt such evil."

"Indeed! And if I have another child, I shall bring him back." The continued cries of a terrified mother from the other room sent daggers of pity through my very heart. "I must leave now; the day is passing quickly; but- what of Selena?"

"She will be all right my son. I will see to it. I will make some coffee. No more teas- for any of us."

I got up from the chair. "I will make it grandma."

"Non, Henri." Her voice was firm, her formidable nature having returned. She rose, ordering me to go. "There is no time left." I kissed her on the cheek and (glancing at my poor wife, cradling and rocking our newborn son), I started to leave. I could not stand to see Selena in such a condition. She had always been so strong for me.

Yet, I remembered one more thing I had to make sure of before I departed.

Grandma-ma was already making her usual strong coffee. I went into our bedroom and kissed Selena goodbye. "Bring him back, Henri. Bring Marcel's twin brother back."

"I will ma petite, I will." I casually felt for the hiding place under our bed where I had put the portrait in the invisible cloak. Bon, it was still there. The witch had missed that. It just might be my ace in the hole, later.

I had not gotten ten paces out the door when down the road a reckless horse-and- buggy was careening carelessly towards the house, obviously out of control. I recognized the handsome black carriage. It was from Sans Souci, along with the two huge dapple grey horses which the driver, noticeably, was not able to handle. Holding precariously onto the reins was my precious tiny Juliette! And she had completely lost control of the animals and carriage.

Deftly, I jumped in front of the fast moving horses, barely managing to grab the harness railing and halt the speeding steeds, using my own strength and force. A feat, I may add, no ordinary man could accomplish. Braking so suddenly, they almost toppled over on me.

"Juliette! What are you doing?" My voice cracked with alarm for the young girl and what might have happened. I could tell she was scared out of her wits; her face flushed, her eyes red from crying.

"Oh, Master Henri!" She exclaimed as I helped her down from the carriage. Our embrace was furtive. "Oh Henri," she repeated, noticeably leaving out my title.

I spoke calmly to her. "What has happened, my dear? Why are you here?"

"Master Gerard, my grandpa-pa... they need you! They need your help. Sans Souci is..is..," at this point she broke down into tears. I held her gently while allowing her to sob, but I gathered from her a complete mental picture of total destructive terror. Sans Souci was being burnt- the mansion, the fields, the land, even the livestock! Slowly she collected herself together somewhat, her strong resiliency shining through for me. I held her at arm's length, encouraging her to speak calmly.

"I suppose it was some sort of she-devil. I was upstairs on the balcony when she appeared in the distance like a black cloud; her face a black cloud of smoke; slowly enveloping the whole sky. She approached on the wind; the land was, suddenly, all afire in every direction; the blazes moving towards the mansion. Most of the other slaves had already ran away, but many were running around screaming and hollering in panic. Immediately grandpa-pa," her sobs still were choking her a little, "he told me to escape- to find you. That all would be lost unless you returned in time." Her look, her eyes, drifted off into the distance as she painted the horror in explicit terms- a horror a young girl like herself should never have to witness. The wild disorder of the slaves, whirlwinds of fire; trees that came alive trying to stop her and the carriage; demon voices and laughter all around her, louder than thunder. And as they raced away, she saw behind her, boulders and rocks of fire soaring down from the sky upon the mansion. In her frightened state, she instinctively put her head on my shoulder, sobbing over and over, "Poor grandpa-pa, poor master Gerard." Then suddenly she looked up into my eyes- her own filled with tears of despair. "What sort of creature is that? Is she a…god?"

That I could not answer. Then as we both looked towards Sans Souci, the voodoo drums reached an ungodly supernatural tempo, climbing to a crescendo, achieving their climatic point. She covered her ears; I wanted to for it was very painful to my hearing, but I did not. Grandma was standing at the open door to the cabin, listening in shock at the mysterious sound, and then suddenly.. with no warning.. the drums stopped. It was over. All over. And I had not been there to help.

Letting go of me, Juliette crumpled into a heap of hopelessness on the ground at my feet, weeping and weeping over again in fear and trembling- "Grandpa-pa, Sans Souci," she repeated. "They are gone. Even Master Gerard. They are all gone. All gone."

Yes, I thought to myself. Gerard has lost the battle. He is defeated. Gerard- the one loup garou like myself, the one man I could love- was now gone forever from this earthly plane. My mentor, my master was dead.

6

"Tread careful my son," was the final admonition from grandma-ma as I left the cabin and called for Montesquieu who appeared like a ghostly steed materializing out of thin air. Just before we flew off, going into the unknown, I looked back to see the three women in my life. They were huddled together in the doorway staring towards us with concerned looks; their fear and worry co-mingled with the hope for my success and safe return. As I looked back at them, they appeared small, helpless- even the stalwart old one seemed diminished.

There was Juliette, still staring with wide eyes from what she had just been through; staring with anxiousness for the fate of her grandfather, her tears barely dry. She was now part of our household, for she would surely be killed if she were to return. I sensed that the girl would play an important role in all our lives; and in my life if I survived. Of course, Selena and her grandmother accepted her readily without question as I knew they would.

Juliette did bring a very important article with her. After relating the story of her treacherous and harrowing escape, she pulled out a carefully wrapped parcel containing some large and heavy item. "My grandfather was instructed by Gerard to get this to you, safely and intact. He enjoined him to guard it with his life. Of course, grandpa-pa had to give it to me for I was the only one able to.. leave." Her tears began to flow again. I wiped them away with my handkerchief. She visibly gathered her youthful strength and continued. "I knew it must be important, for I sensed that the witch was after me- I mean to say- she was after me because I carried this particular package."

I knew what it was before I untied the twine around the wrapped package and yes, there it was- the book that could save us all from Satine- save our whole world as we knew it. It was the book of the dead. Did that mean Gabriel had returned with the sarcophagus?

There was also a small leather pouch containing a man's ring of black onyx. Engraved into the stone was a silver fleur-de-lis; unique in its design, it was partially composed of two snarling wolf's heads on either side in profile. A symbol, no doubt, representing Gerard and myself. "According to Grandpa-pa, that is to be- or was to be- the plantation crest for Sans Souci. At least, that was Master Gerard's intention." She wanted to cry, but held it back for later when she would be alone. Putting on the ring, I vowed that Sans Souci would be rebuilt and this would be the plantation crest, as my mentor had wished.

I then spoke with Selena and her grandmother. Selena was at the door holding Marcel who was still on his mother's tit. I kissed him on his forehead. Selena had calmed down considerably. The once unflustered strength she used to possess; the female fortitude I had fallen in love with- was returning. She knew, without words, I would bring back our other child- or die in the attempt. "Tristan."

"Tristan?" I asked.

"Marcel's twin."

"A British name!" Selena knew my hatred of the English. "Why Tristan? A British knight?"

"Because he will be like that- pure of heart, great in virtue, brave in stature gracious in bearing. One day, if we survive-" she tried to speak with her usual casual confidence. I saw Grandma-ma squeeze Selena's hand. "One day he will save the whole family." She looked off towards the large river. "For some reason I know it to be his destiny." Then her eyes turned sadly down upon Marcel in her arms.

"Well," was all I could say at that declaration. Grandma-ma again squeezed her hand. "Well- then his name shall be Tristan." Of course, I had no choice but to comply. "And I will bring him back, I promise."

"He must be raised by us and no other." Selena spoke in earnest. I helplessly kissed her- deeply, shamelessly, I must admit- not proper in front of the others. I sensed Juliette's embarrassment- or was it rather, envy?

I turned to her. "And I promise you, ma petite- to bring back your grandfather, also."

"If he.." She half-sobbed, not being able to finish the

sentence.

I lifted her chin with one finger, requiring her to look up into my eyes. "We both know how resourceful and capable he is. No one is the better. I am sure he found a way to survive."

"And Master Gerard?" Her eyes looked deep into mine, searching for..asking me something. Did she know? Did she know about Gerard and I? I did not intrude upon her thoughts for I cared too much for the girl. She continued, "I fear we have lost."

"Not for long!"

"You do realize my son, you can not defeat the witch by yourself," grandma-ma's voice was solemn, full of heartfelt worry for me.

At once I stepped over to her, kissing her, reassuring the old one. "I know grandma-ma. But I must go find Toussaint and Pierre and bring them home with the child. I need to see with my own eyes the destruction and perhaps, Gerard is still alive or held captive. We will come back and then.." I stopped, not wanting to reveal our plans for battle.

Grandma-ma leaned down close to my ear, whispering so Selena and Juliette would not be able to hear. "Plot your revenge carefully, yet conduct it quickly when the time comes. You will need to visit.."

"Marie. Yes, grandma-ma I know. Gerard and I have made much plans, but you must not know any of it for your own safety, comprendre? " I turned to leave. "I shall know what to do and when to do it."

"I hope your friend, Gerard..survived." I nodded thank you. She knew. She knew everything about me; everything about Gerard's and my relationship. Nothing escaped this blind lady.

"Tread careful and well, my son. Tread careful."

All the while, as we flew fast for Sans Souci, my mind was cluttered with so many varied thoughts and fears. My first aim was to rescue my son and friend: yet, I knew well that I was not in any position powerful enough to make demands on Satine. I also had the extreme need to find out what actually happened to Gerard and the plantation. I could not allow her to take from me what was rightfully mine. It was, after all, my plantation also.

So, for the first time, I acknowledged to myself that, yes- I considered Sans Souci mine! I wanted it to be my home; I required making it my own. With my family, Toussaint and Juliette, with our new home in the northwestern corner- I would indulge my pleasure in working the land, fields, the bayous and streams. It was my land as much as anyone's. And I swore I would have it back! Besides, I knew Gerard wanted it to be so.

Also, I had to confess my desire to be near Gerard. Even after our last encounter, I knew I could not live well without him. He was part of me, as I was of him. I had chosen him as much as he had fallen in love with me. Together we were whole and complete- together we could survive for countless ages making Sans Souci into that magnificent thriving plantation of our dreams.

My strongest worry right now was that he was gone and the witch had won.

However, that was only the first battle in this war. Now I was determined (and angry enough) to stage a second. Whenever I thought upon that poor crucified boy and the witch's unmerciful cruelty, my blood boiled. My power was growing still and I was confident enough to confront her.

We landed far down the shady oak alley, away from the house and I alighted. Montesquieu obediently, immediately, hid himself away, ready at any moment to come to my aid. I walked slowly, out in the open as if a welcome visitor. Moving towards the home, my first

with the other, raised a pistol and pointed it at my heart. I knew the bullets were silver.

"Kill him."

"No Pierre. Put down the gun and come with me." I tried to speak calmly with reassurance, while motioning gently with one hand, for him to come to me. I repeated, "Put down the gun and we will leave together."

"Shoot him. Kill him." My poor friend's arm started shaking uncontrollably. There was a battle of wills raging within himself; a struggle that one of us three was going to have to lose.

"Pierre please. This is your cousin, your friend Henri. Listen to me, mon ami." Were my baby boy's cries becoming even louder? "Put down the gun." She began shouting over me. "Do not listen to her!"

"Shoot him, now. Aim for the heart. Maintenant! Shoot, Now!" Still he hesitated, but I could see his will weakening; he was losing the war within and I knew he had to release the pressure or die. He used to be a perfect marksman. I would require perfect timing, in order to dodge the deadly bullets.

"No Pierre. You are strong. You do not have to do anything except come here to me."

"Shoot! Shoot!" Her voice rose to a screech, like some giant bird. A shrill that shot daggers of pain in my ears and head. "Shoot you fool! I said shoot!"

And he did. In a flash, before I could turn into a werewolf and save us both, he turned the gun upon himself and, shooting through the temple, my best friend, my childhood companion and playmate, collapsed to the ground so much like Mercutio had done before him. Gone, past forever.

"Pity." Satine registered no remorse at having lost her lover, yet she did show surprise at her failure to command him. "That was impossible!" She threw a quizzical, angry look at me. "What sort of power did you hold over him?"

"Something you had not considered. A power infinitely more potent." Now it was my turn to pause for effect. "Something called friendship. Pierre would rather be dead than hurt me. Love.."

Another shriek pierced the air and she began to levitate.

Transforming completely in an instant, I was ready to act, her force field no longer able to hold back my fury. Making one considerable leap, my fangs were within inches of her throat, when some mighty force, a supreme blow of unknown origin, hit me in the chest and sent me hurtling through the air a tremendous length, all the way back to one of the largest oaks in the alley, where I slammed against it solidly with my back. Howling in pain, I could not react soon enough and the tree- coming alive- held me captive; its branches and roots wrapping about me violently, quickly, cutting deep into my wolf's thick hide, encircling all of me; in seconds- literally covering my entire body, save for the eyes.

Satine floated over to me, her feet only inches above what used to be soft lush grass that now was dust. She gloated over me, rising higher in the air. I struggled yet could not move within this cocoon of wood; My wolf's strength not powerful enough to burst free; but what if..perhaps.. I tried to recall something of importance. What was it from that dream?

The tree and the earth beneath began to tremble and I realized, I was being slowly dragged under; to be trapped deep beneath the giant oak's enormous roots. I glimpsed Satine already turning away, flying back to the torched house, leaving me to my fate. I still heard my baby's cries. In a matter of seconds I would be eternally engulfed. I had to think- act quickly; I needed to remember- some memory from a daydream when I was similarly trapped.

Suddenly, I felt an extreme cold; a unique cold for it should not have been there; a coldness not unlike that which haunted the grandfather clock at Sans Souci. Was it Gerard? Was he able to come to my aid?

Yes! Now I knew what must be done. With astonishing clarity, the dream came to my mind in its entirety. Gerard had helped me recall the dream.

Within me was a mighty dormant power from the lightning stroke, which I had to summon into existence. This seemed to me like an impossible task, but it was my only chance of escape. I had to try- and believe it possible.

Therefore, using all my supreme will, all my supernatural strength and witch's abilities- my body gradually began to glow and burn- white hot- without consuming itself! The tree immediately reacted trying to crush the life out of me further; trying to pull me further into the earth to smother my flame. But I grew even hotter- into an incendiary!- so, with an instantaneous burst, erupting through and from my entire body (and mind), the tree was sent up into flames like so much dry kindling and the thick roots which had held me, broke apart, crumbling into cinders and hot ash from the violently intense combustion.

I heard Satine's banshee cry of shock and disappointment as she turned to see me gain my freedom and the giant fireball of a tree that had been her evil creation. Howling for revenge, I bounded with all my speed towards her for another attack. She hastily flew into what was left of the house and just as I leaped up onto the landing, she appeared high in the air above me and the ruined, still smoking mansion. To my terror, she held my little baby boy- my Tristan- in her arms!

All I could do was helplessly watch, as they disappeared across the tree-tops, flying fast upon a strong wind that whipped up suddenly all around us- blinding me with dust and debris. Even Montesquieu with all his great speed, would not be fast enough to catch her. Abruptly after, all was calm and quiet. I heard birds chirping in the trees. The wind and the evil had gone and with them went my child.

My anguish expressed itself with despairing wolf howls; if any human heard, they could only believe that the hounds of hell themselves had been released. Satine had escaped and I was left with a ruined mansion and my dead friends!

I heard movement behind me. Was it her? No, the scent was human. I transformed back, complete with tattered, torn and charred clothing. It was Toussaint! He was peering cautiously around the corner from one of the sheds near my workshop. I ran to join him.

"Toussaint! Thank God." I cried with delighted relief.

"Master Henri!" We embraced warmly, as friends.

"You saw what just happened?"

"Everything. If only Master Gerard were here, then perhaps the two of you could have defeated her. But each of you alone.." his voice trailed off. "She is the same witch my father faced with Gerard on the island?"

"The very same." I paused. "And she will return here soon. However, next time we meet I will be prepared."

"She wants something else besides your boy and Gerard's death." He apparently had given this some thought. I wondered about the mummy. "The sarcophagus, perhaps?"

"Toussaint! You know?" I searched his mind, finding out Gerard had indeed, confided in him when handing over the book of the dead for safekeeping.

"Yes, the master said I may be needed when the time came- to read the incantation." If the book allows him to, I thought. "However, I do not know where Gabriel hid the ancient one." That- I probably knew, now that I recalled the dream completely. Yes, I had an idea where the gargoyle had secreted the mummy. "Come, we have tasks to take care of before going to my home." We walked towards the front of the house.

"And my little one- Juliette? She arrived safely?

"Yes, she is perfectly well. Scared and shaken, but safe and well. She will be so relieved to know you are alive. I will have to leave you there for I must seek out.."

"Marie?"

"We need her help now." My mind went back to what had just passed in the last few minutes- Pierre's torment and the substantial friendship he had for me. If he had loved me less, he would still be alive. I thought of the senseless destruction of the plantation and our poor slaves held in chains. "I must bury my friends before we go." A light drizzle began to fall.

"I will help you retrieve Gerard's body, Master Henri."

"No, Toussaint. That is my responsibility." I looked upon him with sincere affection. "Merci, Toussaint. You have always been a true confidante and I will never forget out friendship."

"And there is something more I must do."

I had already given thought of plans for the slaves from Sans Souci. "Is there a safe haven you can take them, temporarily, somewhere relatively safe from the witch; somewhere nearby away from the prying eyes of humans out for bounty?"

He nodded. "The large barn in the pecan grove was sparred her fire storm. The grove too."

"Bon. Take them there. Later, Juliette and you can bring them medicine, food. We will rebuild and if they stay and work for me I will grant them their freedoms. Comprendre?"

"Of course, Master Henri. We will reclaim Sans Souci one day." He turned towards the slave cabins where the wretched lie chained and bleeding.

I turned to the extremely unpleasant task of having to bury my poor dead friends.

Pierre's body lay like a pile of bones in a heap. He had been unrecognizable from the vibrant, energetic, fun-loving boy I grew up with. The sadness of losing both him and Gerard would have been unbearable, save that I stayed my mind on one course- focusing on one thing- my ultimate revenge. Hopefully, with Marie's help, I might be able to bring back Gerard for a time- for the battle. He must be waiting for my call. It was necessary for me to find Marie quickly.

The drizzle turned into a steady shower as I dug three plots- for Pierre and Gerard, then a tiny spot for the horrible bloody carcass of Mercutio. I selected a small rise not far from the house, for the plantation cemetery, from which they would be able to see the distant river flow for eternity. It took only a small effort (physically speaking) and in no time I had them buried. It seemed so much of the time I was having to bury someone. Retrieving Gerard's body was the most difficult for me and I tried not to let my human side dwell upon the ghastly work fate had called me to perform.

Gathering his remains, I noticed he had on a ring matching the one Juliette had brought me which I still wore on my dirty hand. Toussaint approached as I was finishing a silent prayer. A solitary tear fell from my eye upon the freshly turned damp earth. I wondered how many more graves I would have to dig and pray over before this was all finished.

Montesquieu was impatiently waiting for us, but I wanted to view what was left of the upstairs to see if any manuscripts were left untouched by the fire. It was of no consequence if Toussaint learned about them for he already knew of the book of the dead. However, first he had to show me one more thing.

He led me to my workshop, saying there was something here which Gerard had hidden away, though Toussaint did not know what. We went inside, yet saw nothing other than my tools and clock parts. The last timepiece I had been working on was still disassembled as I had left it that day not so long ago. Everything looked undisturbed except for being badly covered in dust. My foot hit an unseen object and then I understood. I lifted one corner of the invisible cloak. (At this point it mattered little what Toussaint knew; in fact, he needed to know most everything, in order to protect himself and the others during what I had begun to consider as retribution upon the witch). I was thinking as Gerard- she must pay!

What we found meant nothing to Toussaint- I read his mind- some looking-glass wall mirror and a lot of what looked to him to be very old books and papers. He did recognize the portraits of the doctor and Julian Fontenot. There were some other items of which it is not important to describe here.

"Master Gerard placed special emphasis on these items for some reason. Of course," he nodded at me, "you understand."

"Yes," letting the corner of the cloth drop down, the floor filled again with apparent emptiness. "Gerard is really very clever. I will say that. I should not be surprised at anything he does." I was believing he had planned all of this- that Satine had simply played her role as expected. "Come we must hurry."

Montesquieu was waiting outside the door, anxiously prancing about; he knew well the imperativeness of our leaving now and he was eager to fly. Soon we three were back at our friendly cabin. There was no need to introduce Toussaint to grandma-ma.

"I know of your grandmother very well. Even many miles from here her name is mentioned. She is practically a legend, like Marie." I believed the two old ones would complement each other very well indeed.

After his tearful reunion with Juliette, I left Toussaint to explain all that happened at Sans Souci; I kissed Selena (who was controlling her anxiety over Tristan very well), and said adieu. Grandma-ma pointed me in the direction of Marie's (even she did not know the exact location of where the voodoo queen dwelled, for they say it was on an island that moved). The cemetery I wanted to visit was along the way.

Bon, I thought to myself as I set off on foot. Montesquieu followed. Turning back, I petted his large long face and told him- not this time, that he was needed back at the cabin to help Toussaint get food and medicine to the slaves.

I turned to start off on my journey again, but he still followed me- nudging my back and tugging on my dirty shirt with his teeth. He wanted me to ride him; to take him along. 'No Montesquieu, go home. I must do this alone. Go back.' I ran on, even though he was the faster of the two of us. Yet he still would not turn around and go home.

Finally I stopped and, turning, demonstrated the anger which was surfacing within me. With that, he stopped and departed back to the cabin, (however reluctantly), and I continued on in a dead run. Of course, I could never be angry with my familiar.

Marie told me I would know when to contact her and then together we would raise Gerard's spirit. To find her, I would have to depend upon my wolf's sense as I did some months back when seeking out Gerard for the first time. I also must be cautious to ensure Satine did not follow me or discover what I was about.

Though there was some daylight left, I transformed into the wolf and with lightning speed came upon my first destination within minutes. I did not sense the witch near, but knew I had to be quick for she must not find me here in the graveyard.

The thin showers were becoming heavier as I slipped into the Fontenot mausoleum, sight unseen, closing the thick door behind me. I could tell immediately that someone had been here not so very long ago; in fact, quite recently. How strange to return to what was once my cage- where I resisted becoming a werewolf. Now I came willingly, as a werewolf and glad of it. No longer a curse to dread and fear, I now positively believed I could use it to my best advantage- with judicious control over my powers and hunger. Especially after learning all of Gerard's witchcraft. I was not evil!

The slabs of stone were placed atop the two stone coffins, as usual. Pushing aside the one slab, I reached inside to trigger the secret panel and I descended the stairs (after replacing the slab back to its original position and closing the bottom panel). Everything must appear normal in case of an intrusion.

It was dark as a cave, but I had no problem seeing with my night vision. I followed the tunnel, slowly along, searching and feeling on both walls for the entrance or some mechanism to open the door to the secret room. Going through the tunnel, inch by inch, the walls wet with moisture and mold, it seemed an eternity and then- suddenly I faced the stairs to ascend- I was already at the end!

Were my instincts incorrect? Was I foolish to follow the dictates of a dream? Non, it had to be here. I had overlooked it somehow- just as Pierre and I had overlooked it before.

I went back through the tunnel, taking even more careful scrutiny, when not much further down, I found a latch down below where the wall met the dirt floor. Feeling above it, I discovered that this part of the wall, was not made of rock and earth like the wall should be. It was a solid piece of carved stone, similar to the large slabs and panels above in the crypts. It seemed impossible! How had I failed to notice something so obvious. Is someone else's witchcraft involved here?

I flipped the latch with my foot and the door cracked open slowly with an annoying grating sound. The dream had been right! I had found what I was looking for.

Opening the door further (it swung out into the tunnel), I entered the chamber, hoping that the object I was seeking would be there. Smelling resin, I noticed a torch ready to be lit on a nearby wall, yet there was nothing to light it with. I wanted to get a better look see and examine the artifact thoroughly. Its power was unmistakable- palpable.

It dawned on me to try and summon the fire power within myself, as Henri and not as loup garou. Transforming back into human form, I reached up to the torch and concentrated on fire- my own fire power. It took a long minute and I wondered if the power would have acted sooner if I had been loup garou. Sparks started, virtually, flowing from my fingertips and the torch came to life. An amazingly easy feat actually- my witch's ability assisting.

As the room filled with light, I turned. There before me stood an enormous, tall magnificent piece of ancient Egyptian art- the mummy's sarcophagus. Encrusted all over with gold and precious metals, it reflected the torch's light as if it had been made yesterday. Dark onyx eyes looked down at me with an indifferent countenance. The value must be worth several fortunes.

My glee was hard to disguise. Gerard and Gabriel (with Dr. Fontenot's help) had accomplished the near impossible! So if all goes well for us, the combination of our powers will enable us to capture the witch and this old lover of hers will keep her prisoner forever.

I dared to touch the relic- I had to be positive he was the one. Its supreme power was contained within, yet I could still feel it with out. Marie's description from her spirit world, was accurate. There must be no other creature on earth, as powerful and strong as this timeless, changeless being. A being, horrible to behold; inexorably stalking its enemies; once a king among kings- this one could save Sans Souci and my family. Or, he could possibly destroy us all, if we do not control him as described in the book. I discovered some writing in a dead language on one side of the sarcophagus, but I hadn't the time to decipher the meaning.

The incense burner was in the corner just as it had been in my dream. It would seem that Gerard had planned well and secretly; now it was up to me to contact him and we begin our detailed plans for enticing the witch to this chamber.

I snuffed out the torch, replacing it in its holder. Just as in doing so, I felt that same intense cold pass through me again, (though the room was warm and dank), and I imagined a distinct movement behind me. "Gerard? Is that you?" I called out. "Or some one else?" Perhaps my heightened senses were playing tricks on me; always hearing and feeling the supernatural, confusing it with the real world.

Standing absolutely still, I detected nothing further- no movement, no sound, no cold. Just as it had been when I entered. Whatever it was had left. Exiting, I closed the door behind me, trying to be as silent as possible. It sealed itself so well, the door was barely detectable. Who had created this magical place? The Fontenots? Gerard himself? What witch had invented this secret chamber?

I went out the stairs leading up to the grave on the far side of the cemetery, closing all panels. My name was still morbidly carved into the tombstone. A thick fog was rolling in and at first, I ignored it, but then realized it was sent from Marie and meant to lead me to her. It would also serve to disguise my route from the witch, so as not to be followed.

Along the way, I gave serious thought concerning Toussaint's and my own observation that Satine wanted something more from all of this. At first consideration, it would appear that the mummy and his power is what she was after, however on deeper reflection I believed it was not. Instincts told me it must be something else. Yet what? More appropriately, who?

She had taken my boy from me already and (in her mind) Gerard had already been dealt with. So who could it be? Myself perhaps? That did not seem plausible. As Marguerite, she could have destroyed me easily and she almost had. What a fool I had been!

What about Marie? Satine saw her merely as an inferior local voodoo charlatan- no competition; an annoyance she could stamp out easily at any time. It had to be someone else.

Soon the fog was so thick that even my keen sight could barely see a foot ahead of me. However, I did not worry, for the fog itself started pushing me along, avoiding trees and obstacles; in fact, after a time, it had lifted me, carrying me a few feet or so above the ground, much as it had when rescuing me from the hounds. And we made good speed, traveling fast through the forest/swamp, the fog rolling with its own unique form of life. It was, oddly, not moist- rather, the fog was dry, wrapping itself around me like a warm blanket. I had the feeling of being with a friend. I wondered how it might treat Marie's enemies? A familiar like this- a particularly special form of creature- was practically indestructible.

Now we were crossing over water, building speed ever faster; narrowly skirting dead tree trunks, as it carried me forward, deeper into the basin. Yet, all the while I felt safe and secure. I did lose all sense of time and place though and our journey, despite it seeming a short time, must have taken me many, many miles away (unless of course, we were traveling in circles). The swamp appeared limitless and then finally, in the cloudy distance, I saw a tiny light ahead- a soft light as if burning from someone's window. Approaching nearer, I eventually distinguished the outline of a small cabin between tall cypress trees- a cabin much like my own, but built upon a little piece of island, completely surrounded by swamp. The fog slowed and I was gently guided into a pirogue- apparently, I was to arrive at Marie's under my own power. The fog stayed thick all around me, but it was not as it was before. The familiar had other work to do! Yes, the witch was searching and Marie and I must remain carefully hidden.

I transformed back to myself and rowed quietly to the

pier. It was actually enjoyable to be in this area- wetlands and basins such as this were my happy home now. (If this was real and not an illusion.) This particular swamp was certainly the largest inland body of water I had seen so far- in this 'new world'.

I tied the pirogue at the end of a long narrow pier leading to her island cabin. As I walked up from the pier, the fog allowed me, through occasional thick drifts, to see a tall shadowy female figure in the doorway. With the light behind her, I could not make out her features, but it was definitely Marie. I would recognize the regal majesty of the voodoo queen anywhere.

I must take some time and effort at this point in my narrative, to briefly describe her home on this secluded island, for it produced the most marvelously profound effect upon me. Everywhere- descending from rafters above the pier, hanging in the trees, spread out over the grounds- everywhere- were the signs and charms, the gris-gris of voodoo and, many other ancient religions- some native to this land, others I recognized as Catholic, Egyptian, Babylonian- most probably everything from around the world. Magical symbols and diagrams covered the entire cabin- there was a pentagram or two; red clay dust circled the entire island- to ward off those who would do harm and welcome only that which meant well.

However, what really held me was the feeling I gathered from the place. As if I were witnessing one of the most spiritual and beloved shrines in the world. I felt a sacredness in this place; and I was a privileged intruder.

And there was magic! Immediately, with my very first step on her land, light appeared about- everywhere- as if a thousand candles had been instantly lit. It was so beautiful and I was so astounded- all I could do was just stand there like a dumbfounded fool.

"Bonsoir Henri. Entrez, s'il-vous plait." She beckoned me inside.

"Bonsoir, mademoiselle," or was it madam, I did not know. I was always so flustered whenever in her presence. The only light in the cabin was the bright warm glow of an oil lamp on a side table. The place itself was small, maybe three rooms at the most and I wondered as to how she lived.

"Do not worry about the lights outside. The evil one will not be able to see us." I believed her. "This is a special place," she added.

The house was furnished with very little, but along one wall were shelves full of bottles and containers; no doubt her supplies and ingredients for voodoo potions, remedies and love spells. She obviously lived simply and unadorned; in contrast to the way I imagined a powerful, respected high priestess would live, for surely she had plenty of income from the local populace who would seek her out for advice, help and to perform both little and large miracles.

"This island is a very special place," she repeated as she had me set at a center table.

"Yes, so I noticed. I am honored." And somewhat intimidated.

She sat across from me. "There are other such places in the world, (not many), though she will devour them one by one if given the chance."

I observed, whereas her cabin may have been lacking in articles and household ornaments, her dress was the complete opposite. Beautifully colored in vivid oranges and greens, the gown she wore showed off a long slender, yet voluptuous figure and, as always, she was immaculate, even fastidious, in her look. That is the only way I have ever seen her; the only way she probably allows anyone to see her. The auburn hair was coiffed high on her head, wrapped up in a crimson African scarf. All held up by her lovely long brown neck. To put it simply- she was an extremely handsome woman- desirable to any man. Even I, with my urgent need to contact Gerard and make battle, was distracted by her allure.

Also, noticeably, she wore a pentagram on a necklace, but I knew instinctively that she wore it- not for protection- but in honor of Gerard and myself.

She lit a red candle which was directly in the middle of the table and we were ready to begin the seance. There was no time for simple conversation; it was important to establish contact with Gerard as soon as possible.

"Are you sure you can bring his spirit back?" I naively asked- The- high priestess of all voodoo practitioners, as she sat composed and stately across from me.

"As sure as I can be." My look of bewilderment and doubt must have been obvious, for she explained further. "What I am saying is, yes, I- we- can call him back." She paused, "However, we must be positive, it is really Gerard we summoned and not a different spirit wanting to return to the world- a spirit pretending to be him. Or that we do not accidentally allow in other- undesirables- from the spirit world."

I had no idea a seance could be so problematic. "Will not your spirit guide- the old one you contacted before at the previous seance- would not he make sure it is our Gerard?"

"We shall not need him tonight." She explained further to me in simple terms, (but not in any way with a condescending manner). "We needed him for the other seance, because we had a difficult question that only he could provide an appropriate and adequate answer for. This seance is different- we are to summon up someone we both know well and try to bring him back to us for a brief time."

"How long is a brief time?"

"He will remain with us, corporeally, only until the task at hand is completed. Then he must return to the spirit world."

"The task being the destruction of the witch."

"Exactly." Did I detect a hint of pleasure in her voice at the thought of Satine's demise? She stretched out each of her arms on the table, the hands palm up. I joined them with my own.

"I feel he is eager and ready for us to beckon him home."

"Yes, I sense the same. He is already at the door. Now do not break contact," she paused, "nor say anything unless Gerard asks you to." I wondered just what door he was waiting at- the door to heaven or the one to hell. If there were such places. Perhaps he would be able to tell us.

Just before starting the ceremony, she leaned forward, searching deep into my eyes. "You miss him very much, yes, mon cher?"

And I admitted to her (and perhaps for the first time to myself) that not only did I miss him, but I missed his confidence and masculine strength; the touch of his physical beauty. "I love him," I replied simply.

"Bon. Then this will be that much more easier." She closed her eyes, but then opened them back up- and wide. "There may be some- thing- he may ask you. And your reply will be most important. The secrets between the two of you are the links to bringing him back here to us. Now clear your mind and think only of Gerard and our purpose here and now." She again closed her eyes and started chanting in some foreign language, probably long dead, which I had never learned or come across before in Gerard's library. I closed my eyes also and concentrated with her, hoping that not too many secrets were revealed tonight in her presence.

During this seance, she neither swayed nor rocked, but sat tall and still- regal as if a statue, and after some time she switched to French asking to speak to Gerard.

"Gerard, are you here? Available to us? We know that you are near and want to communicate." She paused as if an answer might come with the wind. Then she spoke more pointedly. "Henri is here, with me." Another pause but no response. "He very much wants to speak with you." Another pause, "and to see you." Still no answer and I was about to despair."Henri needs you Gerard. He needs you badly." She went on to add, "in order to defeat the one that you both call enemy. The witch and succubus- Satine!"

At that point, the candle flickered, though there was no breeze and that same extreme cold sensation I had felt recently, was now present- appearing from nowhere- prevalent all around us. Gerard was here- back with me! I must remain calm.

"Gerard, if it is you, show yourself." A pause. "Gerard your presence is needed, required for our success. Gerard.."

Just then the door flew open with a loud crash. Reflexively, I turned towards it, opening my eyes, but kept our hands in contact. A solitary male figure stood in the shadows, the fog behind him swirling like a ghost itself.

"Gerard!" I exclaimed without thinking. She squeezed my hand for silence; she too now had her eyes open, observing.

She spoke a command to the spirit. "If you are Gerard, make yourself known and step into the light." The dark figure raised an arm. The candle and the dim lamp in the corner, both blew out, snuffed by an invisible hand. Marie leaned in towards me and whispered, "I feel he wants something from you; he needs your.." she shrugged, "Je ne sais quoi."

"I know what it is," I whispered back.

"Then pray say it and quickly. Give him what he needs to return. Maintenant! Before he is called back."

I spoke loudly to the spirit at first. "Gerard, I...I forgive you." My voice consequently sunk lower, as did my head and shoulders in admittance. "I have always forgiven you. I forgave you a long time ago."

There was a firm hand upon my shoulder, a man's strong hand. The lights turned up, brighter than before and looking up- I found myself gazing into the dark blue eyes of the only man I could ever love. He was whole and alive; corporeal- human.

Gerard had come back to me.

7

Our embrace was so long-lasting, so intense and heartfelt, we did not even take notice when Marie discreetly left the room, leaving us alone for our intimate reunion. Gerard and I were too absorbed in one another to notice anything else. We said nothing to one another, as we kissed all the while, never releasing the tight hold we had on each other.

Stopping for breath, I whispered how I had missed him so; he whispered back that he thought he had lost me forever- that he believed I would never forgive him.

How could I not? "For I love you," and as I said the words, joy spread across his face. And, as if it were possible, we clutched one another even tighter. Through our clothing, I rubbed my stiffness against his.

"We do not have time."

"We have tonight," I replied. We must make time, for afterwards- if we survive- he would be taken from me again (perhaps this time forever)- the spirit world will have to take him back. "There may be little time then and we must make the most of our time together now. Besides dawn will be here in a few hours and we can spend the day preparing for the battle. We confront her at dusk, correct?"

"Yes, when the moon rises. We should start making plans now." He still dissented.

"And we will- afterwards." I licked his ear, his neck. He still had his wolf scent and it made the desire in me grow that much more- uncontrollably so. My wolf's needs, my human desires, were all coming to the fore. I wanted us to embrace each other completely unclothed; to feel his brawny hairy chest against my own; to watch our muscular arms entwine and grasp and clutch each other; to touch each other in that special way, yet again.

The warm fog enveloped us as we walked outside, hand in hand. Finding a soft grassy spot among the reeds, we undressed one another and lied down, resuming our strong embrace.

Surrounded by magic, we made love; Marie's familiar kept us hidden- safe to be ourselves. The air was thick with the fog as it swirled about us, warm and inviting and, (it may have been my imagination), but it seemed to join in with us, acting as a comfortable sheet enclosing itself around us. It grew warmer as our passion increased.

"Non, non, mon cher. This time, this way." Gerard turned over onto his stomach and, as he gave himself- totally- to me, I felt the fulfillment that can only come from loving, completely, the one man in the world that is the same as myself. He made me- created me- fashioned me into what I am today. It was inevitable that we become lovers.

Yes, that was what truly made our loving intense- we were the only ones of our kind; exactly the same; no one else could share what has passed between us- as men or as loup garou. I would not be here as I am writing this, if not for him. For many hours, we loved each other that night.

As I described earlier, Marie's fog gives a distortion to reality- in particular, the sense of time or the passing of time. That night was no exception. Perhaps half the night, maybe more, we lay there together in the soft billows of clouds, nude, our muscular bodies touching affectionately- then again, aggressively. The matching male beauty of our bodies- against one another, holding each other- was enticing, alluring, exciting. Finally, we kissed and lay across one another, and started to discuss, in silent telepathy our plans for battle.

Gerard began. She must be lured out.

I think I know of a way.

You have her portrait?

Oui.

That should work. However, she is very clever.

Not so much as you and I together.

Overconfidence can lead to a downfall, Henri.

It is her overconfidence which will result in her downfall.

True, she always underestimated me.

And she does not know you have returned.

That shall be the surprise. I must appear at just the right moment.

She has my child.

I know. He caressed me close. Do not fear. She has not harmed him. We will save your baby boy. Not to worry.

Yet there is something else she is after also, n'est-ce pas?

Yes, I believe I know what- or to be precise, who it is.

You are speaking of..

Julian.

Of course!

She wants his power. Then she could possibly be unstoppable- forever.

So, if she finds him before we do..

He will not be found by anyone- unless he wants to be- or at least, that is my impression. I wonder-

Yes, Gerard?

If we trick her into thinking Julian is below..

In the crypt where the mummy is…

And then she will descend..

To meet her doom in the mummy's clutches.   I

paused with doubt.   Sounds too easy mon ami.

Well, we will have to play it out very carefully and be prepared for any contingency. If only we had a way to disguise thoughts, to make appearances deceptive, unclear and distorted. A way to confuse her.   The fog grew thicker, warning us that dawn was coming soon. We will need special weapons and tools, Henri. You must fabricate them yourself.

Yes, I know what we need and how to make them most powerful.

Forged with your magic fire?   I nodded.   They must be made of inert materials. Not made from hemp rope or any plant matter. Remember, she can command and break living substances.

The weapons most likely will only work for a time, before she adapts..

Her power. However, they should give us the time we need and provide a decided advantage. Gerard, looking at me tenderly, caressed my goatee and chin, then held my face in his hand. Our eyes were close; I felt his breath upon my lips.   You must lead the attack with Montesquieu.   My surprise made him laugh. I had no idea he could keep a secret from me. And I foolishly thought I could keep one from him.   That is his name, is it not?

You know of my familiar?

Ever since that first night in the carriage. Maybe even before that, mon ami.   Gerard's extrasensory perception was beyond what I had previously believed.

Yes, we will lead the attack. And you and Gabriel?

We will follow at just the right moment, after you have weakened her. It should be quite a surprise for her.   We paused in our thoughts. The night was ending quickly- and so was our time alone together.

Gerard- the lightning strike gave me a power- a fire power. Just as you thought it might.   My silent voice was proud.

I know. I could feel it all during our sex. I feel it now, holding you. It pulses through you like crashing waves. It is magic.

I am still learning to control it.

It will be there when you need it. Not to worry.

And Gabriel?

Now that I am back, alive, he will be also. He was, most likely, flying this night, leading Satine away from this sacred isle.

The dagger will be dipped in the same poison she used against me- the one that turned me permanently into a wolf-man.

Bon! Use her deadly magic against her. How befitting. Then she will become her true self forever..as..

A centuries old succubus. The dagger must find its mark-

In her heart. We echoed the thought in unison.

He squeezed me tight. It was time to leave, to prepare for our dangerous quest. We dressed quietly- trying not to dwell upon what might go wrong and the dire consequences; trying not to think that this night might be our last together. The fog revealed a glimpse of the moon as it made its way for the sun. Already the first signs of a new day were appearing. We sensed Marie waiting for us at the pier.

She kissed us each on the cheek; in greeting, in farewell. "Gerard it is good you are here. The witch must not be allowed to stay in this land."

"We will see to it, one way or another, mademoiselle. And thank you for performing the ceremony that brought me back. Because of you, I am whole and ready to fight."

"And ready for other things as well," she replied subtly, knowingly; and I believe, I saw Gerard blush for the first time. But in less than a heartbeat, she turned to me and presented me with a small item wrapped in a purple cloth. I could tell from its feel that it was a heavy necklace of some sort. "This is for you Henri. You must wear it around your neck and keep the amulet close to your heart constantly during the battle. It is a most powerful talisman- no witch can harm the bearer as long as he is wearing it."

"It protects even from one such as she?"

"Even from one such as she." I started to open up the tissue, but she stopped me, telling me to look at it later. "It is from the natives of this area and contains great powers from the spirit world. To ward off all evil."

She turned back to Gerard. "And for me? Do you have some talisman for my protection?" He asked in his half-joking manner as was his endearing way.

"You do not need such protection. You are of the spirit world now. But beware- she will try to send you back."

"Yes, I am prepared. I can dematerialize and reappear at will." He gave us a demonstration, vanishing completely (I then felt the same extreme cold as earlier, but it disappeared when he rematerialized). "I may re-main corporeal as long as I desire."

"Until the task is completed." I had to add a serious note.

He put a comforting hand upon my shoulder. "Yes it is true, I must return after the witch is destroyed." We all were silent for a moment. When next he spoke, it was as his light-hearted self. "I can command wind and rain, earth and fire- the elements."

"Remember," (we always listened carefully to Marie's words, but never so much as that night.) "Remember, the uniqueness of this witch. She is a creature of fire- a true Phoenix. Only the earth can snuff her powers out completely."

"At least for another one hundred years," Gerard commented.

"That is her legend." Marie slowly walked back with us to the pirogue at the end of the pier. Her familiar would follow us to shore- cloaking us from unseen eyes. She turned to me once more just before I got in. "The material you seek for the weapons is in the northwest corner of the lake."

"Oh? But that is out of.." I started to say, but Gerard stepped in.

"Yes, Marie I know that area well and we will see to it. Never fear, Marie. We will win."

As she waved, she shouted at Gerard, for we were traveling fast: "I must speak with you about the world you just came from, Gerard. I have ..questions."

"I am afraid I remember very little, mademoiselle," he shouted back. I could barely see her- all the magical lights were diminishing. "I would be honored to discuss with you what I do remember- and felt. I am your servant, Marie- available at your summons."

"Merci, et bonne chance!" Her voice floated with the fog, bodiless. "I am confident I will see you both again."

As we sped rapidly to the shoreline, near where the forest was that she had directed me to, I pondered- like Marie- about the spirit world and what it must be like. Was it peaceful? Did Gerard know now of heaven and hell? Did there exist the dark one and was it he who gave us these powers which we could use for good or evil?

Those questions would have to wait. Exactly what material am I looking for, Gerard? You will know it when you see it, he replied. Trust in your instinct.

As dawn made herself known, we landed and, after an intense parting between us, he dematerialized into the wind to search for Satine. But we both knew where she was or would be upon the rising of the moon- back at Sans Souci, waiting for me- waiting for me to try and take back my son. However, she shall meet with some surprises.

Several feet in from the lake, I entered a forest of dead trees. At first I did not take notice of just how different this forest was. Then the instinct Gerard told me to trust, caused me to halt in mid-step. Right before me stood the remains of a tree, long dead; a large trunk of a tree almost as tall as myself. I touched it- the tree was rock! Then I realized the property or material Marie wanted me to use for the weapons. Petrified wood!

Hundreds, maybe even a thousand years old- this forest used to be living- now it was completely stone. The perfect composition for a weapon against a witch like her; against one who commands and uses living plant material. Hopefully, when the stone/wood makes contact- pierces her skin and enters into the blood- it will react violently and inflict great damage on her.

The long dead petrified trunks were standing about, mixed with living trees and brush. There was even a great deal of heavy petrified logs lying about on the ground; broken pieces, growing ever older as time marched by. On close inspection, the rocks appeared semi-precious like quartz or carnelian. How beautiful it all was. They could be worked into lovely jewelry, but now they were needed for more serious business.

I selected one particularly large trunk still standing (I believe it used to be a palm) taller than myself- and using superhuman strength, I pulled it completely from the ground. Even some of the roots remaining were petrified. This would be plenty of material for the weapons and equipment I had in mind. Carrying the heavy load on my shoulders, I ran as a wolf all the way around the lake and back to our cabin- instinct directing me while avoiding all human contact of course. There was no time to lose for much had to be done. I arrived as the others were still having breakfast.

I did not stop to eat. All that morning- and into mid-day- I worked upon fabricating and forging the weapons and tools we would need:

  − a long chain of strong magical links made of the petrified stone and forged from my lightning fire;
  − a sheet of chain mail- armor for Montesquieu- again made from the petrified wood and imbued with my

495

magic;

    – blindfolds for Montesquieu and myself- for the witch would surely change into the Gorgon sometime during the battle. At which time, my familiar and I will have to communicate telepathically;

    – a bundle of arrows, tipped with petrified wood and forged in magical fire. I would probably make most use of these, from a distance, when leading the attack. As part of the spirit world, Gerard really has no need for these concrete, solid weapons;

    – a large and heavy sword fashioned from the same material, that would be able to cut and break the limbs and branches that she commands;

    – a giant shield to deflect her red fire power;

    – Satine's portrait- to be used as a lure. Already Toussaint had placed it in the chamber near the sarcophagus, cloaked in secrecy;

    – and of course, I had the talisman for protection. However, I was seriously thinking of leaving it with Selena for her own protection;

    – Last but not least, there was, perhaps, the piece de resistance. A dagger of petrified wood, stained with the very same poisonous tea which Satine (Marguerite) had used to make me revert permanently into a werewolf- my cursed self. With grandma-ma's help we found the formula, and hopefully, if even a drop enters into the witch's blood system, then she too will revert into her own specially cursed self- permanently! And, consequently, also be unable to change into her other forms.

    Yet, with all these preparations, there were still so many variables and imponderables. Innumerable ways each scenario may play out. We would have to be ever alert for even the smallest opportunity to inflict damage- and it must be as swiftly as possible.

    The rest of the day Montesquieu and I practiced riding and shooting. At first, we rode without the armour, then, after putting a heavy blanket over him, we added the chain mail. It was somewhat heavy, but for my strong Montesquieu it mattered little. He could still fly and react quickly as always. It did interfere some with his long powerful hind legs when leaping, so I modified the armour suitably.

I practiced with the bow and arrow, and using my wolf's eyesight and warlock's concentration, I found my mark every time. With just one strike, the extremely heavy sword could cut through (with bright white sparks) the thickest tree branches. Toussaint (joined hand-in-hand with grandma) came out to watch us practice- applauding us when we succeeded and offering hints of help. Such as, when Toussaint observed that I tend to leave my left side vulnerable, or when I take too long to reel back. "Speed will be of the utmost importance," he advised. "I saw first-hand how fast and ultimate her power is- she destroyed Sans Souci in only minutes."

"Gerard is back?" Toussaint asked as Montesquieu and I took a break and I wiped us both down from our sweaty strenuous exercise.

"Yes, but..," I felt the need to explain, "Of course, he is still a spirit, only appearing as Gerard for short times. He should be here soon for the day is fading fast." Again I paused, "Toussaint," I addressed him seriously. "We must enlist your help."

"If you need me for the ceremony, the answer is yes. I will help." He read my mind.

"We will need you to read the incantation from the book at precisely the right moment. We must all be in the crypt at once and, if our plan works, Satine will be below when the mummy wakes and.."

"I should say the incantation," grandma-ma interrupted.

"Non, non!" Toussaint and I echoed each other. He continued, "It should be me. I promised Master Gerard."

"I still say it should be me who recites the incantation."

Grandma-ma was being her firm self.

"The book will allow me to read from it. I feel sure of it." Toussaint was confident.

"Grandma-ma, it has been decided.."

"And it can be re-decided. I should say the incantation," she repeated herself.

"With all due respect, grandma-ma, even if the book allowed you to, you..you cannot.."

"See? Read?" She laughed heartily with her wonderful 'whiskey-filled' throatiness I had grown so fond of. "You have the words, my son, non? Then, I can memorize it also."

"Yes, but the slightest inaccuracy, the tiniest mispronunciation.."

"May mean failure. I understand." She paused, then spoke slowly in her wise way. "I firmly believe the book will tell me or communicate in some way the words I need to know. I also believe it will be important that I be there when the time comes. For some reason, I know I will be needed." Her portent sent shivers up my spine.

Toussaint tried once more to intervene. "But I assure you there is no need, ma cherie. No, it is better that you stay here with Juliette and Selena. We can accomplish this ourselves and not have to worry about.."

"A woman!" Her voice displayed amusement, but she was serious. "All you men and your creatures against that one woman, that one witch!" Toussaint and I were both embarrassed. "Remember, the witch tried to eliminate me. She wants me out of the way. I will be there." Her voice was becoming more strident with each syllable and I knew what that meant.

"Now, grandma-ma. There will be no need."

"Now my son," she mimicked me. "How can you be so sure?"

"Maddie!"

"Tous!" Toussaint and grandma had obviously become even more 'acquainted' than I had originally thought. Perhaps, there was a history between them which I knew nothing of. I did not intrude by reading their minds; though it would please me very much if they were to become close.

"Tous? Maddie?" I had to ask.

"Short for Madeleine." She hesitated, her eyebrows questioning me. "You do remember my first name, do you not my son?" She laughed again. "You think of me only as grandma-ma!" We all had a good laugh at my expense. Then she became serious again. "Bon. It is settled. I will be there at the ceremony."

"And so shall we." It was Selena approaching along with Juliette, who was cradling my Marcel. She and Toussaint were definitely part of our family now.

"Really Selena," I started to disagree. "Someone must remain behind, here."

Toussaint echoed my concern. "Juliette, it is much safer for you to be here."

"Safer yes, but I feel my place is beside you grandpa-pa." She nodded towards me. "And beside you too, Master Henri."

"Now we spoke of this before, Juliette. I am no longer your master; you must call me Henri." She bowed her head a tiny bit to hide the blush in her delicate young light brown cheeks.

"We are not afraid, Henri. You must give us the chance to help." Selena pleaded with me.

"Of course, you ladies are very brave, but.."

"She has my son!"

"I know my darling, and that is why you must stay behind- here, safely."

"Besides, Juliette and I hate that witch. She has tormented us both." Selena looked fondly at tiny Juliette; a sisterly affection was developing between them which I was happy to see.

"But.." Toussaint and I tried one last attempt to dissuade them, however, the two of them stood stubbornly, stolidly together, holding hands, determined to be of some help. Toussaint and I looked to grandma for aid. Instinctively, the old one knew to take the reins.

She came over close to Selena and, taking both of her hands in her own, grandma-ma spoke softly in their native patois. "Selena, my little child. You and the babies are my last blood relatives in this whole world. When the time comes and we are performing the ceremony- all of us there in the cemetery will be in extreme danger. The witch will not spare even one of us." Selena started to interrupt, but bit her lip, thinking better of it, and allowed her grandmother to finish. "Therefore, you must understand the importance for you to remain here, safe and sound." She took one hand free and reached for Juliette. "And for you too, my dear. You will both be needed here, for when Henri brings back Tristan." A few tears loosened themselves from Selena's eyes and trailed heavily down her cheeks. "We require you both to remain here, praying for our success. The reason I'm going is because I am positive my presence will be a necessity." Selena wanted to speak, but again stopped herself; she believed in her grandmother and her intuitions- as did I. Was there something she felt or knew that I should be made aware of? Grandma-ma continued with emphasis, "I also know, positively, that you and Juliette must stay behind. I am sorry my dears, but- I insist. Your father and mother would want it this way, Selena. "

They all three embraced and there were no more tears. My ladies were strong and determined- born from pioneer stock. And I silently promised we would all be free, out from under that witch's heavy hand of evil.

After a moment, I broke the silence. "Bon, then it is agreed. Toussaint and grandma-ma- Madeleine- you must see to it that everything is ready at the appointed time."

"And the signal?" he asked the question I did not quite

have an answer for.

"You will know when the time comes." He looked hesitantly at me. I patted him on the shoulder. "Trust me mon vieux. Be at the cemetery, cloaked in invisibility and watch for when she enters the mausoleum. Gerard and I should be entering in from the other end of the tunnel. We might already be waiting for her."

"Then we will enter and begin the incantation."

"Yes, just repeat it over and over and make sure plenty of the special incense is prepared and lit. Both for above where the coffins are (there you and grandma-ma will be) and for below where the sarcophagus is- and the scene of the final battle." I felt my voice being called on the wind. Gerard was near and it was time to say goodbye. "Hopefully all will go as planned," I added optimistically.

I turned to Selena and took her aside for a moment; she was now holding Marcel. I gave him a peck of a kiss on his little forehead. He was sleeping- so calm, so without worry, knowing nothing of the unfolding events and possible tragedy and destruction which might occur around him. "I want to give you this." I took Marie's gift off my neck and handed it to her. "This is a most powerful talisman that protects the bearer from any witch. Wear it around your neck and keep it over your heart."

"I know what it is. Did Marie give you this?"

"Yes." She put the talisman back into my hand and closed my fist around it. "But Selena, I want you.."

"Non, mon cher. You must wear this until the right time and then use it to protect our baby, Tristan." She looked deep into me with her moist almond-shaped eyes. They pleaded with me. "Please, Henri. For Tristan."

"Mais oui, bien sur, my love." I took the relic back, and we kissed, holding each other for a long moment. Out of the corner of my eye, I saw Gerard, in human form, walking across the clearing towards us. Toussaint and Juliette went to greet him; she practically ran to the man-the man who once was her master.

Our lips parted. "Be courageous and careful, my dear Henri."

"I will. You must be careful, aussi." I hesitated. "If we fail," my words were hard to say, "if we fail, you and Juliette must seek out Marie. The witch will eventually come for all of you, including Marie. Remember, no matter what happens to me, we will always be one- always together, for we are never apart." Slowly, we dissolved our embrace; I wiped a solitary tear off her cheek and then wandered over to join Gerard, who had just finished his parting with Toussaint and Juliette. Montesquieu, who had been waiting patiently, followed a few paces behind me.

"Come back safe with our son, mon cher!" Selena shouted after me as she was joined by the others.

"I will my darling. I will."

"Are you ready, mon ami?"

"I am." The sun was setting fast.

"And your weapons?"

"All prepared. Montesquieu is carrying them in an invisible satchel." I myself had the bundle of arrows and bow over my shoulder; The poisoned dagger was in its sheath on my hip.

The barest glimpse of a full moon was rising.

"Bon, then it is time."

"Yes it is time." I mounted Montesquieu as Gerard dematerialized and all three of us flew off together towards Sans Souci. I glanced back at the five of them; leaving my loved ones behind was not at all easy; with none of us knowing who would return whole. Or if this would be the ending of us all.

The last lingering rays of the setting sun gleamed across the swamp-forest, as Montesquieu and I rode to Sans Souci. Looking down, I could still see the shadow of us flowing upon the verdant land and water. The invisible form of Gerard was ahead. My thoughts drifted back to how much this place, named after a king of France, meant to me. This area has become my home; I have made it my own; it gives me comfort. A serene and dangerous wilderness where an abundance of fish and wildlife gave one a rich place to live and make a living- with its wild fits of weather that reminded man, he is not king here, but subject to nature's whims. The grand buildings and plantations- designed by the white man and built by the enslaved- were picturesque and beautiful monuments to, at one and the same time, the creativity and cruelty of mankind.

I hoped to see this land free of slavery. Perhaps it will evolve in the years to come. I had to survive this contest. For if she won, this scene could change and her evil would dominate- devastate my family, Sans Souci, the surrounding country. Gerard spoke of her as the harbinger of war- the bearer of destruction. He and I, along with the others, were all that stood in her way. This was the last chance to conquer what I had begun to think of as an evil Egyptian goddess.

Yet even Gods can fail. And fall! Brought down, toppled by their own supreme arrogance and overweening conceit. She will underestimate us and we must use that to our advantage.

Armoured with my shield and weapons, Montesquieu in his cloak of chain mail, our blindfolds at the ready- we sauntered slowly up the oak alley resembling, I am sure, one of the knights I had read about as a child. The trees were alive and bent down towards us, yet did not attack.

Trying to scare us, they let us know we were being watched. Night had just fallen (as it always must) and the moon was rising, full and close. Feeling its power surge throughout my body, the moon brought my wolf's senses and powers to a peak. Was tonight the night of the total eclipse? I reminded myself to be diligent with my thoughts; careful what she might read from my mind. She must gather only that which I wanted her to.

I approached the poor, half-burnt, dilapidated mansion which had once stood in wondrous glory and I called her out. "Satine! I have returned witch. Satine!" I paused- for there appeared to be no one about. I continued nonetheless. "I have come for my child- My son!" I demanded she show herself.

Montesquieu startled and I sensed movement behind me. Strolling down the oak alley was Satine- self-possessed, confident, acting the part of a French colonial plantation matron; a delicate full-brimmed hat in one hand, a basket of flowers in the other- with no other concern than maintaining her own beauty.

Dressed in a very light pink pastel dress of cotton and lace, Satine's particular dark beauty still struck me- even at this stage of my hatred. Trailing several paces behind her was a female slave, carrying my Tristan in her arms. The girl looked to be oblivious to her surroundings, walking like one of Satine's zombies.

"What a shame, what a pity," were the witch's first words, as she approached closely to us. "Sans Souci was such a lovely place. And after all those delightfully gay parties I had heard about." Her laughter chimed lightly in the breeze. She started to walk past us. "But I will rebuild it my way. That trunk of riches should come in very handy. Very handy indeed. Though I do not really have need of such things to accomplish my goals."

"That gold was meant for me and my family."

She turned back to me and replied, with a snake's hiss, "And now it is mine, to do with as I see fit. Just as the boy is mine now." She looked at Montesquieu as if seeing him for the first time. "What a magnificent steed." She held her hand out as if to pet him, but he snorted at her and backed away. "And all decked out as if for war." Her laughter this time was louder, serious, full of venom. "It will be of no consequence. Pity he will have to be sacrificed. Such a waste." She paused. "That is if you continue on the course you have set for yourselves. . "

I interrupted, "You can keep the gold. Merely give me my boy."

Her smile widened, bright with even young teeth. "Since when do I take orders from you! You obviously come here to do harm. I carry no weapons, simply a basket of flowers. Shame on you Henri, to try and frighten a poor damsel into giving up her rightful due. I thought you more of a gentleman." She pointed back down the alley, "Now leave, before I lose all my charm!"

"Not without my son." I spoke firmly, strongly, but it was of no matter to her. She turned away from us and started towards the ruins.

"I have your portrait!" My voice came to a shout. I was foolishly allowing my anger to surface. I imagined her hesitating for a moment in her stride, but she continued on. "My son, for the portrait."

"There is no bargaining here, Henri. Now go."

"Only I know where it is and I shall destroy it."

At that she turned to me. "I do not need that picture. It has a life of its own and cannot be destroyed." She turned away. "You exaggerate its importance to me."

"I do not think so, mademoiselle." She continued to walk away. Montesquieu and I trailed at a discreet distance. "Then if I cannot destroy it, I can paint over it, modify it. Make you look like the thousands-year old witch you actually are!"

That threat did achieve a response from her, as she spun around to face us, her anger no longer contained. "You think you know my real self, Henri?" she practically screamed the words at me. "You want to see me as I really am? Then so be it." Laughter echoed through the treetops. "I will show you then- little wolf. You pitiful example of a warrior. I have defeated much deadlier and stronger creatures than yourself, Henri. You are a sheep in wolf's clothing, little man, and you will die for your foolishness- tonight!" She raised her arms and the moon turned red, as Gerard had warned me. Blood on the moon was the beginning. "Regardez, Henri and watch true uniqueness; true power. But be prepared for the consequences!" Her shouts were on the wind which had risen with her voice. However, Montesquieu and I were ready.

Instantaneously, her body completely burst into red and yellow flames; the heat scorched us even from the distance we kept ourselves. The slave girl finally found her legs and, taking my child with her, ran for the nearest shelter in the broken down mansion.

The burning figure before me hardly resembled a person. It instantly took flight soaring high and away. She was the firebird, the phoenix herself! All wings and claws and beak- her feathers were actually red hot flames; it was rather- quite beautiful- only the emerald eyes let me know it had once been Satine. As it soared up and around, over us and the trees, I thought how like a small dragon it was, only this creature was entirely made of fire. And admittedly, I was terrified; not since, as a human, when Gerard first attacked me, have I felt such terror. But I must not hesitate when the time comes.

As I watched, she started to soar down, swooping towards us for an attack- screeching like a harpy. Flames shot out from the firebird's wing tips, but my Montesquieu was quick. His leap was grand and her first shot missed us, yet scorched the ground all around. A second shot of fire, came immediately after and caught us in mid-air, my magic shield deflecting it only at the last second. With no pause, the bird whirled about and soared higher, in order to fly in for another attack. I had my bow at the ready, as Montesquieu leapt to meet the enemy.

This time the firebird threw fiery lava-like rocks (just as Toussaint and Juliette had described), falling all around us- on the grounds and what was left of the house where hopefully my son was unharmed. One bomb hit Montesquieu squarely, and though the chain mail protected him, it gave us a severe jolt, and we tumbled in the air, losing our balance for a time. "Steady, mon ami! We must never be unawares." I shouted encouragement as he gathered himself, so I could aim carefully for the bird as it flew in a circle, closing in towards us for a kill.

My shot hit the phoenix- only in the shoulder- however it did injure her noticeably! Tipped with the petrified wood and forged with lightning fire, the arrow caused the firebird to halt herself, visibly, in mid-flight, but unfortunately, she recovered before I could launch another arrow, and proceeded to fly further in, continuing the attack.

I shot another arrow, just as her fire hit us solidly-forcefully- on our left side and we crashed to the ground, more stunned than injured. I smelled burning flesh. Ignoring the scorching pain, I gathered myself up quickly in order to see if the arrow had hit its mark. Montesquieu and I were now separated.

It had! My arrow had hit the witch in the heart and she had fallen to the earth. Yet, she still had not reverted into her human form and so therefore, with no time to lose, my final arrow must find its mark before she had the chance to recover.

The firebird stood, obviously weakened. I shot- yet in that one flash of a second, the bird vanished and my last arrow missed. Turning around, I saw that she had reappeared behind me, no longer in flight, approaching me- lumbering menacingly- like the large pterodactyls that used to roam the earth millennia ago.

With no arrows left, I reached for the sword of petrified wood. It and the dagger were my last arsenal. Excepting, of course, my own fire power. The heat was scorching as she sent a missile of fire. Behind the protective shield, I summoned my willpower, and met the fire with my own- a white lightning heat. The impact was a shock to us both, though we both remained standing, facing off to each other. She sent another missile and another; I managed to deflect them with my shield and then for one moment, between her firings, I succeeded at throwing a tremendously long bolt of my own energy and I watched with delight as the fire eagle screeched in pain and fell, briefly, to the ground. Frankly I was astonished at my success, but she had left herself open and I took advantage of it.

Then, in the next instance, a fire ball, seemingly coming from nowhere, hit right at my feet- the impact throwing me hard upon the ground. I tried to recover as quickly as possible, but discovered I had suffered a severe fire wound to my chest. Montesquieu had also fallen; the shield was lost and I was so weak I could not raise myself off the ground. What was worse: the talisman that Marie had given me was gone; the chain must have broken from my neck sometime during the firebird's attacks! It could be anywhere.

And so now, Satine took advantage of my weakened state.

She approached my prone body. Now, she was as herself- human, composed and arrogant- apparently recovering quickly from the wounds I had inflicted. I lay still on my back, trying to encourage all my regenerative powers to heal my body rapidly for I knew she could deal a death blow any second. Now was the time for Gerard to appear. Where was he? And where was my talisman? I tried to raise my head to look, but I was too weak. I had miraculously held onto the sword- if only I could find enough strength to use it.

"So little warrior, you did well. Though not well enough!" She stood above and over me, then- ever so slowly- she stretched out her arms to the trees and sky; the wind promptly rose following her command and dark clouds swirled above, obliterating the red light of the moon. "Do you not realize who you are dealing with?" She glowered down at me, smiling like a hungry panther. "I am a God compared to you, Henri. I can kill you with a single thought."

The pain seized me dramatically in every joint of my being; my whole body convulsed, racked in torment. She was slowly crushing me to death with her own supernatural will. Where was Gerard? Gerard hurry! If only I had strength enough to raise my sword. "Tell me, where is the portrait?"

Wincing through the excruciating pain, I was able to sigh: "Let me go and I will tell you."

"I will ask you only once more, Henri, little fool. Where is my portrait?" In my pain, I allowed one word to escape from my mind for her to read- mausoleum.

Precisely at that moment- in a flash- Montesquieu attacked! All I saw, from my disadvantaged position, was his large hoofs pounding upon her small frame and head, as he leaped past her, causing her to fall, bleeding, on the ground.

She could not recover fast enough. Now I was able to jump up to join Montesquieu. The winds were continuing to whip everything about, causing confusion and unsteadiness. I noticed she raised her head, but seemed too shook to fully rise. But all she needed to do was raise one hand to give a command.

And with that one command, the ground trembled beneath Montesquieu and giant tree roots reached up, grabbing his hind legs before he could fly away. Using my sword to free him, for each limb I cut, two more sprouted up from below in its place, until we both were caught in their ironclad grip. Gerard- Where are you?

I saw Satine stand up and though weak, she was fastly recovering. And she was furious. The wounds Montesquieu had inflicted were open deep gashes and her pretty pink pastel dress now had streaks of dark red blood stained on it.

As she approached us, the direction of the winds changed. She looked up, obviously surprised that her power over the wind had dissipated. Some one else now was controlling the elements. Gerard had finally arrived!

His invisible force, his intangible spirit, was sensed rather than seen; flying like a comet, it spiraled down and around until it found the witch; and it whirled about Satine causing her to become even more angry. Montesquieu and I were still captive, struggling with the tree; however, now the witch's concentration was preoccupied with Gerard and the roots were weakening enough so that Montesquieu and I managed to sever the last of the wicked tree and we broke free. Satine had underestimated me.

"Get yourself from here, spirit. I command you. Whoever you are- this is not your fight." The sky had returned to being cloudless, yet the 'blood moon' was still red and ominous. "I command here; I command you, spirit!" Satine shouted above the wail of the wind. "I am ordering you to return to your grave."

"You do not command; you have no dominion over me. Non! Not with me!" I recognized Gerard's voice echoing from a long empty tunnel.

"Who is that? Some witch-hunter you conjured?" Satine looked at me accusingly. "You think you are clever, yes?" Gerard left her and started to slowly materialize beside Montesquieu and me.

Then abruptly, there was a loud roar-primordial/prehistoric- as Gabriel (wonderful Gabriel!) awoke and came to life. Satine and I looked over at the huge statute which was now already in flight, and then, she turned back to me, knowing this meant only one thing. "Gerard!"

"Yes, Satine. I have returned, if only for one thing. To destroy you completely- forever!"

"As a ghost you cannot conquer me. You and your wolf lover! I will turn you all to ash!" The pronounced hiss of the last word, lingered as she started to float up into the air, the trees moving behind her like giant beasts.

But before she could make her next transformation, Gerard and I launched a double blow. In a flash, I sent a lightning bolt of fire at her chest, which sent her reeling, off balance. Gerard soared straight for her and, delivering his own blow, threw the witch back down, up against the empty plinth where Gabriel once sat close to the house.

She hit the stone slab heavily with a clearly audible crack to her skull and having fallen so hard, I believed that we had finally achieved a strike of some merit. She was, visibly, having difficulty recovering herself. If we deliver another mutual blow to her as quickly as possible, we might break her enough to be able to wrap the chains around her.

But as it was, she deflected, weakly but successfully, another bolt of white energy I sent at her; she floated up, gathering speed and my second strike missed. Gerard's blow had better luck, yet she countered using her strengthening force field which threw him back towards me. Landing roughly on the ground, he was visibly injured, coughing from the supernatural blow that would have killed any ordinary man.

At this point in the battle, I heard the hiss and rattles of the snakes; we had to move quickly! Gerard and I transformed immediately into loup garou, but before I could attack I had to blindfold myself and Montesquieu. Gerard, who was already dead, and Gabriel, who was already stone, were the only ones who could look upon the medusa without repercussions. We all four separated- each to surround and distract the witch.

Though I could not see it, my psychic abilities (my

mind's eye) showed me a female gorgon that rose almost two stories high, with a gigantic snake-like body- a horror of a monster. And I knew this battle would entail the ultimate test of our abilities- a trial of tactics and coordination. Gerard and I leaped at her, fangs and claws ready to tear her tough reptilian-like hide apart, but we each received a severe blow from her that tossed us far back into the oak alley where the trees swiftly grabbed us and held us tight so she would be able to deliver further blows even more disastrous. Gerard was able to simply vanish to rematerialize elsewhere. I could not.

Reacting quickly, I summoned the lightning force within me and broke the wooden bonds. It was at that particular, miraculous moment when I just happened to look down and spied the magic talisman glowing in the red moonlight. I grabbed it firmly in my wolf's claw.

Gerard and I both called out to our familiars, for each had their own task to accomplish at this stage of our clash, while he and I kept the gorgon occupied.

"Now, Gabriel!" "Now, Montesquieu!"

Gabriel promptly retrieved the invisible bag of magical chains from Montesquieu as my familiar leapt up to the broken down landing and, without delay, entered into what was left of the mansion and in the next moment, came out, carrying a baby's blanket in his mouth, containing my Tristan all bundled up. Montesquieu stood for a second, silent and successful on the empty plinth where Gabriel sits during the day. However, he was far too close to the monster medusa for my comfort.

Gerard and Gabriel (with his one claw) were encircling the gorgon, each carrying the other end of the long chain, trying to wrap the magically wrought fetter about her, but they were having a rather difficult time of it. She could not break the chains, yet repulsed, with her strong writhing limbs, their every attempt to shackle her.

With the sword in one hand, and clutching the talisman in the other, I attacked the gorgon from the rear.

Cutting and slashing, I inflicted only minor wounds against her tough reptilian skin; while avoiding her strong tail which whipped about in a deadly frenzy. Finally, I was given a chance and with one tremendous exertion, I stabbed her tail completely through, pinning it to the ground.

Not a mortal wound, it gave, however, Gerard and Gabriel the moments needed to gain a hold of one her arms and begin successfully containing the monster. Her banshee shrieks were deafening, piercing all our ear-drums, but we had to ignore the bleeding pain and continue for we had the decided advantage. I had hope for a moment that the first part of the battle would end in our favour. It was then, as I approached Montesquieu to retrieve Tristan, when our first tragedy struck.

Montesquieu had paused for only an instant on Gabriel's concrete plinth, yet in that one sliver of a second, his blindfold slipped and my wonderful companion, my first familiar, the one who had helped me become accustomed to witchcraft, met his fate. One sideways glance of the Medusa was all it took and my Montesquieu was now and forever frozen in stone.

His large stallion body slowly, steadily froze and cracked as gradually he turned into a statue. At the last moment, I managed to feel flesh, to pet his neck and head once more just before he died. He spoke to me also, one last time, as I took Tristan from him. A small neigh to say goodbye and that he was sorry he had failed me. I replied silently, that he had not failed, that Tristan would now be safe, and the witch would be defeated because of his help.

And then my friend was no more.

There was no time to grieve, that would have to wait. I rushed Tristan to a safe spot out of the way, trying to be some distance from any trees and bushes and put the talisman around his neck, placing it over his heart, snug under his blanket. This would protect him from her evil familiars. In fact, I paused briefly to watch as roots grew searchingly upwards for my child, as branches crept close to him, but upon sensing the protection of the talisman they silently withdrew. I knew then he was perfectly safe; though what was really remarkable, was that in all this time, with all the noise surrounding him and the rough jostling, he never cried out once, unlike the day earlier. Just as Selena had known instinctively- this boy was born a warrior. Would his twin be the same I wondered?

The gorgon was now completely chained and as she groveled and hissed on the ground, she screamed, "I will break these chains, as I will break you both!" It was time to make our next move with all haste. I handed the magical dagger, dipped in the witch's own poisonous brew, to Gerard. I wanted to plunge the knife into her heart myself, for what she had done to Pierre, Montesquieu and the rest of us, but this was Gerard's privilege.

He approached her without caution, his fangs bared, able to look upon the Medusa with no ill effects. Her green eyes stared him down; she was barely recognizable as Satine. He raised the knife which dripped with the poison she had used on me. The same super poison that had rendered me into an uncontrollable and permanent werewolf- and now she would fall victim to her own clever devices.

Gerard, still in wolf's form, bent down near to her and whispered that he now held her fate in his hands. "Never," she hissed, "it will take much more than the two of you to defeat me."

"Tell me Satine. Do you remember Andre? My lover that you turned to stone in my very arms?"

"Ha!" She spit on him. "Sodomites!"

Gerard snarled and growled that she would die this very night. "Never," she hissed again at him. "I will never die. I am timeless and will always survive in one form or another."

"I do not think so, Satine. Not this time." He looked about. "Where are your gods now, Satine?" Hurry Gerard- I sent the thought to him, though he had every right to gloat. "Your sun god seems to have deserted you. After all these centuries, he has finally forsaken you. Did you abuse the power he gave you, or", the snakes on her head hissed and tried to bite him as he leaned closer to her, his sharp teeth clenched in a vengeful grin of hate. "Or perhaps he was jealous of you taking all the credit for the destruction around you."

"Pitiful fools!" She almost choked on her venomous wrath. "I will survive you all!"

"Then let us find out." He howled loud and long enough to be heard for miles away. "Take your own medicine- witch!" And he plunged the dagger deep, deep into her heart.

Her shrieks of agony, mixed with disbelief at being foiled, sounded her death knell. Gerard pushed the poisonous blade further into her bosom and then- just as it had been with me- step by excruciating step, she transformed into her true supernatural state- a centuries old succubus! And this time it was Gerard and I who watched with wondering amazement and anxiousness as the poison slowly worked itself on her and took its toil.

After some impatient moments, standing before us on weak and unsteady legs, was the old crone from my dreams; the aged hag from Gerard's island home- a decrepit and shriveled succubus from old Egypt. The chains had slipped off the diminutive, infirm body she now possessed. Her strength visibly ebbing, she let out a screech of despair and hatred at losing her vigour and beauty. There was even an element of surprise in her cry: surprise that she had been defeated so, especially by the use of her own magic. The moon suddenly lost its blood-red hue and changed back to normal, signaling that she had lost most of her powers and it was time for us to use the final chess pieces in our arsenal- the portrait was next. She would require it in order to regain her abilities, not to mention her beauty. Gerard and I both thought of the cemetery and the secret room in the mausoleum where the portrait was concealed.

She had read our thoughts (as we knew she would) and, not unexpectedly, she floated up into the air and away, using what power she had left. But Gerard was not ready to let her go just yet. "Not so soon, Satine," he yelled, as he managed to grasp onto her wrist. She still was able to float above us. I leapt also, but could not reach her. Instead I grabbed Gerard by the waist, as the succubus pulled him higher, and I tried to pull them both down. Slowly and steadily she began to weaken and just when I thought we might capture her again, she made the most desperate move- the only move possible to escape our clutches.

With whatever power she had left, she reached down with her free hand and placed it on her arm just above where Gerard's strong wolf's paw clutched her. From where I was below, holding onto Gerard, I could not see the fire she summoned, though I smelled the burnt flesh and heard her painful scream as she severed her own hand and Gerard and I fell to earth.

The blood dripped profusely down upon us and the ground as she floated higher. For such a withered figure, it was astonishing how much she bled. I was hopeful this last desperate act would weaken her further. However, she called to her familiars for help and was carried away across the treetops by a gentle wind.

"The portrait! She is going to the cemetery," my growl could not disguise my anxiety. I transformed back into my human self- Gerard did the same.

"Good, that was what we wanted. This time I choose the battlefield." He threw away the disgusting hand which had withered away into nothing but bone.

"We should get there first. To prevent her from

516

regaining her powers."

"I believe it is of no consequence; her ancient gods have deserted her." He spoke with the utmost confidence.

"For now. She may yet strike some bargain. We must.."

"Did you cover the sarcophagus with your magic cloak of invisibility?"

"Yes. She will only sense some immense power in the chamber, but not know what or whom. Gerard," I had to express my apprehension. "I do not trust that she is all that weak - or helpless."

"She will regain her original beauty, but she will never be as strong as she once was. It will be her own curiosity and quest for power which will undo her."

"If she finds out the mummy is there, she will not enter." I still had doubts as to the effectiveness of our deception.

"She will enter, if for nothing more than to retrieve the portrait."

"We must make sure she does not leave with it."

"Yes, however she will not leave until she finds the source of that power."

"I understand. Like a moth to the flame! She will think it is Julian and his power of invincibility."

"Correct, but instead she will discover.."

"Her long dead lover, come back." I hesitated- again with doubt. "But if she escapes before he can grab her.."

"Then he will hunt her down. There will be no escape for her once he has risen."

"If only we could wound her more. Cloud her mind with pain."

"Hopefully Henri, we might have some aid in that respect. Our allies know we must win and they are observing the battles. Come we must go now." I did not gather exactly what he meant by allies and help. There were so many contingencies- so many ways this last battle could finally play out. But there was no more time for discussion. "I must take Tristan home to his mother. Then we will meet at the cemetery."

"Bon. Quickly then!"

"Until soon, mon ami."

Even though I ran all the way, I would have made better time with Montesquieu. Oh how, I will miss him! I deeply hoped we would lose no one else, for whereas Selena and Juliette had finally agreed, reluctantly, to stay with the children at the cabin- while the ceremony was being conducted- there was absolutely no persuading Grandma-ma to not participate. Of course, I had no time to watch the tearful reunion as Selena held for the first time the son no one believed she had given birth to. When I carried my boy inside, I was as Henri, but as soon as I left, (leaving the talisman with my boy), I transformed and went with all haste to the cemetery where would lie the scene of either our victory or our defeat.

There was a cool mist in the air, heralding a change in seasons, which became thicker as I approached the graveyard. Yet, when I actually entered the property, a thick, wet fog developed. Thicker than when Marie saved me from the evil potion of Marguerite's or even when it cloaked Gerard and I in secrecy as we made love.

I realized what Gerard had meant earlier about aid from our allies. Marie had sent her familiar to help us: to blind the witch, to disorient her and prevent her from reading anyone's thoughts. Hallelujah! I was filled with confidence that we would succeed. My strength was at an all time high. I could not see the full moon, but its silver light- reflecting within the fog- gave a surreal atmosphere as I walked among the graves. What was it

Gerard had told me about tonight's eclipse?

I met him at the far end of the graveyard, where my 'tombstone' was displayed. He had watched as the wounded and bleeding Satine slowly, cautiously entered into the mausoleum at the other end of the cemetery. We would enter from this other vantage point. Toussaint and grandma-ma were hidden from view, cloaked by my magic and the fog, and they would enter- only- after Satine had crawled into the tunnel and discovered the secret room. The two of them were to perform the ceremony from the main room where the stone coffins and chains in the wall were. How so very different this was from that fateful day when I was sealed in that cell!

"You noticed the fog?" Gerard asked me. We were both as wolf-men.

"How could I not."

"Non, mon ami. I mean, do you notice the difference in this particular fog?"

"Not exactly. It is much wetter than before. Moist, misty, not warm as previously."

"Precisely."

"I don't understand."

"We should be able to see what she does from a distance."

I could not comprehend his meaning or gather the exact thought uppermost in his mind. "I still do not understand."

"Read, Henri, read the fog's telepathic sense. It is communicating to us even now- telling us her every action, her very thoughts."

I allowed my mind to be clear and receptive, then.. "Mon Dieu! I perceive it now. It gives us another advantage. Thank God."

"Thank Marie. She is watching." We crept stealthily and ever so quietly into the tomb and descended the stairs, failing to close the panels behind us. Our first mistake.

"See, the fog even permeated the tomb and tunnel." Every few steps or so, we stopped to view in our mind's eye just where Satine was and what she was feeling-thinking.

She was in great pain, and gravely fatigued. I could sense that easily. She literally crawled on her one hand and knees through the foggy mausoleum to the coffin which led downstairs. She held on tightly to the emerald scarab necklace which she carried in her one good hand, all the while praying passionately to her venerable gods.

'Sun god, Ra, please listen to your servant, Satine. I have been most faithful to your desires and have supplied you with scores and scores of souls for many centuries. Great Ra, grant me the ability to restore myself in order to perpetuate your glory; to destroy our enemies completely; to annihilate all those who dare to stand in our way. Those creatures that would prevent me from fulfilling my obligations to your great and glorious self. Please all powerful sun-god, do not abandon me, your devoted follower. Lead me to that profound destiny which is rightfully mine. Send your life-giving rays of power to me.'

She barely could climb into the coffin and open the panel to slowly creep down the stairs. We stayed at our end of the tunnel.

'What if her gods help her?' Gerard and I communicated entirely through telepathy when so close to the witch.

'Let us hope they do not. If so, we must immediately intervene. Especially if she conjures a magical fire and begins to pray into the flames.'

"We should intervene now."

'No wait, mon cher.' He held his arm out, physically restraining me. 'Let us observe her next action.'

She was in the other end of the tunnel now, making her way through the foggy corridor. She took notice of the misty fog and the wetness on the hard dirt floor and walls. 'It is from that voodoo queen, who thwarts my every move. This fog is preventing my contact to the fire god. I should have disposed of her a long time ago. I must find that portrait.' She began calling to her gods again. "Help me mother, Isis; give me strength, father Osiris- guide me safely to the secret chamber. This time is not my time yet."

It was then as she approached the room and was about to open the door when she hesitated for what became- for me- an anxiously long moment. She sensed some thing other than the painting within the chamber- a strong, unknown, power source. To her mind, whatever it was, its purpose must be to protect the portrait. Who else could it be, but Julian?

As far as I could tell, Satine never conceived the thought that she could become trapped there below the earth. Her thoughts were clouded, muddled, by the pain; the fog caused her to be disoriented. Yet, her immediate need for healing was her primary thought. She had to get that portrait before whatever guardian power in the chamber could respond.

'She wants to badly defeat us; her two loup garou who dare to challenge her. She is obsessed with creating our destruction. She senses us nearby.'

'She is in awe, even fearful of Julian.' I had to ask myself: Why? Had she previously met Julian? She seemed to know more about the Dr.'s creation than either of us. 'She believes that she can actually succeed at not only possessing the portrait, but Julian's power as well.' What a maniacal ego!

Determined to go on, she used the remainder of her physical strength to open the loud grating door, not knowing what to expect inside. Aware that this was a snare, it was also her only means to recover (unless the god Ra, or Anubis himself, performed some miracle). It was unclouded inside the room for a moment, but then the fog rushed in as if it were being inhaled by some great beast. She floated in with the fog using what little of her power was left. To whoever was there, she must appear strong and not as the wounded witch and old succubus that she actually was.

As Gerard and I followed the fog towards the open door, I sensed something else prevalent in her. She was obsessed with power. To her mind, if she had Julian's power she could then permanently become a phoenix; a fire-witch with no chance of destruction. No chance of ever being the old crone again. She would live for centuries more with no one on earth able to supplant her; no one in heaven able to suppress or challenge her. She would never have the need to be reborn from her own ashes. She intended (Mon Dieu!) to create armies of Julians for her dark lords and her reward would be to live as a god! Then she would be truly immortal!

At the point of entering, having sensed two torches, she brought forth what little fire power she had left. Raising her hands, the torches spurted and lit themselves; Immediately- promptly- the wet fog dissipated, escaping from the room. Gerard and I were now alone in the battle- until the mummy was raised.

We were not far from the open door. 'Should not Toussaint begin the incantation?' I asked.

'One moment more.'

'She sees the portrait.'

In one corner, the last of the mist lifted, revealing her old portrait. She felt stronger just gazing upon it. Glancing about and- surprisingly- spotting no one, she rushed as fast as her feeble legs could carry her and, grabbing the painting, held it to her heart. So weak she could barely stand, but upon touching the portrait, it began to emit a glow- the eyes aflame with its old power from time long past. From where we were in the tunnel, we could see the supernatural light.

'When the light dims, I will block the door and you give Toussaint and grandma-ma the signal to begin.' I nodded in agreement.

We saw her (with our mind's eye) transform in a mere moment. Now she was as young as ever, a girl again, her exceptional beauty restored. And we could also sense that her power was steadily increasing.

'We must move now, Gerard. Now!' I was impatient. I did not want her to gain back her strength.

'Yes, now. Rush upstairs. Tell them to light the incense and begin the incantation.'

I did as directed and stopping below at the bottom of the stairs leading to the mausoleum, I whispered a growl to Toussaint- one word- "Begin." From the torchlight upstairs, I saw his head as he peered briefly, down into the coffin. He nodded in response, knowing what to do.

I rushed back to the open door, the light only fading slightly. Gerard still kept himself hidden in the shadows. But...

"Come in you two. Join me. Gerard- Henri. I know you are there."

We appeared in the doorway. The entire room was brightly lit and she, herself, seemed to be the source of the light- radiating a brilliance like an angel of evil.

I silently chastised ourselves for allowing her to gain some of her strength back- too easily, too much, too soon.

She was dressed in the same flowing dress as before, no longer soiled with blood; the severed hand had been restored; her dark beautiful complexion and teenage youth renewed- a beauty that would captivate any man. I knew Gerard started to think of his island home and the intimate times he had spent with her. I grabbed his wolf's paw in mine and brought him back to the present. For now, we changed to human form, still holding hands.

Her chandelier laughter echoed and chimed through the chamber as she carefully placed her portrait down in a corner and she began, casually, searching about the room. She felt the presence of power but did not yet know it was cloaked. Perhaps- she thought- there was another room, concealed and secret, where Julian kept himself. Across the hall, maybe?

However, she continued searching. It would be any moment now in which Gerard and I would have to make our move- for she had found the cloaked sarcophagus.

"What sort of object is this? Hidden from sight with your amateur spell. Do not tell me you think you found some powerful relic? You cannot get rid of me so simply, Gerard." She kept speaking even as she removed the invisible cloak with one swift movement. "You should know better..," she stopped in mid-sentence, observing, in disbelief, the beautiful sarcophagus; the coffin containing the mummified remains of her lover from hundreds of years ago!

"No! You don't know what you have done. No, Gerard!" Her scream reverberated like a high pitched tin drum throughout the underground chambers. I instinctively covered my ears. She stared at us, her emerald eyes wide with actual fear, perhaps for the first time in centuries. "You have foolishly been communicating with that madman who calls himself a doctor!" Did that mean she knew- or knew of- Fontenot and his creation?

Gerard waved one hand and the incense in the room lit by itself and began filling the room with its heavy per- fumed smoke. My super hearing detected Toussaint's soft voice as he recited the incantation slowly.

Satine heard Toussaint also and looking about, up and around, she shouted at the top of her voice: "You fools! You cannot comprehend in the least what you have done. He will destroy us all!" She raised her arms as weapons. "Stand aside and let me by. Or else!"

"Or else what, Satine?" Gerard replied. "You have used up all your bags of tricks."

A small whirlwind rose about her and she floated up, above the top of the tornado. This caught us off guard and almost threw us out the door, but Gerard hastily dematerialized and soared about the room to counter her wrath with his own power- when suddenly all our action ceased and the three of us remained still- noiseless and apprehensive. For we all had heard the heavy thump from within the sarcophagus.

He was alive!

"NON!" She screamed again. "You fools. Idiots! We must all leave this instance. If he wakes, and we are here.." She put her hand to her mouth, demonstrating genuine terror; her cat eyes ablaze with ancient atrocities.

"What was it, Satine, that you did to make him hate you so?" The bodiless voice of Gerard taunted her.

"You imbecile," she looked anxiously about screaming at his apparition. "You have no idea of what you are dealing with!" She turned to look directly at me. "Idiot! Let me by. I am warning you!" She glanced up at the low ceiling. "Stop reciting that incantation. Stop it now, I say!" I thought I heard Toussaint's voice waver and falter, but he recovered in the next moment.

I felt the fire before I saw it. She extended an arm of flame directly at me and threw me against the wall near the door; yet I recovered in a heartbeat, and met her force with my own version. Only this time, when calling up my fire (summoning so deep inside of me it hurt), I tapped into a well previously unknown. My whole body felt electrified; it all came to me so naturally and uninhibited; I shined with strength.

Reflexively, I shot back a flash- a bolt against her own red fire. Mine deflected hers aggressively, sending it back upon her. The jolt sent her to her knees (surprising us all!) though she was not injured. We were about to exchange more discharges, for it was imperative she remain there until the mummy awoke fully- at any cost to Gerard or myself. Her arm raised, I assumed my stance- but that was the only volley between us, for just then…

The door to the sarcophagus opened slightly with a tremendously loud crack, sounding as if the very earth had ruptured. Satine, still on her knees, now looked as if she was saying a prayer. "Quick!" Gerard spoke to me. "Get to Toussaint. She is trying to interfere with the ceremony- entering his mind. Be swift- Now! I will try to distract her here."

"Be careful, Gerard." His ghostly form started to circle about Satine, attempting to destroy her concentration, but I saw no immediate effect upon her. As swift as lightning, I rushed headlong, down the tunnel and up the stairs into the crypt and saw poor Toussaint rolling upon the floor in agony, grasping his head with both hands. Satine was succeeding! The book of the dead lay open on top of the other stone coffin near a dim lantern. The incense was not burning. "Get out of his head, you witch!" I had never heard grandma raise her voice before; she sometimes spoke firmly, yet it was still in her normal 'soft whiskey' voice. "Leave him alone. You have no right! You do not command us!" Her majestic forcefulness was awe-inspiring as I watched her clutch Toussaint close to her bosom. He was still trying to say the words, remember the incantation, but he was losing the cerebral battle. A minute or so later he collapsed prostrate upon the floor in a complete mental collapse.

"You will not win, witch!" Grandma-ma shouted out into the shadows of the poorly lit tomb; her strong will echoed through the slightly ajar door and into the cemetery. I lit the incense with but a thought and supposed I would read the incantation, but Grandma kept shouting. "I will not let you trick me again. I am prepared for your evil this time." She grabbed hold of the sacred book and, (it might have been my imagination), but I swore its light grew brighter and the pages glowed with an incandescence stronger than when the book acknowledged me. Beginning the incantations over again, she repeated the words by rote, sensing the ancient phrases; the book, perhaps, giving her the ability to see the print in her mind's eye. It was then, watching grandma-ma's strength and determination, when I knew we would win- or at least, succeed in raising the creature. What happened after that, I could not foresee. Would grandma be the only one able to control him?

Unexpectedly, I heard Gerard shout- to alert me to an approaching danger. In one leap I was back downstairs in the tunnel ready to do battle as a wolf-man. However, instinct froze me there for some reason and I listened closely. In the next instance, I heard that danger- it was scratching at the walls, creeping up the steps, and I realized what other evil Satine was carrying out. She was raising her zombies! And the danger was above! Toussaint and Grandma-ma had forgotten to close the door securely and now the creatures were staggering in!

In another leap, I was upstairs. Three of them were already inside the crypt approaching grandma-ma and the incapacitated Toussaint- yet scores more were outside the door, about to enter in. Acting as fast as possible, I first ran to seal the door- and pushing the rest of the zombies out and away, I (with some effort), managed to bolt the door firmly against their foul-smelling figures. At that time, I happened to glance at the full moon and noticed that the eclipse was beginning. With no time to give it any thought, I turned then, upon the other zombies inside who were dangerously close to my loved ones (grandma-ma still continued with the incantation regardless of the danger to herself). Carefully avoiding their deadly bites, (for I didn't know what the consequences would be even for a werewolf if bitten), I whipped about like a tornado- slashing and cutting, knocking them aside- crushing their skulls in with my fists and cutting off their limbs with my sharp talons. Yet there was a scream- Selena's grandmother- I had missed one of them!

A male zombie of some size had got past me and

had placed his hand on grandma-ma's shoulder in an iron-clad grasp. Though in obvious pain, she still kept up with the incantations. Nothing was going to stop that woman! It would be easier to halt the wind and rain. About to intervene, I suddenly felt very weak and light-headed; so drained of energy I thought I might faint. I recovered after a few seconds but my hesitation had dire consequences.

Toussaint had come to and (though hardly conscience), ran to grandma's aid before I could and he grabbed the zombie. They struggled, the zombie letting go of his painful death grip on grandma-ma, but Toussaint, still being weak, was easily overpowered by the strong zombie. It pinned Toussaint down against the stone coffin, and in that one instance of time, before I could cut off the monster's head and smash it against the wall, Gerard's and my faithful companion and overseer became our second tragedy in this supernatural struggle. Toussaint had been bitten!

"Mon Dieu! Toussaint!" I grabbed him, noticing his look of astonishment at being a victim, before he fainted in my wolf's arms. "I can make a magic salve to put on that wound, but it must be done right away, with no..."

"There is no time, Henri." Grandma-ma interrupted her recitation for an urgent moment. "The other end. The other end of the tunnel!" And again I heard Gerard's shout.

Leaving the two of them up in the main tomb, (knowing Toussaint had only a short time before turning), I jumped down the stairs and rushed to Gerard. I felt horrible about Toussaint, but right now our priority was to destroy the witch. I briefly spied Satine still on her knees in the secret room. Gerard was at the doorway, making sure she did not escape. Her zombies had entered into the tunnel and were approaching from the far end. Gerard was all that stood between the hungry zombies and myself.

"It is better I take care of them." He spoke with the authority and confidence I had come to depend on- and love.

"But.."

"I am already dead. They cannot harm me; I will force them out."

"But- upstairs..," He read in my mind that Toussaint would soon join the ranks of the living dead.

Laying a comforting hand upon my shoulder, he said, "We will have time to say goodbye, later. Now we must continue the battle. You must see to it that the ancient one is released. Stay here at the door and make sure she does not invent some new trick in order to escape." In a flash he dematerialized.

I heard his whirlwind and the grunts and squeals of the zombies as he destroyed most and forced the others out with his invisible energy. I could smell the blood everywhere, sense the puddles of body parts. The witch was successfully separating us; keeping us occupied so as to... A loud and colossal crash came from the chamber and the earth trembled violently beneath us for a moment. I knew without seeing- our mummy had risen!

Peering cautiously into the chamber, I realized that of all the barbarous horrors, evil and savage death that I have witnessed in the last several months, I would never be able to erase this particular gruesome picture from my mind. It would haunt my dreams for more than a century.

The beautifully bedecked sarcophagus lid had been completely removed; it lay upon the floor, cracked and broken in two by some tremendously powerful force. Satine was on her knees, looking up in stupefied horror at what had once been her lover from centuries past. A piercing scream of terror issued throughout the room and corridors- its source unknown. The shriek reverberated from deep within the earth; from old Egypt, perhaps from hell itself. Satine's lips could not have formed any sound. Towering over her, the creature, with one mighty hand, had her throat in a death crunching clutch. His other hand was raised to strike.

I will try my best to describe this monster that defies description. My fear was if I came close to his grasp or looked into his eyes, I would go to oblivion with the two of them.

His frame was over seven foot; his bulk that of a great titan; bandages of rotten cloth were wrapped about him, covering him almost completely save for the eyes. Mouldering away from decay- centuries of slow decomposition- the cloth was peeling off like a skin, showing a mummified dusty shell beneath. But that was a mere deception; he was strong as ten loup garou. From where I was I took a glimpse at his green eyes, yet I did not want to stare for I remembered Marie's admonishment that to look into his eyes would make one his slave. A thick dust drifted everywhere in the room- along with the stench of decayed death. The smell of ancient dust and death made me nauseous. The power and forceful strength of the mummy was palpable in the very air. There was none he could not conquer- a leviathan stronger than any other supernatural being that I could imagine. Grandma-ma was the only one who could command him- perhaps not even her.

Describing Satine's agony gives me the greatest pleasure. For the first time in centuries she was now experiencing- not just fear- but true speechless, unquenchable horror. If I did not hate her so much, I might would feel compassion. The witch must now meet her fate for all the tragedy she has brought on us- on Gerard and those we have loved. Not to mention the scores of men's souls she has sent to the darkside. Dust is to be her destiny- Literally.

She looked directly up at the thing, her face full of choked blood and terror. He could easily snap her neck with a simple twist of his grip (and I wish he had), however instead, he released her, throwing her to the ground as if in eternal disgust with this woman- this lover who had betrayed him so long ago.

Coughing, choking and struggling for air, blood dribbled between her full luscious lips, yet she waited not a second before pleading with him. "Ahmed, do not harm me, please. I never meant to betray you." At that his mouth dropped open to release the most unearthly roar that made the entire mausoleum tremble. Satine instinctively covered her ears, more in dread than pain.

She continued pleading though, now crawling on all fours to reach his feet in sublimation. "They forced me to give you up. Oh Ahmed, I did love you, I have only loved you." He let out another roar of unrelieved endless anguish, shaking the room so hard, this time timbers began to fall from the chamber's ceiling.

"I was weak, my love. I am weak. They said if I did not confess they would bury me alive." She paused and looked up at his implacable countenance. "I am sorry Ahmed. They offered me power beyond my wildest dreams. My love, if you let me go, together we can conquer worlds.."

This time his roar made the earth tremble so violently, the roof started to collapse. And when his roar stopped, the earth still continued to shake. This was to be the end.

"NO, my love. NO!" She pleaded still while the walls started to crumble, with the ceiling falling down around them. "Please, I beg you, it is not my time yet. Ahmed, I love you." She had to scream to be heard above the noise of the quake. "Listen to me." She grabbed his thick legs, the rotten rags falling off of him. He backhanded her, slapping her down, then grabbed her roughly by the arm ready to take her to oblivion.

It was precisely at this moment where I made my mistake. Instead of leaving them to their fate, I had to watch to satisfy my need. The need to make sure she was consumed by the Egyptian sands of time which had started to swirl about as the mummy raised his powerful arm. Satine looked directly at me- her last hope. "Henri, help me. Help me please." Then it was as if he noticed me for the first time. His evil reptilian eyes stared me down, locking with my own. I could not turn away. He was warning me not to intervene.

I stood at the door, perfectly still, captivated, transfixed upon this horrendous scene. A scene of revenge for ancient betrayal. The sand blew in my face, stinging me. The wind increased as the secret chamber was crumbling to bits- filling with sand and earth.

Satine reached out her arms to me, making one last desperate plea. "Henri, please. You must save me. You must!" She had to scream above the din of destruction. "Henri, I carry your child!" At that moment of shock, I should have gathered my wits and left with all haste. I heard Gerard at the end of the tunnel calling me to hurry and join him upstairs.

The mummy's glance towards me had now turned to obvious hatred. His supernatural fury struck me through to my soul. How dare I be insolent enough to make love to his queen, but to impregnate her also! With an arm that seemed to stretch into infinity, he grabbed me by the shoulder and started to pull me into the maelstrom. Satine's wicked maniacal laugh mixed with the crash and crumble of the room. I could see nothing before me, except the hatred of his eternal green eyes and feel the extraordinarily excruciating pain of his clasped hand upon my person. Instinctively, I tried to change into my wolf's form, but I could not. I felt faint and sick like previously upstairs- my super strength totally exhausted. The eclipse! It was because of the eclipse- which must be total at this very moment. What catastrophic timing! And, just like Satine, I had no fire power because of the mystic ancient sand.

"We all go together then! And poor Gerard loses another lover!" She laughed as a mad woman. And there was nothing I could do. I tried to fight his will, but it was useless. I was to die with them! I heard Gerard behind me shouting and yelling- what, I could not make out clearly. The sands were approaching up to our necks. I prayed to some supreme being for help; some god or devil- whoever would answer. What does a loup garou pray to?

Then, just before I thought I would expire- or worse, be locked forever into nothingness- I saw a different hand; the white hand of a man, slender and slim, almost effeminate, (it was not Gerard's); a hand I had seen before- somewhere, sometime long ago. It reached out to grab the mummy's hand which still had its fierce grip on me and slowly it forced the creature to release his grasp. Whoever it was had to be immensely strong. The mummy's eyes registered surprise at this unexpected stranger and then I glimpsed another white hand, clenched into a fist, slam itself forcefully and directly into the mummy's shriveled face, knocking out ancient dust, bits of broken bones and preserved flesh into the sandy storm. I could not see just exactly what was happening for the sand was so blinding, but I was given a sudden forceful shove back out of the room (with Gerard pulling me from behind) and the door slammed in front of me closed. I was free! Free from the mummy and his maelstrom to nowhere.

I found myself outside in the tunnel, standing by the door, Gerard by my side. We stood silently in awe as we heard Satine's scream from the sealed room- hollow and soulless, it attained a deafening pitch. The earthquake and the gales of the tempest reached a crescendo- a climax and then- all was silent. The only sound we heard was the trickling of sand falling out from the cracks around the door- and soon that ended. They were all gone; all three gone to their own purgatory. Her emerald scarab necklace lay on the ground by the closed door. Gerard picked it up. Her sun god had truly deserted her.

For a long, long moment, we could say nothing; trying

to regain our breaths and normal heart beats; trying to tell ourselves the war was actually over. I looked at Gerard with deep affection. Thank you.

"It was not I who saved you."

"He is now gone forever with the other two."

"Locked in eternal, immortal combat."

"Who would sacrifice themselves so? For me- Henri LeBlanc? Only an angel.."

"Do you not know? Can you not guess? Henri- Regardez!" He grabbed me by my shoulder and pointed across and down the tunnel, where a small flickering light escaped from another hidden room- a room none of us had ever discovered- sensed, yet never found. Another bewitched room!

I peered inside the dimly lit chamber. Gerard lit more candles so we could inspect the room thoroughly (our wolves abilities were gradually returning with the full moon). The place was furnished with all the creature comforts of home- a bed, armoire, dresser; it included a settee, a few upholstered chairs, a private desk and an impressive library. A warm brandy and a still smoking cigar were on a side table. "Julian!" was all I could say.

"Yes," agreed Gerard. "It was Julian."

9

"So he was here right under our very eyes all this time."

"But why sacrifice himself for me. I do not understand."

"Perhaps we will never know." Gerard and I were in Julian's room, looking about, searching for clues to understanding this mysterious man. "He certainly enjoyed his comforts."

"As do we." We exchanged knowing glances and I realized I had little time left with him. Grandma-ma, with Marie (who arrived suddenly, intuitively knowing her friend needed help), had already left. Together they would fashion a voodoo doll to represent Toussaint as a zombie and insert a large pin in its head, through the temples. They could not bring themselves to do it any other way. He would then be at peace. In the interim, he was chained to the wall in the upstairs crypt as a precaution.

"Maybe there is an answer in here somewhere."

"If there is you will have to find it, mon cher." He flipped through the pages of one of Julian's books left open on a night stand. The book was about witchcraft-spells and potions. "Interesting. He obviously practiced witchcraft."

"So Satine did sense him and his power."

"Apparently. Dr. Fontenot might be able to answer a lot. From what I gathered Julian hated his creator with a passion."

That made me remember once hating my creator also, yet it definitely turned to passion. "Do you believe he was that bored with immortality? Or did he simply hate his existence: being soulless- a man-made creature of dead human body parts?"

"Yes, I can understand it." He let out a large sigh. "One day you may be able to relate Julian's story." He helped himself to a brandy, then poured one for me. I accepted readily. "Perhaps Julian knows of a way back."

"Let us pray the others never find a way back."

"So," he stared at me directly and changed the stream of conversation. "When did Satine trick you into having intercourse, or- were you a willing victim?"

"It was in a dream- or what I thought to be a dream." Sensing his jealousy, I walked closer to him, and kissed him fully on the lips. "And no, I was not willing. Her familiars had me pinned."

He put his hand on my cheek gently, fondly. "It is no matter. How silly for a ghost to be jealous of a werewolf." We both laughed. Our last until..? "Je t'aime."

"Je t'aime, aussi." I never said those words to anyone else but Selena. There was a pause before I became serious again. "What are you going to do now that you have no vessel to possess?"

"I will seek out the good doctor and we will create another being- using my spirit as the life force."

"Here at home? At Sans Souci?" I sounded hopeful.

"Most likely. Whenever- wherever I can persuade him to act. The vessel must be very handsome, though. Be sure of that."

"You will persuade him with money?"

"Yes and if that does not influence him, I may have to force him to comply." His voice was becoming softer, fainter. We hadn't much time.

"I will rebuild Sans Souci."

"Of course, it is yours now. In my will you are sole heir." He hesitated for the next words seemed so strange to utter. "My remains are buried on the rise with the others?" I nodded. "Now with Toussaint. He was a good friend and comrade." Our sadness was hard to disguise, but I was unable to cry. "You know, Henri, you will have to keep that voodoo doll in a secure place. If the pin is removed or falls out.."

"He will return as a zombie." I wanted to talk about us. "How much time do we have?"

"Only a few minutes. I feel them calling me now."

"Who?"

"I do not know exactly. My mother, Andre, others."

"So you are all together again."

"It is a peaceful place whatever it is called." His figure was starting to fade and then rematerialize.

"Gerard you are dissipating!"

"I know mon cher. Hold me." Our embrace was tight. I did not want him to go and pretended to myself that if I hold on hard enough, he would not be able to leave me. Yet unfortunately, uncontrollably, his body started to vanish.

"Don't go Gerard, fight it! Stay with me and we will lie down together- here in Julian's bed."

"I want the same, my one and only, but.." He faded completely for a moment, then came back into my arms.

"You must come back as soon as possible. You must! I cannot thrive as well without you. I am not complete when you are gone."

"You are strong now, Henri. You will do fine. The time I will be gone will seem short. For immortal beings like us time should be of no consequence..." His voice faded out; I was losing my hold over him. We had only a moment left.

I kissed him solidly on the mouth, our lips demonstrating what would become a centuries-life-long passion for one another. "You must come back soon, Gerard..Do you hear me?" He was almost completely gone from my grasp. I held eye contact until the end, staring deep with true affection into his dark blue eyes.

"I will..return..", his voice was but a whisper. Then he was gone and I was holding onto nothing- holding onto a memory only.

"Henri." I looked up- his voice was all that remained- it floated in the air; the words so faint, they seemed to reach far from the other side of the world. He spoke with much effort. "Be diligent, Henri. There will be more bat-tles- wars- for you to face, large and small, and I will not always be.. there for... Je t'aime.." And with those last words, which I will never forget, Gerard left me completely. He would return one day- some year- a century?- from now and we will be lovers again. Yet there was the lonely, eternal thought that he might never return.

I sat there in that tiny comfortable room for some long moments, reflecting on the last few days and hours.

Feeling sad at losing my friends- feeling pleased that we had bested the witch. I would always make sure that door was bolted securely and I'll disguise it, making the door blend in with the rest of the tunnel. I can use Julian's witchcraft; the spell is probably among his papers on the desk.

I thought of Pierre and how he and I would get drunk and seek out the girls back in our childhood home; I reminisced on how I first met Montesquieu and the elation I felt when riding the skies with him; then there was my dear friend Toussaint and how much he taught me about plantation life and the ways of Gerard.

My memory turned to that wonderful study at Sans Souci, (this room of Julian's gave me a similar comfortable feeling), and how Gerard and I would laugh at silly Mercutio's antics; and then my thoughts turned into desires, as the memory of that first night when I met Gerard, flooded my soul- of how I joined him in his bath, freely- and the long nude embrace we shared.

I needed to go home and join my family. To see if Marie and grandma-ma had succeeded in putting Toussaint to rest. I would, sadly, take a look at him on the way out. Poor Juliette- she will be beside herself with grief. We will be the ones to take care of her now and I will comfort her. I noticed the scarab necklace of Satine's on a center table where Gerard had left it. I placed it in one of the drawers in Julian's desk. The wall above the desk was empty. That would make a good place for his portrait. Another blank spot across the room is where Gerard's enchanted mirror could go. Yes, I think I will make this room my own, my little sanctuary. There was no clock- I will have to select just the right timepiece. I suppose time did not matter much to Julian or perhaps he disliked noting the passage of time.

As I turned away from his desk, I noticed a large box or crate in the corner covered by a Persian-style rug. It seemed oddly familiar and my instincts (and curiosity) told me to take a look at it. I tossed the rug off and yes, Yes! There it was- the trunk of treasures Gerard and I had taken from that stagecoach on our last hunt. Opening the lid, it looked to be all there save for some coins and jewels..

But how did it get here? I thought Satine had hid it somewhere or it was back with what was left of Sans Souci. When did Julian obtain possession of it and how? Could.. I thought this possible before.. could Julian and Satine have met previously? Did she know Julian before the experiment, when he was an ordinary man? There were so many questions, and I had even more imaginings. However, I thought as I put out the lights and closed the door behind me, I have years in which to find the answers.

Upstairs I found Toussaint slumped over, still chained to the wall. There were no signs of life; I felt for a heartbeat. He was dead to our world- and the next. Marie and grandma-ma had succeeded.

Making sure that all the panels were closed at both ends of the tunnel, I said adieu to the spirits within, unlocked Toussaint from his chains and, cradling my dead friend in my arms, I exited the mausoleum, securing the door behind me. I rather enjoyed my walk through the quiet night of the graveyard. Perhaps, like Julian, I felt comfortable being among the dead (as I carried one of their own all the way to San Souci for burial). The full moon still shone brightly, but daybreak would be soon. Transforming, I arranged Toussaint's body over my back and ran the rest of the way. It helped clear my mind and that very night I began to make my plans for rebuilding Sans Souci.

*   *   *   *

The restoration of my Sans Souci took more than five years to complete in its entirety for I not only resurrected the original mansion, but also built new slave cabins (furnishing my people with 'livable quarters') along with other buildings, barns and pens for more thoroughbreds, a bigger workshop for myself, an expanded kitchen and two garconnieres for my boys when they become older. Much of the fields were burnt and we had to wait for planting season. Nature, given encouragement, cures slowly and steadily, and only after two harvests (mostly cotton and sugar cane) production already surpassed earlier figures and Sans Souci became very prosperous and well-known over time, with me purchasing even more neighboring acreage. I managed the plantation with an easy grip trusting in my wolf's senses and used my witchcraft only when necessary. And soon the house was ready for us to move in to. Even grandma-ma moved with us, renting out her old cabins.

When rebuilding, I kept the original floor plan, save for adding more square footage to each room and I also added a secret windowless back room, downstairs, (hardly bigger than a closet), which could only be entered in by way of the study. It was here I stored my books and notes on witchcraft and the supernatural. Kept here also was the book of the dead, wrapped up carefully in an invisibility cloth and then placed in a wooden box and sealed with a curse on anyone who opened it without permission. The voodoo doll of Toussaint was also safely hidden here. Only I knew where it could be found. Also hidden within these walls were Satine's emerald scarab necklace (who knows what potential power it provided) and Marie's talisman used in 'the great battle' (my usual reference to that nightmare). It was arranged so that, the door to the room was hidden behind a bookcase. A simple button, when pressed, released a latch, allowing the 'bookcase' to swing open, revealing the door. This secret room was created to replace the original one of Gerard's, that had been upstairs and was destroyed completely. I am still ever so grateful that Gerard, remarkably, saved almost all of the original papers and manuscripts. I would read and reread all night, still needing no sleep. Over the years I collected many tomes and my study and secret room overflowed with literature. I tried to keep Julian's library separate and eventually I used his room as a sort of laboratory- working on spells, potions and the like. Sometimes I remained for days in that little room in the graveyard, lost in my research.

The crepe myrtles, that were around the back patio, had to be replanted and the trellises replaced. In fact, I had crepe myrtles and flowers planted all over San Souci and because we had so many blooms all year round, including the naturally found iris, our home became regarded as one of the most beautifully landscaped plantations in the area. On the porches and balconies of the main mansion, I added more columns and dark, green wrought iron replaced much of the wood banisters. All the friends I had buried, including Pierre, were reinterred, given appropriate above ground tombs on that especially beautiful rise which became the family cemetery. Of course, Gerard's remains were properly placed in a suitably grand crypt.

Looking over all this and the work being accomplished all around him, was my giant Montesquieu (along with his companion in stone, Gabriel). Would I get a new familiar now that he was gone, I wondered? If so, what type of creature would it be? But I was too busy to dwell long upon such things.

The original slave cabins were not tore down after the new living quarters were built and occupied. That was for appearances only. I really did not care if neighbors or citizens spoke of me as 'foolishly benevolent' or worse- that I was setting 'a dangerous precedent', yet I did attempt to make some impression that I was a slave owner and not 'spoiling the darkies' or being a negative influence for other plantation slaves.

When manumitting my slaves, I did so gradually over

time, so as not to raise suspicions, however I took care of my people and made sure they were never in want for food, clothes or medicine. Of course, the house slaves had to be freed first, for Selena would have it no other way.

The proper paper work had to be filed in 'la cite'. Actually, I had to make several trips into the town, primarily to claim title to Sans Souci. Gerard's will left all to me with his death certificate simply stating he died in the fire. I was not above using witchcraft or the forgery abilities Gerard taught me, but- in this instance- I had delays but no problems establishing ownership. Legally, in the eyes of the local government, I was now sole possessor of Sans Souci. I searched the minds of many of the citizens and- particularly- the officials (and non-officials) in the land and deeds office, and as far as I could tell, no one was suspicious of the fire or what had happened at the plantation.

Going back into the town (often taking Selena and Juliette), we would pass- on occasion- the old saloon where Gerard and I had dispatched our victim. It was still an active enterprise; however, seeing it triggered the hunger in me. Being so busy, I had not felt the need to feed for some time, but the next time I was required to sign papers or produce some document in town, I arranged to come late in the evening by myself.

That night I went to that same particular saloon to select my victim, but other times I could be at any number of small rowdy drinking taverns which were plentiful and I would frequent them, avoiding as much as possible any familiarities with the servants or patrons.

Feeding did not necessarily have to happen monthly for me (at the full moon or no). I controlled the hunger- as long as I answered its occasional beckoning. Starting the plantation back up and rebuilding, took so much of my time and energy, my mind was usually always preoccupied. Then one day, something would jolt my senses and I would suffer the beginning pangs of hunger and would have to plan accordingly. The victims were, for the most part, transients of the sordid type- with no connections or family. Of course, I never tortured or toyed with them as Gerard would; their ending usually being quick with little suffering. Disposing of their remains, however, was sometimes problematic for me, especially since I had neither Montesquieu nor Gabriel to help. More than once I had to devour the entire evidence. And again, I would wonder when, (or if), I would be given another familiar. Gerard said I would- eventually. Perhaps they only appeared when danger approached.

Then there was one very important- major- addition to the plantation. In the northwest corner, near a scenic man-made pond, ten or so miles from the main mansion, I built a small cottage just as Gerard and I had talked about. It was a tiny place (only about a third the size of the main house), but it resembled a grand plantation home on the outside, with one-story columns and large floor-to-ceiling windows and all around it were gardens and flowers. It was originally meant as a guest house or a home for Selena's grandmother or even a type of garconniere for the boys, but as it turned out, it became the perfect place for my new overseer.

For the time I owned Sans Souci, when slavery was legal, I seldom purchased more slaves. My easy-going generosity as a taskmaster, kept my people loyal, with me rarely resorting to witchcraft to influence them. Never once did I use the whip. I did make a purchase (of sorts!) when I required an overseer to replace my Toussaint and there were none already at the plantation whom I believed capable. I was not about to hire some local Frenchman, for I knew what they were capable of from my dealings with other plantation owners. I had to find- somehow- a loyal, competent, preferably middle-aged male- one who was not a stranger to plantation life and the workings of the seasons and crops; one who could command respect from the other slaves and who, perhaps one day, might even gain my confidence as Toussaint had.

This was certainly a tall order to fill and I realized there were none who could actually take Toussaint's place. However, I had to try to find someone suitable, even if it took months (or years) of searching. And so, I went to auction after auction, plantation after plantation, small and large; reading the minds of black slaves and white owners trying to find anyone even remotely eligible; and had no luck- until one day, after about a year or more- I finally found the one man I thought to be perfect for Sans Souci.

He was quite tall, extremely dark and brutally muscular, yet I sensed in him, a great deal of intelligence and, (for lack of a better description), common sense. No ignorance or superstition showed itself. Reading his mind, I discovered he (amazingly) understood most English and French and, for a short time, had help command a banana plantation in Central America. He could neither write nor read, but I could easily teach him that, along with mathematics. He was un-fearful, had a calm disposition- and I believed he had great potential. Most importantly, though, the slave was a proud man of integrity and, (for the master who treated him rightly), if he gave his word, he kept it. That was exactly what I was looking for in an overseer.

When I first saw him, he was barred inside a wooded cart, shackled and chained with about a dozen others- mostly males, and I asked the auctioneer (we were out in the streets at the time) when he would be put up for sale. 'Oh, sorry monsieur, he and the others are to be taken north to an English colony. They are owned by that slave trader..' He pointed at such and such. I forgot the name, but I knew the trader he was referring to- an Irishman, particularly known for his dislike of the negro. I spoke to the strange looking red-haired, red-faced man about purchasing the slave or even the whole lot of them, (if need be), in order to have the one. 'They are already spoken for', he brusquely answered and, though I was dressed as a gentleman, he shoved me aside as he took his place on the cart and started the horses. That was a definite mistake on his part.

I knew the route they would take and where the turn off was to go to Sans Souci. I followed, discreetly, in the woods. I was riding Porthos, who had become my favorite for she never shied from me; never minding my wolf's scent. We took a shortcut ending up a few miles ahead of the cart and came to that particular fork in the road where they would turn to go north. Here, in a certain bend, the setting sun would be in the slave trader's eyes. I tied Porthos to a tree in the near distance and waited.

As they approached, I transformed and almost immediately, his horses sensed me and they hesitated, refusing to go further and he was having a hard time controlling them. I seized the chance and (to the slaves in the car), I was but a blur- a blur of some type of wild animal that had attacked the trader and dragged his body off into the swamp. I had to tear his heart out quickly, for the horses had bolted and the cart was careening carelessly.

I could run faster than any horse, even in my human form, and so I did, running hidden in the woods and when I passed them up, I jumped out into the middle of the road and managed to halt the horses and, with my witch's effort, calmed them down. However, the gasps, shouts and pointing of the slaves surprised me until I realized I had much of the man's blood on myself and my clothes. I hastily explained in French that I had killed the animal (I did not elaborate on how or what) but, unfortunately, the trader was dead. I further gave them the choice that they could either work for me at my plantation near here, and I would give them their freedom after a year of service, or they could take their chances now, on their own, in the wilderness as runaways. Of course, they all chose to take their chances with me, especially with their slave trader dead, but I did sense the deepest skepticism in the one I had selected to be my overseer. However, as I drove the cart back to get Porthos and then proceed onward to Sans Souci, he (and the others) began to grow hopeful about their future.

When the slaves saw the night beauty of the plantation, the dense and lovely oak alley and all the restructuring being done, I could feel their gratitude, for they had heard grave reports about the mean master they were to belong to. Each one had their papers in order in a satchel by the driver's seat and I unshackled each one separately, in turn, assigning them different tasks and cabins. The papers- I would burn- after duplicating them with my name as owner. It was all accomplished easy enough. In those early years at Sans Souci, I never was concerned about the authorities. In fact, as the plantation and, (consequently my name), grew in stature, I achieved a certain sway- power- over many officials, just as Gerard had done. However, I always made sure all was in order legally.

The cart and horses were never found- lost, supposedly, in some boggy bayou with the slaves escaping or drowning. The trader's remains were found- an alligator, fortunately, helping himself to what I had started and the poor colonial planter up north lost his investment. Rumors were he had quite a bounty set upon the head of each slave, but with the lack of cooperation from local French officials, he had no recourse and eventually gave up the hunt. Bounty hunters were a constant danger; many were slave traders; those were the people I did have to worry about; and I dealt with them as only a warlock would.

It was getting late as I told each one to get some rest and be ready for work in the morning. I saved the one slave I wanted as overseer for last, and taking him to

Gerard's cistern, I let him bath while I sat on the edge and talked to him. His skepticism returned, for no master allows his slaves to wash in his private bath. Yet, at the same time, his astuteness told him I was a different sort of master.

His name was Sebastian, "But they call me 'Bon Temps'."

"Pour quoi?"

"Because I have always entertained my masters with song and dance. I play the ukulele. I play it well." He was friendly enough, with some innocence left from his youth that his previous owners had not completely destroyed. He paused in his bath to display a proud, broad chest full of muscle as he continued. "I also can grow grapes and make wine." Excellent, I thought, for I had wanted to plant a larger vineyard by the cottage.

Bon Temps was approximately thirty years of age, we guessed, for he did not know his date of birth or what happened to his mother. Born into slavery in Panama, he had never known any other life. He was still cautious with me as we talked and when I asked him if he thought he was capable of one day being the overseer of my large plantation and slaves, he responded, at first, with heart-felt enthusiasm, then his circumspect nature surfaced again. I read in his mind that he suspected I had other motives behind my friendliness. I could not help but notice his extra large male anatomy.

"I will give you your freedom in exchange for your hard work and fidelity to me. As foreman, you may have your own separate cottage in which to live and you may, if you wish, even select a wife from the females here at Sans Souci. I will also arrange for you to earn a salary- if-you stay here long enough." His dark eyes grew bright with delight. I had won him over. "We have extensive acreage and grow everything from pecans and grapes to cotton and sugarcane. With plenty of livestock, Sans Souci is self-sustaining." I paused before asking him again, "Do you think you are capable of assuming the responsibility of being the overseer to such an enterprise?"

That time he did not hesitate and he answered me with complete confidence that yes, he was capable. And so that is how I 'acquired' Toussaint's replacement and eventually Bon Temps and I became close confidantes. I let him become aware of my practicing voodoo, (which was commonplace), but not of my werewolvism.

Of course, Juliette was the first to be given her freedom and she rapidly became part of our family, being destined to become closer to me personally. And Bon Temps moved into his cottage, which he called Bonheur. And soon, surrounding the chateau were vineyards and all types of flowering bushes and trees. It was one of the most idyllic scenes on the plantation.

So life was full of hard labor, yet we went without serious worry, establishing a true Sans Souci haven together. And it was the norm for many years until Selena's next pregnancy and the tragedy it brought to all of us.

* * * *

When the boys were about six or seven, Selena finally carried a child for the full term. She had tried several times before, to become pregnant, but severe and painful miscarriages were always the consequence. We both felt this was a direct result of Selena consuming the previous poisonous tea Marguerite had supplied her.

As for myself, I noticed she was becoming weak and sickly- not her usual vibrant self, but she insisted she was fine. Even her grandmother mentioned to me that Selena did not seem herself. It was after the main house was completed and we had moved in, when she announced- proudly- that she was three months pregnant.

I was overjoyed (mostly for her) because I knew how

548

deeply and desperately she wanted another child of mine. I still had trepidations about my children inheriting the curse or some form thereof. However, the boys did grow up at a normal human pace, for which I was very thankful- yet I kept a watchful eye on both for any sign of the loup garou. Grandma-ma and Marie said not to worry, though I read- deep, back within their own minds- of doubts they themselves had.

This pregnancy had a normal nine month gestation period, which made me very hopeful for a normal child. However, Selena had a hard time of it, being bedridden much of the time. All our medicines and remedies were of little effect. Marie, who now visited Sans Souci regularly, gave Selena particular potions, but even that only worked temporarily and eventually was useless. The pregnancy was definitely not as it should have been and when the pains began, all I could do was hope and pray that all would be well and over soon. At the time, I actually gave little- if any- thought towards the child she was carrying. My only concern was for my wife and first love.

As it turned out, the labor began one long hot summer evening, the sun still bright in the sky, and it lasted for many hours with grandma-ma and Juliette shut up with Selena in our upstairs bedroom. (Selena and I had claimed the large bedroom across the hallway from where Gerard's room had been; my 'old bedroom' be-coming grandma-ma's and Juliette's shared room, with the boys sleeping in the room that had once contained the secret panel).

Bon Temps and I anxiously waited outside on the balcony or in the hallway; he sat smoking his pipe, as was his custom now, while I mostly paced to and fro like a nervous wolf. We would bring fresh linens, hot water or medicines as the perspiring and fatigued Juliette would peek her head out the door with their requests. The clean towels and sheets were exchanged for some which were alarmingly bloody and my heart sank as she handed them to me. Once, she put her delicate hand to my cheek and gazed fondly at my worried and harassed countenance. Her eyes and voice told me not to worry, but in my weakness, I read her mind and knew the situation was seriously grave indeed.

Finally, we heard a baby's cry and not being able to contain my wolf's impatience any longer, I burst through the double doors leading from the hallway and saw Juliette cradling a tiny bundle in a clean blanket; grandma-ma was sitting on the bed, washing my poor Selena's flushed and sweaty face and arms with rags in cold water. Upon seeing me, Selena wanted to sit up, trying to prop herself up with damp and soiled pillows. Her grandmother had to help her and it was obvious that the birth had taken its toll on my beloved, though I had yet to fully realize the consequence. Selena managed a weak smile and motioned towards the baby.

Juliette tried to show me the little girl: "Madeleine." They had named her after grandma-ma. I glanced at the bundle, but my thoughts and concern were only for Selena. Somewhat offhandedly, I waved the crying infant away, but grandma-ma stopped me before I could get close to the bed.

She whispered softly, "Be quick my son," and put her hands on both my shoulders, bracing me, telling me to be strong, as her vacant eyes stared into my own shocked and pleading ones. It cannot be true, I thought. "I am sorry. It is time for you to say goodbye, mon fils." Her blank eyes, now full of tears, turned hastily away and she and Juliette, taking the baby, exited the room, to leave me alone for Selena's last moments.

I kissed my love on the cheek, as I sat down gently beside her, taking her hand in mine, "She is a healthy girl, Henri. Did you see?" Though these were her final minutes, she was smiling and happy.

"Yes, my dear, I saw."

"Madeleine. I wanted to name her after grandma-ma. I

hope you don't mind."

"Of course not. It is a sweet gesture, quite appropriate." I paused. "Why don't we just sit here quietly while you regain your strength?" I felt her pulse slowing: she was slipping from me even as we spoke.

"No, I must say something." She looked so tenderly at me, but she was strong, not a tear in her eye. "Do not blame her."

"Blame who? I do not know what you mean." I only hoped I would be as strong as she.

"Don't blame your daughter for.." Suddenly her whole body stiffened and she stared vacantly at the ceiling. I was about to call out to the others for I believed I had lost her, but then she recovered: her breath coming back, though shallow, her body relaxing a bit. She blinked a few times, trying to dispel her pain, then she turned to me, reaching weakly with one hand to caress my face, my lips tenderly. "Do not blame our baby, Madeleine, for what happens.. here."

My sensitive ears listened to the whispers beyond the door:

"There is nothing that can be done?"

"Non. Nothing." I heard Juliette's sobs above the tiny cry of the infant.

"Then it will be.."

"Only minutes from now." A pause. "Bon-Temps- get the boys, please."

"Are you sure they should see their mother like this?"

"It is time I had a talk with them about life and death."

"Henri should.."

"Non. He will be too- preoccupied. I can do it." I heard grandma-ma take a deep breath. "I have done it before."

"Henri, are you listening to me?" Selena got my full attention back.

"Yes, ma cherie, my heart's delight. I am listening."

"Tristan is the strong one, the survivor. It will be Marcel who will need your guidance and your . . .

understanding." She began to cough and could not stop and just as I reached for a glass of cool water by the bed, the coughing stopped suddenly. She struggled to speak. "Kiss me, Henri. Kiss me now." Her voice was urgent.

Our lips met, I held her to me, never wanting it to end. Yet end it must

And when we parted, she spoke for the last time. "Every kiss is .." and then in the next instant, her body went limp- her eyes staring vacantly at nothing. Her life force, the spirit was gone from me forever. I gently closed her eyes with my hand, letting my fingers linger on her beautiful serene face.

"Yes my darling. Each was like our first."

My howl of pain and anguish became legend. Heard for miles around, it disturbed humans and animals alike. Gigantic flocks of birds, nesting for sunset, flew out- startled, frightened- all at once from the trees, blackening the skies. It was taken as a portent of the end of the world by the voodoo fanatics in the parish and talked of for years afterwards. I never- never again- let my emotions go so completely like that. But then, I would never be so distressed either.

We buried my beloved Selena in our ever growing populated plantation cemetery, near to all my other friends and lovers.

* * * *

I kept my desolation private, too private. During the day, I functioned as the overlord of a fastly growing, thriving plantation- going through the motions quite like one of Satine's zombies. But every evening, for near to three months, I stayed to myself- drinking, smoking in Julian's room which had now become my private sanctuary. A sanctuary for my mourning, a place for me to waller in pity. Sorrow at losing Selena. Sorrow at losing both my lovers. Will the years ahead, the endless centuries which stretched before me, be always this way- full of pain and longing, death and suffering? The true curse of the werewolf?

So I drank and drank some more, never seeming to become really inebriated. Oh, but how I wished and prayed for sleep, blessed sleep and somehow to be able to forget. I even smoked opium for a time, yet even that did not alleviate my sorrow, my anger. Would that I could cry, but that simple act had become impossible for me.

No one dared disturb me when I was locked up with my wretched solitude. Once, when working outdoors on a fence with Bon-Temps, he tried to speak to me in confidence (I think at grandma-ma's urging) about how I must recover myself, mentioning my responsibilities to the children and how I was not the only one going through the pain of losing Selena. Yet I ignored his admonishment and actually, treated him and his genuine concern with rudeness. I could not even take an interest in repairing any timepieces. I had no honest interest in anything, including my children- especially my daughter. I could not even lay my eyes upon her, much less hold her- she had taken my true love away. For those few long months I had no heart.

And so, I hunted mercilessly. On any given night, I killed without discretion, slaughtering the innocent as well as the guilty; women as well as men- whoever happened to be unlucky enough to cross my path. Most of the time, I did not even feed- I just wanted to destroy. It was anger and wrath which I felt, not hunger. One murderous night, I pulled a couple out from their carriage, tearing their bodies asunder (and also breaking their horse's necks). Then after my destructive wrath, I heard a baby's cry in the carriage. Inside was a tiny baby girl wrapped up tightly in her blanket. She appeared to be the same age as my child and I reached in with my giant wolf's paw to permanently silence her whimpers, but I stopped myself at the last second for whatever reason I still do not know to this day. I left her to her own fate.

Then one evening, near the autumnal equinox (if I recall correctly),I downed a complete bottle of absinthe and in my angry disappointment at not being totally drunk, smashed the bottle against the wall (narrowly missing Julian's portrait) and I thought I heard a tiny, yet distinct voice say 'ouch'. I put it down at the time as to my half-drunken imagination and continued to pour myself some other sort of alcoholic concoction. Sitting down heavily into one of Julian's comfortable chairs, I accidently turned it over and subsequently, sprawled out onto the floor.

While lying on the floor there by the upturned chair and my spilt drink, I heard, without mistake, another voice or rather what sounded like.. .giggling! It was not my imagination this time, so I confronted whoever was spying on me and invading my private misery.

"Who is it? Who is there?" I challenged the empty room. "If there is some spirit come to taunt me, you had better reconsider, for I will banish..."

At that moment, I heard more giggling- tiny laughter as if from a child, yet it seemed to be more than one. Angry at being teased, I overturned the furniture searching for I knew not what. "Spirits be gone, I will not be trifled with." However my search revealed nothing and resulted in only a wrecked and disturbed room.

"Show yourselves, cowards. Show yourself!" I demanded, and then to my complete astonishment, on top of the desk, from behind some books, appeared one by one, three tiny little figures- three little people no bigger than a thimble. They jumped around on Julian's desk, dancing and twirling like wind-up figurines.

"What sort of joke is this?" My patience had all but disappeared, replaced these last few months with only anger and despondency. "What- who- the hell are you and why do you disturb me? I have no time for trivial games. Return to your forest or playscape and leave me be."

"We cannot Henri." They spoke in unison. One resembled a small fairy, with silver wings and a chartreuse dress. She flitted about in the air, above the other two. The second miniature was a male- dressed in a strange emerald green tunic and red trousers. In all respects, he looked like a leprechaun, complete with a little beard and a conical hat. The third figure was another female, but with no wings. Instead she carried a miniature bow and arrow and was dressed as a huntress, in light brown. She stood solidly and strongly in an amazonian manner, facing me- the obvious leader of the three.

"Who are you? And where do you come from?" My curiosity was growing, though I still mostly wished to be left alone. Perhaps if I changed into a werewolf and scared them away. "Why do you plague my solitude?"

"We are your familiars, Henri." Their voice was one.

I almost rolled with laughter. "C'est impossible. This must be some sort of joke. How can you help me? You could not assist me in any battle."

The one with the bow and arrow- the serious one- stepped forward and spoke alone. "Oh, but we can. We are here to help you with one particular battle you are now involved in."

I was growing impatient again. "And what battle is that?" I scoffed.

They each replied in turn. The tiny fairy was first. "There are many battles," she started, then the leprechaun spoke, "that a werewolf who happens to be a warlock, must fight." The huntress finished the thought, "And many of those battles are from within." I could think of no quick retort to their logic.

"Well then," I stood a chair back up and sat in it (rather clumsily still). "Introduce yourselves. Demonstrate what value you are to me- Henri Le Blanc- the werewolf who became a warlock."

The girl with the diminutive wings started first. "My name is Papillon and I can bring back physical images from your past." Her voice had a vibration, a trill. It was almost musical, soothing actually. She flitted about as she spoke.

"Images? Physical?" I was so full of doubt about their usefulness.

"Yes, images of people. What I call vibrations. With them, I can show you a peaceful, serene way to live."

I snorted loudly and rudely at her. The huntress scowled at me. But really! How could three tiny people such as these be of help to a being like myself- a being who helped defeat the mighty Satine. "Well," I professed impatience, "go on, show me. Go on!"

Waving her Lilliputian hand as if it were a wand, she twirled around in a circle and disappeared- then in her place, miraculously- in front of me- were hundreds of tiny yellow butterflies. They filled the chamber with their beauty. Reflexively, I stood up and they floated over to me, flying all around me, lighting upon me. I was covered, yet I did not mind. In fact, overwhelmingly, I felt the most profound feeling of peace and contentment; emotions I had been longing to experience all these last few months; feelings I had almost forgotten could exist. And all in my life was tranquil, care lifted away from me, like Gerard had always wanted life to be. Like he had tried to teach me to be.

But, remarkably, her demonstration was not over. The butterflies, leaving me, regrouped over in the corner near the desk by Julian's portrait and gathering cohesively together they formed a human figure- that of a woman. Then in another second- and to my utter surprise- the butterflies were gone and in their stead, they had left behind (or perhaps heaven had composed) my beautiful and stately Selena, in the flesh, standing before me. She raised her arms beckoning me.

In my newly found happiness, I half-ran to her.

Holding her solid form, kissing her- it was just as if she had never left me. I stopped our affection for a moment and had to step back to regain my reality, literally shaking my head to clear it. I was feeling giddy, dizzily happy. Yes, it was Selena, my first love and she was wearing the same dress as on our wedding day! "Oh Selena, mon amour." We resumed our lovers embrace.

Again, in another heartbeat, I was holding onto nothing but a swarm of magical butterflies- caressing me, hovering all about me. Yet, for some supernatural reason, (or spell?) I still felt the same absolute sense of happiness. My sorrow and pain from the last weeks, was quickly becoming a memory. Then the butterflies too, were gone. The little fairy gave me a huge smile.

"Bon, je compris. I understand, now. And I appreciate you, Papillon." I hesitated. "Can you.."

"Yes, anyone from your past- mother; father...Pierre."

"And...Gerard?"

"Unfortunately, his- essence- is still roaming the earth- at this time."

Here the other female interrupted with an authority I would come to respect. "Papillon can only produce for you the images of those who have passed onto the other side." She nodded to the leprechaun; it was now his turn.

"I am called Tourneaux." Announcing himself, the little gleeful fellow bounded towards me, turning somersaults, laughing all the while.

I looked down at the tiny man on the desk. His belly, fat and round for his size, jiggled with his small contagious laughter. "You are certainly a happy one. Are you what they call a leprechaun, which I have read so much about?"

"I am- if that is what makes you comfortable."

"Can you find the pot of gold at the end of the rainbow, then?" I was being sarcastic. Still cynical, it was hard for me to take all of this seriously.

He laughed and rolled around on the desk some

more, ignoring my skepticism, doing his somersaults and handstands. The other two laughed with him. "Oh no, silly! I am Tourneaux and I can help you by allowing you to relive actual events from your past."

"Time travel?" My skepticism increased and I am sure it showed.

"Only events from your past," he repeated. "I can turn the clock back. Shall I?" he looked towards their leader who gave her nod of approval.

Without warning, and with but a wink of one tiny green eye, I found myself back at my old home as a child. I was outdoors with Pierre and we were playing fetch with our pet dogs. I had not thought of that particular scene in many a year, but pondering it further- I had been reminiscing on my childhood and my time with Pierre growing up. Had he somehow taken a memory, seized it from my mind and now- I was reliving my past?

I was a boy again and I joined in the game, kicking the ball about, wrestling with our pets and laughing as only ten-year olds can do, without a care in the world. I heard my mother call my name and turning I saw her figure in the doorway. I felt happy- no more than happy- I felt safe and secure.

Then, with a blink, the secure feeling left me, for I found myself aboard a ship- the same ship which carried us away from my homeland. Pierre was by my side and I relived the depleting fear of the unknown. And the supreme anger of losing control over my life, over my destiny.

In the next particle of an instant, I was transported to Sans Souci, sitting under the beautiful bright crepe myrtles, enjoying my daily breakfast with Gerard and I felt that wonderful security again- and love. He was across from me hungrily devouring his usual helping of rare red meat and I reached out for him, wanting to touch him again- to feel his strength, hoping it would then become mine.

But in that flash of a second, the scene shifted to a more recent memory. I wanted to leave it immediately and go back to happier times, for it was a scene of extreme sadness. I was now at Selena's death bed and she was telling me some thing of import, words I had completely forgotten. "Do not blame the child," she repeated. "Don't blame our little girl."

At that point, I was back in the present- in Julian's room with the three of them. I sat back down, heavily, into my favorite overstuffed, comforting chair, astounded-speechless- believing what had just happened and then not believing. I did not know whether I felt happy or sad- anything- other than incredulity! The little man just stood there grinning at me with his silly clownish self, his hands on his hips.

"Tell me, Tourneaux- Pourquoi? Just what was the importance of my reliving all that." I realized I was breathing heavy from exertion- and anxiety. "Especially the last scene? Pray tell me." Yet even as I asked the question, I knew the answer. It was time for me to stop indulging in my self-pity. Perhaps immortals do feel emotions to the extreme. Of course, that was no reason to continue this desolate solitude. I must become the father Selena wanted me to be; the man Gerard wished for me to be.

Tourneaux gave no reply, just giving me what would become his recognizably typical grin, as he stood on his hands and somersaulted back around to be behind the huntress who now stepped forward and answered my next question before I could ask it.

"I am called Artemis."

"The moon goddess?" I was already impressed.

"No, I am not," she bowed her head slightly, "thee goddess. But I am a moon child." She curtsied to me, gracefully with honour and I knew instinctively that she was probably the one of the three whom I would rely on the most. The one whose abilities I would, most likely, find indispensable. What those abilities were I had no idea for I could not read her tiny thoughts.

"And what tricks can you perform? How can you serve me?" I immediately regretted my rudeness.

"I do not 'serve' anyone," her pride was obvious, "but I can help you."

"And how is that mademoiselle?"

"I will help you realize your full potential. To capture as much power from the moon as possible."

"I have already learned that. Gerard taught me all he..."

She interrupted me. "Even he did not achieve the greatness possible for the right loup garou. The right moon child." I shook my head slightly with doubt, but she continued. "Can you control the moon instead of it controlling you? Can you turn the moon a different colour as the witch could?"

I thought back to the battle and the blood red moon Satine had conjured. "Show me this thing then!" I was definitely more than curious, however still skeptical, for these three 'familiars' were absolutely not what I expected. Not at all like my Montesquieu. Then again, the first two had proven their worth.

Papillon and Tourneaux quickly skipped and flew out of the room and into the tunnel, laughing and playing with each other all the way like little children, ever so happy-go-lucky. For small folk, they traveled very fast. I placed Artemis upon my shoulder and we followed behind them, us two obviously being the more serious ones.

Outside, the graveyard was clearly lit by the full moon and I immediately thought of feasting, though it was not hunger which drove me, but rather desire- the need for some sort of satisfaction. Artemis looked up at me while the other two circled about me, flying and laughing, doing tricks and acting foolish. I could not read any of their minds like I could with Montesquieu. However, it was obvious that they could easily read my thoughts.

Artemis said to me, simply, "Stare at the moon and concentrate."

"Concentrate? On what- turning the moon red?"

"Oh no!" Her tiny voice exclaimed. "You will see. Concentrate all your current feelings of sorrow and lost, of sadness and melancholia- your immediate feelings. You have had much pain in your short life, Henri LeBlanc- losing both lovers and experiencing all the horrors of the battle and there will be more horrors yet to come. Let your pain and anger flow out- focus it upon the moon!" She put her miniature arm around my neck with genuine affection and I realized then that these three were going to be, not only my familiars, but my friends and companions, just as Montesquieu had been.

I did as she directed. All the aching and sorrow of the last few years; the stress and worry of rebuilding Sans Souci, all the barbarity of Satine's acts; the outrage of losing my loved ones and friends to her and the battles we fought; and then, most profoundly- my loneliness without Selena and Gerard- my lack of direction and strength with them gone- all this was focused upon my ruler- the moon.

What happened next was the most miraculous, extraordinarily sensational feat I could have ever imagined- even over and above my remarkable fire power. I never dreamed I could actually command the moon itself.

The silvery sphere turned a distinct shade of blue!

All three of my little people danced, clapping and shouting, "Hurrah! Hurrah!" And I now knew what Artemis meant. I still had more to learn, power to gain- and there was even more for me to learn about life with humans. For though I was immortal and technically not human, I lived and breathed among them- destined to marry them, love them; to have children by them; to laugh and argue, celebrate and fight with them. To share in their despair and misery- and experience their deaths.

"And so one day, all the power of the moon.."

"Will be yours." Artemis concluded.

"Will be mine!" I felt refreshed again- complete and strong. I was almost as giddy as those three.

"So now you understand," Papillon began.

"And you will prosper ..." Tourneaux added.

"And use your power wisely." Artemis finished the thought. The three were as one. "Yes," I agreed, "and I must return to Sans Souci now." And I meant that figuratively as well as literally. I sat Artemis down on the ground. "I have something- someone- I need to take care of."

"Until soon, Henri." Papillon and Tourneaux were already leaving. Artemis had one more thought to share. "Only you, Henri- only you- know what you lost with Selena's death and what you have gained. Do not lose your capability of love, Henri LeBlanc. Adieu, mon ami."

"Adieu, Artemis. Mon ami." It was most strange how much, at that very moment, she reminded me of Gerard.

Back at Sans Souci, I crept into Selena's and my bedroom. A small nursery had been created in one corner of the room and I heard my little girl crying softly. Grandma-ma was trying to comfort her, rocking in a chair, but the child would not quiet herself. I gently took her from her great-grandmother and held my baby for the first time, looked upon her for the first time since her birth and it was as if I were gazing at Selena- they had the same features and almond shaped eyes, the same cafe-au-lait colour. She was a beautiful child. How selfish I had been! Forgive me, my little one.

Remarkably, as soon as I had lifted her, the child grew quiet, peaceful. "All she needed was her father." The old one rose and, going to the door to leave us, she turned to say, "It is good to have you back, my son. I knew you would." She closed the door behind her letting the two of us become acquainted, together, alone.

I rocked my baby girl in my arms, gently, putting my

finger on her tiny button of a nose and touched her little wet lips. She laughed and wiggled with my caresses- her eyes bright, big and lustrous with life. I turned around for I thought I had heard the giggles of my familiars, but I was mistaken.

We walked over to the window. The moon still shined bright and blue. Concentrating with sharp exactitude, I waved one hand over it and the moon turned back to its normal full and silver orb. "And now my little Maddie, you have a father who will lasso the moon for you, if you so desire. He will do anything for you- all you have to do is ask. After all, not just any father can turn the moon blue."

Sitting down, I rocked my child into a peaceful sleep and we stayed that way until the early morning.

*   *   *   *

"I believe you will need a pinch more of that last ingredient."

"The bark? I believe you are right, Artemis." She was helping me (as she often did) with a new formula. This potion was one that would render the consumer invisible for a short period. She was quite knowledgeable at creating voodoo recipes. We were in my secret room off the study with Papillon and Tourneaux playing on the floor with Madeleine ('my little Maddie'), who had just turned five. Their laughter was infectious. My daughter almost always wanted to be with her daddy and we seldom were apart. Sometimes, I even took her with me on my rounds in the fields. Madeleine had become the light of my life and I would not know how to live without the child.

Maddie had always been a happy girl, laughing and cheerful, scarcely ever sullen, never melancholy- and the only one on the plantation (save for Juliette) who knew of the hidden room and my familiars. It was daddy's and hers 'little secret'. Her look and style told me she would

563

grow into a beautiful woman one day, like her mother. In fact, every year she came more and more to resemble Selena- at least I thought so. And not only did she physically favour her mother, but I was positive Maddie had inherited Selena's telepathic abilities and we practiced our psychic mind reading whenever possible by playing 'mental guessing games'.

Most likely I would teach her about voodoo when she came of age (if she so desired).

She already showed a great propensity for reading, languages and music and caught on quickly to any new educational material; her elderly tutor was a French lady from the east coast. Maddie was quite astute for her age.

Juliette and I had married about a year and a half after Selena's death. That was another reason for my extreme happiness. She had kept her beauty and youthful figure well and our sex was not only extremely passionate, but quite experimental, lasting for many hours at a time. What had once been a purely innocent slave girl, was now an accomplished woman. Juliette was also perfect for Sans Souci and she took her responsibility as the matron of a large and prosperous plantation seriously and made sure the household was run efficiently to perfection. I could not ask for a better mate.

She and I had a silent agreement, though, for us not to have children. There was no keeping what I was secret from her and so on the day I proposed, I told about my wolf's self and how her master had made me; that I was not evil and would never harm her. Without blinking, she asked to see, so I showed her my true self and allowed her to gaze upon me. She showed no fear, but instead, amazingly, was quite curious and after I transformed back to my human self, she came to me with a kiss and accepted my proposal eagerly. I read desire in her mind, sensed it from her person and we made premarital love that night, made that much more exciting because she lost her virginity to what I was- a loup garou. Many times during our marriage, as she reached climax, she would became almost as wild as myself.

I never asked how she prevented having children, but of course, she consulted with Marie quite often. Because of legends and folklore we did not want to risk having 'the blessed curse' transferred to our offspring. And so we, as a family, kept a very close watch on the twins, for they were quickly maturing, coming of age and puberty.

A loud boom went off. "The boys are target practicing again," Artemis said with a sigh. "Even at night."

"I know. I told them to do that out in the southwest forest, yet they seldom follow my directions."

"Tristan does."

"Yes, he does. It is Marcel who.."

"Is the rebellious one."

It was true. The boys, though twins, were quite different from one another. Marcel, the older, was not as dutiful and dependable as Tristan. He was a bit of a loner, quiet even sullen much of the time, with more than a touch of sadness (and ill-temper) about him. I believed, he had particularly taken his mother's death hard. Growing up he was less than average at his studies and athleticism, showing little interest in things new and had a poor attitude towards work.

Tristan however, (though also quiet like his brother) was a young example of manliness and I suspected him to grow up to accomplish great things- just as his mother had predicted. He was almost too perfect in everything he did; it appeared as if he never made a senseless or false move, yet had a thought behind every action; showing strong presence of mind. Whereas, Marcel was careless and simply reacted to whatever circumstances life presented to him.

Tristan was also different from Marcel, in that he had a peacefulness about him, within him. He was quite the mature gentleman, possessing a southern charm and solicitousness (much like the knight he was named for). All in all, I was closer to him than Marcel, which I suppose, was mostly my fault, for Marcel and I definitely had our differences. At times, he would argue with me- our 'discussions' becoming quite heated and he had difficulty controlling his anger. To be truthful though- I saw a great deal of myself in him.

Another loud shock went off and then another right after which shook my equipment.

"Thunder," quipped Tourneaux as he and Papillon played hide and seek with Madeleine. The little girl giggled so, anyone could find her hiding place.

"Nonsense," countered Artemis. "There is not a cloud in the sky tonight." A full moon beckoned me outside and I thought I would feed after testing our concoction.

"On a human or yourself?" she had read my thought.

"Most likely I will test it on Maddie's cat or one of the horses."

"You will need more of the potion for such a large animal." Usually more serious than not, Artemis paused in thought. "Gerard would choose a victim."

"Yes, I know exactly what he would do." The mere mention of his name sent pangs of longing through me. I needed his male companionship; I wanted his maleness near.

Just then there were some more loud thumps in a row which startled even my little girl. Papillon began floating about nervously and whispered something to Tourneaux whose beady little green eyes grew wide. He immediately came over and said something to Artemis that even my super sensitive hearing could not detect.

"Again, nonsense," exclaimed Artemis. "Stuff and nonsense, I say."

I was on the verge of asking what they were alarmed about when several more of the jolts shook the whole house. The storm (or whatever) was coming closer.

This time even Artemis showed surprise and then, I

discerned a profound sadness fall over her, which I had never seen in her before. "It is time, Artemis." Papillon trilled. "It is time," Tourneaux echoed.

Artemis' gaze fell to the floor. My Maddie began to softly whimper in her hiding place in the corner behind a chair. The two others went over to comfort her. Did she sense something I did not? "What is happening Artemis? Time for what?" I disliked this feeling of cluelessness.

"It is time for us to leave." Her eyes could barely look upon me and I saw the strong little moon child/amazon cry for the first time.

"Leave? Pourquoi? I do not understand."

"Your new familiar has arrived." More thumps shook the house and I realized- they were footfalls!

"We must leave, now, quickly." Papillon and Tourneaux spoke together at once. The tiny fairy flew over to me and, kissing me on the cheek, said, "Remember to remain happy, Henri." Then, a hundred butterflies appeared surrounding us and, just as quickly, they vanished into the air.

"But surely you can stay and introduce.." I was interrupted by a roar as the clock in the study chimed the hour. The roar was like that of a tiger- a primordial sound. My bewilderment was embarrassing, for I had been priding myself on the control (and peace) I had experienced since the three of them were here.

"I am sorry, Henri, but I must follow. Avoir, mon ami." Tourneaux handed me his Lilliputian hand and I extended a finger out to shake it, as he gave me a piece of good advice. "I have helped you relive your past, but remember Henri- you and only you- make your own tomorrow." With that he somersaulted away disappearing much like the way he had first arrived.

It all happened so fast, and I was so dumbfounded, I had not the chance to say farewell. I turned to the moon child. "Artemis?" My question was just that.

"We will be back when you need us. For now you

require a different sort of familiar." She looked about. "Changes are coming to Sans Souci, extreme changes and you must be prepared- cautious. They are..they will be..," Another roar, another thump interrupted her.

"Come let us go outside and say goodbye, then I must leave so you can greet your next companion." She lifted her arms and I placed her upon my shoulder as we always had. She affectionately put her arm about my neck holding on to my shirt collar. Taking Madeleine by the hand, we went into the study, closing the secret room behind us. Juliette was waiting in the hallway. She had heard the noise and understood without being told.

"Now Madeleine, it is late and past time for you to be in bed." She looked at me with a mother's slight disapproval. "You always keep her up too late, Henri."

"Goodnight, papa." I bent down and she kissed me on both cheeks. "Do not be afraid." She was my brave little girl.

"I won't ma cherie. As long as I know I have you by my side." Her fat tabby cat was mewing at our feet; she picked it up, holding it awkwardly; ready for bed. Juliette gave us a wide smile, then looked at me questioningly, her eyebrows arched. She spoke to me with her mind asking if this was my new familiar arriving. I replied, yes. Then all will be right, she assured me- it was just another step in this my long life. "I will be up later, my dear." I kissed Juliette gently on the lips and went outdoors to the front lawn with Artemis still on my shoulder, while my two girls went upstairs to bed.

The fog was so thick I could not see the moon or even the treetops and it moved about, billowing- though there was no wind. Marie's familiar was announcing (I suppose) the arrival of this familiar, who must be very special indeed. It had to be huge. "But why? Why need of a giant?" I wondered out loud.

Artemis had no answers, but said simply, "I must go."
"I will miss you, I think, more than the others."

"We will be back one day when there is a need in your long, long life." Did not Juliette just say something of that sort? "You have a gloriously full life ahead of you, yet you must remember..?" she paused.

"Yes, the power I have from the moon; and, my power to influence the moon." I wanted to ask what sort of creature I would be facing in the next moment or so, but she pecked me on the neck with her tiny kiss, saying- "Je t'aime, Henri,"- and so she was gone from me. Another loss, another gain? I whispered aloud, "Je t'aime aussi, Artemis."

Marie's fog appeared to be getting thicker, closer; it started to quickly breeze past me in a windless wind; and I saw ahead the large looming shadow of some thing coming this way. However, there was no shaking of the earth, announcing its arrival. It walked softly, yet was as large as an elephant. And though I could not make out what sort of animal it might be, what was immediately obvious to me, was the surprising grace and feminine style and delicacy the creature possessed, especially considering its immense size.

As it neared, more and more I noticed its elegance; its poise, finesse; its light-footedness- and I immediately thought of a cat, a large female cat to be exact. But I also thought I heard the rustle of wings like with Gabriel. Then suddenly, when I could see clearly I realized I was partially right- it was an enormously large lioness with the head of an eagle! And what were those?.. On its sides? At once, the fog vanished and she was revealed to me in all her glory.

What a magnificently special creature I beheld before me! A creation unlike any other in the universe. And it was for me! It kneeled in front of me like a sphinx, in respectful regard and servitude. And it was endowed with wings! Enormous feathered wings.

Bowing its huge head in acknowledgement and deference, this creature- this familiar- was more like my

Montesquieu in that we could read each other's minds. But of course, I could only read that which she allowed me to read.

I was thrilled with excitement- enchanted beyond belief at the mere sight of this supernatural flying feline and its majesty. What wondrous adventures it must be here for! Then logic made its way into the mind of my young boy's heart and I realized that with such adventures must also come the threat of danger. Why was it so necessary to have such a strong and mighty familiar?

How are you called, I asked silently.

Cassandra.

I was impressed that much more. And like that namesake you..

Foretell the future. With a snarl, the sleek and light-brown 'lioness' let out a sharp low growl and its wings wriggled and shook as if to unfurl and take flight. How I wanted to fly again! Like I had done with Montesquieu. Only this time. . .

And what powers do you possess? How can you be of use to me? I hoped my questions were not taken as disrespect, for I admired her so already.

However, this time her growl was more like a shriek. This familiar had even more pride than Artemis did. And so she told me. As your familiar I am here to protect and serve you; to give you advice and guidance; to aid in your battles. My powers are great and many. She laid her feathered head down on the earth in a gesture of intimacy. I hope to be a good companion also, as those familiars before me. I heard a distinct purring sound, though it was only for a moment.

I am positive- in time- we will become the best of friends. I then put forward my first question to her about the future. And how much time will you and I have together?

This shriek was loud enough and forceful enough to

let me know that any information about the future comes only when she permits.   I can only divine that which is revealed to me. The pause between her sentences was obvious- she had to weigh her words carefully.   I can say: you will have many difficult tasks ahead and some are quite- unsavory.   Did I catch that eagle smiling? This familiar might have a sense of humor. She was definitely the most knowledgeable.

I petted her majestic head, touching her for the first time. Her feathers were soft and felt more like fur; she purred like Maddie's cat, but with a giant sound. I spoke out loud to see if she would do the same; to know if she actually had a voice. Montesquieu had had none.

"By tasks, you mean.. my boys?"

Yes, all four children actually.   She responded to me only telepathically.

"Madeleine, also?" I noticed that the griffin-like creature had miscounted, yet I did not correct her.

One day you will have to do the impossible to save her.

"What could that possibly be? Can you be more specific- what do you mean?" Anything concerning Madeleine made my apprehension rise.

That is all I know. All that is revealed to me- I reveal to you, Henri. I hold nothing back. One day she will require from you the impossible.

I hesitated in thought.   And the twins?

One brother will seduce and murder the other.

I was so shocked, I exclaimed: "What? How can you say such a thing?"

Unless you profoundly change the circumstances, that which is revealed to me will not be altered.

"I dare say, I will change it." Again, a thought occurred to me.   So by your meaning, I can prevent (or alter) what you foresee.   My statement was really a question.

She answered me with a statement I heard earlier from another familiar.   You, and only you, make your tomorrows. Be diligent, Henri, like Gerard and Artemis cautioned you.

Her straightforwardness would be part of what I must accept- and appreciate. "What of Gerard? Will he return soon? Where is he and was he successful at finding a vessel to live within?" Once started, my questions and concern about him were released like water from a dam.

"Slow down, Henri." The winged-lioness did have a voice! And, what I took to be a short laugh followed. Her voice was low and quiet; a wonderful soft purr of a sound. It charmed the very air around her. She did not seem to mind my flood of questions concerning Gerard and I knew we would quickly become fast friends. "I do not get any impressions- revelations- about the one who made you; however, I can say, for it has been revealed to me, that one day soon I will take you to meet the creator of the one who saved you from the mummy's grasp."

"Dr. Fontenot?" That raised a whole host of questions within me.

She nodded with her noble eagle's head and a purr. But now, tonight, we fly.

"Fly!" My excitement with this familiar grew by the second.

"With me, you can travel thousands of miles, across a continent-- if need be. And you will see great and wondrous things, Henri. You are blessed with this 'curse'." Her voice was so soft, yet compelling, that any one listening to her would have to regard her as an oracle. Perhaps that was exactly what she was.

"And tonight..?"

"No where in particular, however..," I transformed into my loup garou and in a leap, mounted this lioness who seemed so unreal as to be out of some mythological tale. As she rose up on all fours and spread her imposing wings, I felt a tremendous energy purring- her power roaring- beneath me. I was thrilled as a young school boy would be; similar to when I was with Montesquieu. If you wish, I can show you a battle far from here, but which will come treacherously close to your doorstep one day.

Madre, was all I could think. I knew the war she was speaking of. It was between the British and their former colony, which our land (for better or worse) would probably become involved in. However, like the land and water which we were so much a part of, the French in us would never die (especially for this immortal). "Yes, Show me!"

She leapt into the air and we took our first flight together. The giant oaks bent in obeisance from the forceful beat of Cassandra's giant wings. Stronger than Gabriel, she was faster too. We flew so high, the moon no longer cast our shadow on the earth below.

And once again, I now have the opportunity to view the land I love from a unique (and privileged) perspective. Sans Souci was more majestic and beautiful than ever. The moon's rays skipped across the swamps and bayous; the mighty river that coursed through the land- also coursed through my heart. And I would defend my property, home and family from all intruders- human or inhuman.

I yelled out to the universe, "Yes, This is Henri LeBlanc and I am back. Demons beware for I am the werewolf who became a warlock. Witch slayer. Conjurer of specters and spirits. I have worlds to see and evil to conquer." Cassandra released a cry in agreement. An eagle's cry of superiority. My long life was just beginning.

And despite the frightening future Cassandra had foretold, I was ready. Prepared to do battle; to help my children with whatever 'curses' happened their way; to defeat any monsters, any demons, that threatened from without- or from within.

I was Henri- one of the super-immortals! Henri LeBlanc- LOUP GAROU!

THE END

VOLUME ONE OF HENRI LEBLANC'S MEMOIRS

About the Author

Born in South Texas, the author currently resides in Austin, working as a master clockmaker.

Loup Garou

CPSIA information can be obtained
at www.ICGtesting.com
Printed in the USA
FFOW02n1617031013
1952FF